YELLOW TAPE AND COFFEE

PAT LUTHER

For Dr. Chantel Saban

With thanks for unending patience and encouragement and liking every one of my Facebook posts while I was writing this.

ACKNOWLEDGMENTS

This book, like all such works, was not written in a vacuum. I could not have done it alone. I had a great deal of help along the way. I'd especially like to thank the following:

James Sutter, for valuable early feedback on my first draft at PaizoCon when I was just starting.

Rhiannon Held and Grá Linnaea for all of their feedback on an early draft at the OryCon Writers Workshop.

For that matter, to all the organizers of OryCon and the participants in the ORCs and writing panels therein.

My editor, Kaitlyn Keller.

Stephen Goldin, for introducing me to Nellie Bly in the first place.

Bonnie Henderson-Winnie, for answering my questions about silver smithing.

Gerald Del Campo, for answering all my questions about firearms, and for being Saladin lo those many years ago.

And all of my beta readers, whose feedback greatly improved the final product: Iris Blackburn, Allison Chambers, Zack Dubnoff, Vijay Lakshminarayanan, Thomas Marsh, Charlotte Mueller, Makaela O'Rourke, and Jorden Peery.

CONTENTS

ONE

THE HOUR OF THE WOLF

"Dammit, Sandra, just go to sleep," she told herself again. She looked at the clock. 3am. If she fell asleep right now, that would give her a solid three and a half hours. She didn't dare set the alarm any later. She'd already received two warnings about being late. Her boss made it clear there would not be a third.

She was fucking everything up again. Problems with her car had cost her her last job, and how was she supposed to get it fixed without an income? She felt she was letting everyone down. Mary. Her dad. Even Sid. She'd driven away the one close friend she'd made out here. She wanted badly to apologize to Mary. That was a stupid falling out, especially over trying to defend her relationship with Sid. Mary had since moved away to who knows where. She couldn't even reach her through Facebook since she'd been blocked.

And Sid. God, what had she been thinking? He hadn't threatened her, not really. Not exactly, but it had been enough to freak her dad out.

She turned over again and looked at the clock. 3:15. When he visited last month, her father urged her to move back home.

She'd told him she wouldn't. She didn't need him to protect her. It was safe. Sid wasn't even around anymore. Last she'd heard he moved to Seattle. But sometimes people came back from Seattle...

Maybe she should move back home. Try again in a year or two somewhere else. Save up some money first so the slightest problems didn't bring everything crashing down. She turned over again and squeezed her eyes shut. She would find a way to make it work. She loved everything about Portland. Except how damn expensive everything was.

And that was when she heard it. A soft click. The door to the back patio closed quietly. She had locked it. She knew she had. Hadn't she? She froze where she lay in bed.

Someone was in the house. Could it be Sid? She'd warned him not to come back. He'd said then that they'd be together forever. Maybe she should have gotten that restraining order after all. She'd told her dad she would but hadn't gotten around to it. She had at least taken the gun he'd given her, although as she'd pointed out at the time, she hadn't fired one since she was a little girl.

"Schedule some range time then," he'd told her. She promised she would. She hadn't gotten around to that either.

She thought Sid was too much of a coward to actually break in. It appeared she was wrong. Or maybe it was just a burglar. Just a burglar. How fucked up a thought was that?

She cursed silently to herself as she slid out from under the covers. She felt for the bathrobe on the nearby chair and shrugged into it. Only then did she carefully move to the closet to get the gun. She loaded it as quietly as she could, then slid the safety off and started stealthily toward the hall.

If it was a burglar, they'd find out the hard way they picked the wrong house to break into tonight. She tried to sound tough in her thoughts. If it was Sid, well, they'd see what happened.

Could she actually shoot him? She didn't know. If he tried anything... maybe. At the very least, she'd give him a good scare, it would serve him right.

She carefully opened her bedroom door and peered into the hall. A faint light shone from the kitchen. The bastard was raiding the fridge? She stepped into the hall. Froze, took a couple more steps, and froze again. She thought she saw a shadow move. *Okay, now I'm just scaring myself*, she thought. But it was another long moment before she willed herself to move again.

She crept, carefully, gun gripped in both hands, to the kitchen. The refrigerator door was hanging open. By its light, she could see what looked like a pile of shredded clothing on the floor in front of it. A naked burglar? Or Sid's idea of romance. Why would they be shredded? And how? Whatever was going on, there was definitely somebody here, and she was rapidly moving from scared to angry.

Footsteps behind her, from the living room. Fast, across the carpet. She whirled, raised the pistol, and peered past it into the darkness. She stepped forward and reached for the light switch, feeling along the wall. "All right, asshole, I know you're there. Step out slowly, hands where I can see them, or I'm blowing your fucking head off."

She was answered by a low growl. She could see him now, a shadow, low to the ground, moving toward her, crawling. "I mean it," she said again, desperately trying to keep her voice calm, to show no trace of her fear, over-enunciating "I am armed, and I will shoot you."

No answer to that, but the figure still advanced. Her fingers found the switch and the room blazed into light. She recoiled at what she saw. It wasn't a burglar, or even a man at all. She tried to scream, but no sound came out. She raised the gun and pulled the trigger. The noise was deafening in the small space.

The figure twitched but still advanced. She pulled the trigger twice more. Two more loud reports. It leapt.

The weight of the creature hit her, knocking her to the ground, teeth at her throat. She tried to scream, but the jaws were already clamped down too tightly. She could feel something warm trickling down the sides of her neck, over her ears. Then there was only darkness and silence.

"OTHER SIDE OF THE TAPE, Ms. Rosen," Police Detective Michael Diaz called out to her about half a second after Veer ducked under the tape to get a picture.

Dammit. Just a few more steps and she would have seen what the yellow flag on the ground outside the broken window was marking.

She quickly ducked back to the right side of the tape.

"Is this another dog mauling, Detective?" she called back to him.

He didn't answer her, though.

"Why is homicide here? Shouldn't Animal Control be involved?"

Veer knew she wouldn't get much but hoped for at least something. Five years of working the crime beat in Portland, off and on. It wasn't what she wanted to do, but it paid the bills and allowed her to work on the big stories, the deep-dive exposes that were the real reason she'd gone into journalism in the first place. And now that she was sitting on the biggest one yet, for almost three years, it seemed all she could do was sit. These attacks, though, if her guess about them was correct, might be exactly what she was waiting for.

And she was being thwarted by this police detective. If only he knew what she knew. Of course, she could never tell him. In the years she'd been here, she learned who she could cajole a bit of information out of and who would just blithely ignore her. Who would likely be angered into shutting her out completely if she stepped over a line, and who would just recognize it as part of the game as long as she didn't actually interfere with anything. Diaz was one of the latter.

"I have no idea what you're talking about, Ms. Rosen," he responded to her question. "Do you know something that I don't?"

"Two people killed in two days, both badly mauled?" she responded. "You don't think that establishes a pattern?"

"How do you know this guy was mauled?" he asked her. He seemed genuinely surprised.

Dammit. She shouldn't have given away that much.

"I have my sources," she responded.

She was hoping he'd be amused, but instead he just got annoyed. "Not really in the mood for games tonight, Ms. Rosen," he responded.

"So tell me what you've got, here. Some guy roaming the neighborhood with a big dog?"

"We don't know what we have here yet. I just got here myself. We don't even know if this case is connected at all to the one from Friday." Seeing the look of skepticism on her face, he continued, "How about you answer a couple of questions for me? How do you know about the mauling? How did you get here so much faster than your fellow vultures?" He indicated the news crews just arriving and unpacking their gear.

"Let me in, and I'll tell you."

He laughed, not entirely without mirth. "I can't do that. Even if I did want to."

"What about the reports of shots being fired? Did the killer shoot the victim before he was mauled?"

He gave her a strange look. Instead of answering, he turned

back toward the house. "She," he said before heading inside, leaving her on the other side of the yellow tape.

DETECTIVE MICHAEL DIAZ walked into the controlled chaos of a busy crime scene inside the house. Two people were bagging the body for transport to the morgue. A couple of other officers were measuring the three bullet holes, marking and laying down measurements for the crime scene photographer who, having finished with the body, moved on to the rest of the house.

The living room and kitchen seemed to be the only parts of the house affected by the violence. The victim, deceased, had been found by the doorway between them. A shredded pile of clothing, like at the last scene, was lying on the kitchen floor. The CSI team were still taking prints in the rest of the house, but if their suspect had been anywhere else, he hadn't left any obvious signs.

Despite what he had told the reporter outside, Detective Diaz was fairly certain the killings were related. Both had had the same mauling pattern, with the victims' throats torn open by large teeth, and bites and scratches over the rest of the body. The shredded clothes were similar to the last one. Sweatpants, T-shirt, sandals. He was willing to bet that they weren't in the victim's size.

No signs of forced entry, and in both cases the doors had been locked. So, the victim let the killer in, and... and, what? This one at least distrusted the killer enough to have a gun handy, and by the looks of things had gotten a couple of shots off, wounding the killer pretty badly before his dog got her.

Did the dog owner even do any of the killing himself? He didn't even know if it was technically murder if someone trains a dog to kill someone. Fortunately, that wasn't his responsibility. It was up to the DA to figure out what to charge the guy with. He just had to catch him. Though if this was a burgeoning serial killer, and there was every indication it was, the latest victim may have put an end to it. There was enough blood on the floor that the killer couldn't have gotten very far. So far, the police searching the nearby area hadn't turned up anything. Nor had alerting the local hospitals. But it was still early.

It was even possible that all the work they had done gathering evidence would only be used to confirm the identity of a corpse found in some back alley days from now. Wouldn't that be nice?

Detective Philip Lee walked in the front door, carrying two drink trays full of steaming paper coffee cups. For several seconds he was the most popular guy in the room. They all knew it was going to be a long night.

"They got you fetching coffee now, Phil?" Michael asked him, taking one of the cups for himself.

"It was on my way," his fellow detective answered him.

"What, Powell's?" asked Detective Lauren Boyd, noticing the label on the cup she had taken. "There's closer coffee." She'd made detective only a week before but was already fitting in as if she'd been there forever.

"I was coming from the other side of the river," Phil responded.

"He just likes the barista there," Officer Don Avison said, looking up from his camera.

Phil looked to Michael for help but found none there.

"What, the short pudgy one with the wolf tramp stamp?"

"Hey, she's not..." Phil started, but was saved from the conversation by the arrival of a uniformed officer from a back room.

"What've we got?" Phil asked him as he came in.

"Jones," he introduced himself. "We responded to a call about shots being fired at this location."

"Wait a minute," Michael interrupted him. "Was that how dispatch reported it?"

"Yeah, as far as I remember, why?"

"No reason, go on," he told him.

Phil stopped him with an upraised hand, though. "What is it?" he asked Michael.

"The reporter, Vera Rosen. She knew there were gunshots because we reported it over the radio. She must have been listening to a police scanner and just gave me the mysterious act about it so I'd bite and give her more information."

"Clever," Phil said.

"I almost fell for it, too," Michael responded with a slight smile. He turned back to Jones. "Sorry, go on."

"When we got here, there was no sign of disturbance," Jones continued. "We knocked and got no answer, then my partner spotted the deceased up against the wall there." He indicated the spot where the body had been.

"We both drew our weapons, and I kicked the door in and entered while he covered me. It was locked before I did so. I tried it. The girl was obviously dead, so we secured the rest of the house and called you guys."

"And you didn't touch anything else?"

"The front door, the doorknob to the bedroom, and a couple of light switches. Didn't move anything around of course. Found the bullet holes and the blood, weapon knocked out of the victim's hands." He indicated another pin flag where the gun had been found.

"What do you make of it?"

"You ask me. Your killer picked the wrong target this time. Got himself shot, but not fatally. Ran off while, or after, his dog tore the victim up. Door probably locked on its own while closed."

"I'll check that. Thanks."

"No problem. There was also a stolen vehicle reported about fifteen minutes ago a couple of blocks from here, so you'll have that report on your desk soon as well."

"Great. Let's put an APB out on the vehicle, just in case it is related."

"Already done."

Michael supposed it was just as likely that the killer went out the back door as the front. When he checked it later, it also wasn't bolted, and could have been locked before it was closed.

The press demanded a statement before he left, so he gave them the usual no comments and "We're still investigating." They didn't expect anything else, veterans all, though they knew they needed something to show their audiences. TV crime shows had led everyone to believe the case should be cracked in an hour, though truthfully he knew he might be starting an investigation that could be open for years.

God, he hoped not. If the latest victim had wounded the killer enough to end the guy's career, he would be eternally grateful.

Rosen, he noticed, was not among the crowd of her fellow reporters demanding a statement.

VERA ROSEN WAS MAKING A REPORT, though not for her editor. That would come, hours later, but what went into it depended a lot on what happened in this room tonight.

There was danger enough here, speaking to Victor about such things. He was known to the public at large as Victor Stumpp, president and CEO of Stumpptown Systems. And he was that. But to a very small group of people, including both of the others in the room, he was more than that. And currently he was not acting in his capacity as head of Stumpptown Systems. Instead, he was speaking as the Alpha of his region.

The other man standing near Victor's desk added an extra unknown element, though. She guessed he was Gregor Theissen, Alpha of Southern California and she happened to know Victor's original mentor. His presence here lent strength to a suspicion she had about the deaths.

"Hello, Veer," Victor said brightly as she entered the room. "What did you learn from the crime scene?"

His use of her familiar name along with the cheerful attitude she knew would not be an accident. It was a signal to Gregor that she was a friend and not just a flunky —a way of letting them both know that she had his trust and his support.

She let herself relax, just a little bit. "Not much more than I told you before I went," she replied. "I wasn't able to get in. By the time I arrived, the police were already there."

"And you didn't try sneaking in?" the other man, standing by a filing cabinet, asked. He looked to be in his early eighties, though Veer was sure he was much older than that.

It was a stupid suggestion. And although Veer knew better not to say so in so many words, she would not kowtow to him, either. Victor may have to answer to him, but she only had to answer to Victor. That carried its own ironies, but that was a thought for another day. It would be dangerous to even consider that right now, lest either of the two men realize what she was thinking.

"Like I said, there were police all over the place. No way to get in without them knowing," she replied instead.

"No way a Human could get in, perhaps?" Victor put in. Which was really just too much.

"I should have transformed right there? Because a wolf

nosing around in the middle of the city, at a crime scene where the chief suspect is a large dog wouldn't have raised any notice at all?" She tried to sound more amused than confrontational, to let him know his suggestion was no better than a joke.

She was already tired of these petty power games, keeping her standing while giving her report, questioning her. Doubting her. From Victor, she could take it. He had earned her respect. He was, after all, her Alpha. This stranger, Alpha or no, had no such claim over her. She didn't like him, and she didn't like the way Victor followed his lead.

She continued, "You weren't there. Don't try second guessing my decisions from the safety of your armchair."

"Look," she immediately gentled her tone, but still chastised her elders, "I'll get the information you want, but I'll get it my own way and in my own time. I'll use my own judgment while I'm out there about when to proceed and how."

Victor looked amused, which was better than angry she supposed. Gregor looked like he was about to say something.

"No," she interrupted before he could start, "This isn't a negotiation. If you don't like it, do it yourselves. Or get someone else to go for you."

She kept the fear out of her voice as she spoke. She was all too aware of her danger. She hadn't been able to find proof - yet - but rumor held that people who had angered either of these two men disappeared in the past. But she had to establish her place early, and firmly. To do any less would bring its own dangers.

Despite her words, she desperately didn't want to take the risk of them giving the task to someone else. If she got the information from the police, or even worked with them, she might yet be able to turn this whole situation to her own advantage.

"Do you have a plan?" Victor finally responded. She knew he could sense her relief, but she didn't let her guard down.

"Yes," she replied simply, but didn't elaborate.

Gregor glared at her, and then took a step toward her. She met his gaze. From what she understood, it would be a breach of protocol for him to do anything here, in Victor's territory. She hoped her understanding was right. He was stopped in his tracks by the laughter of the man behind the desk. Gregor reeled back in that direction.

"Hell, you asked for that, Gregor!"

"The fuck," the older man said. "You give your people far too much leeway, Victor."

"Ah, kids these days," Stumpp replied, leaning back in his chair behind his desk. "What are you going to do?" His tone was mocking, and the other didn't miss it.

"You keep them in line is what you fucking do." He'd forgotten about Veer, and leaned toward Victor now, putting both his hands on the desk. "If you'd done that, I wouldn't be here!" He stalked back toward his chair, turned but didn't sit down.

That didn't seem likely. She decided to assume her earlier deductions were correct and see where that took her.

"Shouldn't we wait to see who it is before making that assumption?" she asked him. "After all, didn't the killings start in your territory?"

Both men turned to look at her in surprise.

"One in San Diego and another in Stockton. And then one in Ashland last month."

Victor looked to Gregor. He hadn't known.

"In that order," she told him. "The first was the night of the full moon last month."

"Weeks between each, then?" Victor asked.

"Yes. But then two killed back to back up here. Any idea why?" She directed the question to Gregor.

To his credit, he hesitated only slightly before giving a

slight shake of his head. "I didn't even know about the one in Ashland."

"Is that all of them, then?" Victor asked, turning his attention back to Gregor.

"All that I know about for sure," Veer responded. "I've found some others that may fit the pattern and I'll follow up on those. Of course, there could easily be another dozen we'll never hear about."

Nobody said anything for a moment. Then Victor brought it back to the important point. "We've got a Werewolf, running around killing people blatantly, and leaving evidence behind. He seems to be working his way North. Maybe hitchhiking up I-5?"

"Or she. Or they. There might be more than one," Veer added. "It could just be coincidence that they seem to be in a line."

"Oh, now that's a comforting thought," Victor said. "Let's assume it's all the same person. Why change his pattern when he gets to Portland? And he's being loud about it. Almost as if he wants to get caught."

"Maybe someone who's trying to reveal us? Know anyone who wants to do that?" Gregor asked.

"Only about half the clan," Victor replied. "Same for you, I take it?"

"They know better than to do anything," Gregor replied testily.

Veer knew there were Were who were unhappy with the strict code of secrecy - she'd spoken to several who'd expressed as much. That there were so many, and that the Alphas knew, but were unconcerned, was a surprise. Perhaps this was nothing new - just one more thing they were used to dealing with. That would be something worth following up, but at a later time.

"Kids these days," Victor echoed his earlier sentiment. "What if we have a rogue? Somebody who's creating more either on purpose or accidentally? Newly awakened, no training, no control?" he asked.

"You think the killings could be done by his victims? The pattern could be different because the actual perpetrators are different."

"I hope not. But it is a possibility," Gregor said. "Whatever it is, it has something to do with Portland. They were more or less careful until they got up here."

"Well, we'll have police evidence soon. That means DNA, hair samples, prints, whatever they can find. We'll be able to tell if both the Portland killings were the same person," Victor said.

"And it doesn't bother you that your police will have all of that as well?" Gregor asked him.

"If it becomes a problem, we'll find a way to make it disappear." He had already confirmed that he didn't have anybody within the police department. Veer wondered how he'd manage to pull that off. She wondered if even he knew. Could he be less confident than he sounded?

"Besides," he continued, "I'm kind of curious about what the analysis will find."

"Other than who it is?" Gregor asked.

"For one, will it be human or canine DNA? How deep does the change go?"

Gregor merely raised an eyebrow in response.

"There must be some mechanism for the change, even if we have no idea what it is," Victor explained. "I'm curious if our overall mass changes as well. It seems to, but I can't imagine how."

Veer was used to this from Victor. It was one of the things she liked about the man: his insatiable curiosity. God, what an ally he'd make. All she'd have to do is convince him to betray everything he'd sworn to protect and go against everything he was. Right. But then again hadn't she been doing exactly that herself for the last three years?

"Seriously? This is what concerns you?" Gregor asked him.

"Don't you wonder what we are? How it all works? Where we really come from?" Victor pressed his mentor.

"We're Were. Inheritors of a power passed down to a chosen few since the dawn of pre-history. Given superior intelligence and strength and longevity by the great wolf Fenrir. Who cares how it works?" Gregor responded.

"I do. Why don't you?"

"There's no science to it, Victor; it's magic," Gregor replied.

"Bullshit. There's no such thing as magic."

Gregor laughed aloud at that. "No such thing as...Victor, you're a fucking *werewolf!*"

TWO

THEFT AND LIES

It was easy enough to set up a distraction to get Diaz out of the precinct building quickly. A simple favor from a friend who placed a call from a phone booth across town asking to meet him, promising information. When nobody was there to meet him at the assigned spot, he'd come back. Another minor mystery that would never be resolved.

Fifteen minutes after she'd sent her friend the text letting him know she was in place, Detective Diaz rushed out the front door of the station. Apparently, it had only taken that long because he had to hunt down a working phone booth so it couldn't be traced back to him.

The operation would be risky, but this whole situation might be exactly what she needed, if she were bold enough and clever enough to take advantage of it.

Once inside, she started toward the front desk, then raised her gaze and let a relieved smile cross her face. She hurried over toward a waiting area where several people were already milling about. Hopefully the simple ruse would be enough to convince anyone watching that she'd seen whoever she'd come to see, and they didn't have to worry about her checking in now.

Veer had been in the police station a few times before and was familiar with the layout. On the ground floor there were holding and processing areas as well as a waiting room with a coffee pot. An exit toward the back presumably led to the underground parking garage. Along one side of the interior there was a raised section, just a few steps up, with an antique looking wooden railing around it. Likely it was part of an adjoining building with a higher floor whose connecting walls had been removed decades ago when the precinct expanded. It was big enough to hold half a dozen desks and a couple of small conference rooms. These desks would belong to the detectives. There were a few extra chairs that could be moved around to allow a guest to sit at a desk, usually witnesses or low risk suspects being interviewed or otherwise processed. Nobody was using any of them now.

This raised section was her target, and where it could get tricky. She'd have to find his desk, then get into his files, without drawing any attention to herself, in an area where she probably wasn't supposed to be.

She walked over to where the extra chairs sat against the wall, trying to hide her nervousness and act like she belonged there. She picked one up and started into the room. It only took her a moment to find the desk with the detective's nameplate on it. She set the chair down next to it and took a seat.

She pulled out her phone again and pretended to be reading it, while looking up every few seconds and fidgeting, trying to convey an impression of someone waiting impatiently. A detective across the way glanced up at her, but then back to his own paperwork, ignoring her. She kept an eye on him while pretending to look at the phone, and carefully opened a file drawer with her other hand. The file she wanted was the first one. She pulled it out quickly and laid it flat on the desk. Pretending to ignore it again, she scanned the room, while feigning interest only in her phone and the front door.

The detective was looking her way again. She didn't acknowledge seeing him at all. She scowled at her phone and looked toward the front door again, right through the detective watching her. Finally, he looked away, and she flipped open the file. Making certain the phone's sound was off, she took a picture of the first page. She repeated the process several more times. Glance at the door again, wait for the detective to look another direction, then flip a page in the file and take another picture. If he suspected anything, he didn't try to interfere. After a few more minutes, he got up and walked away.

Finally, she reached the end of the file, closed it, and slid it back into the drawer. Relieved, she stood up, put the phone back in her pocket, and walked out of the station into the city.

To make sure she wasn't being followed, she first turned away from the direction she'd parked her motorcycle and walked down the street. She passed the same detective who'd been watching her inside the station, sitting in an unmarked car. Did he know? Most likely he suspected something. He couldn't be sure, though. If he knew what she'd been up to, she'd be under arrest now.

She continued past the car. He was studiously - too studiously — looking at something on the car's laptop computer's screen. She suppressed a smile. Was he intentionally mocking her earlier attempt to be sneaky? Or was he hoping she hadn't noticed him? As long as he only suspected, she was good. Now she'd just have to keep him from learning anything more. She decided to take a walk. If he wanted to follow her, he'd have to earn it. Plus, it was a nice day: overcast, with just a light mist in the air. Perfect Portland October weather.

He started the car and drove up the street directly away

from her. She cut to the right and walked another block. In a couple of blocks she was at waterfront park. She'd been hoping for a bigger crowd, but not really expecting it.

She walked through the park for a couple of blocks, hoping to lose him under the bridge. She didn't see him when she got there, but just to make sure she took the stairway up to the bridge and started across it. She did her best to blend in with the few other pedestrians doing the same thing. At the top of the stairway, she stopped to do a few stretches, as if she was a jogger about to get started. The movement let her look around while hopefully not looking like she was trying to look around. She started across the bridge. A quarter of the way there, she turned and hurried back the way she came. If he had followed her this far, he'd be committed to crossing. She would be long gone by the time he could get back.

She didn't see him the rest of the way back to her bike.

WHEN MICHAEL GOT BACK to the precinct, Phil was on the phone. But he waved Michael over to him when he saw him.

"So why don't you just arrest her now?" he was saying to whoever it was he was talking to. "I guess. What do you hope to learn?"

He listened for a moment then replied, "I'd assume it would be for her paper. But if you think there's more to it than that, then go ahead," he added. "Michael just walked in, I'll fill him in. You sure you don't need backup?"

Michael raised an eyebrow in query and Phil filled him in. "You had a visitor while you were out."

"A visitor?" Michael asked, a little confused.

"That reporter, Rosen."

"She seems to be popping up a lot recently. What'd she want?"

"Apparently, to see your desk. She didn't speak to anyone, and left before you got back."

"And that's probably what that call was about," he said. He rushed over to his desk to check if anything was missing or out of place.

"What call?"

"About half an hour ago, I got a call from someone who said he had information about the murders. When I got there, there was nobody."

"She may have gotten hold of one of your files. Sam's tailing her now."

Michael could guess which file.

Phil led him into the conference room before calling Sam back. He put the phone on speaker and set it down on the table between them.

"She hasn't seen me yet," Sam's voice said over the speaker. "She tried to lose me under the Morrison bridge, but I played a hunch at what she was doing, and came back, switched cars, and caught her doubling back. Oh...now that's interesting..." he said.

After a few seconds of silence, Michael prompted, "What's going on?"

"Sorry - recognized the building she parked in front of. Stumpptown Systems."

"Don't know it," Michael told him.

"Renovated historic building attached to the White Stag building," Sam replied.

Michael had been in Portland long enough at least to recognize the name, even though the sign had read simply "Portland, Oregon" since he'd lived here.

"Yeah, she's going inside," Sam said.

"What would she be doing there?" Phil asked.

"She went there from here, whatever the reason," Michael answered.

"I think she read through one of your files," Sam said.

"Phil told me. Pretty sure it's the serial killer," Michael replied.

"Anything in there to connect Stumpptown?"

"Not unless she saw something I didn't. Nothing in it to connect anybody," Michael responded.

"I'd give anything to see who she was meeting with right now, or what they're talking about," Sam said.

Michael retrieved the suspected file from his desk and brought it into the conference room. They paged through it as they waited, but he didn't see anything useful. Lots of raw data from the crime scenes, but nothing to indicate any connections to anyone specific.

"I didn't see which file she actually got," Sam said. "Could it be something else entirely?"

"I doubt it," Michael said. "She was at both the last two scenes."

"She's coming back out," Sam finally said. Michael had been poring over the file. Michael waved to Phil to come back into the room.

"She's heading West now, not toward her home. Looks like she's got another stop to make." Michael and Phil listened quietly as Sam narrated.

"Yep, west, she's getting onto Sunset." Highway 26, Michael translated, one of the main roads out of town. They kept listening and turned their attention back to the file as Sam occasionally narrated his drive. "Beaverton. Hillsboro. Heading up into the hills."

"So...she breaks into your desk, reads your files, visits a tech company, then...heads to the coast?"

"Oh wait, she's turning off. Road's not marked. Just says 'Private Drive' and Google doesn't show a name for it," Sam said.

"Okay, be careful. It's probably someone's house she's going to, and they're going to see you if you get close to it. Likely they don't get a lot of visitors."

"She probably wouldn't recognize me. If anyone asks, I'll just tell them I got lost and am trying to turn around. Fortunately, this road winds a lot. Can't see more than maybe a hundred feet ahead at best, so she can't see me back here. Of course, I can't see her either, but there's nowhere to turn off yet."

For several more minutes, all they could hear was the sound of the car on the gravel road. Then Sam spoke again. "Oh, hey, parking lot. Hold on... There, I backed up a bit."

They could hear him turn off the car.

"Looks like a small office building of some sort. No markings on the building, but there's a big stone wall. I'm gonna take a peek over it and see what I can see."

A car door opened and closed, followed by the sound of Sam walking on gravel.

"Only one other car here," Sam said, and read off a license plate number. Michael wrote it down. "I'm going to put you in my pocket for a bit. Keep quiet; I'll let you know when it's safe to speak again."

Phil hit the mute button on the phone so they could talk without broadcasting anything.

"I don't like this," Michael said.

"Should we call him back?"

He thought about it for a second. "Let's give it a few more minutes. He's smart enough to leave if there's any real danger."

"It looks more like a business than a house," Sam said again. "I don't see anyone around. Just a yard and an expanse of woods on the other side of the wall. Okay, trying the direct approach." They heard knocking.

"No answer," he said. Then, a few seconds later, "Door's unlocked."

Michael was about to say something about that, then remembered Sam wouldn't be able to hear him.

"Hello?" they heard him call out. "Anyone there?" He waited a moment then spoke to the phone again, "Yeah, looks like an office. A couple of chairs against one wall. Counter with a window - dark in here, nobody home."

"Another door with a window." They heard the rattle of a knob. "This one's locked. Dark in there, too. Metal table in the middle of the room, buncha machinery around it. Medical facility of some sort?"

Phil and Michael exchanged a look. "No idea. No major medical facilities around there that I'm aware of," Phil said.

"Okay, last door," Sam's voice continued. "This one's open. Hallway with a bunch of lockers, benches down the middle. Hm. Showers over here, like a gym. No signs. I don't know if this is the men's or women's room, though. Most of the lockers are open, and empty, and...a set of men's clothing in one of them. So, that answers which...wait, no...bingo," he said a few seconds later. "It's what she was wearing. Guess she changed here. As did whoever she's meeting. No bag or anything, just all her clothes in the locker. No locks on them. She left her phone, keys, wallet, everything."

"So... Gym?" Phil said.

Michael shrugged. "Awful long way to go to work out."

"Let's see what's through door number three," Sam said. "Back yard. Little wooden deck. Too small to be anything more than a landing. Bit of bark dust yard, then a trailhead into the woods. Private hiking spot? Whoever maintains this place they sure like their privacy. That wall's gotta be eight feet."

Michael hit the mute button. "I don't like this," he said. "Come on back, we'll check into it later."

Sam must have turned the volume all the way down on his end, though, because he didn't respond, just continued his narration.

"Heading up the trail." They could hear him breathing and walking along for maybe ten minutes. Finally, he spoke again. "Lotsa woods, but the trail's maintained," he said. "Wait...What's that? Holy shit!" he yelled, and it sounded like he was running.

"Sam? Sam, what's going on?"

All they could hear was Sam's heavy breathing. Then, "Shit, which way was the front?"

Something heavy crashed into underbrush. Sounds of a scuffle. Then a scream.

"Oh god! Oh god, my leg!"

"What? What is it? Get out of there!" Michael yelled, forgetting for a second that Sam couldn't hear him. He leapt to his feet.

"The wall!" They heard from the phone. Phil was carrying it in front of him as they both ran toward the door to the parking garage.

"I... Oh my god. Made it to the top. Hah! Take that, scruffy!"

Michael and Phil both paused at the door. Michael wanted to move, but they'd lose contact with Sam if they went any further.

"Holy..." they heard him cry out, then a scream of pain. A loud crash and some kind of terrible thrashing sound.

Sam's cries grew weaker, then stopped. There was silence for a second, then some kind of low animal growl.

"C'mon," Phil said, and they headed to his car in the underground garage.

When they re-emerged, Michael tried to call him again, over and over, with no success. Phil radioed for backup as they drove, heading toward the highway.

THE TILLAMOOK COUNTY sheriff already knew of the location, and guided them in. The local police had already found Sam's body and the coroner removed it. His car was still parked down the road and aside from police the parking lot was empty.

"I'm sorry about your friend," the deputy told them when they'd stepped out of their cars. "But it doesn't look like a murder. Your friend stumbled into a private wolf sanctuary. To all appearances, it's a wild animal attack."

"A wolf sanctuary? I didn't know we had one up here."

"They're not open to the public. Apparently, they're privately funded."

"Is that even legal?" Michael asked.

"Guess so. They get regular visits from a vet in town, and a guy from the government comes out once a year to inspect the place."

"You said it was privately funded?" Phil asked.

"Yeah."

"By who?"

"Dunno - some company. No idea who owns it or who works for them, other than Walt."

"Who's Walt?" Michael asked.

"Caretaker. Lives up in Manning, but we haven't been able to reach him yet."

He led them not to the front door of the building, but up a path into the woods. After a short while, it curved back and ran into a tall stone wall. "We found the cell phone just on the other side. Body was further in. Dragged off."

He wondered if Sam had been dead by then, or if he was dragged, injured and terrified while the wolves tore at him. A horrible way to go.

"I'd like to see the inside."

The sheriff offered his hands as a step to boost Michael to the top of the wall.

"Take a peek, but don't go in. Don't touch the wire." He stepped into the cupped hands and pulled himself up to where he could see over. A well-maintained path covered in bark dust led up to and along the wall. The covering was disturbed directly under where he was. Blood stained the ground.

Eight feet, Sam had said, and Michael saw he was right. And if it enclosed the entire area, that'd be a lot of stone.

"Hell of a wall," he said.

"Gotta be to keep the wolves in."

"They just roam free in there? Isn't that dangerous?"

"Only to people who go inside. Which is why they don't have visitors."

"How many wolves are there?"

"Maybe a dozen? You'd have to ask Walt for an exact account."

"I'd like to talk to him."

"I'll give him your number next time I see him."

He let it go at that. He was outside his jurisdiction here, and didn't want to antagonize anyone who could help him.

"Do you see Walt often?"

"From time to time. I've helped him load roadkill deer into his truck for the wolves sometimes."

That was interesting. Made sense though. They had to eat, and the area they were confined to was probably far too small to sustain maybe a dozen wolves.

IN THE END, the sheriff wouldn't allow them onto the grounds. Even though an officer had died, they were not treating it as a crime scene, which meant they'd need a warrant to go in any further.

The next morning, back at the precinct, Michael was at his desk on the phone with the coroner's office when Phil came up the three steps to the detectives' landing and pulled up a chair to his desk.

"They've confirmed the cause of death as animal mauling," Michael told him after hanging up the phone.

"Bullshit," Phil replied. "I checked into it. Do you know how many people are killed by wolves in this country?"

"Tell me."

"Twenty."

"Is that per month, or year, or...?"

"Ever."

"What do you mean 'ever?'"

"I mean, in the entire history of the United States, there have been a total of twenty people confirmed to have been killed by wolves. It almost never happens, especially to adults. And half of those were probably murdered and then literally thrown to the wolves. And wolves on a preserve wouldn't be either hungry or rabid, which is the only reason wolves ever attack humans. Maybe Sam was killed by wolves, but that doesn't mean it's not murder."

"I agree," Michael said. "Too much of a coincidence. Shot, poisoned, stabbed, car accident, even breaking his neck after falling off the wall, I might have bought. But mauled to death, like the murder victims? No, he found something."

"Hey, Diaz," a voice called from behind him. He turned to

see Detective Boyd coming toward the stairs. She nodded back the way she came. "Captain wants to see you."

He glanced and Phil and they both went down into the captain's office.

Police Captain Frank Billings sat behind his desk. A short stocky man, he looked perfectly at place behind his desk, on which piled papers nearly overwhelmed his keyboard and mouse. A well-stained coffee cup sat on an empty spot on one corner, half full, and Michael didn't even want to guess how old it was. His door was open, and he looked up when the pair entered.

"Ah, there you are," he told them. He motioned to chairs then swiveled the monitor most of the way around so they could see.

"What is it?" Michael asked.

"Footage from the camera in Sam's car," Billings said. He started the video. It was the low-resolution black-and-white view of security camera footage, showing the inside of a police cruiser. The car was parked, on a forest road, and the lights were off.

As they watched, Michael thought he saw a brief blur of movement in one corner. A second later, the dome light came on. An arm reached into view, followed by a bare shoulder and the back of a man's head. There was broken glass on the driver's seat - the man must have smashed the window to get into the car. He slid fully into view and they saw he was completely naked. He was in his early thirties perhaps. He obviously cared a great deal about his appearance, from the well toned muscles to his short perfectly coiffed hairstyle and carefully trimmed beard.

He picked up a notebook that had been sitting on the passenger's seat, riffled through it briefly, then carefully tossed it behind him, out the door. He spent the next few moments doing a quick search of the car, checking under seats, behind the visors, and in the glove box. Finally, he reached up, looked directly into the camera, and reached for it with one hand. The image went dark.

"We have the car back. They're searching for prints now," Captain Billing said. "He found the camera and pulled it loose. No idea what he did with it, but the recorder's a separate unit. He missed it. He must have picked up Sam's notebook and taken it with him as well. For now, we are assuming he is somehow connected to the murders, and to Sam's death. And yes, despite what Tillamook says, we're still considering this a murder."

"And Rosen was just moments ahead of him."

"So, how is she involved in all this?"

"I intend to find out."

MICHAEL TOOK HIS OWN CAR. No need to upset the neighbors, he figured. He found Vera Rosen's house easily enough: a modest building, it looked like one or two bedrooms, in a quiet Northeast neighborhood just off Klickitat street. He parked on the street nearby and walked up the driveway to her front door. As he approached, he could see her through the large living room windows. She was sitting at a desk, facing a pair of large computer screens in front of her. From his approach, he couldn't see what was on them.

Rosen looked up before he knocked, setting down her coffee cup, and stood to answer the door. She adjusted the large bathrobe she was wearing as she did so. He realized that this may be early morning for her. Covering the crime beat, he could easily imagine her working mostly nights.

"Officer Diaz," she greeted him. She seemed pleasantly

surprised to see him, but he didn't buy it. An appearance of friendliness could be a tool. In her line of work she would be as much an expert in getting information from people as he was. "What brings you by?"

"I'd just like to ask you a few questions, Ms. Rosen," he replied.

"I suppose turnabout is fair play," she said with a smile. "Come on in. Call me Veer." Her tone was still pleasant, as if this were a social occasion. They both knew it wasn't.

"Michael, then," he said. Normally he'd encourage, if not demand, the use of his title and last name. It subtly reinforced his authority. In this case, though, he decided that playing along with her casual routine might be a better tactic.

She stepped back as he entered and closed the door behind him.

Next to where her desk was set up in the front room, he looked over the bookshelves. Though neatly arranged, they didn't seem to be sorted in any particular order. Modern politics sat next to Civil War history. A couple of travel guides next to three different biographies of Nellie Bly, a name that seemed vaguely familiar though he couldn't place it at the moment.

"Coffee?" she asked, heading toward the kitchen. "Just made a pot. I'm afraid all I have for it is milk."

"I prefer it, actually. And thank you." The thought of poison flashed but briefly through his mind. He thought she might excuse herself to go change into something more than the bathrobe. She did not. She seemed utterly unconcerned with her state of dress. Not seductive or sexy. Just a complete lack of self-consciousness. Did she intend to make herself seem more vulnerable? Her manner of acting did the opposite, though. He took his cup and seated himself at the kitchen table, across from her.

"How do you know Victor Stumpp?" he opened with,

hoping she'd be caught by surprise. If she was, she didn't show it. She'd been ready for the question, he realized. She must have figured out she was being followed, so she would know they knew of her visit to Stumpp. She hesitated before answering. Just long enough to think up a lie, or to consider one then reject it.

She answered, "The wolf preserve is owned by Victor Stumpp. I had an idea that these killings may have been done by a wolf, not a dog. So," she continued, setting down a mug of coffee on the table in front of him before taking a seat opposite him, "I wanted to talk to someone who knew something about wolves. I knew of this place from an earlier story I had done, so I went there first."

"And what did you find?" he asked her. He carefully sipped his coffee, keeping his composure no more tense than if he'd been discussing the weather.

"Nothing. I couldn't find the caretaker. Or anyone else. So, after a while, I gave up and left, figuring I could come back later," she replied, just as calmly.

"And that's it? You went all the way out there, stood around for a few minutes, and left?"

"Pretty much. I went inside, looked around a bit, realized I was walking alone into the woods with several wolves, and got a bit creeped out, remembering Little Red Riding Hood. So, I came back."

That wouldn't explain why she'd changed clothes. She was lying, but he wasn't sure how or why yet. He decided to try a different tack.

"You never saw or heard Sam?"

That one drew a slight reaction. But she quickly covered it up. It was enough to let him know there was something there - but it might have been as innocuous as a completely unexpected question.

"Sam?" she asked, apparently puzzled. He had to fight back his own anger now. Sam had been a good cop, and she had, wittingly or not, led him to his death.

"Sam Bailey. He was a police officer. He was killed yesterday at the preserve, after following you there." He deliberately used "was killed" not "died" to see her reaction.

"I'm sorry," she sounded like she meant it. "If I'd have known I was still being followed..."

He cut her off. "You'd have done exactly the same thing." He tried to keep the anger out of his tone. He couldn't afford to alienate her, not at this stage. She knew something. Or suspected something. And whatever she knew and wasn't telling had gotten a good man killed. There'd be more to come. He knew it.

But how to get the truth out of her? She was an experienced investigator and would probably know all the same tricks he did. Unless he could get her into an interrogation room, she couldn't be threatened. Probably not even then. Perhaps an appeal to compassion might work?

"Ms. Rosen," he began, letting a tone of earnest pleading into his voice, "if you know anything at all, I need to know. As I'm sure you're aware, the girl the other night wasn't the first to be killed. And I don't think she'll be the last. Any information you can give me could save lives."

"I'm sorry, detective. I really can't tell you anything. All I have is hunches and ideas myself, nothing solid at all."

Now we're getting somewhere, he thought.

"Then tell me your ideas. Maybe there's something worth following up. Or something that meshes with other data." He told her.

"Did you get any prints at the crime scene?" she asked him.

"You saw the report," he replied in a neutral tone, as if reiterating a known fact.

She acknowledged the point with a brief smile and slight nod. "I only saw a photograph of a single paw print. That won't be enough." She ticked the points off on her fingers, "Wolves and dogs have nearly identical paw structure. They both have four pads, and the same alignment of claws. You need a set of them to tell the difference. Dogs' front legs tend to be farther apart than their rear legs, so there would be prints next to each other. Wolves tracks, on the other hand, will be all in a line, but their stride is longer, so they'll be farther apart laterally."

He wasn't sure if such measurements had been taken. He'd have to check in the morning and order them if they had not.

"I thought you said you couldn't find the keeper," he said. It was almost a question.

"I didn't."

"Then where did you learn all this?"

"I googled it this morning,"

He laughed at that. "All right, Ms. Rosen, I've taken up enough of your time. I know you read that report. And we both know that alone is a crime. I suppose you were just doing your job. I'm willing to overlook it this time, on two conditions."

"Which are?"

"One, you don't release any information from there that we don't release," he said.

"Agreed, granted that the condition is lifted once the case is over," she added.

"Fair enough," Michael replied. "But over is when I say it is. Maybe once we've made an arrest. Maybe only after a conviction."

"Good enough for now," she accepted. "And your second condition?"

"You share anything you learn in your own research," he told her. "Even if it isn't conclusive, I'll decide what's worth following up."

"I'll continue sharing if you will," she told him, ignoring the fact that the initial "sharing" of his data wasn't exactly his plan.

"All right, as long as you accept there will likely be some things I can't tell you," he told her.

"That works, as long as I get full access to the finalized report," she replied.

"Okay," he said, "I can accept that. And you stay out of my files until then." He had a good idea that her promise would mean more to her than any threat of law.

WHEN HE HAD RETURNED to the station, he pulled the file out of his desk drawer and found the picture of the single paw print. He had remembered it correctly after all. Dogs and wolves both have four pads, she'd said. So why did this one have five?

THREE
TAKING THE FIELD

Grant Talman set down his morning paper. He considered for a moment getting a television so he could see what they were saying about him on the news. TV wasted too much time, though. It was for unimaginative people with nothing important to do. In the paper, he could skim the articles and search for mentions of himself. Today, they weren't hard to find; he was front page news.

They claimed the police could find no connection between the "victims." That's because the police would be looking for motives for murder. What they didn't know was that he didn't mean to kill any of them. It was just so hard to control himself when in wolf form. The others, before he'd come home to Portland, they had been meant as food. But he wasn't looking for food here. He was looking for disciples. But they were so fragile.

Maybe he should go back to San Diego. Hunt down the creature that had done this to him and make him explain it. He'd come back to Portland searching for his old crew. Maybe biting some of them, giving them the same gift he'd been given.

Even in ten years, the city had changed. His old hunting ground was now called The Pearl and full of the same people who ten years ago would never deign to cross the hills and go out in "that" part of the city at night, and all his old friends had moved away years ago. Screw them. He didn't need them anyway. He'd always been faster, stronger, and smarter than those around him. The wolf blood had only increased all that. Even in human form, he found he could see better, hear better, and even taste so much more than he ever could before.

There must be others like him out there, somewhere. After all, one had made him, hadn't they? But the only other one he'd ever met had been in San Diego. He stopped at that thought. As far as he knew, anyway. Nobody recognized him for what he was. For all he knew, he'd met hundreds of others without knowing them. That was almost an intolerable thought. It was also, he quickly decided, unlikely. He'd been scouring the papers for any story of dog or wolf attacks. Aside from a couple he'd found in which witnesses clearly identified the dog in question, the only reports were of him.

It amused him to see the complete befuddlement of the police. A serial killer who brought his dog with him to do his killing? That was their best guess? He laughed out loud. The world was his for the taking. He was something new, something so far outside the limited experience of their little minds they'd never be able to figure it out.

What should he do next? Stay in Portland for a while, he thought. There was no limit to what he could get away with. He'd try again to make some more. A companion, but someone he could control. Maybe a girl. Yeah, that was it. He'd find a house with two or three people in it. Maybe a parent or two, and a teenage girl. Perhaps after eating the parents he'd be sated enough not to kill the girl. She'd be scared, confused, not understanding what was happening to her. And he'd be there to explain it all. Somebody rich, too, so that after winning her to his side, he'd have access to the family fortune. That would do it.

He put on his "working" outfit - sandals, stretchy sweatpants, and t-shirt, and went out on the hunt for what he needed.

———

"IT'S A WERE. It's gotta be a Were," Carl said again, watching the report on TV. He turned his chair toward Kevin and Shelly, who were sitting beside each other on the couch.

"You're probably right," Shelly responded. For a moment he felt triumphant about that, but it was short lived.

"Maybe," Kevin said. "But maybe not. In any case, what good does it do us?"

"There's gotta be a way we can use this! Hell, the cops are looking for this guy. If they catch him..."

"Then they'll probably kill him. Sicko like this isn't going to be easy to take alive."

"But what if they do?" Carl insisted. "And if they find out..."

"How're they going to catch him? They're looking for a guy with a big dog," Kevin answered him, then in a mocking voice, "Uhh, gee, officer, I don't got no dog! Oh, well, better let you go, then. Sorry for the inconvenience."

"We could tell them..." Carl started.

"Talk to the police?" Shelly answered, obviously horrified by the idea.

"Why not? Like you said, they'll never be able to catch this guy on their own," Carl started again and was again interrupted by Kevin.

"What're you gonna say? 'Hello, officer, I happen to know

that the guy you're looking for is really a werewolf.' How do I know? Oh, well, I am one too, you see... Hello? Hello? I wonder why he keeps hanging up..." He mimed looking in confusion at an imaginary phone in his hand.

Carl hated this about him. About most people, actually. Just because he couldn't immediately imagine how something could be done didn't mean there wasn't a way. He usually remained silent when people were like this. This was important, though, so he gathered his courage and spoke up.

"It's...it's an idea, not a plan," he said. "I don't know how to do it yet, but isn't that what we said we wanted to do?" They both looked surprised at his vehemence. He was a little surprised himself. But he pushed forward. "How...how are we ever going to reveal ourselves if...if we just dismiss every possible opportunity that comes along?" He raised his voice a bit more, overriding Kevin's attempt to speak, "Maybe this isn't it. I'm not saying it is, but shouldn't we...I mean...I don't know, maybe at least consider it?" His voice lost its force at the end, petering to nothing.

Kevin started to speak, but this time it was Shelly who interrupted him, to Carl's surprise again. "No, maybe Carl's right. There might be a way we can use this." When nobody immediately said anything in response, "The cops have got to be busy, right? And Stumpp's gotta be losing his fucking mind searching for this guy."

Carl hadn't thought of that last. Of course the Alpha would know about what was going on. There's no way he would not be monitoring news of anything that looked even vaguely like a rogue Were.

"So we attack while they're all distracted?" Kevin asked, without anyone interrupting him.

If he was going to take it seriously, Carl was prepared to forgive him. "What do you mean?" he asked.

"The cops are looking for this guy. The Alpha's looking for this guy. What if we do what we were talking about earlier, like right now."

"What were we talking about earlier?" Carl asked him, confused.

"Not you - Shelly and I were discussing it before you got here,"

"I don't know if 'discussing' is the right word," Shelly interjected.

"Well, whatever. If we just turn a few right now, it's perfect. If anyone finds out, they'll assume it's related to this killer guy, and nobody will come looking for us. We won't end up like Stan."

Carl hadn't known Stan well. Kevin and Shelly had known him longer. It was only a few months after Carl was turned that their friend, after being denied permission to turn his girlfriend, went ahead and did it anyway. Less than a month later they were both dead in what the police ruled a murder-suicide, but everybody here knew better.

There was a flaw in Kevin's idea, Carl thought, and he voiced it. "Wouldn't that go both ways?"

"Both what ways?"

"Won't they also assume that the killer is related to us. Or is us?"

"Who's nay-saying now?"

"I'm not nay-saying!" he objected, eliciting a snort of laughter from Shelly. Dammit, she was supposed to be on his side.

"So we're careful not to get caught," Kevin said.

"Who do we turn?" Carl asked. Everybody he knew was either already Were or was someone he didn't want to become Were.

"I say just a bunch of nobodies. We'll take 'em, drag 'em out to the woods, bite 'em, and let 'em go."

"Umm..." Carl started but wasn't sure how to object. Shelly did it instead.

"You can't just grab people off the street and throw them into the back of a van!" she said.

"Why not?" Kevin asked. "I've got a van. We're not going to hurt them. Maybe they'll be scared for a few hours. They'll get over it. We bite a few, then they bite a few, then they bite a few..." he said.

"And in ten iterations, everyone in the world is Were," Carl finished for him.

He didn't know about the whole grabbing people off the street thing, but if that's what it took to move forward...

"But the cool thing about this is eventually the cops, or the press, or somebody, will find that there are werewolves. And this killer rogue will give them a reason to be looking for them, so, especially if we push it a bit behind the scenes, it'll be impossible for them to ignore it or cover it up."

Ideas aren't plans, and plans aren't victories, Carl reminded himself. He didn't remember where he'd first heard it, but he liked the saying. After talking about the idea for more than a year, it looked like it was finally starting to move into the realm of a plan.

"IS ALL THAT FROM THE MAULER?" Phil asked, pulling up a chair to Michael's desk. There were open folders, stacks of papers, photographs, newspaper clippings, all in various piles on his desk.

"Afraid so. And please tell me we're not calling him that," Michael responded.

"I think you're going to need a bigger desk," Phil said.

Michael didn't laugh. "Or find a wall to start pinning things to. Take a look at this." He handed Phil the folder from CSI of the Sandra Clark scene.

"Okay," Phil said, thumbing through it. "What am I looking for?"

Michael pulled out the paper-clipped bundle of pages with the picture of a pawprint on top. "Five pads," he said, pointing to it. "Wolves and dogs both have four."

"So..." Phil asked. "What does that mean? Some other animal?"

"Or a mutant maybe? I'd like to get a closer look at those wolves on the preserve. Maybe it's a family trait."

"That won't be easy. Apparently, there's a bit of a political situation developing."

"Political how?"

"Dunno - but you probably want to talk to Billings before you go anywhere."

"They only have the three?"

"Yeah. Looks like the killer left by the back door, unfortunately, not a lot of bare dirt. The rest is grass and sidewalk."

"Not dog?" Phil asked, pointing at one of the photos. It showed a tuft of what looked to Michael's unpracticed eye to be dog hair caught in a shrub.

"Protein analysis says human." Michael read the note below it. "They're sending it off for DNA"

"Great. If we ever get a suspect, we can positively match him at least."

They had a lot of evidence. Possibly enough for a conviction. All they were lacking was a suspect.

"C'mon," he said. "Whatever's going on is tied to that wolf preserve. Let's go talk to the captain then see about heading up for a closer look. And when I get back, I'm commandeering that conference room," he added, pointing at the larger of the two. "We're gonna need a war room for the duration."

"YOU WANT a warrant to search a wolf preserve?" Captain Billings asked him from behind his desk. Michael noticed the coffee cup seemed to have lost ground against the paperwork since he had last been here. He and Phil stood on the other side of the desk, facing Billings.

"Yes," Michael responded. "With a team to take pictures, castings, measurements, and an animal control unit to..."

"No," was his captain's quick response. The abrupt dismissal caught him by surprise.

"What do you mean no?" Michael asked.

"What part of 'no' don't you understand?" At least he'd kept his sense of humor, such as it was.

"The part where this is our best lead," Michael told him.

"How is this a lead at all?" Billings asked. "What exactly do you expect to find out there?"

"A five-clawed wolf." He explained about the abnormality on the prints from the latest crime scene.

"Let's assume for a moment that you did find your wolf," Billings responded. "Then what? What if they all have five claws? Even if they don't, who owns it? Who's giving the orders?"

"Vera Rosen?" He didn't believe it, and he could tell the captain didn't either. "Okay, no. But she definitely knows something."

"Agreed. She led Sam to the preserve. Chances are, if she's not your killer, she knows, or suspects, or has some kind of relation with whoever is."

"So why can't we get a warrant for the preserve?" Michael asked.

"One police officer was already killed there," Billings responded.

"I'll be careful," Michael interrupted.

"I'm sure Sam was careful too," his captain continued, "but that's not the point. I got a phone call from a rather livid lawyer this morning. Want to guess what about?"

"Something to do with the preserve?"

"Our man was where he shouldn't have been, and because of it-" He raised his voice when Michael tried to interrupt him. "And because of it, the entire pack had to be destroyed."

"What?" Phil exclaimed.

"They killed and ate a human being. We don't put up with that from animals. No way to tell which ones were involved, so they all had to be put down. And no, they're not happy about it, so no, they're not going to be giving us the carcasses to study."

"Already?"

"The order was given. I don't know if it's been carried out yet."

"Probably for the best. They're dangerous."

"Don't ever let your reporter friend hear you say that. The last thing we need is for Portland to be flooded with animal rights activists protesting the police. This is already causing a minor storm on social media. It's only a matter of time before the mainstream news notices it."

"All the more reason to get in there now before it looks like retaliation."

"I'm afraid it's too late for that. You're going to have to settle for whatever the coroner can find."

"But..."

"No. That's it. Finding the wolf, if it even is a wolf, is less important anyway than whoever's setting it on people. I think your efforts would be better concentrated on the reporter. I'll authorize continued surveillance, and ask the judge to include wiretapping and a keylogger for her computer as well."

That caught him by surprise.

"You're worried about public outcry, but you want to tap a reporter's computer?"

"If nobody finds out, there won't be any outcry."

I LOVE MY DAUGHTER, Gordon Chandler reminded himself as he looked over the mess in the kitchen. Barbara's a good kid. She's staying in school and getting decent, if not great, grades. She doesn't use drugs. What's an occasional milk carton left out? Or a bit of cereal on the counter? And on the table. Okay, she could do better in the boyfriend department. At first it had seemed sweet that he'd come by early in the morning and walk her to school. Then he realized he was getting a free breakfast out of it and leaving Gordon with the cleanup. But that, occasional bouts of poetry, and idiotic politics expounded with all the arrogance of youth weren't the worst vices a 16-year-old boy could have.

Barbara hadn't approved of everyone he'd dated in the six years since her mother had left them, either. Considering his last brief relationship, it wasn't without cause. He closed the milk carton and stepped over to the refrigerator to put it away and heard the crunch of cereal underfoot. I love my daughter and she's a good kid, he reminded himself again as he got the broom.

He had time for a quick breakfast of toast and coffee himself before he headed to his car, ducking his head against the rain as we went. Pulling out of the driveway, he had to stop and wait for a man walking down the sidewalk behind him.

The guy was looking intently at the house as he drove away. Something about him seemed creepy. He was in a t-shirt, sweatpants, and sandals, with no jacket on such a cold and rainy day. Gordon circled the block, just to double-check. When he got back, the man was already past his house, making his way down the street. Whatever he was up to, he was moving on, which was good enough. Gordon headed in to work.

"HER CAR'S still in the driveway," Detective Aaron Schmidt said from the back seat. Phil was sitting beside Michael as he drove the unmarked car. They'd chosen this time of evening specifically because they thought she'd be out working now. In the October twilight it was dark enough that they might not be noticed, but still early enough that three people showing up at someone's doorstep would not be suspicious. A late mid-week dinner party is all. He supposed the bags Schmidt was bringing along could conceivably be carrying food.

"The car doesn't mean she's here," Phil answered him. "Day like today, after all the rain we've been having? She'd have taken the bike."

Michael hoped he was right as he pulled the car to stop on the side of the road in front of her house. One more bit to avoid suspicion. A car on the street and the occupants might be heading to any nearby house. But if he'd pulled into the driveway, there'd be no ambiguity at all. Aaron took the lead and headed to the door alone, while Phil and Michael stayed in the car, close enough that they could see the door from their location. Since Aaron was the only one who Veer hadn't met before, he'd be the logical choice to check if she was home. If she was, he could offer a plausible excuse, and they could wait until she left before going in.

A couple of minutes later, he demonstrated the other reason, as the door swung open and he walked in as if invited, after turning to wave to them indicating the house was empty. Michael and Phil grabbed his bags and headed up the walkway to the front door.

The first thing he did when entering was to close the blinds in front. Aaron went immediately to the computer. When he wiggled the mouse, the screen turned on and showed a login prompt. "Figured it wouldn't be that easy," he said and pulled a small device from one of his bags before sliding under the desk.

"Oh, yeah, she hasn't checked down here for at least a year," he said, looking behind the computer sitting on the floor.

Michael left him to his work and went to search the rest of the house. Opening a kitchen cabinet, he was surprised to see several expensive-looking liquor bottles, all unopened. A collector, then? Or a series of gifts?

Back in the front room, Aaron was out from under the desk. Michael found him and Phil at the end of the short hall inspecting a closet that turned out to contain a hot water heater and a bunch of cleaning supplies. "Perfect," Aaron said and grabbed his bag, squeezing into the tiny space.

The two doors at the end of the hall led to a bedroom and a slightly smaller room apparently used for storage. In the storage room, a couch sat against one wall and a pile of cardboard boxes and a couple of suitcases against another. Pushing them aside, Michael discovered the smaller of the two, about the right size for an airplane carry-on bag, wasn't empty like the larger one was. He opened it on the floor and found mostly what he'd expected - a couple of sets of clothes, one considerably nicer than the other, a toiletries bag, several empty notepads, and a handful of pens. In one zippered compartment was a small bag containing a passport and several hundred dollars in cash. Ready to head out at a moment's notice, he thought. For work, though? Or to flee something? Maybe both.

From the hall, Phil called out "Five minutes!" Damn. He hastily stuffed everything back into the suitcase, in what he'd hoped was a close approximation of its original layout. With the clock ticking, he made a hasty once-over of the bedroom across the hall. In the drawer of the nightstand was a small handgun sitting on top of a concealed-carry holster and next to a box of ammunition. He made a mental note to check if Rosen had a permit.

"Wow, check this out!" Phil called, lifting a large scoped rifle from the closet. Michael didn't recognize the model.

"It's a tranquilizer gun," Aaron said from across the room.

"What...how do you know that?" Michael asked him.

Coming out from behind the dresser, Aaron pushed it back into place before taking the gun and looking it over.

"It's similar to the one my wife uses." He pointed out the Pneu-Dart logo on the side of the barrel. At the querulous gazes from the other two cops, he continued, "She's a biologist. They use 'em to sedate bears for tagging."

He took a box of ammunition from the shelf next to where the rifle had been sitting. "See?" He showed them the darts in the box - about a dozen of them in a box made to hold twice that many, with shiny silver needles on the ends. "Thirteen millimeter cartridge to accelerate it." He picked one up, moved it toward his hand like it was in flight. "Hits the bear, this part stops." He indicated the front part. "The rest keeps going, drives the needle in like a syringe. Knocks it out in about a minute."

"I wonder what she'd need something like that for," Michael said out loud.

"Maybe she's more involved in the wolf preserve than she lets on," Phil said.

Michael couldn't think what she'd need to be sedating wolves from a distance for, but either the box came half-full or she had used half the darts at some point.

TWO HOURS LATER, Michael entered his new war room. Aaron was hooking up a computer he'd scrounged from somewhere as Michael and Phil pinned up the photos he thought relevant on a cork board next to a large map of the city. Each cluster of labeled photos had a string leading to a pin on the map, showing the locations of the murders. Only Sam didn't have a pin, though his picture hung to the far left side of the map. He looked over the locations: a house out past the Hollywood district, an apartment on Belmont, and another on Powell. Finally, the house on 72nd. The last house and the two apartments were rentals and the first was owned by its occupant.

"No obvious pattern there," he said to Phil, stepping back to look at the board.

"Deliberately scattered, maybe? To avoid giving away his home?"

"Or there's some connection between these victims we're missing."

"I think that's got it," Aaron said from the other end of the room. He moved back around to the front of the computer. One screen was split into four sections - two of which were showing the inside of Rosen's house. One was in the living room, looking into the kitchen, showing the table where he had sat and had coffee with her just a few days ago. The other was pointing down the hall from the other direction, looking into the living room.

"I could only get three cameras," Aaron told them. "But the feed is live now. There's sound as well, though of course, nothing to hear right now. The third window," he indicated the dark one in the lower left, "Is behind the dresser in the bedroom. No vent in there, so I couldn't find a good hiding place where it can see the room, but we'll still be able to hear and tell when the lights are on or off."

"And the fourth one?" Michael asked him.

"Nothing there. The software I'm using just gives you four windows."

Probably just as well there was no view from the bedroom, Michael thought. This wasn't his first surveillance op, but it always felt like an invasion. This time it was even more so, because he knew the subject, not just as a suspect.

"What about her computer? What were you doing there?" He asked.

Aaron indicated the second monitor, which was currently blank other than a text window dominating the screen. "That's the keylogger the Captain told you about. I just put a transmitter on the USB port between her keyboard and the computer so anything she types will show up here. Everything's tied together with the Wi-Fi router I installed behind her water heater, so we have our own network inside her house. It transmits here with a cellular hotspot."

"That sounds expensive," Michael mused.

"Not as much as you might think," Phil responded. "Aside from the keylogger, which I had to build myself, everything's off the shelf - I picked most of it up this morning at Fry's. Discounting the monthly cell fees, the whole setup's under four hundred dollars."

"Nice. Too bad we can't see the monitor."

"Once she types her password, which should be the first thing she enters, we can go in and install a mirror, or whatever we need."

"Sure beats the hell out of the old days, when we'd have to be nearby sitting in a cramped van or watching through a telescope," Phil said.

Michael agreed. "Something else I just thought of, too, while you're here?" Michael began.

"Shoot," Aaron answered him.

"You got into her place pretty easily," he said.

"Yeah, the dead bolt gave me a bit of trouble," he answered. "But only a bit."

"Are they always that easy?"

"Some more so than others, why?"

"We've been assuming the victims knew the killer, or otherwise invited him in..."

"I see what you're getting out. Yeah, maybe our guy just knows how to pick locks? It's not that hard to learn, takes maybe a couple dozen hours of practice to get good at it. They have kits you can order online."

"Is that legal?"

"That's how I learned," Aaron replied with a broad smile.

HE WORKED the lock with pride. The hours upon hours of painstakingly patient practice had paid off. Less than five minutes on the back door, then he had nothing to do but wait.

No beer in the fridge. That annoyed him.

A box of cheerios sat on the counter. He opened it up and got annoyed again at the tightly rolled bag inside. He opened that, too, and took a handful with him, eating them as he wandered about the place checking to make sure nobody was home. He ended up back in the kitchen and was about to pull his shirt off then decided not to this time. Not yet. He needed a good place to wait, and didn't want to alert anyone to his presence before he was ready.

There were two bedrooms in the house, both upstairs, and a study downstairs. The man and his daughter lived here alone as far as he could tell. The upstairs rooms were at opposite ends of the landing. He went through the girl's first. There was an old iPod shoved in the back of her underwear drawer. He went through the stack of panties but didn't find anything that turned him on, which was disappointing. Maybe that would change when she was his.

In the man's room, he dug out a pair of pants that could fit him, and an old t-shirt. He took them out the back door, crossed the yard and quickly vaulted the fence. He opened the back door of the empty house behind theirs. Stepping inside, he thought it over for a moment, then, smiling, he switched clothes and left his own, including the sandals, on the back stairs. He laughed, anticipating the man's fear as he confronted him wearing his own clothes. Then he'd transform and revel in the terror before beginning to feed. Maybe the girl would be frozen in fear. Maybe he'd get to chase her through the house before biting her. That'd be fine, too. He'd have to concentrate hard, to just wound her without killing her. It was hard to control the wolf, but he knew it could be done. He knew it. Maybe others couldn't control themselves, but he was special. He knew what he was.

Maybe it would be easier after feeding. He'd be calmer, more himself perhaps.

He'd see. If not this one, the next. He would figure it out.

He crossed the yard barefoot in his stolen clothes. He had a few hours, he knew, from watching the place these last couple of days. She'd get home first, then, a couple of hours later, her father would show up. He had watched them for three days. They were utterly predictable and boring people. He could save her from that life. He dreamed of all the fun they'd have together. Tonight, shortly before dawn, she'd wake up, probably far from home, naked in some field or park or something with no idea how she'd got there. Maybe she'd go to the police first, or the hospital, or somewhere. But eventually, within a few more days at the most, she'd make her way back here. Where else could she go? She wasn't strong enough to leave familiar territory and strike off on her own like he did. Not yet. He'd teach her. When she returned, he'd be ready. The only one in the world who would understand her and could explain what she was going through. He could teach her to be strong. To use the gift. And they could hunt together, reveling in the kill. Make their way east, traveling across the country and baffling small town cops across the nation as they went.

He wandered back up to her room and went through her dresser again. He picked up a bra and tried to imagine the girl in it. Nothing. He tried to picture pulling it off of her. Still nothing. The image was too ill-formed in his mind to be exciting to him. He thought of it ripping into shreds as she transformed into a wolf, the shreds flapping away behind her as she ran forward. That brought a smile to his face. He tossed the bra onto the corner of her bed. Let her be embarrassed at finding it there, and thinking she'd forgotten it, sitting out in the open where anybody could see it.

He went back downstairs and checked the fridge again. He hadn't missed the beer, there really wasn't any. The best he could do was a can of coke and some left over potato salad. He took both upstairs, settled on the man's bed, eating it and dreaming of the future. He knew from watching the house that she'd come home first. He chose her father's room as the least likely place she'd go when she got here. Unlike her bedroom, this door had been firmly closed when he arrived. He closed it again. When she got there, he would hear her. He'd sit, and drink his Coke, and listen to her as she moved about the house, and imagine what she was doing, without her having any idea that he was here the whole time, listening and waiting.

FOUR
NEAR DEATH EXPERIENCES

Veer ducked under the yellow tape still strung across the door to the building that served as the entrance to the preserve. This was the second time in a week she had come here. Behind the front building was a gate leading to a short driveway for delivery vehicles. Another gate led from it into the preserve proper. She parked her motorcycle in that driveway but went back to the front to enter the main building to change before entering the preserve. She was grateful that the small parking lot was empty of other vehicles. This soon after the full moon, she wasn't expecting there to be anyone else, but you never knew. The full moon, and a couple of days before it, was always the most common time for transformations. Any Were who couldn't get out of the city for a nearby weekend would come here, so she could expect half a dozen people in any given month. Nobody would want to change again this soon after, though. Almost nobody, she smiled to herself.

She was still on edge, so it took all her concentration not to transform as soon as she was undressed and through the door, despite having changed only a couple of days before. There was a light rain, which was perfect. Too much and this wouldn't work, the mud would be too thick. But the ground being slightly damp would help her.

Not even the keeper was around, though that wasn't unusual. She could count on one hand the number of times she'd actually seen him in the last three years. Somebody kept these paths up, though. All the main paths had the underbrush neatly trimmed back and were lined with bark dust. She wished she'd thought to wear sandals at least as she stepped on it. Soft and comfortable under shoes, it was a little prickly to bare feet. For that matter, she should have picked up something expendable to wear on the way in. Normally, she'd have changed before getting this deep into the woods of the preserve. Wandering naked along the paths, she felt especially vulnerable.

She doubled back twice just to make absolutely sure she wasn't followed this time. She had brought her phone, because she would have need of it. There was a second one in the locker that she could use to track it if she couldn't find it where she left it later.

Finally, she found what she was looking for: a large spot of bare dirt, near a good sized tree with a sturdy bough in which she could lodge the phone without fear of it being knocked loose. She tested the damp ground with her bare foot and photographed the footprint it left. Then took several more of the area before placing the phone as high as she could reach into the tree.

Walking to the center of the muddy patch, she bent down, letting herself fall forward, hands outstretched as she finally let the change sweep over her.

Her front paws hit the ground, and she raised her head. The distant smell of some prey animal reached her. Instinct took over, and she ran joyfully toward it, through the mud and into the underbrush.

IN THE END, Carl mused as he drove up the gravel road, nothing was really decided. Kevin was stuck on this idea of choosing just a few people, then grabbing them off the street, taking them somewhere where they couldn't hurt themselves or anyone else and biting them. It was a simple plan. Too simple maybe. While Kevin had accused Carl of over-complicating it, Carl had insisted there were parts they were over-looking. The fact that he couldn't say what those parts were didn't help his case.

He hadn't changed for over a month. He'd think more clearly after a good hunt. He always did. It was a crappy enough week as it was. He had just lost another job. Another contract that didn't get renewed. He was used to it, as a programmer. The whole tech industry was like that: hire a bunch of coders on short-term contracts when you need them and let them all go when the work slows. Just a bunch of disposable cogs in the great machine of capitalism. At least it paid well when he was employed, and the unemployment insurance paid his rent, so he only had to use his meager savings on luxuries like food and electricity.

What good was being a Were if he couldn't even meet his basic living expenses? The Alpha, who was supposed to take care of them, even owned a tech firm, but in the three years Carl had been a Were he had been consistently passed over for jobs there. He'd expected his life to change after Kevin turned him, but instead it had just gotten crappier. Just one more thing he had to deal with. He kept an eye on the Dodge's heat gauge. It was steadily climbing upward as he ascended the mountain road. He thought he could still make it to the preserve, and if he was there for a couple of hours, that should give it time to cool off enough to make it back home, especially if the light rain continued.

Crappy car. Crappy job. Crappy life. Fuck it, he'd go along with Kevin's plan. At least it would change things. He'd drive the van for them. Nobody would get hurt, and maybe when it was all over he could leverage his abilities somehow instead of keeping it a secret from everyone forever. He had no idea how he could do that, or what exactly would change, but it couldn't get any worse, right?

The parking lot was empty when he pulled in. With luck, he wouldn't see anyone else the whole time he was here. He loved this place and felt a little gratitude toward the Alpha for maintaining it for them. It would be nice if it was a little closer to town or easier to get to. He'd have to fix his car by summer, or it would never make it this far in the heat. And then what would he do? He could probably catch a ride with Kevin or Shelly but that would take away half the joy of being here, running alone and free beholden to nobody's schedule but his own.

He undressed and stuffed his clothes into the same locker he always used and walked out through the open back door and off the porch. For a moment he stood, savoring the sweet smell of the forest air, the feel of the grass under his bare feet and the cool October air against his skin. Then, taking a deep breath, he reached out to the wolf. It was always there, at the corner of his mind, and he called it to him now.

THE WOLF TORE into the underbrush joyfully, reveling in the wash of smells around it. It was only after running for a time that he stopped and sniffed at the air to sort them out. There was prey, many kinds in many directions. But there was something else, too. Something that didn't belong here. In the back of his mind, he knew it was the scent of something he should avoid. There was a strange kind of danger there, but curiosity urged him forward. He crept up until he saw it: a human slowly making its way up the well-trod path. He stepped out from the underbrush. The human froze in its tracks. He lowered his head and snarled at it, hoping it would run so he could give chase. It did not disappoint.

MICHAEL PARKED in the small gravel parking lot of the wolf preserve. Billings had only told him he couldn't have a warrant for the place, he didn't say he couldn't go there at all. If he managed to get permission to enter, then he didn't need a warrant. The only other car in the lot was an old green dodge that had obviously seen better days. He quickly wrote down the license and proceeded to the door. There was no answer when he knocked at the front door. He wasn't really expecting one. It was unlocked, so he opened it. Stepping in, he found the same reception desk and office behind it that Sam had mentioned.

"Hello?" he called out, to no response. "Anyone here?" He continued through the lobby. He stopped at the door across from the office. Peering into the dark room through the window in the door, it looked much like the examination room that Sam had guessed it was. This was probably where the vet the sheriff had mentioned examined the wolves when needed. The door was locked. The room probably didn't get a whole lot of use.

He followed in Sam's steps, through the locker room. None of the score or so of lockers were locked. Most hung open and empty. Inside one, he found a set of men's clothes, and a towel.

Jeans and a t-shirt. Sneakers. They didn't match either Sam's description of the "fancy" outfit, or the sweatpants and sandals they'd found at the crime scenes. Another locker contained a set of women's clothes, and a cell phone. The phone was locked and nothing on the screen gave any indication about its owner. He left it alone.

The far exit, he knew, would lead into the preserve itself. He stepped through the door.

The yard, and the tiny porch, and path into the woods were all as Sam described. There was no doubt this was exactly the way he had come. Michael followed the path. It was tended, and covered in bark dust, obviously made for human use. He checked the small canister of mace in its holster, behind his gun. If he ran into any wolves, he didn't want to kill them, but he didn't want to be defenseless against them, either. He looked for prints. On the path, he could tell none would be found. He couldn't even see his own footprints. And off the path, the vegetation was just too thick. He continued on, into the woods, unsure at this point what he was seeking.

And then he heard a noise.

There was a rustling in the underbrush, off to his left. A wolf? *The* wolf? They shouldn't attack, right? Here on the preserve, they should be well fed, and stay away from humans. They shouldn't attack. But they had. He suddenly felt aware of exactly where he was. Regardless of how idyllic the path, he was in the woods surrounded by wolves. Wolves who had already killed a man.

Billings had said the pack was scheduled to be destroyed, but that may not have happened yet. He wasn't sure if it was even true.

Turn back, he told himself. This is stupid. It's not necessary. We have a picture of the paw, we have DNA, and we'll have surveillance on Rosen. You don't need to do this.

There was no reason to continue, and every reason to turn back.

He continued.

He touched his canister of pepper spray and his firearm, making sure they were in place. He looked for climbable trees. He called himself an idiot.

He pressed on.

Another rustle in the bushes. Something moved quickly, right beside the trail.

He froze, staring into the underbrush and finally saw it. A rabbit. He laughed out loud in relief. "Ha! You scared the shit of me, little fellow," he told it.

At the sound of his voice, the rabbit bolted, vanishing into the woods.

That's when he saw the wolf. Just one, standing in the middle of the path. It had just come around the bend in the path and stood there, watching him.

He froze. It crouched down as if to charge and let out a low growl.

He turned and ran. It followed. A dozen paces back the way he'd come, a tall elm with branches low enough to reach. He leapt up and caught one, pulling himself onto it, as the wolf's jaws closed on air below him. Not sure how far the beast could jump, he scrambled up to another branch, then another.

The wolf hurled itself against the trunk. As large and sturdy as the tree was, he could feel the impact from his perch fifteen feet off the ground. He felt like an idiot, hiding in a tree, but at least he was safe here, while the wolf paced back and forth on the ground beneath him. It was large and dark grey, almost black. A beautiful animal, but he didn't want to see it any closer than it was. Eventually, it would give up and go away, looking for easier prey, right?

He watched it pace and settled his back to the trunk. "I've got all night, fluffy, how about you?" he said out loud.

At the sound, the wolf froze, then turned toward him and cocked its head slightly. He almost laughed out loud at that, it looked like it was actually considering his words. It was almost dog-like. But it's not a dog, he reminded himself. It's a wild animal, a predator, quite possibly the same one that killed Sam.

A moment later, it walked back over to the trunk of the tree, then standing on its hind legs, stretched its front legs up, as high as it could reach, and sunk its claws into the trunk, hugging it. Holding on and pulling itself up the tree, it began to climb.

It was slow, but it kept coming, shuffling its way up the tree trunk. Using its forelegs, it pulled itself up as high as it could, then sunk its hind claws into the trunk. It let go with its front legs just long enough to reach upward and repeat the process.

Michael scrambled up to a higher branch.

Slowly, inexorably, the wolf kept coming. It was slow enough that Michael could easily out climb it, but soon he would run out of tree. The branches were already getting thinner and he wasn't sure if he could trust the higher ones. He stopped at a steady perch and waited for it.

It kept coming. This close, he could see the great claws it was using - all five of them on each foot. He was sure a normal wolf couldn't climb a tree like this. Not only was this one a mutant, it was trained. Trained to climb, and trained to kill. But by who? And why? Genetically engineered, maybe? Was he dealing with some mad scientist, testing his creation?

Nonsense.

The wolf was getting closer. He tried to quiet the trembling in his hand as he reached down and carefully slid out his canister of pepper spray. He aimed it and pressed the activator to release a jet directly into its face.

The wolf gave a loud high pitched yelp and tumbled to the

ground. It lay below him, writhing and whining in pain, desperately pawing at its eyes. *Don't rub it, it'll just make it worse,* he thought. He didn't say it out loud, though. Didn't want to give it any ideas. His own eyes were watering just from the proximity. He almost felt sorry for the beast. Almost.

He was hoping that it would give up then and run away. But when it stood up and looked at him, it didn't look frightened. He hadn't scared it, he'd just pissed it off.

Shit. Now what?

The wolf stared directly at him and growled. The orange dye streaked the wolf's face, making the visage even more terrifying. Michael pushed back, as if he could meld into the tree trunk. He was just about to get ready to try those higher branches after all when the wolf, after taking a few steps away, charged straight toward it and leaped.

And what a leap it was, enraged, teeth bared, and foreclaws extended. Its impact shook the tree and Michael nearly lost his grip on the branches he was clinging to.

And then it started again, its slow shuffle up the side of the tree.

Maybe I shouldn't have come here after all, Michael thought. At least I found the killer. Then again, Sam probably did too.

He aimed the mace at it again and the beast snarled at him. At this distance, its teeth were frighteningly large. Trying to ignore his fear, he released another burst aimed at the wolf's eyes. But it turned its head at the last second and took the spray on the side of its neck. It snarled again in anguish but didn't release its grip. His own eyes were stinging from being so close to the repeated sprays.

It snarled again and swiped at him with one great claw. He scrambled up and out of the way, barely, but dropped the canister in doing so. He heard it strike a limb below him. He never heard it hit the ground. As fast as he dared, he pulled himself up to a higher branch. The wolf was still coming. Aside from the dye staining its fur, there was no sign of damage or lingering discomfort from the spray.

He balanced himself on one branch, holding onto the tree with his left hand and reaching for his gun with his right. He could kill this thing. The fallout would be immense. There would be lawsuits. An investigation. He'd almost certainly be fired. He was here without a warrant, against direct orders from his captain.

Drawing his weapon now could save his life, but it would almost certainly end his career. Balance that against almost certain death if that thing reached him. This beast was trained to kill. If he stopped it now, at the very least he'd be saving the lives of all those who it would otherwise attack in the future. Wasn't that worth one career? Worst case scenario, the wolf would be dead, he'd be unemployed, and whoever trained it would get away. Maybe Phil would catch him.

He took aim and squeezed the trigger. The sound of the gunshot was swallowed up in the forest. The wolf barely twitched. It stared directly at him and snarled, as if daring him to shoot again. Before he could, though, another wolf bounded out of the underbrush. This one was smaller and grey on top fading to almost white toward its paws. There was no mistaking its destination as it sprinted directly toward his tree. He aimed at the first one, hoping to dispatch it quickly before the other joined to help.

He fired again, this time paying close attention to exactly where the bullet hit. Again, the wolf twitched, then gave a slight shake of the head as if to clear it. Blood flowed down the wolf's face, mixing with the orange dye from the pepper spray, but it soon stopped and the wolf advanced.

The other leapt. Instead of climbing, though, it landed

heavily against the tree trunk, its jaws closing around the leg of the larger black wolf. Together, the two tumbled to the ground.

They fought. A ball of teeth and fur and claws and snarls and yelps of pain. Leaves and dirt flew around them, obscuring sight to where he almost couldn't see which wolf was which. Although outclassed in size, the light grey one proved faster and much more agile, rolling, flipping over, and ducking around the wild lunges of the other. He held his weapon but didn't dare fire. He didn't want to risk hitting the smaller as it seemed to be his savior not another murderer. Trained to defend people, maybe?

Could it have been following a different training regimen than the larger one? To what end? And who was doing this? It had to be a complete program, not just one person. Stumpp owned this place, Rosen had said. If he managed to get out of here alive, he'd have to look into his involvement. At the moment, that was a big if. Even if the smaller one won this fight there was no guarantee it wouldn't turn on him next.

Michael holstered his firearm, having no desire to shoot either of them if he could avoid it. He thought about trying to escape, dropping out of the tree and making a run for it, but he wasn't sure the two combatants wouldn't forget about each other the moment he was on the ground.

The fight continued, the smaller one gradually gaining the upper hand. The other was clearly tiring and beginning to slow down. Eventually, it rolled onto its back and lay still, the smaller one triumphantly standing over it, its teeth on its throat. The defeated wolf began to whimper as the winner squeezed. Michael didn't want to watch what was to come but couldn't look away. Whatever he was expecting, it wasn't what happened. The wolf on the ground began... turning. There was a weird shift as it seemed to turn in on itself, or over and inside out at once. And where the large black wolf had been there was a man - a scrawny young guy, couldn't have been more than 25, laying naked on the ground with a wolf's teeth at his throat.

Michael felt dizzy. It made no sense at all. But it did. It explained everything, but it made no sense. When the transformation was complete, the wolf let go of the man and he scrambled to his feet and ran away without a backward glance, disappearing into the woods. The wolf looked up at Michael, then ran off in the opposite direction. The look it gave him, though. Such intelligence in those eyes! And anger. A warning.

He didn't have to be told twice. He half climbed, half slid to the ground and ran as fast as he could back toward the entrance of the preserve. He didn't slow down until he'd come to the parking lot. All the way there, he refused to acknowledge the word that was threatening to push its way into his conscious mind, each time bearing down and running harder when it got close.

GRANT HAD SETTLED BACK DOWN on the large bed. He was getting bored. And angry. He had long since finished off everything in the house to snack on, and had searched thoroughly without finding the liquor or even any beer. He'd made himself turn off the TV half an hour ago so that the sound wouldn't give him away. He was staring at the ceiling, trying to think of what else to do when he heard the door open downstairs. Finally!

"Barb?" a man's voice called from downstairs. "Are you here?"

Dammit, what was he doing here? The girl was supposed to get home first. The man wasn't due until a couple of hours afterward. He stood up, not sure which way to go. Any minute now, he'll come in, and the whole plan will be ruined.

"Barb? What is this mess? I just cleaned..."

He was a little insulted at that. He'd been careful not to leave any signs of his rummaging. This guy must have been one of those anal retentive types who noticed any tiny thing out of place. That explained the state of the house, spotless and sterile, like nobody lived here. He could hear footsteps coming up the stairs now. His hearing was superior, especially since he changed. A lesser man might not have heard something as subtle as footsteps on carpet. He quietly moved over to stand beside the door.

"Barb, honey? Are you here?" the man called again. He was moving away from his own room, where Grant stood and went to the door at the other end of the landing. There was a knock. He was knocking on the girl's room? In his own house? Obviously one of these emasculated modern men. A mindless drone, going about his pointless life. Probably aspiring to nothing more than middle management in some large company. Interchangeable with a million others just like him. The world wouldn't even notice his passing.

Getting no answer from the other door, even after opening it and yelling in, he finally headed to his own room. Grant moved to stand directly in front of the door. When it opened, he was standing on the other side of it, smiling.

"Who are you?" the man asked, predictably. "And what are you...?"

At that moment, the front door opened downstairs. "Dad?" a girl's voice called from downstairs. "Sorry I'm late, I..."

"Barb! Get out of here now! Go to Mrs.."

No! This wasn't supposed to happen like that! They were ruining everything. He lunged forward through the door while changing, before the man could finish.

His frantic call ended in a scream as the wolf's teeth sank into his shoulder.

THE RICH WARM taste of human blood flooded his mouth, and he shook his prey then dropped it where it lay still and quiet. Another human's voice was shouting something, and he could hear it running up toward him. It froze when it reached the top of the stairs and the sweet smell of fear washed over him. He growled, a deep menacing noise as he paced toward it, head low, ready to spring. It turned and ran down the way it had come. He chased after it. Something nagged at the back of his mind. Stop. You're supposed to... what? It didn't matter. The creature was afraid and running from him. He knew how to react to that. He ignored the other feeling and sprang forward, his leap knocking his prey down. Together, they tumbled to the bottom of the stairs.

He sank his teeth into it then, savoring the taste of blood and fear. It was only when it stopped moving that he listened to the voice in the back of his mind telling him to stop, to run, to flee. He fled.

The door was closed, he sprang through the window. Glass and wood splintered, cut into him. He ignored it. By the time he had leapt over the back fence, the wounds had already healed.

MICHAEL MADE it to his car, slammed and locked the door, breathing hard. The green dodge was still in the lot. Its license plate was in his notebook, but he ignored it while he drove, as fast as he dared, back toward the city. Halfway there, he pulled over and, finally, gave voice to the word he'd been trying to suppress.

"Werewolf," he said aloud, alone in his car along the side of the road. "Werewolf!" he said again, with a mirthless laugh.

"Werewolves," he corrected. The second one had to be one, too.

No. It's a trick. An elaborate hoax. A stunt of some kind. Smoke and mirrors. But... why? And how could someone have planned this? Was he being followed? How did they know he'd be here? He hadn't told anyone his plans. If they followed him, how could they have set all this up in the time it took him to walk a hundred yards?

And what was the alternative? A conspiracy of mad scientist nudists breeding super-wolves? And then staging the scene to throw him off the trail? To what end?

How large was the conspiracy? Was Rosen a member, or was she investigating it, too? If she was treated to the same stunt, it could explain why she didn't tell the police. We'd all think she was crazy.

There were too many questions. He wanted answers. He called Phil.

He kept his voice as calm as he could when he answered. "Hey, can you do me a favor and run a license for me? I'm in my own car."

He gave Phil the number and waited while he pulled up the information.

"Some guy named Carl Jablonski. Here, I can send you the picture."

A minute later, a text arrived on his phone with Jablonski's driver's license photo. It was unmistakably the man he'd seen in the preserve who'd changed from a wolf.

"That's him," he told Phil. "What can you tell me about him?"

"Let's see... age twenty-five, address on southeast eighty-fourth. Looks like he's been in Portland about three years.

Wisconsin before that. Listed occupation as a software engineer."

"So... probably moved out here for a job right after college?"

"Could be. He's in the system. Nothing major. A couple of speeding tickets, and a citation for driving on a suspended license after not paying the tickets. Contempt of court charge after that, which was dropped. A couple of arrests last year. Drunk and disorderly and indecent exposure. Is this our guy? Where did you find him?"

"Maybe." The priors were all petty stuff on the surface, but it spoke to a deeper disrespect of society. Usually, these types grow up and out of it. Looks like this guy had graduated to murder instead.

"Should we bring him in?"

"He's not at home. I just saw him at the wolf preserve." He didn't say any more than that. He was skirting the edge of his orders, if not the law, by going there. Phil didn't push the issue. When he didn't say anything, Michael added, "Let's get a warrant for his place and see if we can go through it before he gets home."

"Okay. What's the grounds?"

That was a good question. The only way it held together would be if he were a werewolf. He couldn't say he saw him transform from a wolf to a human while at a preserve he wasn't supposed to be at. "Anonymous tip," he finally replied.

There was a pause. "Okay," Phil said. He'd trust him enough to go along with it, but he'd want an explanation later. That was fine. He'd give him one as soon as he figured out how.

"I'll meet you there," he told him after getting the address.

He was just past the 217 bypass when his phone rang again.

"Answer," he called out to it, and Billing's voice came over the speaker.

"Where are you?" was the first thing he asked.

He wasn't ready to tell him about the preserve. "Highway twenty-six, just past two-seventeen, headed East," he responded.

There was only one reason he'd be out that way, and they both knew it. But Billings didn't say anything. A lot of that going around. He'd have to come up with some really good explanations later. He hoped he could.

"Good. You're already close, then. There's been another one." He gave him an address in a housing complex in the West Hills.

An ambulance was just speeding away as he approached, its lights flashing. He parked along the street nearby and approached the scene on foot, ducking his head against the pouring rain. It was coming down harder in the late afternoon. The house was in an older complex, built during a previous growth spurt a couple of decades ago. Rows of identical homes stood along steep winding streets, each with a tiny, manicured lawn. He stepped past the yellow tape that was just being put up at the edge of the sidewalk. Uniformed police were directing traffic away from the house. He was almost surprised not to see Vera Rosen standing nearby.

Phil greeted him at the front door. "Guess our man wasn't as wounded as we'd hoped," he said as he entered. Phil led him to a corpse laying at the base of a set of stairs leading to an upstairs landing. He explained what had happened as they went. "Neighbor may have scared him off this time. He heard a scream and came to investigate. He let himself in - he had a key - and found victim number one, there." Phil indicated a teenage girl on the floor at the base of the stairs, her throat torn open.

God, she was just a child. He quickly pushed down his reaction. There'd be time for that later. Right now, he had to focus on his job.

"Victim number one?" he asked Phil. "How many were there?"

"Two. Number two is on his way to the hospital now. They don't know if he's going to make it or not."

If he lived, that would be excellent news. An eyewitness. Speaking of. "Did the neighbor see anybody?" he asked.

"See? No. Heard, though. A large crash." He steered him through a dining room, with what used to be floor to ceiling windows. The glass was shattered outward, littering the wooden deck and yard past it. A trail of blood, enough of it that the rain hadn't completely washed it away yet, ran across the grass, all the way to a back fence.

"Who's in that house?" he asked, indicating the one on the other side of the fence.

"Empty," Phil responded. "Owned by some multinational. They own half the houses in this neighborhood now." There was a hint of bitterness in his voice as he said it. Michael ignored it. It wasn't the time for that, either.

"It would make a good hiding place..." he started.

"Yeah," Phil agreed. "Think our perp might be there now?"

"It's possible. Let's go."

"What, just you and me? Shouldn't we get some backup?" he asked.

"There may not be time," he responded. "As far as we know, he's not armed, and is probably naked and injured." In truth, he would have liked nothing better than to let as many people as possible see this. But a breaching team would have their own leadership and would probably use their guns. He wasn't sure that bullets would stop this thing. But pepper spray had been proven to at least slow it down. Werewolves or no, the simple fact was if anything weird happened he'd be the one most prepared to deal with it, just because he was the only one expecting something weird. He didn't say anything to Phil.

There was no way to say it in a way that would do any good. It was just too unbelievable.

"Think it's this Carl Jablonski fellow?" Phil asked on their way there.

Michael shook his head. "He couldn't have gotten here in time. He might not be working alone, though."

Phil looked startled at that. "What did you learn out there?"

"I'm not sure yet. C'mon."

They were too late to catch their suspect. He had been there but had left before they arrived. Strangely, they found the accustomed sweatpants and sandals, but they were intact, sloppily folded on a table near the back door.

"We don't know why he tears them up, and now he just leaves them. Maybe he was planning on doing it after the kill, but got scared off this time?"

"Last time he got shot and still managed to do it."

"There you are, detective. You're going to want to see this," one of the CSI people called when they came back to the house.

After telling them to add the house in the back to the crime scene, he followed the man upstairs. "This" was obviously the scene of the attack of victim number two. The one who might live. Here was the torn clothing they'd found at the other scenes, only this time it was slacks and a dress shirt. He found the size tag on the remnants of a collar and on a hunch pulled one of the shirts out of the closet. It was a match.

"What the hell?" Phil asked, joining him. "So... what, he shredded the victim's clothes this time instead of his own?"

"And left his own in another house. Intending to go back for them, and wear them home, maybe?" Michael mused. Which made perfect sense. If there was a reason he couldn't be wearing them in the meantime. If, for instance, he was a werewolf

FIVE

LAMENTATIONS ON THE PRECIPICE

"Ah, good, you're back," Aaron said as Michael entered the war room. He picked up a folder from the stacks on the table and handed it to Michael. It had been sitting on the folder of Rosen's articles on the dog mauling case that Michael had looked through earlier that morning.

"Preliminary results of surveillance on Rosen," Aaron told him.

Michael glanced up at the computer screen. It was still showing the four-way split. Two of them showed empty rooms. He sat down at the side of the table and opened the report. Aaron took the seat across from him.

The first page at first looked like just a jumble of text. It took him a minute of staring at it to realize this must be the keystroke log that Aaron had mentioned.

The first line read simply "sicTr4nzit."

"What is this?" he asked.

"Password, most likely," Aaron replied. "Would have been the first thing she entered when she started. If you want, we can now go in and install a back door giving us full access any time we want."

"Cool," he said, genuinely impressed. "Maybe later."

"Those six minutes there." Aaron pointed to the times listed in a column along the left side of the paper. "She was making a pot of coffee while the computer came up. I thought you might be interested in the next bit."

The second line was "news.g" followed by two icons representing downward-pointing arrows. "What's this, then?" he asked.

"Down arrow. The address she was typing was already in her cache. Looks like she was doing a news search. It's what she was searching for that was interesting."

"Dog mauling," he read out loud. "If she's just now getting around to searching for news on other maulings, I'm gonna be disappointed with her."

"Keep going, then," Aaron said with a smile.

The next word, though, was what got his attention: "Ashland."

"Ashland? Why Ashland?" he asked.

"Your guess is as good as mine," Aaron replied. But he was beaming as he said it. This was something new, whatever it was, and proved the value of the key logger he'd installed.

Next was a string of searches, variants of "Dog attack" "Dog mauling" and, interestingly, "Wolf attack," each followed by "San Diego."

"What is she on to? Have there been attacks in those cities?"

He noticed the next entry was over an hour later.

"What's that gap?" he asked.

"She's reading the articles - taking notes in a notebook."

"Who's Dianne Searley?" he asked, as that name was the next thing typed, presumably more searching.

"I had that same question," Aaron answered him, reaching for another folder. "I checked into it. First hit was a woman killed in San Diego a couple of months ago. I called them and they faxed over the file."

Michael looked at it. It was disappointingly brief.

"So... not a murder?"

"Animal attack. Mauled to death, possibly a dog, in her apartment. They never caught the dog, but the door was open, so they assumed it came and went that way."

"And they didn't have anything to connect it to so never investigated it any further."

"That'd be my guess," Aaron replied.

"How'd she know?"

"No idea, but it means she's got information she hasn't given us."

"She spent a lot of time searching for attacks in Ashland, too."

"No names there," he said, scanning the rest of the log.

"No," Aaron agreed. "Probably found what she was looking for without having to do any additional searches. They're compiling a report of all animal attacks in the last two months and will send it up when ready."

"How many can there be? It's not that big a city."

Phil came in at that moment. "Checking in on our Ms. Rosen?" he asked. Michael and Aaron both replied in the affirmative. Michael laid the file open on the table, turning it so Phil could read it too.

Aaron pointed to the next section. "The real smoking gun, though, is the email. Check it out."

"V<TAB>" it started.

"Autocomplete," Aaron explained. "She's starting an email to someone whose name begins with V."

"Damn. I'd give a lot to see the rest of that name."

The very first sentence made his hair stand on end. "The killer is almost certainly a Were," it said. He felt dizzy, as if he was standing on the edge of a great precipice. She knew. He'd suspected, but this was confirmation. The problem was, he was the only one who understood it.

He fought to keep his voice from shaking. "A Were?" he asked, pointing to the page. Could they see it as well?

"Aware, probably?" Phil suggested. It was more a question than a statement.

"Typo," Aaron agreed.

But he knew better. He read the rest.

"There's been an incident," it continued, followed by a line of what Aaron explained were backspace characters. Then "Something happened" followed by more backspaces.

"She was going to report something, wasn't sure how to say it, then changed her mind," Aaron supplied.

He read the next few lines

"There is news. And we may have an ally. I trust him."

"I also have questions. I'm coming over to your office now."

"Please be there" followed by a bunch of strange characters that Aaron told him meant she'd deleted "Please," leaving only "Be there."

"Guess she changed her mind about how polite to be to whoever V is," Phil said

"And she left right after sending this?"

"About ten minutes later. Changed and headed out the door."

"GREGOR'S BACK IN SAN DIEGO?" Veer asked.

"Were you hoping to share your findings with him?" Victor asked with a slight smile.

Veer gave a snort of laughter. They both knew that's not why she asked. She sat at the small conference table in his office and opened her laptop. "It took me the better part of an hour to find the same spot again," she began as it booted up.

"Here it is," she said when she'd loaded the first picture. It showed a muddy spot of ground with several paw prints. She'd included her own foot next to them for size reference. They were larger than she'd expected them to be. She wished she'd taken a ruler to take actual measurements with. She was sure she could find average sizes of real wolves online.

"Wolf prints, I take it?" Victor said.

"Werewolf. It's me. These are my prints in wolf form. The footprints next to them are my foot as a human."

"What am I looking for here?" Victor asked her.

"Try this. Here are some real wolf prints I found online," she said. She swiped across the screen to show those images. "And here's the ones from the crime scene. Notice anything different?"

"Is it the number of claws?" he said.

"Exactly." She showed the two images side by side. "Wolves have only four paw pads. The killer and I both have five. I'm willing to bet that's true of all Were."

"The killer's a Were," Victor said. "Though we suspected that already."

"Not only that, but it shows we're not real wolves. Whatever we turn into, it looks like a wolf, but it isn't really. According to the report, the DNA is human, at least by the time it gets to the crime lab."

"I've suspected as much," Victor replied. "I wonder how many other differences there are? I would guess there's a number of small things that someone, say, four hundred years ago would never have noticed."

"What about in the meantime? How come nobody's noticed this before?"

"Maybe they have," Victor said. "We're a secretive lot. Who knows how many discoveries over the centuries individuals have made and kept to themselves?"

"But surely they could share among the Were. There's no stricture on..." she stopped. "There doesn't need to be," she said in response to her own unasked question. "Of course, the code of secrecy tends to keep people from asking too many questions, or from sharing answers when they do, lest others suspect them of planning to reveal the secret."

Victor gave her a meaningful look.

"I wonder how many discoveries have been made. Maybe even now there's some scientist hidden away recording their findings, waiting for the day they can openly publish. Imagine what new knowledge mankind might gain if we come into the light."

"And imagine what horrors they might unleash with such knowledge. If the secret ever is revealed, it will have to be far, far into the future, when mankind is more enlightened than they are now," Victor replied.

"Then again, if the cops knew what they were looking for, they might have caught this guy by now," she said.

"Or perhaps, as is too often the case, simply rounded up everybody like him."

She couldn't argue with that. Imprisoning or killing entire groups of people for the crimes, or even perceived danger, of a few among them seemed to be the one constant throughout human history.

"That might get tested. The police know the killer's a Were," she said.

Victor looked up sharply at that, but didn't say anything, giving her time to explain.

"One of them does at any rate," she said. "The lead investigator, Michael Diaz."

"This is the ally you mentioned?" he asked her.

She nodded. "If he hasn't figured it out yet, he will soon. I imagine he's wrestling with all the implications now. He saw one of us transform."

"Who?" Victor asked immediately.

She didn't want to finger Carl. She had no particular liking for the boy but didn't desire to see him sanctioned because of her.

"A boy. It wasn't his decision. I forced it on him after he'd chased the detective up a tree, on the preserve." She let that sink in. Whatever measures he'd taken to keep the police away from the place hadn't worked. In this version, she was the hero who'd salvaged the situation and possibly found a way to turn it to their advantage.

She hoped he'd see it that way and ignore the possibility that she'd caused a greater disaster.

The silence dragged out as Victor contemplated the news. "Do you want to turn him?" he finally asked.

It was an offer that brought its own peril. Doing so wouldn't help her, though. Fortunately, she could be honest when she answered. "No. I think he'd hate us for that. He's more useful as he is."

"Can you trust him to keep quiet?" Victor asked. She had anticipated the question.

"I believe so," she answered, again honestly. She didn't add, *at least as long as I do.* "I think if I explain to him what the situation is, and what's at stake, he'd be more likely to keep our secret than he would if he figured it out on his own." Again, it was the truth, just stated in a way to suit her own purposes.

It had, after all, worked for her. Understanding the dangers, for humans and Were alike, and how they'd worked in the past to discredit those who would expose them had kept her quiet for three years. But it wouldn't work forever, and there was opportunity here as well as danger.

He didn't accuse her of projecting, but she knew he was thinking it. To some extent, he may be right, but she was also convinced of the truth of what she'd said. Diaz would keep digging until he'd found the truth, one way or another.

"Most importantly," she said, "together we have the best chance of catching your rogue." The phrasing of course was deliberate: it was the Alpha's mess, and she was working on cleaning it up. *Everybody look at the crisis, and pay no attention to any hidden agenda.*

There was also a protocol here that she was invoking, and Victor realized it and granted her what she'd hoped.

"Inform me if you need assistance, then," he said. "Otherwise, as long as he stays quiet, I'll leave his fate in your hands."

"WHAT'S THIS ONE?" Michael asked, taking out the next page. It was a list of addresses. He recognized a couple of them and looked up at the map pinned to the far wall.

"Yeah. Locations of all the attacks," Aaron said when he saw where he was looking. "Nothing new, though - just the ones we already have. Probably she was looking for a pattern, too."

He walked over to the map and started tracing them in order. The most recent attack, at the Chandler's house on Butner Road, far to the west, almost in Beaverton. The one before that on the other side of the city, 85th and Halsey. Something caught his eye. An icon on the map indicating the local train system. There was a major Max transit hub just a few blocks away. He looked back over at the Chandler one.

"Hey, check this out," he said. Phil and Aaron both came

over to see where he was pointing. "Chandlers." He touched the head of the pin indicating their house. "Sunset Max station." He tapped the map showing a light rail stop about four blocks away. He continued, tapping the map with each new location. "Bendt, sixty-second and Hoyt, three blocks from the last MAX stop before it crosses eighty-second avenue. And Walstone." He indicated the first murder. "Fifteenth and Lafayette. Max stop three blocks away."

"So..." Phil said, looking at the map. "Maybe there is no connection between the victims. Our killer's taking the train."

"Not sure how that helps us with a pattern, though," Aaron said. "The train goes everywhere."

Michael had caught it, though. "Yeah," he said, "And everywhere it goes, it has cameras."

"We know exactly when most of the attacks were. Let's check out some train schedules and give TriMet a call. I have a feeling we're going to have a lot of video to start digging through."

THE NEXT DAY, there was a knock at the conference room door, and Michael turned to see Detective Alice Johansen stepping inside.

"Hi," she said, and handed him a USB thumb drive. "They asked me to bring you this on my way over."

"Ah!" Aaron said gleefully and took it from Michael's hand while he was staring down at it. "Is this the TriMet footage?"

Michael let him take it over to the computers and turned his attention back to the detective.

"On your way over?" he asked. "If not that, then what brings you down here?"

"Temporary reassignment," she told him. "They seemed to think you could use some help down here."

"That we can," Aaron told her before Michael could answer. "Pull up a chair, looks like there's a couple hundred files on this thing for us to look through."

She sat down at the table while Aaron started the first of the videos. "Great. What are we looking for?"

Aaron looked to Michael. "A man and a dog?" he suggested.

No dog, Michael thought. Just a guy who turns into a wolf. He couldn't say it. They'd think he was joking at first. If he insisted, then they'd think he was crazy. They'd spend all their time arguing about which while the killer was getting away. There had to be a way he could convince them. Head back to the preserve and hope to run into another one? And... what?

"No, guys, seriously, this wolf will turn into a human. All I need to do is, uh, wrestle it into submission." There had to be a way. But for now...

"How about a guy in sweatpants, sandals, and t-shirt?" he suggested. The outfit should be unusual enough for the cool October evenings that there shouldn't be too many people dressed like that. He hoped.

While they watched, Michael filled Alice in on what they knew so far. The multiple suspects they found and then discarded.

"Vera Rosen?" Alice exclaimed. "I know her. Crime reporter, right? I mean, I don't know her, but I've seen her around. Is she a suspect?"

"Not directly," Michael said. "But we have reason to suspect a conspiracy of some sort, involving multiple people and she is somehow involved."

"Shit. This is bigger than I thought. What are you doing about her?"

Aaron indicated the other computer monitor, with its split screen showing the inside of Vera Rosen's house.

"Is that...?" Johansen started.

"Yep," he said. They both knew what she meant. Surveillance of this extent wasn't undertaken lightly, and especially not against a member of the press.

"Who else knows about this?"

"Just those of us in this room, and one other," Michael answered her. "And the Captain of course," he added.

"What about that Jablonski guy?" Johansen asked, scanning the big board.

"He's involved, but has an airtight alibi for the last killing," Michael said.

She turned her attention back to the video playing on the computer screen. "Okay, what about this Sid guy the second victim's father mentioned?" she asked while she watched.

"We tracked him down to Seattle," Michael responded. "He's in jail awaiting trial for an unrelated domestic violence case. Has been since before the first murder."

"So, violent fuck, but not our killer."

"Afraid not."

"And Naked Car Man?" she indicated the man who had broken into Sam's car after his death.

"No ID on him yet. He's our best suspect so far. Even if he didn't kill the others, he may have killed Sam."

"Detective Bailey? He was murdered? I'd heard he was attacked by a pack of wolves."

"We think that occurred after he was killed."

"Shit," she said. He knew how she felt. "So why is car guy naked?"

Because he's a werewolf. He probably just turned from wolf to human and hasn't gone back to the locker room to get dressed yet. How would she react if he said it? A wry laugh?

Stunned disbelief? Slowly inching away from him until she could demand to be transferred back to her own precinct? Depends on how he said it, he supposed. Maybe she'd believe him, and they could get on with stopping them. Somehow, he doubted that.

"Hey, check this guy out," Aaron said and paused the video playback. Michael turned his attention back from Detective Johansen and back to the security video from the trains.

Aaron had paused it and they both saw immediately who he was referring to.

"Geez, someone call central casting," Johansen said.

The man was dressed in dark blue sweatpants, a greenish t-shirt with what looked like some obscure metal band's logo on it, and cheap sandals. Late 30s, maybe early 40s, doughy, with thinning hair he'd combed over from one side, and an angry, disapproving scowl on his face.

"Yeah, I think even if I didn't know who we were looking for and someone showed me this picture and asked what his hobby was, I'd guess serial killer."

"Serial killer, or internet troll," Aaron agreed, "Could go either way."

"No reason it has to be one or the other."

You couldn't go to court with that, of course, but it was certainly enough to warrant investigation. The idea that the murderer would be the person you'd least expect was purely an invention of Hollywood. Nine times out of ten it was exactly the first person you'd finger.

"Get me a printout of that," Michael said. "The hospital says Chandler will be awake soon. We'll see if he recognizes him."

By the time he was about to leave, Phil had come in and joined the search through the video archives. They'd found several more pictures of the same man. He had no doubt they'd found their suspect. They'd sent it down to the lab to run an image search to see if they could match it with a name.

It did. They printed it at the front desk and Michael went down to get the papers, gathering them into yet another folder to add to the piles on the conference room table.

He opened it for all to see and pointed to the first page. It was a mugshot from about ten years ago, but it was unmistakably the same person. Grant Talman. "Looks like he served a year in prison for burglary in Portland." He pointed out. The next page, though, was the clincher.

"Will you look at that," Aaron said, with a low whistle.

There were two arrests in San Diego.

"How'd she know?" Phil asked. It took Michael a moment to realize what he meant. One of Rosen's first queries was about wolf attacks in San Diego.

"That's a really fucking good question," he said. "And it might be worth bringing her in here to get an answer."

Both the San Diego arrests were for assault. There was an open warrant out for him for not reporting to his court ordered anger management class.

"Burglary and assault. A real winner," Johansen said.

"Skipped town and came back home, it looks like," he said. "Unfortunately, the last local address we have was before he went to jail."

There was no doubt of it. They had their man. Now all they had to do was find him.

"THAT BITCH!" Grant swore out loud, tossing the paper aside. Digging through several papers, looking for news of himself, he'd come to realize that several of these articles had the same byline: Vera Rosen. At first, he was excited. She was interested in him, whoever she was. Indeed, for the last two weeks she'd written about nothing else as far as he could tell.

But the last couple...she'd mentioned "growing mountains of evidence." Bullshit! He hadn't left any evidence behind! There was nothing they could have found. She didn't say what this so-called "evidence" was. She was probably just making it up. He did leave his clothes. Sweatpants, t-shirts, cheap sandals, but those could belong to anybody. They sell them at the dollar store.

And her characteristic of him. She made him look like a pathetic loser who was intentionally killing young girls. That wasn't true at all. Sure, that's who he'd killed but that wasn't because he was a coward. She didn't understand. He stopped at that and a broad smile crept across his face. Yes. She didn't understand. But she would. He'd make her understand. He'd find her and turn her into the same kind of creature he was. Then she'd know. Then she'd be sorry she wrote all those horrible things about him.

But he would be magnanimous. She could join him. He'd spare her life, and she could learn what it really meant to be a werewolf. She'd repent of thinking him a coward who only went after young girls. She could understand he was trying to recruit, to make a new one, but she alone was lucky enough to get turned that way. The wolf form was raw, powerful, uncontrolled. And he wouldn't have to say anything more than that, but she'd understand not to make him angry, not to invoke the wolf against herself. Oh, he couldn't wait to turn her. He was going to have so much fun. He'd bite her and she would have no idea what had happened, and then he'd show up at her door a few days later.

"Hi," he'd say, with his suavest smile. "Remember me?"

She'd be scared at first, but he'd just smile again and tell her that it's Okay. It's more than Okay, it's better now. *You're* better.

And then he'd tell her the rules. You don't have to wait for the full moon. You can change at any time. If you bite other people they'll change. It's a whole new world, and she could share it with him.

He needed to find her. He knew someone who could help him, but it would cost. He hadn't hit a house for money for a while. Not since San Diego. He'd cased that place carefully, but the woman was home and when he grabbed her, she'd changed form and attacked him. It was only through his strength of character and extraordinary willpower that he was able to survive. Flee. Recover.

It was only later that he realized what he was, and what power he had now. He could do anything he wanted. Nobody could stop him. Nothing could harm him. But for now, he needed money to pay an acquaintance for an address. He grabbed his jacket off the hook on the back of the door. Time to go hunting again. A day. Maybe two. And then, he thought, Vera Rosen will be mine, one way or another.

"VERA ROSEN," Carl said. "I'm sure of it."

"Vera fucking Rosen," Kevin whistled. "The Alpha's right hand. You didn't mess up small." He and Shelly were both sitting on the couch opposite him, facing him as if in judgment.

Shelly shot her boyfriend an annoyed look, for which Carl was grateful. "And you're sure this human saw you change?" she asked.

"Yes, I'm sure he saw me," Carl answered again. "He was like twenty feet away from me, up in that tree."

"What would a human be doing in the preserve?" Kevin asked him. What, did he think he was lying or something?

"How the hell do I know? What does it matter anyways?
He saw me change."

"Why were you following a human anyway? You should
have just stayed away from him," Shelly said.

"I don't know. I just was. I was in form, Okay? It's too late to
change that now." How could they miss the point so spectacu-
larly? "The question is what do I do about it?"

"And why would Rosen attack you?" Kevin asked, as if he
hadn't even spoken.

"I don't know!" he said, raising his voice again.

"Obviously to stop him from killing the human," Shelly
said. "Maybe she saw him before she changed, or perhaps she's
just better at remembering the rules when in form." He bristled
at the mention of the rules. He knew damn well not to attack
humans. So... why did he?

"I still don't get why you changed in front of the human
instead of just running off," Kevin said again.

"She made me. She held me down and kept her jaws
around my neck until I did."

"Huh," Kevin said. "That changes things a bit."

"It does?" he asked, caught off balance by the sudden
reversal.

"Sure. Say she reports you. Maybe you'll be in a bit of trouble, but not as much as she will. Who do you think the Alpha's
going to come down hardest on, the person who changed or the
person who forced them to?"

"I'm not so sure about that," Shelly said. "They're close.
Like, really close. He'd probably forgive a lot for her that he
wouldn't for anyone else."

Shit. "What about the human?" he asked.

"What about him? He saw you change. So what? Who's
going to believe him? Without proof, everyone's going to

assume he's either lying or crazy. Haven't you ever seen the X-files? That's how it always goes."

This seemed somewhat shaky reasoning.

"You're probably right about that," Shelly said. "It wasn't someone who you recognized, right?"

"No, but..."

"Then he probably doesn't know who you are, either." That seemed shaky reasoning at best. There always seemed to be a lot more people who recognized him than he recognized. But she continued, "Even if it ever does get back to Stumpp that a human saw someone change in the preserve, how would they ever know who it was?"

That made him feel a little better. But it still seemed a thin hope on which to bet his life.

"I just wish we knew who the human was," Shelly said again.

"Well, we don't!" Carl shouted, getting frustrated again.

"Calm down, I'm just saying we could maybe use this somehow."

"What? How?" Kevin asked.

"Look, we got this killer on the news, and now a human saw Carl change. We want to reveal ourselves, right? Maybe we should all change in front of humans. We should turn more, and encourage them to change, too."

"We shouldn't change ourselves," Kevin said. "If the Alpha catches us, it'll be over before we start."

"So, we go back to your original plan. Grab a few people, change them, tell them what's what, and let them go off on their own to do their own thing. If we do a few, and they do a few, and so on, it won't matter if a bunch of them get caught, as long as there's more who don't."

Carl didn't like where this was going. But... something had to change. He had a close call today - his life could have been forfeited through no fault of his own. It still might be. The preserve was supposed to be a safe place for them. If it wasn't, then nowhere was safe. And never would be as long as there were Alphas who could rule a territory and impose their every whim upon them. If the secret was out, if everyone knew of the existence of the Were...

"All right," Kevin was saying. "Let's do it, then. I can get a van and a cabin in the woods. You in?" He looked to Carl.

He hesitated, but only briefly. If this worked, if they would really overthrow the secrecy themselves... wasn't it worth the cost? Never again having to hide, to live in fear of the Alpha finding out he'd changed in front of the wrong person or violated some rule. For there to be no more Stans, murdered just for falling in love with the wrong person.

"Yeah," he answered. "Yeah, I'm in." He looked up and met Kevin's gaze. "What do we do?"

SHE'S GONE, Gordon thought to himself for the hundredth time this morning. She won't come visit. She wouldn't be at the house when he got home. He'll never see her again. She didn't run when he said. Instead, she'd come up to check what was wrong. Of all the times...

That was one of the first things they'd told him, after he woke up. Woke up this time, he thought. Apparently, he had woken up several times in the last few days, but he didn't remember any of it. Days. He had been in and out of consciousness for days. He'd had some kind of psychotic episode the first day he'd been brought in. Trashed the room, and they'd found him lying naked on the floor, his gown shredded. They'd transferred him to a different room and kept him sedated since then, to "aid in his recovery." Physically, he felt fine, but they wouldn't let him leave. He had a feeling that if he insisted, things would get worse.

So, he sat. And he waited. And he wandered about the room, and every few minutes, or hours, he'd sit down on the chair or the bed or the floor, and cry and wonder about Barbara. He'd been unconscious when she'd been killed. Murdered. By the same man... man? It wasn't a man. He thought of the "psychotic episode" and the torn gown and... no. He wasn't going to think about that. That way lay madness.

They told him a policeman had been asking about him, and he very much wanted to speak to him as well. But he wasn't sure what, if anything, to tell him.

He was lying in the bed when the cop arrived and decided to stay there.

"Mr. Chandler?" the man asked, after a nurse let him into the room. "Detective Diaz," he introduced himself. "I'm deeply sorry for your loss. I know this isn't a good time for you, but I need to ask you some questions."

Right to it then. Not even a mention of his condition or where he currently was.

"Are you the cop looking for her killer?" Gordon asked him.

"I'm the head of the task force, yes."

This was a surprise to him. "A whole task force? Is that usual for a murder like this?"

"It wasn't the first. We believe someone is using a trained dog, or maybe even a wolf..."

He made his decision. "It wasn't a dog," he said. After a pause, he continued. "It wasn't a wolf, either." He hesitated again. Finally, after a long silence, he said it. "At least, not at first."

The cop's surprise at that was unmistakable. Surprise, where there should have been confusion.

"You know something about this man." Gordon meant it as a statement, not a question.

The police detective hesitated only the briefest fraction of a second. "Yes. Like I said, we've been investigating for several weeks now."

"But it's more than that. Tell me."

Again, the hesitation. "Okay. I will, but first, tell me everything you remember."

Not good enough. "Promise me first. Promise me you'll tell me the truth."

The detective was silent for a long moment, then finally said, "I promise." He took a seat, and Gordon began to talk.

"He was in my room standing in my door when I got upstairs," he began. "He was dressed sloppily in clothes that he'd pulled out of my dresser. And then...and then, he kind of shifted, like he turned sideways only sideways wasn't him, it was...whatever it was, it shredded the clothes he was wearing, like they couldn't contain him anymore. The clothes fell to the floor, but the man...the man was gone and in his place was the wolf."

The cop just sat there, quietly, letting him continue. He was so hard to read. He didn't seem to regard his story as the ravings of a madman, though, which had to mean the police knew something.

When Diaz didn't respond, he continued and told him the rest. Barbara came home. He yelled to her to run, and the wolf leapt at him, knocking him down. He remembered teeth and jaws and tatters of cloth fluttering away behind it. The next thing he knew he was in the hospital, and somewhere between surgeries he had been lucid enough for them to tell him that his daughter was dead.

For a long time, nobody spoke. They sat and looked at each other. Appraising.

"I'm not crazy," Gordon finally said.

"Didn't say you were." The detective opened his briefcase and passed him a photo of a young white man, probably in his early 20s. "Is this him?"

"No," he responded, disappointed.

"Are you sure?"

"I got a real good look at him. He was at least ten years older, a bit of grey and a paunch." They were both ignoring the more fantastic part, the important part, of his story. The cop handed him another picture. Another man, mid to late 30s, but slight, athletic build, like a dancer.

He shook his head. "Who are these guys? Are they...?" he didn't want to say it. He forced himself to anyway. "Were-wolves, too?"

To his credit, the cop hesitated for only a second before answering. "I... I think so. The first one, Carl Jablonski, at least. I watched him transform from a wolf to a man just a few days ago."

"How long have the police known?" Gordon asked him. He could feel his anger rising and could tell he didn't fully keep it out of his voice. "How long have you been covering it up? Who else knows? Just how high does this conspiracy go?"

"I don't know." Diaz held eye contact. "I've only learned it recently myself. I don't think anybody else in the force knows. I'm honestly not sure that I'm ready to accept the existence of werewolves. But I can't think of a better explanation."

Could it be true that the cops only now are learning of these things at the same time he did?

"Either way," he said, "I'd think about getting some silver bullets."

"I'll let you rest." Diaz stood up to go. "If you feel up to it, I'll send a sketch artist over to get a description. If you can describe both the man and the wolf, that could help immensely. You might want to consider implying they're not one and the same."

"These people are killers, detective. Don't keep their secrets for them."

"Not for them." The cop responded. "I mean to bring them down. But I'm not ready to be branded a madman yet. Are you?"

Gordon didn't have an answer for that

SIX

WATCHING, THE DETECTIVES

Michael was sitting at the table in his war room, watching Vera Rosen type. In his hand he held the dart he'd taken from her closet, turning it over and over. He finally realized, too late, what had struck him as so unusual about it. The needle was not made of surgical steel, as would be customary for such a projectile, but of silver. Which now made sense. He hated that it did, and still didn't know what to do about it.

He looked back over to the wall with the big map on it. Earlier, he'd added the picture of Carl Jablonski next to the unknown man who'd ransacked Sam's car at the preserve. A string from Jablonski's picture led to a pin on the map with a red X next to it. The address from the DMV had turned out to be out of date, and there was no forwarding address. They'd debated releasing either image to social media to see if they could get citizen involvement in identifying or locating their suspects but decided against it. They didn't want to tip them off that they were being searched for. He couldn't even get an arrest warrant for Jablonski since he couldn't tell anyone what for.

In one of the four windows of the computer monitor, Vera Rosen was sitting in her bathrobe at her own computer in her living room. She was typing furiously, occasionally pausing to stare at the screen and take a sip of her coffee. Every time she typed something, the text appeared on the smaller monitor here. She was writing an update to the "dog-mauling" stories. He was sure she knew better. He looked down at the silver-needled dart in his hand. Yeah, she definitely knew better.

The article was focusing on the victims. It was fascinating to see how slowly it was entered, all the false starts, deletions, entire sections being re-written. She used cut and paste a lot. Moving sections around, maybe? Trying to improve the overall flow of the article? This was a lot more than relating facts - the presentation was important as well. It was a fascinating process to watch.

She'd conducted interviews with the neighbors. The girl, Victim Two, Barbara, seemed to be well thought of in the neighborhood. Many of them seemed genuinely distraught about her death. She had babysat for half the families there. "Cheerful" and "Always willing to help" were some of the quotes used. The news piece could double as her eulogy.

Rosen had also spoken to Gordon Chandler sometime after Michael had. No mention of werewolves, though he didn't know whether that was because Chandler had kept quiet about it when speaking to her, or because she had decided not to put it into her article. All the hints were there, though, for someone who knew what they were looking for. She mentioned that he was expected to make a complete recovery, and much faster than previously estimated. He was planning on leaving the next day, which was even more impressive given that the doctors initially weren't sure he was going to survive his wounds. There was no mention of months to years of physical therapy before he could function at 100% again.

He thought of the wolf he'd shot at the preserve. He had been certain at the time he had hit it dead center. Later he'd decided he must have just grazed it. Perhaps his initial impression was correct. In all the movies, werewolves healed almost instantly from any wound not caused by silver. And they became werewolves by being bitten. Chandler had mentioned that they'd found him naked on the floor. Did that mean he was one of them now? Did he even know himself? He had accepted the idea a lot quicker than Michael had, he must at least suspect as much. But if he thought he might be a werewolf, wouldn't he want to keep quiet about it? Don't keep their secrets for them, he had told Michael. But if he was one of them...

The door opened, interrupting his train of thought. Phil entered, bearing a hardcopy of the picture of Grant Talman.

"Still don't want to spam this out to social media?" Phil asked him, as he took it to pin up on the board.

"No. I'm afraid he'll just leave town and pick up somewhere else if he knew we were this close to finding him," Michael said. He didn't say that he was worried some other town wouldn't be prepared to deal with werewolves. Whatever was happening, it would have to be stopped here in Portland or it might never be.

He stuck it up next to the one of Jablonski.

"Thought we'd ruled him out as a suspect," Phil said.

"He didn't do the last attack," Michael said. "But he's definitely involved somehow."

"Involved?" Phil echoed. "We're investigating a conspiracy now?"

"I'm beginning to think so," Michael responded. "Even if there's only one killer, there's a whole lot of people who seem to know more than we do. Vera Rosen, for one, and Carl here."

"Sounds a little paranoid."

"Yeah? Who's Rosen reporting to?" He indicated the card labeled simply "V" connected by string to Rosen's.

"I didn't say you were wrong."

"WHAT'S THAT?" Phil said, pointing at the top right window.

Michael looked up at the kitchen feed. The door was slowly swinging open. As they watched, a man wearing a baggy T-shirt and sweatpants inched his way in. Michael picked his phone up off the table, and with his left hand opened her file, searching for her number.

"It's him!" he shouted unnecessarily. He turned to Phil. "Get everything we have in the area to Vera Rosen's house now. The killer's there right now."

Phil was already out the door heading to his desk, on the radio to dispatch.

The man, a serial killer, a werewolf if that was to be believed, had slid into the kitchen. He froze as Rosen's phone rang.

She continued typing, ignoring it.

"Pick up!" he shouted at the screen. The man in the kitchen cocked his head to one side, as if thinking, trying to decide what to do.

The phone went to voicemail. He immediately dialed again.

The man began to advance again.

Rosen glanced at her phone, looked puzzled for a second, then finally answered.

"Hello?" she said.

"Veer! Get out. Get out now!" Michael shouted into the phone.

"What? Detective Diaz?" She sounded confused.

"The killer. He's in your house. You've got to get out of there."

She stood up and looked about. Phil came back in. "A black and white will be there in four and a half minutes."

On the screen, Rosen was moving, but not toward the front door.

"No!" He shouted into the phone, "There's no time! Just run out the front door, police are on their way."

She stopped and looked around. Dammit. He'd just blown the surveillance. But worse than that, she still wasn't leaving.

She headed down the hall, toward her bedroom.

On the screen, the killer stepped into view of the hall camera. He was unmistakably the same man from the photo he had hung up not ten minutes ago. His smile of anticipated pleasure sent shivers down Michael's spine. Veer stepped out of the range of the camera, and he could hear a door close. On the bedroom screen, the light turned on. They could hear movement but could see no more than that.

"Get out, get out, get out!" he thought intensely at the screen. Phil stood beside him, equally mesmerized, radio in hand.

They could hear a closet door slide open. "No!" he thought again. "There isn't time. Just go!"

"She went for the tranq gun, maybe?" Phil suggested, "Not the pistol in the nightstand?"

Michael hadn't even thought of that. He glanced down again at the silver-tipped dart. *She knows what she's doing. She's prepared for exactly this.*

The bedroom door slammed open. A man's voice spoke. "Big gun, little girl. But do you really think you've got the..."

Whatever else he was going to say next was cut off by the

sound of a rifle shot. It was accompanied by a scream of pain, and loud cursing.

There was a crashing sound, followed by the sound of shattering glass. Michael and Phil both stared at the empty screen the noise was coming from. They heard a loud thud and wood splitting. A grinding sound of furniture sliding roughly across a floor ending in a reverberating slam. Then another crash and a scrape as metal against wood and splintering glass. And in the midst of it all there could be heard a low animal growl and a sudden canine yelp of pain.

"The dog!" Phil said, then shifted his gaze to the other windows on the screen. "I didn't see it. Did you?"

Michael just shook his head. There was no dog. What there was, they both saw walk down the hall. But it was a human when it did.

There was a sudden loud crash, of splintering wood and glass, followed by a few seconds of quiet whimpering, then silence. They both stood where they were, both staring at the screen. A moment later they could hear the sound of a siren approaching.

Michael hung up the phone and slid it into his pocket. "Let's go," he said to Phil, and turned toward the door.

TWO SQUAD CARS were already parked in front of the house, lights flashing. A street-facing window near the end of the wall had shattered from the inside, taking part of the frame with it. Even if he hadn't already known where the bedroom was, he'd have recognized what made the final loud crash he'd heard over the computer. They'd already taped off the yard and sidewalk in front of the house, and a crowd was beginning to gather. He almost looked for Veer among them, but obviously she wouldn't be there. He was afraid of what he'd find inside the house. Phil parked the car behind one of the marked vehicles and left their own light flashing to signal that they belonged here.

A woman came out of the house and down the steps to greet them.

"One of you Diaz?" she asked when he and Phil got close.

"That's me," Michael answered her.

"Leanne Washington, detective, fourth precinct," she said, holding out her hand.

"Detective Phil Lee," he said, introducing Phil.

Detective Washington lifted a stretch of tape and they followed her in. "We got here maybe ten minutes ahead of you. Looks like a big fight in the bedroom, but nobody's inside."

"Nobody? Where's Rosen?"

She shrugged. "Not inside. A couple of officers are searching the neighborhood now. Neighbor said he saw what looked like a couple of wolves fighting on the lawn, then they both ran off behind the house."

"A couple?" Phil broke in.

"No people?" Michael said at the same time.

She picked up on the implication of Phil's statement immediately. "Wolf doesn't surprise you, but two does?" she asked.

"Fill you in later," Michael said.

"Well, nobody back there now. Probably jumped the fence and took off who knows where. If anyone's seen a pair of wolves running through town, though, nobody's called it in."

Michael looked up when they were halfway down the hall. Even knowing where the camera was, he couldn't see it from here. Phil, following his gaze, gave it a quick smile and a wave.

Washington shot him a puzzled look, but it was Michael who answered.

"We've got the place under surveillance. We thought Rosen might have been connected somehow to our killer."

"I'm guessing you were right. Did you get him on video?"

"Yeah. I think we got a pretty good shot of him. I'll have someone pull a still from the recording and send it over."

"On it," Phil said and pulled out his phone, hanging back as they proceeded to the end of the hall.

She was right about a fight.

There was blood splattered across the closet mirrors, which were both shattered, and one of the sliding doors hung limp, off its track. The footboard of the bed was broken in half and even the mattress had been torn. The rifle lay in the ruins of the closet, next to Rosen's robe.

Must've been a hell of a fight.

"Looks like she hit him once," Washington said. "But didn't put him out. He interrupted her reloading for a second shot. Bolt action's not the best choice for home defense." She gave a sort of half-smile at her observation.

Michael found he didn't want to open the nightstand to check if the pistol was still there. He didn't know this woman and she didn't know Rosen, but he didn't like her thinking she was stupid to go for the rifle when there was a handgun available. And he couldn't explain why a silver dart would be better than a lead bullet. He'd have to find a way to tell everyone else, somehow, and without everyone thinking he was crazy. He needed proof. Damn Aaron for not trying harder to get a working camera in the bedroom anyway.

"That's weird," Washington was saying. She directed his attention to a pile of shredded clothes near the damaged dresser. T-shirt, sandals, sweatpants, it looked like.

"Don't touch them!" he said reflexively. She gave him a withering look. Of course she knew better. "Sorry. They belong to the killer," he said. "We found the same at the other crime scenes."

"Why are they shredded?" she asked him.

That was the question, of course, that couldn't be answered.

"We're working on that."

"I'd love to see the surveillance footage from this room," she said.

He shook his head. "Camera in this room's behind the dresser. Didn't catch anything but sounds."

"Bummer that."

"Tell me about it. I'm gonna take a look around back. You good to coordinate with CSI here?"

"Not a problem," she said.

He headed outside by himself. Based on witness reports, Washington had guessed the wolves - two of them - had jumped over the back fence. On a hunch, though, he took a closer look at the hedge. About halfway back along the house, it was broken and pushed aside, as if something had run through it. Peering into it, he found there was an old fence on the opposite side that appeared undisturbed. Not through it, then, just out of it. Someone - some *thing* - had hidden in the hedge, then came out when it was clear. But out to where? A bunch of shorter bushes lined the other side of the narrow walkway, along the house. He peered closer into them and saw it. Along the wooden fronting of the sill wall, a section covering what used to be an access port had a small gap in it. On a hunch, he pushed it, and it swung open. He dropped down and crawled in, allowing it to swing back closed behind him.

He saw it lying on the ground near a central pillar and recognized it immediately. The gray coat fading to white down the legs, with a patch of black on her forehead. This was the wolf from the preserve that had attacked Jablonski and saved his life.

A wiser part of him was shouting: Wounded animal! Dangerous! He ignored it. There was blood on the ground nearby, but he could see no obvious wounds. He guessed they had healed already. A handy ability, that. The wolf was sleeping now. Carefully, he took off his coat, remembering the boy in the woods, and her own discarded robe, and laid it out over her. The wolf stirred slightly but didn't wake. He settled back, sitting on the ground, resting his back against another pillar. He could hear the footsteps of the people above.

After several minutes of sitting and waiting, his radio squawked. He thought about ignoring it, but only for a second.

"Diaz," he said into it, adjusting the volume to keep it low.

"Hey, you around anywhere?" Phil's voice asked, "You Okay?"

"I'm good. I'm following up another lead. I'm going to be offline for a bit. I'll fill you in when I get back."

It was a breach of protocol, and Phil was too good a cop not to notice it. He was also too good a friend to push back. Again. He was going to have a lot of explaining to do, at some point. He turned off the radio and waited for Vera Rosen to wake up.

VEER WOKE WITH A START. There was someone else here. There was a moment of panic, and she sat bolt upright, clutching the blanket to her chest as she did. Then she realized it wasn't a blanket, and she wasn't in bed. She was under her house, sitting on the hard ground, and detective Diaz was sitting here, waiting for her. She looked at him, then toward the exit and. He had positioned himself so that he would not be blocking her way out. That would not have been by accident.

He intentionally didn't want her to feel trapped. She realized also that it was his coat she was currently under.

She repositioned herself so that her back was to the pillar she had been lying next to. He quickly looked away as she moved. The gesture was neither necessary nor expected. After years of changing along with others, she was used to nakedness by now. But those were Were. Diaz was human.

"Thank you," she said, indicating the coat, as well as letting him know she was settled. He hadn't spoken, but he nodded an acknowledgment.

"So," she said, but didn't continue.

"So," he agreed.

"So," she wasn't sure what to say, but didn't want to leave it there. "How long have I been under surveillance?"

It took him a moment to answer. He seemed almost in shock. Understandably so. It wasn't an easy truth for a rational person to accept.

"A few days," he finally said. "Since Tuesday." There was another long pause before he spoke again. "How long have you been a werewolf?"

And there it was. She only thought briefly of denying it. She wasn't a werewolf, she was just hurt in the fight and decided to crawl down here. Naked. Without a scratch on her. Ignore whatever you saw on your surveillance cameras... Denying it would have been insulting as well as fruitless at this point.

"Just over three years," she answered.

Silence again. She could hear faint footsteps overhead. She was about to ask about them when he finally spoke again.

"So now you're... what? A rogue werewolf, leading a lonely war on your own kind to avenge their wrongs against humanity?"

She almost laughed. She could tell he wasn't entirely serious, though the question wasn't quite in jest, either.

"Not quite." She smiled as she said it. "The Were you're
hunting is the rogue. We're only looking to stop him."

"So, Victor Stumpp is like, what, your boss?"

"No, he's..." she began to reply, then noticed the expression
on his face. Just for a moment, then it was gone. But it was
enough to let her know she'd fallen into the trap. He hadn't
been sure about Victor. He was now. He wasn't quite as out of
the loop as he seemed. It wasn't just her they'd been investigating. It was done well and if she'd been more awake and not
sitting naked under her house after being attacked she wouldn't
have fallen for it so easily. She liked to think that was the case at
least.

She gave a slight smile and a nod to acknowledge the point
and continued. "He's the Alpha of this region."

She watched as he processed that.

"Where are the cameras?" she asked after another long
pause.

"What?" He was shaken out of his contemplation. She
didn't suppose the answer would actually be relevant. She had
to assume that it was unsafe anywhere in the house.

"Did they record... everything?"

"No." That was unexpected. And cause for a glimmer of
hope. "We had them in the living room, kitchen, and hallway.
Unfortunately, the one in your bedroom didn't show anything.
Just the microphone worked."

No camera in the bedroom. Where the fight had been, and
where she'd changed into form. That was good. That was more
than good. That simplified everything. She decided to deliberately lighten the mood.

"Unfortunately? You were maybe hoping to catch me

changing?" She said it lightly, but she knew he'd understand she wasn't referring to her clothes.

"Just did," he responded with a gentle smile. "But no, there's no video evidence. I still can't tell anyone without them thinking I'm crazy. That's how you keep your secret, isn't it? Avoid cameras, discredit witnesses?"

"Pretty much."

"It can't last."

"It has for over four hundred years."

"We haven't had digital cameras in everyone's hands for four hundred years. There hasn't been continuous ongoing footage of every public building, or an international way of communicating the information if there had been. Eventually, you'll be caught."

"We already have. Lots of times."

He was as surprised to hear it as she had been.

"Then how come I haven't heard any of this?"

"Like you said, would you believe it if you had?"

He had no answer to that. But she continued; she needed to make him understand what they were up against. "Search for 'real werewolf' on YouTube some time. You'll find hundreds of hits. How many claim to be real? How many actually are?"

"And... four hundred years? What happened before then? How come the history books aren't full of werewolves?"

"Who says they aren't? But contemporary accounts of werewolves from the dawn of the seventeenth century are even less credible to modern people than YouTube videos. Four hundred years ago, Europe was ruled by the church. They decided we were possessed by demons and tried to wipe us out. There were werewolf pogroms across Europe. In the early sixteen-hundreds there were tens of thousands of trials in France alone and they were all recorded. You can still look a lot of them up today, even read the original transcripts, if you can read seventeenth century French."

He was silent for a moment before finally responding. "It's all right there, and nobody believes it. That's depressing."

"Because you can't tell anyone."

"We've got a killer out there somewhere. We're going to catch him, but when we do, what the hell do I tell the DA?"

She had an answer for that, but she could tell he wasn't ready to hear it. Not yet. There would be no trial. Peter would be called in, and the man would disappear, or maybe seem to take his own life.

"He's got to be nearby." She said instead, "He couldn't have gone very far."

"Maybe not. Maybe. He's gotten away so far."

"I hit him point blank with a very strong tranquilizer. The silver in the needle will keep the wolf from metabolizing it away. Five, ten minutes tops, he'd have passed out, and be out for the better part of a day."

"Damn, that's great news." He thought about it for a second. "I need to let them know, and I can't stay away for too long anyway. You ready to come out?"

It wouldn't really matter what she answered. She knew she had to go with him, ready or not.

"I can have someone take you down to the station, or a hotel, or something."

"A hotel would be nice, actually. I assume my entire house is still a crime scene?"

"'Fraid so. If you need anything from inside, I can have it brought out."

"My laptop, it's in a satchel in the kitchen. And there's a small blue suitcase in the spare room that'll have everything else I need."

"I know the one," he replied.

She barely suppressed a shudder. "I can't say I'm not a little creeped out about that. I assume you had a warrant?"

"We did," he answered, not looking back as she crawled out of the access hatch behind him. "I can get you a copy if you want."

"Eventually, yes." She stopped when they rounded the corner, shocked by the site that greeted her on her own front lawn. Several police cars, lights flashing, yellow tape blocking it off. She finally succeeded in getting to the other side of the tape, she thought absently. No flags on the ground over here, though.

A uniformed police officer came over to escort her to a waiting ambulance. "I'm fine," she told her. "I don't need medical attention."

The woman glanced at Michael for confirmation. He nodded. "We just need to find somewhere to put her up for the night."

"I think I can arrange a safehouse after we get her statement back at the precinct," she responded.

"Perfect," Michael responded. "Let's do that. Give me a minute to get your stuff."

The officer led to her a police cruiser and Veer slid into the passenger's seat, carefully keeping the coat around her as she did.

When Michael brought the two bags out a few minutes later, there was a strange expression on his face.

"What is it?" she asked.

"I'm sorry. It's nothing. Best thing is to get you out of here."

"You wanted to ask me something."

"Not sure if you'd know. But, yeah. Can you give us a moment?" he asked the officer. This time she looked to Veer for confirmation, then stepped a few paces away, out of easy earshot.

"How much silver is in those needles? And how much does it take?"

"I don't know." She wasn't sure what he was asking. "It's enough to stop the healing factor from counteracting the drug, if that's what you mean."

"CSI," he nodded toward the house, "tells me he may not have gotten any of the drug."

She was puzzled at that, and it must have shown, as he continued. "It looks like you fired from only a few feet away?"

"Less, I think. He was charging straight toward me."

"Those rifles apparently are designed to be fired from a considerable distance. At such a short range, the whole thing may have just shattered rather than get injected. All you'd have is a really inefficient bullet in that case. They're checking for residue."

"And that's why you wanted to know how much silver."

"Yeah. I wanted to know if our suspect might actually be wounded, or if he was going to heal within minutes."

"I'm afraid I really don't know. I've never actually shot a werewolf with the tranq before. The guy who had it before me always did so from a longer distance." She realized what he was saying. "And that's why you're so eager to get me away from here."

She would prefer to stay. Most of them had no idea what they were dealing with, and she could help. But getting them to accept that fact would take far more time than they currently had. If she stayed here now, she'd only be causing more confusion.

"Fair enough. Once you find him, though, come see me. I have questions, and there's information you need to know. Doesn't matter how late it is. I don't expect I'll be sleeping much tonight."

SOMEWHERE BEHIND THE CLOUDS, the sun was beginning to creep over the horizon by the time Michael got to the safe house. He stopped at a coffee shop down the block to pick up the four cups he was now carrying in a cardboard drink holder. He stopped by the unmarked car posted across the street to drop one off. The officer took it from the carrier gratefully.

"Thanks," the cop said. "Don's on inside duty. Whoever this guy is, he's not going to get by us."

Michael hoped not. But what could they do if he did show up? Nobody here was equipped to deal with the monster. Veer could probably get away again. Hopefully the creature would chase her and not the cops on duty. God, what a horrible thought.

Don was in the living room, reading a book on the couch, when he entered. "All quiet," he reported. "She's been in there for a few hours now."

"A few?"

"Working late." The officer indicated the laptop computer sitting open on the small kitchen table, its power cord dangling across the gap to the wall.

Michael gave him another of the cups of coffee and sent him out to wait with his partner.

THE HOUSE itself was small and uncluttered, plainly decorated. A couch in the front room faced a small TV across a coffee table. He set the drink holder on a fake marble counter that separated the kitchen and pulled out one of the cups for himself. Taking a seat at the opposite end of the table from the computer, he picked up the folded newspaper. He was tired, but he could wait for her to wake up. Werewolf or not, someone had just broken into her house and tried to kill her. He ignored his own long night. He took another sip of his coffee and noticed the paper had been turned to her article, the one she'd been working on the night before.

And there'd be another one in the afternoon edition, he guessed. She'd been up all night writing it. In some professions "somebody broke into my house and tried to kill me" would be a valid excuse for missing a deadline.

He finished his cup of coffee and eyed the remaining cup on the cupboard. No point letting it get cold. Feeling only slightly guilty, he picked it up. Feeling a little more awake now, his thoughts turned toward food. He checked the fridge. It looked like someone had stocked it, expecting the place to be occupied for a few days. What did werewolves eat, anyway? Bacon and eggs, he decided. He found what he needed and set to work. When he heard her stirring in the other room, he started a pot of coffee, tossing out the dregs from the previous night.

He had finished dicing an onion and was stirring it in with the olive oil and basil when she came out of the room, dressed in an oversized T-shirt and a pair of sweatpants that he'd seen in the suitcase in her spare room. It was hard to believe it had only been a week since then.

"What's cooking?" she asked, taking a seat at the counter.

He found a mug in the cupboard and filled it from the coffee pot before handing it to her. "Breakfast," he said.

"Well, hell, if I'd known these places had this kind of service, I'd've gotten into trouble sooner."

"I have a suspicion you have." He meant it to be light-hearted, but she fell silent as he said it. Damn. He didn't want to alienate her before he got the information he needed.

"Not really," she said quietly, staring into her coffee. "Maybe not as much as I should have."

He was about to ask her what she meant by that when she looked up. "You never found him." It wasn't a question.

"No," he told her. She realized that he would have mentioned it first thing if the killer had been caught. "We will. We have pictures; we know how he gets around. We sent the photo to San Diego to see if we can get more information."

"San Diego?" She looked surprised at that. "You've done your homework."

"I'm afraid I just copied yours."

"Teacher's gonna be mad." She took a bite of her eggs. "These are really good. They teach cooking in cop school now?"

"Interrogation 101," he said with a smile, glad the mood had lightened. Her face fell as he said it and he immediately regretted it.

"I'm sorry. It's been a long night. My dad taught me. Mikey," he fell into his imitation of his father's accent, "you're not much to look at, and none too bright. You better learn to cook, or no woman will ever love you."

She laughed at that, but it was strained. They both knew the first was the more honest answer. She had asked him here with the promise of information. Then she realized what he'd said. "Have you slept at all since I last saw you?"

She was quick, even just waking up, she understood the subtext he didn't even mean. He'd have to watch himself.

"No," he replied, "Been a little busy. There'll be time later. You've been busy yourself," he said, indicating the paper. "I read your article."

She picked up the paper in her right hand and the mug of coffee with her left. "They edited it," she said, after a second.

"Not much," he said, and immediately realized his mistake.

Her slight tightening of the lips announced that she did as well. "I'm sorry," he said. "I just..."

"No," she set down the paper and looked him in the eyes, "you were just doing your job. I understand that. It just feels like..." she paused, fishing for the word.

"A violation," he finished for her. "I know. I've done surveillance before. Like you said it's part of the job, but when it's someone you know, it's different. It can seem a little...creepy. I mean, we're not exactly friends, but I...I understand it can seem like I betrayed your trust, and for that, I am sorry."

"Perhaps we could be," she offered. "Friends, I mean. And I suppose turnabout's fair play. I was cribbing off your homework long before you stole mine." He hadn't forgotten about the files she'd copied. Obviously, she hadn't expected him to.

"Will you be willing to testify?" he asked. No reason not to lay all the cards on the table. "When we catch this guy. We've got the evidence, but the defense attorney's going to kill us on the bite marks. There's video of him in your house, but not of the attack."

She took another bite of her breakfast. Stalling. Or thinking it over. "I can say he attacked me. If I say he's a Were - a werewolf - the prosecutor's going to have my testimony laughed out of court."

He didn't like it, but she was right.

"Maybe we can prove to them there is such a thing..."

"There doesn't have to be a trial," she told him. "You could let us take care of him."

"I'm afraid that's not how we do things," he began.

She cut him off, "There is no way to do things. The Portland police have no standard protocol for dealing with werewolves."

What she said was true, but wrong. You don't turn to some

nebulous conspiracy to eliminate a suspect. That wasn't justice that was just...making a problem go away. But could there be justice? Was prosecuting a werewolf killer even an option? How could they ever convince a jury, let alone a judge, that that was what they had? Even if they had someone come in and turn into a wolf right there in court, could they convince the court it wasn't a trick? Even after he saw it the first time, he wasn't convinced it was real.

"So is your dad the reason you became a cop?" she asked him, in an obvious attempt to change the subject. He actually laughed out loud at that.

"No. He wanted me to be a plumber like him. He came around by the time I'd finished training, though, and I never saw him prouder than at my graduation from the academy."

"Where is he now?"

"Passed. Too much of his own cooking."

"I'm sorry."

"It's Okay. It was ten years ago. How about your folks?"

"Both alive and well back in Kansas."

"Kansas? I never pictured you as a country girl."

It was her turn to laugh at that. "It isn't all wheat fields, you know. There are actual cities in the Midwest."

"Did they want you to be a reporter?"

"Oh hell no. I don't think my mother's forgiven me for it yet. Their plan for me was to marry a minister, or at least a doctor, settle down, and give them a bunch of grandchildren. They were horrified when I told them I was not only going to college, but to Los Angeles, the biggest den of sin and iniquity they could imagine."

"Hah! How'd you end up there?"

"I blame my Uncle Joe. Being the subversive bastard he is, he gave me a copy of Nellie Bly's *Ten Days in a Madhouse* for my twelfth birthday. I read it, and then everything else I could find by and about her, and knew by the end of the year that that's what I wanted to do with my life."

"Be committed?" he asked. He smiled as he said it. Obviously, there was more to the story than a woman who'd been committed to an asylum.

"Nellie Bly was a reporter in the nineteenth century. Women reporters back then, the few that there were, were supposed to cover fashion, society events and the like. When a newspaper editor wrote that they couldn't cover real news, she bought a one-way ticket to New York to prove him wrong. She faked insanity and had herself committed to an asylum to write about the abuses there. The articles appeared in the paper over ten days and led to widespread nationwide reforms in the treatment of mentally ill women."

"Wow! In the nineteenth century? I can't even imagine the kind of courage that would take."

She agreed. "She spent a career exposing abuses and corruption of all kinds. She once had to flee Mexico after reporting negatively on President Porfirio Diaz."

"That name I know," Michael responded. After a second, he added, "No relation."

She laughed softly at that.

"She sounds like a remarkable woman. Like someone with a real thirst for justice." The last was aimed at her of course, and he knew she'd pick up on it. If this person was a hero of hers, perhaps comparing the two would convince her to do the right thing. The only thing that assuaged his conscience of the cynicism was his assumption that she'd understand the hint. "And I'd never even heard of her before," he added.

"She was my idol. But it is weird. At one point she was one of the most famous people alive. There a time when everyone in the country was discussing her latest exploits. And now, barely over a hundred years later, hardly anyone even knows her name."

"Like werewolves," he mused. "We forget our history."

"But not entirely. Thanks to the internet, she's made a bit of a comeback over the last decade or so. People are finding her writings and putting them online, and her books are available on Amazon after being out of print for so many decades. Some of us remember werewolves still as well. The secret's been kept for over four hundred years. For good reason. It's not just for our protection, but yours."

"Our protection? How does that work out?" He almost pointed out that the current crisis was hardly protecting anyone but didn't think it would be productive.

"Were have a reputation, even today, of being violent, uncontrollable..."

"Is it entirely undeserved?" he asked. So much for not pointing it out.

"Most of us aren't like that. Attacking humans is pretty much our number one crime."

There was a revelation there, too, and he couldn't ignore it. "You don't consider yourselves human, then?"

"I... that's not the point right now..."

"I'm not sure about that," he said. "I admit my experience is limited, but out of the three werewolves I know about, one's a serial killer, and another tried to kill me on the preserve."

"You were where you weren't supposed to be," she said, which surprised him. Not that she knew it had been him on the preserve, but that she'd admitted it openly. Was that a mistake or a trap?

"And this guy you're hunting," she continued, "is an anomaly."

"I want to believe you, I do. And I haven't forgotten that you saved my life there." He meant it. There must have been a cost to doing so that he wasn't even aware of.

"I didn't know you realized that was me," she said. "Or did I just fall into another trap?"

"No trap. I recognized you in wolf form, under the house, before you...transformed?" He fumbled for the right word to use.

"I was in form when you found me?" she asked. "Did you... did you give me your coat before I changed, then?"

"Yes," he answered her. "Your modesty is intact."

She smiled softly at that. "That's...that actually means a lot. You found me in form, looking for all the world like a wounded dangerous beast, and risked approaching, for all you knew risking your life, just to preserve my modesty. Thank you."

He hadn't actually believed she was dangerous at the time. At least, not very. But he understood what she was saying. "You're welcome. Maybe you're not all violent, but what you're telling me is I've got a secret society in my city, who live by their own laws, and they're willing to kill to preserve their secret. They may not all be psychopaths. I don't think you personally are. But even you just now casually offered me an assassination to avoid revealing your secret."

"I...I'm sorry." Now it was her turn to apologize. "But you can't hold him. Even if you catch him, he'll transform, break out of any handcuffs, shatter bulletproof glass, and laugh at any attempts to shoot him."

"Police cars don't have bulletproof glass," he said because he couldn't think of how to answer the rest of it.

"That's what you pulled out of all that?" But she laughed when she said it.

"And there are ways, there must be. Silver bullets? Tranquilizers? Steel cages? Hell, I don't know, you tell me, but he's killed too many people, and he will be brought to justice."

"Justice doesn't always mean the law," she replied. "Even if you do catch him and hold him, you're going to tell the DA he's a werewolf? Even with video evidence and a dozen witnesses, you'll be a laughingstock."

She was almost certainly right. "I don't know what else to do," he said.

"I've offered one option."

"No. There's got to be a better way."

"There's more," she said. "I told you before that it wasn't just for the protection of the Were that they keep secret. Even if you could manage to convince everyone there are were-wolves, even if I helped, it'd just lead to more deaths. I want to reveal them too. But if handled badly, it could even mean war - Were against humans, each feeling justifiably threat-ened by the very existence of the other. If what reveals the Were is a psychopathic killer, that'll almost certainly be the result."

"I don't know, Ms. Rosen — Veer — I really don't. This is so far beyond me. I'm too far out of my depth in this."

"I know. Believe me, I know. I understand how you feel."

"You've covered up for them." It was sympathy, not judg-ment. He was sure she understood that. She had had to make exactly this decision herself. He understood her choice, though he could not agree with it.

"You've told me how you became a reporter," he said. "How did you become a werewolf? Were you attacked?"

"No. Very few Were are, actually. I don't know of any - at least not recently."

"How recently is not?"

"Victor was attacked in Germany, during the war."

"Which war was that?"

"World War Two."

"World...but that'd make him..."

"He was twenty-five at the time. He's nearly a hundred now."

"I wouldn't have put him much past sixty. Are you immortal?"

"No. But we do heal fast, and seem to be immune to all disease."

"It doesn't sound like too much of a curse."

"It really isn't. It's...It's hard to explain."

"More coffee then?" It was the only thing he could think to say.

"Please." She pushed her empty cup across the counter to him. "And let's move into the living room."

He brought both mugs into the living room, taking a seat on the chair across the coffee table from her. She sat on the couch cross-legged, holding the cup in both hands, savoring the warmth of it. She stared into it for a long while before speaking. He gave her time to gather her thoughts.

"It was three years ago," she began. "I'd already been in Portland for a couple of years, trying to get established up here. I'd heard some rumors of some unsavory business practices from Stumpptown Systems, Victor's company. And some rumors about him, too."

"What sort of rumors?"

"Secret back doors in the software. Blackmail. Fraud. Mob connections. Exploiting third world labor. And a strange secrecy surrounding several 'hunting trips' involving large numbers of people.

"I did some digging and found he'd come from nowhere, forty years ago. No past before then. But he had money already. Computers were just getting started. Apple and Microsoft were new, and he'd decided they were the future. Everyone knew how he'd built his company up, but nobody knew anything about him."

"The Howard Hughes of computers," Michael said, remembering a phrase he'd seen the paper use about the reclusive mogul once.

"Exactly. So, I decided to find out. I faked up a resume, under an assumed name. Nellie Bligh. I changed the spelling and thought I was being clever."

"He recognized the name?"

"Almost a hundred, remember? He remembered her from his childhood."

"Oops."

"Yeah. So, I got the job, but he was watching me from the beginning. He was friendly, drew me out, I couldn't believe my luck at the amount of access I was getting. He caught me searching the records on his computer late one night."

"What'd he do?"

"He invited me on the next hunting trip. Told me he'd give me full access, answer any questions I wanted to ask."

"Oh, that's not ominous at all."

"Yeah, so I thought I was going to die, but was equally afraid to say no. The opportunity outpaced the fear. I agreed. Turns out they really were hunting, only all the hunters were Were. I was freaked, thought I'd be the main course."

"What happened?"

"He kept his word. Told me all about Were society. There were no back doors in the software, no blackmail. His hold over the others was just that he was the Alpha. He's well connected. He can arrange introductions and meetings, conversations, help people find work or funding or projects to fund. They like to do business with other Were when possible. He told me he could use someone like me and offered to make me one of them."

"An offer you can't refuse," Michael said with a wry grin. Her description sounded very much like what the head of an organized crime family did.

"No - he told me if I didn't want to, I could go on my way. Write whatever I wanted, they wouldn't stop me."

"And you believed him?"

"I did. I know now he would have let me go unharmed if I hadn't agreed. Of course, if I tried to reveal their secret, they'd protect it. If simply writing about werewolves didn't do it, they had ways of discrediting people."

"Or eliminating them."

"Yes. If necessary."

"But you agreed. You joined them."

"Long life, heightened senses, no injury or disease, what's not to like?"

"Loss of humanity?"

"I'm still human," she protested. "Still everything I was before."

He wondered about that. She had earlier made a distinction between "Were" and humans. He didn't say anything though.

"Still. To voluntarily turn yourself into a...a..."

"A monster? It isn't like that, not really."

"And I've got about a thousand questions about how that all works. But first, tell me what happened next. What about your big exposé?"

"I wasn't going to go to press with 'Victor Stumpp's a werewolf' of course. I'd never be published outside the lunatic fringe. But he kept his word, full access. Like I said, the blackmail rumors weren't true. And his only hold over so many people is that he's the local Alpha. The Chinese sweatshop was true. One of the factories he'd outsourced to had some rather unsavory labor practices. I found memos and reports and took that to the paper."

"Even knowing what you knew, you crossed him like that?"

"That was our agreement." She said it so matter of factly.

"He must've been pissed."

"No. The bastard had a press conference over it. Confirmed everything I'd written. Vowed to stop, move the jobs back to America. And he did. Opened up a new fab plant in Hillsboro and got a 10% bump in stock almost overnight. Tons of free press, which I'd given him."

"Shrewd."

"Yeah. I was pissed. He used me. I stormed into his office and told him exactly what I thought. He admitted it - he knew what I was taking to the paper. He pointed out that I'd done exactly what I'd set out to: expose a corrupt business, shaming them into improving. Even cut me a final paycheck for the time I'd worked there. I tore it up and threw it back at him."

"Damn. So how come...?"

"Why are we still friends?"

"Yeah."

"I calmed down. The whole thing turned out to be a big boost to my career too - after all, I'd shamed a famous businessman into making positive changes. I talked to him several times after that. He's turned me on to a couple of big stories. He's a valuable resource."

"So, no regrets?"

"I kinda wished I'd kept that paycheck. Turns out executive assistants to major computer magnates get paid a lot more than freelance reporters do."

She said it as a joke, but he thought of the implications. "You could have stayed," he said as he realized it. She was a reporter. It wasn't just a job for her, any more than being a cop was for him. It was her identity, who she was, even more than a werewolf. If she was helping them keep their secret rather than expose it, there had to be a damn good reason. He thought of what Chandler had said: Don't keep their secrets for them.

But she wasn't keeping their secrets. Not from him. Not

right now. She'd recently had a shock, and no matter how in hand she was taking it she had to be shaken. And this was something she couldn't talk about with anybody. He had to learn as much as he could while she was in a mood to talk.

"How's it all work, then?" he asked. "Do you all know each other? How many of you are there?"

Them, he thought, when he saw her reaction to the question. He should have said how many of *them* are there. But she answered.

"In the Portland area, maybe a few hundred. I don't know all of them, though Victor does."

"Because he's the Alpha. So aside from knowing everybody, what exactly does an Alpha do?"

"Mostly he's in charge of enforcing our laws, and as much organization as we have, he does it. He presides at gatherings, sometimes settles disputes between Were, that sort of thing. And, of course, nobody can make more Were without his permission."

"And now we're back to scary."

"What do you mean?" She looked genuinely confused. *Did she really not see the implications here?*

"Where to start?" he said. "Enforce your laws? You already offered to have someone killed. Is that what he does when someone threatens to expose your secret? Is that what'll happen to me if you can't convince me to keep quiet? Will you do it yourself, or is there someone whose job it is?"

She was quiet for a moment and looked down at her coffee. "I don't know," she finally said, her voice sounding smaller than he'd ever heard it before.

"You don't know?" he asked, feeling himself grow genuinely angry.

"It's more complicated than that." She shifted in her seat. "I've basically claimed you, brought you under my protection.

Nobody will do anything to you - kill you, turn you, whatever - without my permission." She looked up then and met his eyes. "But yes, if they think you're a genuine threat, I think they'd have someone kill you regardless of my objections."

"It's good to know you'd object at least," he said bitterly. "What about biting me, making me into...one of you? Surely it's occurred to you that I'm more likely to keep your secret if I shared it."

"It was discussed," she said.

He didn't like that at all. It meant she'd already talked about him to the rest of them. He was in deep now.

"But you objected," he replied, trying to keep the fear and anger both out of his voice. His fate had been discussed, and decisions about his very life were made completely without him even being aware of it, let alone having any say. She claimed that they weren't monsters, but it sounded pretty monstrous to him.

She obviously got the gist of his meaning. She took a long breath before replying. "I won't make you - turn you into a Were. Not without your permission. And neither will anyone else."

"So how does it work? Through biting, like in the movies?"

"Yes. That's one of the few things the movies got right. It doesn't work every time, and it may be more effective under the full moon - or maybe that's just superstition. Nobody really knows. There's a lot we don't know, actually."

"What do you mean?"

"What we really are, for one. We're not wolves when in form. We look like them superficially, but the morphology doesn't match up. Five claws, and the DNA is still human."

"Now you've been copying my homework," he said.

"Teacher's gonna be mad at us both, I guess."

The organization and capabilities, these he needed to know

for the good of the city. There was one question that was more important to him than any of these, though, so he finally asked it. "Who killed Sam?"

She dropped her gaze again. Again, that faraway wistful look. She looked back up before she answered, though and met his eyes. "I don't know," she said.

It may not have been a lie. She probably didn't know who did the actual deed, but she had her suspicions, and he had a feeling they both knew who gave the order.

"He wasn't murdered by your rogue," he said. "Someone within the organization killed him. Whoever it was was at the preserve with you that day. They broke into his car and stole his notes. He wasn't a threat to anyone, only to a secret. And he died for it."

She didn't say anything in response.

He stood up and took his mug to the kitchen.

"I've got a lot of work to do today," he said. "And I suppose you do too. You've got a story to write, and I don't envy you trying to write it. And I've got a killer to catch. I'll be sending over some pictures for you to look at. Your cooperation would be appreciated. If there's anything you need, let me or one of the officers know and someone will arrange it. Don't try to leave the house, and don't try to contact Victor Stumpp."

She nodded, but didn't say anything, just watched him go while she sat on the couch holding her cold empty coffee mug in both hands.

SEVEN
PREDATORS AND PREY

The pain was overwhelming, but the wolf knew he had to keep moving. Flee. Run. Hide. He couldn't fight. Flight was the only option. Every step was agony, but each put more distance between him and the house, and the source of his pain. Loping through the neighborhood, everything was unfamiliar. He had no goal, no destination in mind, only away. Escape.

Somewhere, a human screamed. It was nearby - prey, he caught a whiff of its fear as it fled. It would ease his hunger, help him heal. But he wasn't strong enough to pursue it, not yet. Keep going. Flee. Run. Hide. A vehicle swerved, blaring an alarm as it passed. There were more ahead. Avoid them. Run. Hide.

But something deeper inside overruled his instinct. Something recognized it, though formed no words to convey what it was, other than a possible way to relieve the pain, to seek safety. He took two more steps and reached for the human within, pulling it forth. It struggled, it didn't want to come, it feared the pain. But it knew it was the only hope. It came.

GRANT FELL ONTO THE STREET, splashing down into a puddle, barely catching himself with both hands. Headlights appeared out of the rain and a car swerved around him with a loud honk but didn't slow down. He was naked, lying on the road, and there was an excruciating pain in his side. For some reason he hadn't healed where the reporter had shot him. He pulled himself painfully to his feet and stumbled to the side of the road. A young woman looked at him, shocked, asked him if he was okay, but turned and ran when he just growled an obscenity at her. He took several more steps, down the sidewalk. At the end of the block, a taxi was sitting alongside the road. Step by painful step he reached it. He opened the door and fell into the back seat. "Seventieth and Alberta," he told the driver. "Hurry"

But it didn't move. "What the fuck, man? You drunk?" He glanced back at him in the rear-view mirror. "You don't look like you got any money on you."

"Got money at home. Go!"

The man turned to look at him more directly, and obviously noticed the blood.

"Whoa! You okay? Someone shoot you? Hold on. I'm taking you to the hospital."

"No! No hospital! Home! Please," he added when the car did not immediately begin to move.

He felt disgusted, begging from this lesser man, but it was the only way. He had to get somewhere safe. Shift back into his wolf form so he could heal. He knew he could heal almost anything as a wolf. For some reason he hadn't this time, but he couldn't think about that now. He'd figure it out once he was somewhere safe. He wanted to kill this man for seeing him like this. For arguing with him. He knew he wasn't strong enough to do anything about it though. Not yet. For the first time in a long while he wished he had a gun. God, the pain though. It was nearly unbearable. But he would bear it. He would recover. Once he got home, he could heal, then he could make the taxi driver pay. Him and the reporter. He had made it a rule to never go back to the same place twice. That was how stupid people get caught. But there was an exception for every rule, right?

The car was moving, bringing his salvation closer with every block it wound its way past. Or so he hoped. It was impossible to tell where he was, staring out the back seat's window through the darkness and the rain, but he had made sure the driver understood, in no uncertain terms, what would happen if he was taken to a hospital, or anywhere else other than where he'd been told, or if he ever spoke about this to anybody.

GORDON LAY in his hospital bed, reading about Barbara in the newspaper. He'd only had to ask a couple of times, then demand it a couple more, once he found out such an article existed, before his doctors decided he was strong enough to see it. They were astonished at how well he'd recovered, but still wanted to keep him for a few more days for observation. He was able to use that, a vague threat of leaving on his own if he didn't get his way. The truth was, though, he didn't want to go home. He didn't know how he could ever face the house again. Everything in it would remind him of Barbara. He'd never again come home to a barrage of questions raking him over the coals for every tiny infraction of whatever noble cause she'd picked up this week. No more two dozen text messages when he was in the middle of a meeting. No more stepping into the kitchen to the sound of a lone Cheerio crunching underfoot.

He had thought about calling the office earlier that day, but there had already been a message in his voicemail from his boss. They'd all heard about what had happened of course. "Anything you need, let me know," the message had said. "Take as much time as necessary. Your job will still be here when you come back." He was lucky. Ten years ago, his manager wouldn't have been so generous.

The card and flowers arrived that afternoon. "I'm sorry for your loss," most of the people signing it had written. A few more offers of help, as if there were anything anyone could do, and some longer messages of condolences. The words, long or short, were meaningless. How could any words ever bridge that gulf? Mere language wasn't capable of conveying the enormity of the loss. Compared to the immensity of what needed to be said, all words fell equally short. The meaning came through: you are not alone. The world may seem dark and empty but there are other people in it, people who care about you.

The newspaper article had quotes from some of his neighbors. They all had nothing but praise for Barbara, of course. That, perhaps more than anything, made him believe she really was gone. The fifth time he read the article it didn't say anything different, so he set it down and laid back and closed his eyes. He was startled awake what seemed a moment later by the door opening and the light from the hall hitting him in the face.

He knew something was off about the man in the white smock as soon as he saw him. He stayed silent, motionless.

"Sorry to startle you," the man said. "I've just brought some more medicine. It'll help with the pain."

That didn't make sense. The nurse had been here just an hour ago, and they were supposed to be tapering off the medication.

"It's okay," he said, as calmly as he could. "I'm not in much pain right now. I don't think I need anything."

"Doctor's orders, I'm afraid," the man smiled apologetically. "Trust me, this one's pretty mild, but when the other stuff wears off, you'll be glad to have it." He produced a hypodermic syringe and approached the bed.

"Okay, then, if you think it's best," Gordon said, and offered up his left arm. The man ignored the shunt they'd placed in it. Gordon caught the unmistakable sheen of silver on the needle, which confirmed his suspicions. All of his suspicions at once - who this man was, and what he himself had to be. It felt like a punch to the gut. It seemed fantastical but it was the only thing that made sense. As the false nurse looked down to his arm to plunge the needle into it, he made his move.

He knew he couldn't let up. He had to move as fast and relentlessly as possible. This man would win in anything resembling a fair fight, so he had to take him off guard quickly and keep him there. Reaching across with his free hand, he grabbed the man's wrist. His other hand he slid under his opponent's elbow and pushed up, twisting, trying to aim the needle back toward him. He'd hoped to drive it into his flesh wherever he could reach, but the man twisted and broke free. The needle flew out of his hand and went skittering across the floor. Gordon rolled from the bed, yanking hard on the bed covers to pull them free. He hurled the blanket at the man's face, hoping to confuse, entangle, and blind him. His assailant batted it easily away, but it was sufficient for a momentary distraction and in that moment Gordon sprung. He lunged forward, using his own body weight to slam the man against the far wall.

Time was running out. It'd only be a moment before someone heard the commotion and came to check. He wanted to be gone by then. He struck hard with his elbow, then drew back and punched forward as fast and as hard as he could, landing his fist in the face of his assailant one, two, three times before the man could get his hands up to defend himself. On the fourth swing, he caught Gordon's wrist and pulled. Gordon let him, moving toward him then twisting to come around behind and smash the heel of his other hand into the back of his head as hard as he could. The man staggered forward, and Gordon helped him on his way, slamming him face-first into the foot of the bed. And then nobody was between him and the door. He stepped backward then turned and ran out, slamming it shut behind him.

He sprinted down the hall, grateful to find it unoccupied. A door behind him slammed open. He assumed it was his assailant but didn't dare turn to check. He kept running. Past the elevators. Into the stairwell. Halfway down the first flight, he vaulted the railing, landing hard on the next flight. One of his slippers flew off his foot as he did so, hitting the wall and coming to a rest on the steps half a flight up. There wasn't time to go back up to get it, but it gave him an idea. He took off the other one and hurled it further down the stairway. Then, as quickly and as quietly as he could, stepped through the door to the floor he was on. Once through, he ran into the closest room and closed the door behind him.

For several heartbeats he stood at the door, his back to it, ready to spring into action again if it opened. Another second went by and he heard nothing from the hallway. Had his ruse worked? And for how long?

"You're not a doctor," said a man, lying in a bed across the dim room, hooked up to a number of monitors and tubes.

"Neither's the guy chasing me," said Gordon. "I just want to hide here for a minute, okay? I won't hurt you."

The man frowned at that, then looked toward the closed door. Finally, he gave a little shrug. "All right. Not like I'm getting any other visitors."

"Thanks," Gordon said, and stood at the door, listening for anyone approaching.

"Why's this guy chasing you?" the man asked.

He couldn't think of a good lie, so he told the truth. "He's a werewolf. I think he's trying to kill me," he replied.

"Oh," the man in the bed said. He looked again at the door. He obviously didn't believe him but didn't seem overly frightened by a strange man in his room telling him a werewolf was trying to kill him. They were both quiet for a long while.

"So... Why's this werewolf guy want to kill you?" the man finally asked.

"Because... I think it's because I'm a werewolf too."

"Oh." The guy wasn't much of a conversationalist. But he wasn't making any noise or attracting any attention. And Gordon didn't really feel much like conversation at the moment either.

After another long pause, he asked, "If he finds you, are you going to kill him?"

Gordon thought about it. He didn't want to. His assault a few minutes ago had been brutal and could have killed a normal man. But he'd stopped as soon as he had a chance to flee.

"No," he answered. "I'm just trying to get away. The cops are after him - I'm going to let them handle him."

That seemed to relieve the man a bit. Just a stupid lunatic, not a dangerous one then. Gordon smiled slightly, still facing the door.

Several more long moments went by, there seemed to be no alarm in the hall still. Hopefully that was a good sign. Perhaps his trick with the slipper worked and his assailant had given up and left. Gordon decided to stay just a few more minutes before doing the same.

"Werewolf, huh?" the man in the bed asked.

"Think so," Gordon responded, still watching the door.

"Do you know any vampires, then?"

"No. Sorry. Maybe try the phlebotomy lab?"

The man actually laughed at that. Then got quiet again, "Too bad," he said.

He held up his hand when he heard footsteps in the hall. He braced himself. Hit hard, run fast, he reminded himself. If he could spin around, maybe he could make it to the stairwell again. He shouldn't have waited even this long. He should have found a better hiding place. He checked the door. There was no lock on it. He guessed it really wouldn't make sense for there to be one.

The footsteps receded. Just someone passing by. He let out a breath he hadn't realized he'd been holding, then turned back to the man whose room this was.

"Why's it too bad I don't know any vampires?" he finally asked.

"I thought if I asked maybe one could bite me and turn me into one."

"Why would you want to be a vampire?"

"Super-powers, eternal life, sure I couldn't go out in the daylight, but at least..." he trailed off.

Gordon turned his attention away from the door and fully to the man in the bed.

"Why no visitors, uh..."

"Bill," he answered. He started to lift a hand but then let it fall back down.

"Gordon." Gordon nodded.

"I don't really know anyone out here. Just moved here about six months ago. Supposed to be a new start, ya know."

Gordon could understand that.

"I got a contract-to-hire job, but then I got sick. Diagnosed about a month ago. I knew something was wrong, but I was waiting for the insurance to start before seeing a doctor. Sixty day waiting period to make sure I didn't have any preexisting conditions," he said with a bitter laugh. "Guess they made a good choice."

"What... what are you in here for, Bill?" he asked, afraid his guess was correct.

"Cancer," Bill confirmed it. "Started in the lungs, spread all over now. I got maybe a month. Two if I'm lucky."

No wonder a vampire sounded better than the alternative. "I'm sorry," Gordon said, finally.

"Yeah. Me, too." Bill laughed. "They could give me another six months maybe with chemo, but..."

Gordon could fill in the rest. Insurance hadn't started yet. Now that he was diagnosed, he couldn't get insurance. Which meant no chemo. His contract to hire position wouldn't have benefits until he was actually hired, which was obviously never going to happen now.

"I'm sorry, Bill," he said again. What do you say to a man facing his own inevitable death, all alone?

"I'm really just worried about Danni," Bill said. Gordon felt a hand clutching at his heart at that.

"Danni? Is that...?" he almost didn't want to say it.

"My daughter. Guess she'll have to go back to Minnesota now. Live with her fucking mother. I guess it's only for a few years."

A new start, he'd said. Must have been a bitter divorce. He knew how that was.

"Ah, she can't be that bad. She married you once," he said. Someone had told him that after his own divorce. It hadn't cheered him up either.

"Nice of you to say, but the woman's crazy. Not like you. Mean crazy. She always resented Danni, even more than me."

"I..." Gordon started, not really sure what he was going to say.

Bill interrupted him, "Her last words to Danni were 'Good riddance you fucking whore.' Who says that kind of thing to their own daughter?"

The hand around his heart clenched harder. Leanne hadn't been kind to him during the divorce, but she had never taken it out on Barbara.

"She's a good kid," Bill was saying. "Maybe a little wild, but she's fifteen. You know how kids are at that age."

Tears filled Gordon's eyes. He could no longer hold them back. She's a good kid. You love your daughter.

"Yes," he sobbed. He sank back against the door and wiped angrily at his face with his hand.

"Hey. Hey, uh, Gordon, you okay there?" Bill asked. Then a moment later, "You got a kid?"

Gordon nodded. Then a second later shook his head. "Barbara," he said, forcing himself to say her name out loud. "She... she would have been seventeen in a couple of months."

"What happened?" Bill asked, in a soft voice.

"She was..." he hesitated. He didn't want to say it. Saying it made it real. "She was murdered. Same bastard that put me in here."

"Ah, fuck, man, no wonder you went crazy. A man oughtn't outlive his own children," said the man who knew for certain that he wasn't going to.

Gordon stood back up. Calmer now, but with tears still

flowing. He didn't know any vampires. But if anything he knew about werewolves was true...

"Bill," he said, "I'm going to try something. I don't know if I can do it, and if I can, I don't know if it'll work. But if it does..."

"What? What're you talking about man? You're scaring me."

"No. Listen. I have to go. You won't see me again after this, but if this does work, you're going to have to keep it secret. If they find out, they'll kill you." He started moving toward him.

Bill leaned over and hit the nurse call button as he spoke, "What are you... Don't..."

He cut him off. "Yes. Yes, call the nurse. That's good. Maybe they can help you. On the off chance this does work... You take care of your daughter. You raise her up and you tell her you love her. Tell her you love her no matter what." The tears were flowing freely again as he thought of Barbara and all the chances she would never have. He could barely choke out the last words "Even if she never, ever, puts the milk back in the fridge."

Bill shrunk back into the bed as he advanced, though there was nowhere to go. He was hitting the call button over and over now.

Gordon didn't know how it worked, but he knew what he was, and the man who'd attacked him had changed when he wanted to. He could feel the wolf pressing around him, wanting in.

He let it in.

SOUND SURROUNDED HIM. A cacophonous symphony from all the machinery in the room. Smells nearly overwhelmed him. Fear from a human in front of him, and sickness. So much sickness.

He wanted to flee, but there was something he had to do. He jumped up to where the human was, and it screeched in alarm. It tried feebly to get away from him. He knew he was supposed to bite it. At this distance, the smell of its sickness was almost overwhelming, but he stretched forward and sunk his teeth into its soft shoulder. A collar bone crunched under his jaws and warm blood sprayed his face, and down his throat. He didn't rend. Instead, he let go and pulled back. He was already beginning to turn away when he heard the sound behind him. There was a sudden opening in the wall and a new human was standing there, frozen in fear. He jumped past it, brushing it easily aside. He ignored the food/prey smell from it. He was already feeling sick from the blood he had swallowed. He stopped and retched in the hallway then quickly gathered himself to sprint to the end and hurl himself against the door. It popped open and led to stairs, which he ran down, taking whole flights at a time. When there were no more stairs, he threw himself against another door and then he was outside. He kept running. Pavement turned to grass then to brush and he hid himself in amongst it. Exhausted then, he lay down and went to sleep.

VEER WAS STILL SITTING on the couch, holding her coffee cup when the officer, Don, came back in.

"Ms. Rosen? Everything okay?" he asked, then added, "I mean, other than... well, everything."

She laughed at that. It was as good a way as any to put it.

"Yeah. Yeah, I'm fine," she said. He was obviously not convinced.

Don fidgeted awkwardly for a moment, then finally said, "Um... Hey, Lieutenant Diaz is a good guy. He can be a bit of an ass sometimes, but he's a good guy. All he wants is to keep you safe."

"No," she replied. "He wants to catch his killer."

"Well, uh, yeah, that too. But that guy did try to kill you."

"Don, if I ask you something, will you promise to tell me the truth?"

"Sure. I mean, you know, if I can," he replied.

Good enough, she supposed. "My house was under surveillance," she began, and could tell by his reaction that it was news to him, but she continued with her question. "Was I bait?"

"What? No!"

"You sure about that?"

He took the chair opposite the couch so he could look directly in her eyes on the same level. "Yes. Yes, I'm absolutely sure about that. The lieutenant wouldn't do that. He can be an asshole, and insensitive, but if we catch this guy - when we catch this guy," he amended, "It'll be a clean bust. Diaz wants him bad, but he won't step an inch outside the law to get him."

And that really told her what she wanted to know. There was the law, and there was justice, and sometimes the two were not the same. But she couldn't count on the police to recognize that fact. Could she still work with Diaz? Bringing this secret out, would he be willing to do it carefully, in a way that might actually work? Or would he just destroy this chance with his zealous pursuit of a conviction for a single man who could never be convicted? Could she make him see the larger picture?

"Thanks," was all she said.

"Yeah, here, let me take that," he said, reaching for the empty mug. She handed it to him. "Thanks," she repeated. "Is there any left?"

"It's cold. I'll make a new pot."

"Thank you," she said again. "I need to get to work."

Back at the end of the kitchen table, she barely registered when Don set the new cup of coffee on the table next to her. She stared at the blank document on her screen for a long time, trying to decide what to write.

MICHAEL WAS ready to drop by the time he got home. His latest meeting with Rosen didn't go as well as he'd hoped. Perhaps he should have played it straight rather than trying to be charming.

Still, he had learned a lot. Enough to know that there was a hell of a lot he still didn't know.

He wanted to sleep, but first there was something he had to do. It had been a while since he had done any reloading, but he still had all his equipment in the basement workshop. Before he'd come home, he'd done a bit of online research and made a few shopping stops. He intended to take Gordon Chandler's advice. The most obvious need of course was the silver. A quick trip to a pawn shop near his house furnished him with a small quantity of jewelry - all he could afford. He had no idea of the purity of any of it but hoped it would do the trick. A stop at a hardware store yielded a MAPP gas torch. That would provide enough heat, but the melting pot he would normally use for lead would never stand up to silver's significantly higher melting point. The sites he'd found had suggested a "foundry crucible," which they didn't sell at the hardware store. A bit more online searching and a few phone calls later he'd learned it was just a high temperature ceramic crucible, which he found in a hobby shop on Alberta Street.

With his new tools, he set to work. The torch melted the silver easily enough and kept it consistent once he'd figured out how to properly flux the melted pool, which alone was a couple of hours of online searching, shopping, and experimentation. Normally when loading cartridges, he'd use the liquid lead itself to heat the molds - pour the first couple of bullets in, then dump them back out to be re-melted instead of used. He decided that wouldn't work with silver, though, with the significant temperature difference. But using the same torch to preheat the mold seemed to work well enough. He may need to buy a new one once this was all over. He had no idea how much internal damage he was doing to it by repeatedly heating it up to such a high temperature.

The moment of truth - using the tongs that came with the crucible, he poured the molten metal carefully into the mold. Once they were cool enough, he opened the mold and revealed a couple of passably bullet-shaped lumps of silver. There were weird bluish-purplish stains in the metal, which he hoped wouldn't affect its ability to... do whatever it was it did.

The problem came, though, when he tried to press them into the sizing die. They were too small. All of them. He dug out his caliper and measured their diameter. Each one was over a hundredth of an inch too small. How had that happened? He thought it through, going over the whole process in his head. He hadn't missed anything. The mold had definitely been full, to the point where the sprue plate had something to shear off the end, and had actually taken a noticeable extra amount of force to do it. Maybe he could force them into a squat enough size by sacrificing a bit of length and just pushing really really hard on the press. But he was taking enough chances as it was. They wouldn't do any good if they ended up jamming his gun or exploding in his hand. But why were they smaller? Another quick online search provided him the answer: silver shrinks more than lead as it cools. Not enough to be noticeable to the naked eye, but enough to make these bullets too dangerous to use. Any gaps that large and they could do more damage to him than whatever he was shooting at.

A hundredth of an inch. Such a tiny amount to fail by. He couldn't make the molded bullets any bigger. But... maybe he could, after a fashion. The 9mm rounds he had cast had come out too small to fit securely in the casing. But a sabot round might be a little more forgiving. He wouldn't be able to use the rounds in his service pistol, which was 9mm, but he also had a .45 caliber revolver. The bullet would fit inside the plastic casing, the sabot, that in turn could fit inside a .45 caliber shell. The plastic would be more deformable and less damaged by the action than the brass would be. He had a large box of blue sabot sitting around from a failed experiment in creating hunting ammo several years ago. He found it and took it out of the cupboard.

He set everything aside and started over, including melting down his newly created bullets, and then turned the torch on the 9mm mold. Getting everything right went much faster the second time around, and within a couple more hours he had a dozen 9mm silver bullets ready to be attached to sabot.

There were no published guides for 9mm silver rounds in sabot in .45 casings, so measuring the powder took more guess-work than he was truly comfortable with. Too much and the gun could explode in his hand. Too little could cause a jam. He'd have to be careful with these and make sure he knew where each round went before firing the next.

He filled his revolver with six of the new silver bullets, and a quickloader with the remainder. Twelve shots. That would be all he'd get until he had a chance to make more. Better make them count.

THERE WAS no answer when he tried to call the room, so he called reception.

"Hi, this is Detective Michael Diaz," he told her. "I'm trying to reach Gordon Chandler in Room 702."

"Chandler? Hold on. Let me check..."

There was some muffled discussion that he couldn't quite make out in a rather frantic tone, then a familiar voice came on the phone.

"May I ask who's calling, please?"

"Phil?" he asked.

"Michael? Is that you? I've been trying to reach you all day. The fuck you been?"

"Working," he replied.

"Yeah? Well, you're gonna have a lot more. Get your ass down here now. I'll fill you in when you arrive."

"On my way." He hung up and grabbed his coat, stopping just long enough to drop his new loader into the pocket. He hurried up the steps and out.

Fifteen minutes later, he was in the hospital talking to Phil and a nurse.

"McDonald," the nurse said, offering his hand. He went immediately into his story, "I was on rounds in oncology. six-oh-two - that is, the patient in room six-oh-two - hit his call button, so I headed to that room..." he began.

"Wait... six-oh-two? So that's down a floor from Chandler?"

"Umm... Chandler was on the seventh floor? So, yes, one floor down."

At a look from Phil, Michael continued. "Okay, thanks, go on."

"Well, I heard him screaming when I got close, so I ran the rest of the way. I opened the door and saw what looked like a dog on the patient's bed. It turned toward me and growled. It was huge. I swear it might have actually been a wolf. It jumped off the bed and slammed me into the door frame, hard. It ran off and pushed open the stairwell door at the end of the hall!"

"The exit from the bottom of the stairway was also open," Phil said, "which set off the alarm."

"The wolf opened the doors?"

"They're both panic doors, designed to be opened with any pressure against them," McDonald said. "I did what I could to treat the wound, and they took him down to surgery."

"The wound?"

"Yeah, the thing had bit him, tore open his shoulder."

"Wait, surgery? So he's alive?" This would be excellent news. For the patient of course, but also for the case to have a second living witness. He only felt a little guilty for thinking of the latter first.

"Looks like he'll be fine. I mean, from the injury at least. The thing missed his throat."

"Lucky him."

"Well..."

"What? Is he okay or isn't he?"

"Sixth floor is the cancer ward," Phil said. "He's terminal."

Well... shit.

"Thanks, we'll be in touch," Phil told the nurse, then to Michael, "Let's head up to the room."

"What do you think?" he asked Phil as they waited for the elevator. "Come to finish his work, then get the wrong room?"

"The wolf, maybe. But I think the guy got Chandler."

"Wait... what?" Michael asked, confused.

"Missing. I'll show you." Inside the elevator, he hit the button for the 7th floor.

"Six, isn't it?" Michael asked.

"Chandler was on the seventh floor. We're going there first." He continued as they rode the elevator and walked down the hall, "Patient down the hall said he heard some crashing noises.

He assumed someone had their TV up too loud and put his pillow over his head and went back to sleep."

There was already a line of yellow tape over the doorway, and a uniformed officer posted outside who nodded to them as they ducked under the tape to enter the room. The source of the "crashing noises" was immediately obvious. An IV had been knocked over, as had a wheeled metal table containing several dishes, the remains of an earlier meal. The bed had been knocked to one side, sitting askew against the wall and the linens torn off and scattered on the floor.

"Looks like he put up a fight," said Michael. He didn't say that he had a good idea what had happened: Chandler had transformed. He'd wrecked his own room trying to get out, and somehow made it down a flight of stairs to 602. The first thing he did was attack another patient before leaving the hospital. So much for Rosen's assertion that werewolves aren't inherently compelled to attack humans.

He looked around but didn't see what he was expecting. "They find any clothes up here?" he asked Phil.

"Not that I know of. We can ask the nurse on duty, though she swears nobody touched a thing, other than unplugging the heart monitor. The flatline squeal was disturbing the other patients."

"I bet," he said. He was about to say something else, then spotted something under the edge of the cart. Taking a handkerchief from his pocket, he reached down carefully and picked it up.

"What's that?" Phil asked him.

Michael showed him the hypodermic needle, still full.

"Dropped by the killer?" Phil said. It obviously wasn't the kind of thing they would have just left here, even sitting on a cart. Someone else was in the room. What really got Michael's attention was the fact that the needle was made of silver. Just like Rosen's darts. Clearly there was something more than met the eye after all.

"If he's using poison now, he's branching out," Phil continued.

"Ten to one no doctor prescribed whatever's in this," Michael said.

EIGHT

CABIN IN THE WOODS

In the end, they'd decided against kidnapping anyone, which was a relief.

Kevin and Shelly had borrowed a white cargo van from someone. It had no back seats, but plenty of space. There were already a few sleeping bags and a cooler piled on the floor in the back along with a couple of grocery sacks.

"Oh. I didn't bring anything," Carl said, seeing the gear they'd loaded.

"No worries," Shelly told him. "The place is supposed to have bedding, but we brought a few extra sleeping bags just to be sure."

"Who'd you convince to become Were?" he asked her. "And how?"

"Oh, they don't know about that part yet," Kevin said. "They think it's just a camping weekend. That'll be a special surprise."

In response to Carl's skeptical look, he said, "Don't worry about it. We'll be sure they don't cause any problems and don't get hurt or lost. And, if worse comes to worse, I've got this."

He pulled a sheathed knife from an inside pocket of his

leather jacket. It was a pretty weapon, with a wire-wrapped handle and a rounded pommel. It looked like a reproduction from some fantasy movie or another. He slid it out of its decorated sheath and looked at the shiny grey metal blade. "Is that silver?" he guessed.

"Yep. Just got it yesterday. Pretty, isn't she?"

"It is that," Carl said, sliding it back into the sheath and handing it back to him. He wondered how much silver was really in it. He'd looked into it in the past and everything he'd found online seemed to indicate that silver was far too soft to make a weapon. Silverware and jewelry were usually made of sterling silver, which he had no idea if it would be useful against a Were. He hoped he never had to find out.

After they'd picked up the first two guys, Ross and Mitch, Shelly asked him to take over the driving so she could sit in the back and talk to them. Kevin took the front seat, navigating them to the last house.

"Oh, how nice, you pick me up in a rape van," the girl said as she approached the passenger side window. Given what they were planning, her comment hit a little close to home.

"Hah," he said, trying to sound casual. "It was the only vehicle we had big enough for everybody."

He didn't mention that they hadn't even had it at all until that morning.

"Whatever," she said, looking in the sliding back door that Kevin had opened for her. Shelly was sitting on the floor using a large duffel bag as a backrest, along with the other two guys they'd already picked up. Seeing the lack of seats, she said, "I'm calling shotgun."

Carl shook his head. "I need Kevin up here to navigate."

"Gimme the address," she said, pulling out her phone.

Kevin stepped back from the front door, gave an exaggerated bow and held it open for her. She climbed in and took the seat, tossing her bag in the space between them.

Kevin got into the back and closed the sliding door behind him. Standing, bent low under the van's ceiling, he made the introductions. "Carl, Toni. Toni, your pilot today will be Carl." Indicating the people seated behind him he continued, "You've already met Shelly, and this is Ross and Mitch."

Ross waved and smiled.

Mitch gave a slight nod.

Kevin took a seat on the floor next to Shelly and read an address off his phone that Toni entered into hers.

"Three and a half hours," she said. "Go forward. Looks like we're taking the Banfield."

"Okay... where's that?"

"I-84?"

"Got it," he said.

"I can only see out the back window," Kevin's voice came from the back. "So, I'll let you know after you've gone too far."

"You're friends with Shelly?" Carl asked her after they'd merged onto the highway.

"Umm..." She hesitated a second, as if she didn't know how to answer. "I guess?"

"You don't know if you're friends?" Carl asked. Though come to think of it he wasn't really sure if he and Shelly were friends either. He was friends with Kevin, and had been for years, but he'd always thought of Shelly as Kevin's girlfriend, not his friend. Certainly the only time he ever saw her was with Kevin.

"I mean, I've really only met her a few times, at work," Toni said, interrupting his musing. "We've had like half a dozen minute-long conversations across the bar."

"Oh, you're a bartender?" he asked.

"Barista," she corrected. "I work at Powell's."

"Oh, yeah, I know Powell's. I go there all the time," he said. He didn't want to say that he'd never noticed her there. He had spent a lot of time in the bookstore, but only rarely ventured into the cafe.

It was Shelly, leaning forward into the front part of the van, who brought up werewolves. She made it seem so natural, the way she just came up and mentioned it like it was casual conversation. It was almost like magic the way she could do that, move conversation to a topic she wanted without making it seem clumsy or forced.

"Gods, that'd be awesome," Toni said in reply. "Being able to turn into a wolf, run free under the stars. Hunt what you want... Of course, it'd depend on what kind of werewolf. If you're compelled to kill people that wouldn't be as much fun."

"As much?" Shelly commented.

"Depends on the people doesn't it?"

"So, what would you do if you were a werewolf?"

"I guess I'd try to make sure I was locked up somewhere every full moon so I couldn't hurt anyone. Or surrounded by people who deserved to be hurt - you know, terrorists or Congress or something."

"Sounds good to me," Carl said. Shelly stepped back to sit down. Once she was seated, with her back to the rest of the passengers, she caught Carl's eye in the rear-view mirror and, with a broad smile, gave him a quick thumbs up and a wink, then pointed toward Toni. He quickly turned his eyes back to the road but smiled softly to himself as well.

BONNEVILLE DAM LOOMED large in the distance when Toni, still navigating, told him to take the next right. Off the highway, the asphalt eventually gave way to gravel, which turned to packed dirt after another turn. The forest shaded the rough road and Toni rolled her window down.

"Smell that," she said.

He rolled down his as well, despite the cold. The air had a crisp and fresh smell to it.

"It's beautiful," he told her, and meant it. She smiled at that. He liked her smile.

"If that's actually a road, I think it's the one we want," she said, pointing to a dubious looking path to their left.

"You sure?" he asked her.

"No, but can't hurt to try," she said. He shrugged and turned onto the road. It could hurt to try it, if they got stuck somewhere with no way to get out or ended up on the private property of some crazed loon who thought shooting them all would be an appropriate response to inadvertent trespassing.

He smiled at the last, imagining some country bumpkin holding a shotgun at them. He'd step forward, followed by Kevin and Shelly, while Toni and the two guys stood back, quivering in fear. The expression on their faces when the shotgun fires and he falls back, but only for a second. Instead of falling down and dying, he changes and leaps forward, and the gloating sneer of the landowner turns to a scream of fear as he falls on him.

That is how they should react to threats from humans, not hiding, cowering, in order to protect their secret.

"What?" Toni said, apparently seeing the expression on his face, but not understanding it.

"Nothing," he said. "Just thinking."

"About what?"

"Nothing important," he responded. She wouldn't understand. Not yet. "Does anyone know what the place is supposed to look like?" he called back.

Kevin came forward and stood hunched over, hands on the

back of both of the front seats to keep his balance on the uneven road. "Yeah, this looks right. Should just be another couple of miles."

He held on as the van bounced with every bump and dip in the road. As bad as it was up here, Carl figured it must have been worse in the back, without seats or seat belts. He hadn't heard any complaints, though, so he decided not to worry about it.

The road widened out and came to an end in front of an old dilapidated cabin.

"Damn, does this place even have electricity? Or running water?" Mitch's voice came from the back. Carl had nearly forgotten about them. Between his conversation with Toni and the road noise, he hadn't heard anything from the back of the van since they left the highway.

"I know what you mean. I half expect Jason to jump out at me waving a machete," Ross answered him. Carl winced just a bit at that. My god, I'm the monster in the cabin in the woods. Then he smiled at the idea. This could be fun.

He had been wondering how they were going to do it. Shelly had assured him that she and Kevin had a plan. His job was just to keep everybody else distracted.

"So... there's like two beds total?" Mitch said when they had entered the cabin and scoped it out. There wasn't much to scope. A living room with a single couch and rustic wooden chair, connected via a small island to a kitchen, and a bedroom with two beds in it. "Didn't really think this through, huh? With six of us?" he added.

"Guess one of the people sleeping on the floor can spread some blankets out or something," Toni responded. "Dibs on one of the beds," she added, tossing her backpack onto the far one.

"I..." Carl began. He wasn't sure what to say. It didn't really matter, he supposed. There wasn't going to be a whole lot of sleeping going on.

"Wow! Complete with a spooky basement!" Ross said, from the kitchen.

"Really?" Shelly replied, heading that way. She gave Kevin a quick look before she dropped her bag on the couch. "Let's see."

"I'm gonna go get my stuff out of the van," Kevin said with a glance at Carl and a nod toward the other two in the room.

He wasn't ready. What was he supposed to say?

"Basement?" Mitch said.

"Oh, uh..." he started, with no idea where he was going. He approached the bed Toni had claimed, "If I'm going to be sleeping on the floor, can I have the comforter for padding?" It was the only thing he could think of to redirect attention from the basement. He guessed it wouldn't do for everyone to go down there at once. That must be what they meant when they'd told him to distract the others. They should have filled him in better so they could have planned it out.

However lame his strategy, though, it worked.

"Yeah, I guess, sure," Toni said, and moved to pull it off her bed. Mitch, he'd noticed, had quietly moved to the other bed to set his backpack on it, effectively claiming it and, more importantly, not going into the basement. He had assumed by the looks and the minimal instructions he'd been given that Kevin and Shelly wanted them in the basement only one at a time. It seemed like that's what was happening. Score one for selfish opportunism. He heard the front door open, then close as Kevin went out, but then the basement door opened, and closed again quietly a moment later. Kevin had snuck downstairs to help Shelly with Ross. Now there were only two to separate.

Toni handed him the large comforter, and he looked at it

stupidly. Now that he had it, he wasn't quite sure what to do with it. Dropping it in a corner of the living room would be the obvious choice - it was where there was the most floor space. But he didn't want to leave these two alone in a room together. Focus, he reminded himself. They had a purpose here.

He headed out to the living room and a moment later Toni joined him, followed by Mitch.

He didn't know what to do now. Any moment they were bound to notice half their group was missing.

It was too late to suggest exploring outside the little cabin. They really should have planned this better. It wasn't fair that he got stuck watching both the others while Kevin and Shelly were both downstairs. He looked over the shelves on the back wall.

"Hey, they got Cards Against Humanity. Anyone up for a game?" he asked and picked up the small box.

"Sure, why not?" Toni said. "I haven't played that in forever. Where'd everyone else get off to?" she asked, looking around to see how many players there'd be. Dammit, that had been the wrong thing to suggest. Mitch got up as if to go look. Carl had just begun to panic when Shelly appeared around the corner from the kitchen.

"Well, basement's a bust," she said. "Dirt floor. No ancient tomes. A couple of broken bottles, though."

"You in?" Toni asked her, holding up the deck of cards.

"Sure. Kevin too. Lemme check on Ross," Shelly replied.

She stepped back toward the kitchen, then, behind Toni's back, caught Mitch's attention. Laying a finger aside her nose, she nodded back toward the kitchen and shot him a questioning look. He nodded and stood up.

"I'll, uh... be right back," he said, and hurried after Shelly.

Toni looked after him, then stood up as if to follow. Not yet, crap!

"Hey look over there!" Carl exclaimed.

She turned to look. "What?"

He wasn't actually expecting that.

"Uh... " he said, pointing out the window. Hey, look at this distraction. "An animal. Big. Big animal," he said instead. Smooth.

She looked skeptical.

"Like a moose or something."

"A moose?" she said, with a mocking smile. "Sure it wasn't a wolf?"

"Uh... a what?" he asked, confused. How could she know...

"Never mind," she said, and came to the window. She didn't know. She was just... making a joke? Referencing their earlier discussion about werewolves maybe? It was such a transparent ploy, but he guessed if there was no reason to suspect anything nefarious she might not be watching for it.

"So where is this 'moose' of yours?"

"Elk, maybe?" he said, looking out the window with her. "Are there those around here?"

"Maybe. Right state at least. I don't see anything out there."

It's a don't-look-in-the-basement, he didn't say.

"Must've wandered off." It felt lame as he said it.

"What's going on here?" she asked, looking around the room, "Where'd everybody else go?"

"I... uh..."

She turned quickly away from him and headed toward the kitchen. He followed her, and as she got to the basement door called out, he hoped loud enough for Kevin and Shelly to hear, "No, wait!"

She turned to face him, her hand on the doorknob.

His mind spun furiously, trying to come up with a reason why she shouldn't proceed, but he couldn't think of anything. When he remained silent, she pushed the door open. He hesitated only a few seconds before following her into the basement. The stairs descended then turned at the far corner. He couldn't see anything past the turn. By the time he got to the door, though, she had already reached the basement and was obviously spooked by whatever she saw there.

"Stop her!" Kevin shouted as she ran back up.

Carl stood near the top step and spread his arms, trying to make himself seem large and imposing. He had no idea what he would do if she actually got up there and tried to pass him. It didn't matter. His presence was enough to make her hesitate, which was enough for Shelly, then half a second later, Kevin, to reach her and grab her arms.

"Go lock the front door!" Kevin ordered him.

He gladly fled up the stairs as Toni cried out from below demanding they let her go.

———

ONCE HE'D LOCKED the front door, Carl took a deep breath, steeling his courage to go back down.

When he returned, their three "guests" had leather manacles, hand and foot, chained to brackets set in the concrete wall. The brackets looked old and rusty, Kevin and Shelly had obviously not recently installed them. They must have been here for a long time. Carl didn't want to think about what use they'd originally been intended for. There was also some kind of loose-fitting leather harness around each. It didn't look like it would hold a person, and Carl realized it wasn't intended to. The harness would be for the wolf.

When Toni saw him enter, she looked up at him with a look he couldn't parse. "Carl?" She said. "Please. Don't. Whatever you're doing, you don't have to..."

"Relax," Kevin interrupted her. "We're not going to hurt you."

"Then let us out of here, you freaks!" Mitch said.

"Fuck you! You guys are so dead! The second I get my hands on you, I'm going to fucking kill you!" Ross was a little more direct.

Toni just glared directly at him. He looked away. It would be best to just get it over with. Couldn't Kevin see that nothing he said was going to calm them down? We should just change, then do it. Then they'll understand that everything would be okay.

But Kevin was still talking. "You can't see it yet, but you will. Twenty-four hours from now, you will be back at your homes. But your lives will have been forever changed," he went on, ignoring their pleas. "You were chosen to be the first of a new breed. Something that the world hasn't seen for a thousand years. Free Were. For centuries, our leaders have betrayed us. Kept us weak, our numbers few. They have done this out of fear! Fear of humans! But we have nothing to fear from them, it is they who should fear us!"

"We're humans, just like you, dumbass," Mitch snarled at him, pulling against his restraints.

Doesn't he know that that's exactly the wrong thing to say to Kevin.

But Kevin just smiled, a patronizing I-know-something-you-don't-know smile. "Soon, you will be like us. You'll find that even in your man-forms you're faster, stronger, smarter, more aware of everything around you. Better in every way. Most importantly, you will have the power to make more like you. You can choose to use this power on anybody you wish. You will be the first of a new breed, but not the last. We'll make more. You'll make more. And when the time is right, we will reveal ourselves, rise up, and take on our natural roles as the rightful rulers of humanity."

Rulers? Was that the plan? He looked over toward Toni but had to look quickly away from her hard glare. She hadn't spoken since he'd turned away from her, but her look said everything.

"Bullshit!" the other man said. "You think keeping us chained up here, brainwashing us into joining some kind of freaky cult is going to work? What will you do if we refuse?"

Kevin shook his head in a mockery of sadness. "You won't be chained for much longer. There'll be no brainwashing. There's no cult." His smile broadened even further. "Though things might get a little freaky. We're not going to try to convince you of anything. We're going to show you. And we're going to show you right now."

At that, he began unbuttoning his shirt. Shelly began doing the same, and Carl almost missed the cue. Fortunately, he was wearing a T-shirt that he could quickly pull off over his head. He glanced over at Shelly, who had taken off her shirt and scowled at him. He should be focused on the task at hand, not watching her. He looked away and finished undressing. He nearly tripped over his jeans as he took them off, remembering at the last second to kick off his shoes. There was a scream, and he whipped his head up to see that Kevin had already changed. He was in form and across the room, sinking his teeth into the shoulder of Ross.

All three were screaming now. He realized chaining them like this would probably scare them all by itself, when they didn't understand what was going on. But it was for their own protection. If they were free, they could hurt themselves in their misunderstanding of what was happening to them. A second later, the large grey wolf that was Shelly leapt onto the other man. Toni stared at him, didn't move and didn't say a word. Did she understand what was going on? Did she want it? She'd said earlier that she did, right? He stepped out of his jeans.

Slowly, he thought to himself as he changed. That's the way to do it. *Slowly, and don't kill. One bite. Don't kill.*

THE SMELL of fear filled the small room. His prey was trapped in front of him. He could move slowly, take his time. The others had begun moving away from their own prey, but they left his to him. He knew he shouldn't kill it but didn't know why. He approached slowly as it thrashed noisily against its trappings. There were loud noises coming from all directions now, and an intense level of fear and... something else he couldn't recognize. He heard and smelt everything, but his eyes were focused on the human in front of him. Trapped. Easy prey. Bite it.

He bit it.

The curious sensation went away as he did so, and he could smell only fear and hear cries of pain and terror. One of the humans whimpered and emptied its bowels as it died. That was wrong. Something was wrong. He grew afraid without understanding why. He wanted to run, to flee. And this... these prey captured, not moving, that was wrong too. He wanted to hunt, to find moving prey to test himself against. He longed for the joy of the chase.

He let go of the human, and ran, away from the rest, up and out of the small room. He could smell the forest nearby. But there was no way to get to it. Something was happening, and he didn't understand it, and it was wrong, and he was trapped, and humans were screaming he couldn't get out...

Yes he could. There was a way out. Instead of waiting to

sleep, he reached for the human now and brought it into himself.

CARL WOKE up on the stairway, laying naked in front of the door out of the basement.

From below him, he could hear Kevin's voice, though he couldn't see him around the corner. He crept, slowly, back down the stairs. Shelly was sitting at the bend in the stairway, wrapped in a blanket. She looked up at him with an unreadable expression. Where did she get a blanket? How come he didn't have one? He stepped forward, past her and poked his head around the corner. One of the men, Mitch, was looking directly at him. "Please! I'm bleeding! I need help! What the hell is going on?" The last was almost a whimper.

The other lay still, unmoving, blood pooling beneath him. Toni was turned at a weird angle, pressing her bleeding leg against the concrete floor, in a desperate attempt to staunch the flow of blood. Carl was glad she was facing away and couldn't see him. He wanted to help her, use some of the clothes piled nearby as a bandage or something, but didn't dare. This was part of the process. He'd done the same thing, laying on the ground in the high desert of Central Oregon, hands pressed desperately against his own wound. Moaning in pain as the sun slowly sank beneath the horizon. He looked away from her and towards his clothes lying in a chaotic jumble on the floor. He found it hard to bring himself to go farther into the room. One of the men still hadn't moved. Was he dead? He didn't want to know.

Kevin was pacing, seemingly oblivious to his own naked-ness, in front of the captives. If he noticed Carl's arrival, he paid no attention to it. "Don't worry," he told them. "You'll be okay.

The wolf can heal almost any damage. One of the nice little side effects. Well, you'll be okay anyway," he said directly to the conscious, pleading man. Then, without looking at either Carl or Toni, "I don't know that I've ever seen anyone change after being bitten in the leg before. Interesting choice. I'm curious to see if it works."

Shit. Did he just doom the girl? If the wound was deep, but wouldn't heal... She could die without ever transforming. He looked back over to her, but she was studiously looking away from all of them. He took two more steps forward, scooped up his clothes, and ran toward the stairs.

He hesitated at the top, before opening the door.

"You are Were now." He could still hear Kevin's voice, "You should already feel the edges of the wolf, forming, gathering around you. Soon it will be fully formed. Call it to you, enter it, and let it enter you. Then you'll see the torn flesh for the blessing it is."

Shelly stepped up behind him, still wrapped in her blanket. She saw Carl standing there, clutching his clothes. She nodded toward the door and gave a slight eye-roll, though whether she was indicating Kevin's speech or Carl's state he wasn't sure. He opened the door and stepped through it. She followed and let the door swing shut behind her.

Carl stopped in the kitchen to get dressed. He had just finished when Kevin came up and walked past him, neither carrying nor wearing the clothes he'd had on earlier. Carl followed him to the living room where Shelly was sitting on the couch, still wrapped in her blanket.

"That went well," Kevin announced.

"Except for you killing that guy!" Shelly retorted.

"He's dead?" Carl blurted out.

Kevin just looked a little sheepish at that. "He wouldn't stop squirming." He held up both hands. "Hey, the other two are fine. Two out of three ain't bad. And if Carl's leg thing works maybe we should all try that next time."

"Are you just gonna hang around naked like that?" Shelly asked him.

"Why not?" He spread his arms wide. "We're young, we're wild, we're free, and we're in the middle of nowhere. No one's here to see." When neither of them responded, he turned to Shelly and, with a nod toward the bedroom, said, "You wanna..."

"No," she replied, her tone flat.

"All right. I'm gonna go for a walk," he said, and strode out the front door without getting dressed.

Carl sat back down again when he'd gone, in a chair across the room from Shelly. Neither of them spoke for several moments. When he couldn't stand the uncomfortable silence anymore, he got up and wandered into the kitchen.

Mercifully, he hadn't heard anything from the basement. What did that mean, though? Would he have heard any noises if there were any? What if they'd found another way out? How long should he wait up here? There's a dead man down there. That didn't seem real. Nobody else was doing anything about it. Should he? If so, what? If the guy was already dead, it was too late to do anything, but where did that leave them? Lacking any other ideas, he began looking through the cabinets in the kitchen.

"Hey, there's hot chocolate," he announced his find to the other room. His voice seemed uncomfortably loud to him in the small space and he cringed when he thought of the people downstairs hearing him. "Want some?" he asked, just a little quieter.

She was quiet for a while, as if thinking it over. Then finally, "Yes. Please."

He found a couple of mugs in another cupboard and filled them both from the tap before sticking them in the microwave.

He glanced toward the door to the basement again. He still couldn't hear anything from there. Was that one guy really dead?

He continued checking the cupboards while the microwave ran. He found a box of crackers in one. It was still sealed and when he checked the use by date, he was pleased to discover it was nearly a month in the future. He dug the cheese out of the refrigerator and started slicing it. Still no sound from downstairs, and no sign of Kevin. What if he'd run into trouble? How long had he been gone? Should they go out and look for him?

He didn't say anything about his doubts to Shelly. He went back to the front room and handed her one of the plates of cheese and crackers along with a mug of hot chocolate.

"Thanks," she said, taking both and sitting up on the couch, awkwardly pulling the blanket up as she readjusted her position.

"Think we should check on the... uh..." He didn't know what to call them. Recruits? Victims?

"They'll be fine," she said, sparing him having to continue, then added, "hopefully."

"Maybe next time we should bring some bandages or something," he ventured.

"Think there'll be a next time?" she asked.

"Why not?" he responded.

She gave him a look of utter disgust at that. Oh, yeah, the dead guy.

"I mean. We can do it again," he said, trying to cover his embarrassment. "We'll just have to be more careful. It's still a good plan, basically."

"Basically?" she asked.

"Well, making more. Break out of control of the Alphas." The way he said it made it more a question than a statement.

"Should we? Are we any better?" she asked. "We just... those people," she nodded her head in the direction of the door to the basement, "They didn't have any choice. Doesn't that make us just as much tyrants?"

He didn't have an answer to that. She was wrong. She had to be wrong. He just wasn't sure how.

He was silent for a long while.

"What do you want out of all this?" she finally asked.

He thought again of his humiliation at the preserve. I don't want to be the bottom rung anymore. He didn't say it out loud.

"I dunno," he finally answered, then continued slowly, "It's kind of a nice idea, though, isn't it? Not having to hide? Being part of normal society?"

"I'm not so sure what normal society has to offer," Shelly answered.

He didn't have an answer to that either.

"I think I wanna take a nap for a bit," she finally said. "You gonna be okay?"

"Yeah. I'm fine," he responded, surprised by the question. Of all people, why wouldn't he be okay?

She stretched out on the couch under her blanket, setting the plate with its untouched contents on the floor beside her, next to the empty mug.

Carl sat, sipping his chocolate, and finished the cheese and crackers without really tasting either.

After he finished his drink, he got up and wandered back to the kitchen. Dropping the dishes in the sink, there was nothing better to do than explore the rest of the cabin, moving about as quietly as he could so as not to disturb Shelly. There wasn't much to explore. The one bedroom, Toni's backpack still sitting on the bed, a linen closet, which must have been where Shelly got her blanket from. He didn't want to face the downstairs on his own. He found a stack of old magazines on one shelf, selected one and took it back to the one chair, aside from two barstools at the kitchen island. The cover article was about all the robots currently exploring Mars. He would probably have found it captivating if he was reading it while alone at home. As it was, his attention was divided between Shelly sleeping on the couch and watching for any signs of movement from either the front door or the basement.

He started when the front door opened, nearly dropping his magazine. Kevin stepped in, with the same broad smile he'd had when he left. Shelly awoke immediately and sat up, clutching the blanket.

"Have a nice walk?" she asked him. There was a disapproving tone in her voice.

Kevin ignored it. "Not bad. A little cold." He smirked at his own joke. He still hadn't gotten dressed. "Any word from our friends downstairs?"

"Uh..." Carl started. He felt like he'd been caught at something. Or caught not doing something he had been supposed to.

"We haven't been down there yet," Shelly answered for him. She gathered her blanket and stood up.

"C'mon," Kevin said and headed toward the door. Carl followed them.

The two captives lay still. Carl's gaze went over to the dead man and he couldn't look away. His neck had been ripped open and his shoulder almost torn off. There was no way he would have survived that. This wasn't a simple bite meant to transform someone. What had he done to make Kevin so angry?

"Please... help me," came a voice. It took Carl a second to realize it came from the other man. He took a step back.

Kevin, on the other hand, stepped toward the man.

Shelly hadn't moved.

Carl followed her eyes and saw that the girl was awake as well, glaring at Shelly with a strange mix of emotions. She had her thigh pressed hard against the concrete floor still, though it looked like the wound had stopped bleeding. That was a relief. It was almost certainly due less to the awkward pressure she was putting on it than to the dawning wolf.

His attention was torn back to the man when he spoke. "Please, just let me go. I don't want to die here."

"That's good. I don't want you to die, either," Kevin answered him. "But you're going to have to heal yourself."

"I need medical attention!" It was nearly a sob.

"Sorry, no," Kevin said. "They'd just ask a bunch of questions that you really don't want to answer. But don't worry, you can do it. You just need to learn how."

"I don't know how! Just tell me!" Carl noticed the man kept saying "I" not "We." Didn't he care about his fellow captives? Carl hated him a bit for that, fully aware of the hypocrisy in doing so.

He looked back at the girl, but looked away as soon as she turned her gaze toward him. Toni, he reminded himself. She's a person and her name is Toni. And the man is Mitch. And the one who died... He looked back over at him. He didn't even look real. Like a Halloween prop. That used to be a person, he thought. A person with dreams and aspirations and goals and... and now he's not. Now he's nothing. A mistake that's going to have to be dealt with. He wondered if anybody would miss him.

But Kevin answered his question. "You should feel the wolf by now," he began. "You'd be dead if he wasn't there. Just reach out. Feel its presence. Enter him. Let him enter you."

The man mumbled something about "mystical nonsense" and what could have been "fuck you."

"C'mon," Shelly said. "You just saw us all change into wolf form and back. What else will it take to convince you?"

Carl looked back over at the woman just in time to catch the expression on her face. A thoughtful look with a sudden realization. Just when he realized what was happening, she changed.

Her wolf form was dark grey, almost black, except the face and feet. Smaller than he was expecting. More lithe than any of them accounted for, she slipped the harness easily and leapt toward the stairs.

"Stop her!" Kevin yelled, and Carl moved to intercept her, realizing as he did it that he wouldn't have time. Not in his current form.

He pulled his shirt off and tossed it aside, but that was all he had time for before she was past him. He transformed and gave chase.

At the top of the stairs, he caught up to her and tried to circle around to cut her off. She shoved past him, slamming him into the wall, and barreled through the open door. He followed. Her scent hung in the air. A complex mixture of anger, fear, and... joy? The room was thick with all three. He ran through the small opening and saw her leaping against the door to the outside. It didn't open. He could smell trees and soil and prey outside and longed to run free. He knew she smelled it too. She turned. The window. She leapt toward it, but he intercepted her flight. Both wolves tumbled to the ground. Something wooden crashed and splintered underneath them. She rolled to her feet and he did the same, blocking her path to the window. He lowered his head and growled. She wasn't intimidated. She was enjoying this, this contest, as much as he was. She darted forward. He blocked her. She leapt back and tried from a different angle, but he leapt up onto the couch, slamming into her, deflecting her course. They both landed on their feet. She darted forward again, straight toward him, but then spun around at the last second. His jaws closed on air. Her spin had landed her in the opposite direction, and she was moving directly away from him. She was heading for another exit, across the room, smaller and higher up. He leapt again, onto the back of a large piece of furniture. It began to fall, and he kicked off of it, hurling himself forward, knocking it over behind him. He caught her mid-leap, his jaws clamping on a rear leg. The two wolves tumbled to the ground, rolling forward to smash into a wall. She twisted, trying to pull free, but he moved with her. He turned his jaws sideways and was rewarded with a loud snap, a yelp of pain, and the taste of warm blood.

She spun on him, teeth seeking his throat. He released the leg to defend himself. They fought, rolling over and over on the floor, each seeking advantage. She was faster by far, but he was the larger and the stronger. By the time he'd gained the advantage, her leg had healed. He pushed forward again, heedless of her teeth, using his larger size and brute strength to push her down. His jaws closed about her throat, his whole weight behind them. But he didn't rip or tear. This was dominance, not hunting. He held tight. He would force her into the lesser, the weaker form.

But something pulled him back. Some tiny voice crying in the back of his mind cautioning against cruelty, against humiliation. The thought was strange to him, but he listened to it, and pulled back. The other wolf lay still, carefully watching him as he retreated. He settled down onto the floor, laying his head on his forelegs, his eyes never left her. She curled up and closed her eyes. It was over. She would remain here and out of danger. And there were others here now - he could hear and smell them behind him - who could help if needed. He closed his own eyes and drifted into sleep.

WHEN CARL WOKE UP, Kevin and Shelly were in the room, now both fully dressed. He surveyed the room. The girl was still asleep in wolf form, lying on the wooden floor nearby. She would wake up in a few minutes, he knew. He looked around. The big chair had been knocked over and the couch was bumped out of line, but the only real damage seemed to be the coffee table. It was smashed into splinters.

"Bout time," Kevin said quietly, when he saw he was awake, but he smiled when he said it.

"We're going to go check on our friend downstairs," he continued. "You gonna be okay up here?"

Carl looked over at the sleeping wolf and decided he could handle it if she tried to escape again. He nodded in response to the question.

"Here," Shelly said, and tossed him his shirt. "I'm afraid that's all that's left."

"Thank you," he said, and meant it. He pulled the t-shirt on as she left. Somehow, wearing the T-shirt but nothing below the waist made him feel even more naked. He looked around and spotted the blanket Shelly had wrapped herself in earlier on the couch. He wrapped himself up in it and settled down on the couch and watched the girl. He knew it wouldn't be long now.

A few minutes later, she changed, and a few minutes after that she woke up. She opened her eyes but didn't say anything. She didn't move at all, just looked around the room. He gave her what he'd hoped was a reassuring smile but wasn't sure what to say. For several moments, they watched each other in silence, he wrapped in the blanket on the couch and she lay naked on the floor.

Finally, she spoke. "So... I'm, what? A werewolf now?"

"A Were, yes," he agreed.

"What happens now then? Next full moon I go all wolfy and eat my roommates?"

He thought she lived alone. Shelly had assured them that nobody would notice she was missing for a few days at least. But that wasn't the most pressing thing to talk about right now.

"No," he said. "It doesn't work like that. You don't have to change. I mean, you do eventually but you can control when." He fumbled for the words. He almost wished Kevin was here. He was so much better at this kind of thing than he was. He could hear dim shouting coming from downstairs but couldn't make out the words. The man must have reverted back to human as well. The door was closed, and nothing was crashing against it, so he decided not to worry about it.

"It's kinda like sleeping, right? You can put it off and go without, but only for so long. And when you do change, you don't have to kill anybody. You're still you." He caught her skeptical look. "Well, kind of," he amended.

He wasn't sure how to describe it. "You're you but not you." Good job he thought. Brilliant.

He craned his neck, trying to check the wound on her thigh where he'd bitten her. Misreading his intent, she hurriedly put her hand down between her legs and gave him a hard glare.

"No!" he stammered. "I mean... your, uh, leg. Where I bit you."

She turned, exposing her thigh but keeping her hand in place. Carl found it hard to take his eyes off her to look down at the wound. There was the faintest trace of a scar, as if it had healed years ago.

"Hell of a bite you got there," she told him, as she ran her hand over the new scar. She quickly moved it back when he shifted his gaze, though.

"I'm sorry," he began, quickly raising his gaze to her eyes. "I..." he trailed off when he couldn't think of anything to say.

"What happened to my clothes?" she asked.

"Gone. I'm sorry, the transformation..."

"Figured as much. That's why you guys got undressed."

He nodded affirmation.

"How about a blanket?" she asked.

He hesitated for a moment, then unwrapped the blanket around himself and tossed it to her. Conscious now of how little the shirt he was wearing was covering, he tugged, embarrassed, at the hem, trying to pull it down as far as possible.

She wrapped the blanket about herself and stood up.

She looked around the small space. Finding the toppled chair, she righted it then sat down. "So now what?" she asked.

"What do you mean?" he said.

"What happens now. I assume you didn't go to all this trouble just to kill me, so what are you going to do with us now?"

"Nothing," he said. "We'll take you back to town tomorrow, like we said."

"Just drop me off and fuck out of my life like nothing happened?"

He didn't answer and she didn't wait.

"Why did you do it? What was supposed to happen?"

That was the question, wasn't it? "We... Just like Kevin said, we wanted to make more Were. A lot more."

"So, you've done this to other people? This is your idea of a fun weekend?"

"No. You're the first. We just thought..."

"I doubt that. I'm guessing not a lot of thought went into this at all, did it?"

She wasn't wrong. He glanced at the door. There was no sign of Shelly or Kevin.

"No," he answered her. "You're right. We didn't really think it through. We just wanted to make more Were - we'd hoped we'd make more, then you'd make more, and soon there'd be too many to..." He trailed off. He wasn't sure how much he should say. He glanced at the door again. No help there.

"You honestly think that after what you just did to me, that I'd respond by running off and doing it to someone else?"

Now that she said it, it didn't seem likely.

"And what do you mean? Too many to what?"

"To silence," he said, quietly.

For a second, her expression softened. She sat back a bit in her chair. "What do you mean, too many to silence? Who's trying to silence you?"

"The Alphas," he said. She didn't say anything, so he continued, "Our society, Were society, is outside human law. We're ruled by a bunch of tyrants - the Alphas. Law in any region is whatever they say it is at any given time. Except for one: Keep the secret. Humans can't find out we exist."

"And you're... what? Rebelling against them? So that's why you want to make more? More who you think won't be in favor of the Alphas?"

He just nodded in response. It seemed so childish now.

"I never asked to be part of your rebellion," she said. "You had no right to drag me into it."

"I'm sorry," he said. "I really didn't want to hurt or scare you."

"Well, you did," she replied.

He reeled back. He wasn't expecting that. He wasn't sure what he was expecting, but not... not that. He couldn't think of a response.

When he didn't say anything right away, she continued, "You did both those things." She paused for a second, then continued, "You could have just told us what you were planning."

"What would you have said?" he replied. "Really. If I told you that could turn you into a Were? You would have thought I was crazy. You never would have agreed."

"If you told me? Maybe not. But you could have shown me. You can transform any time you want, right? You could have shown me what you could do. Taken the time to explain it. At the very least you could have asked."

She was right, of course. Did they really need to be in that much of a rush? The plan could take years. An extra week or two trying to make contacts, convince people... Hell, even if they wanted to wait until the next full moon, they could have.

"Would you have?"

"Said yes? Maybe. Probably. I mean, it's still a hell of a trip, isn't it? But I would have liked a choice. Instead, you took... you took something from me that I never even knew existed. There's this amazing, wonderful thing that I never thought could be real, and right when I found out it was, you ruined it for me forever."

There was nothing he could say to that. Kevin and Shelly saved him by coming upstairs. The man from the basement followed behind them, wrapped in a sheet and wearing a sullen expression.

Toni pulled the blanket more tightly around herself when Kevin looked her way.

"Good to see you're all getting along. We were just filling Mitch in on what's what."

Mitch glared at him at that. Carl could guess how that conversation had gone.

"Same," he said without moving from his position on the couch.

Kevin had wandered into the kitchen and was firing up the stove. "Hamburger?" he called from the kitchen.

"Yes!" Carl called back. As hungry as he was, he was perhaps more motivated by an escape from the conversation.

"You talking to us, too?" Toni asked. She stood up and walked toward the island to the kitchen.

"Of course. You especially," Kevin replied.

Carl stood up as well, tugging again at the bottom of his t-shirt.

"Here," Toni said. "You look ridiculous and I can't move. Trade me."

It took him a second to catch what she was referring to. He took hold of his t-shirt, then hesitated, looking around. The small room seemed very crowded all of a sudden.

"Oh, for fuck's sake," she said. "We've both already seen each other naked. After everything you've done, don't pretend you're shy now."

Fine. He pulled off his t-shirt and tossed it to her. She put it on before she handed him the blanket. He pulled the blanket around himself. She wasn't much shorter than he was, but the shirt hung halfway to her knees. She took one of the two stools at the island and he took the other. Shelly started a pot of coffee while Kevin busied himself at the stove. Mitch hung back near the end of the counter. He looked back and forth and shifted his weight repeatedly from one foot to the other.

"With cheese or without?" Kevin asked.

"With," Toni replied. "And bacon if you got it."

"Sorry, didn't bring any."

"Are you fucking kidding me?" Mitch finally exploded. "These guys chained you in a basement and tried to kill you and now you're all buddies with them?"

Shelly turned and took a step forward. But only a step.

Toni turned to face him and answered. "Well, I wouldn't go so far as to say buddies..." she began.

"Chill out man," Kevin put in unhelpfully. "You've been given a great gift."

"A gift?" he said. "You bit me in the neck!"

"Actually, she did that," Kevin indicated Shelly with a jerk of his thumb. "And it was mostly the shoulder."

The other man did not seem amused. "I could have died!" he yelled.

Somebody did die. Carl was acutely aware that there was a corpse just below him that nobody was talking about.

Kevin was unmoved. "Coulda. Didn't. Want a cheeseburger?"

"No, I don't want a cheeseburger." He sat down on the couch, pulling the sheet tightly around himself. Carl wanted to say something. Reassure him. Tease him. He didn't know what.

He went and took the other seat at the counter, beside Toni.

"What about potato salad?" she asked Kevin.

"On a cheeseburger?" he responded with an easy smile, "Gross!"

Carl envied him that - his easy way of knowing the right thing to say to lighten the mood.

"On the side, dumbass," Toni replied. "This is a campout, isn't it?"

"You said you'd take us home?" Mitch asked, from his position on the couch.

"And we will," Kevin answered him from the kitchen. "In the morning." He tossed the patties he'd created onto the grill. "Sure you don't want one?"

"I'm not hungry."

"Liar," Kevin said with a smile. "You've just changed into Form then back out without eating. You're ravenous."

Mitch just glared in response to that.

"Hey, it doesn't make any difference to me," Kevin continued to press it. "They're here if you want 'em." He flipped the burgers and put a slice of cheese on three of them. Carl's stomach growled at the smell of cooking meat.

"There's crackers in the cupboard," he told Kevin. "As a side, since we don't have any potato salad."

Kevin found them. "Oh, sure, potato salad, wheat crackers, practically the same thing." But he handed Carl the box before he began pulling out condiments and setting them on the counter in front of Carl and Toni.

He took a handful out and passed the box to Toni, who did likewise before setting it back down.

Mitch stood up from the couch and began to pace, which made Carl nervous in such a small space. He was distracted, though from the arrival of the hamburger patties. "One or two to start with?" he asked Toni. He gave a pair each to both of them and one to Shelly before he turned back to the stove and tossed another batch onto the grill.

Toni looked over at them between bites of her burger and asked, "Why do you say Were instead of werewolf?"

Kevin replied, "I dunno. Just do. Everyone seems to say it, though."

"I wondered about that myself," Carl said. "Were just means 'man'"

"It does?" Kevin asked. Pulling off a couple more burgers and handing one of the plates to Shelly. "In what language?"

"Old English."

"How do you know that?" Kevin asked.

"I was curious, so I looked it up."

"Well, that's great," Toni said. "I can't wait to update my Facebook: 'Today I am a man.'"

Carl wanted to laugh at that but wasn't sure if he should. Nobody else did.

She took another bite. When she'd swallowed she asked, "So are you guys like at war with vampires or something?"

Shelly laughed out loud. "There's no such thing as vampires," she said.

"Are you sure?" Toni said immediately. "This morning, I would have said the same thing about werewolves."

That was a good point. Could it be possible? Surely, if vampires existed, someone would know about it, right? Maybe somebody did and just never told him. Why would they?

"I'm making more if you want one," Kevin called out to the front room.

"Why? What'd you put in them?" their "guest" asked from his position on the couch.

"Don't want one just say so," Kevin responded. "Don't have to be a dick about it."

"How can you just sit there and calmly eat with them?" Mitch turned to demand Toni.

"I'm not saying I'm cool with the kidnapping and murder," she said. Carl winced at that. "But I'm eating because I'm hungry. As for them turning us into..."

"Into what? Into what they are? A bunch of psychopaths with no regard for human life?"

"We're not human," Kevin said coldly, facing Mitch. "And neither are you anymore."

"No. No, I'm not, am I? I'm a..." He stood up. He never finished the sentence. Instead, he stood up, took one step toward him and changed. The sheet fell to the floor and where the man had been, a wolf fell to all fours.

"Hey," Kevin began. Carl and Shelly both jumped to their feet, ready to change as well. Toni swiveled the stool around, slid off of it and backed up so as not to get between them.

But instead of attacking, the wolf turned and leapt, away from them, off the couch, and through the front window, shattering glass behind it.

"No! Let him go!" Kevin yelled when Carl dropped his blanket.

He and Shelly both turned to look at him. "He's made his decision," he said. "That's what this was all about. Each of us is free to live how we want. He doesn't want to stay here with us, hear what we have to say, fine. He can go off on his own." He shook his head and went back into the kitchen.

Carl picked up the blanket, then looked toward Toni and found her looking toward the broken window. She gave a slight shake of her head then pulled herself back onto the bar stool.

Kevin looked back toward the front window, too. "So much for the damage deposit, I guess." Then, raising his voice, "The door was unlocked, asshole!" he yelled into the darkness.

NINE
INTO THE FIRE

Veer sat in front of her laptop at the kitchen table in the safe house they'd put her in, staring at the blank document on the screen. *Reporter Vera Rosen was attacked in her home last night by the serial killer she'd been writing about,* she started. She deleted the last bit and replaced it with *...the serial killer she had been tracking.* She didn't mention the killer was a werewolf. She added a few more details about how the police had intervened. She didn't mention they'd been watching her because they knew she was connected to him. They didn't know, and she didn't write, that it was because she was a werewolf too. The killer had escaped. Because the police weren't prepared for him to turn into a wolf. She was in a safe location now and vowed to keep covering the story. Except she'd keep leaving out the most important part, because she was too much of a coward to come out and say it.

So where did that leave her? What was she doing if she wasn't reporting the truth? Why bother writing at all in that case? She might as well have stayed in Kansas.

She opened a new document to start again.

A rogue Were, she started writing. *But before I tell you what the killer is, I will have to tell you what I am.*

What am I? A liar, a coward, a fool?

Victor Stumpp has been like a father to me, she started again. *No, too soon to bring him into it.* She erased the line.

For an hour she wrote, erased, wrote more, erased more. Finally, she selected everything but the opening line and hit delete with a disgusted grunt and got up from her chair.

"Not going well?" the detective on duty, Rebecca Abrams, asked her when Veer walked into the living room. She had been sitting on the couch reading the book that Veer had lent her.

"That obvious, huh?" she asked, taking the chair and rubbing her temples.

"Yeah," the officer told her. "Wanna talk about it?"

"Not really," she replied. She did, badly, but not to this woman.

"S'aright. I'll still be here if you change your mind."

"This has got to be difficult for you, sitting around watching me all day," Veer said.

"Eh. I've had worse assignments," she said. "You're not the first witness I've had to protect."

Witness. Is that what she was? Doesn't a witness testify? Tell what she knows?

"What happened to the others?"

"The other witnesses? After they testify, you mean?"

"Yeah."

"Look, I'm not going to lie to you. I don't know what you're involved in, but it's obviously big. This house, round-the-clock protection? All that ain't cheap. And the captain wouldn't have authorized it if he didn't think it was worth it. So, if you're trying to decide whether to testify or how much..." She looked at Veer expectantly.

"Something like that," she said.

"Yeah, everyone in a big bust goes through that. But if you were the one they were after, you wouldn't be here, you'd be in a cell. So if you want my advice, tell them everything you know. If you've done anything illegal yourself, talk to the DA, work out some kind of immunity, but tell them everything. You got a lawyer?"

"No."

"That speaks well of you. But I will tell you one thing - these other guys who went through this - big-time cases - not one of them went happily back to their previous lives. It's a life-changing event. Some people you thought were friends, you're gonna find out they're not. Same with family, maybe. It ain't gonna be easy, but it'll be worth it."

"They really didn't tell you anything about what it's all about?" she asked her.

"Well..." she hesitated, as if this was unsafe ground, "I know that it has something to do with Diaz's serial killer, and there's some kind of big conspiracy involved and there must be threats against you specifically or you wouldn't be here."

"That's it? Aren't you curious about what's really happening?"

"Curious, sure. But my job is to guard you, not question you. We've got strict orders not to ask you about anything related to the case."

That made sense. This officer was probably already being more open and friendly than she was supposed to be.

She was about to ask further, but at that moment the cop's radio clicked twice.

"Inbound friendly," she told Veer and moved to the door. She checked through the window first before opening it. Detective Diaz stood on the front porch holding two brown paper grocery bags. So much for no questions.

"Ready for a break?" he asked Abrams, once she had let him

in. She looked back over at Veer, who gave her a reassuring nod.

"You'll be okay" she said to Veer before she left.

"How are you doing?" he asked her, taking the bags he was carrying to the counter. By the way he emphasized the second word, she knew it wasn't just an idle question.

"Okay," she said, following him into the kitchen. He began unpacking the bag.

"You brought dinner?" she asked.

"Thought you might like some."

"Looks fancy. You must have a lot of questions," she said.

"I do," he replied.

Well, at least they knew where they stood. But it was just as well. "We have a lot to talk about," she said. "I've been thinking about our earlier conversation."

He stopped unpacking and turned his full attention to her. She sat down at the kitchen table and turned the laptop so he could see it, where she had written:

"A rogue Were. But before I can tell you what the killer is, I need to tell you what I am."

"I'm afraid that's as far as I've gotten," she said.

"It's enough," he told her.

"No," she said. "It's not. But it's a start." She didn't say, but they both knew that she couldn't publish yet anyway. Until the killer had been caught, they couldn't risk tipping him off that the police knew what he was. "If you do this, and think you can get enough proof to convince a judge, I'll back you up any way I can."

"Does that include testifying against Victor Stumpp?" he asked.

"Yes," she said. It wouldn't be easy, but she'd made her decision. She'd made her decision three years ago and had just been waiting for the right time. No more waiting, she decided. If it wasn't now, it was never.

He accepted the single word answer. He seemed to understand the weight behind it, and that fact gave her the courage to continue, "But I want to talk to him first."

"No. Bad idea."

"Don't care," she replied. "I won't have him learn I betrayed him by reading about it in the paper. After all, when I betrayed my real father, I did it to his face."

She let slip too much with that. The fact that she saw Victor almost as a father figure was something he could use against her. He picked up on it. "You betrayed your real father?" he asked.

Was he just making conversation, or pressing for useful information? "Just his principles, I suppose," she answered.

He looked at her but didn't respond. She appreciated that. There was a lot about him worth appreciating. She'd have to be careful.

She decided to tell him the story, and only hated herself a little bit for being aware that doing so could deepen a bond between them that she might be able to use later.

She picked up an onion he'd set on the counter. "How do you want it?" she asked.

"Diced, please," he responded, then passed her a chef's knife.

She set the knife down and began peeling the onion as she spoke.

"I told you my parents were pretty conservative, and didn't want me going to journalism school, right?"

"Right." He took two potatoes and started washing them at the sink.

"So..." she started, "I applied anyway, my senior year in high school. I sent them everything I'd written for the school paper.

When they finally responded, I was so proud of getting the scholarship, I went to show my father."

"But he still didn't want you to go?"

"I assumed that once he saw it wasn't going to cost him anything, he'd change his mind. He never had a lot of money, but the money was never the point."

"What happened?"

"He tore up the letter and grounded me."

"What?"

"Like I said, college wasn't his plan for me."

"Still - I can't imagine not wanting your kids to go if they're interested in it. Especially if they got a scholarship already."

"They weren't against it for their 'kids,' just the girls. Both my brothers had already gone. My oldest brother, William, had just graduated with a business degree from Bethel."

"Wow," he said. "So, when you said conservative..."

"Think Victorian era."

Funny how things can seem so normal, until you see them through other people's eyes. The degree of strictness and constant presence of anger over the slightest infraction never really seemed horrifying to her until she talked about it with someone else.

Michael remained quiet while he opened a package of chicken he'd brought and began preparing the fillets while sauteing the mushrooms.

"But you did end up going," he said, "didn't you? How'd that happen?"

"Yeah, well, the next day I had to call them to tell them I wouldn't be coming. You ever have someone completely change your life, and you never even catch their name? For me that was the woman who answered the phone in admissions. I was nearly in tears when I talked to her and she told me I can still come if I want. At eighteen, I was technically an adult - my life was my own."

"Wow. Good for her. She could have gotten into a lot of trouble for saying that."

"Huh. You know, I never really thought of that before. Now I really do wish I'd known her name. Maybe let her know how things turned out. Especially after I told her I didn't have the letter anymore, it got torn up, and I didn't know what to do."

"What'd she say about that?"

"She laughed! Oh, my poor dear," she caricatured the voice of a kindly old woman. "The letter's just to let you know you were accepted, we don't need it. Your information's all in the computers. If you want to come, come. Everything's waiting for you when you get here."

Even now, a decade and a half later, she could feel tears threatening to come out at the memory of her relief and the kindness of a stranger who was just doing her job. She pushed the tears down. It was not nearly safe enough here for that.

"So obviously you made it to... where was it again?" he asked.

"UCLA," she responded.

"Wait... you got a full ride scholarship to UCLA?" he seemed impressed by that.

"Yeah," she said. "I had no idea what to expect there. I didn't know how to choose a college, or even that you were allowed to apply to more than one. I just chose the farthest away city I could name."

"I guess it worked out," Michael said with an astonished grin. "Were you scared, jumping off into the unknown like that?"

"I don't think I've ever been as scared as I was then. I snuck out of the house in the middle of the night. Dragging a suitcase behind me down the dirt road to meet Jim at the corner."

"And Jim was?"

"He was my boyfriend. He had a car."

"True love," he said, which was a rude dismissal.

"It wasn't like that at all," she replied, with just enough ice in her voice to let him know he was out of line. But she continued, forestalling any apology, "So my father caught me sneaking out, of course."

"Oh! I can't imagine that went well," he said. The insult had been forgotten, by both of them, as she decided, she wanted it to be.

He turned his attention back to the potatoes, cleaned and peeled, he quartered them, and tossed them into a pot of boiling water. While they boiled, he began melting butter in a pan on the stove.

"Oh, there was yelling, and screaming, and crying," she continued her story. "But things had changed. This concept of my life being my own was new to me, and I wasn't going to let it go. He thought he still had power over me. He told me running away wouldn't solve anything, I told him I was an adult and when an adult does it it's called moving out. He said if I left now then don't ever come back. I said that works for me and left."

"Wow." Michael was quiet for a moment, then asked, "Did you ever see him again?"

"Eventually. After that first year I finally called them. We've come to terms - to some degree at least. It probably helped that a couple years later my sister went off in the opposite direction - to business school in New York. I went home several Christmases in a row, from LA and later Portland. We're in touch, but we're not what you'd consider close."

She remembered what he'd told her on his last visit about his relationship with his own father. That kind of closeness with family was so alien to her.

"God, I can't even imagine what that would have been like. Completely on your own at eighteen. It's a wonder you didn't end up..." he broke off. Veer wondered what he was going to say. End up what? A criminal? A serial killer? Technically, she was the former. Did he suspect her of being the latter? Or somehow in league with him?

She let it go. There was too much risk pursuing that line of questions. "At the time, it was actually a profound sense of freedom," she said. "Barreling down Interstate seventy in Jim's Oldsmobile, with no ties behind me and everything I owned in the world in a suitcase with a broken wheel in the trunk. We were both young and free with nothing holding us back. I had a full scholarship to UCLA to study journalism and he was going to be an actor - or maybe a musician - he hadn't decided yet. We were both going to do great things and change the world and be together forever."

He gave a soft laugh at that, and she didn't hold it against him. She smiled at the memory herself.

While the chicken cooked, he dropped the skinned and boiled potatoes into a large bowl for her to mash. Then tossed in half a stick of butter, that melted as she stirred them around. When he came over with a couple of cloves of garlic to add she had to comment. "Okay, now I know I didn't see a garlic press in here earlier."

"Most of this I brought from home. They say these places are fully stocked, but they never really are," he said. "So, what happened?"

It took her a moment to realize what he meant. "The relationship lasted longer than the car," she said with a smile, teasing him for his earlier remark. "But neither survived the summer. Every once in a while, I find myself looking up his name on IMDB, but I haven't found him yet."

"Guess we don't all get to live our dreams."

"Is that what I'm doing?" she wondered aloud. "I wonder sometimes what happened to that girl, though. The girl who was willing to jump first, then try to figure out where to land on the way down."

"Grew up, I suppose."

"Maybe. Got older at any rate."

"There is something to be said for looking before you leap."

Diaz arranged the two plates with the mashed potatoes and green beans and spooned the mushrooms over the chicken. She half expected him to produce a bottle of wine, but none was forthcoming. Nonetheless, "I could get used to this," she said, after taking the first bite. "This is good. I mean really good. I rarely cook much myself, and when I do it tends to be something I can make in a single pan, or a slow cooker."

They ate in silence for several minutes. Then Diaz spoke again, "How much trouble will you be in when this goes public?"

"A lot," she answered honestly after only a brief pause. "It's not just Victor. We'll be bringing the whole organization down on us. They'll do their best to discredit us both, or kill us if they don't think that'll work. I'll have to go into hiding for a while. You'll be in danger as well. Do you have any family?"

"No," he replied. "What about yours?"

"I don't think they'll go after them."

"You sure about that?"

"Victor wouldn't, even if we weren't friends. But the council... I don't know. If they don't see any other way to get to me, maybe."

"I'll see about offering them some sort of protection."

"No, don't. The cops wouldn't be able to do anything, and they might draw attention."

He nodded in agreement. He hadn't been too sure about it either, obviously.

"Speaking of Stumpp..." he paused. She let him finish the thought. "You can't protect him."

"I know," she said, and thought she did a good job of keeping the anguish from her face.

"Okay," he said. "As long as we're clear." But they both knew that Victor wasn't the real target here.

"Things are going to get interesting," she said in an attempt to lighten the mood. It didn't work.

"They already have," he told her. "I think Chandler is a werewolf now."

She looked up sharply at that.

"He's missing from the hospital," he said, and then, after another pause, "A nurse reported a wolf attack on another patient one floor down from him."

He looked at her expectantly. He was waiting for a reaction. It took her a second to realize what he thought the implications were. Chandler had turned, and the first thing he did was attack another patient.

She thought hard before answering. This could be delicate. She'd have to convince him without seeming like she was trying to convince him. "That doesn't make sense," she said at last. "I've talked to his neighbors. Chandler was never a violent man. You don't become homicidal just because you're a Were."

"So you've said," he replied. He obviously didn't believe her. She was about to respond to that, but he continued, "He may have been hurt or confused and it's possible it wasn't even him."

That surprised her. She cast him a querulous look, so he continued, "He was attacked in his room. We found a hypodermic on the floor, with a silver needle. They're analyzing it at the lab now. Any idea what's in it?"

She shook her head. "What makes you think Chandler was the wolf who attacked the other patient, then?" she asked. "Couldn't the killer have gone after him, too?"

"For one, we showed the picture around at the hospital, and nobody recognized him."

"But obviously he'd been there. Someone tried to kill Chandler." She was just assuming the needle had been poisoned but drugging him wouldn't make any sense. He was already in the hospital. Unless they intended to move him somewhere? She wondered if this was Victor tying up loose ends. And if he would tell her if she asked. Probably not. Most likely, asking him about it would just tip him off to what she knew.

"Do you think it's likely that Stumpp knows who this guy is?" Michael asked.

She thought for a moment that he meant Chandler, or possibly whoever attacked him in the hospital, but then she realized he meant the rogue. "No. It wouldn't make any sense. He asked me to look into it. I can't see him doing that if he already knew who it was."

"Throw you off track, maybe?"

She thought about that for a second, too, looking down at her plate so he couldn't read her face. *Was it possible?* She'd guessed a lot from the way he'd asked, and the fact that Gregor had been present. He couldn't have known exactly what that would reveal, but he was clever enough to realize any conversation could reveal something. "No. Just keeping quiet would have been safer. There'd be no reason to involve me at all."

"I'll buy that," he said. "But somebody knows. Someone had to turn him into this, right?"

"Yeah, somebody," her tone indicated the difficulty of ever determining who that somebody was. "Maybe you can ask him once he's caught. There haven't been any more, though. Or if there have, they've been very quiet."

"You sure about that?"

"As sure as you are," she said. Hopefully he'd understand what she meant: if there were any more like him running around, the police would know about it the same way they knew about this one.

"How'd you know he was from San Diego?" he asked.

"The Alpha of Southern California is in Portland. I've spoken to him."

For a second, she expected a bigger reaction. But of course, he didn't realize what that meant.

"Southern California? How many of these 'Alphas' are there?" he asked her.

"In North America, fifty-six," she told him. It had taken her over a year and a dozen conversations with Victor to learn that fact. It was sitting in a folder in her computer in an encrypted file, against this day. It felt good to say it out loud. "That includes Canada and Mexico. I don't know about world-wide. Other places organize differently."

"You're all over the world, then?"

"As far as I know. There are even some villages in Europe and Africa where they're actually well-known, and the whole town keeps their secret from outsiders."

"Why would they do that?" he asked, as she suspected he would.

"In some places, they're seen as village guardians. Holy warriors sworn to protect their people. There're at least a couple of small towns in America that do the same thing."

"How could everybody possibly not know about that?"

"Well, a lot of small towns are pretty insular. They don't tend to have a lot of trust in outsiders. And outside America... I'm sure a lot of anthropologists have heard of them and just chalk it up to local superstition. People ignore what they don't want to believe."

"So how can we ever convince the jury that the killer's a werewolf?"

"That's the question, isn't it? I've been looking for an answer for three years."

"You don't have to wait for the full moon, right? You can change at will?"

She understood where he was heading. She'd had the same thought herself. "And a decent defense attorney could find a stage magician to do the same."

"Can that really be done?"

"I've seen it at the Magic Castle in LA."

"Damn," he said out of frustration. She knew exactly how he felt.

"Maybe we won't have to," she said. "Maybe the evidence you have here will be enough to convince a jury."

"Maybe," he said. She could tell from his tone that he didn't believe it, though. He was committed to going forward even without hope of doing it without exposing the Were. Good enough.

She wanted to follow up on that, but then his phone rang. He looked at it apologetically. "Sorry, gotta take this."

"Yes?" he answered it. Then, "Are you sure" a pause, "Now?" another pause. "Shit. Okay, do your best to stall them until I get there.... Shit. Okay. On my way." He stood up and grabbed his coat. "Sorry," he said to her, "I gotta run."

"What is it?" she asked.

He hesitated for a second, then answered. "They've found Talman. Tracked him to a hotel room and have a swat team on the way."

They both understood the implications of that. The swat team would be killed. "I'm coming with you," she said.

"Like hell you are. Sit tight. Finish your meal. I'll be back."

"We both know your men can't stop him."

"I can," he said. "Silver bullets if I need them."

"You gonna stop me from coming?" she asked. "You already sent my protection home."

"Dinh is still outside. I'll send him in."

"I can identify him," she tried.

"Already been identified," he countered. Of course he had. Dammit, this was taking too long.

"I'm still coming." She grabbed her own jacket from the back of the chair it'd been hanging on.

"No, dammit," he replied. "It's too dangerous."

"I know. That's why I'm coming. You're still under my protection, remember?"

"No, you're under mine," he argued. "And you'll stay here where it's safe."

This was starting to sound familiar, and fuck that. "I'm going, one way or another. You can either give me a ride, or explain to everyone why there's a wolf chasing after you."

"Dammit," he swore again. But realized he had no choice. If he was going, there was no way to stop her. "Fine. But you do what I say, and if I tell you to run, you run."

"No promises," she told him, and headed out the door, leaving him to catch up.

He stopped briefly at a car across the street. "I'm taking Rosen," he told the man who must have been Dinh. "Keep an eye on the place. If anyone even glances at it, I want to know."

PHIL WAS WAITING for them on the street when they arrived. Three cruisers and a van were parked outside the small run-down apartment complex just off Alberta street.

"Second floor," he told Michael. "Halfway down the hallway."

"Shit," Michael swore. It was exactly the worst place. There was no way to evacuate the civilians without tipping him off and risking him taking hostages.

"The good news is, he may be wounded," Phil continued. "Looks like you got him," he said to Veer, who Michael hadn't noticed had come up directly behind him. "Should she be here?" he directed the last to Michael.

"No. She should definitely not be," he answered.

"Okay, then." Phil didn't ask for any further explanation.

"Has there been any contact?" Michael asked.

"No. Landlord responded to our fax from yesterday. The suspect came in three days ago, dripped blood all over the hall. Hasn't gone out since."

If he was still wounded, the silver needle must have worked after all. Otherwise, it would have healed by the time he'd gotten here.

"If he's been here since Thursday, he couldn't have attacked Chandler at the hospital," Veer said.

A good point. He wanted answers. "Well, let's go in and see what we find. Tasers and mace if we can. I want to take this guy alive."

Phil seemed surprised at that, but acquiesced, drawing his taser. Michael did likewise. His service 9mm was loaded with standard rounds, but he also had the .45 revolver with the silver sabot rounds, just in case. He didn't have time to explain now, so didn't mention it.

He heard the utter pandemonium in the hall before he opened the door. A man rushed toward them but stopped when he saw the weapons and raised his hands in the air, backing against one wall. "He's down there!" he shouted. He needn't have bothered. Halfway down the hall was the largest wolf Michael had ever seen. It was standing over a man lying on the floor, its nuzzle buried in the man's open belly. The victim's mouth was moving, as if trying to talk, but no sounds came out.

"Go!" Michael yelled to the man who was still standing against the wall and nodded to the stairway behind him. He stepped past him without seeing if he obeyed, raising his weapon. Phil was already a step ahead of him but had switched to his service weapon. Obviously, he thought that the desire for capture was for the man and didn't apply to his pet wolf. There wasn't time to warn him before he aimed and fired directly at the beast's head. It twitched slightly, then turned its attention from the corpse it was devouring to Phil and leapt at him. He had time to fire once more before it was on him.

Michael stepped forward, trying to get a clear shot where he could hit the beast and not his partner. Phil was on the ground under the wolf. He had lost his weapon in the attack and was trying to hold the massive wolf off, pressing both hands against its head, which was lowering toward him with jaws wide open. Michael fired his taser.

It jerked its head up, howling in pain. Despite the electrodes in its flesh and Michael's thumb holding down the power button as hard as he could, it leapt straight toward him, knocking him over. The taser was knocked out of his grasp. Inactive without a hand on it, it spun off out of his sight. He was dimly aware of Phil struggling upright behind the wolf.

He fought as Phil had done, trying to avoid the beast's jaws. Suddenly, his whole body jerked with the pain of electrical shock. The wolf howled again, raising its head. It jumped off of him and straight back of Phil who had somehow gotten his taser out and was hitting the wolf with it. Michael turned over, barely. His limbs weren't responding right yet. He saw Phil in the same stance he had been in, with his taser in hand, the two wires leading directly to the wolf, and his thumb pressed hard against the activation button.

For the third time, the wolf leapt, and Michael saw both it and Phil go down, the massive jaw closing over Phil's arm.

Blood splattered across the floor. He rolled up onto his side, willing himself to move, forcing uncooperative limbs to pull him upright. Phil was down and unmoving, and the wolf turned its attention back to him. Before he could react, another wolf, sleek and grey, had tackled the larger one. Veer had joined the fight. Phil crawled to the side, nursing an injured arm. It was bleeding profusely and possibly broken.

The two wolves rolled around, biting, snapping, clawing at each other. A single ball of roiling teeth and fur. He raised the revolver but couldn't get a clean shot. He brought up his other arm to steady the gun. Phil sat unmoving, mesmerized by the spectacle, the two beasts directly in front of him.

They fought, while he tried to track the larger one with his gun. He could already feel strength returning to his limbs. He hadn't gotten the full jolt from the taser, just been in contact with the wolf when Phil had hit it.

Eventually, the big wolf came out on top. It lifted its head in triumph and Michael fired his weapon, twice. The beast shook with the impact, blood splattered against the wall behind it. It turned toward him, and he fired again. And again. The smaller wolf got unsteadily to its feet and ran off down the hall. The larger wolf advanced on him, obviously hurt and barely moving. He fired once more, and it fell to the ground. The beast itself seemed to sink into the air and dissolve and leave in its wake the man he'd recognized from the surveillance footage from the Max and the photos taken in Rosen's hallway: Grant Talman. He lay still and naked in a slowly spreading pool of blood.

Michael dragged himself to his feet and went over to where Phil sat, looking stunned. He took out his radio and called "Suspect is down. Officer injured. We need medical up here now." Then turned his attention back to Phil.

"Nice shot," was all Phil said to him.

A pair of paramedics entered the hall at that moment. One went to the suspect and the other to Phil. He immediately went to work to stop the bleeding. They must have been already on their way. Two more uniformed cops came with them and entered the apartment. Michael already had a good idea what they'd find, and what they wouldn't.

"Can you walk?" one of the medics was asking Phil. "If you want, we can bring a stretcher up here."

"I can walk," Phil said. "In a minute." He turned his attention to Michael. "Let me see your weapon."

Michael hesitated but then he handed it to him, butt first. Phil took it in his good hand. He opened the cylinder and spilled the remaining cartridge to the floor. He set down the gun and picked it up.

"That's the ugliest round I've ever seen," he said, indicating the lump of metal embedded in the blue plastic. "Silver?" he asked.

Michael nodded in response.

"Silver bullet," Phil said accusingly. "Either you're secretly the Lone Ranger, or you knew what this guy was."

"I..." Michael started, unsure of how to respond.

"You've got some explaining to do."

"Yes," he agreed. "You go get yourself fixed up. I'll fill you in back at the station."

"I want everything. *Everything*." He emphasized the word the second time.

"You'll get it, I promise."

Phil looked at him skeptically for a moment, then finally nodded. "All right. See you at the station." And let the paramedic help him down the stairs.

After he had gone, Michael asked one of the uniformed officers to secure the scene, telling him that he was going to check out something else. He didn't tell him what. He still couldn't.

The apartment would be empty, but somewhere nearby there would be another werewolf, and this one would need his help.

He found her clothes, shredded as he'd expected, in the stairwell. He gathered them up and felt only a twinge of guilt over the destruction of evidence. He pulled out her wallet and her phone. How do they normally do this? From the locker room at the preserve, he guessed they didn't, usually. Not without preparation. It must be a rare thing indeed for them to change unplanned like this, or she wouldn't keep such things in her pockets.

He looked at the stairway. She'd come in here, but which way had she gone? There were cops watching the ground and they hadn't reported any sign of a wolf. So up it was.

He found her, still in wolf form, curled up on the roof. This time, the wolf was awake and watching him warily. There was blood nearby and in its fur, but her wounds seemed to have healed. He took off his coat and draped it over her, and sat back, shivering in the cold October air and waited for her to change back into human form.

A couple of minutes later, she did. She took a moment to take in the situation, then said, "We've got to stop meeting like this."

He smiled but didn't say anything.

"Did we get him?" she asked.

"Yeah," he responded. "We got him. It's over."

"Good," she said. And that was it. He understood how she felt. He just wanted to go home and sleep for a week. But he'd just shot and killed a suspect. Even if he hadn't been a were-wolf - a Were - there'd be a lot to deal with. He still had to figure out how to tell the rest that that was what he was. His phone rang and he saw it was a member of his task force. With an apologetic nod to Veer he stood up and took a couple of steps away to answer it.

"Congratulations, Detective," Alice Johansen said on the phone. "I hear you've bagged our bad guy."

"I got one of them, yes. Unfortunately, he's now deceased, so can't give us any information beyond whatever we find in his hotel room."

"What hotel?" she asked.

He gave her the address. "Meet you down here?"

"I'm on my way," she said. "It was Grant Talman, right? Not suspect One? And you know it was him?"

"It was definitely him, but we're pretty sure he wasn't acting alone." Something she said had rang an alarm bell, though. "Hold on, I'm with somebody who might be able to identify Suspect One. Can you send me a picture of him before you go?"

"Sure thing. You'll have it in a minute."

When he'd hung up, he saw that Veer had heard part of that. She had stood up, his coat closed around her, and now stepped forward. "Suspect One?" she asked.

"Maybe the guy who killed Sam," he said.

The phone beeped and the picture came through. He saw that Johansen had just pointed her camera at the picture they had of him hanging in the war room. Good enough for a quick ID. "Recognize him?" he asked, showing the picture to Veer.

She was silent for a long moment. Much longer than he felt comfortable with. It had to mean she was sorting through facts, trying to decide what to tell him. Finally, she answered.

"Yes," she said. Another pause. "His name is Peter. He works for Victor."

"Shit," he said. It wasn't over. He had a feeling it was barely beginning.

TEN

LOST IN THE WOODS

"You can drop me off at my apartment," she said. Toni had taken the front seat in the van. She was still wearing Carl's shirt, and before leaving the cabin she'd commandeered Kevin's jacket as well. Carl and Shelly were sitting on the floor in the back, while Kevin drove. "You know where it is, right, from when you were stalking me?"

"Researching," Kevin corrected her with an easy grin. "You wanna come back up with us to clean up in the morning?" he asked.

"No thanks," she replied. There was no warmth in her voice, or trace of amusement. "Right now, anything goes down and I'm firmly in the category of victim. I think I prefer that to accomplice."

Kevin kept his smile. Carl didn't see how he could. He looked over at Shelly, who seemed to be ignoring the whole interchange. Didn't they see what she was saying? Kevin and Shelly may not be worried about Human law, thinking themselves untouchable by it. He wasn't so sure. Sure, it'd be easy for a Were to escape arrest, but once they knew your name, it was all over. Maybe for a minor offense they wouldn't bother searching for you. But for kidnap and murder? They would come.

He remembered being told early on not to get arrested. Were didn't go to prison. He supposed that there was some sort of legal assistance, bribes to the right person, getting charges dropped, that sort of thing. They obviously couldn't risk a Were being incarcerated. What happened when someone changed in a cell, in full view of Humans and security cameras? And if locked up for more than a month or two, they would eventually change whether they wanted to or not. Rule One is Secrecy. He'd heard that more times than he could count. The Alpha had to have some way of disposing of any Were foolish enough to get himself committed to even a relatively short sentence.

And as for Were law. Carl had no illusions there. All four of them could be killed for what they had done.

Toni didn't owe any allegiance to either Human or Were authorities. He had a feeling she was used to being at odds with the one, and would have no idea how to contact the other. But she owed no allegiance to Carl or his friends, either. She was making that clearer with every word. Why didn't they see that? Would she call someone the minute she was out of their sight? Not the police. And not the Alpha. Her boyfriend maybe. As calm as she seemed, as accepting of the whole thing, she'd want to talk it over with someone. No telling what they'd say. What advice they'd give. He made a hasty decision.

"Can I come with you?" he asked her. "I mean, we could... talk, or... whatever," he added as she turned an amused expression to him.

"Whatever?" She quoted in a mocking tone. Her smile didn't reach her eyes. He carefully didn't look at the other two in the van. He didn't need to see their amusement at what they almost certainly believed was a clumsy attempt to hit on the girl.

"You might have questions," he said. "And there are things you should know."

She thought for a moment — at least she didn't laugh — and finally said, "Sure, why not?"

She must have noticed his relief. "You're not getting your shirt back," she added. He laughed at that.

Kevin stepped out of the van. "Are we picking you up here in the morning, or...?"

"I'll meet you at your place," Carl replied. The safest option. His car was already over there anyway.

———

TONI'S APARTMENT was up a flight of stairs in a complex just off Northwest 23rd avenue. It was a tiny place, beyond a small bathroom, kitchen, and a single bedroom. A futon sat under the lone window, which overlooked an alley. A small stuffed couch was opposite it, backed up against a closet with no door. Carl took a seat on the couch.

Toni reached past him and pulled a couple of things out of the closet behind the couch.

"You wait out here," she told him and headed into the bathroom. A moment later, he heard the shower start. He looked around but there wasn't much more to the place. A small bookshelf standing next to the window was the only other piece of furniture. Even as small as it was, he wondered how she could afford it, in this neighborhood. She'd probably been here for a while, he guessed. Did she say she had a roommate? The couch didn't look big enough to sleep on...

The bathroom door was half open. Did she do that on purpose? Was it a test to see what he'd do? He laughed to himself at that, at his own paranoia. Maybe that was just what she normally did, to let the steam out of the room. It doesn't have to mean anything, he told himself.

Several long minutes later, Toni came back out wearing sweatpants and a sweater. There was no sign of his t-shirt or Kevin's jacket.

"Still here?" she asked him when she came out. She took a seat on the futon opposite him. He wasn't sure what to make of that, either.

"Did you... were you not expecting me..." he stammered.

"Relax," she told him. "For somebody who's got this awesome secret power, you're awfully uptight."

"Secret power," he replied. "I'd never thought of it that way before."

She got up and went into the kitchen. "What else would it be?" she called back. "My god, I feel so... alive?" She thought for a moment. "Hungry," she finally said as he heard the refrigerator open, then close again a moment later. "I don't got shit in here. Wanna go out for a pizza?"

"Umm... sure... I..." He still wasn't sure what to say. He was having trouble keeping up.

She shifted gears again, sitting back down on the edge of the futon. "Why are you here, anyway?" she asked him.

Carl was taken aback by that. "What? What do you mean?" he said.

"I mean, why are you here?" she repeated. "Are you supposed to keep an eye on me? Keep me from going to the authorities? Do you think you could stop me if I wanted to leave?"

"I wouldn't. That's not why I'm here," he explained. "I just thought you might have questions. Or maybe we could just, you know, talk. Get to know each other a bit." He was still unsure himself. Having turned her, he felt some responsibility. There was so much she didn't know, but he didn't know where to start.

"No. I wouldn't stop you if you wanted to go," he said.

"What if I told you to go?" she asked him and stood up. For a moment, he was afraid she would do just that, and prepared to stand up himself.

"I'd go. You're not.... You're not property. You're supposed to be free. That's the whole point."

"I don't get it," she said. "Free? You mean you're not?"

"Not exactly. Me, Kevin, Shelly, all the rest, we're supposed to answer to the Alpha. And I'm supposed to answer to Kevin because he turned me."

"But you turned me, and I don't have to obey you?" She sat back down again on the futon, her legs folded under her.

"No. Because we didn't do it right." She looked startled at that. "I mean, you turned okay, there's nothing wrong with you or anything..." he trailed off for a moment. Nothing wrong with you at all, he wanted to say, but thought better of it. "It's just that there are rules. We're not supposed to turn people without the Alpha's permission."

"What about the permission of the person you're changing?" she asked him.

He looked down at his feet. "That's usually asked for, too," he admitted.

"Usually. But not always," she replied. It wasn't a question.

"No. But there are other rules, too. Secrecy, mostly. They hardly ever make someone without their permission because there's no telling what they'll do - if they'll agree to all the other rules," he explained.

"What about you?" she asked him.

"What do you mean?" He was lost again.

"Did you get a choice? Or did Kevin kidnap you like you did to me?" The accusation was back in her voice. He couldn't blame her. It had made sense when their plan was an abstract idea. When she was an abstract idea. But now, talking to her, she was a person. And they had done this thing to her against her will. He wasn't sure how he felt about that. He felt like a rapist. The thought made him sick to his stomach.

"No. I chose. Kevin told me about it ahead of time, then invited me to a convocation. I was turned there with a couple of other people."

"Convocation? What's that? Some big gathering of werewolves?"

"Yeah. Exactly. They have them a few times a year," he said. "Most Were get turned at them. The Alpha and his council and their friends have their meetings and they usually organize a hunt or two, and parties and stuff like that."

"So, do I have to go to those now?" she asked him.

Did she really misunderstand her position that badly? Or was she teasing him again? If she didn't understand, whose fault was that?

"No. No, you can't. They can't know you exist," he tried to explain.

"Because of the secrecy rule?" she asked. "So your little group has the same rule, only it applies to the rest of the werewolves as well as everyone else."

Carl didn't like the accusation of hypocrisy, but she wasn't entirely wrong.

"No, because you're not supposed to exist. We broke the rules when we turned you. The Alpha'd punish us for that."

"Punish how? I don't like the sound of that."

He thought about it for a second, then replied, "They'd probably just kill you outright to get rid of you. Probably me, too. It's happened before." He could see the shock in her face at that. Perhaps he could have worded that better.

"They'd actually do that?" she asked. "Just because you

broke some rule, I get the death penalty if they ever find out?" She stood up again, took a couple of steps toward him, turned, paced back toward the kitchen, then sat back down on the other end of the futon.

"What am I?" she finally asked.

"You're a Were. Like me," Carl responded.

"Am I a person anymore? What happens to me now?" She was serious.

"Yeah. I mean, yeah, you're different now. But nothing's taken away. You're still who you were before."

"Are you sure about that?" she asked him, looking directly into his eyes. "Are you sure that you're what you were before?"

What was she talking about? "I... I think so. I mean, I guess I wouldn't really know, but, yeah, I'm basically the same person, just, you know, faster, stronger, better."

"You kidnapped me, chained me in a basement. I didn't know if you were going to kill me, rape me, chop me into pieces, or if you were going to be wearing my skin by morning. Fuck, you killed a guy in front of me and left me chained up next to his corpse. These are not the actions of a normal person, Carl."

"I..." he began. He hadn't really thought of it. He didn't want to say that, though. He wasn't sure what to say, but Toni cut him off.

"So, I gotta ask you again, were you always like this? Or is this a result of being a werewolf? Who thought last night would be a good idea? You, or the wolf?"

He couldn't meet her gaze. "I never wanted to hurt anyone," he said quietly.

"Yeah?" She hurled the words at him. "Well, you did, didn't you?"

"Nobody was supposed to die," he replied, lifting his head, "Kevin just..."

"Don't," she interrupted. "Don't even try to defend that little psychopath."

He smiled at that. He couldn't help himself. "I wasn't, actually. I was going to point out that it was Kevin, not me, who killed the other guy."

"The other guy? He had a name. He was a person, and you left me chained up, wounded and bleeding, next to his corpse. That doesn't make you much better. I'll tell you the truth, Carl. I've had better nights."

He had no answer to that.

"Nobody was supposed to die," he repeated.

"What did you think was going to happen?" she asked him. "Did you think that after everything, we'd all just get along and be grateful for this great gift you'd given us?"

He had mostly thought that, as much as he'd thought of it at all. He didn't think it wise to admit that now, though. He hadn't really thought of their reactions. He felt ashamed at that fact. Was that him or the wolf? Could there be a difference?

"I... I don't know," he said finally. It sounded lame even to him.

"Well, that's something, I guess," she said. He wasn't sure what she meant by that, either.

Another long pause. Toni just sat and stared straight at him. He finally met her gaze.

"How do you feel?" he finally asked. He realized it was the question he had come here to ask. And he meant it sincerely despite not being able to say the words and not think of them as a quote from Star Trek.

She picked up on his tone though and pondered it for a moment before answering. "I don't know," she said, which wasn't encouraging. "Do you mean, am I angry at you? Yeah. You violated me, in a way you had no right to do. I'm not forgiving that. And I'm kinda numb, and sort of strung out and strangely amped. I feel like I've stepped into another world that I never even knew existed. And maybe I'm a little scared, about what you turned me into, and what I'm still going to become. I know you insist that I'm no different now, or nothing less, but I don't know. Even if you believe what you say, your judgment may not be the best."

He sat still, trying to take in everything she'd said, and looked directly at her as she paced nervously. That's a lot for not knowing how you feel, he thought, but remained silent. He was trying to think of something to say in response, but she continued.

"And I'm hungry. Ravenous. But I don't really want pizza. I want to turn into a wolf again and, I dunno, maybe chase down a wildebeest and eat it raw. And I never really noticed how dinky this fucking place was before. And..." she hesitated, then continued, "and every time I look over at you, I want to leap at you, teeth bared, and I honestly don't know if it's to jump your bones or tear your throat out."

"Well, if I get a choice," he started before thinking better of it.

"You don't," she cut him off. She didn't smile when she said it.

"And your friend Kevin's a psychopath, and I'm not sure if you're one or not or maybe you are and just not as bad. And was he always like that, or is that because he's a werewolf? And you seem like a nice enough guy. Kinda stupid, but not evil. But you've done some evil shit, and is that because you're a wolf or because you're stupid? And if it's because of the wolf, am I like that now? Or am I going to turn into some crazy little girl who thinks kidnapping people and chaining them in the basement in a cabin in the woods sounds like a fun way to spend a Friday night?" He started to open his mouth, but she continued, cutting him off. "So, I'm a little scared about that, too, and there's nobody I can talk about it with but you, because none of my friends would understand and I don't want to accidentally turn into a wolf and kill them," she finally finished. "Does that answer your question?"

"Yes. It does." He didn't apologize again. He still felt guilty, but a little more relieved. He didn't know what to say to all that, or how to make it right. "I'm not quite sure what a wildebeest is exactly, but if deer and stuff'll do, there's a place we can go."

"Really? Let's go now." She sprang to her feet.

"It's a ways away. And my car's at Kevin's," Carl told her.

"I've got a car," Toni replied.

Sure, Carl thought, why not? There probably won't be anyone there now, right? What could go wrong? "Okay," he said.

She changed in the bathroom again, coming back out wearing jeans and Kevin's coat. She went straight to the front door. "Coming?" she looked back at him. He got up and followed her out the door.

———

GORDON CHANDLER SHIVERED in the cold October air. He was lying naked on mossy ground. He rose to his feet, and realized it wasn't a struggle. He sprang up easily. When was the last time getting up from the ground required this little effort? He felt better than he could remember feeling for years. A feeling of elation washed over him, quickly replaced with a wave of guilt. This was wrong. Barbara was gone. He had no business feeling good after what had happened.

He looked around him. Trees, as far as he could see. Where was he? How far had he gone to end up in a forest? He had to figure out where he was, and how to get back. Get back where? Home? The hospital? No point going back to the hospital. He'd

have to answer a lot of questions and make himself a target
again. He didn't want to go home, either. How could he ever
face it? Plus, that would be the first place they looked for him
once they found he wasn't in the hospital.

He started walking. Might as well start by figuring out
where he was. Give him time to think about where to go.

Someone had tried to kill him. Twice. Two different some-
ones. The first one killed Barbara. Perhaps that one had just
been a random burglary, but the second one had targeted him
directly. They, whoever "they" were, knew what he was and
wanted to keep anyone else from finding out. It was the only
explanation he could think of why they would attack him in the
hospital like that. So, this mysterious group - and it had to be a
group, there were multiple coordinated individuals - were well-
organized, not above committing murder, and likely had at least
some of the police working with them. It couldn't have been a
coincidence that they'd struck only a few hours after he told
that policeman what he knew.

He came upon a small footpath. He didn't think it was an
animal trail, though he was no expert. It was too well-worn. Or
maintained. Forest Park. It must be. Ever since he'd moved to
Portland, he'd been meaning to check it out. It seemed like a
good hiking spot right in the city, but he hadn't gotten around to
it yet. He regretted that now. Maybe if he was more familiar
with it, he could figure out where to go.

Wherever he went, he'd have to find something to wear.
If people started reporting a naked black man coming out of
the woods the cops wouldn't take long to respond. Then
again, were the police even a threat to him now? In wolf
form, he could easily outrun them. Even if they shot him, he
could heal any damage. Of course, if it got to that point, he'd
be a hunted fugitive. Although, wasn't that what he was now?
He had an image of himself on the run, traveling from town

to town across the country encountering problems that
somehow could always be resolved by turning into a wolf,
always one step of the one dogged lawman who nobody
believes when he tells them of the monster he's chasing. And
what would that make Barbara? His tragic backstory? The
girl in the fridge, as she would have put it? No, she deserved
better than that.

He had to figure out a way out of this. He had this super-
power, but so far it was more liability than asset. Maybe it could
come in handy, and maybe he could just ignore it and never
change again. Before he did anything else, though, he needed
more information. He had to stay out of sight until he figured
out who was trying to kill him and what allies they had. He had
a good idea where to start for that, and it wasn't with a cross-
country road trip.

The path he had been following met a larger well-maintained trail, and this one had a signpost designating it as the
Wildwood trail. A direction marker told him it was 2 miles to
Lower Macleay Park. That was one he knew. Once there, he'd
be in the city proper. He started heading in that direction. He'd
have to be careful, there was a real possibility of other hikers
along the way, despite the damp weather.

There was another possibility he'd have to consider: he
could just be crazy. It was the simplest, most logical explanation. A burglar had murdered Barbara in front of him, he had
been unable to do anything, and he went mad from grief and
shame, exactly like the patient he'd attacked had said. There
had been no assassin in the hospital, just a nurse who had been
trying to administer medication, probably a sedative because he
was dangerously violent. He had attacked the nurse, then ran,
somehow losing his hospital gown in the process, and his
fevered mind had conjured up all the imagery about werewolves to explain it to himself. In that case, the best thing to do

would be to get back to the hospital and turn himself in for treatment.

The problem with doing that, though, was if he wasn't insane he'd just be placing himself into their hands and would be unlikely to ever come out again. That cop didn't seem surprised when he told him. Was that because he already knew, or because he didn't want to upset the crazy person? If someone's completely nuts, isn't telling them the polite thing to do? He couldn't rely on what anyone else told him, he had to find a way of comparing his perceptions against objective reality. He also needed to find some clothes.

Half an hour later he came to the entrance to Cornell road, and by then he had figured out how he could do both at the same time. There was a Goodwill store on 23rd and Burnside, and at this point he wasn't more than another mile or so away. A naked man wouldn't be able to make that distance through the city without someone questioning him. But a wolf might, if it was careful enough. The wolf wasn't entirely mindless, and part of its mind had to be his own. Could he find a particular destination in wolf form? There was an easy way to find out, he thought, as he stepped out of the woods and onto the road, and leaned forward, changing as he went.

THE SMALL PARKING lot was empty when they arrived, much to Carl's relief. On the first night of the full moon, there were usually at least a few people here, but for about a week afterward, he'd found, he could usually get to the whole place to himself.

"How does this work?" Toni asked him as she parked the car near the edge of the small gravel lot.

"What do you mean?" Carl asked.

"Well, I'm not supposed to be here, right? So how do we get in? What do I say if someone sees me?"

"Shouldn't be a problem," he replied. "There's supposed to be a caretaker who keeps track of who's here, but I've never seen him. If we do see anyone, nod politely and keep moving. They shouldn't ask any questions. If they do, just tell them you're visiting from out of town."

She looked dubious at that, so he added, "We're tend not to ask a lot of questions, or volunteer information, with people they don't know, so it really shouldn't be a problem."

"That makes sense, I guess. If you don't want people to even know you exist... you're gonna be pretty quiet around strangers and get used to everyone else being the same."

He nodded as they walked up to the front door.

"The door's not locked?" she asked, as he pulled it open.

"No, it's mostly just to keep the wolves in," he replied.

She seemed surprised at that. "Wait — you mean they're real wolves here, not just werewolves?" she asked him.

"Yeah. This place is legally a wolf preserve. It's privately owned," he replied.

"You can own a wolf preserve?" she asked.

"If you're rich enough, I guess," Carl answered her. "The Alpha owns it. Pretty good deal, I'd imagine - gives us a place to go, and gives him a nice tax deduction."

They passed the front lobby, and he opened the second door into the locker room.

"Who's this Alpha guy anyway?" she asked him.

"Victor Stumpp," he started.

He was about to continue when she broke in. "Stumpp? The computer guy?"

"Yeah. You know of him?" he asked.

"I've met him. I tempted at his company a while back," Toni answered.

That stopped him in his tracks. He held the door for a second.

"What?" she said.

"Wait, really? I've only ever seen him at gatherings and such, but never up close. It's just... weird that you know him."

"I wouldn't say I know him. I filled in for his secretary for a couple of weeks at Stumpptown Systems. Though if I'd known then that there was such a thing as werewolves and you asked me to point one out, he'd probably be my first guess." She paused as if in thought for a moment, then said, "I wonder if he'd remember me. Maybe I'll introduce you some day."

She walked past him through the door into the locker room and he hurried to catch up.

"Yeah, there's a terrifying scenario," he said. "I've tried to work there, but they've never hired me." They'd stopped again. "Okay, the preserve's through that door. You can... uh..." He was embarrassed again and tried to plow on ahead as casually as possible, as if it was an everyday thing. "You can put your clothes in any empty locker..."

Toni looked around her. "There's just the one room?" she asked him.

"Yeah," he answered. "I mean, it's no big deal, right, like you said? We're just kind of get used to changing around each other." On her skeptical look, he turned away from her. "If it helps, I'll face the other way," he said as he did so. Wasn't she just a few hours ago telling him not to pretend to be so shy?

After a moment, she spoke from behind him. "So, is this whole thing just so you can repeatedly get me naked?" He turned back, startled so see she was almost finished undressing. He'd barely started.

"Well, not just," he said, trying to match her tone, and hoping she wouldn't notice he was quoting Star Trek again.

She tossed the rest of her clothes into the locker.

"'This door?" she asked, walking over to it, showing no signs of self-consciousness. He found all he could do was nod. She opened it and stepped through. Then she turned back to him, with an enigmatic smile and said, "Catch me if you can." And let the door fall shut behind her as she ran towards the woods.

He realized he had stopped undressing while watching her, and quickly finished, throwing everything haphazardly into the locker and sprinting out the door. He saw no sign of her. He began running in the direction he'd seen her go, letting the wolf come over him as he did so.

THREE STEPS LATER, he landed hard on four paws.

The wolf sniffed the air, caught her scent, and was off. She'd left the path almost immediately, charging through the dense underbrush.

He followed, sniffing excitedly at the ground and the air. Originally, there'd been fear and uncertainty mixed in with her scent. Now there was only joy. He picked up the pace, following the trail. It wound its way through the woods for several minutes, and then, the scent trail grew stronger. He must be close. He sprinted forward even faster but then the trail came to an abrupt end.

He stopped, confused. Vanished? How could that be? He sniffed around, testing air and ground, searching for the lost trail. There was no sign other than the trail he'd been following. It just stopped there. He felt a growing urgency, a demand from deep within his mind. It was trying to tell him something, but he couldn't understand what.

He turned, ran back the way he'd come. At the place where the trail had increased in intensity, he stopped again, and sniffed around the area. The sudden change in the trail was still there. It hadn't gotten stronger at this point because she was so close, but because she'd doubled back. There were two trails on top of each other. He cautiously sniffed at the ground around the area. There it was, a smaller weaker trail leading off to the side. He headed down the new trail, more carefully this time.

The trail veered suddenly again. This time, he sniffed around carefully before following the new path. It wasn't long before he found her. She was in a clearing, harrowing a deer. Running in circles around it. Each time it would turn and try to go a different direction, she'd be there, nipping at its shins. It tried to kick, but she'd dodge out of the way. It would lower its head, and she'd run to its side. It tried to turn, and she'd be there in front of it. All the while, jumping in, nipping at it, then leaping back out. Some feeling again from deep inside told him not to interfere. He stood at the edge of the clearing, watching.

The deer was beginning to tire, but the wolf didn't even seem close. The deer was already wounded and bleeding. It wouldn't be long. The wolf was faster, stronger, and more agile. The outcome was never in doubt.

A lunge, a feint, and then she got in close enough to get a good grip on a foreleg. With a pull and a twist of her head, she pulled the leg out from under the beast. Bone snapped. It was down. The wolf sprang for its throat. Her teeth sank into it and held the creature's neck down as blood flowed across her jaws and onto the ground. Moments later, it stopped thrashing. He moved in then, slowly. She turned to look at him when she smelled his approach. He took another cautious step forward. She turned back to her prey and when she didn't drive him away, he walked up and joined her in devouring the beast.

He'd eaten his fill and laid down near the remains of the carcass of the deer, about to let himself drift into sleep, when a new scent reached him. A subtle shift in the other's emotional state. He didn't recognize it at first, but snapped instantly wide awake and alert. She was walking away from the remains, back toward the tall trees of the forest. He took a couple of steps, slowly following her. She turned and let out a low growl. He lowered his forequarters to the ground and replied with a happy growl of his own. She turned and ran toward the trees. He leapt into pursuit. He'd recognized the new smell: desire. He caught up with her just at the edge of the new growth and leapt upon her, bringing her down. She rolled, though, got out from under him, teeth bared. The scent of desire from her was almost overwhelming, but she was going to make him work for it, prove his worthiness.

They both leapt again, almost simultaneously. For the next several minutes they wrestled, but she slipped away every time he thought he had the upper position. Twice she twisted away only to end up over him, her teeth on his throat, and twice he escaped only to come back at her again. Over and over they rolled, each seeking the higher position.

She was faster, and more agile, but he was larger, stronger and, most importantly, more experienced. Somewhere, on some level, he recognized that and that she'd learn quickly. This may be the last time he could ever win against her. He fought with renewed vigor. Once again, he barely avoided her attack, and rolled to his feet.

And again she sprang, knocking him over. He allowed himself to follow the motion, landing belly up despite every instinct warning him against it. She came in low, teeth going for his exposed throat. At the last second, when she was unbalanced from the movement, he flipped back over, taking her with him. Surprised to find herself on her back, she turned over and tried to rise. But he was on top of her then, his teeth sunk deep into the fur on the back of her neck. He held her here and was overcome with her scent.

He mounted her then, in the way their kind always had.

She let him, moving with him, and when he was spent, he pulled away, walked just a few more steps away from her toward the edge of the trees. When he saw she was following him, he lay down and together they drifted off to sleep.

―――――――

WHEN CARL WOKE, it was still dark. Toni was already awake, sitting naked on the grass nearby, her arms wrapped around her knees, drawn up to her chest against the chill October air. He looked up to meet her eyes, but she was looking past him, at something farther off in the meadow. He turned to follow. In the middle of the field below them, half a dozen wolves were gnawing at a deer carcass.

"That's our kill, isn't it?" she asked.

Did they kill a deer together? He vaguely remembered waiting.

"Yeah. Yours, at least, I think. Huh. Didn't know they'd eat meat that someone else killed."

"Wolves are often scavengers in the wild," she said. "Pretty much all predators are."

She moved up against him, the warmth from her made him realize how cold the October night air really was. He didn't react. He didn't want to say or do the wrong thing, lest he scare her away.

"They're beautiful, aren't they?" she asked.

He looked back over at the wolves. He'd seen them in the reserve in the past, but generally tried to avoid them before, feeling a little bit scared of the wild animals. Calmly watching them going about their own business, he didn't feel afraid. He found he didn't want to scare them away, either. A flock of crows was beginning to move in now, as well.

"I'd never really noticed just how..." he fumbled for the right word, "how majestic they really are before." He felt stupid, and sappy.

Toni didn't laugh, though. "It's the hour of the wolf," she said. He didn't understand. She must have sensed it, and explained, "It's what my mom called it. The hour before the first light of dawn, when the stars are still shining bright. All the night creatures have gone to sleep and the day creatures are yet to stir. The hour when you lie awake overwhelmed by all the troubles in your life, all your bad decisions and missed opportunities. The should'ves and could'ves and the might-have-beens. She described it as being consumed by a beautiful sadness."

"I've heard the phrase before. There's a song by the band Mozart's Bitches. Part of the lyrics are 'Dancing, dancing, dancing, under a full moon. It's the hour of the wolf and we're all dying soon.' I wonder if that's where they got it from."

"Probably," she said, with a strange smile. "It's an old phrase, but not too common. It's mentioned in a Babylon Five episode as well."

"I never knew what it meant. It's like... like being connected to the world." What the hell was he talking about? He felt like an idiot.

Toni turned toward him without moving away. He was acutely aware of their state of dress. Placing her hand on his shoulder, she guided him gently down onto his back. He didn't understand what she was doing at first, until she swung one leg over to straddle him.

He didn't understand. Why...?

She leaned down and kissed him, full on the mouth. The ground was almost painfully cold against his bare back. We should get back, he thought. I should get ready to go meet Kevin and Shelly.

"I don't think..." he began.

"I didn't ask you to," she replied, placing her finger across his lips. And then she was on him and he could feel her pressing against him. He tried to push up, to roll her underneath him, but she pushed his shoulder back down. Surprised, he tried again, and again she shoved him down flat, keeping him on his back. She was not gentle. "No. You stay there," she said.

He wasn't sure he was in the mood. He didn't want it like this, this feeling of helplessness. But after all he'd done, he didn't feel he had the right to say no. The hour of the wolf. And when she rose above him, and arched her back, silhouetted against the stars, he found he did want to after all. Incongruously, he found himself wishing he had his glasses on. But they were back in the locker, a world away.

Afterward, they slept again, arms and legs wrapped around each other. The sun was just beginning to peek over the eastern hills when Carl woke up again, shivering. He'd had fleeting and disturbing dreams, but they all seemed fragmented and jumbled up. Toni was standing, looking around. He lay still for a moment, watching her. Looking at her. Finally, he pushed himself up. "What is it?" he asked.

"Just trying to figure out which way to go back to where we came in," she answered.

"Oh. Back that direction." He pointed into the woods. "There's a trail there that winds back to the entrance."

Normally after a night of having changed, acutely aware of his lack of clothing, Carl couldn't wait to get out and dressed. This morning, though, he found he was in no hurry, despite his shivering in the cold.

He stood up to lead the way. Impulsively, he reached out to take her hand. She let him but drew back when he tried to pull her closer and dropped his hand. He wasn't sure what to make of that.

They found the path within a few minutes of searching. Carl used his usual strategy - head in a random direction until he found something. The underbrush that had been so easy to run through in wolf form was full of branches and stickers to poke and scratch humans, making the going slow. He didn't remember if he'd had that much trouble in the past. The path itself, once they found it, was smooth, though the ground well-tended and soft to the step. He mused that someone must be maintaining it for the humans who would be walking through here on bare feet. One of the duties of the caretaker, he supposed. It must be a lot of work. There were a lot of paths. He had never thought of it before: Somebody did this, it didn't just happen. This path didn't naturally occur, it was the result of somebody he didn't know and had never even thought of before spending hours upon hours working at it for the benefit of people he'd never met. That seemed somehow a profound realization. Everything around him seemed fraught with significance.

"So now what?" He found himself asking Toni, walking beside him.

"I kinda want to find those showers we passed on the way in," she replied.

"No, I mean..." She just looked at him with an unreadable expression, waiting for him to continue.

"I mean..." He was still scared of chasing her off, but he decided to just plow ahead. "What about us? Do I get to see you again?"

She stood quiet for a moment. Thinking it over? Fear vied with hope. He could feel his heart pounding. At least she was thinking about it. He could certainly understand that. He had no claim on her, but found he didn't want to let her go.

"I'm sorry," he said. The words were too small to cover everything he was sorry for. But he continued, "This whole thing can't be easy for you..."

"Easy?" The sharpness of it startled him. "No. No, it can't be easy for me. You tricked me into going with you to a remote cabin in the middle of nowhere, chained me to a wall in the basement, left me injured and bleeding next to a guy you killed in front of me. I didn't know if I was going to make it through the night. And... and I don't even know if what you did earlier counts as rape."

When she said it, he realized they had made love in form. The flashes of memory danced at the corner of his mind. It was only a vague impression. Did she remember it more clearly than he did? He wanted to ask but didn't dare. And... rape? Was it? They were in form. He didn't even know what the rules were there. As far as he knew, he'd never done anything like that before. Didn't she want it? Was their play beforehand a form of consent?

Her voice was more controlled as she continued, in the face of his silence. "And now... and now I'm standing here, bare-ass naked in the middle of the woods, woods filled with wolves mind you, with the guy who did all that. And you want to know if you can see me again, like we're on some kind of fucking date? Did I miss anything?"

"Well," he started, and realized that anything he could say at this point would be incredibly stupid.

"Oh! And I almost forgot to mention the big one! Right! I also found out that werewolves are real, and then I got turned into one, without anyone even bothering to ask if that's what I wanted. And, of course, since I didn't get turned in the normal way, I'll be murdered out of hand if anyone ever finds out. Now did I miss anything?"

"I didn't mean to act like it was a date," he replied, lamely, after she'd stopped. She'd looked like she was expecting him to say something. She just raised her eyebrows at him.

"I mean, yeah, I'm sorry. I fucked up. Major big time. I completely fucked your life up probably in ways that I'm not even aware of yet. And there's nothing I can do to undo it." He told her.

"You're about to say but," she said.

"Yes," he admitted. "But first an and. And I've not been thinking at all about how fucked up that is, other than I didn't actually want to hurt you at all."

"But?" she prompted.

"But I know I wasn't considering how everything would affect you, and how... evil... what we did actually was. But I do like you and maybe I have no right to and maybe it's just fucked up stalker speak but I do and want to see you more and spend more time with you. I think we could at least be friends. But I do get it, and if you want me to leave you alone and never contact you again, I realize it's entirely on me and I won't blame you, and I will. And, uh, won't." He said, almost in one breath.

They walked in silence for a long while after that. "You're right," she spoke, breaking the silence. "You have no right at all to like me. Or to say any of that to me. What you did to me was beyond fucked up. Maybe evil."

He looked down at his feet. She was right, and he felt himself flushed with shame, and with loss, and felt even more guilty for hating himself more for driving her away than for hurting her in the first place. And then felt even worse for noticing just how close, and still naked, she was in front of him. He could feel himself begin to stir. He kept his gaze furiously down and away, desperately trying to think of anything but her.

"Well?" Toni finally said. "Aren't you going to say anything?"

"I..." He looked back up, quickly meeting her eyes. "There's nothing else to say. One thing, though: when we get back inside, I want to give you my number. Not in case you change your mind. I'll leave you alone. But there's a lot you don't know still. If you have any questions, or need anything, or get in any kind of trouble, or... well... anything, you can call me."

"Okay," she said in an even tone, and walked on. He followed at a short distance, trying to keep his eyes down at the path.

"I don't hate you," she said after a while. They were nearly back to the clearing behind the entrance. His gaze snapped up at her. She spoke without turning around, "Maybe I should. I can't think of any reason not to, but I don't. So maybe I'm just a fucked up person since long before you met me. Or, I dunno, maybe I have Helsinki syndrome or something."

Stockholm Syndrome, he almost corrected her, before thinking better of it. But things were Okay. She didn't hate him. She was still adjusting to being a Were, but Carl thought she'd be okay. All was right with the world.

And then, "Of course," he thought to himself, as it all came crashing down.

COMING out of the building as they approached was Andrew Hudson. Carl had seen him with Victor Stumpp several times at gatherings, though he couldn't recall if he'd ever actually spoken to the man. Hudson paused and looked Toni up and down in a way that made Carl want to tear his throat out. Then he looked puzzled for a moment. "Hey, don't I know you?" he asked. For a second, Carl thought he was talking to him. But then he continued, to Toni, ignoring Carl's existence altogether. "Yeah, you temped at the office a while back, didn't you?"

Toni simply nodded and tried to cover herself with her hands. Carl seethed silently at her side.

Hudson continued, "Huh, I thought the agency had sent you over. Victor never mentioned you were a Were. Funny."

They tried to push past him. He couldn't fail to notice they were in a hurry.

"Anyway, gotta run," he said, with an amused smile. "See you around. You, too... Carl, right?" he said, finally turning to Carl.

"Yes!" Carl squeaked. He looked straight ahead and barely moved a muscle as Hudson stepped past them. After he'd passed, Hudson turned one more time to leer at Toni. Carl was certain he was going to make some comment, and Carl steeled himself, not sure what he would dare to say or do in response, but Hudson just smiled and turned away. An instant later, he shifted into wolf form and was gone.

"Shit! Shit shit shit shit shit!" Carl swore as soon as they were both inside.

"Calm down," Toni told him. "It can't be that bad." She didn't seem convinced herself, though.

"Yes," he replied testily. He pulled his clothes out of his locker and tried to put them on as fast as he could. "Yes, it's that bad. This is exactly the worst thing that could have happened. He recognized me. Worse, he recognized you. He's going to talk about it to Stumpp. We are so fucked. Oh god. I'm so sorry. I fucked you bad. I..."

"Shut up," she said sharply. He did. "You did that earlier. And it wasn't that bad," she said with a slight smile. He registered her meaning but couldn't access any part of himself that could do anything about it.

"It's not funny," he said. "This is serious. They are going to kill us both. Dead. As soon as he talks to Stumpp, they'll figure out what happened. They'll probably question me first, learn about Kevin and Shelly. And Mitch."

"What, you'd give over your friends? Just like that?"

"No, not just like that! But they'll use torture. Everyone

talks under torture. Everyone," he said. He could hear his voice climbing up an octave as he said it.

"Now you're just being melodramatic," Toni said.

"No." He took a long deep breath. In a calmer tone, he said, "No. I'm really not. These people are outside the law. They will do anything they feel they have to to keep their secret, and they've been doing it for thousands of years."

"Okay," she replied. How could she be so calm? "These people want us dead. Panicking isn't going to help. If they do kill us, it won't be because I rolled over and let them. So, what can we do about it?"

"I don't know. I really don't know what to do. I'm sorry." The tone of panic was beginning to creep back into his voice.

She looked directly into his eyes. "If you say you're sorry one more time, I will rip your throat out with my teeth, and I won't turn into a wolf first," she told him.

"Okay, first thing is let's get the fuck out of here." He said.

"Agreed," she replied and turned back to getting dressed. When they'd both finished, they headed for her car.

There was now another car in the parking lot, which must have been Hudson's. Carl thought about sabotaging it in some way, to at least slow him down a bit, but decided against it. He didn't know what to do to a car to stop it and didn't want Hudson coming out just as he was doing it. As soon as they rounded the corner, Carl gave voice to his thoughts. "We can't stay in Portland. They'd find us. Even if we avoid our current residences."

"Run and hide?" she asked. Her tone told him what she thought of that. "Is that your solution then?"

"You got a better idea?" he asked her. "Because I'd love to hear it." He looked over at her, she was staring straight ahead at the road. "That wasn't sarcasm," he said a second later, "I would seriously love to hear a better idea."

She slowed the car and came to a stop. "Yeah. Yeah, I do." The way she said it chilled him.

"What will that guy be doing right now?" she asked him.

"Same as us," he started. Then, off her look, "Not that! Hunting, I mean."

"And after that, sleeping?" she asked him.

"Well, yeah..." he answered tentatively.

"You're sure about that?" she asked.

"No," he admitted. "But most everyone does. The change takes a lot of energy, almost everyone needs to sleep after they've eaten to replenish it." He wasn't sure where she was going with this, but suspected he wasn't going to like it.

A moment later, she confirmed his suspicion.

"Can you kill him with this?" She withdrew the knife that Kevin had had at the cabin. He must have put it in his jacket pocket. The jacket that she was now wearing.

Kill him. Kill a man. Could he? He was already accessory to one murder, as Toni had repeatedly pointed out. This would be different. This time it wouldn't be a human, but a fellow Were, and it wouldn't be an accident.

"I'm not sure," he finally responded.

"You'll have to be sure," she said.

"Wait a minute... why me?" he asked.

"I've never killed anyone before," she told him.

"Neither have I!"

"I'll help," she conceded. He realized he wanted to. For the way Hudson had looked at her, and for the sake of both their lives. He found appeal in the idea of being seen as her protector. Stabbing a man in his sleep wasn't exactly slaying a dragon, but it was still an act of bravery, wasn't it? Could he do it? He was terrified.

"Okay," he finally said. He held out his hand and Toni placed the hilt of the knife in it.

"Shit," he said, looking at the knife. Its silver edge gleamed in the moonlight. "Okay. Let's do it." He was trying to sound bold and determined. As one of his D&D characters might when setting out on an adventure.

He could tell Toni was trying hard not to laugh and loved her for it. He almost felt like laughing himself. Almost. He was going to take a man's life. He knew then that he was going to do it.

"You know this moves you out of the category of victim and into accomplice, right?" he asked her.

"And the alternative is, what, living the rest of my life looking over my shoulder, never knowing when I'm going to be killed?" she answered him. "I mean, it's not like I can go to the police for protection, right?"

He could imagine the headline. "Kids commit murder. Claim victim was a werewolf."

"No," he answered. "One of the first things Kevin told me is that we don't go to jail. Don't commit any crimes, he said, because there's no way to hide what you are in prison. If you do get sentenced, they'll find that you either killed yourself or died in a tragic accident on the way there."

"So, if we don't kill him now, he'll kill us later. Hell, from what you said, he'd have me killed simply for existing. That makes him pretty damn evil in my book. So, yeah, I really don't have a problem with killing this guy."

"Then why am I the one doing it?" Carl asked her for a second time.

"I have even less of a problem with you killing him," she replied.

"Gee, thanks. If anything goes wrong..." he started.

"I'll be right there with you, accomplicing."

"I was thinking maybe we should call Kevin," he told her.

"No," she cut him off.

The sharpness startled him. "I just meant..."

"I don't want anyone else to know anything. Especially not Kevin. I don't trust him."

"I don't trust him either, but he is a friend," Carl responded. If she noticed he was quoting Star Wars, she didn't say anything.

"C'mon, we can do this. Just like you're playing Dungeons and Dragons, kill the monster, save the girl."

He felt she was making fun of him again. He ignored the fact that he'd just made the same comparison five minutes ago. "In D&D, we use dice, not knives," he told her.

"So, it's a LARP," she responded. He was surprised but immensely pleased that she knew what that meant. He forewent arguing that even in a live action role-playing game he wouldn't be using a real knife.

"Okay, so how do we do it?" She asked him.

She was looking to him to come up with a plan. It wouldn't be complex. "Find him. Stab him. Hopefully, while he's sleeping," he said.

"How're we going to find him, then?" she asked.

"Same way I found you. Follow the scent trail," he responded.

She looked skeptical. "So, what, one or both of us need to be in wolf form?"

"No. With a bit of practice, you should find that you can do the same thing in human form now," Carl told her.

Tori looked at him. "Seriously?" she asked.

"Well... yeah," he replied, then paused. "Why would you think that's weirder than everything else?"

The truth was, though, she wasn't the only one who thought so. Stumpp had told them about the possibility during their initiation. There was nobody who could actually teach him, and most Were seemed to think it was some kind of joke on the part of the Alpha, but with enough practice, he had been able to figure it out. It made it easier that he started with the belief that it was possible. He rejected the notion that it was a joke on the assumption that Stumpp had no sense of humor. It had been frustrating that even after doing so, he had been unable to convince Kevin or Shelly that it was possible.

"I can't really remember all the details of being in wolf form," Toni began answering his question. "It's kinda hazy, like a dream that you barely remember. But I do kinda vaguely remember being completely surrounded, awash in scents and sounds. There's nothing like that now," she said.

"There is," he replied. "I've heard that our senses are enhanced by the change. And that might be true. I'm not sure, though. We're surrounded all the time by a medley of scents, even in human form. We've just learned to ignore them. Our eyes are so good, and so precise, we tend to rely on them exclusively."

She thought about it for a second. Then said, "Short answer, you can track him by scent."

"And so can you, if you try it. It's not the same as in wolf form. It's less conscious of a single scent, more instinctual, the way the wolf operates."

She was quiet for a moment, a puzzled look on her face. He was about to ask what was wrong, but then she replied. "Maybe later. If you think you can do it, that's good enough for now."

"All right," he agreed. And she put the car in gear and started heading back up the main road.

"Is this wrong, what we're doing?" she asked him, after a few minutes of silence. Carl had assumed she was trying to concentrate on focusing on other senses and didn't want to disturb her.

"It was your idea," he replied defensively. "It's not too late to turn and run." He found himself almost hoping she would. She didn't say anything, though, so Carl continued, "I don't think it is, though. Wrong, I mean. It's not just Stumpp, every region has its Alpha. I don't know how wide their reach is, or how hard they'd search for us. But our lives were forfeit the minute Hudson saw us. He will cause our deaths. Maybe not out of malice, maybe he's not actually evil. But it doesn't matter."

"It makes sense, but..." she started, then trailed off.

Was she really struggling with the moral implications of this? She was the one who'd pointed it out: The man was a threat. There was only one way to eliminate that threat.

"I asked you before if I was still human. Now I'm wondering. I don't think I would have even thought of killing anyone yesterday. Is that the wolf in me making that decision, or the human?" she asked.

He looked over at her. She was staring straight ahead at the road. It had begun to rain again. He was glad it waited until now. "Wolves and humans aren't that different, though, really. A lot of behaviors are shared. We evolved together after all, since long before either species was in its modern form. Both species learned from and influenced each other. They say you won't do anything as a wolf that you wouldn't do as a human. That might be true, but I think a lot of people underestimate what a human will do. Maybe you've never contemplated killing someone before, but maybe that's just because nobody ever actually wanted you dead before. Even if they did, yesterday you could go to the police, or get a restraining order, or even buy yourself a gun for protection. Now, none of those'll work. The law is us, or nothing," he said. She had remained silent as he spoke, concentrating on her driving without looking at him.

Carl wasn't quite as confident as he'd made himself out to be about his tracking method, as the two of them walked side by side down the path in the rain. He couldn't smell anything. Trust your subconscious, he reminded himself. The trick wasn't to find the scent, the trick was to just go in the direction that felt right. Let the wolf decide which way that was. It was difficult to quiet his mind enough to listen to it. Let go of conscious thought and let the wolf do its thing. They crept along as quietly as they could, following his uncertain lead.

Even with the light rain, it was getting warmer, fully dressed and with the sun climbing over the hills. He was about to suggest a break when they found him. The game trail they'd been pushing through opened into a clearing, in the middle of which was a dead deer and a solitary wolf, light grey and thin, eating it. Was that the same deer? Had he driven the real wolves away? Or had they left already by the time he and Toni had? Was this even the same place? He was thoroughly lost again.

The wolf looked up when they approached, but when they dropped back into the trees, he ignored them and turned back to his meal. They fell back and circled around the small clearing, coming at it from another angle a quarter of an hour later. When the wolf spotted them, they fell back again, and repeated the maneuver a third time from yet another path. Carl figured a Were would be used to others being around and in wolf form would ignore anyone who was not an obvious threat. The air was too still for any direction to be considered downwind. But if they spaced their visits far enough apart, Hudson was likely to forget about them in the meantime. At least that was his hope. Toni followed him without asking him to explain what he was doing. He was slightly disappointed with that. He'd been eager to impress her with his cleverness. But either she'd figured it out, or she trusted him enough to follow his lead.

Eventually, though, she placed her hand on his shoulder, stopping him. "I think we're developing too much of a pattern," she said. "He's getting suspicious."

"I don't..." Carl started. He was going to say that the wolf memory shouldn't be that long. But he wasn't sure. "You might be right," he said instead. "It won't hurt to give him an hour, or even more. He'll probably sleep for a couple of hours at least, once he falls asleep. We can stay nearby and come back then."

They found a spot nearby that looked inviting enough. There was enough cover from the trees that the ground here wasn't wet yet. Sitting next to Toni, Carl wanted to say something, reassure her, anything, but couldn't think of the words. He checked his phone again, noted the time and made sure once more that the ringer was still off.

"Crap," he said quietly, when he saw the text messages. "I was supposed to meet Kevin and Shelly half an hour ago."

She looked at him like he was an idiot.

"I'm not going to go, but if I don't at least let him know, he'll wonder what's up - maybe come looking. I'm gonna text him to let him know I won't be there."

"What're you going to say?"

"I dunno. I guess, 'Not going to make it, will explain later.'"

She smiled at that. "What'll you tell him later?"

"Dunno. I'm sure there'll be time to make something up once this is all over," he said.

Throughout the hour, he continued checking his phone. Finally, after 50 minutes, he'd decided that was enough. His nerves would kill him if he waited any longer. He checked again that the phone was silenced.

Hudson was in the same small clearing he'd been in earlier, sleeping toward the edge of it. Toni hung back at the edge of the woods as Carl crept slowly forward, Kevin's knife in his hand. Twice, three times, he stopped as the wolf twitched in its sleep. He smiled silently to himself, trying to laugh at his own nervousness. He forced himself forward. Three more steps. Then two. Put everything out of his mind but the task at hand. Another step. One more step, and he'd be a murderer. He took the step. He crouched low over the sleeping wolf, raised the knife in both hands and, taking a deep breath, plunged it downward toward the beast's neck.

It was the sharp breath that was his undoing. The wolf reacted, eyes opening and beginning to roll over. His knife sunk, not into its neck as he'd intended, but deep into its shoulder. It howled in pain but made it up to its feet. Somehow, Carl kept hold of the knife, widening the cut as it withdrew. He jumped back as the jaws snapped at him. He took another step backwards and held the blade in front of him with both hands. It seemed small and inadequate. He brought the knife closer to himself, keeping one hand outstretched. He looked for an opening. How would he recognize an opening?

The wolf's paw swiped forward at him. He turned, but not fast enough. Flesh tore from his forearm. He swung the knife again and cut only air. The wolf leapt straight at him. He managed to turn aside again, this time keeping the knife outthrust. Blood splashed across his jacket and face. He slashed again wildly, and felt it drag alongside the beast's hindquarters. It landed, twisted, and leapt again. He swung the knife around just in time to meet its lunge. It knocked him to the ground. Claws raked and tore his flesh and clothes. But the knife bit into something hard, he could feel the impact as he fell.

The wolf howled again in rage and pain as it tore away. Kevin's knife was pulled out of his hand and went spinning into the underbrush. The wolf ran in the opposite direction. Carl stood, frozen in indecision. His every instinct was screaming at him to transform. Become the wolf and heal his wound. Or chase down his enemy. A more rational part of him knew he had to get the knife and finish what he'd started. What he really wanted to do was find Toni, get in a car, and drive very fast away from Oregon. That option was taken away from him by a streak of gray fur. Toni had shifted to wolf form and was chasing after Hudson.

"No!" he cried out as she passed. She wouldn't stand a chance against him. Carl might be able to help in wolf-form, but Hudson would heal too fast from any wound either of them could give him. Aside from leaving town and going into hiding, their only hope was to finish what they'd started. But for that, they'd need Kevin's knife. He could hear the sound of fighting, not too far off into the trees. His arm was agony where it was bleeding. He pulled his right arm out of the jacket sleeve and did his best to wrap it around the wound, creating a crude makeshift bandage.

He continued searching, trying to ignore the nearby sounds. She would have to keep him busy for just a little while longer. He saw the glint of silver at the same time he heard a shriek of pain, followed by a whimper. Then silence. Again, he froze, wanting to run immediately to her aid in wolf form. Instead, he took two more steps, swooped down and grasped the hilt of the bloody knife, then sprinted toward where the noise had been coming from.

He found the two wolves on the trail. Hudson was standing, but with obvious difficulty, leaning forward and panting heavily. His heart sank when he saw Toni laying still in front of him. There was so much blood pooled nearby. She was still in wolf form, though, which meant she was still alive. The larger wolf reached toward her, teeth bared.

This time he didn't hesitate. Carl sprang forward, screaming in rage and fear and pain. He leapt onto the larger wolf, using all of his momentum to plunge the knife into his side. He didn't bother to aim for any precise spot, only intent on doing as much damage as possible, plunging the knife in, cutting, tearing, before drawing it out again. He was aware of the beast moving beneath, then around, and above him. He kept cutting, stabbing, slicing. He could tell that it had cut him several times. At least nothing will happen to me if I get bit, he thought, with an edge of hysteria. He lost all sense of time and of pain. Raise the knife, lower it, slice, cut, stab. That was all he could remember for what seemed like an eternity. Exhaustion finally took him, and he rolled onto his back. The wolf pulled away as well. Still going. What the hell does it take?

It only managed a few more steps. Carl could barely move. He tried to raise his hand. He thought he'd gotten it a couple of inches off the ground, but that might have been his imagination. Shock, he thought. I'm going into shock. What am I supposed to do? Keep warm? That's going to be hard lying here on the ground. Maybe he could go find a blanket. He chuckled at the thought, and a new pain shot through his side. Broken rib, maybe? He looked down and was astonished to see how much blood there was. He couldn't put it off any longer. For the third time in less than a full day, he called the wolf down into himself and transformed.

THERE WAS pain in his chest, but it faded quickly, even as he struggled to his feet. He took a couple of steps forward, and caught a scent - enemy, danger, fear - and death. He approached it slowly. It was dead. The threat had gone. He moved away. He walked back to where he'd come from. His mate was there, sleeping. He circled around the area. There was prey nearby, but no threats. On the far side of his circle, he could smell the corpse. He felt an odd sense of relief as he moved away. The dead thing had been the only threat nearby, and it was gone. He walked back over to his sleeping mate and lay down beside her, and soon drifted off to sleep himself.

HE WAS AWAKENED by a pressure in his side, and a voice calling from far away. The voice repeated, calling his name. Carl opened his eyes. He was lying on the ground, its cold seeping in through his bare skin. Toni was standing over him, prodding him in the side with her toe. He was glad that his ribs were no longer broken, if indeed they had been. He didn't seem to be bleeding anymore, either, which was nice.

"Come on," she repeated. "Get up. We've got to get out of here." She was wearing Kevin's coat again. She must have taken it off before she changed. Smart. He wished he'd thought to do that. He blinked again. "Hudson?" he asked and was surprised to find how dry his throat was, how raw his voice. He struggled to his feet.

"Dead," she replied. "And I don't want to be anywhere near here when anyone else finds out."

"Agreed," he said, following her. He rolled to his side and up to his feet. "Did you... I mean... Oh, god, I really fucked that up."

"You did fine," Toni replied. The October air suddenly didn't feel quite so chilly, "I.." This time it was she who was at a loss for words. She had a strange expression on her face. It was soon replaced by her usual enigmatic smile. "I can honestly say I've never seen a murder committed with more style and finesse."

He registered the word murder and again felt a brief shiver of fear. But the compliment made him feel like he was walking on air. He followed her in what he assumed was back toward the entrance.

"Shit!" he swore, stopping in his tracks. "My keys and wallet are in my coat. If they find them..."

"Relax," Toni interrupted him. She drew his wallet out of her coat pocket. "I got 'em while you were sleeping.

Carl breathed a sigh of relief. "Did you get the knife, too?" he asked her.

"Couldn't find it," she answered. "Can it be traced to Kevin?"

"Maybe. I doubt it. He just got it. I don't think he'd shown it to anyone else. If someone else shows it around, though, he'll probably recognize it as his."

"Which means he'll know we did it," Toni said.

He nodded. "Can't imagine him volunteering that information to anyone, though."

"Okay, good," Toni replied. They continued on, leaving Kevin's knife somewhere behind them in the underbrush.

When they got back to the front building, Toni immediately started checking lockers. She quickly found what she was looking for. She tossed Carl Hudson's clothes. "Here, put these on. You'll attract less attention."

While he was struggling into them, he noticed her going through Hudson's wallet. She removed a sum of cash and tossed the wallet back into the locker. A second later, she apparently reconsidered, and took it back out, shoving it into her jacket pocket.

"I wanna dump this stuff somewhere far away. With luck, the wolves'll eat him, and nobody'll even know he was here," she explained.

"You're taking this awfully well," he told her as they walked out the front door. He felt a mess of nerves, constantly thinking they were going to get caught. As if someone else was about to stroll out of the woodwork.

"What am I supposed to do?" she replied angrily, as if his words were an accusation. "Fall apart? Break down and cry? Run around in circles screaming? Do you want the list again?

It's too much. Aside from the kidnapping, torture, getting chained in a basement, bitten, wounded, transformed into a mythological monster, the maybe-rape, now I'm an accessory to murder. I have no idea how to deal with any of that other than to deal with it."

He was taken aback by her vehemence. "I didn't mean it as an accusation," he said.

Neither of them said anything while they finished the walk to her car. There was nothing funny about anything she'd said. But the absurdity of it, of them being here, and what she'd alluded to earlier, and he could barely keep from laughing out loud.

He must have been too obviously trying, because she finally turned to him and said "What?" in an angry tone.

He knew he shouldn't answer. Especially given the one accusation she actually did make earlier. He assumed she'd remember, and it would be unwise to say what he was thinking. But she was looking at him expectantly.

He couldn't get away with saying nothing so, unable to think of a good response, he told the truth. "It's just... that's a hell of a lot, I was just worried. How the hell am I going to top that for our second date?"

She could hit surprisingly hard when she wanted to.

ELEVEN
THIEVES AND LIARS

Moments before there had been screaming and fear and fleeing humans. Now, it had grown quiet. A few whimpers and stinks, but only a few. It had been an easy journey to get here, he was able to avoid most of the humans, and it was a short run. Once he was inside the building, there were a great many of them close together, but most of them fled shortly after he arrived. He knew he had to get here, but now that he had arrived, he didn't know why. This was not a hunting ground, nor a place of shelter. He didn't know what to do. So he slid back into the darkness, pulling the human into his place.

GORDON WAS behind a rack of clothes when he woke up. He was lying on a thin carpet in what looked like a store. He stood up and looked around. It worked! He recognized the goodwill. He looked hastily around him and didn't see any other people. Had there been screaming? He had a fuzzy memory of a general panic. That must be the wolf's memory.

He couldn't reach it when trying to recall it more thoroughly. There was a rack of men's pants just a couple of aisles over from where he stood. He hurriedly grabbed the first pair he found in his size and put them on, ripping off the tag and shoving it behind the rack. He ducked into the next aisle and grabbed a t-shirt printed with some band he didn't recognize, then found a pair of tennis shoes and put them on. A quick glance around and he still didn't see anyone else nearby. He decided that a jacket would make him look less suspicious, given the drizzly weather. He chose one hastily and shrugged into it, then stepped out of the front door into a spotlight and a police cordon.

He raised his hands in the air and stepped toward the light. "What's going on?" he asked when a uniformed police officer stepped forward. His gun was in his hand but wasn't pointed at him. He preferred to keep it that way.

"This way." The man gestured with his free hand and led him toward a cruiser parked on the streets with doors open and lights flashing.

The last thing he wanted to do was get stuck talking to the police, especially if they learned who he was. He was surrounded, though. "Oh, god, I gotta sit down," he said, feigning a slight stumble and putting his arm out as if to catch himself.

The officer took the bait. "Here," he said and guided him to the curb. This was a little better, more police between him and the store than between him and an exit. He could breathe for a moment before deciding what to do next. "Is there anybody else in there?" the officer asked, once he was down.

"Yeah, I think so," Gordon replied. "A couple of others maybe. What's going on?" he asked again.

"I was hoping you could tell us. We got reports of a wolf attack."

"An attack?" He felt a cold chill. He didn't want to, but he had to ask, "Was anybody hurt?"

"Not as far we know." That was a relief. "What did you see?"

"Not much I'm afraid. Everyone was screaming and when I looked, I saw something big and furry on the other side of some racks. That was enough to convince me not to come out into the open. I hid behind the mattresses until things got quiet, didn't see anything when I peeked out, so I came out."

The officer looked disappointed that he didn't have any more to tell. "Is it over?" he asked him. "Can I go back in? I think I left my phone in there."

"I'm sorry, I'm afraid it'll be a while," the officer responded. "If you need to call someone, though, we can probably find you a phone to use once forensics gets here."

"Forensics?" he asked, not needing to fake astonishment. "What... wasn't this just a wild animal? Why would forensics be needed?"

"Wasn't just an animal," the officer responded. "Or, well, it was, but it could be a wolf that someone trained. Killed a couple of people."

"I thought you said nobody was hurt."

"Not here. But it attacked other people earlier."

"Shit. And you think that's the wolf that I saw?" Gordon asked him.

"Pretty sure. How many wolves are going to be running around downtown Portland at any given time?"

You'd be surprised, Gordon thought.

The officer continued, "I hope you understand if anything inside gets stuck in evidence for a while."

"Yeah," Gordon answered him. "Yeah, I'll find some way to make do. It's okay to tell me this?"

"Sure, why not?" the officer responded.

"Dunno. Maybe I just watch too much TV, but I was expecting more 'move along, nothing to see here.'"

"You were already on the inside," the cop pointed out. "Besides, once the yellow tape goes up, people are going to gather and ask questions. Nothing for that, and I'm not telling you anything that's not already been in the news, which honestly is all I really know myself."

Gordon shrugged. "Is there someone I can call, later, about getting my phone back?"

"You can call Detective Diaz, or anyone on his team, probably, if you don't want to wait."

Gordon struggled to keep his tone calm when he heard the name. "I'll do that. Thanks, officer, I'll give them a call tomorrow."

The cop wrote down the information for him and he tucked it into the pocket of his stolen shirt. Then he got away as quickly as he could. Diaz would almost certainly recognize him if he saw him and that would raise far too many questions. Or worse, answer ones he didn't want answered right now. He still didn't know who was involved, but right now Diaz was his number one suspect for whoever let the assassin know where he was.

At least he had more evidence of his own sanity. Others had seen the wolf, it wasn't just his imagination.

He had to walk down to fifth street to catch a train. The bus was closer, and would have gotten him closer to his own house, but the bus driver would ask for payment. On the train there was a decent chance of getting there without anyone noticing he didn't have a ticket. Barbara had explained how it worked to him just a few months ago when he'd grounded her for getting a fine for riding the train without one. If only she could see him now. If only.

He made it to his stop without running into any fare inspectors and walked the last half mile to his home.

His house loomed before him. This was the first time he had seen it since... since before. Yellow tape still surrounded his yard. If there had been any crowds, they were long gone. They may come with the tape, as the cop said, but they don't stick around as long. He didn't see any signs of anyone else watching the place either but circled the block to be sure. The house behind his, which had been empty for as long as he had lived there, had police tape across its front door as well. Taking a cue from that, he went around it to its back yard, then climbed over the fence into his own. If there was anyone watching his house, hopefully the simple trick was enough to elude them. He had planned to get the spare key from under a pot on the back porch, hoping Barbara had remembered to return it since the last time she forgot her key at school.

When he got there, he saw that the key was moot. The entire back window had been broken out, along with part of the frame and the wall it was attached to. Someone had put up a sheet of plastic over the hole and duct-taped it into place, keeping the rain out. He wondered if the police had done that, or a kindly neighbor. Foregoing the key, he pulled up one corner of the sheet and ducked under it and into his dining room. He made his way upstairs, then froze in his steps. The carpet on the steps crunched when he stepped on it. It was saturated in dried blood, and the stairway, hall, and upstairs landing were dotted with evidence markers. Worse yet, right at the top of the stairs was a chalk outline.

He put his arm out to the wall for support. That's where she died. Right there. The last moments of her life. The police had drawn the line around a corpse, but it had been Barbara who'd laid down there. Fallen down? Been knocked? What was she feeling? Pain? Terror? Did she call out to him, only to be met with no answer?

He stared at the chalk marking, unable to pull his gaze away. In his mind's eye, he saw her stumble back, sink to the ground and lie still, neatly into her outline. And he was there. He had been right there and could do nothing to stop it.

Why did she have to die? He could feel the anger rising now. He knew in some detached part of his mind that this was expected. When you're grieving, you want to find someone to blame. It's natural. Only in this case, there really was someone to blame. And that someone was part of a larger organization. Whoever they were, he would get his answers. Focusing on that, he took another step up the stairs. Then he would tear their organization apart. He didn't know how, but he would make sure that they remembered Barbara, and regret what they had done.

He shook himself out of it. Stop it, Gordon! This isn't a comic book, you're not The Punisher, and Barbara isn't your tragic backstory.

He couldn't stay here long. He didn't know if they were watching the house, whoever "they" were, but he didn't want to tempt fate. There were things he would need if he was going into hiding. With an internal shudder, he forced himself to step over Barbara's outline toward his bedroom. He had an ATM card in his dresser, kept there against the possibility of losing his wallet at some point.

He took it and filled a backpack with clothes. He planned on going into hiding. Use the card once, to withdraw the maximum daily amount, then not use it again except at the direst of need. Anyone tracking his finances would know he'd been here, but that would be the end of the trail. He could leave town but decided against it. Whatever he was going to do, it would be harder from farther away.

On the train, with a legitimate pass this time, he stopped by a Fred Meyer's to pick up a pre-paid credit card and put three quarters of his money on it. It would look less suspicious than paying for a hotel room with cash, but still be untraceable. Even if they pulled the security footage of this transaction all it would confirm is that he had been there. It was part of his reason for going out of his way to go to the store before heading downtown.

Sitting at one of a row of computers at the downtown library, he noticed he wasn't the only one in the place with a large bag. He wondered what all the rest had them for. Travelers from out of town? Homeless people? He thought briefly about getting a sleeping bag and camping out under the Burnside bridge. But he really didn't know the first thing about surviving on the street. He might end up more conspicuous there than holed up in a cheap hotel. But it was an option if it came to that.

He found the cheapest hotel he could and booked a room for a week online with a fake name and his new card, then spent the next few hours searching for information. Detective Diaz had apparently told him the truth about the death of the man who had murdered his daughter. Searching for his name brought up an article with the prosaic headline "Suspected Killer Slain in Motel Shootout." The article was by Vera Rosen. He did a search for her name and found a slew of other articles, including ones about the other attacks Diaz had mentioned.

Her other articles he found noteworthy as well, especially in contrast. They were a mix of small petty crime stories and longer deep-dive pieces, one of which, about Stumpptown Systems and their overseas labor practices, he remembered hearing about a few years ago. Even the crime stories, he realized, were each tied into some larger theme, a discussion of the overall context and a call for justice or suggestions for ways to reform the system to avoid or minimize similar events in the future. The articles on the recent killings were different. She'd been following the attacks from the beginning, and every article listed just the facts of the case.

There were no calls for reform, no claims that the police should be doing their jobs better, not even any suggestions for what people could do to protect themselves. There were no direct references to werewolves, of course, but all the information was there. Each house had no signs of entry, but all had massive damage to windows and sometimes even their frames on exit, "as if a large heavy object had been thrown through it," though no heavy objects were ever found outside.

In two instances, she mentioned piles of shredded clothing that were found. Anyone looking for signs of werewolves would have spotted them immediately, and he wondered if that had been intentional. She had to know. She was an investigative journalist, she could have found out any time during her career. He decided to look her up as a possible source of information. He would have to be careful, though, as he had no idea what side she was on. He could come back tomorrow to research more about the reporter, but it was getting late, and he had plans for the morning.

Fifth Precinct, he remembered the cop saying. He looked up the address before he left the library.

<hr />

IN THE MORNING, he bought a bus pass back to downtown and was still trying to come up with an excuse to be visiting the detective as he entered the building. A uniformed man made eye contact, inviting him to approach the desk he was standing behind. He did so and asked where he might find detective Diaz. The officer started to point toward the back of the building, where a short flight of steps led up to a landing containing several desks, but then interrupted himself. "Oh, there he is now."

Diaz was just descending the steps to the main room when he looked up and saw him. His eyes opened in surprise. Too late, Gordon realized the implications of him being here, now, when he should have been still recovering in the hospital. The last time they met, someone had attempted to kill him three hours later. They must have suspected what he was then. Now he had just confirmed it.

Diaz took a step forward.

Gordon turned to bolt toward the entrance. At that moment, several police officers, with a handcuffed man between them, were making their way in through the door.

"Hey," Diaz shouted, and it seemed like all eyes in the room turned to him at once.

He glanced around. There was another door to his right that looked like an exit. He sprinted across the room toward it.

"Wait," he heard Diaz shout.

He didn't dare. One moment's hesitation, and a dozen cops could get between him and safety. He slammed the door open and ran down the staircase on the other side, with a weird sense of deja-vu, and pushed through the door at the bottom. It opened into a small underground parking garage, tight spaces with large concrete pillars between many of the spots.

What was he thinking coming here? Cops all around and he thought he could just walk into the middle of them and...

He ran across the garage, following the uphill slope. He was most of the way toward the entrance when he heard the door open behind him. He immediately ducked behind one of the pillars.

"No farther!" he shouted toward the detective, poking just

his head around the pillar, ready to duck back behind and run if he saw a weapon.

Diaz stopped where he was. "Mr. Chandler..." he started. His hands were empty, held out in front of him in a gesture of peace.

So, he was willing to talk. He could talk where he was.

Gordon stepped fully out from behind his pillar but didn't step away from it. "You know I can kill you, right? That even armed you couldn't stop me?" It wasn't what he'd planned to say. But it seemed like everybody else had the upper hand. He had to remind them he wasn't a helpless victim to be carelessly put down.

"Is that what you want to do?" the detective asked him.

"No," he answered immediately. "Not unless you make me."

"Then I won't make you," Diaz replied.

They regarded each other in silence for a moment.

"What do you want?" the detective asked him.

"Answers," Gordon replied, raising his voice to be heard across the distance.

"I don't have many," Diaz told him. "I'm nearly as much in the dark here as you are."

Gordon thought about that for a moment. He glanced back at the opening out of the parking garage, making sure it was still unblocked.

The cop apparently noticed. "Look, if you want to go somewhere and..."

"No," Gordon cut him off. He didn't know what trap might be laid elsewhere. Here, at least, was a place nobody else was expecting. Nobody chose this location. "How long have you known?" he asked the detective.

"About werewolves?" the other man replied. "Since last Saturday. You found out before I did."

Was he telling the truth? It was an awfully callous way to

put it, considering how he'd found out. He pushed that memory down. But it did raise his opinion of the cop's honesty. If he was lying, surely he'd say something Gordon was more likely to want to hear. But it still didn't hold up.

"What about the rest of the cops?" he asked.

"I'll be briefing a team this morning."

"This morning? *This* morning?" he repeated in astonishment.

The detective nodded but didn't say anything.

"But..." he started, unsure of what to say.

Diaz waited patiently, letting him continue.

He blurted out, "I was attacked, just a little while after talking to you."

Again, the policeman was silent for a long moment before answering. "Tell me what happened," he finally said. His tone made it an invitation, not a demand. But Gordon felt a flush of anger.

"You tell me. Who attacked me?" he asked. He tried to repress it, but he could hear the anger in his own voice.

"We don't know yet," the other man said.

"We?" he asked.

"My task force. We're looking for him."

"You really don't know?" He still wasn't sure whether to believe him or not.

"We really don't. I'm sorry, but I did tell you that in many ways I'm more in the dark here than you are."

He still didn't know if he was being lied to or not. He wanted to trust the detective but didn't dare too much. He checked behind him. It was still clear. There was one other door out of the garage, but he didn't know where it led. Another level perhaps, or a separate building.

"So how did he know where to find me?" he asked, watching the reaction to his question carefully.

"We don't know that either." The detective's face gave nothing away.

"What about the other guy? The one who..." he almost choked on the word, "...murdered my daughter?" he wanted the words to hurt, to show the other man what was at stake, and what his stake in it was.

Again, the officer showed no reaction. "What about him?" he asked calmly.

Anger flashed again. And again he pushed it back down with effort before responding. "What's the connection? Who was he?"

The policeman looked uncomfortable for a second. "We hope to know that soon. We're trying to ID him now."

"ID? You have him?"

"He's dead."

Dead. He should be glad. But it was too easy. And a lead cut off.

"What happened?" he asked.

"I took your advice," the policeman said.

He wanted to ask what he meant. There was just too much he didn't know, but at that moment, the second door opened, and two uniformed police officers stepped out. This was too many. One of them saw him and turned, about to say something. He couldn't risk it. He ran.

The cop shouted, and Diaz simultaneously shouted for him to wait, to come back, but he didn't dare. He ran up the ramp and out into the city streets. He glanced behind him. He could hear angry shouting but there seemed to be no pursuit. He settled down into a quick walk, trying to blend into the crowd of pedestrians on the sidewalk. He cut across to the Fifth Avenue bus mall, got on the first one he saw, and let it carry him away, his head folded down, pretending to relax.

"YOU FUCKING..." Michael started, then caught himself. It wasn't the officer's fault. "Sorry," he apologized immediately.

"Want me to go after him?" the officer offered.

"No. He's done nothing wrong. He's just..." he trailed off, not wanting the say the word.

"A werewolf?" came Phil's voice behind him.

Michael turned to see Detective Philip Lee emerging from the stairway. "Was that the survivor from the hospital?" he asked. "Guy with the kid?"

"Yes. To both," he answered.

"Wait," the other officer spoke up. "Which question did you answer there?"

"What?" Michael was confused.

"You mean, is he really a werewolf?" Phil offered.

"Yeah. I mean, I've heard the rumors..." Rumors, since last night. That was faster than Michael had expected. "But you're telling me you actually believe there are such things as..."

Michael interrupted him. "It doesn't matter what I believe. If they aren't werewolves, they believe they are. Or want us to believe it for some reason. We do know for sure that they're organized, believe themselves above the law, and have already killed several people, including one police officer."

The officer thought about that for a second then asked, "But if he's one of them, why are you letting him go?"

"Because what Michael told you was the diplomatic answer," Phil answered him. "It'll probably be a good one to give the press when they start hearing about this, but it's not really true."

The cop looked surprised at that, but no more so than Michael.

He was about to say something, but Phil continued,

silencing him with a look. "These guys are dangerous. Anyone likely to cross them, which is soon going to mean all of us, needs to know the truth. The truth is, they're real. There are people who can turn into wolves, and they're immune to ordinary bullets. We're going to dismantle their organization, but we've barely just started. Eventually, they're going to notice what we're doing and strike back. I don't want any cops facing these things without knowing how to defend themselves." Any more cops. Michael shifted uncomfortably at that. Phil still hadn't really forgiven him.

Phil turned back to the officer. "He let him go, I suspect, because even though he's a werewolf, he's not part of the organization. In fact, they tried to kill him. They failed, but he got bit. So now he's a werewolf too. Is that correct?"

The last was directed at Michael.

"Yes," he replied. Then he continued, "Whatever it is that turns people into Were, it's transmitted through biting. Fortunately," he indicated Phil with a tilt of his head, "It doesn't always work."

"Fortunately," Phil repeated, without looking at anyone in particular.

"We're gonna need to come up with some kind of education program for these guys," Phil said a few minutes later, after they'd headed back upstairs. "I hope I wasn't overstepping my authority back there, but I really do think..."

"No," Michael interrupted him. "No, you're right. They will be coming after us, and while I'd prefer keeping it all quiet, as long as possible, I don't want to put any cops in danger because they lack information. We should see about distributing at least a few silver loads to everyone we can as well."

"Good," Phil said. "Because we just got a possible lead. He's over in Gresham, someone brought him into the psych ward.

They were going to release him, but he wanted to talk to the police first."

"So why us?"

"Well, he's changed his story, but when they first brought him in, he had been wandering naked in the woods, and swore that a couple of guys had kidnapped him and turned him into a werewolf."

THERE WAS laughter in the briefing room.

"You expect us to take this seriously?" Detective Lauren Boyd asked. "Werewolves?"

He couldn't blame her skepticism. She must be wondering what she did wrong to be stuck with the crazy guy on her first assignment after making detective. Boyd was the youngest member of the task force, though she had actually been with the Portland police longer than he had, by about six months. Three and a half years on the force, promoted to detective in near record time, she had seemed to be going places. And now she was stuck here. Hopefully, it would work out for her once she realized what they were really up against.

She was seated at the conference table next to Detective Don Avison, who had been a police officer in Seattle before transferring to Portland something like five years ago. This was his first assignment after being promoted to detective as well.

Billings had assigned both of them to his new task force. The others he knew already: Alice Johansen's transfer had been made indefinite, an event she did not seem disappointed with. She already knew about the realities of what they were facing. Phil and Aaron of course had both been with him from the beginning.

He looked up toward the front of the room before answering. Grant Talman's picture still hung on the board next to the big map, but somebody had drawn a thick black X through it.

"I do. And yes., Michael replied finally. He nodded to Aaron, who clicked something on his laptop. The body camera footage of one of the members of the SWAT team began playing on the large TV mounted on the wall next to the map. With the increase of responsibility came an increase in funding, and this was one of the first things Aaron had asked for. Lauren and Don both glanced back at Phil, who was leaning against the back wall near the door, his arm still in a sling. On the screen, he discharged his weapon, firing point-blank into the wolf, with almost no effect.

"This is Talman, in his wolf form," Michael told the group. This was mostly for the benefit of Don and Lauren. He'd filled Alice in the night of the events, and of course Aaron had learned all about it when editing the footage. There was another expression of disbelief from Detective Boyd.

"Our witness joins the fight," Michael continued narrating as Veer entered in wolf form. His audience was captivated despite their doubts. Even Phil winced, watching himself roll away from the big wolf, his torn arm pooling blood.

"And, finally, I get a clear shot. Note the difference in ammunition." The wolf twitched as the bullets hit it. The room was silent as they watched it fall, struggle to its feet, then finally collapse again, bleeding from its wounds. A few seconds later and the wolf shifted - the strange twist in on itself no more comprehensible on video than it was in life. In its place lay the naked dead form of Grant Talman. The other wolf had run off.

"Is this a joke? A hoax? I don't understand," Boyd said. A good beginning, he supposed. At least she didn't storm out, thinking there was some kind of trick being played on her. Skepticism was to be expected, and he wouldn't want someone who easily believed what they saw, but the process of convincing someone could be tedious. All he could think was to go with it over their objections and let them learn the truth for themselves in time. Avison, on the other hand, sat quietly. Obviously not convinced, but willing to wait to see how it all played out.

Michael pulled one of his silver bullets out of his pocket and held it up. "And this is what killed him," he said, before handing it to Detective Johansen, who passed it around the room.

"I made this one myself," he said, "two days ago. I've got a friend of a friend working on loading as many shotgun shells as they can. You'll all be issued as many as we can get." There were more murmurs of disbelief at that.

"Wait a minute," Boyd asked again. "If the guy's dead..." She didn't need to finish.

"Tell them how many there are," Phil said from his position by the door. Michael could tell he still hadn't really forgiven him for keeping quiet about the Were once he found out. If he'd been warned, been able to prepare... He was just glad Phil was still wearing the sling. His arm hadn't healed yet, which in its own twisted way was a good sign. He'd been bitten on the night of the full moon. Not everyone changed, Veer had told him, but some things, like the full moon, increased the chances. If Phil had changed into one of them, though, his arm would have healed by now.

"Probably around ten thousand or so on this continent," he told the assembled police. There was a general chorus of astonishment at that.

"How could that many dangerous creatures stay hidden?" Detective Avison finally spoke.

"They're organized," he said, "And operating with a strict code of secrecy."

"But even so, with so many..."

"There are nearly six hundred million people living in North America," he answered. "That means about one in sixty thousand is a Were - that's what they call themselves. If you haven't met sixty thousand people, it's quite possible you've never met a werewolf. Even if you have, you would probably never know it. Most of them are no threat. For the most part, they've assimilated into society, and are harmless. But," he nodded to Aaron, who brought up the image of Peter on the TV, "there are exceptions.

"This is Peter, last name unknown, formerly known as Suspect One," he raised his voice again. "In all probability, he is the man who killed Detective Sam Bailey." Boyd and Avison were both silent. He continued with the next bombshell. "He may be working for Victor Stumpp, who our informant claims is the Alpha, or chief werewolf, of this region."

"Stumpp?" Boyd asked incredulously. She knew who he was of course. Everybody knew who he was. "Do you have any proof of this?"

"Unfortunately," he responded, "we have no hard evidence of Stumpp's involvement at this time. All we have is hearsay that he knows this man. Keep your eyes open, but we're not currently moving forward with the Stumpp connection. Once we have our suspect in custody, we can hopefully use him to get whoever hired him."

He had chosen to interpret her question as being about Stumpp's involvement and hoped she wouldn't notice that he had no proof of the very existence of werewolves either, but she was too good of a detective to let him get away with that.

"I'm going to need proof of what you say. I can stick around for a little while, but I'm not staking my career on this nonsense without knowing what's really going on," she said.

This was good. It might make her hard to work with in the

short term but would make her a more valuable asset to the team. Billings had chosen his people well.

"You'll get it," he said, though truthfully, he had no idea how. "For now, though, any questions?"

He was surprised when Phil spoke up. "What would have happened if I had turned?"

"What do you mean? From what I understand you'd know by now," Michael said, puzzled.

"We're likely going to be confronting more of these things," Phil said. "What happens if someone on our werewolf squad here gets bit? Do we kick them off the force? Lock them up?"

"I don't know. I haven't really thought about it," Michael admitted. He should have, he realized. There was so much he should do. "From what I understand, the person should still be able to do their job. I don't know if it's true they can control themselves when changed, or how violent they actually become. Or how much it varies from person to person."

"Not much of an answer," Phil responded.

"No. I suppose it's not. I think if it does come up, we'll have to take it on a case by case basis. At least for competence..." he trailed off.

"What other than competence?" Detective Boyd asked, seeing where he was going.

"Loyalty," Michael said, after a brief pause. "Will a werewolf necessarily be loyal to their own kind more than to the friends and acquaintances he had before?"

"Why wouldn't they?" she asked.

"We don't know. Our informant insists that their personality doesn't change, but we don't know how much that's true."

"Shit."

He knew how she felt. "Just one more new thing that I hope we never have to deal with," Michael told the squad at large. "Then again, if we had our own werewolf, we could maybe use them for undercover work. Infiltration isn't really feasible currently."

"You keep referring to this informant," Aaron spoke up for the first time. "Should the rest of us know who it is?"

He didn't want to say anything. He never made any specific promise, but it would still be betraying his confidence. But his loyalty had to be first and foremost to his own people.

"Vera Rosen," he told them. "The reporter."

TWELVE
TRUTHS, FACTS, AND OTHER DECEPTIONS

"That," Victor said, "is the knife that killed Andrew."

Andrew. Andrew Hudson. She couldn't remember ever hearing Victor use his first name before. He was always Hudson, but now that he's dead it's suddenly Andrew.

Veer looked down at the knife lying on an unfolded cloth on Victor's desk, its silver blade still stained with blood. It was a ridiculous thing. Overly gaudy, it looked like it would be more at home in an old B-movie than used as an actual weapon. The caretaker had found it on the preserve near Hudson's body. The preserve was supposed to be a place of refuge, of safety. She had used it herself a number of times. It could never be that again, now. Even if Were continued to visit it, they must always consider the possibility of being attacked, murdered in their sleep. She felt a sense of loss over that even more than the death of a man who'd been an acquaintance for three years.

The preserve was also supposed to be outside human authority. That would need to change now, too.

"We're going to have to involve the police in this," she said.

"No," he replied. "With two deaths in the same place so

close together, the police will not believe it is a coincidence. Your detective Diaz would ask questions that I don't wish to come up with answers for right now."

"But police resources..."

"No." His tone was final. "We're going to have to do without them. We will find the ones responsible on our own."

She wasn't sure if she was covered in that "we," or if she was suspected of being the one responsible.

"So, who..." she started, but he interrupted her.

"I'm starting by showing this knife to some of our more senior Were - the ones I know I can trust."

That answered that question. The ones he knew he could trust. Which, despite being one of the newest Were, obviously included her. It made what she had to do that much harder. He would have realized that, of course, and factored it into whatever calculus he had done in deciding to show it to her.

"I'm going to ask the others to keep their eyes and ears open. Someone knows about this knife."

Going to. Which meant that she was the first one he had talked to. He would have known she would catch that, and he wanted her to be aware of that fact. He wanted her help.

"Was this a message for you, then?" she asked.

"Maybe," he said. He'd obviously already considered the possibility. "But not a very clear one. It's also possible that we have a wolf killer on our hands. Could it be Detective Diaz?"

"I don't think so," she replied. "He has silver bullets, for one. He wouldn't use a knife. He'd also be more likely to come at you with a search warrant than with a weapon."

"One of the other police, perhaps, who learned about us, and made it his mission to hunt us down? Could they have their own rogue now?"

"Still doesn't seem likely. It's just too..." she searched for the right word, "careless. If Michael did tell someone else about us, they'd also have access to silver bullets. And more careful planning than to just stab someone and drop the knife."

"So, we're back to unknowns. It had to be someone who knew there were Were at the preserve, and they obviously intended the knife to be found. He was covered with dozens of small scratches as well as a few deep wounds. I'd like to know why."

"Long fight, maybe?" she guessed. "Or he was in wolf form when it happened. A CSI technician who knew what they were looking at could probably tell you."

He just gave her a look. She didn't really think it would convince him, but it was one more argument for coming out. If she could eventually convince him...

"We could still use some of their resources," she said, offering a compromise. "Michael already knows about it. He could probably get some analysis done - maybe trace the origin of the knife or see if it's really Hudson's blood."

"It's his," Victor cut her off. "I saw the body."

Veer could imagine what he meant but was saved from answering by the chime of the phone on Victor's desk. He tapped a button on the phone and the voice of the woman who had let Veer into Victor's office spoke. "Sorry to interrupt," she said, "but we don't seem to have Ms. Rosen's address in our records. As long as she's there..."

Victor looked annoyed. Veer was about to answer, but he beat her to it, "Yes, that's by design. Why do you need it?"

She shot Victor a querulous look, but he held up one hand to forestall her question.

"I was going through the list, for the... uh... the funeral, and preparing to mail out..."

"You can give her card to me," he said. "I'll make sure she gets it, and in the future, never interrupt me when I'm in conference."

He hung up without waiting for an answer and turned to Veer, "Sorry about that. I really miss Andrew," he said with a sad smile.

"She's new," Veer offered. "She'll learn."

"You didn't take this long when you were there," he replied.

"I had Hudson to orient me first," she pointed out. Then on another note, "He was very thorough. I'm almost surprised he didn't make all the arrangements already."

"Guess there were some things even he didn't anticipate."

"So how are you going to have a funeral if you can't officially say he's dead?"

"Why would I have to officially claim he's dead? The funeral home doesn't check for death certificates. They don't even need a body to have a service."

"But..." Veer tried to think of all the possibilities. "I know people who've had people close to them pass, and there always seems to be a great deal of paperwork, even when it wasn't murder."

"Most of that, I imagine, is just to prove he's dead. Inheritance, creditors, insurance, and so forth. If we don't need to prove it to anyone, it'll be a lot simpler. I can make sure his property taxes are paid for a while, and we have access to his accounts through our payroll system. If nobody makes a claim against his life insurance, that's not a problem. You might be surprised how easy it is to hide a death if everyone who knows the deceased cooperates. The only hard part is disposing of the body."

"What about next of kin? How do you deal with them?"

"It turns out we are his next of kin."

"Wait, what? We who?"

"He listed me as both emergency contact and sole inheritor or, if I predeceased him, then you."

"Me?" she said, taken aback. "Why would he do that?"

"Were you not close?"

"I've never even seen him outside of the office or the gatherings."

"That is interesting. Perhaps... Hm."

Whatever he had figured out, she didn't follow. He obviously wasn't planning to share now, though. She made a mental note to follow up at a later time.

"So why wasn't I supposed to be in the records?" she asked instead.

"I didn't want you involved, should anything happen," he responded. He must have read her puzzled expression. "I didn't want anything leading to you, in case our records were compromised. Rival groups, the Council, Hunters, the police," he explained, stressing the last one pointedly.

She decided to ignore that. "Nosy reporters," she continued for him.

"Especially those," he agreed with a grin.

He was trying to protect her. Of all the people in his organization, he was trying to protect... her.

CARL TOOK the beer Kevin handed to him and sat down on his usual chair, facing the couch.

"So how come you didn't bring your girlfriend?" Kevin asked him, just as Carl had taken a sip.

He nearly choked on it. He tried to hide his annoyance at Kevin's timing, but didn't think he succeeded.

"She's not my girlfriend," he replied when he had recovered. She had told him exactly that herself. But they had made love, he'd pointed out. "We fucked, Carl. Don't make a big deal out of it."

"But you have been seeing her every day," Kevin responded, interrupting his musing.

This took Carl by surprise. It was true, but he didn't know how Kevin was aware of that. "You been spying on me?" he asked him.

"You bet," his friend responded. Carl had expected him to deny it, then perhaps come to admit it only after a lengthy argument. He wasn't sure what to say to this frank admission.

"Well, uh..." he stammered.

"Sorry," Shelly interrupted him. "But we had to know what you were up to. For our own protection."

"Your protection? What did you think I was going to do?" He asked her.

"We didn't know. That was the point," she said.

Kevin chimed in, with a smile that belied his tone, "You didn't call, you didn't write..."

"And then you killed that guy with Kevin's knife," Shelly said, shooting Kevin a dirty look.

"Oh, yeah. That," Carl responded.

"Oh, yeah, that?" Kevin echoed. "You murder a man, in a way that implicates *me*, and all you have to say is oh, yeah, that?" Carl couldn't tell whether he was amused or angry.

"Wait," he just realized what Kevin had said, "implicates you? How?"

"The Alpha's been showing people my knife and asking about it," Kevin replied.

"Shit, how'd he know it was yours?"

"He doesn't. That's why I'm still alive, dumbass."

"If he doesn't know it's yours, then it's fine. He..."

"Not the point! Why'd you do it?"

"Sorry," he replied, "but we didn't have anything else..."

"We?" Shelly interrupted him again.

Carl knew she knew the answer, but he wasn't going to say it. "I had help," was all he said.

"But why did you leave the knife behind?" Shelly asked him.

"I didn't mean to," he said. "After it was all over, I couldn't find it. Things were kind of... confusing."

"Confusing, how?" Kevin asked.

"Just... kind of... hectic. It turns out, it's not really that easy to kill someone with a knife, especially in form. And he kept running away..."

"Wait, how'd you even use the knife in form?" Kevin asked him.

"No," he responded. "Hudson was in form..."

"Hudson?!" Shelly exclaimed.

"Yeah. You didn't know?" Carl answered her.

"Who's Hudson?" Kevin asked, looking back and forth between the two of them.

"No wonder the Alpha's so pissed," Shelly mused.

"Who the fuck is Hudson?" Kevin sounded more frantic now.

"Oh, nobody important," Shelly told him. "Just Victor Stumpp's right-hand man."

Kevin whistled softly at that. "You killed the Alpha's... damn. No wonder you didn't want to stick around."

Carl caught Shelly's frown at that. Was she playing prosecutor in this little impromptu trial here? And if so, was Kevin the defender? So who was the judge? Whichever it was, he had a feeling a verdict had just been reached.

"It's just a good thing that nobody else recognized the knife," Shelly said then.

He resented that. It sounded petty. He was glad Toni hadn't wanted to come with him. He didn't know what she'd say to that, but he doubted it would be constructive.

"You did say you'd just gotten it," he said in his own defense. "So, I guessed that nobody else had seen it yet. And," he continued quickly to forestall attempts at interruption, "if anyone did find it, I was pretty sure you wouldn't tell anyone it was yours without checking to see what had happened first." He lifted his bottle to his lips as he finished and took a big swig of the beer, watching them over the top of it.

Kevin smiled, more amused at the obvious flattery than flattered by it, as Carl had hoped. It did happen to be the truth, though.

"So, what have you been up to?" Carl asked Kevin and Shelly. The matter of the knife, and the murder, had been left behind, at least for now. It was too late to do anything about it. There was no talk of replacing it. Kevin didn't ask, and Carl didn't offer. They both knew he wouldn't be able to afford it.

Shelly deflected the question back to him. "Have you turned any more?" she asked.

"Not yet," he responded.

"But you're planning to?" she pressed.

"Yeah. But, uh, differently. Only people who've agreed ahead of time. We've got a few candidates, but we're still working out the details."

"What details? You bite 'em, they change. It's pretty easy," Kevin said.

Which was almost exactly what he'd said to Toni when she'd first proposed her idea. They'd argued a bit about it at first. She kept wanting to add what he thought of as, and called in so many words, "a bunch of mystical mumbo-jumbo," including an involved fake history of the Were.

"Look," Toni had finally exploded, "I know it's bullshit. You know it's bullshit. But it works. Give people something bigger than themselves, or even us. A grand mystery stretching back hundreds of generations. They'll feel that they're part of something huge and grand and secret. If there's an ancient unassailable institution that they can never know everything about, they're less likely to think they know everything and do something stupid."

He worried about what would happen if anyone ever discovered the truth, but she'd had an answer for that, too. "Oh, some will. Definitely. There's the beauty of it. If anyone actually looks into history and calls bullshit, we can just explain that the whole thing's really metaphor anyway, and now that they know that, they're even more on the inside."

"Huh," he'd said as he had thought it over. "How'd you come up with all this anyway?"

"It's been done before," she had replied. "I went through an Aleister Crowley phase a few years ago." He had no idea what she'd meant by that, but let it go for now. He seemed to be doing that a lot lately.

He wasn't completely sold, but was intrigued enough by her ideas to see how it went. He explained as much to Kevin and Shelly. "We're doing our first 'initiation' on the night of the full moon," he concluded.

"You're, what, starting some sort of weird werewolf cult?"

"No," he said, although he wasn't sure how it wasn't. "If you want, come see for yourself. We're having a sort of party next weekend to kind of feel them out a bit more, make sure of who we want to invite. Probably winnow it down to about a half a dozen or so initial candidates."

"Sounds like fun," Shelly said at almost the same time Kevin was saying, "I don't think so."

"What?" they both asked each other. Carl laughed out loud at that.

"If I'm not mistaken, we have plans for the full moon," Kevin said pointedly to Shelly. Carl could guess what his plans were. He wanted to plead with him to stop. Don't do it, not that way, but he knew it wouldn't do any good.

"Not for the initiation thing, but we can make the party," Shelly responded. She looked to Kevin, "We can help Carl out, give our input on his guests."

"Okay, fine," Kevin conceded. "We can do the party. But I'm not joining Carl's freaky little cult."

"You don't have to," Carl said with a broad smile, "You're already initiates of the deeper mysteries."

He changed the subject. "Have you heard anything about Mitch?"

"Nothing. Dude seems to have disappeared off the Earth. We've been checking on his apartment, but as far as we can tell he hasn't been there. Car hasn't moved at all either."

"Watching me, watching him. When do you two find time to sleep?" Carl asked him.

"We aren't alone. We turned more last week," Kevin responded. "A few more have joined us."

"Joined you? Joined you in what?" Carl asked him.

"In our grand quest, of course. A free and open Were society." Kevin responded, but he smirked as he said it.

"Three joined?" asked Carl. "Were there more? What happened to them" Carl was afraid of the answer, but the question had to be asked.

Kevin confirmed his fears. "One died. One, the change didn't take, and one of the guys wanted nothing to do with us afterward."

Carl was taken aback with the casual way he said "one died." He looked to Shelly, but she didn't seem to notice. Or at least she didn't react in any way. One had died that night - was it really only two weeks ago? - that they tried to make three new Were in the basement of a rented cottage. He felt a pang of guilt when he realized he'd barely even thought of him since then. Come to think of it, even when Toni mentioned him it was always "a corpse," as if he had never been a person at all.

"What about...?" he started, then realized he couldn't even remember the guy's name.

"Who?" Kevin asked.

"Ross?" Shelly supplied. That was it.

"Yeah. Hear anything about him?"

"Pretty sure he's still dead," Kevin replied.

Shelly shot him a look at that. "If anyone's even noticed he's missing, they don't seem to have reported it," she told him. "We haven't found anything online or in the missing persons notices."

He hadn't even thought to check. He didn't say anything. It was too late to do anything about it now.

There was something else bothering him, too. It had taken them almost two weeks to find three candidates, and the three of them had barely handled them. "How'd you find people to turn this time?" he asked the other two.

"Yeah, Kevin, tell him what we did," Shelly said with a strange smirk.

"Yeah, okay..." Kevin said as if he didn't want to answer. Finally, he smiled and said, "We used Shelly's original idea."

"What, just asked people if they wanted to be Were?" Carl said.

"Pretty much," Kevin admitted. "We spent all Friday night at Pioneer Square approaching various people who seemed likely. We came up with a couple of minutes of wind-up, then told them that werewolves were real, and asked if they'd like to be one."

"And people just agreed to that?" Carl asked skeptically.

"Shockingly, yes. A few at least. Some just looked at us like we were crazy, and some told us to get lost, but enough agreed. We drove out to the woods the next day."

"What about the one guy?" Carl asked, concerned. "And Mitch? Aren't you worried that they'll tell someone? Go public?"

"Isn't going public the whole idea?" Kevin retorted.

"Well, eventually, yeah, but... I mean, what if the Alpha finds out what you're doing?"

"How would he find out?" Kevin said, "We're not using real names, I'm James, she's Joyce, and those guys don't even know there *is* an Alpha, let alone who he is or how to contact him."

Carl didn't know how to answer that. He didn't know of any specific way that anyone would find out, but he also hadn't given it much thought, and apparently neither had Kevin. There would always be something they overlooked. He resolved to discuss their own plan more with Toni, specifically to think of ways they could be discovered. Just because he couldn't think of any didn't mean someone else couldn't. Fake names sounded like a good idea, though. If either they or Kevin and Shelly got caught... he guessed it was good there were two separate groups operating.

Shelly saved him from having to answer by changing the subject again. "Why'd you kill the guy, anyway?"

That wasn't the subject he wanted to deal with either, but he didn't feel like he had much choice. He owed Kevin that much at least. "He saw us," he said. "Toni and me. At the preserve."

"You killed him just for that?" Kevin asked him. "What, you were afraid he was going to turn you in? There's no way he would have drawn the conclusion that she was an illegal Were from that. He doesn't know every single one. Hell, he probably wouldn't even recognize you."

Carl could see the imagined scenario playing out in both their minds: chance meeting with Hudson, and little Carl, panicked, afraid of his own shadow, grabs the knife and leaps to the attack. Still scared he's about to be found out, he drops it and runs, never thinking to pick it back up. The thought was intolerable. He responded, forcing his tone to be as light as he could manage, "No. He didn't recognize me, at least not at first. He recognized Toni."

"Wait..." Kevin said, taken aback. "What? How do they know each other?"

He enjoyed his surprised look and decided to prolong the suspense for a few more moments. "She used to work for Stumpp," he told them. He got the stunned response he'd been hoping for.

"Wha... how is that possible? She worked at Powell's. We all saw her... She didn't choose us, we chose her. How could she have..." Kevin started, confused.

Carl laughed. It would have been fun to let him continue, but it had been enough. "Relax," he reassured him with a laugh, "It's nothing like that. She used to temp. Office work. She did a gig at Stumpptown Systems a couple of years ago."

"Oh. Shit," Kevin said with a sigh of relief. "I thought for a second they were on to us."

"They might still be," Carl mused.

"What do you mean?" Kevin asked, at the same time Shelly said, "What else happened?"

"No. Nothing happened," Carl answered hastily. "I'm just saying we might not know right away if anyone's been watching or spying on us. They could totally be, like, biding their time and waiting to spring their trap."

"You've seen too many movies," Kevin responded.

Or maybe you haven't seen enough, Carl thought. Just because you're not aware of something doesn't mean it's not happening. But he didn't say it out loud.

"BUT YOU ORIGINALLY SAID YOU were a werewolf," Michael said.

The kid, Mitch Douglass, was sprawled in the large chair facing the couch in the small living room of the safe house. Michael sat on the edge of the couch. Two weeks ago, this man had wandered out of the woods naked and asked for a ride back to Portland. He said at the time that the people he'd been staying with in a remote cabin had turned him into a werewolf. But now...

"That was the drugs. Whatever it was they used, it fucked up my perceptions, okay? I don't know what actually happened."

"Then why did you say werewolf?" Michael asked again.

"I don't know! There may have been a dog there, but I can't tell for sure, because it's all jumbled up. Because of the drugs. That they gave me against my will. Are you gonna find these guys or not?"

"We're doing our best. Unfortunately, so far, you're our only witness."

"So, what are you doing here? I already gave your sketch artist the descriptions. You can't just keep me here forever."

Michael took a deep breath before replying. "Nobody's keeping you here at all. You're here for your protection, but if you want to take your chances out there, you're free to go whenever you want. You're not under arrest."

The kid glared at him but didn't say anything.

"If you're willing to cooperate, we need to know what happened. You mentioned a cabin somewhere? Can you tell me where?"

He sat quietly for a minute before speaking. "I don't know where - somewhere up in the mountains, there were a lot of trees. Sorry, I was riding in the back of the van and couldn't see out real good."

"Van? There was a van? Can you describe it? Did you get a license?"

"White. No windows or seats in the back, we sat on the floor."

"We? How many people were there?"

"Just the three of them and three of us."

"Did you at least get any names?" Michael asked.

"There were Toni, me, and, uh, Ross."

"Were they both turned into werewolves, too?"

That earned him a disgusted look. "I already told you, I don't know what really happened. They slipped something into my beer or something. Next thing I knew I was chained up in the basement next to Toni and Ross and... and I think they killed Ross. I remember a lot of blood and he wasn't moving and, uh, somehow I got loose and the next thing I knew I was waking up naked in the woods with no idea where I was."

It sounded like werewolves to Michael. He couldn't really blame the kid for not wanting to admit it. It wasn't too long ago that it would have sounded crazy to him, too. But now? He wasn't sure what to do. It was possible the guy had actually convinced himself that it was just drugs, and maybe there really were some involved. Hospital toxicology reports had come up negative but he didn't know if that meant anything. Veer said they could control the change. Was it possible to just never change? Could there be werewolves who never knew what they were, and it never affected them?

Those questions didn't matter yet. Now, he had to concentrate on the organization.

"What about the others?" he asked. "The ones that did this to you. What were their names?"

"Shit, I dunno. It was Shelly something, and I think her boyfriend, and Carl, who drove the van."

He recognized that last name. "Hold on," he said and

reached into his jacket pocket and pulled out the picture of Carl Jablonski that Aaron had printed out for him. "How about this guy? You recognize him?"

"Yeah, that's him. That's Carl," Mitch replied immediately.

"You sure?"

"Definitely. I spent a couple of hours with him, didn't I?"

"Thanks, you've been a big help."

"Good," he replied, leaning back in the chair again, crossing his arms across his chest. "That guy fucked me up real good. They could have killed me. I hope you nail that bastard hard."

THIRTEEN
THE STORIES WE TELL OURSELVES

"Remember that he's the victim, not a suspect," Phil said after Michael had filled him in. He sat in the passenger seat, his arm still in a sling. "Do you think he's really a werewolf?"

"No doubt," Michael said. He put the car in gear and started forward. "The only argument against it is that the entire notion is ridiculous. But we know they're real, so we're going to have to let go of that kind of thinking."

"But you still think there's something he's not telling us? Aside from admitting he's a werewolf?"

He looked away from Phil as he made a left turn and answered him with his own question. "Who gets in a van with five strangers without even having any idea where they're going?"

"But yet it's not him you're mad at." Phil knew him too well.

"No. I suppose not. I'm really angry at myself. I believed her. How could I be so thoroughly taken in?"

"Wait, her? Her who?" Phil asked.

"Rosen," Michael replied. "I'd hoped she was an ally in this at least, if not a friend."

"What's she got to do with any of this? I thought she was pretty much your entire source of information about these guys."

"Exactly," Michael replied. "I relied on her, and she lied to me. If she didn't lie, she at least didn't tell us the whole truth." When Phil didn't say anything, he continued, "One of the first things she told me is that Were don't attack humans, and don't make more without permission. And here, the first other group of werewolves we've heard about, and he's attacked and made more. And this time it's not some lone rogue - there're three of them."

"Let's not jump to any conclusions here," Phil replied, "I'm not exactly president of the Vera Rosen fan club here, but think about it: we've got Talman, and this Jablonski group, right? And we met them within weeks of each other."

"Right." Michael wasn't quite sure where he was going with this. He merged into the traffic on MLK and looked past Phil for a chance to move over.

"And they've both ended up with victims that've surfaced on our radar," Phil continued. "One, with several."

"Right." Michael got it. "And if werewolves always attacked people..."

"We'd have heard about them long before now."

"Fair enough. These guys have stayed off our radar, all of our radar, worldwide, for four hundred years, so why are they coming out of the woodwork now?"

"Only two so far, right? Rosen revealed herself to you."

That was true, though that obviously hadn't been her plan.

"So, what's the connection here? Two of them being this blatant this close together isn't a coincidence. Was Jablonski working with Talman?" he mused.

Phil stared out the window in silence for a moment, taking

in the view as they crossed the Fremont bridge back toward the precinct.

"Maybe," He finally said. "Or inspired by him."

"That's one more thing that Rosen knows that she didn't tell us. She claims to have no idea who Talman was, but she can't deny she knows Jablonski."

"What do you mean? How do you know she knows him?"

"Remember at the preserve, when Jablonski attacked me?"

"Yeah."

"Veer was the other wolf."

"The one who saved your life."

"Yeah."

"And then she did it again when she attacked Talman."

"Okay, point. Doesn't sound like the actions of someone working against us."

"Right. If you had died in the preserve, that would have been the end of the investigation right there. Certainly, I never would have come up with werewolves."

"So we keep Rosen as a valid source for now?"

"With eyes wide open, but I'd say yes."

"Okay. I'll talk to her, see what she knows about the kid."

FOR TWO WEEKS, Gordon had been scouring the internet and learned nothing new. He picked up a paper again, saw the same article that was there the last time he picked it up, about the death of the so-called "werewolf killer." He had traced the origin of that moniker online. If his theory that Vera Rosen knew about the werewolves was true, the name would have started with her. Interestingly, she only started using it a few days after the incident, and the first time she did, it was to mention that someone in another paper was using the term. He had found the original reference, and it had indeed been out for a least a couple days before her. He didn't know if that invalidated his theory or if it just meant she was taking great pains to be careful.

This was getting him nowhere. He needed a break, some fresh air to clear his head. He walked out the door of the hotel, and into the city sidewalk. He ignored the usual barrage of requests for spare change and wandered in a random direction. He had no idea where he was going, or what he hoped to find. He just knew he had to get away from the computer for a while and think of something other than werewolves and their secrets.

Maybe he should stop. Just forget the whole thing and go back to work. "Take as much time as you need," his boss had told him. That obviously wasn't unlimited. Perhaps two weeks was more than long enough. He hadn't seen any evidence of anyone still looking for him. His house had been undisturbed, and if anyone was staking it out, they were doing an exceptionally good job at hiding it. He hadn't dared go in again but was it because he was honestly afraid of someone trying to kill him, or was he afraid to face the house where Barbara died. She would laugh at him for that. She'd want him to go on... no, that wasn't right at all. She wouldn't want him to go on, she'd want him to just get over it so he could focus on her. That was his daughter. Not the saint portrayed in last week's memorial service or the stories in the papers, but flawed, self-involved, possessed of the infallible arrogance of youth, and utterly, beautifully human.

She was his daughter and he loved her. Her lectures, the fight over the concert he wouldn't let her go to because she hadn't done her homework. Her idiot boyfriend. Though the kid had actually surprised him at the funeral. He seemed truly devastated, and yet more focused on how Gordon himself was feeling. He figured the boy would make a bit of a show of it, then move on, with a tragic story to impress the girls. He would move on, it was true. Eventually. And he would have his tragic story, and it would give him status in the bizarre little world that was high school social politics. But there was no harm in that, no malice. He would not dishonor her memory. The thought comforted him. There would be a great many people who carried memories of her with them. Some would be kind, some less so. She had moved through the world and touched many lives. That's what he should have said at the funeral.

He was shaken out of his thoughts by a woman's voice. Loud, pleading, and close. Followed by a man's chuckle. No, two men. He rounded a corner toward the sound. He reached into his pocket for his phone before remembering he'd left it back at the hotel. Where was he anyway? He wasn't familiar with the neighborhood, and he hadn't been paying attention to where he'd wandered. He must have been walking for a couple of hours. Shit, this was stupid.

There were three men, surrounding a single woman. She looked scared and didn't look any less so when she saw him. The three men ignored him.

"Hey!" he shouted, trying to get their attention.

It worked. Briefly, at least. They glanced over at him, but quickly dismissed him and turned back to their prey. One of them grabbed her arm.

He noticed her outfit. Short skirt. No jacket. What was she doing out here dressed like that at this time of night? He could almost hear Barbara's chastising tone. "A woman should be able to walk down the street naked and drunk after turning tricks all night and still not have to expect to be raped," she'd said once while lecturing him on "rape culture." He'd dismissed the senti-ment, wondering what pamphlet or school lecture she was parroting the statement from. It wasn't her opinion, but it had been delivered with all of the self-righteousness that only a teenage girl could truly muster. He reconsidered now. Maybe it wasn't originally her opinion or her words, but she'd adopted them and maybe she was right. Perhaps this is exactly what she meant by "rape culture." Not that anyone was in favor of rape - that was patently ridiculous — but this casual acceptance of it as inevitable. Maybe the men weren't intent on rape, but whatever they were after it wasn't inevitable tonight.

"Hey!" he shouted again. "I don't think she's comfortable with your actions!" It was the first thing he thought of to say. He thought Barbara would approve. The words might have been directly from her lecture. Was that talk longer than he'd remembered? Or had there been more than one? They'd probably talked of it several times, it was in the media a lot these days. Whatever the source of the statement, it got a reaction. The two closest to him turned to look. They were both younger than he'd thought at first. One with scraggly hair down to his shoulders, and one with a stupid looking beard he was trying to grow.

"Piss off, old man," the one with the stupid beard said.

"Let her go," he replied, taking another step forward. He wasn't scared, not really. He had one secret weapon here. He almost hoped he'd have to use it.

Unfortunately, stupid-beard didn't look scared either. He took a step toward Gordon, puffing out his chest. He didn't even look back to make sure his friends were still with him, which is what Gordon had been hoping he'd do. It would give him a chance to attack if needed.

From behind his opponent there came a loud grunt as the guy who had his hands on the girl's arm cried out in pain and stumbled back away from her. She had taken advantage of the momentary distraction to wrench free of the man holding her with the aid of a sharp kick.

"Run!" she shouted, then took her own advice. The man

she'd kicked recovered and ran after her. The one in front of Gordon didn't react at all. Long-hair glanced back, made his decision and stepped up behind stupid-beard.

His friend pulled something out of his pocket, then slid it open with a "snikt." For an instant, Gordon thought it was a switchblade, then laughed softly when he saw that it was a box knife. It could still hurt him, even kill if the guy got lucky, or was any good, or if the two of them could pin him. They wouldn't pin him. He knew he couldn't run. They'd both be quicker than him.

"Let me go!" The girl shouted and he glanced over that way to see the guy had caught up with her too. Out of his peripheral vision, he saw him raise an arm, and heard the slap when it came down. She cried out in pain.

"You're attracting a lot of attention," Gordon told him, standing his ground. There was more noise coming from the struggle ahead. "It's not too late..." He was interrupted as the knife wielder lunged forward. He stepped back and the knife missed him by a foot. They stepped in again quickly, trying for the man's elbow. He made contact but couldn't get a good grip as the kid twisted away, dragging the tip of the razor down Gordon's forearm. The cut wasn't life-threatening, but if it had happened two weeks ago, it would have required stitches.

But things had changed since two weeks ago. The guy with the knife crowed, "You picked a fight with the wrong guy, old man." His friend remained expressionless behind him, silently ready should he be needed. Gordon didn't like that at all.

"I'm forty-one," he addressed stupid-beard. "Forty-one's not old," he added when he saw his opponent's puzzled expression.

The kid made another swipe with the knife that he barely avoided by jumping back. He still hadn't reacted to the blood dripping from his forearm. The kid wasn't scared off by the blood any more than he was by the noise. He'd done this sort of thing before.

But Gordon knew what he was and had an inkling of how it all worked. It was a new moon night, but he didn't want to take any chances. A man like this was dangerous enough. He mustn't become a werewolf, too. It only took him a second to decide. He took a step backward, then lunged forward, shifting as he did.

His prey made no noise as it fell before him. It didn't have time. He felt something cold and metal touch him and wetness grew where it touched. He barely felt it and ignored the sensation as his jaws closed on the human's neck. He held it tightly and shook. Bone popped and blood sprayed his face and chest. He dropped the corpse and spied the second creature running from him. He gave chase and in the seconds it took to catch up to him, his wound was already healed.

"I HEAR we've got two more," Phil said as he entered the war room. Michael was adding his newest additions to the big map already. A picture of two corpses, taken from far enough away to catch both of them, though not in great detail, and a closeup of a shredded set of clothes. He led a red string from the picture to the place on the map where the bodies had been found, just off 82nd Ave. He added another string, white to indicate an unproven relationship, leading from the picture to the photo of Carl Jablonski.

"You think he might be involved?" Phil asked as he saw what he was doing.

"It isn't Talman," Michael replied.

Phil acknowledged the point with a grunt of laughter. "Address didn't check out?"

"According to the landlord, it used to be valid. He was consistently late on rent until they'd had enough of him and threatened him with eviction. Apparently, he moved out the next day, leaving no forwarding address."

"Cell phone?"

"None registered in his name."

"Damn. I take it you've issued an alert?"

"Only internally. I don't want any of his associates to know we're looking for him yet."

"You think he's carrying on Talman's work?"

Michael shook his head. "MO is different. These two were killed in the street. Witness said he heard a scream and saw a girl running away from the location but didn't see anything else."

"ID on the deceased?"

"Morgue's working on that now."

Michael took a seat at the conference table, and Phil did the same opposite him. He didn't face Phil, though. He was staring at the map. The connections, made tangible in colored string, ran to pins in the map, to Jablonski, to Stumpp, to "Peter" to Rosen. Together, his team had found a pattern there once. They'd broken that pattern only for a larger one to emerge. They'd have to find this one, too, and before more people died.

"What is really going on here? What are we missing?" he asked out loud. Phil didn't answer.

"You look like a pair who could use some good news," a voice came from the doorway of the war room.

They both turned to look, as Detective Lauren Boyd entered the room, carrying a folder. She dropped it on the table and opened it. Taking a photograph from the top of the documents inside, she pinned it onto the board next to the picture of "Peter," formerly known as Suspect One.

Phil reached with his good arm and began looking at the

rest of the documents in the folder as she turned back to them to explain.

"Peter Maxwell. No known occupation, but we got criminal history and, best of all, a current address."

"Nice house, too," Phil said, pushing a page to Michael with what looked like a Google street view photo of the residence, over a map of a West Hills neighborhood.

"Not bad for no known occupation," Michael responded.

"You think that's good, check out the priors," Boyd told them. She walked back to where they were going through the file.

Phil found the page in question, first, and pulled it out and set it on the table so they could all see.

"Manslaughter?" Michael read out. "Two years in prison - looks like a fight, not an assault."

"Trespassing five years ago, charges dropped," Phil said.

"Check this out - another murder three years ago. Charges dropped. The only witness, a small time drug dealer, disappeared before he could testify."

"Convenient that."

"The last one's my favorite," said Detective Boyd.

Michael glanced down to the bottom of the page. "Indecent exposure" he read out loud. The details showed that he'd been arrested for being too close to a high school when he was found naked. He claimed he'd been mugged and was eventually let go.

"Sounds like a werewolf to me," Phil said, indicating the charge.

"Maybe," Boyd replied. "But it's Portland. You can't just assume every naked person wandering the street is a werewolf."

"I think, given everything else..." Phil started.

"You're right," Boyd said before he could finish. "It's a pretty safe assumption all told."

"But you're not wrong," Michael said to her. "We're going to have to find ways of identifying these guys. Turning up naked somewhere that naked people usually aren't is one piece of evidence but won't be able to stand on its own."

"So how do we want to play this?" Phil asked, ending that conversation.

"Surveillance probably won't work," Boyd said. "Dude's a plumber, right? They only call him out when they've got a particular leak fixed."

"Agreed," Michael said. "We don't want to catch him in the act."

"Why don't we just drive over there now and arrest him?" Phil said. "We've got video. Interfering with a murder investigation, destruction of evidence, grand theft - that's a rack of felonies right there. Previous record, even. We wanna get the big bosses, we've got enough to force information from him through a plea deal."

"Okay, let's get a warrant and then, what a SWAT team?" Phil said.

"When it comes to werewolves, we are the SWAT team," Michael said.

"Might be enough. Assuming he's alone when we find him," Phil replied.

"We? I thought you were still on restricted duty," Michael said.

"Maybe a SWAT team's not such a bad idea after all," Boyd spoke up.

"Take too long to prepare them. I meant it when I said we're it. We've all got silver bullets and understand why. I wouldn't trust anyone who hasn't been briefed to respond properly, and they'd need to be issued ammunition we don't have enough of."

"I can at least run communications," Phil said. "This is going to be our first engagement as the werewolf squad. Don't cut me out."

"All right. Let's see what kind of plan we can come up with before everyone else gets here."

"We're going to have to come up with suggestions for rules of engagement, and run them past Billings, probably before the afternoon briefing," Phil said. "Is a man turning into a wolf enough to constitute a clear and present danger?"

ON THE THIRD day of exchanging emails, Gordon finally got a response from one that seemed promising. He'd answered a Craigslist ad the previous day for a group seeking those interested in "wolves and transformations." It had a lot less information than most of the groups he'd found - and he'd found a surprisingly large number of them - but there was something about it that seemed more legitimate, if that was the right word for a secret society advertising on the internet. They didn't spend any space in the ad explaining their beliefs or trying to justify their existence. He'd fired off a quick email and received a response the next day from someone with the unwieldy email address "childofthebrightestnight." It was on gmail, so Gordon assumed it had been set up using a fake name, the same way he had created his own.

The message said that something called "The Order of the Wolf" was looking to induct a few new members and was signed simply "-J." In the reply, there had been a bit more information about the group, and it went on a bit about fighting for freedom and free-thinking individuals, but still none of the angst-ridden whining that he'd seen in most of the other groups he'd contacted. He replied he was still interested and was invited to an informal meeting with a couple of the group members and some other possible new recruits. "Come find us in the garden" J had written, and given him directions to a coffee shop in the Southeast called the Pied Cow.

Gordon agreed, then at the last minute sent an email saying that something had come up, it was important, and that he was "still interested but unfortunately won't be able to meet with you today." Then he got on a bus and headed to the meeting.

He walked up the short flight of steps to the coffee house proper and ordered a simple black coffee before heading back out to the garden. Despite the light drizzle on and off throughout the day, there were a few groups outside, clustered under the trees. A trio, two men and a woman, all in their early twenties, had a hookah and a plate of various finger foods between them. One of the men looked up expectantly when he arrived but turned his attention back to the others when he didn't react. Gordon wasn't ready to reveal himself yet. His goal here was to scope things out, learn what he could before contacting anyone who might actually be a werewolf. He took a table nearby the trio and sat facing away from the group but at such an angle he could watch them from the corner of his eye without seeming suspicious. He took out his phone and tried to look like all his attention was focused on it. With his ear buds in and the phone off, he could hear everything at the nearby table.

"We're still waiting for a couple more people," the man, Gordon assumed he must be the mysterious J, said to the other man at his table.

"There was another guy, too, but he just emailed me to say he couldn't make it,"

Yep, that was J.

"Probably changed his mind," the other man at the table said.

"Could be," J said, "Chickened out, maybe, or decided the whole thing was bullshit."

"Well, it does sound a little fantastic," their guest said.

"His loss, anyway," J said. "As you'll be finding out in a couple of weeks." He tore off a piece of bread and used it to scoop up some of the hummus before stuffing it in his mouth.

Moments later, two women, both in their early twenties it looked like, approached the table. J looked up at them and looked like he was trying to swallow quickly so he could speak.

Before he could, one of the girls spoke up, "You the werewolf guy?" she asked. Gordon nearly choked on his coffee. He had expected more circumspect conversation. Dancing around the issue, nobody daring to say the word openly. "The wolf crows at midnight" or some such nonsense. Not this glib reference to J as "the werewolf guy."

Nor his glib acknowledgment. "Yep. And you must be Lilith and Kim."

"Lily, please," one of the women said.

Her friend gave her a look at that.

"New life, new name," she explained with a shrug.

J seemed to approve of that. He stood up. "Lily it is then," he said. "And you're right about a new life. I'm Carl, and this is Toni and Will." His two companions nodded. "Will answered the same ad as you two." Which must mean Toni hadn't, Gordon realized.

Then Gordon realized why he looked familiar. Carl. That cop, Detective Diaz, had shown him the picture in the hospital, then seemed disappointed when he hadn't recognized him. He had been a suspect in the other killings. But he hadn't been involved with the attack on Barbara and himself. He now knew something the police did not. This could be currency. Even if he learned nothing more here, he could use this to get more information from the police. It also confirmed his hope: he'd finally found another real werewolf.

He sipped his coffee, keeping his face carefully neutral and focused on his phone as he eavesdropped.

The two women sat down at the table and Carl, aka J, pushed the plate of food toward them. They both declined the hookah but picked up some of the cheese and pita.

The group made small talk for a bit. Carl, he learned, worked in software. Lilith-now-Lily, and Gordon wondered what her real name was, worked for Intel out in Hillsboro. Carl had worked there in the past but no longer. Will remarked on the coincidence but Carl pointed out that, "Portland's not that big. If you work in the tech industry at all, it's eventually your turn to work for Intel."

As they talked, Carl reminded him of Barbara's boyfriend, Timothy. The girl, Toni, he noticed mostly kept quiet, occasionally drawing the others out with questions, but saying close to nothing about herself or their group.

Finally, the talk turned to werewolves.

"In the dawn of time," Carl began, intoning the words as if it were a ritual. The girl, Toni, smirked at that, but he continued, "Wolves and humans lived side by side. Men built fires around which they would gather at night, roasting meat from the day's hunt. They would throw the bones off away from the fires and wolves would gather at the edges of the light to carry off their refuse. At first, the men would drive them off, or try to kill them, fearing the fierce beasts. In one tribe, though, there was a woman who realized the wolves only wanted the food, which the people were already giving them freely. The wolves in turn would keep other predators away from the camp."

Gordon watched the others for their reactions to Carl's story. Kim seemed enraptured, while Will seemed mostly bored. Lily kept looking to her friend to see how she was reacting to all this. Interestingly, Carl looked repeatedly at Toni, often paused, and would continue when she nodded. He was an experienced storyteller, that much was obvious, but still looked to her for direction.

"This woman," he continued, "encouraged her tribe to not only allow the wolves to be in peace, but to bring back additional meat to throw to them. This they did, and over the years the pack of wolves who would gather around the fires with humans grew. The humans quickly discovered the mutual advantage. The wolves with their superior senses, would give warning if predators approached the camp. While there were many creatures who would gladly feast on a lone human, there were very few even then that would dare to attack a camp full of humans alert and ready for them.

"And even more, wolves are expert hunters. They can scatter herds, isolating animals and driving them away from the protection of their fellows. Humans and wolves learned how to hunt together, the wolves separating the bison from the herd and driving them toward men with spears."

Gordon smiled at that. He had trouble believing a band of men, no matter how mighty hunters they might be, would do anything but scramble for safety when faced with an angry charging bison. But the core of it was probably right. Man and wolf had been together a long time. The relationship had no doubt been mutually beneficial in a variety of ways throughout time.

"The tribe prospered," Carl continued his story. "Other nearby tribes took notice and began treating their own local wolf packs with kindness and emulated their success. Decades went by, and the woman grew old and came to be respected far and wide for her wisdom. And one day, a new tribe came into the area. They were powerful and warlike, and had no wolves of their own, killing the beasts wherever they could find them.

At first, unused to the tactics when wolf and man worked together, they were beaten back and stymied in their attempts at raiding. But they were experienced in the art of warfare and soon adapted, focusing at first on only the smaller, weaker groups.

"The other tribes saw what was happening but couldn't decide what to do. Those closest to the raiders wanted to band together, put an end to it, but others didn't see why they should send warriors from their own land to engage in a fight that they weren't involved in yet, and may never be. Eventually, word of this reached the wise woman, who decided to travel alone to talk to the raiders."

Carl paused for a moment and was interrupted by one of the girls - Kim, if he remembered her name correctly.

"Not so wise, then?" she said, with a smirk.

That earned her a scowl from her friend, and an amused smile from Carl.

"She was old, near the end of her life, and more concerned about the fate of those who looked to her for guidance than for her few remaining years. But, as you've guessed, she was indeed attacked. She wasn't alone, though. Although she'd forbidden anybody from accompanying her, wolves are not so easily controlled. Several followed her on their own. When the raiders approached, with their stone spears at the ready, two great wolves emerged to stand before her. The raiders attacked immediately, throwing their spears in an attempt to kill the wolves." His voice rose, and his cadence quickened here. He was getting caught up in his own story. It worked, though, as Gordon could tell the others were as well.

"But the wise woman leapt between them, throwing her hands up, trying to show that neither she nor the wolves would attack." He paused and took a sip of his coffee. But only a sip,

He didn't want to lose his audience. He spoke again, "Both spears hit her."

"What?" the man, Will, said. He had been listening after all. This was not what Carl's audience was expecting. Gordon caught himself almost reacting along with them.

"When news of her death reached the tribes, they went wild with anger. They decided to unite together to put an end to the invaders who would do such a thing. The wise woman knew that her death at the hands of the enemy would unite the tribes. And that was the real reason she went. But she didn't die."

His audience reacted to that. They'd been had.

"As she lay on the ground, two wolves at her side, the day grew dark and a full moon rose over the valley. An apparition appeared to her. At first, she took it for the spirit of death, come to escort her to the next world. But when it drew near, she saw it was a mighty wolf. It spoke to her then, praising her bravery and her wisdom, and especially the kindness she'd shown all her life to his kind. For all that, he said, he would give her a gift. He bestowed upon her the ability to take either form - the human she was born into and grew up as, or that of the wolves, who she had loved as brothers and worked with all her life. Further, when she did transform, all her wounds would be healed. And lastly, she could pass this gift on to others of her choosing."

It took Gordon a second to realize that was the end of it. He wanted to know how it got from there to the current situation. Apparently, that was a story they were saving for later. Maybe this "initiation" they'd hinted at earlier.

"Nice story," Kim said when Carl had finished. "How much of it is true?" That earned her another dirty look from her friend, and a snort of laughter from Carl, which in turn earned him a dirty look from Toni. The two looked at each other, and finally the girl smiled as well, as if conceding some private point.

"The essence of it," she said.

"We don't... uh... that is, it's been handed down orally since, well, since the dawn of time," Carl fumbled out. Gordon almost laughed and raised his now empty mug to his lips to hide his smile. This guy certainly didn't seem like any kind of hardened killer. Still, he was a werewolf, or at least connected to them, and the police were looking for him.

"The thing is, it's real. The story of how it happened may not be a hundred percent accurate - probably isn't... but, uh..." he stammered again, trying to find the words, "Like Toni said, the essence is true. Werewolves are real. We are them, they, whatever, and you can be too. It's not a metaphor, it's not a game, it's an actual transformation."

"I'll believe that when I see it," Kim said again.

Toni smiled at that. "Then you'll believe it after the next full moon. We're doing initiations then. You'll see it if you're interested and be given a chance to join us."

FOURTEEN
MEETINGS AND ANNOUNCEMENTS

The meeting reached a conclusion, and the others began to leave. Gordon brought up the camera on his phone, double-checked that the sound was off, and took several quick pictures of the group, over his shoulder. He made sure to get Toni and Carl sitting at the table, and the two girls and Will, standing, as they were about to leave.

He knew the police were interested in Carl for some reason. He didn't think they knew about Toni, though, or about their plan to make more werewolves. *Why would anyone voluntarily make themselves into such a monster?* And yet here were three who would. *This can't be normal, though.* If every werewolf made more every full moon, Portland would be overrun with them by now. Something new was happening, but what? He was beginning to think the cop, Detective Diaz, had been telling the truth when he said he'd only recently found out. He was toying with the idea of talking to him again, or at least telling him what was going on, and was trying to figure out how to attach the pictures he'd just taken to an email when the girl appeared at his table and sat down.

He looked up sharply, startled.

"Did you enjoy the story?" Toni asked him. She took a sip of her drink from a paper cup.

He looked around. No sign of her friend. But he had to assume he was around somewhere nearby. "How much of it is true?" he asked her, echoing the earlier question, trying to buy time to figure out what to do.

"The essence," she repeated her answer. But then she continued, "Werewolves are real, if that's what you mean." She paused, considering for a second. "But you already knew that, didn't you?"

"Yes," he admitted.

"You work for Stumpp?" she asked him.

That took him off guard. "Who?" he asked.

"The Alpha?" she prompted.

"I'm afraid I don't know what that means," he told her. He kept looking around, scanning the garden, watching for anything ready to jump out of the bushes.

She ignored his frantic searching. "If you're not Stumpp's, who's are you? Are you one of Kevin's?"

Another new name. If he talked to the cop again, he'd definitely have more information to barter with.

"I don't know who that is, either," he replied with a sad shake of his head.

"How can you..." she started, then switched questions. "How long have you been a wolf?"

Gordon thought about it for a second, and decided that he could get useful information from her, so he might as well trust her with the truth. At least a little bit. He wasn't fooled by her smaller size, and her age – he guessed 25 at the oldest, probably a couple years under that – but if she could turn into a wolf... he didn't know what could happen. *Could they hurt each other in wolf form? Would he heal from injury done to him by another werewolf?*

He didn't want to find out. She seemed willing to talk. Or she was just stalling so Carl – or any other friends she had nearby – could get into position. Into position for what? If they had wanted to attack him, they could have done so as he was leaving – they didn't need to distract him first. He decided there was such a thing as being too paranoid after all.

He decided to be honest with her. "Since the seventh of last month," he answered her question.

She looked surprised at that. "The seventh? Not the thirteenth?"

The thirteenth was the day he fled the hospital after someone tried to kill him.

"No," he said, trying to keep his voice calm. "Why? What's special about the thirteenth?"

"The full moon?" she asked. Gordon hadn't even thought about that at the time. Then she dropped the other bombshell. "That's the day I was turned."

"That recently?" he asked her. "Did... was Carl the one who... what... bit you?"

She fell silent at that, then looked directly into his eyes. She seemed to tense up before she answered, almost whispering the word, "Yes."

There was a significance to that that he was missing.

"How..." he hesitated. Is this a thing that should be asked? "How did it happen?"

She thought about it for a second, then shook her head. "You go first. If you're not Victor's and you're not Kevin's, who turned you?"

He considered for a moment, trying to decide what to tell her, or how. Could he even mention Barbara to this girl? Should he? "I never got his name," he finally answered.

When he didn't continue, she said, "You're going to have to tell me more than that."

"He broke into my house. I... I don't know who he was. He..." Gordon took a deep breath and continued in a rush, "He killed my daughter and attacked me. I woke up in the hospital and figured out what I was after another one tried to kill me there."

"Fuck," Toni said, obviously not expecting this. "The killer. The rogue."

"The rogue?" he asked. It seemed like such a mild term for the man.

"Yeah, Carl told me there's a rogue werewolf killing people. The Alpha's all in a tizzy about it apparently. That's part of the reason they thought they might not notice..." she trailed off.

"Notice what?" he prompted. There was something important here. She was silent for a moment, then he got it. "Notice you making more?"

She nodded at that. He felt a rush of anger.

"He isn't going to be much of a distraction for you anymore," he said. "He's dead. At least, that's what the police told me."

She took another moment to think about that. "You talked to the police?" she finally asked, which was not the question he was expecting.

"Yeah," he told her. "Man broke into my house, murdered my daughter. The police are going to get involved."

She fell silent again at that. Gordon wondered about the significance of that. One more puzzle piece. *But did it help fill in what he knew was missing or just expand the board even further?*

"Wait," she said. "Which one was killed?"

"What?" Gordon asked, feeling anger welling inside him.

"You said one attacked you at the house, and one at the

hospital," she clarified. He calmed immediately. He thought she was talking about Barbara for a second and felt ready to leap across the table at her. He had never been this quick to anger before. *This must be a side effect of his transformation. How much worse was it going to get?*

"The one from the house," he answered her. "I don't know about the one from the hospital. Actually, I don't even know for sure that he was a werewolf. He came prepared to kill one, though."

"What do you mean?"

"He had a silver hypodermic needle. He knew what I was somehow."

"So maybe Carl's right," she replied, half to herself.

"Right about what?" he asked.

"He told me they don't like werewolves being turned without their permission. They kill the ones who are."

"Shit."

"Tell me about it."

He caught the implication of what she'd said right before that. "You didn't know if your boyfriend was telling you the truth?"

"He's not my boyfriend," she responded too quickly. She reminded him a bit of Barbara, the way she said it. He smiled softly but didn't say anything. She caught it, "It's complicated." She seemed to relax a bit, though. He reminded himself not to trust her, nonetheless.

"I don't think he's lying to me," she replied, "But I don't know how much of what he believes is actually true."

"Your turn," Gordon said, "Tell me about them. How about starting with who are 'They'"

"'They' are the Were," she replied. "The main group of werewolves."

"There's more than one group, then?" he asked her.

"At least three, that I know of," Toni answered. "And I'm guessing that the guy who turned you might be from a fourth."

"Why do you say that?" he asked.

"Because he doesn't fit any of the other three."

"Okay, you're going to have to back up and explain who all these groups are, and why he doesn't fit any of them," Gordon said.

"You really don't know," she said.

"I told you," Gordon said, "I just got bitten two weeks ago, and other than the one guy who tried to kill me, I haven't seen any other werewolves. I don't know anything about any of this."

"You got attacked, turned, and figured out what you were, but with nobody to fill you in on what's what," she said. It didn't sound like a question.

Gordon nodded in response, though.

"And that's why you're here," she continued. "You're the guy that said he couldn't make it. You wanted to find out, but you didn't know who you could trust."

"That's pretty much it," he confirmed.

"All right. I had that one advantage at least," she said, "Let's start with Stumpp's group. That's the oldest and largest and best organized. Stumpp's only the local Alpha. There's apparently a bunch of them spread around, each controlling their own region."

"Apparently?" Gordon prompted.

"All I really know is what Carl has told me," she repeated.

"If Carl's the expert," Gordon asked her, "why are you here and not him?"

She shifted uncomfortably at that but didn't say anything. Gordon understood, though. Of course, Carl was here. Nearby, if not in sight. "He's not here because he's the better fighter," he said.

Toni smiled at that, then replied, "Not exactly. Well, he thinks he is, but that really isn't it."

"So, you're, what, feeling me out, trying to determine if I'm a threat."

"Pretty much, yeah," she said.

"And if I am?" He led.

"Then we'll figure out what to do about it," she said. Her tone was calm, but not entirely without menace. Two werewolves. At least. He knew he'd recover from most wounds. The stories of vulnerability to silver seemed to be right. What about damage done by another werewolf? Could these two be a threat to him? He suspected they might, but he also suspected that she was telling the truth. They wouldn't move against him unless they thought he was a threat.

"And what would constitute me being a threat?" he finished the thought out loud.

"Being sent by Victor's people, for one," she told him. "I don't think you are, though. Your story's just too... complicated. If you wanted to infiltrate us, you could have just come to the table, and been in easily."

Gordon wasn't so sure about that. He was nearly twice the age of anyone there. But he didn't say anything, not wanting to raise suspicions where there was no cause for them.

"And that's the group you think the guy who attacked me in the hospital was in," he stated. It wasn't really a question.

"Yeah," Toni replied, "Just because it sounds like the kind of thing they'd do. Eliminate wolves who were turned without their permission."

There was something to her tone. He decided to chance a guess. "And you're worried that that's what they'll do to you," he said. "And you don't really trust Carl to make that assessment."

"For someone who doesn't know anything, you're pretty quick on the uptake," she told him.

"I know a lot more than I did an hour ago," he replied. He did not add "assuming anything you've told me is true."

"Well, you're right," she said. "I have to stay secret for now, because Stumpp's people will kill me if they find out I exist."

"So... why recruit?" Gordon asked her. Either she was lying, or he was missing something. "Meeting in public, making more werewolves? Not exactly laying low."

"And that brings us to the Great Plan," she said.

There was something in her tone as she said it. Laden with sarcasm, but there was also something more. She was pinning a great deal on this plan, but didn't want to seem to be, in order to mask her expected disappointment.

Gordon suspected she'd experienced a great deal of disappointment. He found himself wondering where her parents were. Was she originally from here, or was she one of these young people who seemed constantly lured to the city these days?

"Okay," he asked her out loud, "I'll bite. What is the Great Plan?"

"The question you didn't ask," she began, "is why would Stumpp be so zealous about hunting down and killing unauthorized wolves."

"I presume to keep their existence a secret." he said.

"Exactly," she replied. "And that's pretty much what we're trying to accomplish. We want to reveal the existence of the wolves, but before we can do that we need more numbers. A couple of us, they could silence. A dozen? Maybe. Probably not a hundred, though."

"And that's why you're recruiting," he said. "To build your numbers up before going public?"

"Why else?" She said.

Why else indeed? Certainly not to share a remarkable gift to the rest of the world.

"What if they can? What if they've got enough connections to bring in the national guard, call you all threats, and have us all killed?"

"They wouldn't do that," she said. "That'd reveal their secret as surely as anything we do."

"I don't know about that. I don't know what kind of resources these people have, and I don't think you do either. For all we know, they've got nuclear bombs planted in major cities like this to be used as a last resort to keep their secrets." He felt like a hypocrite. Wasn't he just a couple of weeks ago urging Detective Diaz not to keep their secrets for them?

"That's too much," Toni said. "If they're that strong, then we don't have a chance either way so we might as well try. Maybe we'll get lucky, or maybe all we'll accomplish is giving somebody else a better chance at doing it some time in the future, but I refuse to believe it's that hopeless."

"Let's hope not, then. And you're probably right. If they were that powerful, then this one 'rogue' werewolf wouldn't be so worrisome to them. Sounds like the police did this Stumpp fellow a favor by killing him."

"Possibly literally," she said. "I still don't know how much influence he has. If he has a man on the force, or if he owns them and the mayor as well."

"Then you're taking an awful risk telling me all this," he realized.

"Yes," she said, "I am. But I think you can help us. Even if you don't want to join our group, knowing a friendly outsider could be useful."

"Useful how?" He didn't like the sound of that.

"I don't know yet," she said. "Perhaps just having someone who knows what happened, in case we fail."

She was talking about dying. "In case we fail" meant in case she and all her friends were killed and their message never got out. In that case, he would be her backup plan.

He didn't know how to handle that, so he took the cowards way out and changed the subject. "You told me about the Alpha and his people, and you and Carl, and it sounds like the guy who... put me in the hospital was acting on his own. Who else is there? This Kevin guy you mentioned?"

"Kevin and Shelly, yes. Carl was working with them, then he and I split off."

"And they're trying to recruit more, too?"

"As far as we know, yes," she answered him. "But I believe I was the first."

"Wait a minute," he said. "I thought you said Carl was the one who... what is the word? Sired you?"

"That's vampires," she said.

"Shit. Are there really vampires, then?"

"Not as far as I know," she said. "But yes, Carl turned me. Like I said, they were working together originally." She told him the story, about how she'd gone with an acquaintance and four strangers to a remote cabin, how she'd been chained in the basement with two of the others and left there, wounded. How one of them had died. Gordon shuddered at that.

"You expect maybe I should go to the police after that?" she responded to his look. "Tell them some guys just turned me into a werewolf?"

"You could maybe leave out that part, and still report the murder," he said. But he wasn't sure he believed it himself.

"So far, one hundred percent of the werewolves I know who talked to the police had someone try to kill them shortly thereafter," she said, pointedly looking straight at him.

He had no answer to that. "But if he did all that horrible stuff to you, why did you go with him anywhere after that?" He had a sneaking suspicion he knew what her response would be, and he was right.

"He's really not that bad," she said.

"He is," Gordon said firmly. "And don't tell me he isn't the kind of guy who would do that kind of thing. He did, so by definition..." He was surprised at the vehemence in his own voice. He could see by her reaction that she was, too. He recognized where it came from, though. He was still trying to protect Barbara. This girl wasn't her and he couldn't allow himself to think of her protectively. She was a werewolf and not only that but was making more of them.

"Look, we've all done stupid stuff," she began.

He cut her off. "Believe me, I've done my share of stupid things when I was younger, but kidnapping and murder aren't among them."

"I needed answers, and he was the only one around who had them," she said defensively.

"That still doesn't explain..." he started.

"Doesn't matter," She cut him off, an edge of anger in voice. "You're not my father, or my boyfriend, or anyone else who needs to be judging my actions."

"Okay, fair enough. You're an adult, you make your own decisions." He knew he sounded patronizing as he said it, but he didn't care. What these kids were playing with was dangerous. People had already been killed. It wasn't just Barbara. There was that other kid whose name Toni didn't even mention. All so that they could... what? Change the established power structure. Maybe this Stumpp guy had the right idea after all. Sure, he'd tried to have him killed in the hospital, but he wouldn't have been in the hospital in the first place if one of this girl's friends or someone like them hadn't attacked him. Killed Barbara. Turned him into this... thing.

She apparently saw the angry expression on his face. "And

now you think we're a bunch of irresponsible kids playing with powers we don't understand." She said.

"Am I wrong?" he asked.

"Yes."

"My daughter is dead," he said coldly.

"And I had nothing to do with that!" she replied, matching his volume.

"You killed someone else, though," he said.

She froze for a second then said, "The guy in the basement. I didn't have anything to do with killing him. I was chained up next to him, remember?" She had half risen in her seat, then sat back down, looking around to see who else might have heard. Aside from the two of them, though, the garden was empty.

"But you're working with others who're doing the same thing," he began again, lowering his volume.

She interrupted him again, "Not the same thing. Not at all. We're turning nobody against their will, or without letting them know what they're getting into."

She shifted uncomfortably when she said it, though. She was leaving something out.

"And," she continued, "I know far more than you do about what we're doing. If you'll recall, I was the one filling you in on what the situation is."

"All you know, though, is what Carl told you."

Toni smiled at that. "Kinda proves my point, then, if it were true. But it's not. Some I learned on my own, and I've taught him a thing or two as well."

"You learned that much in two weeks?" Gordon asked skeptically.

"I learned enough my first day as a wolf to know better than to try what they were doing," she said.

"What'd you learn?" Gordon was skeptical, but it seemed

there were entire aspects to his new existence of which he was unaware.

"For one, most people will react badly to being chained to a wall in a basement."

"Well, yeah."

"You say that. It honestly never occurred to them."

"How is that even possible?" Gordon asked her.

"There're competing theories about that," she said with a wry smile.

This confused him even more.

"It's just that they don't consider themselves human." It wasn't really an explanation. She obviously saw the confusion on his face. "They think of themselves as more than human. Above. So they don't tend to have a lot of respect for those they consider beneath them."

"So is that the wolf, or..." he trailed off.

"Yeah, that's the question," she said. "I think it's actually more 'or.' The way they make wolves, or Were as they prefer, they tend to choose people who are like themselves. People who will fit in. And then they fight like hell to keep their secret, basically living outside the law to do so. On top of all that, they've all seen the same movies and TV shows you and I have, and to some degree, try to live up to that model."

"And you don't?" he asked her.

"I came into it a different way," she responded. He understood what she meant. "I didn't get the same indoctrination."

"And this Kevin guy?" Gordon asked. "You haven't said much about him other than that he and Carl originally worked together. Why'd they split up?"

"And Shelly," Toni said. "I suspect that she's really the one behind that whole thing. I disapproved of their methods. In the end, Carl did, too."

Gordon smiled slightly at that. He could understand - he

followed after the pretty girl instead of his old friends. In this case, he probably made the wiser decision. He didn't say anything out loud, though.

"They don't seem to be doing it that way anymore either, so maybe my disapproval isn't entirely meaningless." She said it defensively.

"How do you mean by 'that way?'" Gordon asked.

"I mean, Carl spoke to Kevin and Shelly, and they've agreed not to turn anyone against their will anymore." She replied.

"What? Just like that?" he asked, somewhat taken aback.

"Not, not just like that. I'm sure there was some arguing and recriminations involved. They'll both be at this weekend's party if you want to meet them and judge them for yourself."

"Seriously? You think I'd fit in at your party?"

"Honestly, no. But you don't have to fit in. You'll stand out. Everyone will assume you're some high-ranked muckety muck in the organization. You won't have to lie, just refuse to talk about it. It could work out well for both of us."

"Make you look more like a real organization?"

She smiled at that. He was correct in his assessment. "Exactly."

"I'll have to think about it," he said. "But maybe." He said it sincerely - this was not a polite blow-off, but he really couldn't give an answer until he had considered the implications.

"All right," she said. "But Kevin and Shelly will both be there. And they're both better connected in Victor Stumpp's organization than even Carl."

"Wait... Stumpp? Stumpp is Victor Stumpp?"

Toni nodded. He was beginning to see what he was really up against. The werewolves were even better organized than he had thought. Such an organization would certainly have contacts with the police force. He was certain he'd made the right decision in not trusting the detective too far.

"All right," he repeated, "I'll think about it." Before she could reply, he added, "You can send the information to that same email address."

"Okay," she said. "I'll have Carl do that." And the way she said it confirmed his suspicions of why she was really here instead of him. She needed to be in a place where she could judge the situation directly and make decisions immediately. If Carl had been in charge, she would have said "Carl will do that" or "I'll let him know."

"You've given me a lot," he said. "Thank you. I don't have anywhere near as much information for you, but there's one thing you might not know."

Toni looked up expectantly.

"The police are looking for your boyfriend," he said, looking into her eyes for a reaction.

Her reaction was not subtle. "What?" she exclaimed. "What for?"

"No idea," he confessed, "But when I woke up in the hospital, his was the first picture they showed me."

"The first? There were others?"

"A couple. None of them were the right guy, though."

"Gods. I wonder who the others were. And if they were all wolves."

"Maybe. I know they're specifically looking into werewolves. At least, that's what the one I spoke to told me."

"Wait. A cop actually admitted to you that they knew about werewolves?"

"He knew what I was at that point, but yes."

"Shit. This is big. I mean, this could be huge. And maybe exactly what we need. Or maybe it'll just fuck everything up. Shit. I'll have to think about it."

A lot of that going around. And again, she'd have to think about it, not "tell Carl about it." She was definitely the one in charge here, whether the others, or even she herself, knew it or not.

"Okay," the girl said, with a note of finality. "I've got one for you." Gordon perked up at that. Seeing his expression, she nodded. "It's not quite the same. I have no idea what the real implications are, but I think most of the Wolves get it wrong."

"Get what wrong?" he asked her.

"The change. They don't do it right, or not often enough."

"Not often enough?" He didn't think he liked where this was going.

"Yeah," she said, a note of challenge in her voice. "Think about it. When do werewolves change form?"

"At the full moon," he answered automatically.

"Exactly," she said. "And why?"

"Umm..." he began. Then trailed off.

"Exactly," she repeated. "You can change at will, right? So can I. And Carl. And everyone else, I assume. So why is the full moon so important?" She seemed to be expecting an answer to that. Gordon had no response, so she answered her own question.

"Okay, so here's my theory," she said. "It isn't."

Again, he had no answer, so she continued. "Or, really, it is, obviously, but only because of cultural inertia. Somebody somewhere came up with a bunch of superstitions about the full moon and somewhere way the fuck back in the dark ages, werewolves got rolled into that. It doesn't matter exactly how or when. Some guy who was a big muckety-muck at the time saw a werewolf on the night of a full moon and assumed they were related, probably. And the wolves, they like to think they're separate, see, but they're not, really. They live in the same communities, hear the same stories, so they started believing it. The wolf is always calling, right? It wants in, and people put it off, put it off, until it becomes overwhelming. Or they wait until the full moon and finally let it in."

Gordon nodded, letting her continue. This actually made sense to him.

"You have to transform eventually, and everyone says you should do it about once a month, and the full moon's the traditional time to do it. Now on top of that, they say if you change too much, you start to become more wolf-like. I don't know if that's bullshit, and if it isn't if it's necessarily a bad thing."

"I think you're going to lose me on how this can be a good thing," Gordon told her.

"Okay, how about this? Werewolves are almost exclusively solo hunters. Carl told me he never hunted with another wolf before me."

"You were his first," he winced inwardly even as he said it.

"Ha ha," she said flatly, only her eyes betraying her amusement. "But in a way, you're right. He'd never even considered doing it with a partner, let alone a group." She glared at him as if daring him to make a joke at that. He did not.

"He'd never even heard of anyone doing it before. But," she put up a hand to forestall his response, "real wolves aren't solo hunters. They hunt in packs. And that whole thing about the Alpha wolf ruling the pack, and others constantly competing for dominance? That's all bullshit, too. The concept of the Alpha is from one guy from the 19th century observing wolves in captivity. In the wild, packs are family units, with the mated pair at the head. You know what animal works with an autocratic ruler who has to constantly watch his back for usurpers? Just humans. You know what happens when a wolf gets injured in the wild and can't hunt anymore?"

Gordon had a pretty good idea of where she was going with this. And, as earlier, he wondered how much of it was true. It all sounded like hippie nonsense, glorifying the natural world while ignoring its realities. An extension of the "noble savage" nonsense, applied to wolves. He didn't say anything, though, and let her finish.

"The rest of the pack brings it food and allows it time to heal."

"Sounds very noble of them," Gordon couldn't stop himself from saying.

"It lets it eventually hunt again, contributing to the long term health of the pack. Wolves aren't libertarians, they're smarter than that."

"Okay, so maybe wolves are better in many ways than some humans," he said. "But how does that help us?"

"That's not what I'm saying," Toni replied, and for a moment he could hear Barbara's exasperated tone in her voice. "It all comes back to the full moon. Werewolves fight the change, put it off until they can't anymore, and fear to do it too often. Why? It has nothing to do with any actual needs. It's all based on misunderstandings, superstition, and buying into the popular entertainment based on it."

"Fine," he said, starting to get annoyed with the whole thing. "Even if it's all you said, what does it mean? What good is that? What do you actually do that's any different, knowing all this?"

Toni answered, "You change. Assume wolf form as often as you want. Without fearing how it'll change you."

The thought was horrifying. It obviously showed in his expression.

"Wolves aren't mindless killers. Humans kill things for fun. Wolves just kill to eat. It's not the wolf that makes you a killer, it's the man."

"Didn't you tell me the first thing you did was hunt down a deer?" he challenged.

"Yep." She seemed utterly unconcerned with the contradiction. "And the second, kind of." She had another far away expression for a second that told him there was more to the story than that, but he didn't press her. "But not the third, or the fourth, fifth, or sixth," she finished. "The wolf needs to eat, I think. And when it only comes out once a month, it can get hungry. Wolves are more aggressive than dogs - in fact, that's the primary difference between them. But they only get really aggressive when they're hungry."

"So, if you change often..." he began, not sure where he was going.

"Then the wolf isn't as hungry, and thus less aggressive. And the wolf influences the human just as much as the human influences the wolf, so a human whose wolf is starving and repressed is going to be angry and aggressive. But one who's wolf is happy..." She finished in a kind of shrug.

"Something to think about at any rate," he said. "Maybe it works for you and maybe there're long term consequences nobody has any idea about. Sometimes rules exist for good reasons, even if those reasons have been lost to history."

"And sometimes the reasons have been lost to history because they no longer exist," she retorted.

"Just, please be careful," he said. "And one more thing, before you go." He took his small notepad out of his pocket and quickly jotted down his number and detective Diaz's, then tore out the page and handed it to her. "Top number's mine, Diaz is the cop who's looking for your boyfriend."

"You think I'd turn him in?"

"No. But if you want to expose the werewolves, your goals may be aligned. There might come a time when you both want to contact him."

She nodded at that. "You think I can trust him?"

"I wouldn't go that far, but you won't have to waste any time convincing him you're telling the truth."

"PLACE LOOKS DESERTED," Lauren said.

Michael stepped up next to her and peered in through the window. She was right. There was no furniture in the one room he could see, or any other signs that the house was inhabited.

Aaron went around the side to a kitchen window. "Yeah, nothing - no dishes, no appliances, counters are bare. If anyone ever lived here, they don't know."

"Let's be sure," Michael said. "Aaron, can you get us in?" No need to kick the door in if they weren't in a hurry.

"Sure," he said and went to work on the door.

A quick search of the house showed their initial assessment to be correct. The whole place was empty.

He briefed Phil on the way back to the station.

"What do you think? APB? He's gotta still be in town somewhere."

"Somewhere," Michael agreed. "I'd rather not tip him off that we're looking for him, though."

Phil shrugged in agreement. "Maybe we can draw him out. Any idea how to do it?"

"Maybe it's time to go public?"

"You'll be a laughingstock."

"Not if we play it right. We could drop all the right hints, then suggest we have more. We don't have to say werewolf directly." Michael said, though he had no idea how it could actually be done.

"Think Rosen could be useful here?" Phil asked.

"I don't know. I'm afraid if she was involved, they'd hit her first, and never get to me, and she might be too easy for them to get to."

"Let's keep her involvement secret, then," Phil said.

"All right," Michael replied. "I'll talk to her tonight. Can you arrange a leak of bodycam footage before tomorrow's press briefing?"

Phil didn't even hesitate at the suggestion. "I'll talk to Aaron. Shouldn't be a problem."

VEER WAS ONCE AGAIN in Victor's office. She was seated in a chair she'd pulled over from his conference table to sit beside the desk. They were waiting to watch the live stream of the press conference on the screen that his new assistant, Cate, had just brought in and set up for them.

Of course, the footage from the officer's body camera had been leaked earlier that day. It had immediately become a laughingstock, as she had warned Michael it would when they discussed it last night. It hardly even needed any input from the Were. People were quite happy to mock it as a clumsy forgery on their own.

While they were waiting for the press conference to start, they watched the leaked footage online. The images were shaky, taken from a camera being worn by an officer who was running upstairs and into a firefight, but when the wolf fell, the officer was apparently frozen, facing right at it as it was replaced, through a weird twisting effect, with a naked man lying dead on the floor.

"How many of them are using silver bullets?" Victor asked her, his tone unreadable.

"Just Michael as far as I know," she answered.

Victor just nodded. Any thought he'd had about that, he kept to himself.

When the leaked video had reached the end, another was automatically queued. It turned out to be the same video that someone had remixed, dubbing Michael Jackson's *Thriller* over it. Victor laughed out loud at that.

"Was that one of ours?" Veer asked him.

"Not as far as I know," he said, still laughing. "It seems someone did that one on their own." He got a more serious expression. "Looks like this'll blow over without our help. I was afraid it was going to become a real annoyance."

She wasn't sure what to say about that, so didn't speak at all, though she realized that her silence would tell him volumes.

"Of course, it'll all depend on what your detective says." She didn't have an answer she wanted to give him for that, either.

Once the press conference started, they waited with bated breath for Detective Diaz to bring up the leaked footage, but he didn't mention it at all during his prepared statements. He gave them all the facts: the man's name, Grant Talman, the fact that he had just come up from San Diego, and that he had a string of previous arrests and outstanding warrants. There was no known motive in the killings, and with his death there may never be any. There was no sign of the wolf. Nobody saw which way it ran off to after the firefight. Things were very chaotic at the time and they're still trying to piece together exactly what happened. He warned that if anyone spotted it, they should call animal control immediately. It was likely to only be a danger if it felt itself trapped, though most likely it was out of the city by now. He informed them that wolves have been known to travel up to 30 miles in a single day and often go hundreds of miles before settling in a new territory. Unlike coyotes, they don't like cities. They didn't expect to see this one again.

They were all true statements, but none of them the truth.

"Any questions?" he finally asked, and that's where it really began.

"What can you tell us about the leaked bodycam footage?" one reporter immediately asked.

"I'm afraid I can't tell you anything at this point," Diaz said. "We are still reviewing the footage as well as other sources."

"What about the part where it shows the suspect turn from a wolf back into a human?"

That one was interestingly phrased. She could tell by his look that Victor caught it to.

"I don't know the source of the footage yet, or how much it was altered. But I don't think I'm quite ready to say that werewolves are involved," Diaz responded with a grin.

"He means to expose us," Victor said, turning to her. "Did you know about this?"

This was even quicker than she expected. "What... what makes you think that?" she asked, instead of answering him.

"He's being too clever," he replied. "If he'd said there are werewolves, people would wonder what was really going on. By pretending he doesn't know, he's pushing people to the conclusion that werewolves are real."

"Perhaps he should," she said, though she knew what his reaction would be.

"The fact that the very first thing he did when he found out was to immediately procure silver bullets should tell you something," Victor said.

"And if he'd had them from the beginning, several lives might have been saved," she said, and then, before he could answer, she pressed on, "You carry them also. Lots of Were do." She didn't think this was a good time to bring up the tranquilizer gun she'd taken off the Were hunter they'd encountered last year. "If the police knew what they were up against..." It was the same old argument she'd had with him a hundred times. She hoped that he'd see it that way too.

"It appears they do now. Detective Diaz isn't the only one who knows, is he?"

She should have thought about that and was annoyed at herself that she hadn't. "I don't know," she answered honestly. "It's possible that he told at least some of them."

Victor thought for a moment. "Can you persuade him to keep silent? To work with us?" he asked.

She thought about it. This was the crucial moment of their plan. Everything would depend on her playing her part now.

"Did Peter kill the cop at the preserve?" she asked, breaking an unspoken rule between them.

He thought about his answer before giving it. Weighing all the meanings behind the way she'd chosen to phrase the question, she assumed. She didn't expect him to lie. Not to her.

"I don't know," he finally replied. "He did not tell me he did so, but he often doesn't." He confided more to her in that last sentence than he ever had on the subject before. "It may have been another Were. It may even have actually been the wolves."

Neither of them believed that last.

"Then no," she said, answering his earlier question honestly, setting Michael up as a target. "He can't be persuaded."

FIFTEEN

THE BEST LAID PLANS

"Billings wants to see you," Alice said as soon as Michael reached the upper level of the precinct building. "I don't think he's happy."

She didn't look happy herself. He looked past her into his squad's war room and saw that Aaron and Lauren were in there. All of them should be on other duty at the moment.

"You're here early," he started.

She glared at him. "We're having an early all-hands today," she said. "Assuming you're still here after Billings is through."

She was angry as well. Guess he couldn't blame her. He looked around and didn't see Phil anywhere. Might as well get this over with, he thought, and went back down to the Captain's office.

"What the hell are you doing?" Captain Billings asked as soon as Michael stepped into his office. He continued before Michael could respond. "I don't suppose it occurred to you to ask me first?"

"You would have said no," Michael said.

"You don't know that," Davisson replied.

"And if you hadn't," Michael continued, "you'd be responsible. In this case, we thought that plausible deniability would be more important, even with the perception of undermining your authority."

"Well, it's too late now, so I guess we'll never know," he replied. "'We' I take it refers to you and Phil?"

Michael nodded. "It was my decision."

"I assume this is your plan to draw out this Maxwell fellow?"

Michael nodded.

"Well, you've gone and made yourself quite the target," his captain said, "I'll grant you that. I'll let you brief your team. I'm guessing they're not much happier about it than I am. Better fill me in on the rest of your plan now, though. What if they come after your families?"

"I don't think they will," Michael replied. "They'd have nothing to gain by it. I should be their only real target. Our inside source agrees."

"I see. As long as someone agrees with you it doesn't matter what I think? What about the entire rest of your team?" Before Michael could say anything, Billings continued, "You've made them all targets. You don't have any experience with large organized crime like this, and that's the least of the issues. Who knows what else these people can do? They've managed to keep not just their activities but their very existence secret for god only knows how long. I'm guessing they haven't done that by playing nice. You and Phil have taken a lot on yourselves."

This was true of course. "Everyone wearing the badge is a target, no matter what they do," he said. "I don't believe the risk to them is significantly increased."

"And that's not your decision to make. Don't protect me. I need to be in the loop on this at all times from here on out."

Michael just nodded his acceptance.

"There are werewolves," his captain said. "That fact alone is going to change our whole world and you've put the Portland police department right at the center of it."

"HE TRUSTS ME," Veer told the man she was about to betray. "So, it'll be easy to betray him." She couldn't keep the guilt she felt from showing on her face and knew better than to try to hide it from Victor anyway. If he suspected what she was really planning, though, he didn't show any sign of it. He must have had some doubt, but he wanted to believe her. It would break his heart not to. That's what would make it work. For three years she hated herself for not doing what she was about to do, and now that she was finally about to, she hated herself for doing it.

For a moment, she almost envied Michael, his moral clarity, his lack of self doubt. Everything in his world was right or wrong with no room for nuance. No hard decisions and no betrayal of those he loved.

Her role in the trap was easy. Mark the target, make sure he gets to where he was supposed to. She wasn't supposed to get involved, and she didn't have to. Peter, she had no qualms about setting up, but of course he was only one step in the plan to drag the whole secret into the light.

She waited, watching the front of the police station. Two plainclothes cops were watching her obviously from half a block away, sitting at a TriMet station. From time to time another would approach and they'd exchange a few words without looking at each other. She wondered if they knew of her role in all this. She wished she'd arranged some way of contacting Michael beforehand. It was too late now and would be far too dangerous to call him at this point. She'd just have to trust that he knew what he was doing and had control of the rest of the police. At one point, the roaming cop wandered casually behind her car, stopped for a just a moment, then continued on, jaywalking across the street. Most likely checking the license number, which meant they didn't already know who she was. Hopefully they'd run it and talk to Michael before doing anything. She watched as he continued to the end of the block, crossed back over, then around the corner, probably walking into the underground garage to enter the station unseen.

Ten minutes later, Detective Phil Lee came out of the station and walked down to the bus stop. His arm was still in a sling. She wondered if he really needed it. Surprisingly, he actually got on the bus a few minutes later. She didn't know if he was leaving or just being especially sneaky. Injured as he was, Michael probably didn't want him anywhere near the ambush. She didn't know anything about what Peter had planned. Hopefully, they would try to take him alive, perhaps see if they could threaten him or even reason with him first, and not just lure him to the planned spot and immediately take him out from a distance with a high-powered rifle. They all knew it was risky, but this was the best chance either of them had to get what they wanted.

A minute after the bus carried Phil away, Michael emerged from the building as well. He walked up the street another block and got into his car, which he'd left parked at a meter instead of in the garage. She hoped that wasn't making it too obvious. There was a lot that neither side had told her about their specific plans. With any luck, she wouldn't be needed at all. She didn't believe in luck.

When she saw Michael's car moving, Veer started her own car and put it in gear, but before she could pull out into the street, a gray Toyota a couple of spaces behind her zoomed into the street, cutting her off. It immediately swerved into the left lane and took the next left, as Michael had done. She wasn't sure who it was, but assumed it to be driven by one of Peter's compatriots. It was obviously meant to be seen, so he could lose it and think he'd shaken off the pursuit. The other possibility is that it was police, maybe one of several running interference. She pulled out behind it, trying to keep an eye on Michael's Ford several cars ahead of her.

Another car, a green Subaru, shouldered its way in between her and the Toyota. She dropped back and gave it space. The Ford turned left, and the Subaru followed it, but the Toyota went straight. She made her decision and followed that car instead on a hunch. At the next intersection it turned right, taking it even further away from Michael and his unknown pursuer. Had she made the wrong choice? Maybe this car had nothing to do with Michael. Or perhaps his leaving signaled the end of their shift, and now they were heading home. Or to their next assignment. Or, and she felt stupid for not thinking of it before, they knew she was following them and were trying to lead her away deliberately. Shit. It was probably too late now to pick up Michael's trail. No choice but to keep following the Toyota and hope it panned out.

The Toyota turned again, onto Burnside and started heading up the hill. She spotted Michael's Ford, just a half a dozen cars ahead of it, the green Subaru two cars back.

Were they heading toward Beaverton? She was pretty sure the car she had been following was police. He and Michael would be out of their jurisdiction soon. She checked the rear-view mirror and saw a marked police car, then swore as its lights came on. She tried to look ahead to see where the other cars were going, trying to calculate how far she could go before it became obvious that she wasn't just looking for a safe place to pull over.

There was a pull out, just ahead of her. Damn. She pulled into it and saw the three cars ahead of her take a right, just before the road narrowed to a single lane and entered the tunnel. This part of the hill was a maze of winding roads, private drives, and dead ends. They could be going anywhere. She came to a stop, watching the cars disappear ahead. She had to trust that Michael had laid his trap carefully enough that he wouldn't need her to take part.

"Do you know why I pulled you over?" the officer asked the predictable question.

She resisted the urge to reply, "You were afraid I was going to interfere with your ambush?"

"No, I don't," she said instead.

"You didn't signal until you were almost to the street back there," he replied.

Seriously? That's what he was going with?

"Um...sorry?" she said, somewhat bemused.

She was surprised that he hadn't claimed to pull her over for not signaling, but for not signaling enough. It would never stick in court, but of course that wasn't the point.

She handed the cop her license and registration and watched him go back and sit in his car. He could keep her here as long as he wanted, and would certainly delay her long enough that she'd lose the rest of the cars. Should she take off? Risk arrest as she led the officer to the dual ambushes she knew was waiting ahead? Damn Diaz for not filling her in on the whole plan. Damn her for not asking. She didn't know what side this officer was on, or the drivers of the other cars. The officer behind her might help even the odds. Or tip them against them. She knew Victor didn't have anybody in the police, but that didn't mean that Peter didn't. It was probably too late, anyway. There was no way she could find them now.

Veer had almost given up when the cop practically sprinted

back up to her car. He handed her back her papers and with a hurried, "I'm going to let you go with a warning this time, but drive more carefully in the future," he ran back to his car and drove off with the lights flashing, without even waiting for her to pull out first. It was something big then. She started her car and entered the road immediately after him, ignoring the angry blast of the horn from the driver she'd just cut off.

The car turned onto a narrow road. His lights were still on and occasionally blasted the siren. He was going nearly twice the speed limit, and she followed, keeping up with him. She was gambling that whatever he was heading toward, he would be too busy to bother with her.

He ran the siren again, running through a stop sign. A car going the other way stopped for him, then immediately started again when he passed. It almost hit her as she blew through the intersection herself. Another angry blast of the horn. If anyone was watching, they'd know she was coming. The cop car turned again. She recognized this road, leading up to the old Pittock mansion, a scenic drive, not meant to be taken at 50mph. Her car slid on the first switch back, the rear tire spinning over empty air. She pulled hard on the wheel and gunned the engine, hoping to gain traction. The car leapt forward and caught on the badly paved road. She let out a breath.

Fortunately, the police car ahead still had its lights on, or she would have lost him in the heavy rain. She gunned the engine and continued up the hill. They had turned onto an even smaller road. She could just make out a sign proclaiming it private property.

Around another corner the police car had stopped, lights still on. Michael's car was further up, alongside the road. Another car had struck it at an angle - at quite a good rate, judging from the dent in its side. His car had been pushed nearly through the guardrail, its wheels were hanging over the edge. Both cars were empty.

She scanned around the area, and saw the other detective, Phil Lee, laying on the road, his arm still in a cast, raised over his head as if to ward off a blow. It wouldn't do any good. Peter stepped into the light of her headlights. He was battered and bleeding and was holding a gun in his hand. The wounds weren't severe, and she knew they would heal quickly once he transformed. The uniformed officer was outside his car now, gun drawn, using the vehicle for stability. He was shouting something, but Peter wouldn't care. He might take a bullet or two just to scare him. He began to raise the gun. The cop might get a couple of shots in before he could pull the trigger, but it wouldn't matter. Peter would kill everyone here who wasn't a Were.

She made her decision. There would be no hiding it after this. No more chances. For better or worse, everyone would soon know what side she was on. She didn't hesitate. She hit the horn and the accelerator at the same time. All three men turned, as she'd hoped they would, to see the car approaching. There wasn't much room. Her left tires spun in the mud in the shallow ditch on the side of the road. Her right side scraped against the police car. But she made it through and rocketed toward the two men in the roadway.

As she'd hoped he would, the detective rolled to the side, giving her more room to maneuver. Peter raised his gun and pulled the trigger. She could feel the bullet smash into her chest, and hoped it wasn't silver.

But it didn't matter now. The car had enough momentum. She kept her foot pressed to the accelerator. Her hood struck Peter, carrying him off the road and over the edge, down the steep wooded hill. She tucked her head and went into a roll, leading with her shoulder as the car smashed into a tree. She was hurled forward, halfway into her roll, but it was the wolf who flew through the shattered windshield out into the rain.

SHE HIT the tree hard and lay still for a moment before she realized she couldn't move. The impact had broken her back. She could smell the other wolf close by. His scent was thick with fear and pain. She wanted to chase after him but couldn't move. He wasn't moving either. Just a few more minutes. She growled, low and menacing, and was delighted to be answered with a frightened whimper. But a moment later her sense of triumph turned to dismay. The other wolf had dragged himself up and was coming toward her. Her spine was nearly healed, but it might already be too late. He opened his jaws, took one more step closer, and closed them over her throat. She still couldn't move. She growled in anger, but felt the blood begin to flow from her neck. She was feeling cold now, and the light was growing dim. It didn't matter. All that mattered now was getting up, sinking her teeth into the other wolf. She couldn't move her head. There was something wrong with her vision, and a bad smell of decay, of death, nearby.

Then all at once, it felt like very muscle in her body tightened at once as fire washed over her. She tried to howl in pain but all she could do was whimper. The other wolf writhed and let go and rolled off of her.

A new smell had entered the area. She knew this one. A friend. The smell of its anger nearly overpowered that of its fear. It was attacking the other wolf somehow. Whatever it was doing, it was keeping it back, away from her. It wouldn't last, not for long. She twitched her leg. It wouldn't have to.

There was another loud noise and her foe moved away, backing away at first then turning into a spring. She could move again and climbed shakily to her feet. The human approached cautiously. It was speaking and its words conveyed a warning of danger along with a tone of concern. She moved away from it in the direction it had indicated. The human barked a single loud command at that. She ignored him and sprang forward.

The slope upwards was steep and slick, but she managed it. It was frustratingly slow. She could smell her prey, and another whose scent bordered on familiarity. She crested the hill and saw them, locked in struggle. Colored lights from too many sources lit up the area. Two wolves fought. A couple of dead humans lay nearby. Then a loud noise and sudden bright light descended from above. Behind her, her human friend approached, and its scent was now full of fear. Light and noise and rain and wind buffeted her. She couldn't tell what was going on. The noise was growing louder now, nearly deafening her. She turned and slunk back over the slope into the trees. The noise was still increasing, and the lights flashing around in impossible directions. Dirt and gravel flew up from the ground and pelted her. She tried to move more quickly down the slope and slipped in the mud. She slid out of control to the edge of the cliff and over, plummeting to the ground below.

She lay still, the confusion was too great. She wanted to get away but couldn't. Couldn't remember where. This was too much to handle. Too much for the wolf.

———

THE WHOLE PLAN had gone sideways from the start. He wished he knew who was driving that gray Toyota that had been following him in front of Veer's car. Then when the officer pulled Veer over, he swore, and wished they'd come up with some sort of signal. He didn't know who the officer was and didn't want to risk saying anything over an open line. Maxwell, or one of his people, would surely be listening.

With Veer stopped, the car carrying Lauren and Phil passed her and continued on after him. They'd have to do without her. Veer's job was just to make it easier to spot him, which they obviously had. He wasn't too worried about not springing the ambush anymore. He was just worried about surviving it.

The call from a phone booth claiming they had information and asking to meet him at Skyline Tavern was exactly what he'd been expecting. They hoped to surprise him, and he hoped to surprise them more. He had his entire team coming in four different cars. Lauren had stopped long enough to pick up Phil after he'd jumped on, then right back off a bus to throw them off. Aaron and Alice were already at the lodge, scoping out the inside while Donald sat outside in his car, with an open phone line to Michael. They didn't want to chance anything over the radio.

When the car coming down the hill swerved and ran into him, he barely moved in time for it to strike his side door and not head on. He managed to skid to a stop and avoid plunging over the embankment. He wasn't injured but wasn't sure how he was getting out of the car.

"Shit," he yelled into the phone. "It's here. Right now." He quickly gave the location and heard Donald say, "On our way, hang tight."

Lauren and Phil arrived and approached the other car, both of them with weapons in hand, held low and ready. Lauren was shouting at the other driver to get out while Phil crossed the road to check on him. Rosen had thought that they might actually want to talk to him first. Any assassination would be on the way out of the bar not on the way in, she had said. It looked like she was wrong. The ambush had been sprung halfway up the road.

Then they heard a gunshot. It sounded like it was coming from the thick trees further up the hill.

"Sniper!" he yelled out.

Lauren and Phil both hit the ground. Lauren scrambled back toward her car, but Phil was caught out in the open. Michael's own driver side door was smashed in and pinned shut by the other car. Staying low, he pulled the handle of the passenger side door, then gave it a swift kick with both feet when it didn't open. That did the trick. He didn't know where the driver of the other car had gone to. He hoped to spot him before he himself was seen. He slid out of the car feet first and crawled around to the side to have a look.

Phil was on the ground, trying to scramble to safety, while simultaneously awkwardly pulling out his weapon. Peter Maxwell approached him from the car that he'd crashed into Michael's. Maxwell already had a weapon in his hand and was raising it toward Phil. Michael tried to line up a shot on Maxwell when he heard another car and a blast of a horn. Phil rolled to the side right as Veer's car plowed into Maxwell, taking him over the edge. He scrambled over the edge himself, leaving Lauren to check on Phil. He heard another car approaching from above and hoped it was the other half of his team.

He scrambled down the bank to where Veer's car had crashed into a tree. The entire front end was smashed and the windshield lay askew on the remnants of the hood. Two wolves fought below him, just past the vehicle. He struggled to get a foothold on the steep muddy slope, and finally came to a stop, wedged against another tree. One of the wolves he had seen before, sleek and light grey. It was Veer. He didn't know if he could ever get used to that. The other he assumed must be

Maxwell. He didn't dare shoot him on the chance of hitting her. The taser might put an end to the fight regardless of who he hit, though. He tested his theory.

A few seconds later, the larger gray wolf ran up the slope he had just come down, closely followed by the other. It was getting close to the top when the helicopter showed up. He shouted a warning but was sure there was no way she could hear him over the sound of the helicopter. Could she even understand a warning while in wolf shape?

Going up the embankment took a lot longer than sliding down it. He was almost to the top when the helicopter left. He pulled himself over the guard rail, and saw Veer, naked and huddled behind his car, looking out over the hood. He crouched and ran over to her.

"I think it's safe now," she said when she noticed him approaching. "Looks like everyone's gone."

She gave no indication of embarrassment at her state of undress, but he took off his coat and handed it to her. He turned away as she reached for it.

"Thanks," she said with a smile when she had put it on.

He turned back to her and asked, "So what the hell's going on here?"

"I dunno, but there's wounded. C'mon." She stepped out onto the road.

"Careful!" he said, indicating the woods up the hill. "There was a sniper."

"Pretty sure the helicopter got him," Veer said. "They shot someone up there, and I think they took him away in the van."

He looked out over the scene. There didn't seem to be any movement from anywhere. Four cars littered the road, including his and Maxwell's, and a black and white police cruiser with its lights on, flashing red and blue through the rain. He saw someone half in the passenger door of the fourth car and sprinted to it, leaping over shredded clothing on the ground. When he got there, he saw it was Lauren. She wasn't moving.

"Is she okay?" Veer asked.

"She's breathing," he said, checking. "Pulse seems strong, but she's not..."

"Here," Veer said, stooping to pick up something from the ground nearby. She handed him a dart from a tranquilizer gun. He recognized it from her bedroom closet.

"Friends of yours?" he asked.

"They're nobody I know. Pretty sure this came from the helicopter. Not yours, then?"

"I didn't order a helicopter," he said. "That would have blown half my budget for the quarter. We need to get an ambulance up here. Do you know what this stuff is?" He pulled out his phone.

"She'll be okay in a few hours, assuming they use the same thing. Let's try to get her out of the rain. Aw, shit, over here," she said, running back toward the black and white.

He looked apprehensively at Lauren for a second. There was nothing he could do for her right now. He stepped back up and called in to dispatch for backup and an ambulance.

Veer met him as he approached the police cruiser. There was someone else lying face down in the street. Veer moved as if she wanted to stop him from approaching. He recognized the instinct, but he had to check for himself. The cop was obviously dead. Not all of the shooters were using tranquilizers. He didn't see anyone else around.

"What happened up here?" he asked Veer.

She shook her head. "I just saw the last of it. The helicopter was shooting people, and someone - I think the same people who had the helicopter - took at least a couple of people away in a white van. I couldn't get the license number."

For a second, he wanted to jump into one of the nearby cars and tear off trying to catch up to the white van. He realized that even if he could find it, which was doubtful enough as it was, what could he do once he caught up to it? They had already shown they were willing to kill cops who tried to stop them. Besides, there were people here who needed him. Then it hit him. A couple of people, she had said. He had a suspicion who. He ran back over to where the shredded clothing had been. Veer moved to help him once she realized what he was doing

A minute later he found it, amongst the shredded clothing. "Shit," he swore and held it up for her to see: Phil's badge.

"It takes an hour or more after being bitten to truly become a Were," she said, confirming what he feared. "Did you know?"

"No," he said. "He's been faking his injury since the apartment, he must've been. Could they have gotten to him?" he asked, hoping for a reason other than what he expected.

She considered for a moment. "Not Victor, I think, unless he lied to me, which would mean that he knew what I was going to do before I did. Not entirely outside the realm of possibility I suppose."

"What about the others? The ones from the helicopter?"

"We need to know who they are before we can speculate on their motives. Or what they might have offered Phil, if anything."

He raised an eyebrow at that.

"What's police policy on Were?" she asked. "Could he have had his own reasons for hiding it from you?"

It was too perceptive a question for comfort. "Yeah," he admitted. "I didn't realize it was personal to him at the time. I told him then that I didn't know if we'd be able to trust a cop who became a werewolf."

"He lied to you because you wouldn't have trusted him if he had been honest."

"The irony is not lost on me. I hope I get the chance to apologize. Tranq darts mean they were trying to capture them, not kill them, right?"

"Makes sense."

"Any idea who they are?"

She shook her head. "Whoever they are, they're well-funded, and they know what they're doing. They only took the Were and left the humans."

"Are there werewolf hunters?" he asked.

"Every once in a while, one will show up. They never last long though and are dealt with quickly. Usually, they end up imprisoned for murder."

"How's that work?"

"The ones who hunt and kill Were are the easy ones to deal with. We revert to human form when killed, so what you're left with is a dead person and the guy who killed him. Human law can deal with that just fine. If they tell everyone that the person had to die because they were a werewolf, so much the better. What gives the Were more trouble is when someone makes it their mission to expose them."

They walked back over to Lauren's car while they talked. He put the passenger seat down and together they lifted her into it. It wasn't much, but at least she was out of the rain until the ambulance got there.

"But that's not who these guys are," she said once she was in.

"What? How can you be sure?" Michael asked her.

"Too well-organized. If there was anyone this well-equipped, and this efficient, there'd be a whole lot of dead or missing Were. Someone would have noticed."

"A month ago, I would have said the same thing about the very existence of werewolves," he replied.

She smiled at that. "Not quite the same thing. You didn't

believe in werewolves, so you ignored the evidence even when you saw it. Were are almost paranoid about watching for threats."

"Conceded." He nodded. "What about... what, another Alpha trying to take over? Is that a thing that happens?"

"There does seem to be a lot of internal politicking, but I've never heard of open warfare before, which is what this would be. The council wouldn't allow it."

"There's a council?" he asked. It seemed like every time he talked to her there was some new revelation.

"Yeah. I haven't met them yet, but Victor's spoken of them. He answers to them but was never clear as to how."

She reacted to his look. "They might have the resources, but I can't think of why they'd strike now, like this."

"How do you mean?"

"It doesn't make sense. If they wanted you silenced, they'd demand Victor take care of it first. Why interfere right as he was doing that?"

"Makes sense," he agreed. "They also completely ignored us. They didn't search the area, and we didn't interfere with them, so they let us be. Definitely not the actions of a nationwide conspiracy bent on keeping their secret."

"Which brings us back to another group. Unknown capabilities, unknown motives, but willing to kill or abduct police officers and not worry about witnesses."

Through the rain, they could see red and blue flashing lights approaching, winding up the hillside.

"I've got a spare change of clothes in my trunk," she said, nodding toward her car, over the embankment. "It would raise too many questions if they found me like this here."

"All right, hurry," he said. "With your car here, I don't think I can keep you out of it. But if you need to go into hiding..."

"I might," she said. "I pretty much revealed myself when I plowed my car into Peter. I'll let you know if I need help."

"All right. I'll find someone to get you a ride downtown. You'll have to make a statement, but you can keep it brief if you want. After, get to somewhere safe and call me. I'll come find you."

She tossed him his coat and climbed back over the guard rail, carefully making her way down toward her wrecked car. Michael turned his attention to meeting the approaching vehicles.

———

DETECTIVE DIAZ HAD WANDERED off to the far end of the road, where he was engaged with a woman from CSI. A strand of yellow tape stretched across the road behind him. Somebody had brought him a cup of coffee. She could really use a cup herself. No coffee for the witnesses, though, apparently. Perhaps there would be for the cooperative ones. The ambulance had already left with Detective Boyd.

The conversation with the cop, who still hadn't told her his name, wasn't going as well as Veer had hoped, and she hadn't expected it to go that well in the first place.

"Look, I told you all I can," she said for at least the third time. "Can I go now?"

"No, Miss Rosen," he said, "you can't go now."

"Am I under arrest?" she asked.

"Not unless you try to leave."

"That doesn't even make any sense," she said.

"Leaving the scene of an accident is a felony," the police officer told her.

"Bullshit," she replied, knowing as she said it that it was the wrong thing to say. "Look, I didn't flee the scene. I gave my statement, you have my contact information, you can't just keep me here forever."

"I can keep you here as long as I need to," he snarled. "There's a dead cop, and another missing, along with the drivers of two other cars. Of everyone involved, there's only you left, without a scratch on you despite the state of your vehicle. You can stay here until I find out what you're hiding."

She'd had enough. She'd made a living out of reading people, of saying what they wanted to hear, of putting them at their ease, or off of it, whatever was needed to get them to talk. There was something wrong here. She couldn't quite put her finger on it, but there was an almost palpable danger.

Which made no sense. There was nothing here that could harm her. Only one person, possibly two, would have had silver bullets, and one of them was at the far end of the road, and the other was missing.

The cop was angry. Had he known the deceased, or was he just taking it personally because he was a fellow officer? She could run. She could push right past him and roll over the edge of the embankment. She could even just dive over it and slide down into the bushes. She might break a few bones. The pain would be intense, but only for a few seconds. She would be completely out of sight before she changed. She wouldn't even need to break secrecy.

But there was a story here. She didn't know what was going on, but it was huge. Something even bigger than a botched assassination and a failed trap. She stood up, angrily. "No," she said, "unless you are planning to arrest me," she got no further than that.

Suddenly he was on her, her arm twisted behind her back. It was only because she'd already changed so recently and had just been thinking about it that she was able to resist the instinct to do so as she fell. Her face pressed against the muddy road as the cop used his weight to hold her down.

She felt the cold hard metal of the handcuffs bite into her wrist. He was not gentle.

"Hey!" she cried out as he wrenched her other arm around. She let him.

The man said nothing.

I could get out of this, she thought. *I could change, break these cuffs, get away*. Too many people here, though. Changing now would reveal herself. She didn't laugh at the irony. Enduring the pain and the humiliation in order to keep a secret that she was planning to reveal.

But she didn't dare change now.

The officer was frisking her now, and not being gentle about it, or wholly appropriate. When she pulled away from his touch, he pushed her hands upward, causing the cuffs to bite more painfully into her wrists. Pain shot up her arms.

"Stop it!" she cried. "I'm not resisting arrest!"

He didn't speak. That was more terrifying than if he'd gloated, or even threatened. She found herself hoping Michael would notice what was happening and intervene. And immediately grew angry at herself for wishing it. She wasn't some damsel in distress, and he was certainly not her knight in shining armor. She could get out of this any time she wanted. If he went too far, or caused any injury she would tear his throat out. There was no way the cuffs could hold her. Diaz persisted in being on the other side of the crime scene. No help there. Even if he hadn't been, there was no guarantee he'd do anything, or even take her side. For all their recent cooperation, he was police too, after all.

Eventually the man yanked her harshly to her feet and over toward the police car. When he pushed her inside, she let herself fall, just a bit, to thwart his attempt to bang her head into the car's roof. That earned her another wrenching of her hand-cuffed arms and a sharp kick to the back of her knee. As she fell across the back seat, he grabbed her leg in both hands and twisted it, hard, which forced her the rest of the way into the seat.

He slammed the door behind her, leaving her laying on her side breathing heavily.

At least she was out of the rain.

He is the kind of man who likes hurting women, she began to compose the story in her mind. No, make that, *who likes hurting people.* That would appease the more sensitive among her readers and avoid the common misogynistic trolls who liked to derail the comments section of the online article. She'd have to remember every push, squeeze, twist, every indignity and unnecessary extra painful act for later, and catalog them all carefully so it was clear she was merely reporting on them, not complaining or whining. She'd have to stress how unnecessary each was as clearly as she could to avoid the "Well, why didn't you just cooperate" responses from the usual authoritarians.

He didn't kill anyone, she continued to compose the article in her mind. *There were not even injuries that were serious enough to require treatment. He was careful. Is this how it begins? 'I can twist your wrist like this, causing you to shout out in pain.' And he can get away with it. Nothing can be done there. 'I can spend an extra couple of seconds squeezing your breast while frisking you,' and again, no actual injury is done. But the message is clear: 'I can do anything I want to you and you can't do anything to stop me.'*

Maybe the next person is hurt just a little bit more. Eventually someone fights back, which gives him an excuse to break a wrist or crack a skull and again he gets away with it, as all witnesses will agree the suspect wasn't complying. He may go his whole career without ever committing outright murder. But every person he hurts, even if there is no reportable injury, and every woman he touches inappropriately, even if there is no prosecutable molestation, is one more hurt, scared, angry person who distrusts the police in general a little bit more. Each act drives just a little bit more wedge between the community and the police, makes everyone just a little less cooperative, less willing to deal with the police, less likely to report a crime.

The real question isn't what can we do to stop him before he really hurts someone. The question is, is this really the kind of man we want in the police force? Is this the face the Portland PD wants to put forth? Is this something that we should even tolerate? Why do his fellow police support this kind of behavior? Do they believe this kind of power is actually deserved? That it is good and right that they have this kind of power over the rest of us? And what kind of society, and what kind of relationship between the police and the community does that create, and is that really what we want?

It needed work but writing it in her head helped distract her from the pain and discomfort.

She tried to turn over and sit up, which caused the handcuffs to bite even more painfully into her wrists. She looked out the window and saw the police officer nearby arguing with Detective Diaz.

He's here to rescue me, she thought, then angrily suppressed the notion.

She could get out any time she wanted. *The glass wouldn't be bulletproof.* Michael had told her that in their very first real conversation. The one in which she told him the truth about the world he was stumbling into. There was nothing stopping her from leaving. *So why didn't she? To keep the secret?* She couldn't lie to herself. She wasn't that noble. She stayed for the same reason she always did. The same reason she sat through to the end of that execrable Godzilla movie. She had to see what happened next.

Michael tried to approach the car, but the cop blocked him. She could tell they were arguing but couldn't make out what was said. Finally, he just pushed through him. She could imagine a lot of what was said, as each of them tried to pound the other into submission with their authority.

"If you want to stop me, you'll have to shoot me," he probably said, or some other cliche chest-pounding. "And I doubt you have the balls for that," he might have added.

She smiled at the dialog she was playing in her mind, making them both into schmaltzy action heroes. "The Hero Cop Who Breaks All The Rules!" she laughed out loud at the idea.

He walked up to the front door of the car. The cop who arrested her was a couple of paces behind him. Michael opened the door and leaned in.

"How're you doing?" he asked, and at least had the good grace to look embarrassed.

He's not releasing me, she realized, or else he would have opened the back door, not the front.

"Been better," she replied with a scowl. She saw no reason to cut him any slack.

"All right, fair enough," he said, obviously understanding her anger. "Look, I tried to get you out of here, but this is Jones' little hill and he insists on taking you in."

"Isn't this supposed to be your operation? Aren't you in charge here?" she asked.

"It's more complicated than that. There are jurisdictional issues. We haven't let most of the force know what we're up to..."

It wouldn't make sense to do so now. She couldn't really fault him for that.

"I could stop him," she said.

He seemed to be expecting that. He nodded. "You could. Do you want to?"

She didn't answer that. "Did he know the cop who got shot?" she asked instead.

He didn't seem to be expecting that. "Why?" he asked.

"He seems to be taking the whole thing kind of personally," she offered by way of explanation.

That earned her a worried look.

"Nothing I can't handle," she said, "but I think a police escort might be a good idea."

He thought about it for a moment. "I won't be able to get away from here for a few hours at least... but I'll see what I can do."

"Better yet," she said, "call my editor. Let him know what's up."

"All right," he agreed, and quickly jotted down the number.

She trusted him enough to make the call, and somehow convince Don that it was important without revealing why.

The trip to the second precinct was uneventful. Perhaps Michael did have some influence after all. When they got to the police station, the cop was considerably more reasonable. There was a lawyer already waiting for her there. She recognized her immediately. She wasn't from the paper. She was one of Victor's.

"Vera Rosen?" she asked as Veer was led past, her hands still cuffed behind her. "I am Dianne Solomon. I'm your attorney. The police are going to process you now, but say nothing until after we've had a chance to talk."

She nodded slightly, as her captor pushed her along quickly. The lawyer allowed herself to be pushed back by another police officer.

Sitting in an interview room after the usual fingerprinting

and processing, Veer noticed there was no mirror on the wall. She'd spent her share of time in police stations but hadn't been in one of these rooms before. She supposed she'd expected there to be a one-way mirror on the wall just because there always was on TV. She felt vaguely disappointed.

"That's a pretty fancy lawyer you've got there," a detective Veer hadn't met before said as he entered. "Tell me how a third-rate stunt reporter like you ends up with serious muscle like that?"

"Third rate?" she replied in a reproachful tone.

"It is what it is," he replied insipidly.

"Maybe the paper has a higher opinion of my writing than you do," she replied. "Do you find starting out with insults usually helps you get information from people?"

"Aw, you weren't going to tell me anything," he answered her.

"So why are you even here?" she asked him.

The cop shrugged. "Had to try at least before your expensive mouthpiece got here."

"And yet you didn't," she replied testily.

He looked puzzled at that. Veer thought for a second of saying something by way of explanation but decided not to bother. She wasn't sure if she should mention that she was part of an investigation being conducted by a secret task force in another precinct. She didn't owe this man anything and didn't have anything to gain by educating him. She ignored his unvoiced request for an explanation and instead indicated her hands, still cuffed behind her. "You wanna let me out of these before you send in my expensive mouthpiece?"

He didn't answer, but instead just stood up and walked to the door.

As the door shut behind him, she realized her situation. She was handcuffed here in a room with no windows or recording equipment, and the woman who was about to visit her was one of Victor's.

She leaned back again, trying hard to mimic the posture she'd assumed before. It wouldn't do to show fear. No, confidence was the way to go here. She wondered if she was killed in this room how long it would take for her body to be discovered. *Don't think like that. Would there even be an investigation? Stop it. Show no fear.*

No, this was paranoia. The attorney wouldn't be her judge. Victor would reserve that right for himself. Of course, he might already have done so and just sent this woman to be her executioner. In that case, it didn't matter what she said. She wasn't going to talk her way out of this. If the lawyer used a gun, she might be able to change and attack her before she could fire it. She wondered what the cops would do if they came in here and found two wolves fighting.

If she wasn't here to eliminate Veer, then she was here as a messenger. She thought it over while sitting there. Almost certainly the latter, she decided. Victor would want to hear her side of the story before deciding to have her killed outright. She hoped. Either way, it wouldn't do to show any fear.

"I bring a message," the attorney said as she took the chair opposite her. Veer almost laughed out loud. That removed any ambiguity about her role here. "It is from our mutual acquaintance, Mr. Stumpp," she went on.

Veer did smile at that. Victor might be an acquaintance to the other woman, but to her he was a friend. Well, sort of. Whatever he was, there was obviously a mutual respect still, and she wasn't going to let some minion push her around. It wasn't just pride. If they knew, or suspected, that she had a special relationship with the Alpha, they'd be far less likely to damage or kill her without making absolutely sure that that was what he wanted.

"What's Victor want to tell me?" she asked with a slight tone of reprimand. She emphasized the name.

That took the other woman back a bit. Veer could see the gears turning in her mind. Was Veer unaware of the danger? Or was she truly on a first name basis with the boss? Which it was would make a difference. If the latter, she'd need to be careful, properly deferential, but not too much so. Veer could be a valuable ally, with the ear of the Alpha, but if she showed her too much respect, and she just turned out to be a blustering nobody, then she could lose the respect of her peers, so important to the politically ambitious.

Veer sat quietly, with a slight smile on her face, and gave her time to worry about it. She chose the middle ground.

"Mr. Stumpp wants you to meet him in his office. I trust you know where that is?"

This woman really had no idea.

"I know where it is," she replied. "But I'm kinda busy at the moment."

"That's taken care of," her lawyer said. Of course, she would have waited until now to say anything. Score one for the attorney.

"Interesting," she said out loud, trying to keep her tone neutral. "And he expects I'll just walk into his office for a friendly chat?"

The other woman hesitated a moment, as if she didn't want to say what she was about to. "He said that if you showed any reticence to tell you that he bears you no malice, and that he has need of Nellie Bly."

Veer wondered if the woman knew what that meant. She believed that Victor bore her no malice. That wouldn't make any difference, of course. He wouldn't need it to eliminate her. He could love her like his own child and still put her down if that was the necessary thing to do. He might do it with sadness and regret, but he wouldn't let that stop him. The last half was intriguing, though. She wasn't sure what he meant by it, but now she wanted to find out. Which was, no doubt, the reason for the statement to be phrased that way. He knew her all too well. No surer way to keep her from going into hiding than by presenting an intriguing mystery.

She thought about it for a second. "All right," she said. "Take a message back to him. I'll meet him, but not in his office. Tell him..." She thought about it for a second. Victor wasn't the only one who could send cryptic messages. If he wasn't going to trust this person with too much information, neither was she. "Tell him that I'll meet him tomorrow at the opening, if his hair is perfect."

It was a thin joke. A reference to an old conversation they'd had about their respective times in London, his with Gregor after the war, and hers more recently, during a semester abroad back in college.

"What does that mean?" the attorney asked her.

"He'll figure it out," Veer told her.

"He wants to meet you in his office," she repeated.

"We don't always get what we want," she said with a smile. "Not even Victor." She leaned back stiffly, emphasizing the handcuffs she was still wearing.

She hadn't said it just to elevate herself in the attorney's eyes. She wasn't that important. Her hope was that the message would amuse Victor and remind him that she was a friend, regardless of their current cross purposes.

The attorney was as good as Veer had guessed she was. Someone came in to release her within a minute of her departure.

SIXTEEN
CONCEPTS AND CONCEPTIONS

Toni sat up on the grass beside him and stretched. Carl smiled up at her. She looked down where he was lying beside her. She didn't smile back.

"What?" he asked her.

She didn't speak but stared off into the woods. He gave her time.

"What are we doing?" she finally said.

"What do you mean?" he said, then regretted it. She had already told him - she wasn't his girlfriend: "We just fucked, that's all," she had said. "Don't make it into something it's not." He had made the mistake of calling it "making love." It wasn't that. She didn't love him, and he'd never given her reason to.

It was, though, becoming familiar. Almost every day, heading deep into Forest Park, he never realized how far it went, and how little of it was actually reachable by hiking trails. If he'd known about it before going to the preserve... Well, things would have turned out a lot differently. But they had come here now, seeking out the hidden byways. Changing, running, occasionally hunting, sleeping until they changed back, then, more often than not making love - or whatever it was they were doing. Frantic, emotionally and physically draining, sex, as if it were their last chance ever. Every time. And always the long walk back, naked, cold, and plotting the future.

He didn't know what they were doing. It was confusing and it was intense and as he looked up at her now standing, warming herself in the dawning sunlight, he knew he didn't want it to ever end.

"Turning those people next week? Do we really want to do that? Do we have the right?"

"Oh. That!" He hadn't considered that she was talking about their plan. Tonight would be the warehouse party, the last screening step before they decided which six new wolves to initiate first. They had decided on six as the most they could reasonably change at once. Six people whose lives they were going to irrevocably change and throw into danger.

She turned to face him. "Oh, that?" she mimicked. "Forgive me for thinking it was kind of a big deal. But if you don't think so, hey, no worries, just another day at the office for Carl. Yeah, I'll stop reconsidering and worrying about how much we're going to be fucking up these people's lives, and trying to forestall problems. Just plow ahead and see what happens, right?" She paused for a second, then asked, "Wait. What did you think I was talking about?"

There was no way in hell he was answering that question now. "You think we should tell them the truth?" he suggested, in a desperate attempt to avoid the subject.

"Let them know that there really is no centuries-old conspiracy, you mean?"

"There is. We're just not part of it."

"Not all of us at any rate."

He'd almost forgotten. He had been too caught up in

excitement for their planned future that he hadn't been thinking of their current circumstances.

"The overall goal here," he began, on a different tack, "is to reveal the existence of the were, right?"

She looked out, past him, thinking about it. "And the reason for that is to lift my death mark. Right."

"I don't really like putting it that way, it's not..."

"But aren't we putting that same mark on somebody else? Maybe somebody we haven't even met yet?"

He looked up and met her eyes.

"Only for a short time. Once there's enough of us, and once we're revealed, there'll be no reason to kill any of them. Or anybody else in the future. This isn't all just for you," he continued. He wanted to add that even if it was, he'd still do it. That it would be worth it. "We're building a better life for all Were," he said. "Possibly for generations to come."

She gave him a skeptical look. "Seriously," he continued. "How many people - how many generations - lived and died under the rule of the Alphas? In a society outside the law, whose rules they had no say over?"

"So, you're, what, the Thomas Jefferson of the wolves?" She laughed.

"I wish we had a Thomas Jefferson with us now. We could use one. This may be our last chance for a long while. Maybe ever. Technology is changing like crazy right now. That can't help but change the world. The internet has given us incredible ability to get the word out - to communicate. To organize. And everyone - criminals, governments..."

She snorted at that. They had discussed the blurry line between the two, but he didn't want to derail his point by acknowledging it now. "And the Alphas," he continued. "They're all scrambling to monitor it and control it. It's only a matter of time before they succeed. When only a few large companies own the entire net, they can shut down discussion, stop news from propagating, isolate us and keep any secret they want. If we're going to succeed, it has to be now."

"Okay," she said. "Yeah, we've been through this before. It's just that the closer we get, the more real it seems to become, and the more real it gets, the more fleeing to Montana seems like a good idea."

"God, I've been tempted," he said, "believe me, I've thought about it a lot. The thought of running away with you..." he turned his gaze from her and looked out into the woods. "I don't think Montana would be far enough."

Something caught his eye among the shrubbery.

"Hey, what's that?" he pointed it out.

Something in the underbrush didn't look right. Too flat, too uniform. They walked over to it. Someone had built a small shelter, a lean-to, and covered it, camouflaging it to look natural. If he hadn't been standing fifteen feet away and staring right at it, he never would have seen it.

"What's it doing here?" he asked. It was at the edge of a small clearing where they'd slept, reached only by a tiny game trail.

"Probably built by some homeless guy - a place where he stays so he doesn't have to sleep in the city," Toni said, crouching down and looking into it.

"Shit. If someone was here..." he started.

"I don't think so," she said. "Looks abandoned. Nice, though. Surprisingly roomy, and dry."

Against his better judgment, he crawled in after her. There was enough room that, if they hadn't already slept, they could have both fit comfortably, lying side by side. There was a tarp floor, pulled up on three sides and tied to a crude A-frame. Another tarp was overlaid from the top, and the whole thing covered in greenery obviously gathered from nearby. There was no sign of its inhabitant. They crawled back out.

"There's probably dozens of these, scattered around the park," she mused.

"If it's abandoned, where'd its owner go?" he asked.

"I dunno. Where does anyone go?" she answered him. "A friend offered a couch? Ex-wife let them back in the house? Got a job or got arrested or pissed off the local community somehow and had to move on?"

He hadn't thought of any of that. The builder was as big of a mystery to him as most of the people moving about the city.

"C'mon," she said. "Let's go find our clothes."

They walked in silence for several minutes. She was a few steps ahead of him on the trail when she asked, without turning around, "So you're not having any second thoughts about turning them?"

He was quiet for a moment, considering what to say. He really hadn't thought about it much at all but didn't want to say that.

"I honestly can't think of anything else we could do," he said.

"I wasn't complaining," she said, after a few minutes. "It's just... it's all so weird. It's almost like a dream."

"I would have thought it would have become real after Hudson."

"That was the most surreal moment of all."

He almost laughed out loud at that. "That was more surreal to you than turning into a wolf?"

She smiled at him. "I've always loved wolves. I've always wanted to be able to turn into one." She dropped the smile and continued, "I've never aspired to murder."

"Wait..." he felt like he was playing catch up again. "You

wanted to turn into a wolf before you knew there was such a thing?"

"Sure. Didn't you?"

"I honestly never thought about it," he replied.

"So how did you become a wolf?" she asked.

He had told her before, but he answered anyway. "Kevin turned me."

"No, I mean... why? Or, how. No..." she fumbled for the words. "I mean... you didn't ask me because you didn't think I'd believe you," she finally said.

And the guilt and uncertainty washed all over him again. He couldn't bring himself to regret what he had done to her, and he felt even more guilty because of that. Someone else had died that night, and he couldn't even remember his name. Kevin and Shelly had disposed of the body the next morning. They never told him how. Mitch, who had become a Were, had disappeared. Kevin and Shelley hadn't heard anything from him, either, and that scared him. He could be anywhere, doing anything. And who would die next week? Nobody, he told himself. He wasn't Kevin. Of course, the death of Hudson the next morning had been his own doing. He didn't regret that one, though. Hudson had been a threat to them both.

"What about you?" Toni continued as if she hadn't even noticed he'd been lost in thought. "And what about the rest? How come you believed them, but didn't think anyone else would?"

"That was different," he replied. "I'd known Kevin for about a year. He got permission from the Alpha, and finally approached me. He told me about this whole society and asked me to join them."

"So why couldn't you do the same thing?"

"It would take too long."

"You mean you were impatient. I get the limited window,

and yeah, you're probably right. That window is probably going to close within our lifetime." She paused and watched his reaction, "But not within a year. You could have taken a year, gotten to know me first. Maybe we coulda been... something."

They walked for a while in silence. They found their clothes where they'd left them and got dressed for the walk back to her car.

"So..." he began finally, not really sure what he was going to say next.

"Yeah," she said. "We should tell them everything. It's actually a better myth when you think about it. Instead of joining an ancient conspiracy like you were sold on, they're going to be the first of the new guard, standing up to the ancient conspiracy."

"And it happens to be true," he added.

"Myths always work better when they're true."

GORDON'S first day back at work had gone about as well as he'd expected. He'd purposely started on a Friday, knowing that most of the day would be spent on condolences, welcomes back, and coming up to speed with what had happened at the office the last few weeks. Monday would be business as usual.

The office had seemed surreal after the last few weeks. All these people going about their lives with no idea about what was really going on out there. From the religious, devout or not, to "spiritual," to devoted rationalist, not one of them had a clue to the truth of the world. Or did they? He was realistic enough to know that just because it was a revelation to him didn't mean it was to everyone else. As he had looked around, he wondered how many of these people already knew what he had just discovered. How many were werewolves themselves, keeping their secret from everyone they knew? How many knew even more secrets of the world? Maybe there even were vampires out there somewhere. Maybe even in this very office. Oh god, what if what happened to him hadn't been a random attack, and he'd actually been chosen for... some reason? No, it would be too easy to get caught up in paranoia. He shook his head to clear it as he selected a suit to wear that night. Don't get lost in conspiracy theories, he told himself, then laughed out loud when he considered that he was about to go engage in a conspiracy within another conspiracy opposing an even older conspiracy. If there was a rabbit hole here, he had hit the bottom of it, drank the mysterious potion, and was well into his second cup of tea with the Hatter.

He stared into the closet again.

He chose an older suit, a few years out of style, with a cut that echoed an earlier era still. It should communicate his desired role: an older conspirator, out of touch with day-to-day mundanities. An ageless agent with unknowable connections and resources. He smiled at that. Probably not one of these kids had a lick of fashion sense anyway. The subtleties would be lost on them. Then he laughed at his condescension. Perhaps the part of the out of touch fogey wouldn't be that much of a stretch after all.

He parked a few blocks away from the Northwest ware-house where the party was supposed to be. He looked around. He was pretty sure he'd been to a rave in one of these places about twenty years ago. It hadn't changed much since then, when everything else in the world had. Barbara hadn't been born then. He hadn't even met her mother yet. He walked to the warehouse, ducking his head against the light rain. Inside, there were a dozen or so kids milling about. He didn't recognize any of them. A strange sense of time folding back on itself engulfed him. Like the last twenty years hadn't happened, or

had just been a brief hallucination brought on by too much acid
and flashing lights and techno music. "One you lock the target.
Two, you bait the line," he thought to himself. How many hours
had he spent dancing to that song alone?

There was nobody dancing here, though. No flashing
lights, no blasting electronic music, and he'd be willing to bet
no drugs of any kind. A pair of speakers in the corner were
playing some song he couldn't name but was certain he'd heard
before coming from Barbara's room. The volume was set low
enough to talk over. A few couches had been placed against the
walls and a couple of cheap folding tables against one wall held
various snacks. A counter that looked like it had been ripped
out of somebody's kitchen twenty years ago stood near the back
wall and a young woman he didn't recognize stood behind it,
mixing drinks. Not the kind of wild party this place had likely
seen in the past. Several strands of Christmas lights, hung high
on the walls, provided the illumination. Aside from a few old
posters, torn and fading, scattered around, there were no other
decorations. The kids - and kids they were, he realized, not a
one of them over 25, he'd bet - glanced at him as he walked by,
then quickly looked away.

No sign of Toni or her not-boyfriend. He made his way to
the back of the room and approached the bar and the woman
behind it. She watched him approach, wearing a knowing
smile. A couple of guys hanging out in front of it found reasons
to be elsewhere.

"What'll you have?" the woman behind the bar asked.

"Do you have any whiskey?" he asked. He wondered if she
was selling ecstasy, too. Probably not. He recognized the kids
already present now. These were the uncool kids - the ones
who showed up to parties on time and stood awkwardly about,
trying to have conversations.

She reached under the bar and opened a cabinet to pull out

the bottle. The good stuff, he smiled, recognizing a bottle of blended scotch of a brand he used to purchase when younger and felt like splurging. Some things never change, he supposed.

"I'm afraid all we've got is plastic," she said, taking a red cup off an inverted stack on the bar top.

He nodded gratefully and reached for his wallet, but she waved it off.

"You must be Gordon," she said. He was not surprised she knew who he was. She was obviously connected to the runners of this party.

"I'm afraid you have me at a disadvantage," he said.

She smiled at that. The antiquated phrasing was deliberate. He decided he'd be the airy sophisticate tonight.

"Shelly," she said, offering her hand.

That did surprise him. He took her hand. "Kevin's girlfriend?"

"Is that what I am?" she asked. She smiled an easy smile when she said it. "I'm not a person on my own, just defined by my boyfriend?"

"Ha! You sound like my daughter," he said. The loss was painful, but the memory a happy one. "No insult was intended. I just don't know much about the relationships here. I had just been under the assumption that your group and Toni's didn't see eye to eye."

"Toni's?" she repeated, with a raised eyebrow. "But, no, we have different ways of doing things maybe, but there's no animosity there. We all have the same goal. As for me and Kevin..." she paused for a second. "We look after Carl."

He wasn't sure what to make of that. It almost sounded like a threat. "Speaking of whom..." he started.

"In the back," Shelly said, pointing toward a door leading to the small office in the far back of the warehouse.

This room, if such it could be called, was an obviously amateur addition to the warehouse. The walls went up about eight feet. Probably exactly eight feet, he guessed. The height of a single sheet of dry-wall. On this side the framing was visible, and he could see that whoever had built it hadn't bothered with a roof. Carl and Toni were sitting on an ancient couch against the wall, and one of the girls from the coffee shop was there, as well as a couple of guys he didn't recognize. Everyone in their mid-20's. One of the men, sitting in a chair near the open back door and smoking a cigarette, nodded in greeting. Toni stood up and walked over to him, hand outstretched. A second later, Carl arose and stood awkwardly behind her.

"Gordon! You came. Excellent. I'd hoped you would," she said, shaking his hand.

She turned and made the introductions. "Will." She indicated the nearest smoking man. "And Kevin." The other. He recognized that name.

"Kevin? Shelly's boyfriend?" he asked. He smiled inwardly to himself at that. At least now if they compared notes afterward there'd be symmetry.

"Carl you know... kind of," Toni continued the introductions.

"Ah yes, good to meet you formally." He recognized him from the Pied Cow.

"Dexter," Carl replied, calling him by the alias he'd used in emails. He shook his hand as well. "And Kim, who you've also seen but not met yet." One of the other girls from the coffee shop. He nodded to her in greeting.

"If the goal of tonight was to see who you want to invite, why's everyone back here, instead of out mingling?" he asked.

"Just touching base real quick. Also wanted to make the introductions. What do you think so far?"

"Depends on what you're going for. I don't see any of them

being the particularly ambitious type, or independent-minded. Dunno if you want to avoid or seek out such people, though. I assume more will be arriving as the evening progresses?"

"Probably both," Carl replied, after a moment of thought. "A few go-getters maybe, to help keep things moving. A bunch of sheep to fill out the numbers."

That actually surprised him. He wouldn't have guessed that Carl would have given this some thought already. He could see from their reactions that none of the others had.

"Also," he said, taking on his role, "you should have a tip jar at the bar."

"It's already all paid for," Kevin said. There was a note of pride, and Gordon wondered exactly how that had been arranged. None of these kids looked like they had a lot of money. He supposed that between the lot of them they could probably have scraped together enough to cover rent on the warehouse for a night. It could just as easily have been borrowed from a friend of a friend, or maybe they just broke into it. Given what he'd seen, he guessed that to be unlikely. The most expensive part of the whole thing was probably the liquor and that could have easily been donated from a number of individual private stashes.

"That's not the point," he said. "Look at their reactions. See who tips and how much, and how often. Who tips way over the top? That person is over eager to please - what does he want? Is he a cop? Or an infiltrator who wants everyone to like him? What about the person who doesn't tip at all? Probably can't be counted on to contribute much. Selfish types who think indi-vidualism means not getting along with other people. People who tip just a dollar, but with every drink, they're probably the best socialized - they understand the unwritten rules, but don't go overboard. What kind of money do they have? Someone with a bunch of twenties wasn't prepared for an open bar.

Someone with just a few ones wasn't prepared to leave the house. And the ones who make rude comments about the donation, or sneer at those who tip when they don't have to - well, those are the assholes and it's probably best to weed them out of any group early."

Kevin frowned at that. Gordon was pretty sure he'd pegged him right, then: a self-described asshole and Damn Proud Of It.

"Assuming that's what you want to do," he continued. "After all, if your only goal is to swell your numbers as quickly as possible, the complete assholes might be some of your best recruiters. Just prepare yourselves for having to work with them."

The reactions from everyone in the room was significantly more than Gordon would have expected from a minor joke. There was some significance here. An ongoing argument. But as Kevin was about to say something, Carl stood up. "C'mon," he said, stepping toward the door. "Let's get this party started." Everyone looked relieved at that.

Gordon decided to give them a few minutes before following. Give them a chance to establish themselves before disrupting everything with his mysterious presence routine. It had been a long time since he'd smoked. Before Barbara was born. He wondered if it was even possible for him to get lung cancer now.

"Hey, Will, right?" he said before the kid got up. "You got an extra one of those?"

He took the proffered cigarette and accepted a light before stepping out onto the back patio. "Might as well look the part," he said to no one in particular.

He finished his cigarette in the smoking section out back that he noticed nobody, including the few people he'd seen smoking, were using. When he was done, he figured enough

time had passed to make his appearance. He was just in time
for the drama.

"I said, get out," Shelly, still standing behind the bar, was
saying to a young man on the other side of it.

"You're not in charge here," the man replied. "I was invited..." Then he made the mistake of reaching across the bar
toward Shelly. Gordon wasn't sure if he was trying to strike her,
grab her, or just over-emphasize an attempt to point at her, but
whatever he was doing, she wasn't having it.

She grabbed his wrist in one hand and twisted it, took his
elbow with her other hand and pushed it back toward him, still
pulling the wrist towards herself. He half-twisted around in an
attempt to escape her hold and she moved straight down, taking
his arm with her. If the bar hadn't been in the way, the move
probably would have sent the man to the floor. Instead, it
slammed his elbow into the bar. He gave a short loud gasp as he
struck. She didn't let go but stood holding his forearm tight
against the bar top. The whole thing had taken less than half a
second.

Carl took a step forward while the man struggled to free
himself. Shelly had him well in hand and wasn't letting him up.
Kevin gestured to a couple of other guys and they immediately
followed him to the bar. When they got there, Shelly let go of
her assailant, who was still trying to argue. Gordon stopped
himself from jumping in. He wanted to see how these kids
would handle it. He quickly glanced around. Toni was on the
other side of the room, looking around, as he was. Carl stood
nearby, looking back and forth as if not sure what to do.

The man from the bar spotted him. "Hey! These guys are..."

Carl cut him off. Taking a deep breath and squaring his
shoulders, he looked right at him. "Weren't you told to get out?"

"What, you're gonna let the girl speak for you?" the man

started again. Gordon almost cringed seeing the hole the poor bastard was digging for himself.

"Decision's been made," Carl said. "Why're you still talking?"

It was a good line. Gordon wondered where he'd stolen it from. Sounded like a quote from a movie. A western, probably.

Carl nodded to Kevin who, with a broad grin gestured to his two friends who moved in on the bar guy. He shook them off. "I'm going!" he muttered and walked to the door. Carl went ahead and opened it for him, Kevin and his two friends close behind.

Gordon turned his attention back to Shelly. "Nice move," he said.

"Thanks," she said. "Little party trick I picked up years ago."

He almost laughed at that. He had been happy when Barbara started being interested in Kung Fu a while back. Not just for self-defense, but the overall discipline would have been good for her. Like most things, though, she had soon lost interest and moved on to something else.

The others came back to the bar. "Drinks for the heroes," she said, pouring everyone one. He noticed that Carl looked hesitant, as if he wasn't sure he deserved one. Shelly poured him a rum and coke and slid it across the bar to him without making him ask. And when Gordon looked at her, she poured out another measure of whiskey from the same bottle she'd used when he came in. The excitement over, Toni, from across the room, waved Carl to her and he went to join her and the man she'd been talking to. Kevin wandered about, talking to various people. Shelly pulled an ashtray out and set it on the bar, next to a candle that she then lit. She retrieved a pack of cigarettes as well and lit one from the candle.

Seeing his look, she said, "I don't see any no-smoking signs."

"Hah, finally someone around here breaking the rules," he said with a smile.

"Here," she said, sliding the pack over to him. He took one out and followed her lead, lighting it from the candle.

"There," she said. "Now you can't report me 'cause you're breaking the law too."

They passed the rest of the evening talking, smoking, drinking, and discussing the others at the party. She'd mix drinks as people came up to the place. He would stand and smoke and watch everyone try not to make eye contact. From time to time Carl or Toni or both would stop by and they'd compare notes. "That one's a little aggressive toward his dance partner there," he'd say, or "That one's awfully quiet and afraid to approach anyone." Or "That one's really taking advantage of the free booze, I wouldn't trust her judgment, or even her ability to get home safely."

He noticed Toni had a different set of criteria that would evolve as the night went on and had made the effort to learn their names. "The drunk one's Carrie, she's a computer programmer," she would say, or "Her friend Jacob there likes to work on cars." "Tyler works at Fry's," and "The blonde girl, Cynthia, owns a fifteen passenger van." He didn't know what she was planning and wasn't sure he wanted to. Maybe she didn't know herself and was just preparing for a variety of possibilities.

More people had arrived as the night wore on. Someone turned the music up and some of their guests danced, for a little while. It didn't last long. They could have used a live band.

"Are there any bands with werewolves?" Toni asked when he mentioned it. She had taken a seat at the bar, and he was still standing near the end of it. He'd slowed down on the smoking by then. He knew he'd be craving them for the next couple of days but didn't want to develop the habit again. He supposed lung cancer wouldn't be an issue now. He wondered how the man from the hospital was doing now. If he was out and reunited with his daughter.

"Los Lobos?" He suggested with a smile. "Or American Werewolves."

"I asked about them once," Shelly said. "I was told that none of them are actually werewolves, but at least a couple members of Oingo Boingo were."

The party continued and they winnowed and chose.

"Eight, I think, for our first batch," Toni said. "I think that's already pushing it. I wouldn't want to do more." First batch. He shuddered at that but kept silent.

Gordon looked around the room. Of the three dozen people here now, some lucky - or unlucky - eight were going to be chosen to have their lives irrevocably changed forever. He hoped they knew what they were getting into. He realized they almost certainly didn't. They winnowed and conversed and chose their few, and another dozen "for the second batch, assuming the first goes well."

Eventually the crowd started thinning, and most were gone by now. Carl and Toni were both at the bar. Kevin wandered over with the man Gordon could only think of as his goon. He reminded Gordon of the men he'd killed across town last week. Kevin had killed a man as well. Toni had told him he'd been the one to kill one of the two men she'd been chained in the basement with. Was Kevin thinking of that now? Was he constantly looking over his shoulder, terrified of being eventually caught? Gordon guessed he was not. He'd been terrified himself for the first few days. He'd found the report in the public police activity logs. There was no mention of werewolves, or witnesses, or finding any shredded clothing at the scene. He hadn't been carrying his ID or a phone or anything else that could be traced back to him, and if anyone had seen him sneaking back into his hotel room naked in the middle of the night, they'd never said anything about it.

"What do you think of Daniel?" Toni asked, indicating a man in close conversation with Lily, who Gordon remembered from the initial meeting at the Pied Cow.

"I talked to him a little bit," Kevin said. "He's very full of himself."

Shelly laughed loudly at that.

"What?" Kevin responded with a smirk.

"He's a DJ," Toni started.

"That explains it then," Kevin said. She just scowled at him.

"That means, he's gonna know a lot of people. Which is exactly what we want."

"What about the girl?" Shelly said.

"Kim's friend, Lily." said Toni. "A little flighty but seems nice enough. She's a Wiccan and knows lots of new-age-y people. She's already asked if she could invite another friend of hers in the future. Pretty sure we'll invite both her and Kim to be in the first batch."

"Makes sense to me," Carl replied.

"Looks like things are pretty much wrapped up here," Kevin said, after several more minutes. "I'm gonna take off. It's a late night, and I've got an early morning tomorrow. Sorry I won't be able to swing by in the morning to help clean up," he said. The way he smirked when he said it made seem like he thought it should be funny, but nobody laughed. "You okay to get home?" he said to Shelly.

"Nah, I don't think you guys need me anymore, right?" she said to Carl and Toni. "I'll come with."

Kevin took his "goon" with him as well, leaving only the three of them at the bar, and one remaining couple on the couch. Kevin made it a point to stop and say good-bye to them.

A few minutes later, they followed him out the door, after making their own farewells.

"I think that went pretty well," Carl said.

Gordon wondered if he'd have said it regardless of what happened.

"Looks like you've got your new recruits," Gordon said. "If that's still what you really want to do."

"Haven't changed our minds," Toni said. "Still don't wanna come for the big event?"

"I think this is about as close to condoning what you're doing that I want to get," he answered. "I am a little worried about what those two have planned, though."

Kevin wouldn't tell them what he was planning on doing next weekend, only "Don't worry, you'll find out."

"If it's public, it could help us," Toni said.

"I was thinking the same thing," Carl said, which was a surprise.

"How so?" Gordon prompted.

Carl looked to Toni, then when she didn't answer, he did. "If there are a few public occurrences, even if they're mostly silenced by the Alphas, it can get people thinking about Were... werewolves. Which makes it easier for them to accept us. Kind of like how every time there's a movie with friendly aliens there're people saying NASA is secretly priming us to accept the real ones. Only, you know, real."

He hadn't heard that before, but the kid was perhaps more astute than he seemed.

"Makes sense," he said. "As long as it's a friendly encounter. Violence at this point would be counterproductive at best." He was beginning to think these kids could actually do what the police couldn't, and expose the werewolf organization for what it was. He stood up. "Got any garbage bags?" he asked.

"We'll get it in the morning," Carl said. "I actually enjoy that part."

"The cleanup?"

"Yeah. I know it's kinda weird, but cleaning up after a party is sort of like reliving it. Every half-full cup or spilled plate of food or leftover bottle is its own story."

"You're right. It's kinda weird," but he smiled as he said it. "I'll leave you to it, then. Goodnight to you both." With a slight bow, he left Toni and Carl, who wasn't her boyfriend, alone together in the empty warehouse and headed back to his own home where nobody would be waiting for him

SEVENTEEN
THE BRIGHTEST OF NIGHTS

"Nice place," Toni said as they approached the cabin. "How'd you afford it?"

Carl gave her a sideways look at that. He felt a little insulted at her estimation of capabilities. What made it worse was that she was right.

"Shelly and Kevin lent me the money," he admitted.

She smiled at that, which irritated him. "You're moving up in the world," she said. Her next words belied the playful smirk. "This is much nicer than the place you brought me to."

His heart sank at that. It was only a month ago. He couldn't even imagine now how it had seemed like a good idea. She knew the surest way to hurt him: remind him of how much he'd hurt her. Not that he didn't deserve it. He stopped the car in the large gravel circle in front of the lodge. It was actually nicer than the ad had made it look. Leaving the bags in the car, he walked up the three steps of the front porch. She followed after him, carrying the smallest of the bags she'd brought. He fished the key out of his front pocket and fitted it to the door, sliding open the deadbolt. He opened both of the double doors and stepped back, holding the door open for Toni.

"Fuck," she said in admiration of the place. A huge kitchen and a rustic wooden table easily large enough for a dozen people greeted them as they entered. Two open doorways led from the dining room to the immense central chamber to which three bedrooms and a bathroom connected directly.

"This place is perfect," Toni said, looking around. The complete back wall was composed of large picture windows looking out over the back deck and a hillside sloping gently upward into ample woodland beyond. Those woods, and the fact that their next neighbor was over a mile away, had been what sold him on the place. That, and the fact that Shelly had offered to pay for the place for the weekend as well as cover the deposit. It apparently belonged to some family friend of hers.

Shelly had repeated though, that they still had other plans and wouldn't be joining them that weekend. Carl wondered what they'd be doing instead. She still wouldn't say. He was just as happy to not be involved.

"Holy crap, is there a hot tub?" Toni looked out the back windows then slid the door open to step out onto the wooden deck. Carl hurried to catch up to her, still trying to decide what to do about the rooms. Three bedrooms, and three couches, four if you counted the little short one near the front door. Room easily for half a dozen people to sleep.

He caught up to her outside. He could see why it was so expensive. A covered charcoal grill sat on the deck near the hot tub. A small building offset from the house held a shower and a changing room with a large stack of towels. He wondered why, if Shelley and Kevin had known about this place, they'd opted for the ramshackle little cabin they'd used when they'd turned Toni and the others. It still bothered him that they hadn't heard anything from the one who'd lived. He had definitely been turned, Carl had seen him assume form, and he supposed it was a good thing that he'd kept a low profile since then. He was still waiting for the other shoe to drop on that.

Toni had finished her quick inspection of the outside, and went back in. He followed her.

"Okay," she said upon discovering the master bedroom. She'd already taken a quick look at the other two. "This one's ours, we'll use one of the others as a staging area, and let everyone else decide among themselves where they want to sleep."

He was still stuck on that "ours." He thought for a second that it might be somewhat presumptuous of them to claim the largest room for themselves, then thought better of it. Sure, it was supposed to be a society of free equals without any hierarchy. Except that they were the leaders. Not above them, but "first among peers" as the saying went. He never did understand that saying, and, not understanding it, didn't like it.

"You go unload the car," she said. "I'm going to start setting up."

His suitcase, along with her backpack and duffel bag, he dumped on the large bed in the master bathroom. He was unloading the cooler and grocery bags into the fridge by the time she had finished outside. She came into the kitchen and leaned against the counter. He pulled out a large packet of bacon and looked up at her inquiringly.

"We're not going to have time to hunt tomorrow," she said. "I want fucking bacon on my cheeseburger."

She had asked for bacon at the first cabin, after they'd forced the change on her. She'd said it in a cheerful tone this time, as if she'd come to terms with what they did to her a month ago. As if it didn't even bother her.

"I wonder how all these people are going to turn out," Carl said.

She looked confused at that. No, not confused, but maybe... pensive?

"What do you mean?"

"Well, we're inviting them all into some organization, right?"

"Right..." She wasn't sure where he was going but was willing to follow. At least for a little while.

"But we're not forcing them to, and nothing happens if they quit."

"You're wondering what happens if they do, and where they go," she said.

"Yeah, I mean, that guy who was with you." The one who survived, he didn't say out loud.

"Mitch," she said.

"Yeah. He's pretty much dropped out of sight. But what if he'd gone public, or gone to the police?"

"You're worried that some from tonight will do that?"

"Yeah," he said. He didn't look at her as he emptied the bags full of non-perishables into the cupboards.

"They might," she said.

He looked at her then, meeting her eyes.

"We'll do what we can to dissuade them," she said as she crossed over to help him with the groceries. "But we can't stop them if that's what they want to do. All we can do is try to discourage them and make them understand the consequences if they do, but if we truly want a society of free wolves, we can't dictate their actions. Unless we want to replace one tyranny with another, we have to trust them with their own decisions."

He realized the truth of what she said. It was the same thing he'd said earlier. The same thing Kevin had said at that other cabin. Somehow coming from her it seemed less reckless.

He nodded in response. "And what if any... die." He could barely bring himself to say the word. He concentrated on folding the empty bag.

"That might happen too," she said. "That one's up to us to prevent, as much as we're able."

He didn't have an answer to that. Maybe she was being reckless after all. But she continued.

"I've given it a lot of thought," she said. "It might happen. You told me that the change doesn't always work. So, what happens then? You've got a badly wounded person alone somewhere in the woods, far from civilization. I've brought a first aid kit, and maybe we find them in time. But if we don't, or they're too injured to recover without the wolf? Then, yeah, they might die. Small chance, but not zero."

"So, what do we do?"

"Same thing. We tell them. Let them make an informed decision. At least nobody's chained to a wall in a basement, wondering what's going on."

As usual, he had no answer to that. The enormity of it... how he could have done that. But he did, and he'd have to live with that.

"Fortunately, Kevin's not here," she said. And he looked up at that. He understood, though. So far, all the conversion deaths he'd known about had been directly caused by Kevin being over-zealous in his attacks. Once bitten, it took a few hours for the wolf to take hold and heal the damage. If the wound was bad enough, the recipient risked bleeding to death before it had a chance to do so. If it was too shallow, they might not be turned at all, and remain just human. It was a delicate balancing act, and one made just as one lost control of their senses. Tonight, he would be put to the test. The two of them would have to turn three people each. He'd never heard of anyone turning more than one before. He'd only done it himself one time - to Toni herself. And she never had. Could they do it? It seemed dangerously reckless to try so many their first time.

He almost wished Kevin and Shelly were there, or someone

who could tell him what to do, but Toni may be right. Kevin was reckless, uncaring about the lives of mere humans. It was better that he wasn't here. He still wished Shelly was, though, if only to be one more experienced Were to help with the conversions.

They finished with the groceries and headed back into the rest of the house. Toni picked up the coat rack from the entryway and carried it with her to the bedroom.

"Grab the duffel, will you?" she called over her shoulder.

He knew which one she meant - he'd dumped it in the large room with the rest of the bags. It was an actual old army-style duffel bag, he assumed from some military surplus store.

She'd moved the coat rack next to the bed in one of the smaller rooms. Taking the duffel from him, she unclipped the closings and dumped the contents into the bed. It was a large collection of robes - some white, some black.

"I did some shopping at the local thrift stores," she said. "These are for us." She picked out a couple of the black ones that had been more neatly folded than the rest and tossed them to him.

He unfolded the larger one, holding it up. It was a T-shaped robe, with no zipper or opening in the front, instead needing to be pulled on over one's head. Across the chest, though, was an embroidered wolf, done in a beautiful minimalistic fashion. He unfolded the other robe and saw it has a similar wolf embroidered on it. Same style, but he realized, they were both anthropomorphic just enough to be recognizable as male and female.

"Wow, nice!" he said. She beamed at that. "Where did you find this? Are they all like that?" he asked, reaching for another one.

"No, just ours," she said. "You like 'em?"

"Yeah, they're perfect. What're they from, do you know?"

"What do you mean?"

"I wonder what they were, originally, before they went to the thrift store."

"They weren't. I just bought the robes blank. I made the wolves."

He took another look. "Wow. They look like real made things. I mean... I didn't know you could do that." He knew he sounded like an idiot, but he was relieved he'd praised them before he knew she did them. He would have felt like an asshole if he had asked what the design was supposed to be or something.

They separated out the white and black robes, hanging the white ones on the clothes rack, three or four per peg. Then tossed all the black ones back into the bag. She handed it to him. "Put this in the closet in our room. Whichever of us gets back here first can arrange them somewhere. Either this room, or maybe the porch. Yeah, let's make it the back porch. That way, everyone'll have something to wear when they get back."

"What about the clothes they came in? I thought the whole point of the white robes was to give them something expendable to wear."

"Partly. Also, the symbology. White for purity, black for secret knowledge, all that sort of thing. And there's also something to be said for solidarity in uniform. And so on. But," she forestalled his response, "we don't want to tell them that. And some, inevitably, will simply put their white robes on over their street clothes."

"We could warn them not to."

"We kinda did. We've dropped enough hints, told stories. Did you think I told everyone the story about me having to walk out of Forest Park naked just to amuse them?"

Carl had thought exactly that but didn't want to admit it.

"Some of them - possibly most of them - aren't going to take our warnings seriously. Pretty sure Daniel thinks the whole thing is just a big joke. But he's still willing to go along with it, so here we are. Others are probably going to think we're crazy, or speaking in metaphor, no matter how many times we tell them otherwise. We told them the truth, but maybe they won't believe it until they've actually experienced it. Maybe not even then. So, yeah, some of them are going to be surprised and lose clothing, maybe phones or watches or jewelry. I did. But that'll be their first lesson, too: pay attention to details. This is real, and dangerous, and not everything is going to be spelled out for you."

"Okay, so why use just the one room? Why not have one for men and the other for women? That'd give more of a hint about what's expected, and still not spell it out, wouldn't it?" he asked.

"It would, but I want them all to mix. Enforce the idea of everyone being equals. I don't want to start out by segregating them."

Carl noticed that 'I' she used and felt a bit annoyed at it. Is this what happens inevitably to the whole idea of equals? "Some are more equal than others" already? He didn't say anything, though. Maybe he'd bring it up later, if things got bad. She'd obviously given the whole thing a lot more thought than he had, and he'd agreed to the broad strokes in previous conversations. She hadn't actually tried to give him any orders or override any of his decisions. He just hadn't made as many decisions, or thought of as many details, as she had, which made the whole thing de facto her plan.

"Like in Starship Troopers," he said.

"What?" she said, stopping in her tracks to turn and look at him. She wore an amused smile, which made him want to show off.

"The shower scene. In the movie, not the book."

"Oh. I haven't seen the movie," she said with a note of disdain.

"But you've read the book?" he asked, surprised.

"Yeah, but it's been a while."

"Okay, well, it doesn't matter anyway. The movie's a completely different kind of story."

"Maybe that's why I've never heard anything good about it."

"Yeah, fans of the book never like the movie. I think a lot of people don't get that they're completely different media and you can't just copy from one to the..."

She stopped him with an upraised hand. "I'm all for a good nerd rant," she said, "But what does this have to do with..."

"Oh, right," he said. "There's this shower scene," he started.

"I've heard of that part," she said. She didn't seem happy.

"I guess it's kind of infamous, but the whole point is that there's this group shower, men and women are sharing it together. And nobody says anything."

She looked like she was waiting for him to continue, so he did.

"Nobody says anything. That's the whole point. No one mentions that there are opposite genders naked together, no sexual innuendo, no remarks or anything. It's a depiction of a future end to sexism - complete equality and complete integration of the genders. They're just a bunch of soldiers bantering before a battle."

"That's... uh... actually kind of beautiful," she said.

"Certainly, something to strive for," he said. "But we're not really there yet."

Again, that inquisitive look, which he took for an invitation to continue.

"In our society, women are still taught to be afraid of men. And men are still taught that it's unmanly to not pursue a potentially available woman."

"You think we should still segregate them, then?"

"I'm not sure. I think the ideal is great, but I don't know if we're ready. I think that if we don't, the women are going to be far more uncomfortable and likely to lose whatever they've got than the men are."

"Maybe," she responded. "Some of them might surprise you. I still think it's worth doing anyway. After all, how are we going to get to your perfectly integrated society if we don't take the first steps?"

"All right. If you think it's okay, we'll do it that way."

He realized that once again, they had done what she wanted. She hadn't taken over, or demanded it, or anything like that. They had still discussed it and come to consensus, right? On the other hand, what difference did it make if in the end they only ever did what she wanted? Fuck it. He wasn't going to worry about this now. Things were going well for once, and he wanted it to work too much to let his ego get in the way.

He looked around to see what other setup was left, and didn't see anything obvious. So he asked Toni if she had anything in mind.

"I think that's about all we need to do now," she said. "We can go over our parts later, but for now..." She hesitated a second, then looked up at him. She took both of his hands in hers and said, "Now I think it's time to consecrate the temple."

"What does that mean?" he asked.

By way of response, she pulled him to her and kissed him. Then she pulled his shirt off over his head and tossed it toward the middle of the room. Surprised, he wrapped his arms around her and continued the kiss. After a moment, he pulled her shirt off as she had done to his. She cooperated and continued. Soon they were standing in the large room, their clothes scattered across the floor. Still holding her, he pulled back just a bit, and said, "Shall we... Uh..." And gestured with his head toward the bedroom. He almost laughed out loud at his own awkwardness. They had done this a dozen times, but something was different today.

"How about that one?" she nodded to one of the smaller rooms, where they had hung the robes. The way she said it made it, undeniably, a question.

She was still allowing him to make the decision. He wondered why. Had she sensed his earlier doubts somehow and decided to show him that this was still an equal partnership? That she really wasn't trying to take over? Or was she trying to let him know that what she really wanted was a real man, someone who would take charge. An Alpha male. He almost laughed out loud at that again. No, he had to let go of self-doubt. She wouldn't be here, not like this, if she'd wanted someone so utterly different from him. And didn't "alpha male" pretty much describe Kevin, anyway? Kevin, who she utterly despised. Fuck it. If she was going to reject him just for being a big dork, it would have happened long before now. Like the night they had first "met." God, it seemed like a lifetime ago. In many ways, it was.

He couldn't fix what he had done, couldn't ever make it right. Oh my god, he thought, I helped kill an innocent man. Then directly caused the death of a not so innocent man. Funny he didn't feel guilty at all about Hudson.

But thoughts of Hudson were banished from his mind as well once they'd entered the smaller room and Toni lay down on the bed. He climbed on top and kissed her more, thinking of nothing but the sight of her, the feel of her, the taste of her. It felt almost surreal to be doing something so normal as making love on a bed. Making love. He let himself think the words, though he still didn't dare say them out loud.

Afterward, he lay beside her, gazing affectionately at her laying on her back, the bed covers tangled beneath them.

"What?" she said, returning his smile with her own.

"I'm just..." He wanted to tell her he loved her but didn't dare. "So happy right now." She seemed pleased at that and smiled broadly.

"Me, too," she said. Another surprise. "And..." She hesitated, as if unsure about what she was going to say next.

"Yeah?" he prompted in as gentle a tone as he could manage.

"The girls tomorrow..." she started, then trailed off.

He was confused now. He froze, trying not to think, not to anticipate what she was going to say next. As long as she didn't say it, it wasn't true. He looked directly into her eyes. He willed time to stop.

"I don't want... I mean..." He'd never seen her this hesitant before. He tensed himself, readying for the blow. Was this it? Was she breaking up with him? She couldn't, they were never together. He caught himself holding his breath, but still couldn't let it out. He could feel panic rising.

"I think it's best if you don't touch any of them tomorrow."

What?

"Why would I do that?" he asked without thinking, not caring about how his voice squeaked as he said it. Did that mean...? What did that mean?

He could tell the answer, or perhaps the surprise in his tone, pleased her. She relaxed as he said it.

"You don't really understand your position here, do you?" she asked. This, her gentle teasing tone, he was used to. This was again familiar. Everything was as it had been, whatever that was. There was a lot he didn't understand. She kept telling him that she wasn't his girlfriend. Did this mean she had changed her mind? Did she mean it, or was it just the after-glow speaking, laying there together on the bed after making love?

And again, he found he couldn't think the words to himself without feeling like he was getting away with something.

"What do you mean?" was all he said.

She rolled onto her side, to look him in the eyes. Her amused expression was more serious now. "You're in a position of authority," she said. "Power's attractive. A lot of people will want to sleep with you, or at least be near you and claim a special status. That's going to happen. But it can lead to divisiveness, cliques, rivalries, all sorts of unhealthy dynamics. We can't prevent it altogether, of course, but if you were known to be in a relationship and completely uninterested in anybody else, it'll help. At least, their rivalries will all be with me, and not with each other. I hope."

He thought about it. As far as any of them knew, he was the head of a vast secret conspiracy. "Makes sense," he said. "They say power is the ultimate aphrodisiac."

"Henry Kissinger," she said.

"Who?"

"Kissinger. Evil little troll of a man who ran pretty much every Republican presidency from Nixon through Trump."

"Oh," he said. He didn't want to think about Henry Kissinger right now.

"What about you?" he asked.

"You can touch me," she said with a smile.

He laughed at that. God, that felt so good. He ran his hand over her thigh for good measure. "I mean, you're an authority figure here as much as I am. Won't the guys be wanting to be with you?"

"Yes, and some of the women, too," she said.

Again, Carl laughed out loud.

"But, yeah, same rules apply to me, too."

"Okay," he agreed

"You say that easily now," she said, "but tomorrow when

you're in the hot tub and there's three naked women trying to sit in your lap, you're going to need more resolve."

"Is that really a thing that'll happen?" he asked. He was intrigued by the idea.

She just glared at him in response.

"You're going to be nearby, right?"

"As much as you need me to," she said.

"Then yeah." He continued to caress her thigh as he said it, running a finger up, across, then in her. "It's not going to be a problem."

She smiled broadly at that, obviously enjoying the sentiment as much as what he was now doing with his fingers.

She leaned in and kissed him before rolling back on her back and pulling him over on top of her.

And again, he was in her, moving, kissing, caressing.

He was completely exhausted this time when they were done, and lay on his back beside her, their hands touching. He took her hand and she let him, their fingers intertwined. He turned his head enough to see her, gazing back at him and took her in with his eyes. "Yeah," he repeated. He found it difficult to even form words right now. "It won't be a problem at all."

"THANK YOU FOR MEETING ME," Victor said to her as he seated himself. "Even if you did insist it be... here."

Veer smiled at the disdain in his voice. She had chosen the bar on purpose. Victor despised the place, finding it tacky. She knew she'd be able to convince him to leave shortly after arriving. She'd already made reservations at Mama Mia's, about a fifteen minute walk away. She had been waiting here for over an hour, though that had been her own choice. She wanted a chance to watch to see who else showed up before he did. She came alone, but that was mostly by necessity. Who else could she trust?

"Well, if you don't like it, let's go somewhere else," she said, and immediately stood up.

His face betrayed the faintest trace of bemusement.

"Or we can stay here if you prefer. I hear they make a great pina colada," she said.

He laughed openly at that and sprung quickly to his feet.

She'd already paid for her drink and tipped the waitress well enough to hopefully not mind that she'd sat at a table alone for an hour.

"So where are we going?" he asked her once they were outside. There was a thick mist in the air, not quite heavy enough to be considered rain.

"Do you like Italian?" she said. "It's a short walk."

He came with her out the door.

"Sorry about the cloak and dagger," she said when they'd gone a couple of blocks and she hadn't spotted anyone following them. "I just..."

He cut her off. "Wanted to make sure I didn't have a bunch of people hidden around? Just like your reference to Trader Vic's was meant to remind me of the depth of our relationship so I don't have you offed without thinking," he finished for her. "Do you really think so little of me?"

He sounded hurt. Her instinct was to reassure him, but she knew him too well. As much as she respected, even liked him, she knew him well enough to know that though he could seem like a frail kindly old man when he wanted to, in reality he was anything but.

"I know you wouldn't ever do anything without thinking." It was a back-handed compliment at best, and she knew that that wouldn't be lost on him. "But I needed to know where I stand."

They'd reached the end of a block, she hit the button for the walk signal.

"You stand where you have always stood: wherever you choose to." He paused for a moment to let the implications sink in. On the surface, the meaning was clear: come back into the fold, and all is forgiven. But Victor rarely spoke on only one level.

"Do you remember what the first thing you said to me after you found out I was Were?" he asked her. His voice was still gentle, with no hint of menace in it. But this was treacherous ground and they both knew it. The light turned green and they started across the road.

"After 'Holy fuck,' you mean?"

He laughed, as she knew he would. He could see the evasion for what it was. Of course, she didn't want to be the one to say it, and that itself was a signal. We may end up on opposite sides of the issue, was the unspoken message, but there is still respect.

And the respect went both ways. He was chivalrous enough to say it for her.

"You told me you were going to expose my secrets. To tell the world about me and my people."

"And you told me I was free to try," she finished for him. "I took that as a threat at the time."

"Which was not unwise," he responded. "If you had been a threat to us - one I didn't think I could mitigate - I would have taken appropriate action. At the time."

"You never considered me a serious threat," she said, letting her bitterness at herself over the fact show through more than she had intended.

"That's not through any failing of your own," he told her. He was still trying to reassure her, even now. "We spent four hundred years perfecting the system, you can hardly have been expected to unravel it in just a few months."

They had reached the restaurant and didn't speak again until after they were seated. He seemed surprised, then pleased, when he saw they had reservations already, under the same Sigurdsdottir, another private joke between them.

"You said at the time," she started, almost scared of his answer. "What about now?"

"Now..." he began. Was that uncertainty she sensed in him? It was unfamiliar, she wasn't sure she liked it. "Now, things are changing. I don't know exactly what, but something's happening. You might be able to expose us if you play everything exactly right."

"And you?"

"And I... I could not allow that to happen."

"You could help me."

"You know that that's one thing I could never do."

She didn't know what to say to that. She couldn't turn back now. He wouldn't respect her if she did, any more than she could respect herself. She would try to expose the Were, and Victor would try to stop her.

And as simply as that, with courtesy, mutual respect, and much regret, war was declared.

For several moments, they sat in silence, regarding each other. Veer kept her face calm, nearly expressionless, though it felt like her guts had been ripped out. She wondered if Victor felt the same way. She suspected he might.

"I had another reason I wanted to talk to you," he finally said.

She remembered the message. She had originally dared to hope that he meant he wanted to help her bring out the Were.

"The Nellie Bly thing," she said.

"Yes," he replied. "I have a story to tell you, and a request. If you accept my request, when you are done, you will be in a much better position to expose us, and, hopefully, understand why you should not."

She understood why he had hesitated. This raised the stakes for both of them. "Okay, I'm intrigued." As you knew I would be, she didn't bother to say out loud. "Tell me the rest."

"Last week," he began, "you were involved in an incident on Skyline Boulevard involving multiple vehicles resulting in two disappearances and one fatality."

An incident. That was a mild way of putting it. "Yes. It was widely reported, though I don't believe anyone mentioned the abductions."

"But I didn't see any reports from you. The Journal mentioned that you had been arrested. Surely your editors there must have asked you about it?"

"They did. I haven't answered yet."

"I see. You used the word abductions," Victor said.

"Yes. They took both Peter and Michael's partner, Detective Lee, away in a white panel van," she said.

"Who is 'they?'" He asked.

"I don't know yet," she responded.

"You witnessed this?" he asked.

"I did, but couldn't do anything about it at the time."

"Understandable. If they had known you were there, no doubt they would have taken you as well."

She was confused for a moment. "The helicopter wasn't you..." she started. "But you knew about it?"

"I only found out about it after the fact," he said.

"How?"

"They told me."

"Okay, yes, I'm going to need the whole story here," she said.

He smiled indulgently and began. "They're called Holy Mountain Research. They have a building in a business park in

Hillsboro. Publicly traded, biomedical research, a modest patent portfolio that they mostly license to development companies."

"Doesn't sound like the kind of outfit that would need its own military," she said.

"And lately they've developed an interest in Were."

Genetic research. An interest in Were. She could see where this was heading, and why Victor thought it would convince her to stay quiet.

"How long have you known about this?" she asked.

"Since the day before your arrest," he told her. "They sent a representative to my office, who told me they had a business proposition. I will admit to being happy to work on my real business instead of Were politics for a change. Alas, it was not to be. They were less interested in my embedded microsystems endeavors than they were in my Were connections."

"Wait... how did they know...?"

He held up a finger to forestall her. "I am getting to that. Bear with me. He told me his firm was working on a cure for cancer."

"The regenerative factor," Veer said. "They've isolated it?"

"I don't think so. I think they've only recently learned about it. They indicated they had a subject, who I believe they acquired after he was cured of late-stage cancer."

"They told you this?"

"They told me that a test subject was cured hours after a single application. Bear in mind, this was before they mentioned werewolves. But I gathered from the way he said it, and other things he said later, that they weren't the ones who gave him the cure. They're trying to study him to find out what happened."

"602," Veer said. "It has to be 602."

"What's 602?" Victor asked her.

"In the hospital, where they took Chandler. After Peter stopped by, Chandler visited room 602, transformed, and attacked a late-stage cancer patient there."

"Did you get his name?"

"I did not." Not through lack of trying, of course, but Victor knew her well enough she didn't have to explain that. "Sounds like it worked, though. He disappeared from the hospital and hasn't been seen since."

"You think Chandler was trying to cure him?"

"Almost certainly."

"Then that's interesting. His sudden recovery from a terminal condition may have been what alerted them to our presence in the first place."

"But that was less than a month ago. How could they have all this in place so quickly?"

"I suspect the paramilitary units may have been provided as a turnkey operation by a major investor. The company seems to be expanding rapidly and has made a major turn quite recently."

"Turn meaning research on Were."

"Exactly."

"So... what do you want from me?"

"I want to know what they're doing. They have one Were, quite possibly captive, possibly more. Definitely more, as one of them gave them my name. It occurs to me it may be possible to work with them..."

She was surprised at the thought, and it obviously showed.

"Perhaps they are doing what they say, and seeking a cure to cancer. If we could work with them, without revealing ourselves..."

Her expression said what she thought of that.

"Yes, I know," he replied to her unspoken words of disbelief. "And if their motives aren't benign, we need to know that, too."

"A cure for cancer could be worth a lot of money," she said. "Enough to shift the balance of power. There's very little that a lot of people wouldn't do to get a piece of that."

"I mentioned that," he told her. "I was told the plan was, once they had it, to move it immediately into the public domain."

"That sounds like the most unlikely thing I've heard for a while."

"It wouldn't be entirely altruism. Being known as the company that found a cure for cancer and gave it away to the world? That would lead to a vast increase in the value of every other part of their portfolio. It would also likely buy at least fifty years of immunity from any PR issues."

He was most likely correct that it might put her in a better position to expose them. If they had documents, actual experimentation on Were...

Before she had a chance to say anything, though, she noticed everyone else in the restaurant turning to look out the front windows, reacting to some kind of commotion in the street. The door to the restaurant opened and a man stumbled in, his hand pressed to his shoulder, blood flowing between his fingers and down his shirt, dripping on the floor. A wave of sound hit them from the street, people were running by, fleeing in panic. Had the police attacked another protest? She wasn't aware of any scheduled for today.

A patron helped the wounded man gently to the floor. Victor was already moving toward them.

"Let me through," he told the people in his way. "I'm a medic."

Veer almost laughed at the absurdity of it. He didn't mention that his medical training was over seventy years ago. Veer followed close behind, prepared to render whatever assistance he needed.

"You!" He pointed at the nearest waiter. "Have the chef back there boil water. Toss in whatever clean linen you have and bring it to me after it's boiled for one minute."

The waiter hastened to obey. Nobody mentioned that an ambulance could be there within minutes and only immediate first aid was all that was really necessary.

"What happened?" Victor asked the man on the floor.

"Wolves," he said. Veer had a feeling Victor suspected the answer before it was given. After seventy-five years of experience, he'd probably recognized the nature of the wound as soon as he entered the restaurant. She looked out the window, at all the people running by.

"Where?" she asked him. "How many?"

"Pioneer square. Lots, I don't know. A whole pack."

Another wounded man was brought in and patrons helped him to the floor near the first. Victor and Veer exchanged a look. They both understood. Someone had been moving against them. Her exposé may be about to become redundant. Victor had his hands full, but one of them had to...

"Go!" he told her and turned his attention back to his patients.

Strange our reactions, Veer thought. It didn't matter, and they both knew it. Out of everyone there, it was a secret the two of them shared. Regardless of what kind of treatment they got, within a few hours there'd be no sign they had ever been injured. And by morning, they'd wake up to find their lives forever changed.

"I'll let you know what's happening!" she shouted to him on her way out the door. He simply nodded an acknowledgment and turned back to his patient.

She left the restaurant. Victor still hadn't received the towels he'd ordered.

EIGHTEEN
BAD MOON RISING

The next morning, Carl was already showered and dressed and washing the breakfast dishes when he heard the first car approaching. Toni had left him at the cabin while she took a walk, "to scope things out a bit."

One of their new recruits, Kim, got out of the passenger side of the car. They had chosen her after the warehouse party, but there had been little doubt ever since she first showed up at their initial meeting at the coffee shop. He didn't recognize the man who climbed out of the driver's seat.

"You... uh, didn't come with Lily?" he asked her, standing on the front porch. He let the door hang open behind him.

"She had to work late," Kim said. "She'll be here in a few hours, but I didn't want to wait. This is my boyfriend, Mark."

"Ummm..." he started, not quite sure what to say. "Are you...?" he looked to Kim, who looked a little uncomfortable. She offered no help. He wasn't sure what he was going to say now. "Staying?" "Joining the secret initiations?" "Supposed to be here?"

He wished Toni was there, but she was out looking around the area. Decision time, then.

"Dropping Kim off?" he finished, after far too long of a pause.

The man, Mark, hesitated for a second before saying "I was planning on staying. Seeing what Kim's getting herself into."

That was far too patronizing for Carl's taste. He turned away from the man. "You did get the part where this is a secret society, right?" he said to Kim, emphasizing the word.

"And this weekend is a secret initiation?" he continued before she could speak. "And part of keeping a secret is not telling everyone?"

"I didn't tell everyone," she said. "I told Mark. That's it, I swear."

"Hey, she can tell whoever she wants!" Mark put in loudly.

"He's right," Carl said, still addressing Kim. "That's actually near the heart of what we're doing here. If you want to leave now, you can tell anyone you want anything you'd like. Nobody will stop you. Nobody will hunt you down or do anything at all to harm you." She looked puzzled for a second. This was apparently not what she was expecting to hear.

"Of course, we're under no obligation to share any further secrets with you, and of course if anyone asks, we'll deny everything." This, from her expression, was more along what she'd feared would be said. Carl could see the anger rising in her. He didn't know which way it would be directed - toward him or her boyfriend for talking her into letting him come. He felt like it could go either way, so decided to head it off, letting her know before she committed herself.

"You have a decision to make." He tried to sound authoritative, but his voice sounded more petulant to his ears. "You've made an error in judgment, but that's forgivable. You're not the first and, believe me," he said with a wry smile, "nowhere near the worst. It's too late for your boyfriend to be here. If you want to vouch for him in the future, he can be invited at a later time, and questioned and evaluated the same way you were. If you want to stay, you can. Someone can give you a ride back to town Sunday. I'll be inside. You," he stressed the word, "are welcome to come in if you still want to."

He went back inside and, with some effort, didn't go to the front window to peak out. Instead, he went to the fridge and got himself a Coke. He opened it and drank directly from the can. He considered finishing the dishes, but the kitchen sink was too close to the window that he didn't want to look out of.

A few minutes later, there was a knock on the door. Kim stood there, bag in hand. Her boyfriend was still at the wheel of the car. Carl didn't say anything, nor step aside to let her in. She looked back at the car and waved. Her boyfriend just glared, but started the car, turned it around and sped off down the hill.

"I hope this is worth it," she said as she came in.

"I think you'll find it will be," Carl said. "Is that all you brought?" he asked, indicating her small bag. It didn't even look large enough for a complete change of clothes, let alone any bedding or anything.

"Was there something I was supposed to bring?" she asked. "I'm sorry - I didn't see it in any of the emails."

Carl thought briefly of giving her a hard time about that. Telling her that not everything is going to be spelled out for her. But there'd be enough time for that later.

"I'm sorry if I caused any problems with your boyfriend," he said instead.

"No, it's fine," she replied. "I was invited, and he wasn't. I shouldn't have let him come. I'm sorry."

Let him come, Carl noticed. Not *invited him*. It hadn't been her idea. Good. That made him feel a little better about the whole thing.

"No problem, then," he said.

"So you're still letting me in?" she asked. "This isn't going to cause any issues?"

"Wait - you sent your ride away, stranding yourself here - without even knowing if we were going to let you in?"

"Yeah, well, if you really can do what you say, I figured it would be worth it."

"Wow," he replied. "And, yeah, don't worry. If we dinged people for every lapse of judgment, I'd've been the first one excommunicated. And I meant what I said," he added. "If you wanna vouch for your boyfriend, we'll consider him for next month."

"I dunno," she said. "He was kind of a prick when I told him I'm going to go ahead without him. Fuck him."

"Not my type," Carl responded automatically.

"Oh?" she said with a smile. "Who is your type, then?"

He didn't know what to make of that. Was she hitting on him? What should he say back? He'd already been warned not to touch her. He should say something smooth and sophisticated. "Uh..." he started, then trailed off. The girl just smiled. Was that a slight shake of her head. Dammit. He had no idea how to respond or what she wanted.

"Where should I put this?" she asked.

For that, he had an answer at least. "Just toss it in a corner somewhere. Not in any of the rooms. We'll work out exact arrangements later."

She went to do so, and he went toward the kitchen. "Wanna Coke?" he asked over his shoulder as he went.

"Sure," she said, and, returning, took a seat at the long table. "Am I the first one here? How many are coming?"

"Yes, and I think about eight," Carl replied. "Plus me and

Toni."

"And..." she started, trailing off, like she didn't want to ask the question.

"And?" he prompted. When she didn't continue, he said gently, "It's okay to ask."

"And it's real? I mean, you can seriously turn into a wolf? You, uh, actually believe that?"

He laughed out loud at that. "You're just now asking that?" Seeing her reaction, he immediately apologized. "Sorry. I mean, yeah, it's totally a legitimate question. You mean, is it a metaphor, or are we all delusional, or trying to trick you somehow?"

Kim nodded.

"It's a pretty extraordinary claim. And it's said that extraordinary claims require extraordinary evidence. So, yeah, skepticism makes sense. But, if you want evidence, you'll have it tonight."

"Seriously?"

"Absolutely."

"But how? How does it work?"

"You'll find out."

"Is it safe?"

"No."

"No?" She was obviously surprised at the blunt answer.

"No. It'll be as safe as we can make it. But it won't be one hundred percent."

"That's not really reassuring."

"It wasn't really meant to be," he told her. "But it is the honest answer. There are dangers. And not just tonight. I'm not going to pretend there aren't, or try to hide them from you."

"So... what kinds of dangers?"

"I think we'll wait until the actual initiations to go into that," he replied.

She looked skeptical.

"Don't worry. All will become clear," he said in an exaggerated somber tone. "And you'll have plenty of time to back out if, hearing everything, you decide that's what you want to do."

"What do we do now?"

"Now, we wait. We'll get lunch started once Toni gets back. Then, it's mostly hanging out until an hour or so before moonrise, and we'll prepare you for the initiations then."

"How's it work? What, you're going to turn into a wolf and bite us or something?"

"That's pretty much the core of it. There's also a ceremony, and some information you'll need to know before making your final decision."

"Where are we sleeping? Is there enough space for eight people? Where should I put my stuff?"

"Just out here for now. There are two rooms you can use, with a bed each, and a few couches. We're going to leave it up to you to figure out amongst yourselves. Hopefully somebody thought to bring bedding. After the transformation, though, you're likely to find such things considerably less important."

"What do you mean?" She seemed anxious now.

"Just that your perspective may change. Will change. How much is up to you."

"Is it that big of a change, really?"

"I measure my entire life as either before or after. Yeah. It's a big deal. Even without, well, everything else, it's a pretty big deal. I mean, you turn into a were... wolf." He noticed her reaction to the words "everything else" but she didn't say anything, so he didn't explain. She also didn't question the pause before the word wolf. He was still trying to use the terminology.

Toni had steadfastly refused to use the language of the Alphas and he thought it as a good idea - create a difference, at least symbolically, between them and the society he'd known, and was theoretically still a part of. He'd been thinking a lot about symbolism, after Toni's explanation about the ceremony tonight. By making a ritual of it, it would impress on everyone's minds - including his and Toni's - how important it was. Information and explanations given during the ritual would be more likely to be remembered and considered important. It would also demonstrate everyone's roles within the nascent organization. Establishing a non-hierarchical hierarchy. It was a bit of a paradox, establishing by symbols a stricter hierarchy in an organization of free people than had been established by force under the tyranny of the Alphas.

Toni had attempted to explain the paradox using a metaphor involving a tent pole, but he hadn't really understood it. Even their act of making love yesterday afternoon, not on the bed they'd later slept in together, but in the room where the new wolves would wait to be called, was symbolic of that conception, before being born into their new lives. That was getting more mystical than was strictly necessary, Carl thought. There was a practicality to it, though, Toni claimed: Even though none of the candidates would know, the two of them would share that knowledge, and it would color their thoughts and actions throughout the weekend a thousand different ways and those actions would have subtle effects on everybody else.

Tyler and Cynthia showed up together in the same car an hour later, just after noon. Carl remembered them getting friendly at the warehouse party and guessed they finally hooked up. Hopefully it would be a stable relationship and not a source of drama. He was nervous enough about all the interpersonal dynamics, especially after Toni's warnings and Kim's maybe-flirting. He had to admit he'd enjoyed talking to her while she helped him finish with the kitchen and start to prepare lunch, but was happy that someone else would be here now.

Toni came back, emerging from the woods, up a trail that led from the back yard down to a small stream, right about the time that Will showed up with the two friends he'd invited to the Warehouse party, Caren and Jacob if Carl remembered their names properly. He liked Will. The man was friendly and easy to get along with, and was the very first of their recruits they'd met, at the Pied Cow.

Toni went out to greet them. Carl and Kim finished prepping lunch and took everything out back where they had the grill already going.

They'd finished eating, and most of the group were sitting around the large table talking when Daniel showed up.

"If I'd known you were serving lunch, I wouldn't have stopped on my way up here," he complained.

"Sorry," Toni said. "Coals are still hot if you want any."

"Nah, had a burger on the way up," he said. "Everyone here already?" he asked looking around.

"Still expecting one," Toni said.

"What happens if she doesn't make it in time?" Kim asked.

"Good question," Toni said. "I guess it depends on exactly when she shows up. There are parts of the ceremony that really can't be interrupted, so hopefully she gets here before or after that."

Carl was relieved when he heard a car half an hour before they were planning to start. It had already begun to get dark, though they were timing their ceremony with the rising of the full moon, which should be visible over the house from the back yard within a couple of hours.

WHEN THEY WERE ready to begin, they herded the candidates into the bedroom where they'd made love the previous

evening. *We fucked, and all these new lives are conceived.* He
and Toni went to their own room and donned their black robes
with the embroidered wolves. Now that he was wearing it, it
felt a little silly. He could hear murmured conversation from
the room the eight recruits were in. Toni suggested letting them
sit there for a while in the crowded room to raise the tension.
She plugged a pair of speakers into her phone and set them up
on the dining table in the other room. The soundscape coming
through the open doorways would create a mood as well as
cover what was being said in the larger room. He set up the
chairs, a larger one that Carl would occupy in his role as
"learned elder." The smaller next to it was for Toni. The candidate would stand. In front of them was a low table that they'd
draped with a red sheet, on which Toni had put a pair of
candles and a silver knife. He'd balked when she told him she'd
ordered one online to replace the one they'd lost in the
preserve, but she'd pointed out that its utility could not be
disputed.

The plan was to leave it on the "altar" in front of them in
full view of the candidates but never bring it to their attention
during the initiation ceremony itself. After everyone had
returned to the cabin, they would bring it up and explain both
its practical purpose, as one of the few available physical
weapons against their possible enemies, as well as the symbolic
purpose of its presence, signifying the danger they may now
face, and the importance of being aware of nearby danger even
when nothing is being said about it.

When all was prepared, Toni went to the first bedroom and
opened the door just enough to see into. "Kim Muller, you are
called," she intoned solemnly.

Kim came out and looked around the large room a little
nervously, and obviously impressed with the changes that had
occurred since she went in. Toni led her across to where Carl

was sitting, in his ornate black robe, on what he had come to think of as his throne. They came to a stop and he waited a few seconds before speaking.

"Who have you brought before me?" he asked, carefully keeping his eyes pointedly on Toni.

"I have brought a woman from the city who has come to us seeking to learn the secrets of our order," Toni gave the practiced reply.

As they'd rehearsed it, Carl responded in a similar tone. "I would thank the candidate to step forward," he said, keeping his eyes locked on hers.

"Please state your name," he continued when she had done so.

She looked a little nervous and with a shaking voice replied, "Kim Muller."

"I welcome you, Kim Muller. Is it true that you have come to us because you wish to learn from us the secrets of lycanthropy?"

"It is," she replied somberly. Toni had told him that this would happen. The candidates getting into the spirit of the ritual, and adopting their language to its formal tone, whether consciously or not.

"And do you believe we can teach you these secrets?"

"I sure hope so," she replied, less formally.

"We cannot," he replied immediately. Then paused as she looked startled, as expected. He continued before she had a chance to object. "Our secrets can be passed on. They can be imparted. They can be learned. But they cannot be taught.

"Furthermore," he held up one finger forestalling her questions, "they are not learned easily. Transformation awaits you, and a new life. But like all life, it will be born in pain and terror. Not all survive the process. There exists a very small, but not altogether negligible, chance that you will be among those.

There exists also a possibility that you will be hurt or maimed and not transformed at all. So, I ask you again, do you wish to join us, and learn our secrets?"

"I do," she replied again without hesitation. Carl wondered how much of what he'd said she actually believed and how much she thought was just symbolic.

"Do you swear that you have come here under your own will, and that you are free to do so?" he asked, continuing the questions they'd practiced.

"You know I have," she said with a smile. That was true. He smiled gently in return. She'd taken a chance and made a sacrifice to be here. She deserved that much.

"And do you further attest that you have not come here by request of any group, organization, or individual who wishes to learn our secrets through using you, or who wishes to bring us harm?"

"Yes," she replied this time.

"Then know that these are not idle questions. They are not merely ritually symbolic." He suppressed a smile at the irony of that, couching the questions in ritual and symbolism, then denying the "mere" symbolism of them. "For there are those who do not wish our secrets to be known. Merely by coming here today, you may have drawn their attention. If they learn what you have become, they may mark you for death. We cannot guarantee your safety. It is our goal to create a world in which this is not true, but that is a goal we are yet to accomplish. If you leave now, if you do not become a wolf, and you remain silent, they should have no reason to harm you. So, I ask you once again, do you wish to join us and learn the Mystery of the Wolf?"

"Yes. Yes, definitely," she replied. Carl could tell that Toni was beaming beside him.

"So be it. Please raise your hand and repeat after me."

He paused at each sentence for her to repeat it as he gave her the oath he and Toni had crafted just a few days ago.

"I, state your name," she copied the ritual cadence, filling in her own name, not making the obvious joke that Carl would have. "Do solemnly swear to keep secret all that I learn within the order. To reveal no names, locations, or details involving any gatherings or meetings. To keep secret the existence of the order itself, even under threat of hardship, or of imprisonment, or torture, or death. Furthermore, I swear to not publicly reveal, until such time as the Plan has come to fruition, the secret of lycanthropy, or to even suggest that I am in possession of the secret, even unto denying the possibility that such a secret could exist. And, further," they continued, one after the other, "I swear to privately reveal the secret of lycanthropy only to those who have earned my trust and who I believe worthy to be trusted with this power and invite to join our order only those who have been approved for initiation into it."

She repeated the lines dutifully after him.

"And do you swear obedience to the Order?" he asked, wondering how she'd respond to this part. "To go where you are instructed, to do what you are ordered, to live and to die as the order has decided is needful?"

She stiffened at that. "No," she replied, almost taking a step back. She dropped her hand. "I'm sorry," she said, and Carl could hear the desperation in her voice. She'd sacrificed a lot to get to this point, but seemed ready to walk away now. "I'm not joining a military. Yes, I want - more than anything - to be a wolf, but I'm not signing up to be nothing more than a tool for your rebellion."

"Good!" Carl replied. She looked confused. He continued, intoning the words as he'd practiced them. "You chose your words well. We are engaged in a rebellion. Sacrifices will very likely be called for before the end. You have placed yourself in danger by association with us, but not in servitude. We are first and foremost an organization of free men and women. It is my opinion that we work best together, and that we should do our utmost to keep each other safe, but in all things, you must follow the dictates of your own conscience. It will all be for naught if we simply replace the current order with a new tyranny."

She relaxed at that. "Thank you," she said quietly, almost a whisper.

He just nodded. There wasn't anything in the script for that. "Knowing the dangers, and what is expected of you, and what is not," he said, the final lines of the first part of the ritual, "I ask you a third and final time, do you still wish to join us and learn our secret?"

"Yes. Definitely yes."

"Then you may proceed." He lifted his arm to Toni, who approached and led her away, to the other door.

"There are white robes in here," she told her. "Choose one and change into it, then wait in this room until called." She then said something, quietly, that Carl did not hear. Kim reached up and touched her earring, though, before going into the room.

Toni came back and took her seat behind him. "How're you feeling, oh mighty Saladin?" she asked him.

If it was a reference to something, he didn't know what.

"That was kinda fun," he said.

"That's good. Ready to do it seven more times?" she asked.

"Sure," he replied, finding himself actually looking forward to it. "What did you say to her, at the end there?" he asked. Whatever it was, it hadn't been in the script.

"I, uh, warned her that she probably didn't want to wear anything other than the robe that she didn't want to risk losing," she told him.

"Oh." Carl was confused. She waited for him to continue. "I

thought we'd decided not to tell them that? The whole living with the consequences of your decisions and all that?"

"Yeah. We did. It was a one-time exception."

"Oh." He was still confused, but he let it go.

While Kim waited in the second room, Toni went back to the first. "Cynthia Staten, you are called."

With Cynthia it went exactly the same, as well as with Lily after her. Toni had predicted that Lily would go along with the ritual, having likely done something similar in whatever Wiccan group she'd previously joined. She'd also be the one most likely to know to be completely naked under her robe, which is part of the reason Toni wanted her near the beginning.

Carl was surprised that all three of the candidates so far had balked at the "obey" question. He had figured by the time they got to it they'd be on autopilot and answer in the affirmative. It seemed they were actually paying attention and putting some thought into their answers. He felt good about that. It wasn't until Will answered the question with an "I do," that he got to say it the way he'd practiced it:

"Do not!" he barked at him. He was pleased to see his startled reaction.

"This is no game we are playing. We are engaged in a rebellion." From there, he repeated the lesson about freedom and tyranny exactly as he'd said it the first three times. Toni had begun explaining how it would seem to the candidate that there was a special lesson in there just for them based on their answer when in reality it was just a few words that needed to change. He'd recognized the trick, though, from multiple video games.

Daniel was last. Toni had wanted him in the final placement as she thought he would be the most likely to make the women uncomfortable while changing. Putting him last meant nobody would have to decide how to change while he was in the room. He was also the first to make the joke that Carl would have by saying literally "state your name" when asked to state his name. He smiled at that and just repeated the line. Daniel laughed and got it right the second time.

He was relieved when Daniel was finally led into the second room to don his white robe. He had enjoyed it, but it was exhausting doing it eight times.

"Let's let them hang out there for a bit," Toni said. "We can go out and check how the moon's doing."

THERE WERE a large number of people streaming away from Pioneer Square. "In there. You can get help," Veer told a couple stumbling as quickly as they could down the sidewalk together. It looked like they were both hurt. The couple gratefully headed into the restaurant. Another man saw them and started to follow. Victor was going to be busy for a while. He would be able to help them beyond tending to their wounds. Veer knew he could explain to them what was happening, keep them from hurting anyone else when they transformed, and help them deal with their new lives after. Others would not be so lucky.

The scene as she approached the square was worse than she'd imagined. There seemed to be dozens of wounded. They lay scattered on the ground, their blood staining the brick work. Most holding a wound, moaning in pain. Several were still. She wondered how many would turn. She didn't doubt it would be Were that had done this. There must have been a lot of them. A single bite each on the wounded. Which meant they were trying to turn them. But to what end? Chaos? Exposure? Experimentation? She didn't know enough about this Holy Mountain Research company that Victor had spoken about, but if they had kept such a low profile before, why would they do something so public now?

She scanned around the perimeter of the square. The brick staircases descending into it on one side were deserted. The Were that had done this had already departed. At the corner up the street from her she saw a girl in a short skirt and torn leggings, she looked to be in her early 20s, about halfway up a tree. She looked terrified as Veer approached.

"Hey," she said in as gentle a voice as she could muster. "Come on down. It's safe now. They're gone."

The girl just shook her head, looking around.

"Okay, have it your way," Veer said. Other people had begun moving in, helping the injured, now that the danger seemed to have passed. She could hear sirens approaching. She didn't have long. She sat down on a nearby sculpture shaped like a broken pillar, and looked up.

"Did you get bit?" she asked the girl, who shook her head again in reply.

"Somebody said it was wolves. Is that true?" Veer asked, still trying to keep her voice gentle and as non-threatening as she could manage. The girl nodded.

"Well, climbing a tree was probably a smart move, then," she told her. "Wolves can't climb."

The girl was quiet for a long time after that. "That's..." she finally started, but then stopped herself immediately, as if afraid of what she was about to say.

Veer looked at her, obviously listening, but not pushing. Moments passed. There were police in the square now who were slowly working their way towards them. She had to hurry but couldn't rush the girl.

"That's what I tried to tell Jim," the girl in the tree finally said. She looked on the verge of tears.

"Well, I'm sure he'll be okay," she ventured. Did he get bit, though? If he's a Were now... that'll add a new twist to their relationship. How was Victor going to handle this one? Worse massacres had been covered up in the past, but generally by governments. It had long been Were policy to not get overly involved in politics. The increased scrutiny could lead to exposure, the thinking went. The risk was generally considered to outweigh the benefits such positions could confer. It was a policy that Victor had disagreed with, though of course he went along with it when orders were handed down through the Council.

The girl shook her head at her response, though. To her questioning look, she just pointed. Vera followed her finger to the middle of the square, where the corpse of a young man lay sprawled on the brick. His neck was torn out. He'd never had a chance.

"I'm sorry," she said gently. What can you say to such a thing? The girl didn't dare go to him, and she couldn't bring herself to flee any farther than this. The poor thing was probably wracked with guilt over not doing anything to help, despite the fact that there was nothing she could do.

"Did..." she started, then trailed off to judge the girl's reaction before continuing. "Did you see which way they went?"

"All ways," the girl responded immediately. A little more vigor in her tone this time, which was a good sign. She'd be okay. Eventually. "There were a bunch of them. They ran off in all directions. They said they were going to meet up later."

It took a second to register.

"What a minute... 'They said'?"

The girl in the tree nodded again.

"You mean, before they changed." It wasn't a question. "When they were still in human form."

Once again, the girl silently nodded. Then looked at her quizzically and said, "You don't seem surprised."

"No," Veer said truthfully. "I suspected what they were before I got here, as soon as I heard what was happening."

"You knew, didn't you?" she asked her. There was a note of accusation in her voice.

"I didn't know there were so many rogues," she said. She was aware that she was giving a lot away in that one sentence, to someone with the subtlety and clarity of mind to see it.

"But you knew there were some. You knew there were werewolves. In Portland."

"Yes," Vera admitted. "But they're not supposed to attack people."

"Are you a werewolf, too?" the girl asked her, trembling slightly.

"I'm a reporter," she answered, rather than meet the question with a lie.

"Oh," the girl asked, relaxing slightly. "Are you doing a story about werewolves?"

"Yes," she said. It wasn't the whole truth, but close enough.

"There was one," the girl said, after a brief hesitation, "That just left. I don't know if it bit anyone. It looked confused, like it didn't know what was going on. It walked off slowly - that way." She nodded in the direction, still clinging tightly to the small tree with both hands.

There were two police officers she didn't recognize approaching them now. She glanced in their direction, then looked back to the girl. She didn't want to get caught up talking to the police now.

"Look," she said, "I have to go. I'm going to try to find the... werewolf you mentioned. The police are here, they'll take care of you, okay?"

The girl nodded again, looking scared.

"You don't have to talk to them if you don't want to," she said, not sure if it was true. "If they give you any trouble, ask to speak to Detective Diaz. You can trust him."

"Okay," the girl looked a little reassured. "Good luck," she added as Veer left.

That was awfully generous considering what she was currently going through. "You, too," she replied, and walked as quickly as she dared.

"Hey, you there," one of the officers yelled as she walked away. She took another step, trying to pretend she didn't know he was talking to her. She was about to break into a run, when there was a scream behind her.

"Aah! Help!" the girl cried out. Veer glanced behind her to see the girl hanging out of the tree, holding onto the branch, arms stretched above her. She shot Veer a mischievous smile before looking back to the police. "I'm gonna fall!" she cried. She was distracting them, giving Veer time to get away.

It worked. The cop following her hesitated for only a second before heading back to help his partner. Thank god for street punks. The police wanted to speak to the random stranger who wanted to get away from them. That was enough reason for her to help the random stranger, even in her grief. Veer broke into a run, setting off in search for the Were, though she didn't have high hopes for finding them, with nothing more to go on than a vague "thataway."

Then again, a werewolf wandering the streets would probably not be inconspicuous.

That turned out to be true, but not in the way she was expecting. It was only a few blocks away that the gamble paid off. A group of young men were standing together, guffawing and cat-calling, staring down the street. She followed their gaze just in time to see the back of a naked woman disappear around a corner. She sprinted to catch up to her.

"Hey, wait up!" she shouted down the street. The girl turned and saw her and then started running the other way.

Shit. She continued running. The girl was clumsily trying to cover herself with her hands while she ran. Veer caught up with her after another block.

"Hey, stop," she said, trying to catch her breath. "I'm here to help."

The girl stopped at last, trying to hide herself behind one of the small brass water fountains that dotted the sidewalks in this part of the city. "Here, take my jacket," Veer said, transferring her keys and wallet into pants pockets before handing it over to her.

The other woman took it gratefully. It was a little tight, but she managed to close the zipper.

"Thanks," she finally said.

This wouldn't be one of the victims, Veer realized, it was much too soon for that.

"You didn't stash a spare set of clothes somewhere?" she asked her.

"I did. They were in Bekka's car. But they left without me," she replied, then immediately realized what she'd said.

Veer read the obvious embarrassment on her face.

"It's okay," she said. "I'm Were, like you."

"Oh, thank god." The girl relaxed. "Did Shelly send you?"

"I was looking for stragglers," she replied. It wasn't a lie. Not exactly.

"Do you have a car then?" the woman asked Veer.

"I can get one," she replied. She had passed a couple of the ubiquitous ride sharing cars within the last couple of blocks. "C'mon."

They walked back to the vehicle, and Veer swiped her card over the sensor to unlock it. The girl got in, after a long hesitation. She eyed Veer warily as she did so.

"I'm Veer," she introduced herself, putting her seatbelt on. "And you are...?" she added when the other girl didn't respond.

"Caitlyn," the woman finally answered.

"You're not really with Shelly and Kevin, are you?" she asked as Veer pulled the car out of its parking space. She figured it out. But that was two more names. She repeated it silently to herself, to commit it to memory: "Bekka has a car. Caitlyn the straggler. Shelly and Kevin are in charge."

"No," she admitted as she drove the tiny car down the street.

"Are you... are you with the Alphas?" She looked terrified. What had she heard? Who had told her? "The Alphas" she had said, plural and capitalized. "Where are you taking me?" Her voice rose in panic and she reached for the door.

"I'll take you wherever you want to go," Veer replied. Again, trying to keep her voice calmly soothing. "And no, I'm not really 'with' anybody. I'm just trying to figure out what's going on here."

"Oh." Caitlyn relaxed a little bit. Though she didn't move her hand away from the door handle.

"Look, if you're going to jump out, let me know, so I can stop first," she tried to sound reassuring. "You're not a prisoner and I'm not going to hurt you." She crossed Burnside street, moving into the trendy Northwest district. She asked again, "Where are we going? Did you guys have a rendezvous site set up?"

"Yeah," she responded. "Dante's, just up ahead." Veer knew it. Sounded reasonable. Cheap food, and plenty of it, which they would want, after having changed, but not eaten. Or slept for that matter. And it had large tables and probably not a lot of other patrons at this time of day. Somebody had thought ahead. Though not enough to think to watch for stragglers being picked up by nosy reporters.

"Do you want me to take you there?" she asked her.

Caitlyn obviously understood what she meant by the question. She thought about it for several long moments before finally replying. "Yeah. I need to go. All my stuff's there. My clothes. My wallet."

Vera thought about what could be in the wallet worth retrieving. A few dollars? Maybe a bank card, easily replaceable, and her driver's license. More of a pain to replace, especially if she didn't already have a passport or some other form of ID. There would be danger in this place for the woman if she entered with Veer, as well as for Veer herself, but she had to see these people. This may be her only chance to see who this band of rogue Were really were. She'd be a fool not to seize the opportunity, regardless of the danger.

"All right, want to wait here?" she asked as she pulled the car into a parking space. "I'll find Bekka and see if I can persuade her to come out with her car keys?"

"Yeah, thanks, I really don't want to go in there. I just want to go home..." She seemed about to say more.

Veer let her.

"Oh gods it's horrible. I just want out. I don't want to be a werewolf anymore!"

Veer knew the feeling. She'd had her own regrets after Victor turned her. What she wouldn't do for a story.

"Well, I can give you a ride home, if you want, but I'm afraid you're stuck with the wolf. There's no way to un-make you. But it'll be okay, I promise. There are people who can help you adjust, if you want. It doesn't have to destroy your life." She didn't know if it was true that she'd be okay. The girl was scared, and completely unprepared for what she'd become. Just like so many in the square. Who would help them? Who could? And how would they ever cover such a thing up? Somebody would need to.

She texted Victor before she entered the club. "Were at PS. Dozen maybe. Multiple bites. Following lead to Dante's." The last just so if anything did happen to her, he'd know where to start looking. Then she turned off the sound on the phone so any reply wouldn't give her away. She took a deep breath and opened the front door.

She had dressed for a business meeting with Victor, which made her stand out in the club. She regretted the loss of the jacket, which could have given her a more generic look. She shrugged and headed to the bar to get a drink. It would look better if, while wandering about, she was at least carrying a drink already. It was still early, and the crowd was thin. She headed further in, through a crumbling brick archway, and immediately found what she was looking for.

A larger group of young men and women gathered in the back room. Some were standing, some sitting at the big tables. She recognized one of the women standing at a table, talking animatedly with someone next to her. Shelly. She looked over and saw the man sitting at the table. Kevin. Shelly and Kevin, the ones Caitlyn said were in charge. He was sitting in a lower chair, beer in hand, half a dozen people nearby, all facing him as he gestured enthusiastically, expostulating on something she couldn't hear. The body language was unmistakable, though: He was holding court.

They were Were, both of them, and had been for years. These were no mere rogues; this was a rebellion. She had her information and was about to leave when Shelly looked up and saw her.

"Hey, Veer, right?" she called out, raising a hand. "Why don't you come join us?"

It was phrased as a request, but others began closing in behind her. She had no choice but to move forward, deeper into their midst

NINETEEN
CHILDREN OF THE MOON

"This is your last chance," Carl said to the assembled white-robed initiates lined up on the grass before him. He and Toni were standing on the back porch of the rented cabin, looking down at them. They were both wearing the black robes that Toni had made for the occasion. The weather was perfect. The full moon was just rising over the trees, and there were few enough clouds that it shone through.

"In just a few minutes, it will begin. Once it's started, there's no way to change your mind or stop it. You will know fear, and you will know pain." He paused there for a moment. Toni didn't say anything, though she'd earlier vetoed the line. He was quoting Babylon 5, and she had caught him at it. But he still thought it was obscure enough that hardly anyone would recognize it even if they'd seen the show. He slipped it in now at the last minute as sort of a private joke between the two of them.

"It must be this way," he continued, "for such is the way of all new life." He had pointed out while they were writing the ritual that for the most part it was just humans who experienced excruciating pain at childbirth. Most new life was brought about relatively pain free. She'd kicked him hard, then.

"What was that for?" he'd asked her.

"Think about it," she had replied with a scowl.

He had, but hadn't come up with any answer.

"If you want to back out, go inside now. We ask only that you don't come back out again until it's all over. It won't be safe for you."

Nobody moved. He hadn't expected them to at this point.

"Remember, then, stay away from humans. That's the most important thing. Say it to yourself now. Stay away from humans." He knew they wouldn't understand. Not yet. But hopefully repeating it was enough to get them to remember, perhaps even to repeat it to themselves while they lay bleeding on the grass.

There was nothing more to be said. It was time. They hadn't discussed the change itself, but he didn't want to ruin the robe that Toni had put so much effort into. He reached back and grabbed the collar, pulling it off over his head. She did the same. For a moment, he stood gazing at her standing naked in the light of the full moon. He thought of their first night together, on the wolf preserve, making love while the wolves scavenged the deer she had killed. The others were forgotten, and it was just the two of them standing there. On an impulse, he leaned over and kissed her. Then pulled back, a wide smile on his face. She just nodded and turned her attention to those in front of them. He looked back out now on the others. Bite, then move on, until all had been found, then wake up. He repeated it to himself again as he changed, his smile turning to wolfish grin as he hit the ground.

THERE WAS SCREAMING among the humans in front of him as he charged forward. The scents of fear, mingled with excrement and, from his mate beside him, pure joy. One of them moved forward while all the rest were backing away. He leapt off the wooden porch directly at that one, the impact knocking it backward. His teeth sunk into its shoulder. It cried out as they fell to the ground. He wanted to rip, to tear, to silence its screams. But something told him to let go and to move on. One bite, then move. He did so, and found another one only a few leaping bounds ahead. He took that one down just as easily, ignoring the noise and the feeble blows attempting to ward him off. As soon as the blood filled his mouth he remembered to let go. Leaving that one writhing on the ground behind him, he sniffed the air. He quickly found a scent trail, thick with fear, leading into the woods. He followed, determined to sink his teeth into whatever was at the end of it.

The human was ahead of him, running. Fear poured off of it. He was almost upon it when it noticed him, turned sharply and ran in a different direction. He sprung and his prey turned again. It held something in its hand. It swung it wildly and connected with the side of his head. The impact sent him reeling, but he rolled over and got back to his feet. He approached more cautiously, as the human backed toward a tree, waving its stick in front of itself. A memory of another human in a tree made him hesitate.

The stick swung out again and hit him solidly in the side. He spun with the impact and trotted away several steps. He could run off, but he knew he had to bite this one first. He turned back, hunched down and growling, teeth bared. He was enjoying this game. He inched forward and jumped back, narrowly avoiding the swing of the stick. He tried a different angle, circling to find an opening. He could be patient. The stick jabbed this time, poking straight at him and catching him on the nose. He yelped in pain and moved back again but continued to circle. It was shouting, making human noises at him, with as much anger as fear now. But it didn't matter. He had to bite it, just once, then he could leave to find more. He moved again, jumping toward him then springing away before he could react. If any damage had been done to his nose, it was healed now. He moved to a different side and repeated the maneuver.

The human wasn't as fast to recover. He did it again, only this time, immediately after springing back, turned again and leapt forward, low to the ground. It worked, and the stick swished feebly over him as his teeth closed in on a leg. He stood, lifting it with him, pulling and twisting. The human went down and screamed as bone crunched and warm blood filled his mouth and ran down his fur. He could smell only fear and the unpleasant scent of voided bowels. He shook the leg bone in his jaws, then remembered to drop it as he again charged into the forest, leaving the diminishing cries of pain behind him.

He went back to follow the remaining trails. The humans had scattered in all directions. Trail after trail ended only with wounded humans, and the lingering scent of the other wolf. He was confused as he left the last one, unsure of what to do. He had to hunt down the humans but there didn't seem to be any left. He was done. He called the human down to him. He'd be better equipped to deal with this unexpected development.

CARL AWOKE and sprung to his feet immediately. He shivered, standing naked in the cold October air. He was surrounded by woods, with no idea where he was. Look for the smoke from the chimney, Toni and said, and the lights. All he could see was trees. No smoke, no lights. Crap. He hadn't thought of that. And what about the others? How would they get back, wounded as they were? No, scratch that. They wouldn't be wounded by the time they started heading back. And that wouldn't be earlier than an hour or two before dawn. So, he had a few hours to kill. He had an idea of how he wanted to spend them, and it wasn't wandering lost and naked in the forest.

The others would be out here, scattered around. Maybe some of them had already changed. They'd want to find food, and there was plenty of it in the area from what he'd seen. He hoped they were far enough from any humans that the warning against going near them wouldn't even come up.

He sniffed the air experimentally, then relaxed and inhaled softly, allowing the scents to linger inside the air passages. Don't focus on one scent, let your subconscious do its job, he reminded himself, the same as he told Toni. He pushed into the forest, walking down a narrow game trail, backtracking his own path. He hoped. And what about Toni? How would she find her way back? She wasn't experienced at tracking by scent - not in human form. Nothing he could do about her now, though. He had to find his own way back and just hope she could make it, too. He continued to follow the trail. Game trail, he told himself. Not human made, but created by frequent passing of some animal or some large number of animals. He guessed it would take more than one animal a few passes a day to actually create a trail, even a small one. What, then, a herd of some-thing? Deer? He knew there were some around here. Were there a lot? How many would it take to make a trail? Do they tend to travel the same routes repeatedly?

He realized there was a lot he didn't know out here, and this wasn't even true wilderness, just the bits of forest in between various people's houses. It probably wouldn't be more than a mile's walk in any direction before he ran into someone's home, or another vacation rental. There would be roads all through here as well. Though even if he found one, would he know which way it led? Could he get back to the cabin that way without a GPS? The full moon was still high in the sky. He supposed he could wait until it started to set, then he could tell which way was west. Of course, that wouldn't do him any good unless he knew which way he'd gone from the cabin. Shit, how'd he end up so incompetent at such a basic task? Which road led to where? Where was the cabin compared to any large landmarks? Once he got clear of the road, would there even be any large landmarks? They were up in the mountains a bit - he could probably have seen peaks on the drive up here if he'd thought to look for them.

What was it Toni had said about taking responsibility, figuring things like that out on your own, and not expecting to be told everything? And here he was now, lost alone in the woods. He laughed out loud at the irony.

"Hello?" a voice answered his laughter from nearby. Tentative and strained. He froze, and stood for a moment, silently. "Is someone there?" the man repeated. Daniel, maybe? He wasn't sure who he was. "Please! I'm..." the man hesitated, "I'm hurt. Help me. I don't think I can make it."

You'll be fine, Carl thought, but didn't speak out loud. *If you hadn't been turned, you'd be dead by now.* It was an echo of what Kevin had told Toni, and what's-his-name. He wondered if it was true. He remained silent.

"I know you're there," the man repeated. Carl took one step backward, cautiously. "Help me, you fucking bitch!" the voice said.

Carl could feel anger welling at that, but still he remained silent. Should he speak? Reassure the man that he wasn't going to die? Encourage him to give in to the wolf and end his suffering? He would have, except the guy obviously thought it was Toni here. And the stream of invective aimed her way was only making him angry. He started walking away again, at first as quietly as he could, but quickly picked up the pace. Behind him the curses had turned to sobs. There was nothing there but anger and fear. That and the pain was what was speaking, he reassured himself. The anger should be forgotten along with the pain after his first transformation healed his wounds. Should be.

He decided to keep an eye on him, just in case. He continued down the trail, such as it was, trying to follow the scent trail. Thoughts of Toni filled his mind. Her quirky smile, the way she felt, and the way she smelled. The problem with following a trail like this is, despite what he had told Toni, you could never really be sure you were following it until you found something. It was all done subconsciously, and you couldn't analyze the results as you go.

He had had a lot of success in the past. He had practiced frequently ever since he had heard it was possible, but the wolf mind communicated only in vague desires not in concrete visions. You just had to keep going and trust that there was a destination even if you couldn't know for sure until you got there. It helped to enjoy long walks alone without knowing where you were going or caring how long it took to get there. There was a metaphor in there somewhere. He didn't bother working it out. Let the mind wander, let the subconscious do its thing. He remembered vaguely the advice on meditation from some book he'd read years ago. Or was it something Toni had told him? You are not your thoughts. You have thoughts - let them drift into your brain and through. Don't dwell on any particular one, just let them pass. He did, focusing instead on the sensations and emotions. The way Toni made him feel. He let that feeling grow stronger as he followed the trail.

Eventually, how long was it? Hours, maybe? He'd lost track. Were all the others in Form, out there hunting? The answer to that last question came at the same time he found the house. The woods gave way abruptly to an unkempt lawn. The house was there, he would have recognized it even without the Christmas lights that Toni had put up on the chimney. Lily was lying on the grass, curled up, her white robe stained red. As he approached, he could see she had pulled it up, holding the hem of it to her shoulder trying to staunch the flow of blood. He hadn't been prepared for this. He wasn't sure what to do. Nod politely as he walked by? Ignore her completely? He realized he'd been standing still and staring for several seconds.

"Uh... hi," he finally said. She didn't say anything to him but continued to stare silently back. "How are you doing?" It sounded stupid to him as he said it. He grew acutely aware of his own nakedness. "Ummm..." he started, about to withdraw. He thought of Toni on their first night, leaving her alone in the basement, not knowing what was going on, and stopped. He still didn't know what to say or do next.

Lily started laughing. He just looked blankly. Not sure how to react to that, either. Too much unknown. "I think something bit me," she said, then laughed softly at her own joke.

"I..." he was about to say, "I'm sorry," but stopped himself. He had nothing to apologize for here. She had chosen this, knowing what was going to happen. This wasn't like it was with Toni. He pushed that thought back down quickly. He crouched down beside her to get a better look at the wound. She drew away from him slightly, then cried in pain from the motion.

"It's okay," he decided. "You should be able to feel the wolf now. Sense it, at the corner of your mind, trying to get in. Let it in, and everything will be okay," he said.

"I don't know how," she replied. "I'm scared."

"I know," he said. "But you won't be for much longer."

He thought back on his own initiation and remembered laying in the sage at the end of a hot day, bleeding from the wounds on his arm where Kevin, in Form, had bitten him. Half a dozen others, each bitten by a different wolf, were lying around, moaning or crying or suffering in stoic silence. All the wolves had run off, but Victor Stumpp stood alone among them. Watching. Judging. He'd felt humiliated. Exposed. No, this was better. The change should be a private matter.

"I have to go now," he said, standing up, "But... it's been said that a person of strong will can fight the Wolf. Keep it at bay. But don't. Embrace it."

"What's it like?" she said. He noticed that she didn't ask him for help, but continued to press the robe against her shoulder.

"It's... I don't know how to explain it," he told her truthfully. "It's the most wonderful thing ever. Look," he added. "Hills that way. Stream that way." How did he not notice that until now? "Go downhill, or follow the stream, and it'll come up behind the house."

He wished someone had told him that. Maybe there was a good reason not to. He only found his way back because he knew how to follow a scent trail. And he'd only been able to do that because he'd believed the Alpha when he said it was possible. Most of the other Were he'd mentioned it to assumed it was some kind of a joke. He'd believed it possible and thus learned to do it, but nobody else here had that advantage. The lights on the chimney were worthless. You couldn't see them until you were close enough to see the house. He wondered how many would find their way back? They might have a long wait tomorrow. Well, at least one of them will have a good chance. He hoped the rest of them took notice, unlike him. What if they found some other house instead? Or contacted search and rescue? Or the police? There was so much they hadn't planned for. So much that could go wrong.

"You'll be okay," he repeated. "I'll see you again when you get back."

"Wait..." she said, after he'd taken a step away. "What if I don't change? What if something went wrong, and I stay like this?"

This, at least, was something they'd thought of. "Then after someone else gets back, one of us will take you to the hospital." He said it matter-of-factly, expecting it to sound shocking. He wanted to underscore how dangerous it all was, even after tonight. Especially, perhaps, after tonight, but he could tell she didn't need any more lessons at this point. The pain and the blood was all too real.

"But you probably don't have to worry about that," he told her. "It's possible that the only times the transformation failed are because people have concentrated really hard on keeping the wolf out. That wound? It would be a lot worse, possibly fatal, if the wolf wasn't already there." It was something Kevin had said. He had no idea if it was true or not.

"Just relax and let it in," he repeated. "Then find your way back here in the morning. And remember to stay away from humans."

"Okay," she said, obviously trying to keep her voice steady. "Thank you."

He felt shamed at her gratitude. He just nodded in response and went into the house, picking up his black cloak on the way. He shrugged into it then went into the kitchen. He was ravenous, but didn't want to fire up the grill, not with Lily still out there lying in the yard. He found the large tub of potato salad and heaped some of it onto a plate. When he finished it, he peeked out the window. The girl was still there. He ducked back in quickly, hoping she hadn't seen him. He started forming the beef into patties, found a frying pan and a bit of oil and started cooking one. After it had started, he checked the window again. On the grass where Lily had been was nothing but a shredded white robe.

The patty was almost done when he spotted Toni through the kitchen window, approaching the house cautiously. He tossed another burger patty into the pan, then pushed both to the side to fit a couple of slices of bacon.

"Good timing," he said, pushing a bun into the toaster as she entered the kitchen, now clad in her own black robe.

"Not using the grill?" she asked him.

"Didn't want to wait that long," he said. "Plus, thought I'd save it for the rest of the group."

"Whenever they get back," she said. "How long have you been here?"

"Not long. Half an hour maybe?" he said. "Lily was on the lawn while I was on my way in, but she was gone a few minutes before you got here."

"Oh. Seen any of the others?"

"Heard Daniel. Didn't see him, though. He seemed a little put out."

"Put out?"

"Angry. Like way so. Stream of obscenity - Fuck you, I'll get you, you cunt, whore, slut - that sort of thing. I didn't respond."

"That... sounds a little on the personal side," she said. "Did I bite him, or did you?"

"Pretty sure he was yours," Carl replied. "And he didn't see me - just heard me walk by, so he may well have assumed I was you. Or maybe that's just how he swears when he's stressed."

"Either way, doesn't sound like someone I want to put a lot of trust in."

"Maybe. Sorry. I didn't want to piss you off or put a guy on your wrong side."

"No, it's good that I know. Don't worry, I'm not going to kick him out of the group or anything based on a few words that I didn't even hear. But I am gonna keep an eye on him."

"Okay. I will too, then. Did you see anyone else on the way in?"

She hesitated for a moment and then, as if it were an admission, "Yeah... Kim."

Why hesitate at that? She had talked to her earlier, too, in the first part of the initiation ceremony.

"Oh?" he asked, not sure what was up or how to ask. "How was she?"

"Hurt," Toni replied. "In pain. Scared."

Which was to be expected. Carl found he couldn't speak. His throat seemed to seize up. He was thinking of Toni in the same situation. Except alone, in a basement, chained to a wall and with no explanation given, other than Kevin's rantings, of which she would have had no way of knowing how much was true and how much was utter nonsense.

Toni gave him a strange look, as if she could tell what he was thinking. How could he have had a part in such a thing. It was as if it were another person, another world. A lifetime ago. But it was only a month in the past. She hadn't spoken of it in over a week, but it was there always, laying like a blanket between them.

He met her gaze. She held it for a moment, then looked away. "I talked to her for a bit," she said. One more thing he hadn't done for her. All without her consent. He was disgusted by the thought.

"How'd that go?" he asked. "How long?"

"A while. A long while. I, uh, ended up staying with her until she changed."

"Oh." Exactly what he hadn't done for her. Or for Lily. Should he have? He thought again about his own initiation, lying on the ground with half a dozen others around him, all under the watchful eye of the Alpha. To be by himself, away from the judgment of others? Left alone with his thoughts in that critical time... that's what he would have preferred. But would anyone else have preferred the same? Not everyone was like him, after all. Lily didn't seem to want him to go.

"Something we'll need to talk about," he said, taking his own burger out of the pan.

"What do you mean? Do you think I did the wrong thing, offering her comfort?" She didn't say it, but Carl knew she was contrasting how she was turned.

"No," he said, "I don't know what the right thing is. That's why I want to talk about it. Lily was in the yard when I got back," he nodded toward the tattered robe still lying there. "I spoke to her briefly. But then I left her alone. Part of the reason I didn't fire up the grill was because I didn't want to disturb her. I wanted to leave her to change on her own."

"And you think that's what I should have done?" Toni asked.

"No," he replied, "I don't know if that's better. If it was me... I don't know. I would have preferred to be alone, but I think now that that might have been the company I was in. With someone more supportive, or just compassionate? I don't know."

"What about you?" he wanted to ask her. Chained in the basement, if she would have preferred someone there... But of course, there had been someone. But if she wasn't going to bring it up, he didn't want to. She didn't seem to be angry still and he couldn't figure out why not. Maybe she was dealing with it just by pretending it never happened. Given the circumstances, maybe that was actually the healthiest response.

"Do you think I did the wrong thing, leaving Lily alone?" he asked her instead.

"Can't tell you that, either," she said. "I don't think it makes any difference, really. Maybe unplanned and haphazard is the best way to go."

"I guess. Most of the recruits scattered into the woods and ended up on their own anyway," he said. "Between us, we only met three of them. And then chose three different ways of dealing with them. I don't know which way's right, but it's got to make some difference."

"It's not that it doesn't make a difference. I mean, the whole experience is going to be vastly different depending on all sorts of variables. Including a lot that they bring with them. Trying to control them all is only going to drive you mad. It's just one night. And, from what you told me, you're likely to live, what, another eighty, ninety, maybe a hundred years still? It's like a wedding, right? I mean, some people spend just way too much time and invest far too much stress trying to make everything about it perfect that all they do is make themselves and everyone around them miserable, and forget the fact that it's just one day out of what is theoretically decades to come."

"You're saying we shouldn't worry about it, and just get on with it."

"More or less. Whatever happens, it'll be a memorable ceremony, and that's the most important part. An event that marks a major change in their life. I think we can design in certain lessons, and those who are receptive to such things might gain some insight. Those who aren't won't. But you can't dictate which lessons they'll learn or how. You're painting in broad strokes and letting the initiate sort it out. Plus, that diversity of experience can itself be useful. Gives them all something to discuss later at the very least."

"So now what, then?" he asked her.

"Now, I say we start the grill. We can keep it going or restart or whatever when everyone else gets back."

"Whenever that turns out to be."

"Yeah. I'm not sure what we'll do if some people don't make it, or take too long."

"I guess we can start going out looking for people if they don't make it before we're supposed to be out of here."

"Or contact them again once we're back in civilization."

ANOTHER YOUNG MAN walked over with a few drinks and set them on the table in front of Kevin, who took one without acknowledging him. The man moved to stand beside him. He gestured to Veer, who declined, indicating the drink already in hand. A chair was brought up to her and she took it.

"I can only stay a minute," she told him. "I'm meeting someone here."

How much of this attention was just suspicion at the surprise meeting, and how much did he know? It was quite a stretch to be a coincidence her showing up here right after what had just happened. He'd have to be an idiot not to at least suspect he'd been followed. Here's hoping.

"Meeting someone?" he echoed, raising her hopes.

"Working on a story?" Shelly asked her. Then she turned to Kevin. "She's a reporter, remember?"

Veer didn't like the sound of that last word. She'd been a topic of conversation recently. She was surrounded by rogues who not only knew who she was but had recently been discussing her. This did not bode well. The other rogues were hanging back. More had moved behind her, blocking her way to the exits. All were watching Kevin.

"What kind of story?" Shelly continued.

"Well, I don't want to give out the details yet, but it involves labor practices at a major corporation."

"Sounds boring," came a loud voice from behind her.

Kevin shot a withering look at the man. That was good. He wasn't going to allow any overt aggression unless by his choice. They followed his lead. So, whatever they were up to, it was planned, and his people were disciplined, which could be good or bad. It meant he wasn't going to lash out in an emotional tantrum. He'd only do anything violent if he had more to gain from it than he'd lose. Or if he believed her to be a threat. So, all she had to do was convince them that she wasn't. No problem. They were a bunch of rogues who'd broken the primary law of Were society and could all possibly face death for doing so, and she was associated closely with the people who'd be doling out that punishment. How hard could it be to convince him that she posed no threat?

The alternative would be to convince him that the risk would be too great in attacking her.

She turned to the man who had spoken and sized him up. He was in his early twenties, like the rest of them, and obviously spent a lot of time working out. Well defined muscles, but nothing in his demeanor indicated he knew how to use them. He sat slumped back in his chair with his arms folded in front of him, a scowl on his face. He might be dangerous in a fight, but there'd be no surprises from him. Of course, that'd be as a human. In Form, all bets were off. Her best course of action would be to put him off his game, make him careless and unsure of himself while isolating him from the others. She tilted her head back slightly to look down on him, pulling herself up in the chair to do so.

She trained her best patronizing look at him and said in a soft voice, in a tone that she'd use while addressing a child who had asked her what a journalist did, "Well, yes, you are right. It could be boring. It's a very complex story. Part of my job is not only getting the story but in figuring out how to tell it so people won't find it boring when it's done."

It may have been laying it on a little thick, but she was afraid anything more subtle would be lost on him. He shifted uncomfortably in his chair, his scowl deepening. She heard a short snort of laughter behind her. Apparently, Shelly at least realized exactly what Veer was doing and found it amusing. Good, that would deepen the psychological impact, and possibly sow dissension in the ranks.

She turned her attention back to Kevin. Shelly was standing behind him now, resting her hand on the back of his chair, drink on the table. Ready to spring into action, Veer thought. She also noticed that she was the only one whose attention was primarily on Veer, not on Kevin. A woman's jacket hung on the back of Kevin's chair. The pockets sagged with weight. An experienced Were, then. Kept her valuables separate so they wouldn't get scattered or destroyed when she changed.

"Well, hey, when you're done with that one, I've got a good story for you," Kevin said. "You should write about a secret society of werewolves in Portland."

"That seems to be a popular subject these days," Veer replied.

Kevin scowled, but Shelley widened her eyes at that, inviting her to continue.

Before she did, though, Kevin replied, "There's more. These Were are ruled by a secretive council of Alphas, who make rules and enforce them with no input from those below, enforcing them with an iron fist. Everyone else in this story are second class citizens, only allowed to share their lives with those the Alphas approve. Only working where they allow, living where they say. Living or dying at their whim." He leaned forward as he finished, a challenging gleam in his eyes.

She responded by settling back in her chair, keeping her body language relaxed and unconcerned. "I don't know," she said. "It sounds a little over-wrought. Melodramatic, even. Like a bad novel more than anything else."

"Oh, but wait, there's even more to the story," Kevin said, raising a finger. He wouldn't do anything while he was talking, and neither would the rest of the people in the room. So she needed to keep him talking until she could think of something.

"You see, there's also another group of Were. Several other groups, actually, only peripherally aware of each other. Separate, but working towards one goal: Freedom!" He paused again, obviously expecting a response.

Several groups. That was a major revelation. She ignored it and responded instead with a disdainful tone, "You feel you're not free now?"

"No!" He raised his voice. There was a ripple of reaction across his followers at that. Even Shelly looked surprised. Could she isolate him like she did his crony? What would it take to turn these people against him? These weren't fanatics. How many scared kids like Caitlyn were there among them? Could provoking a display of temper do it? It would make the situation more dangerous if she failed, but she didn't see any other way out.

"Free to do what? What do you want to do that you can't do now?"

"Live free! Make my own decisions!" He was getting close.

"Kill people?" she asked coldly. "You're afraid the Alpha won't allow you to continue your murderous rampage?"

"It's not about killing," he replied. There was a slight hesitation in his voice. She just needed to push a little harder.

"Tell that to Jim," she said, playing to the crowd now.

"Who the hell is Jim?" he asked her.

"One of the people who you killed in Pioneer Square today. He may disagree with your concept of freedom."

"Every struggle for freedom has casualties," Kevin retorted, as she'd hoped he would. He had a casual disregard for human life. She hoped it was not shared by all of his followers. She looked around at them. Not only to see their reactions, which in general were reassuringly wary, but to let Kevin see her looking to them. She wanted to make him hesitant, unsure of his position. She wanted him to be trying to retain his followers. If they saw him doing that, they would realize the question existed as to whether they should follow him or not. It would change the question from whether or not she was a threat to whether or not Kevin was.

"His girlfriend seemed to think he was worth more than just collateral damage," she said.

"His death is... regrettable," he said defensively. That was Good. "But like I said, there's a war on."

"Only to you and your little group here," she interrupted, anticipating what he was going to say.

"There is a war going on, and sometimes people die in war," he finished emphatically.

"Since you're the only ones fighting it, stop and there won't be any need to," she returned.

"We are fighting for our freedom!" he shouted. Losing his temper. Good.

"Shouldn't people have a choice to become Were or not?" she asked, pressing him.

"Everyone here entered it freely," Kevin said.

"What about those in the square?" she asked him. "You didn't murder everyone. A lot of them are going to become Were. Where was their choice?"

"They'll be fine," he said instead of answering.

"That's not what I asked," she reprimanded sharply. "I said where was their choice?"

"We're all Were here - it's not a terrible thing to become. They'll be fine as long as your goon squads leave them alone!"

"I'm hardly a goon squad," she said with a soft laugh. Then she made her tone harsher. "What do you think is going to happen to these people? Changed the way they are with no idea what they are..."

"Oh, I'm sure they'll figure it out!" he said and chuckled coarsely. His comment drew a few nervous giggles, but no general laughter, which was good. Genuine laughter on his behalf could undermine what she was trying to do. She suspected he knew that, at least on some level.

"Sure, they'll figure it out," she replied, her voice as caustic as she could make it. "After they grow irritable for a while, increasingly short tempered as they fight the change, until they finally succumb involuntarily, with no preparation and no training on how to control it," she didn't let him interrupt this time.

"Eventually, after the second or third time of waking up from what they think is a bad dream to find their roommates or boyfriends or children mauled to death, yeah, they'll figure it out. They'll drift, fearful of what they've become, toward the outskirts of society - drifting, running, killing, some of them for years, until someone else eventually figures out what they are, too, and hunts them down and kills them, or they end up taking their own life out of guilt and fear."

She spoke over his attempt to respond. "That's what's going to happen. That's what used to happen all the time. Until we got organized. Until we agreed to help each other out. Until we agreed to teach new Were our ways and how to avoid hurting themselves or others. And those are the days you want to return to? When we all were individually hunted, living short, violent, confused lives? To return to the irrational hatred and cowering fear of the fucking middle ages?"

She focused all her attention on him and only hoped that those around her did as well. She was sowing the seeds of doubt in them. Making the case of the Alphas, of Victor, which she had just been arguing against. She felt no sense of hypocrisy doing so, though. The Were needed to be exposed, to come out into the light of day. But not like this. Not in acts of violence. Doing it this way could only lead to exactly the horrific scenarios that the Alphas predicted in their paranoia.

"No," Kevin said coldly. "That's not going to happen this time. There's more to it than that. We have a plan."

She was about to ask him to explain, when he nodded to someone behind her. Strong hands clasped her right arm. The big guy from earlier. She tried to pull free, but he held her tight. Someone else grabbed her other arm, then she heard Kevin say, "You don't know anything about us."

She turned to look at him. Both her arms were firmly held now. Kevin produced a large knife. Silver blade. A twin to the one that had killed Hudson. It would produce a fatal wound. She was only barely aware of the people on either side of her. Her entire field of vision narrowed to the knife, waving in Kevin's hand.

Kevin was still speaking, his voice seemed to be distorted, as if it was coming from a long way away. "But we know you, Vera Rosen, Right Hand of the Alpha. And we're not yet ready to let you report to him."

She kicked back on her chair as the knife approached, trying to topple it out from under herself and pull the two men holding her in together, tumbling them in between her and Kevin. She was partially successful. She fell halfway to the floor, pulling both men off balance just as Kevin struck forward with the knife. It slid along the arm of the man to her left, deflecting it from her sternum but didn't miss her completely. She felt it enter her side. She couldn't tell how deep. The man let go with a yelp, his arm drenched red. Was that his blood or her own?

I hope he doesn't have anything contagious, she thought as she continued to the floor. Her left arm was free. She swung it across toward the man on her right, twisting her whole body to add to its power. The heel of her hand connected with his nose. Something gave way, but his grip on her arm tightened, rather than releasing as she'd hoped. The knife was approaching again, seeking an opening. More people were closing in. She had to get out of here fast. She frantically pulled down on her trapped arm, pulling herself up.

"Get Kevin!" she yelled at the crowd, hoping to buy at least a second or two of confusion. Her captor was pulling her toward himself, so she let him, pushing forward with her legs and seeking his throat with her teeth bared. He tried to back off and twist at the same time. There was a wet pop as her arm gave way. Kevin's knife slid along her side, tearing clothes and flesh before being thrust forward to explode into fiery pain deep within her as she changed.

THE WOLF'S jaws were deep inside her enemy's neck. She had to open them to pull her head back. She sprung forward onto another person. Her foreleg buckled beneath her. Everywhere around her was light and noise and pain. Scents of fear and confusion washed over her. She leapt forward, pain seared through her side as she did so. Others were around her, getting in her way. They all sprung backwards as she snapped at them. They weren't cooperating. The air was thick with the scents of their fear.

Humans attempted to grab her, and wolves bit at her heels. Pups, inexperienced. She bit hard on a leg and shook with all her neck muscles to teach one a lesson. It fell, whimpering, but there was still real danger approaching. There were obstacles in her way. Escape was imperative - the only important thing. She pushed forward through the crowd again. A step. Another step. Biting, gnashing, pushing forward despite the pain because stopping would be certain death. Finally, there was a break in the crowd, and she sprung forward. Her belly was on fire, but her foreleg took the weight. It was nearly healed. Her midsection was not. It wasn't healing like it should have been. She ignored it in her mad scramble to escape. A door opened as she pushed against it, and the clear sweet acrid smells of the city were upon her.

She ran straight away from the building, a pair of wolves close on her heels. Running into the street, she leapt across it, barely in front of an approaching vehicle. It swerved, leaving its accustomed track - instinct had told her it couldn't do that - and plowed into one of the wolves. There was a loud thud and a scream of crumpling metal, and one wolf crawled away injured. The other was upon her. His jaws seeking her throat. She could barely move. There was so much pain. She'd never felt it like that before. Her vision, her whole body, wasn't working properly. She tried to struggle to her feet. The air grew full of fire. A burning mist stung her eyes and nose. She pulled away and could feel the other moving off, howling in pain. Its face was covered in some bright stinging substance.

A human was beside her now, tugging at her. Trying to get her to move. She didn't want to move. But danger was still near, still approaching. A few more steps. Would it make any difference? It might. She moved. An opening into something lay before her. Leading to the inside of a vehicle. Cars were something to be avoided, entering them was strange and foreign, but something inside her stirred, urging her forward.

She leapt up, wedging herself into the tiny space, as the human pushed from behind. The door slammed shut, trapping her and sending another shock of agony through her with its impact. A moment later the human joined her through another opening and they began to move. She knew somehow she'd finally reached safety. But the wound in her side wasn't healing. This was too confusing and unusual for the wolf to comprehend. For only the second time in her life, she called the human down to her.

———

PAIN FLOODED Veer's senses as her conscious mind returned to her and she screamed, clutching at her side. She was lying in the back of a tiny car, which came to an abrupt stop, throwing her forward into the backs of the seats in front of her and sending another wave of pain over her. She cried out again.

"Are you okay?" the woman in the front seat asked her. Caitlyn. She had given her a ride here, and now she was in the back of the car they'd used. How had that happened?

She almost laughed at the question, though. "No," she managed to gasp. "Oh, fuck, it hurts."

She had heard that a gut wound was one of the most painful injuries there was. Even in her pain, though, she tried to concentrate on what she was feeling, how it felt so she could describe it properly later. After a bit of experimentation, she learned she could breathe without the sudden pain causing her to cry out and lose all her breath again.

"I'm taking you to the hospital, okay?" the woman in the front seat said.

"Yes!" Veer gasped. It could be her only chance to survive. Veer noticed her driver was fully dressed. "You found Bekka?" she asked, though it seemed unlikely. She was very proud of herself at the moment for remembering the name. She wondered if Bekka had been one of the Were inside the club.

"What? Oh, the clothes!" Caitlyn responded. "No. I figured, she drove off and left me behind, I don't owe her anything. I found a rock."

For a second, Veer had an image of the woman threatening another woman with the rock until she handed over her car keys. Then she realized that's not what she meant and laughed out loud. That caused another wave of pain to overtake her. Black spots exploded at the edge of her vision, obscuring it completely until she passed out.

When she came to, seemingly hours later, she was still in the back of the car. Her blood pooled around her and soaked into the upholstery.

"Wait..." she said, barely recognizing the weak croaking voice as her own. "The cleaning deposit..."

There was a bark of laughter from the front seat. "Sorry, I think you can kiss that goodbye. I banged up the outside pretty good, too," Caitlyn said, and the car stopped.

Wait, Veer thought, it was okay. She didn't mean to hurt the car. She can pay for it. Somehow. The door opened then, and she was momentarily blinded by the light. She could feel herself being lifted, moved, something was splashing underneath her. She thought she heard a moan, and frantic voices. What's wrong? Everybody was shouting and gathered around her. There were too many voices. She was trying to sort out which one was hers as everything went dark.

NEWS AND MONDAY BLUES

Gordon exchanged just a few polite words with his coworkers when he arrived, and spent most of the morning in his cube, catching up on email and trying to prioritize his backlog of cases.

Charles had led the way in taking and doling out work that couldn't wait for his return, making sure he didn't lose his clients, so when Gordon took a lunch break to head to the cafe downstairs he didn't say no when Charles asked if he could join him. He almost wished he had when, seated at a table in the corner, Charles asked him, "So... do you think it was a werewolf that attacked you?"

He was shocked at the question.

"Wh... what?" he stammered. How did he know?

"Well, the police said it was a man with a trained dog, but what with the Werewolves in Pioneer Square last night..."

"The what?" The news shocked him even more than the question.

"You hadn't heard? Oh, shit, yeah, a bunch of people

Saturday night in Pioneer Square turned into wolves and started attacking everybody."

"I... no, I haven't seen the news today..." We don't all know each other, he almost said. "And what do you mean, werewolves?"

"Werewolves. Like, werewolf werewolves."

"As in people who can turn into wolves?"

"Man, it's all over the internet..." Charles began.

"Oh, well, if it's on the internet it must be true."

"No, seriously, man, check it out." Charles pulled out his phone, did a quick search and set it so Gordon could see it. There were a dozen videos about werewolf attacks in Pioneer Square. Charles tapped one labeled "ringleader" that showed three people standing at the top of a stairway, calmly watching the chaos below. It did seem strange that they were so calm when everyone around them was panicking.

Then the two on the ends changed into wolves. Right there on camera. There was a weird shimmer and a strange half twist, and the humans were no more. He let out a voluntary gasp. He recognized the motion.

"I know, right?" said Charles. "No morphing or anything. Just a shift, like something's entering from somewhere else, taking their place in this dimension, and suddenly they're wolves."

"But how could they...?"

"Werewolves, man."

"I mean, how come nobody's filmed this before? If there were werewolves, how come nobody saw them until now?"

"I dunno. Somebody's been putting out the word that it's a stealth marketing campaign, though."

"You don't believe it?"

"People have died. Awfully far to go to sell a movie."

"Wait," he said. "Back up to the guys at the top of the stairs. Can you zoom in on that guy?"

Charles did so and showed him the result. It was Kevin, from the warehouse. He was leaning forward, smiling broadly as he surveyed the carnage beneath him. Smiling. This is what he wanted. This was what he'd been planning that he didn't want to tell anyone about. People had died because of him, and he stood there, smiling. Gordon thought of Barbara, dying on the ground, bleeding, scared, like the people in the square, and this monster standing over her, smiling like he was untouchable. He realized his hand was in a fist.

"You know this guy?" Charles finally asked. Gordon had been frozen, staring at the screen.

"Yeah. Shit. I gotta go." He stood up, grabbed his coat, and left Charles behind alone with his half eaten lunch.

"YOUR TIE'S FINE," Aaron told him, catching him adjusting it while looking at his reflection in the conference room glass.

"The tie isn't the problem," Alice agreed.

Michael stopped fidgeting and looked at them both. He knew what they meant. The press conference was in an hour. The public expected an official response from the police. What was he going to say? He'd done his best to hint at werewolves at the last press conference, and someone tried to kill him. What was he supposed to say now that everyone could see the evidence for themselves? Given the magnitude of the attack, this should be a response from the police chief herself, but after speaking to Billings, she'd agreed to delegate communication to them. Great.

Detective Lauren Boyd came in, carrying a folder. She dropped it on the table without bothering to open it.

"The details are there," she said, indicating the folder. "I've checked with every hospital from Hillsboro to Gresham, and Lake Oswego to Vancouver. We've confirmed by first-hand accounts and video evidence that twenty-six wounded were taken away by ambulance from the attack on the square. Eight total arrived at any hospital, plus one DOA."

Michael did the math. "Four dead total and what, eighteen just... missing?"

"More than that," she said. "There're maybe a dozen or two who were there and weren't seen being taken away but haven't been heard from since."

"Shit. That gives us at least eighteen but possibly up to forty? The press is gonna love that."

"Best we got right now," Alice said. "Fuck 'em if they don't like it."

"Yeah, this'll be a fun one. We've got a possible terrorist attack, which nobody's taking credit for, though we do have an official denial from some film company. It looks like werewolves, but we can't admit we think so."

"Maybe it's time to change that last," Aaron said.

"You mean just embrace it and admit there are werewolves?" Michael replied.

"Let them laugh until they find out the truth," he said.

"And if they never find out the truth?"

"Then all of our careers will be ruined, and the werewolves will run rampant over whoever replaces us," Alice said. "No problem."

"It seems like the more we ignore it and dance around the questions the more people think we know something," Aaron said. "That should make it easier once we do reveal the truth."

"Got it. Ignore, deny, dance, there's my strategy." Michael said with a sigh.

Whatever he was going to say next, he was interrupted by his phone ringing at his desk outside the conference room.

"I'll keep trying to track down the other ambulances," Lauren said. "They have to have gone somewhere." She picked her folder off the table.

"I'll give you a hand," said Aaron and followed her out.

Michael picked up his desk phone on the fourth ring. "There's a Gordon Chandler down here who wants to speak with you. Shall I send him up?"

"Yes. Definitely. By all means," he said.

"It's Chandler," he told Alice, who'd followed him to his desk.

He pulled out his revolver and swapped the bullets for silver. Alice cocked one eyebrow at him.

"Just to be safe," he told her, returning the weapon to its holster. She nodded her understanding: Chandler wasn't a suspect, but he could only be trusted so far.

"Mr. Chandler," Michael greeted him when he had been escorted to the detective's desk.

"Gordon, please, or we won't get anywhere," the other man replied. He looked around. "Is there somewhere private we can talk?"

"We can use the war room. C'mon," he told him, leading the way to the converted conference room. "Thought it'd be more comfortable than one of the formal interrogation rooms," he elaborated when Chandler - Gordon - saw where they were headed.

"Detective Johansen is part of my squad," he said as she followed them into the room. "She's been fully briefed."

Gordon hesitated a moment, then nodded. He stopped and looked at the big board at the end of the room. With Grant dead, the investigation was no longer ongoing, so he didn't see any harm in letting him see it. Plus, it could help remind him that they were both on the same side.

"Is this..." he started, then trailed off.

"From the investigation, yes," Michael answered.

Gordon walked over to it, reached out and touched the pin in his own house, tracing the string back to the card with him and his daughter's name on it. He looked wistful for a moment.

"I'm sorry. I shouldn't have brought you in here," Michael said.

"No. No, it's okay," he said, not taking his eyes off the board. "It gives me a bit of an idea what you went through to catch this guy."

Which was exactly the reaction he'd hoped for.

"Who is this Rosen person?" he asked.

"She's a reporter who was working the same case."

"Vera Rosen. Yes. I recognize the name. With the Journal. She popped up a lot while I was looking into... well... everything."

Michael was ready to share some secrets, but he didn't feel her status was his to share. He steered him away from that topic.

"What brings you here today? After our last talk, I really wasn't expecting to see you again."

"You weren't keeping an eye on me?"

"I didn't think you were a criminal, or any kind of threat."

"That's good to hear," Gordon said. "I came about the attack on the Square."

That got Michael's attention. "You know something about it?"

"I'm pretty sure the whole thing was orchestrated by a guy named Kevin, and his girlfriend Shelly."

He knew those names. They had been the ones, along with Carl Jablonski, who'd attacked Mitch Douglass along with two others, one of whom had died. Douglass was currently at the safe house and still refusing to admit he was a werewolf.

"You know them already?" Gordon asked, obviously seeing his reaction.

"Only the names. They were involved in an earlier incident," he replied.

"What kind of an incident?" Gordon asked him.

"I'm sorry," he told him. "It's an ongoing investigation."

Gordon seemed to accept that.

Alice opened one of the folders on the table, pulled out a picture of a group of people from the Pioneer Square attack and showed it to him. "Recognize them on here?"

"That one's Kevin," Gordon said immediately, pointing out the one that they had assumed was in charge, standing at the top of the stairway overlooking the carnage, flanked by two other men. "I don't see Shelly anywhere."

"Do you know if Carl Jablonski was involved?" Michael asked him.

Gordon raised his eyebrow at that. "He wasn't," he replied after a second.

"Are you sure?"

"He was somewhere else this weekend." After another pause, he continued. "From what I can tell, they're old friends. They seem to have broken up into separate factions but maintain cordial relations. I gathered that he and Toni don't approve of their methods. Both groups have been recruiting."

"How sure are you of this?"

"Positive. I was at a party last week with the four of them, along with a bunch of people they were recruiting."

Shit again.

"They're making more? Why?"

"They want to go public, but they're afraid the Alpha will stop them."

"So, we have a motive," Alice said.

"Making more werewolves? Going public? Kind of weak."

"A stupid motive's still a motive," she replied. "It'll make them more predictable."

"The attack on the square..."

"I'm guessing we're seeing the 'methods' that Toni didn't approve of," Gordon said.

"Something spectacular, that couldn't be covered up or denied," Alice finished for him.

"Looks like the Alpha's already making strides toward doing just that, though," Michael mused. "They've disappeared half the victims, and there's a rumor that it's a movie advertising stunt gone wrong."

"I've heard that one. Think it'll work?" Gordon asked him.

"Maybe," Michael replied. "At least this time. It won't help in the long term, though. They'll try again, and probably soon. If the guy's on a mission, he won't stop at this. He's killed people. He's gotta know at this point he'll be hunted by us and the Alpha alike."

Could it be possible to use this to get to Stumpp? They'd have the same goals here - stopping further attacks, though for different reasons. Stumpp would want to keep the whole thing quiet. Most likely, he'd intentionally started the rumor about the movie shoot. Michael didn't think he had enough evidence to get a warrant for him yet. But could he suggest some kind of alliance? Could that convince Stumpp to give up enough information that Michael could eventually use it to bring him in?

Although, for catching Kevin, Jablonski might be the best bet. If he was an erstwhile friend, now on the outs, he might be persuaded to help catch the guy, while also having enough information to track him down.

"Unfortunately, we don't have a valid address for Mr.

Jablonski. The one registered with the DMV is at least a couple of years out of date."

"I've got a phone number and an email address for his alias," Gordon offered.

"That helps. Known aliases are good."

"And I know that his girlfriend, Toni, is a Barista at Powell's."

"Jackpot. If we can get her, we should be able to leverage her to find him."

"Maybe," Michael mused.

"Wait a minute, " Alice asked. "Is this girl short, a little on the thick side, with super short hair and a wolf tattoo on her lower back?"

"I don't know about the tattoo, but the rest seems right."

"It's her. Phil's barista." To Michael's blank look, she continued, "The girl he likes at Powell's, who he buys coffee from."

"Oh, yeah," Michael remembered. He hadn't met the girl himself. "He's going to be disappointed that she's got a boyfriend," Michael said.

"And that she's a terrorist," Alice replied.

"And a werewolf," Gordon added wryly.

"We probably have enough to bring her in," Michael said. Then turned to Gordon, "I once asked you if you'd be willing to testify. I take it by your presence you've decided you are?"

"Maybe," he said. Alice scowled at that. Michael caught it but wasn't sure that Gordon had. "I wouldn't go so far as to call Toni and Carl terrorists. Like I said, there're factions. They weren't involved in the attack in Pioneer Square."

"No, but they were involved in other attacks."

"There've been others?"

"Carl was involved with this Kevin and Shelly pair when they kidnapped and killed a man and turned two others into werewolves. He's not innocent here."

Gordon froze for a second there. Then replied, "Well, damn, and they seemed like such nice people."

There was something there, but Michael didn't think Gordon was ready to reveal it yet. He was afraid if he pried too much he could just shut down. Right now, he was in contact with a terrorist group who seemed to trust him. He could be a valuable informant if carefully cultivated. On the other hand, if he could get to Carl directly...

"Maybe he is," Michael said. "Maybe he just fell in with the wrong crowd and circumstances escalated out of his control. If so, that's a good thing, we can use that. We can cut him a deal if he wants to cooperate. How close is he to the girl, you think? Would he feel protective of her?"

"No. He seems like the type who'd sell out anyone to save his own hide. You might have better luck getting Toni to talk by threatening Carl if that's what you're getting at. I get the impression that she knows more anyway."

Made sense. From what Veer had told him, Carl was a relatively new Were and at the bottom of whatever ranking structure there was. He'd have to ask her about Toni, though. Funny she'd never mentioned her.

"I want to try Jablonski first," Michael decided. "We already know some of the depths of his involvement. He trusts you. Can you arrange a meeting?"

Gordon hesitated at that. Michael hurried to reassure him. "I'm not asking you to set him up, just make an introduction. Someplace public if that makes him more comfortable. I just want to talk, I promise."

SOMEONE WAS YELLING ANGRILY outside her room. Her room? Veer tried to remember where she was. She looked around. Various machines were whining and beeping. Something was attached to her arm, and she felt stiff in her middle. Awareness slowly seeped in. Somehow, she'd made it to the hospital. She'd been stabbed. She was lying in a bed, wearing a gown. Her entire belly was wrapped in bandages.

She recognized Victor's voice. Somebody wasn't letting him into the room, and he wasn't happy about it.

"Dammit," she heard him shout. He was frustrated, but loud, which was rare. It was when he was quiet, though, that he was truly angry. And the most dangerous. "She's a close friend, I'm not here to hurt her."

She tried to call out, let whoever it was keeping him out know that it was all right. They could let him in. She wondered if that were true. Probably if he wanted her dead, he wouldn't be here. Peter, or somebody like him, would be visiting. The point was moot, though, as she found her throat was so dry all she could manage was a coarse whisper. Even if they weren't shouting at each other, they wouldn't have been able to hear her outside the door. On TV there was always a pitcher of water and a cup on a table beside the bed. But she didn't see any here. There was another door that she assumed led to a bathroom. There'd be water in there. It seemed impossibly far away, though. There was still a tube attached to a needle in her arm.

She smiled briefly at the idea of heroically leaping to her feet, ripping the tubes out of her arm. Of course, she didn't have any idea where the other end of that needle was, or what damage it would do if removed improperly. Probably hurt a lot at the very least. Plus, judging how dizzy she got trying to sit up, she guessed that leaping to her feet would be quickly followed by falling flat on her face. A rather unheroic maneuver. This was ridiculous. She wanted to talk to Victor as much if not more than he wanted to talk to her. She couldn't make any noise loud enough to attract their attention. She looked around again for the pitcher that wasn't there, thinking to throw it at the door.

They grew quiet. "No," she tried to say. "Come back." There was still no way they could hear her through the door. She looked around again for anything she could use to make a sound and found the call button. She pushed it, then decided to blame the aftereffects of the medication for thinking of throwing a pitcher first.

There was some more angry shouting a minute later, then "... and you're not going to stop me!" by a voice she didn't recognize. She smiled at that, remembering Michael and the officer who'd arrested her arguing outside the car. Had it only been a week ago?

The door opened and a man came in, dressed in scrubs. A uniformed police officer behind him. A second one stood outside, blocking Victor from entering. She managed to lift one arm to give Victor a wave and a wan smile. He relaxed noticeably when he saw that.

The nurse didn't see it, he was busy dealing with the cop who had come in behind him. "No," he told him. "You wait outside."

"Sorry. Orders. Nobody's alone with the suspect."

"Are you a doctor?" the nurse demanded angrily. "Trauma counselor? Nurse? CNA? No? Then you don't give orders here and you're not needed in the room. So, you wait outside."

They stared each other down for what seemed like minutes. Veer thought it as a good thing she wasn't dying over here.

"Fine," the cop said, looking between them. "We're right outside if you need us," he added. That was big of him, she thought. A lesser man would have forced his way in, or sulked, refusing to cooperate, rather than just accept the blow to his pride and move on, letting him know his help was still available if needed. Funny how that works. If he'd pressed the fight, he probably would have won, then stood there helplessly, being embarrassed at his uselessness. Instead, he backed down, and offered assistance to the man who'd forced him to, and ended up gaining esteem in everyone's view. She could tell from the curt nod of grateful acknowledgment from the nurse that he felt the same way.

He closed the door behind him and approached her bed. "Sorry about all that," he told her. "You're awake. How are you feeling?"

"Fine," she barely managed to croak out.

The nurse laughed at that. "I can tell. Want some water?"

She nodded vigorously.

He opened a small cabinet and retrieved a paper cup and a pitcher. So that's where they kept it! He filled the pitcher from the bathroom sink then filled the cup from it and handed it to her. "Now remember to sip it. Slowly."

Veer took a couple of sips and her throat felt a lot better. It took an effort of will not to gulp the rest of it.

"Are you experiencing any pain?" he asked.

She thought about it for a second, doing a quick survey and was surprised to discover there wasn't much at all. A bit of discomfort in her lower belly was all.

"Not really," she answered.

"Not really meaning yes?" he asked.

"Not really meaning not really," she replied testily. "The pain is very minor and is less annoying than the side effects of whatever you would give me to mask it would be," she added as a longer explanation.

"All right," he replied. "I'll leave it up to you to tell me if that changes."

"Thanks," she said. "Sorry, I've..." she trailed off.

"Been stabbed, then spent three days in a hospital being cut, sewn, poked and prodded at?" he said, smiling softly. "I think we can cut you a little bit of slack."

"Three days?" she gasped.

"Oh. Um... sorry. I didn't realize you didn't know."

"I just remember bits and pieces. A few flashes. Did..." she thought for a second. "Did I get operated on?"

The nurse laughed at that, then quickly stifled it. "Yes." He replied. "A couple of times."

In answer to her look of shock at that, he said, "You seem to be doing well, though, now. It was touch and go there for a while. They had to go in a second time to remove some damaged tissue."

"Am I a prisoner?" she asked him.

He hesitated at that.

"What?" she asked. "What's going on?"

"I don't know, exactly. I mean, I'm not sure if you're a prisoner. Detective Diaz thought..."

"Michael Diaz?" she interrupted him. "Is he here?"

"He's not. He's been checking in, though, and probably will be later today..." he hesitated again. There was something he was going to say. Instead, he asked, "Do you want to see him?"

She thought about it. She wanted to see him, but... "I want to see Victor first."

"The Detective said specifically not to allow him in."

"Why?"

"Somebody tried to kill you," the nurse said. "The police seem to think he might be involved somehow."

"He wasn't." Her voice sounded a little more human to her now. She tried to sit up.

"Who... whoa, hold on. You're better, but you're not ready for that yet. She found her arm wouldn't support her weight. She collapsed back down with a cry of pain.

"Okay," she said, waving him off with one hand. "I believe you."

"Let me get your doctor, okay? He can check you out, and we'll see if you're well enough to have visitors."

"All right," she conceded. She thought he'd leave then, but he touched a badge on his uniform — it looked like something out of Star Trek — and spoke into it. "Doctor Qadir to room five-seventy-five, please." Reflexively, she noted the name and number.

She could hear more commotion at the door now. Finally voices moving off, and the door opened. The same police officer held the door open as the doctor entered. Veer saw no sign of Victor or the other cop. She could guess what had happened. They'd moved Victor down the hall, or possibly out of the hospital entirely, worried that he might cause trouble, or interfere with the doctors. She hoped they didn't remove him entirely. She still needed to talk to him.

"What's going on?" she asked the doctor before she could speak. "Why can't I see Victor? Why are the police here? Am I a prisoner or not?"

"You're a patient," the doctor told her. "Nobody's been arrested. You were stabbed and the police thought someone might try again. Given recent events, I agreed to their request to have someone watch the room to make sure nothing happened."

"Well, if it does, it won't be Victor," she said.

"Are you sure about that?" the doctor asked her.

"Yes." She thought of adding, he wouldn't do it himself. He's got people for that. But instead, she said "I know the guy that attacked me. It's nothing to do with Victor."

"What did it have to do with?"

"I'm a reporter. I was working on a story, and someone didn't like the direction it was going."

"A story about werewolves?" the doctor asked.

She started at that. She looked over at him and at the nurse. The nurse just looked confused, but the doctor looked more concerned than anything else.

"I'd rather not talk about it," she responded.

He seemed to accept that for the moment and proceeded with the exam. When he checked under her bandage, he seemed surprised.

"This is doing well," he told her. "Much better than last time I saw it."

She didn't comment. "So, can I go then?"

"I think it's best if you stay a couple of days at least. I'm going to set up some physical therapy sessions for you as well."

"There won't be any permanent damage?"

"I don't think so, no. Aside from a large scar, I'd say you'll eventually be as good as new. But don't rush it. You'll get there eventually but only if you follow your PTs advice."

"Can I have visitors, then? And get this thing out of my arm?"

He checked her chart and soon answered, "Yes to your second question. I think yes to the first as well, as far as I'm concerned. But it also depends on the police. I'll see what I can do."

After he and the nurse left, Veer tried again to stand up. Moving slowly and carefully, she found she could walk at least as far as the bathroom and back. That was good. Three days in the hospital, two surgeries, and months of physical therapy and they call it 'No major damage.' Ha!

It was almost an hour later when there was a knock on the door. It wasn't Victor, as she'd hoped, but Michael, who entered.

"I was hoping to see Victor," she told him. She was still a little angry at him for giving the orders keeping him away.

"Sorry. I thought it best if we talked first."

She pushed herself very carefully up into a sitting position. "What's going on?"

"What were you doing at Dante's?" he started.

"Who said I was at Dante's?" she asked.

"We traced the car share vehicle you arrived at the hospital in."

"Oh." She should have realized. "Any news on my driver?"

"She left while you were being taken in and abandoned the car a few blocks away. Care to tell me who she is?"

"Just a frightened young woman who did me a good turn," she said.

"We might be able to help her. If we could find her."

She didn't reply. He let it go.

"Wanna tell me why you were at the square? How'd you know about the attack?" he asked. And why didn't you tell me in advance, was the obvious unspoken question.

"I didn't," she told him. "My being nearby was just a coincidence. I ran there as soon as we learned what happened."

"We? Who's we?" he said.

She hesitated for just a second. "I was having dinner with Victor," she told him.

"What? Why?"

"He wanted me to investigate a place called Holy Mountain Research."

"Wait... He was offering you a job? After you attacked his hitman? Surely he must realize..."

"He's known since the day we met that I intend to expose his secret," she interrupted. "He's still hoping I won't. He seemed to think something there would convince me."

"Something where? This Holy Mountain Research place? What's so special about them?"

"They seem to be investigating Were."

He was quiet for a long moment after that, thinking through the implications.

"How do they know...?"

"Remember when you told me Gordon Chandler attacked a man in the hospital?"

"Yeah?"

"It cured his cancer."

"But he diss... oh."

"Yeah," she said. Obviously, he got it. She didn't want to tell him that Victor suspected them of kidnapping Phil as well as Peter. She didn't want him to do anything stupid and alert them that they were being looked at.

"I need to know what's happening," she said. "I've been out of the loop for a few days."

It was his turn to pause. What didn't he want to tell her? "Right now, we're treating the Square as a terrorist attack," he said. "The FBI and Homeland Security are crawling all over it, but as far as I know, you and I are the only ones who know what really happened."

There were a few others, she realized, but didn't say anything to contradict him.

"I had a press conference this afternoon," he continued, "where I had to address pioneer square. I hinted at werewolves but didn't say anything outright. Nobody's tried to kill me since then, though." That lent strength to the theory that Holy Mountain had Peter. It was possible that Victor was too busy with containment to do anything about him yet, but he would have been watching the police response, especially Michael's, very carefully.

"What about Dante's?" she asked him.

"We suspected it was related. No witnesses there, though. Bartender, doorman, and two patrons dead. One server and an unknown number of patrons missing. Wanna tell me what really happened there? We found your wallet and phone amidst a pile of shredded clothes. I've seen you heal from a fractured spine, how come you're here now?"

"Silver knife," she said.

"You remember what happened?" he asked.

"Yes." She filled him in on getting to the square, leaving Victor tending the wounded, then finding Caitlyn, though she didn't mention her name, and finally the fight at Dante's.

"Kevin and Shelly, we know are the ringleaders behind the square," he said. Had this been a test? If so, she supposed she passed. "I don't suppose you know their last names?"

"I can find out," she said. "Probably get you home addresses, too, after speaking to Victor."

"You sure you want to talk to him?"

"Definitely. If I'm going to look into this Holy Mountain..."

"You're planning on going ahead with that? In your current condition?"

She smiled at that. "An hour after I get out of here, I won't be in my current condition."

"Nevertheless, are you sure it's safe?"

"You mean my investigation? Probably not."

"What about talking to Stumpp?"

"If he wanted to kill me, I would be dead by now along with you, your men outside, and anyone else who got in the way, and he'd have an airtight alibi with a dozen witnesses halfway across the city." She knew it would be a blow to his ego, but it was almost certainly true. She hadn't known Victor to use violence often, but when he did, as with most things, he was ruthlessly competent. She could imagine how it would happen. Maybe two men, casually walking down the hall and, at some pre-arranged signal, both stop at once, pull out guns and fire two shots each, point blank, into the police officers' heads. The cops would be dead before they realized they were under attack. The shots would raise an alarm and she'd probably be halfway out of her bed when they kicked open her door and emptied their clips. The bullets would be silver, of course. They'd ditch the guns somewhere, or just drop them there. They'd have no serial numbers, bought on the black market just for this job, and the hitmen would join the now panicking crowd in their escape. Or, possibly, sprint to the nearest stairway and run down a flight or two and casually stroll out with everyone else. There might even be a patient or two in here, prearranged for them to have a legitimate reason for visiting.

Of course, if he wanted to be more subtle than that, he could always either somehow compromise, or replace, one of the officers on duty. That would be more difficult to pull off. A fake nurse, with a syringe full of poison, might be easier. They might even make it look accidental. The nurse had told her it had been a close thing as it was. They'd had to take her in for a second surgery. Nobody had expected her to recover, it wouldn't raise many alarms if she hadn't.

"All right," Michael said. "If you're sure it's safe, I'll let him know."

"He's still here?"

"We sent him down the hall. I didn't want him overhearing anything we said."

"Are your men outside aware of... the circumstances?" she asked Michael.

"They're both carrying silver bullets if that's what you're asking," he replied.

She just hoped that if it came to it, they wouldn't shoot the wrong wolf. She reminded herself that if they entered the room, if she was in wolf form, no matter what else was going on, to change back into human form. She considered changing first, heal up the damage, and feign continued injury, but he'd be too likely to see through that. Besides, the wolf wasn't extremely quiet, and it could cause a panic if someone came in and saw it.

Michael held the door open for Victor as he entered, and glared daggers the whole time. Victor strode straight in, ignoring him entirely. *You are not my rival*, was the obvious message, *You are the doorman.* They can't avoid the macho posturing even now, she wanted to laugh out loud at them.

The second the door closed, though, Victor visibly relaxed, rushed to Veer's bed and hugged her close. Even in his enthusiasm and obvious relief, he was careful not to pull her to him or aggravate her wound.

He let go and stepped back and only then she realized why he was there. He had been worried. He actually cared about her, personally, not just as another detail. Not as a loose end, but about her. In the few years she'd known him, she'd come to respect him a great deal, even like him. His keen mind, and his sense of humor on those rare occasions he'd shown it. And his utter devotion to his duty, to the protection and safekeeping of his "children." It wasn't just his duty he was devoted to. It was his Were, and she held a special place even among them. It made the thought of betraying him that much harder.

"I'm okay," she told him. "I'll be fine, I think, as soon as I get a chance to change."

He seemed a bit surprised by that. "It wasn't a silver knife?"

"It was," she said. "So, let's hear it for modern medicine. The knife destroyed everything it touched, so they cut it all out. All the current damage, if you can call it that, was caused by good solid twenty-first century surgical steel."

"And if they'd known to do that the first time..." he said, seeing where she was going. She was letting him know that she was okay, but simultaneously making a case for revealing the secret. Victor was one of very few people she could talk to on this level. And this was the man she was planning on betraying.

He knew exactly what she was planning and had still come here in a time of crisis because he was worried about her.

She didn't continue. The point had been made, there was nothing to gain by pressing it. He'd agree or, more likely, not, as he would.

"What's happened?" she asked him. "What's going on?"

"How much do you already know?" he asked, taking the pitcher from the table and refilling her water cup.

"Nothing at all of what's been happening since I got here," she said. "Has it really been three days?" There'd be time later to fill him in on what happened before she was brought in. If she decided to do so. "Michael told me the secret's out. Past containment," she finished.

He gave a slight indulgent smile at that.

"Well, Michael," Victor let his disapproval of her use of the first name show plainly in his tone, "doesn't have as much experience at such things as I do. This isn't the first public event of its kind. It's not even the largest."

She was about to exclaim that she'd never heard of such a thing before... but of course, that was the point.

"You'll have to tell me about them some time," she replied. "But how are you keeping it quiet?"

He hesitated. She could tell this was something that he couldn't tell a potential enemy. She knew he was aware that she'd recognized the hesitation, and the reason for it, and this was a measure of trust. This much he communicated with a brief hesitation, his tone, and a quick half-smile. There wasn't anybody else with whom she could share this level of communication. It took both a subtlety and quickness of wit as well as a great deal of trust in the other person.

"We've done our best to work with the paramedics on the scene," he said. "Many of the new Were we were able to remove from the area before they changed. We can take care of them, explain the rules of our society and help them with the adjustment."

"Many..." she repeated the word he'd used.

"Not all," he acknowledged. "Some were brought to local hospitals, including this one. We're asking those few staff who see anything, and it's always less than one thinks, to keep quiet about it. As for the public in general, and to counteract the statements and videos that are out there, the main story is that it was a viral marketing campaign for a new werewolf movie that went wrong. The internet's collective outrage should do a lot of the job for us. Our sacrificial film company has already issued official denials and will eventually be contrite, deeply regret the mistake, the movie will be canceled and the last thing anyone hears from them is that they've been sued into oblivion and never heard from again."

"It wouldn't even take that many people, would it?" Veer realized. "A few phone calls, a press release or two, maybe a few out of court settlements from a lawyer... And if anyone notices that they'd never heard of them before, either they'll just assume that somebody else has and not worry about it."

"That's pretty much it, yes, except for a few details."

She knew from experience that "a few details" involved probably hundreds of things that he would have to keep track of, juggling all those involved, including some she almost certainly hadn't thought of yet.

"Unless, of course, someone with some credibility were to, say, delve into those details in a major newspaper."

"And what would happen then?" she asked. She knew the answer, of course, but needed to hear him say it.

"The results of such an investigation could never be allowed to see the light of day."

And there it was. For all the subtle hints and innuendo and

talking in riddles the man was capable of, there it was in plain terms.

"No matter what?" she said, feeling very small and vulnerable under her blanket.

"No matter what," he responded. There was sadness in his voice.

"Have you considered that maybe they're right? Maybe it's time we show the world exactly who we are?" She had included herself in the group intentionally - a signal to him whose side she was on. If she was going to do this, it wouldn't be as an outsider.

"Not like this. Even if we were to reveal our existence, to start with so much violence and death? No - nothing good can come of this."

"What if it could be turned around? Showing that you care so much about the humans that you're willing to reveal your secrets to cooperate with the police to catch these horrific killers?"

He smiled at that. "You make a compelling argument, but the council would never go for it."

"Fuck the council. Do it yourself."

"Go rogue?" He smiled again. "There has not been a rogue alpha for a very, very long time. Not within living memory. But each new Alpha is told the story, made aware of what happened to the last one, to make sure it never happens again."

"But..." she started. But he cut her off.

"No," he said. "There is no way to use this, and I cannot betray my oaths or abandon my responsibility. I cannot be other than what I am. Even if I could, it would do no good. This situation will be contained. It will not be exploited, and any who try to do so will be neutralized. If I fail to do this, or refuse to do so, the council would then take action. But the point is moot.

Containment has already begun. Most of the evidence has been eliminated, explained away, or discredited as fraudulent."

"Most," she said, again echoing his word.

"The rest will fall in time. Please, I'm asking you, if you still feel you must expose our secrets, wait. Don't do it now. Not like this. Don't let senseless violence be our defining characteristic. You could plunge the whole world into chaos."

"I'm not writing anything tonight," she said, indicating her surroundings. She'd have to start soon, though. Like Victor said, this was a rare opportunity. It would all be a matter of how the story was told. He may be brilliant in his own realm, but this is what she did. "There is one more thing you need to know now, though."

He steeled himself at her tone. He had been honest with her, he deserved the same. She told him what she hadn't told Michael. "The knife used to stab me. It was exactly the same as the one used to kill Andrew."

Victor stiffened. With a low voice, he asked, "Who?"

"Kevin Banks," she told him immediately.

"A matching set?"

"Or from the same catalog."

His look told her what he thought of that.

"I also told Michael." She deliberately used the first name this time. A confession of her divided loyalty that she knew he'd pick up on.

"So, it's a race," Victor said. His tone was flat, unreadable. The chess master was back in control.

She almost pitied Kevin. The poor misguided fool. Caught between an angry Victor on one hand, and Michael and his Werewolf Squad on the other.

THE HOSPITAL DISCHARGED her the next morning. On her way home Veer made one stop, at a grocery store to purchase ten pounds of beef.

"No, I'm going to eat it all myself tonight," she replied when the clerk asked if she was having a barbecue. He assumed she was joking. They both laughed.

She went through the house making sure all the doors were locked and the curtains closed. She thought about the cameras. Michael had assured her they'd all been removed, but she didn't know how much she could trust him. She went into the bedroom, where he had originally told her there'd been no camera that could see anything and undressed there. She looked down at the stitches on her belly. In a few minutes, they'd be gone along with any scar that might have formed.

SHE AWOKE to the sound of the doorbell and found herself lying on the living room floor. She got to her feet and found her robe, still on the chair she'd draped it over. The room seemed to be intact. She'd have to check the rest of the house later, but she glanced in the kitchen. There was a bloody mess all over the floor where she had dropped the meat she'd picked up earlier. The meat was gone, but it would need a good mopping before anyone could be allowed back there.

Out of caution of who might be there - what time of the day was it anyway? The clock above the mantle said 11, but she didn't know if that was AM or PM. She peeked out the window, raising a corner of the curtain, rather than immediately approach the door and look through the peephole. Daylight streamed in. Still morning then. Victor was standing patiently on the doorstep.

Of course, that didn't mean it would be safe. His car in the driveway was a good sign, though. She couldn't imagine he'd come to kill her using his own car and park it right in front of the house. She opened the door.

"How are you feeling?" he asked as he entered.

"Fine," she replied. Realizing it sounded short, she added, "Literally. Good as new." He couldn't have missed the hesitation. She was nervous, unsure of his intentions, and now it showed.

"You were finally able to change?" he asked. He dropped his coat over the back of the couch and followed her to the kitchen. She started a pot of coffee as she spoke.

"Just woke up, actually. Doctors did a good job. I'm seriously a hundred percent again."

"Good to hear," he responded. He started to rise as she fished out a mop and bucket.

"I got it," she told him, waving him back down. She was comfortable enough letting him see this. He'd understand exactly what the bloody mess in the corner of the kitchen floor was about. Changing required energy at the best of times. If the wolf had to regenerate damage, it could take considerably more. All that energy had to be replenished somehow.

She poured two mugs of coffee and they moved into the living room. She took a seat on the couch, perched carefully on one corner, her legs folded under her. Victor took a seat in the chair across from her then lifted the coffee to his lips.

"Kevin and Shelly have an army," she said.

"Hardly that," he replied.

"Do you have a plan for dealing with them?" The question was also a statement of her willingness to cooperate, at least tentatively.

He understood. "Already in progress," he said. "Though I may need your help. Have you thought about my request?"

"I've done nothing but," she replied truthfully. "What I told you three years ago is still true." She chose the wording deliberately, letting him know that nothing had changed, and that she wasn't betraying any trusts. He'd known her intentions from the beginning, but by referring to three years ago rather than a couple of days ago at the hospital, she let him know she was still willing to wait for the right moment. While she could use the events of today, especially the easily disproved cover story, she didn't want to start a war.

"I still think going public would be the best thing for the Were," she added.

"You're not alone in that sentiment." He gestured vaguely with his coffee.

"Kevin," she said.

Victor simply nodded.

"Violence is what I want to avoid."

"As do I," he replied.

"What's your plan?" she asked again.

"You're not going to like it," he told her. "I had a visitor after I left you yesterday, and an interesting trip."

"Oh? Do tell," she said.

He smiled and took another sip from his mug before launching into his tale. "Shortly after I returned to my office, Cate informed me I had a visitor. Another representative from Holy Mountain Research."

She was surprised at that, and let it show.

"He informed me," Victor continued, "that they found out about the attack on Pioneer Square as it was going on and rushed into action. They took as many of the wounded as they could - they had somehow managed to secure a couple of ambulances on short notice and used them to ferry groups of wounded to nearby vans. They had also made contact with the hospitals and were searching for as many of the wounded as they could. As they did so, they learned we were doing the same."

"This must have been a major opportunity for them, to find that many Were at once."

"Indeed, though I was none too happy to hear they'd been taking them."

"What'd you do?"

"They had previously offered me a tour of their facilities. This time I took them up on it."

"What, you went there just then yesterday afternoon? And they let you, without scheduling and preparing?"

"I insisted. The preparation was exactly what I wanted to avoid. I didn't want to give them the chance to clean anything up, hide anything, or worse, prepare a PowerPoint presentation."

"So, what's the belly of the beast like?"

"It's an office building in Beaverton, drab, two-story, indistinguishable from a hundred others in those business parks around Walker Road scattered in between all the Intel and Nike buildings. Inside is exactly what I would have expected from such a place, so not what I expected at all."

"How do you mean?"

"The whole floor was a maze of cubicles, each apparently inhabited by a single occupant staring at a screen. Almost eerily quiet. Hardly anyone even looked up as we walked by."

She liked that part - it would make her job infiltrating the place easier.

"What?" he asked, seeing her expression.

"Nothing," she replied. "So, what happened?"

"I glanced at the monitors as we went by. Lots of spreadsheets, anatomical diagrams of some sort, close up pictures of various injuries, but nothing that was immediately telling. Until I saw Peter."

"Peter was there?"

"It turns out, yes, but I first saw his picture on the screen. Photo attached to some document. I couldn't read the text, but it was unmistakably Peter. He was laying naked on a metal table with some kind of hospital monitors nearby."

"Oh my god."

"Yes. I slowed my pace to allow my guide to get a few steps ahead of me then turned back, walked up behind the woman in the cubicle and demanded to know if the man on her screen was still alive. Poor girl nearly jumped out of her chair."

"I can imagine," Veer said. An angry Victor was something to be reckoned with, especially if he came up from behind with a sudden loud order.

He smiled at her comment and finished his coffee, then got up to go get more. "My guide stopped," he called from the kitchen. "The woman in the cubicle just stammered so I asked again. 'That man there,' I jabbed a finger at the screen in case she wasn't sure what I meant, 'Is he still alive?'"

"She looked to my guide, and he nodded, so she checked. She told me he was downstairs." He brought the pot out to the living room and filled her cup and then his own before setting it down on the coffee table.

"There's a downstairs?" she asked.

"There is. There's an elevator at the back of the room. You need both a proximity card and a code. The code was one-one-oh-nine."

Of course he memorized the code. She repeated it to herself as well in case she needed it later.

"They let you downstairs?" she asked.

"They did. There's a security desk down there, and a number of rooms that look like jail cells. We found Peter's and I made them release him.

"I can only imagine what that involved," Veer said.

"I bet what you're imagining doesn't do it justice," he said with a smile. "They were obviously under orders to keep me happy - apparently they realized I had enough knowledge of Were to be of value to them. It took a bit of convincing, but they took me downstairs. We found Peter, not much the worse for wear, and released him. They were annoyed at him anyway, as he hadn't given them any of the information they'd hoped for."

"What were they doing with him?"

"Some kind of tests - he tells me he didn't see much of the facility. They seemed to have been treating him better than some of the others, only taking occasional blood samples and frequently asking him about other Were. He claimed not to know any, and until I got there, they never knew he'd been lying to them."

"They're trying to learn about Were society as well as physiology," she said. "They have no idea about how we're organized or our numbers."

"No, and I did my best to keep it that way. They suspected I'm a figure of some importance, but if they knew more than that, they never let on."

"Which means Peter wasn't their source," she said. "So, who was?"

"That's a question I would very much like an answer to."

"It sounds like you've established communication now," she said. "Why not just ask them?"

"I didn't perhaps part on as good of terms as it may seem. I very nearly didn't depart at all."

"What? What happened?" She sat more upright in her seat.

"When we first found Peter," Victor continued, "after my first demand that they release him, it seemed they thought it would be better to keep him there, and myself as well. A number of their mercenaries were summoned close for this purpose."

She didn't say anything, but she could imagine where it went from there. Victor picked up the coffee pot and topped off her cup again and then his own before his next words proved her wrong.

"'You don't want violence,' I told them. 'Let's say, somehow you do trap me in here. How many of your people do you think I could bite before you finally managed to drop me?' They didn't like that thought, so I continued, 'And knowing how you treat Were, how loyal do you think they'll be once they've been turned? Even if you manage to contain them all, do you know all of your employees' relationships with each other? How many are friends? Lovers? Care enough to subtly start sabotaging your efforts to get revenge for their comrades being tortured below? How much are you really willing to risk to keep me here when you can get just as much if not more by agreeing to a few simple and entirely reasonable conditions?'" he finished.

"And they bought that?" Veer asked.

"I meant every bit of it," Victor said. "The fact that they hadn't considered such things before made me realize just how new to all of this they really are."

"What were the conditions?"

"First, that they release Peter." He saw the face she made and smiled indulgently. "Regardless of your opinion of him, he really is too valuable a resource to keep locked up. Second, they were to take no more Were without my permission."

"They agreed to that?"

"Oh, yes. Especially when I offered them permission, and the home addresses, of two they could take right away."

She was shocked at this for a second, then realized who he must be talking about.

"Kevin and Shelly," she said.

"I am convinced that if one or both of them did not kill Andrew, they know who did. Even apart from that, their actions in Pioneer Square sealed their fate. They might as well be of some use before they die, and while the good people of Holy Mountain are experimenting on them they might as well ask a few questions on my behalf as well."

"It's dangerous," she said. "If this group is as powerful as you say..."

"Then we can't win in a direct confrontation," he finished.

"But you're willing to work with them..." she trailed off. He shot her a look, but she had already realized what he'd meant. The accusation was unworthy.

"You're willing to use their resources while you stall for time."

"And learn everything possible about them. Which is where you come in."

"You want me to infiltrate a secret organization, one that's powerful enough to have their own military and unethical enough to use it to kidnap people and conduct unauthorized experiments on them."

"Yes," he replied. "That is exactly it. Think of the information you'll get for your big exposé."

She shot him a disgusted look for that.

"I'm not entirely teasing," he said. "If the information you gather, and the situation is overwhelming enough, I might be able to use it to convince the council that it is time for a change."

"Seriously? You think you can do that?" she asked skeptically.

"I can try." He was grasping at straws and they both knew it.

It also occurred to her that once she was inside all it would take would be a simple phone call to have her moved into one of those cells he described, to be experimented on for the rest of her no doubt short life.

Of course, there was never really any doubt about what she'd do.

"All right," she said. "Tell me everything else about your visit there."

What he could tell her was quite a bit. In addition to the elevator code, he had learned the names of some of the tools they used, floor layout, locations of power, emergency exits, and, best of all, the name of the employee recruitment agency they used.

"I know this is going to take a while..." he started.

"Two weeks, tops," she cut him off. She enjoyed his look of confusion.

"You took almost a month to infiltrate my company," he started.

"Yours was harder," she said. "Think about it. Stumpptown Systems is open floor, everyone knows each other because they see each other every day. You can't move around without everyone knowing where you are, and they pay attention because they're friendly and want to help the new girl. From what you described, Holy Mountain is rife with paranoia. That will, inevitably, result in less overt cooperation and more ass covering. Mistakes in an environment like that are only relevant if you get them pinned on you. Everyone's so worried about being watched, they're not watching each other and for the most part not out to help each other. There will be just a few people whose specific job it is to look for intruders, so long as I can convince them I belong, the rest of them should ignore me completely."

"You really think you can do this?" he asked hopefully.

"It won't be without danger. But you're right. It'd be a huge boon to my career. My real career. And if I'm going to be writing about werewolves, big pharma experimenting on them is a better angle for us all than Were killing people in public attacks."

He nodded at that. "Let me know if you need anything."

"A letter of recommendation or two for Nellie's files couldn't hurt."

"I'll have Gregor send them from a couple of his subsidiaries, so they can't be traced back to me."

TWENTY-ONE
FALLING DOWN

"What the hell was that all about?" Jacob asked, moments after Lily had let them into her and Kim's apartment. Carl was already there, sitting at a small round dining room table with Kim and Toni.

He stood as Jacob entered. "I don't know. We were as caught off guard by it as you."

"So you didn't have anything to do with it?" Jacob asked him.

"No," Carl said. "Kevin and Shelly and people they recruited were acting entirely on their own," he said.

"Oh," Jacob replied, turning back toward him. "So why are we getting together?"

"We're trying to decide what to do about it," Lily said.

"If we can use this, or if we should make a statement or something," Carl said as he followed her and Jacob into the living room.

"Use it?" Jacob was horrified.

"Yeah, I voted against that, too," said Kim, coming in to join them.

"I think that's the general consensus," Carl said. There was a murmur of assent and nodding of heads all around.

"Well... okay, good." He seemed relieved.

"I'm thinking we should just stay away from it," Toni said. "If you ask me, we should just continue to keep quiet, see how this plays out. Don't even ask them to defend themselves, just don't talk to them."

"Well, that last part's easy enough," Carl said. "Neither of them have answered my texts or calls since last week. What about Gordon though?"

"What about him?" Kim asked.

"I got an email from him on the way over here, wanting to meet up," Carl told her.

He pulled it up on his phone and handed it to Kim, who read it quickly before passing it to Lily.

"He wants to meet up, talk about what happened at the Square?" she said.

"What else could it be?" Toni said. "Think about it from his point of view. We're the only other wolves he knows. I mean, other than Shelly and Kevin, who just killed a bunch of people in a big public demonstration."

Carl hadn't thought of that, and felt a little ashamed that he hadn't. He'd been focusing on the fact that they'd changed publicly more than the fact that they'd killed people. Under Were law, the former was the greater crime.

"So..." he started. He almost didn't want to say it, thinking it might just sound too cliche. "You don't think it's a trap?"

He almost expected someone to say he'd been watching too much TV. But Toni looked pensive.

"It's possible," she said. "We know Gordon's been in contact with the police. If they think you know how to reach Kevin..."

"Which I don't."

"But you're probably more likely than anyone else, if Shelly's also disappeared."

"Her phone's been going straight to voicemail, too."

"You don't have to convince me," Toni said. "But if that's what Gordon's after, it might be best to go ahead and meet with him to convince him of that."

"What if he's not alone?" he asked.

It was Kim who answered. "You won't be alone either."

AT LEAST THE other man wasn't trying to hide, Carl thought the next day as he came out of the path into the back garden, his drink cupped in both hands. He had left Kim and Lily sitting at a table together inside the coffee shop. Cynthia and Tyler were at another one, engrossed in conversation. Toni was going to be watching from nearby, with Will. The double latte had been a splurge, but he was nervous and it helped calm him down. Besides, tonight might be his last night on earth. If it all ended here, he'd rather have a hot drink in his hand then a few extra dollars in his pocket.

Gordon was sitting at the same table he'd been at last month when he'd eavesdropped on him and Toni. He briefly considered simply turning around and walking out when he saw that he wasn't alone. Then, for a second, he thought it would be more amusing to take his original table, but discarded that idea. His friends, his "Order of the Wolf," were positioned nearby. Secure in that knowledge, he walked up to the table and sat down, perched at the edge of his seat, ready to spring away at any moment. Neither man reassured him, told him to relax, or that they weren't going to hurt him. This was not encouraging.

"Hello again, Carl," Gordon said. The use of his name made

him even more nervous, as if the man was deliberately marking him. He had to restrain himself from looking over his shoulder to make sure that Toni was nearby.

"Carl, this is Detective Diaz. Detective, Carl."

He almost bolted then. But did his best to stay outwardly calm.

"You're a hard man to find, Mr. Jablonski," Detective Diaz said.

"I am?" he said. It was actually a surprising statement. He hadn't spent a lot of time in his apartment recently, that was true. But he hadn't exactly been hiding.

"You haven't been trying to avoid us?" Diaz asked him.

"I don't even know who you are," Carl replied.

"Where've you been for the last several days?" the detective asked him.

"Around," Carl said, defensively. He looked straight at this stranger. "Who are you exactly and what do you want?"

"I just want to talk," he said.

"Is this why you invited me here?" he asked Gordon angrily, "So he could talk?"

"I wanted to talk to you, too," Gordon replied. "And about the same thing."

"And what would that be?" Carl asked, struggling to keep his voice calm.

"What do you know about Saturday night?" the Detective asked him.

"Can you be more specific?" Carl said. It sounded stupid even to him, but he needed time to think. It was one thing to reassure Gordon about his lack of involvement in the attacks, but talking to the police was another matter entirely.

"I think you know what I'm talking about." He was growing visibly angry now. Well fuck him, Carl decided, and fuck Gordon for bringing him here.

"Oh, so we're playing guessing games now?" He turned on Gordon. "Next time, if you want to talk to me, talk to me, don't call the fucking cops, and," he turned to the cop, "you can talk too, if you'd rather do that than play games."

He started to stand. "Wait," Gordon spoke up. He looked trapped. Carl almost felt sorry for him. Almost.

"Why?" he asked.

"We," Gordon emphasized the word, glaring at the cop, "still need your help. Please, just give us a minute here."

Carl thought for a second, then sat back down. "You have until I finish my latte." Coffee, he thought, I should have said coffee. It would have sounded much tougher.

"Look, we know you weren't involved directly," Gordon started. Was Gordon playing the role of good cop here, then, Carl wondered. If so, did he know this or was it a pattern he just fell into? Either way, he wasn't in the mood for it.

"Involved in what?" he said, again letting his voice show his anger. Worried that he might attract attention, he glanced around. Other than the three of them, there was only one other couple in the garden, and they didn't seem to be paying any attention to them.

"The attack on Pioneer Square," Gordon replied.

"Okay, then, there it is. Was that so hard?" he asked. "You have questions? Ask them." He turned to Diaz. "Talk. Like a person. Without trying to bully me or trick me or entrap me. Just ask your questions and I'll answer them."

"Fine," the Detective answered. "Then what do you know about the attacks on Pioneer Square last Saturday?"

"Nothing," he replied.

"We know your friend Kevin was involved,"

"Then you know as much as I do," he replied.

"If you're not going to take this seriously," the cop began.

Gordon looked uncomfortable. No, not uncomfortable... disappointed. Like he'd expected better of Carl and been let down.

"I am serious," Carl began. "I don't know anything about the attacks that haven't been posted online. I wasn't there, and haven't spoken to anyone who was, either before or since. So, yeah, I mean it when I say I know less than you do."

"So where were you Saturday night?"

"That's none of your business," he replied. There was no way he was going to tell him about the initiations, and he couldn't think of a good alibi. He suddenly realized that if the cop was asking, then Gordon hadn't told him. Score one in his favor, then.

"Would you prefer having this conversation downtown in a holding cell?"

"It won't magically make me know anything I don't already know."

"Nonetheless..."

"I'm not going anywhere with you."

"I could arrest you if you prefer."

What would happen if he ran? He could get away, easily. They'd put an APB out on him. He'd be a wanted fugitive, hiding from the police for the rest of his life. He couldn't work - how could he even get a job without a background check? Not in software, certainly. What kinds of jobs didn't check into the person they were hiring? Construction? Bartending? Airport baggage handling? He didn't know how to do any of those. What if he stayed and let them arrest him? Would that be worse? He hoped to avoid either.

"I doubt you could if you tried," he said, trying hard not to sound terrified.

"I've got half a dozen officers, all armed with tasers and sidearms with silver rounds," the cop responded calmly. Carl looked around - the couple at the table he'd noticed earlier were still looking everywhere but toward him.

He realized the implications of that last. He looked back at Gordon accusingly. "What did you tell him?" he said and then realized he'd just given it away. "I... uh..." Shit. Too late to deny anything now. He couldn't hide behind the standard "There's no such thing as werewolves" stance as this cop obviously already knew there were, and that he was one. But if the police knew... that had to mean the Alpha knew what was happening.

"You... you know..." he stammered, trying to buy himself time to think. "That sort of thing's supposed to be secret..."

"Isn't that the point of your whole movement here?" Gordon asked him. "To bring that secret out into the light?"

"How long have you known?" he asked Gordon.

He looked confused at that. "Known about what?" he said.

"Do you work for the Alpha? Was this whole thing a setup from the very beginning?"

"I told you the truth about everything," Gordon said.

"Why let it go this far? Just to see what we'd do? What about the others?"

"I don't know what you're talking about Carl," Gordon said.

"How much was I manipulated? And why meet publicly like this now, why not just disappear me at the beginning before we..." he almost revealed they'd turned a bunch of others. His mind was reeling this was too confusing.

"Relax," Diaz said. "He didn't tell me about you being a werewolf."

That didn't make him feel any better. "So... what?" Carl asked him. "You just guessed and I gave it away?" If that's what happened, he decided, he couldn't be too upset with him. The trap was well laid, and he had no one but himself to blame for falling into it.

"No," the cop said. "I figured that one out for myself, the first time I saw you transform."

"The... what?" Carl was completely confused now. "So... you don't work for the Alpha?"

"No. I work for the police. Which is why we're having this discussion."

Again, the implied threat of arrest. Normally, he'd dismiss such a thing coming from a human. But in this case... how much did the police know? Would they actually arrest him? There were too many of them. He couldn't run and if he tried, the others might get hurt.

"If you're not working for the Alpha, where did you... have you been spying on the Were?"

"You don't remember me?" the Detective asked. "From the preserve?"

It clicked.

"You were the human."

"And you were the werewolf."

"You were following me? Even then? Why?"

"I wasn't. I was following someone else."

"Rosen." It clicked into place. "You know she's like Stumpp's right hand man, right?"

"I know all about her relationship with your Alpha," he said the word with such contempt, as if Stumpp was just some gangster, almost beneath his notice.

"So, you're not working for him?"

"No. I'm not."

"But you seem to know all about them. So, what do you want with me?"

"We want to know about Kevin."

"Kevin?"

"What's he planning? What's his next move? Who else is working with him? Where is he hiding?"

Shit. Kevin never cared about the human authorities or took them seriously. He never understood what they were really capable of. And now, because of him, Carl was caught in the middle.

"I don't know any of that," he said, getting ready to rise, or bolt if necessary.

The cop leaned forward as if he would stop him. Carl looked over at the couple in the nearby table. Both were looking his way. He tensed, made eye contact with the one on the right and jerked, quickly as if he was going to run, but then stopped. They both began to rise but checked themselves half a second after he did. He smiled and relaxed into his seat and looked back at Michael accusingly.

"I told you I had people nearby," Michael said. "Now, are you going to help me, or are you going to make me arrest you?"

"It doesn't matter. I don't know anything about the attacks or what Kevin's doing now. I haven't heard anything from him for over a week."

"So why do you think he'd do something like this without asking for your help?"

"He didn't seem to need my help."

"But why didn't he talk to you about it in advance? It's hard to believe he'd plan something like this without his best friend."

Was he Kevin's best friend? He didn't think so. There was a time - hell, probably less than a month ago - when Kevin had been his. But he didn't know if the feeling had ever been mutual.

The cop leaned back and carefully picked up his coffee. He took a sip without ever taking his eyes off of Carl. "Is there a reason why he wouldn't trust you?"

He almost answered. Almost said he couldn't think of one. This was a trap. The police are not your friends, he reminded himself. No matter how friendly they acted, it was just that, an act, and they wouldn't hesitate to turn on you as soon as they get what they want. It was the mantra of anybody living near or beyond the edge of the law, whether they were criminals, or casual drug users, or just chronically late with the rent. Or a werewolf. Diaz's question was asked only as an attempt to divide Kevin and himself.

But the sudden change in his demeanor had alerted him. He wondered how many other such fishing questions he'd already answered. But why? This cop already knew his one big secret.

"You can't be both good cop and bad cop," he wanted to say, then thought better of it. Let him think he was snowed by his words. It would be to his advantage if Diaz didn't know how easily he saw through his little tricks. He decided to answer the more general question.

"I guess he was trying to protect me. Didn't want to force me into a choice between protecting him or telling you what I knew."

"That seems awfully considerate of him," the cop responded. He obviously didn't believe him. As he said it, though, it seemed likely. Kevin had never really respected him or considered him an equal. He thought of him as a subordinate. But as a subordinate, he'd have an obligation to protect him. He wasn't sure whether to feel patronized or grateful.

"I'm sorry," he told him. "I honestly don't know if I would help you if I could. But I can't, so it doesn't matter."

"Fine. You don't want to cooperate. I probably don't have enough to convict you of conspiracy to commit terrorism. But we still have kidnapping, assault on a police officer, and accessory to murder. That should be enough to send you away for a very long time."

"Kidnapping?" he said, stupidly. Dammit, he might as well have just admitted the other two charges.

Mitch must have gone to the police after all. This cop knew about the Were, so he would have believed his story. And... murder... did they find...? Shit. Or was he talking about the attack on the square? The hint of the thing at the cabin, when he'd turned Toni, may have been another trap. *Drop hints and see if he says anything that would incriminate himself. That was the game, right? Fuck, talking to this guy was dangerous.* He needed to get out of here. He didn't want to get shot by any of the three cops. The three that he knew of, he reminded himself. He'd have to talk his way out of this. He had to find a way. Hudson didn't happen, and the cabin didn't happen, he decided. He knew about the three they changed, and about Pioneer Square.

"I already told you, I wasn't at Pioneer Square and didn't know anything about them ahead of time," he protested hoping it sounded sincere.

"And at the wolf preserve? That wasn't you either, I suppose?"

He glared at Gordon, who looked away, and couldn't meet his eyes.

"Uh... I didn't actually attack you there. In fact, you were the one trespassing. You never said you were a police officer and weren't wearing a uniform." He couldn't read the man's expression, so continued, against his own recent advice to himself. "And what are you going to do anyway? Go into court and tell the judge that I'm a werewolf?"

"Yeah. I might do exactly that."

"You... you'd be laughed out of court."

"I don't think so. I think I've got enough evidence now to prove that werewolves exist, and to show that several people, including yourself, fall into that category."

This was a surprise. He wasn't sure how to react to that.

"No... uh..." he started to rise.

The cop stood up more quickly, as if he was waiting for this. Carl noticed his two friends jump to their feet at the same time. This was going to get real ugly real fast.

"Mr. Jablonski, you are under arrest. Please turn and face the wall with your hands behind your back."

"Whoa, whoa, hey!" Gordon finally spoke up, jumping between them. A little late there, guy, Carl thought.

"Think about it, Carl," he said, still trying to interpose himself between Carl and the detective. "Don't be stupid here. This is what you want, isn't it? The secret revealed? To be part of real society again?"

"Not like this," he replied, still facing them. "I'm not your pawn," he began.

He was interrupted by a large grey and black wolf, leaping through the hedge, shattering the fence as it moved. It barreled directly into the detective, knocking him down. Carl saw his handcuffs spin across the ground.

Shit. No. The wolves didn't need to save him. This wasn't necessary. This was...

It didn't matter. The cop rolled out from under the wolf, which moved on, ignoring him to advance on the other two policemen. They'd both drawn their weapons.

"No!" he shouted to the wolf. He wanted to warn her, run, flee. Let them take me! They had silver bullets! This wasn't worth her life. He took a step toward her before he was nearly knocked off his feet. By another pair of wolves, leaping out of the same bushes, side by side. They knocked over the table and barreled into the two cops. One went down, howling in pain or fear with a wolf's jaws tightening around her throat.

No. Not like this. Don't they understand? This isn't something they can just walk away from. There will be consequences here. They know who I am!

Diaz had got his own gun out by then, and he raised it

towards Carl. "Down!" he commanded, even as he climbed to his feet. "Get down on the ground now!"

Carl raised his hands, and took a step back toward the bushes, thinking to jump quickly through them. He was startled by the sound of shattering glass, when another wolf jumped out through the window, right onto the cop. It seemed to hang in the air as the cop turned slowly toward her, weapon in hand. The two of them fell, smashing the table with their impact. Carl tried to step backwards but he was moving so slowly. There were two sharp reports from the gun. He saw something fly from the side of it to land near his feet, spinning in the dust. Cop and wolf both went down, but Diaz raised himself to one knee. He pushed himself backward.

The wolf raised its head, but then fell. Blood streamed from its mouth. Was it the cops or its own? He tried to move forward. Something was holding him back. For some reason, his leg wasn't moving properly, then the carpet filled his vision. Somehow, he was on the ground on his face. He tried to push himself back up, or forward, but couldn't move his arm either. Someone was shouting from behind. He couldn't make out the words over the rushing sound in his head. A policeman was being dragged away from a wolf, who was struggling to get to its feet.

"Go!" he thought, mentally urging it to run. To stand. To get out of there. There was so much confusion. So many voices yelling or screaming. He thought one of them might be his own, but he couldn't tell which one. There were far more police than he'd remembered.

Some of them were in uniforms. He had an image of the two at the table leaping to their feet and casting off their outfits to reveal police uniforms underneath. That couldn't have been how it happened. There must have been more standing by somewhere. There were too many wolves and too many cops. He tried to count. Where had all the wolves come from? They ran through the garden, knocking over police, spinning and running off in different directions. He couldn't count them. Everything was too confusing, he didn't know what to do.

He continued trying to move to the wounded wolf, who was laying still now, breathing heavily. His arms were wrenched painfully behind him and he couldn't move forward. There was someone there. On top of him. That's what the weight on his back was. He flailed, trying to roll out from under whoever it was. Didn't they understand? That wolf was a person. It hurt. The bullets had been silver, he realized. She wouldn't heal. She hadn't been attacking, just trying to escape. He had to explain. The person on his back pulled his arm around and he felt something sharp and metallic bite into his wrist. He kicked and rolled and flailed wildly. He couldn't be stopped here. This wasn't right.

As Carl watched in horror the wolf changed and in its place was Lily. Her eyes met his. She looked scared, pleading, her chest heaving with labored breath. The last time she was lying wounded on the ground he'd reassured her, and she had been wearing a white robe. Afterward she'd laughed, and thanked him. She'd been wearing a black robe then. She wasn't wearing either robe now. He tried to go to her now but couldn't pull his way out from under the cops. As he watched, her eyes turned glassy and blank and her breathing slowed, then stopped. Nobody was helping her. There were cops all over the courtyard, but nobody was helping her.

A pool of blood beneath her spread, and slowed, and stopped. She was gone. He knew it, but still tried frantically to reach her. He heard a wet popping sound. Dimly, he registered pain in his wrist. He twisted his head around to see three cops on him. One was pulling his arm toward the center of his back, the wrist bent at a weird angle. Several more shapes sprung through the hedge, or down the path from the entrance. Were. Even more. Where were they all coming from? Two of them leapt directly over him, knocking the cops sprawling. He was free.

He tried to crawl toward Lily again. Toni was nowhere to be seen, in wolf form or human. Gordon seemed to have run off at some point as well, or at least found a place to hide. Diaz was crouched in a corner, one arm holding a bleeding shoulder, the other holding a radio he was yelling into. Carl tried to move forward when someone grabbed his shoulder from behind again. He turned, swinging a fist blindly in that direction and stopped when he saw it was Shelly. That didn't make sense. He stood and blinked, unable to process what was going on.

"Come on," she said, "this way."

"I..." he was confused. He turned back to where Lily lay.

"You can't do anything for her now. Come *on!*" she insisted.

"But..." He surveyed the garden. It was almost all cops, now, most of the wolves had gone. His eyes caught the cop, Diaz. He felt full of rage. He wanted to leap at him, tear him to pieces. He should not have been here. This was all his fault. He glared in anger. A promise.

"Come," Shelly repeated. "Go!"

The humor of the contradiction was enough to bring him into awareness of what was happening. There was even more danger here for him than before, especially with the wolves moving away leaving nothing but police in the garden.

He followed her out, keeping low. Once through the hedge, they broke into a run. After a couple of blocks, they slowed to a fast walk. "Doesn't look like they're following us," Carl said, looking behind him.

"They're still probably trying to figure out what happened," Shelly replied.

"What did happen? How'd you get here?"

"We're here to rescue you," she told him, smiling.

"No, seriously - why are you here?"

"You don't believe we'd drive across town to save your sorry ass?"

"I don't believe you knew it'd need saving at this precise moment and this place."

"Oh?" she said. "It's not that hard: Diaz is following Were. We're following him."

"Wait... why were you following him?"

"To make sure he doesn't find us. So, do you have an exit plan here or what?"

The sudden change of topic was too much. He couldn't keep up.

"Exit plan?"

"Yeah - did you and Toni plan a place to meet up in case everything went all cockeyed."

Toni had made him say it, out loud, several times. He repeated it now automatically "Twenty-sixth and Hawthorne - across from the waffle place."

"Okay, perfect, we're halfway there now." She led him forward, as they continued their fast walk.

"Try to hurry. But don't look like you're trying to hurry," he thought, but didn't say out loud. Exit plan. Shelly knew, and had thought of it ahead of time. She even had a name for it, like, of course that's one of the things you'd plan for. Toni had done the same, though she hadn't named it. But she had forced him to say it, repeatedly, as if she'd known he'd have to remember it when he was in no state to think clearly. How had she known? Or was it just one of many possibilities she'd planned for? A contingency that happened to get triggered. Was he the only one who failed so miserably at this whole planning thing? He followed Shelly in silence for a few more moments. He'd almost forgotten.

"Lily," he said, stopping in his tracks. He looked back, but Shelly stopped him.

"No, keep moving. There's nothing you can do back there."

"But Lily... she got shot... she might be..."

"Yeah, I saw. You can't help her, though. If she's alive, she's captured by the cops. They'll get her to medical treatment. We lost one of ours, too. It's gonna happen."

One of theirs. Not even a name, in what must have been the first time anyone spoke aloud of his, or her, death. Just one of the crowd. No significance. But that wasn't true of Lily. She was somebody. She was unique. She had hopes, and dreams. Plans. A future. She had a job, and an apartment, and friends, though Carl had no idea who any of them were, aside from Kim.

He spotted Toni's car when he was nearly a block away. She was sitting at the wheel, apparently reading her phone, but then she put it down immediately and started the car when they came into view.

Carl and Shelly quickened their pace. When Shelly slid into the back seat, Toni just looked back at her through the mirror and asked, "Is this everyone?" Shelly nodded and Toni put the car in gear and started forward down the street.

"What about the rest of your people?" Shelly asked as they went.

"Scattered in different directions. We'll meet up again in a couple of days," Toni answered.

This was news to Carl, also. How many plans were there? Shouldn't he have been consulted, or at least informed?

He tried touching his wrist again. Toni must have seen him wince from the explosion of pain.

"You okay?"

"Yeah. I mean, no. But..."

"What's wrong?" The urgency in her voice almost frightened him.

"Nothing," he replied. "I just think my wrist is broken. It hurts. A lot."

She didn't seem to know how to react to that. He sometimes forgot how new she was at all this.

"It'll be fine. I just need to change soon. I won't be able to use it until then."

She seemed to accept that and turned her attention back to Shelly. "Can I drop you somewhere?" she asked. There didn't seem to be any pursuit.

"That depends," Shelly said, "if you want to join us or not."

"Not yet. Carl and I have to talk," Toni replied with a glance at him.

He nodded in response. He wasn't sure what her plan was, but he had confidence she had one.

"What about Carl? He's going to have to go into hiding. We can help."

"That's one of the things we need to talk about," Toni replied.

Shelly seemed to accept that. "How do I reach you if I need to?"

"Post to Craigslist from a temporary email account. Mention Sandra Dee, and I'll respond."

"But when you reply with a location to meet," Carl added. Here was something he'd thought of earlier. "Swap East for West and add three days to the time. I'll subtract the days and meet you at a place on the opposite side of the river."

"A little cloak and dagger there don't you think?" Shelly said.

"Lily's dead. The cops know who I am, and they think I'm a terrorist. I'm pretty sure the Alpha's hunting me. I'd say a little cloak and dagger is justified."

"All right. We'll do it your way." She seemed to be pleased. Then, to Toni, she said, "Just drop me a few blocks from the nearest Max station, and I'll be good."

After they dropped her off, as soon as they were moving again, Toni turned to him and asked, "Lily's dead?"

LAUREN WAS DEAD.

She'd been a good cop and he'd gotten her killed. This whole mess was his fault. He should have foreseen Jablonski would have had his friends nearby. Michael had placed reserve officers both in and outside the coffee house. Thankfully, they'd managed to clear the civilians out of the area first. He surveyed the damage. Four wounded, two dead: Lauren and the unknown girl. Gordon was off giving a statement to Don, for all the good it would do.

"Too late to help the girl, too," he said, indicating the lifeless form of a young woman, lying on the ground where he'd killed her. He stared at it while Alice handed him a cup of coffee.

"The terrorist," she corrected him.

"She doesn't look like a terrorist. She looks like a kid."

"C'mon, let's get you to the perimeter. Someone needs to look at that shoulder."

"It's fine. Scraped it on a table, not a werewolf."

"Even so," she told him.

He followed her out the front gate. There was an ambulance in the street, but all the paramedics were already busy. He sat on the curb near it and took a sip from his coffee. Aaron joined them and stood nearby. He'd been sitting with Lauren in the garden until everything had gone to hell.

"We need to find these people fast," Michael said.

"You think?" Alice replied.

He ignored the sarcasm. "They're recruiting," he said. "And the different factions aren't quite as independent as we'd been led to believe. That woman who took Carl - she was the one from Pioneer Square. Shelly."

"Shit."

"Yeah."

"So, Carl was basically lying about everything he told us," she said.

"Which raises the question - why did he come?" Aaron said.

"He didn't know we were going to be here," Michael said.

"Which means this wasn't a trap he set for the police," Aaron finished the thought for him.

"Can we be sure about that?" Alice asked.

"What do you mean?"

"I mean, if I was a member of a criminal organization and we'd just committed a huge public act like this, and then out of nowhere an acquaintance, someone I know only peripherally - who knew of the organization but wasn't a member of it - wanted to set up a meeting somewhere, away from my home, in a public place? Yeah, the first thing I'd think of was that it was a setup by the police."

"Seriously?" he asked. "You don't think that's a little paranoid?"

"Why wouldn't these guys be paranoid? Drug dealers tend to think everything out of the ordinary is police, whether it is or not."

"These are werewolves, maybe terrorists, not drug dealers."

"Similar concept, though, isn't it?" she replied. "Stop thinking they're something new and completely different. They're not. What you've got is a loosely organized group of people operating outside the law and trying to avoid getting caught. They need to constantly recruit new members. They're willing to use violence, intimidation, even murder, to meet their goals."

He thought about it for a second. She had a point. Sure, werewolves themselves were an entirely new concept, but that didn't mean they had to throw out everything they knew about policing.

"All right, then, how would you do it?" It was meant to be a challenge and she rose to it without hesitation. She'd obviously given this some thought before today.

"Organizations like this, well it's not really an organization. It's a collection of individual criminals who frequently cooperate. There's going to be internal strife, but they'll quickly unite against a common enemy. They'll build a wall around the group, but they're still each looking out for their own interests first. So, the secret to breaking the wall is to find the weakest point of it. Catch one of them - or have them come to you. Offer a reward - or even a way out. This is big enough to get some federal money backing up requests for information."

Michael looked at Aaron, who was nearly beaming in admiration.

She continued. "The chief difference between terrorists and common criminals is that terrorists tend to be fanatically invested in their cause. But it's still the same - it's just a bit harder to find that one guy who feels like he's in over his head but doesn't see a way out. Give him a way out."

"Yeah, I didn't see a fanatic here before me today. I saw a scared kid."

"Perfect, there you go,"

"Except that when I tried to bring him in, a bunch of werewolves attacked us and now I've got a dead officer and a dead civilian, not to mention four seriously hurt, and no telling how many of them are going to turn into werewolves themselves. If he was scared before, he's going to be more so now."

"Even so," she said. "Do you have a way to reach out to him?"

"Maybe," he answered. "Gordon has an email address, though it's probably a burner. I might be able to get it from him or have him relay a message."

"Get it from him. This is too important to rely on civilians. We don't want him caught in the middle and we don't want the kid thinking he can rely on any of his friends."

He stood up and drew the other two with him a few steps away from the ambulance. He glanced around to make sure nobody was paying attention to them.

"I think you're right, though I might not be able to do anything about it. This isn't going to go well for me," he said. "I'm probably going to be off the case. The werewolf squad's going to need a leader still, you can't let them disband it."

He looked meaningfully at Alice. Aaron nodded his approval. He'd been hoping for that - Aaron had been on the squad longer, but Detective Johansen had more leadership experience, and that's what was needed the most. Aaron looked relieved.

She raised her eyebrows for a second, then nodded when she realized what he was offering.

"Are you up for it?" he asked. A sincere question. "This is going to take over your entire life irrevocably. Of course, there's no guarantee that Billings would even listen to me, but I suspect he might."

She looked to Aaron.

"We both know you're the better choice to lead us," Aaron said.

"All right, then, yes," she replied to Michael.

"Good," he said. "You're going to be in the spotlight here - this is only going to get more public from here on out."

She nodded her understanding.

"These officers - the wounded ones - they're going to need to be watched. Maybe quarantined. If they're going to change, it'll be in the next couple of hours."

"This wasn't just a rescue mission," She said. "They're still recruiting."

"Just remember they're still cops. They aren't the enemy. When they change - *if* they change - they're going to be frightened, confused, and not in their right minds. I don't know how much their personality will change once they're in human form again. I've never been able to get a good answer to that. Rosen says it doesn't. I don't think she's lying, but I don't believe she's objective enough to make that assessment. So you're going to have to be." He looked to Aaron. "Both of you. Keep an eye on them, but don't give them reason to think you don't trust them." Unlike I did with Phil, he didn't say out loud.

To her credit, Alice didn't make any noises about not wanting the position or offer any assurances that nothing would happen to him. They both knew that neither of those things were true.

TWENTY-TWO
SOME ALSO RISE

"What are you going to do now?" Veer asked him.

"No idea," Michael responded honestly. He began pulling cartons out of the bag he'd brought with him. Not having the time to cook, he'd picked up Chinese food on the way over to her house "I figured I'd watch the press conference and hadn't thought beyond that. I'm surprised you're not at it."

"Press briefings aren't really my thing," she said. "My readers expect deeper stories than what you can get from the prepared statements you read us."

Her use of "you" was not lost on him, nor was the implication that she could get better information by ignoring official sources. It was hardly fair, but he didn't want to argue with her while asking for her help.

"Did you know the girl?" he asked. "Elizabeth Rowen?"

"No. She wasn't one of ours. I guess either Kevin or Carl's group turned her," she replied.

"A rogue, then?" he asked to clarify the term.

"She'd be considered a rogue either way," Veer replied. "Public displays like that are explicitly forbidden."

"So, a werewolf can go rogue or be made a rogue?" he asked. "What if they had no say in getting made?"

"Usually, those who get made illegally, whether they agreed to it or not, are sought out and brought into the fold. If they agree to accept our structures, they are welcomed into Were society, the same as I was."

"I can't imagine it would be quite the same," he said. "Weren't you turned by the Alpha himself?"

"That doesn't make as much of a difference in day to day life as you might think," she answered.

"What's Stumpp doing about all this?"

"Trying like hell to find them," she said. "He seems to be getting some flack from the council over it as well."

"Shit. What does that mean?" Michael asked.

"I'm not sure exactly. I'm guessing, he hasn't actually told me anything. Gregor's back in town, I assume at their behest. I heard them arguing. I think Victor's holding them off for now. He doesn't want them involved any more than we do."

"We don't want them involved because...?" he led.

"Their only goal will be to cover everything up, no matter how many innocent bystanders are hurt in the process. If you want any information from Carl, you need to find him before they do."

"You'd think it would be easy," he said. "But in a population of over two million people, even someone who everyone's looking for could blend in, or disappear. Jablonski seemed surprised to learn we'd been looking for him. I don't think he was even trying to hide. Of course, that will have changed now."

"Yeah," Veer responded. "Of course, most people won't be looking for them. Even if someone happens to see any of them, the chances are they wouldn't recognize them, or just quietly turn the other way to avoid getting involved. A lot of people would be more likely to help them than to turn them in."

"You're probably right. I've never understood those people."

"The people who don't trust the police?"

"Yeah. They'll march in their anti-cop rallies, then won't hesitate to call us if they're in trouble."

She didn't answer for a moment. He realized she was trying to figure out how to say it without offending him. He bit back the urge to tell her to just spit it out.

"I think if you check," she finally said, "you'll find quite a few really would never call you. Even so, there's still no real contradiction between saying that police serve a vital function and saying they need oversight."

"Well, we certainly have that," he replied. "Which is the only reason I'm free to meet with you now."

She nodded, dismissing, not conceding, the point. He both loved and hated that about her, the fact that she could convey so much with such a simple gesture.

They brought their plates into the living room and settled onto the couch. He set his down on the low coffee table while she took a keyboard from the end table. Her computer screen was mirrored on the TV in front of them and she opened a window to bring up the press conference.

"Well, Aaron would approve," he said, indicating the wireless setup. "He's always getting on me about my twentieth century technology."

She laughed at that. "It does make things easier. When it all works."

They ate in silence for a moment while they waited for it to start.

She pointed to the screen where Detective Alice Johansen had stepped up behind a podium. "Though for breaking the news of an officer-involved shooting, you could do worse than having it explained by a young woman of color."

He supposed this was true.

"What can you tell me about her?" she asked.

"She's a good cop. Competent. Smart."

"Will she work with me?"

"She should," he said. "She's aware of your role on Skyline, and..."

She picked it up. "She knows of my status, and my position in Were society." She said.

"And about the whole organization, yes," he replied. "I'm sorry, but we knew you were connected somehow to the murders. When we finally found out how, I had to include that in my reports."

"So, she knows everything you know," she said.

"No," he replied, and that seemed to surprise her. "I just told them the facts. But there's always a million tiny things that you only learn through actual experience. They don't - they can't - show up on paper."

She nodded her understanding. "Institutional knowledge. I've often heard of companies worried about losing it when their most experienced members quit."

"Well, I was that, for all the good it did."

"You did stop Grant Talman," she reminded him.

"And then I followed it up by killing an unarmed nineteen year old girl. Second time in my career I fired my weapon at anyone and..." And they were both werewolves, he didn't say.

Veer looked like she was about to say something else, but then Alice began speaking on the TV.

He hated press conferences. He had recommended her for this position. He still felt a pang of jealousy as she began to speak.

At first, she just spoke factually about the attack at the

coffee shop. She couldn't reveal the nature of the operation, but did acknowledge that the heavy police presence was "part of an ongoing investigation." She also acknowledged that the terrorist attack was likely aimed at the police present. She mentioned that three officers had been wounded, which seemed to surprise Veer.

"Three?" she asked him.

"Plus Lauren," he said.

"By Were?"

"Yes."

"Did they turn?"

"I don't know. I haven't been able to find out," he said and was unable to keep his voice from sounding bitter. "It's one of the things I wanted to ask you about, actually. I tried to reach the one wounded officer whose name I knew and was told he was in quarantine."

"That's a new one."

"Yes, but not completely unwarranted. If they're going to change, we need to know about it."

She looked a little apprehensive about that. "What happens if they are?"

"I don't know. We never came up with a policy, and now it's out of my hands."

He looked back to the TV. "The Portland Police department deeply regrets the loss of the life of this young woman," Alice said to the gathered reporters. "We are still looking into the extent to which she was active with the terrorist cell she had been drawn into."

"Oh, that's clever," Veer said in response.

"It's PR speak," he said.

"Exactly. Her family's hired an attorney to look into the shooting and they're pushing the narrative that she was an innocent in all this. She's too telegenic to counter that directly, so they're meeting them halfway. She's still an innocent victim, but of this heinous terrorist group who draws in naive young girls and throws them into the front lines in suicidal attacks on the cops."

"You got all that from her one statement?"

She smiled at that. "And so will everyone else. You'll see. I'm betting everyone will accept that premise, assuming the family is more interested in preserving their daughter's reputation than with the settlement amount."

"Is it true you've issued orders for the police to carry silver bullets?" One of the reporters asked. The camera stayed on Alice, so Michael couldn't see who was asking the question.

"How did they learn about that?" he asked.

Veer just shook her head.

"I've issued no such orders," Alice said in response. That one Michael could see through.

"That's true," he said. "No official orders, and she didn't even suggest it. I did."

"There have been terrorist attacks in Portland," Another reporter shouted from offscreen. "Why are the police looking for werewolves instead of Jihadists?"

"Because werewolves exist here?" Michael suggested sarcastically.

"And Fox News makes its appearance at last," Veer said to the screen.

"I assure you we are taking the threat of these terrorists very seriously," Alice replied. "So far, they have made no statements and there is no known motive. There is nothing to suggest they are affiliated with any specific religious ideology."

There was unintelligible shouting from offscreen in response, and she continued. "I understand you have a specific agenda, but law enforcement has to proceed from facts, evidence, and hard reality. We will not solve any crimes by simply engaging in wild speculation."

"Damn," Michael said. "I would not have expected her to call them out like that."

"I wish more people would. Those people give the entire profession a bad name."

"On what grounds did your officer feel so threatened by a ninety pound naked girl that they had to use lethal force?" another reporter asked.

"Surely he didn't think she was concealing a weapon!" Someone shouted. He felt a flash of anger at that, not so much for the attack on him, but it was a crude joke, and the girl deserved better than the attack on her dignity.

"The investigation into the shooting is still ongoing," Alice replied to the unknown reporter. "The officer involved has been suspended pending the investigation."

The answer stunned him. After the previous answers pointing to terrorists, she had just thrown him under the bus.

"That's about as damning a statement as she could have made," he said.

"It's routine, though, isn't it, in any officer involved shooting?"

"Yeah, and if she'd pointed that out it might have mitigated some of the damage. You know as well as I do that an investigation is as good as a conviction in the public eye."

Veer didn't respond to that. She knew he was right.

"Guess she couldn't say she was a hundred-twenty pound wolf at the time," Michael said.

"Not yet at any rate."

"How does that part even work? How can she be bigger as a wolf?"

"Nobody I've spoken to knows," Veer said. "It does seem to break the laws of physics."

"Fortunately, that's not the law I'm sworn to uphold."

She laughed at that.

She turned off the TV when the conference was over.

"If there was ever a chance of working with him, there won't be now," Michael said. "The narrative is set. Carl Jablonski's the bad guy."

"Isn't he?"

"Maybe," she changed the subject. "You can tell the public he's armed and dangerous and not to approach him," she said, "But with him as public enemy one, how do you keep the police from trying to apprehend him?"

"I have no idea. Everything about this is screwy, and nobody's what they seem. The optics are going to be horrible. Nobody's going to buy Jablonski as a terrorist leader. He looks like he should be living in his mother's basement playing online computer games."

"Maybe you can play up the angry young loner aspect."

"The angry young loner who's a charismatic leader of a group of terrorists? I'm glad I'm not responsible for this mess anymore."

"No, you're not," she said, turning to him.

"No," he agreed, "I'm not."

"She's still following your script of ignoring that they seem to be werewolves. There's lots of talk about terrorists, but she's deftly sidestepping the evidence of Were."

"I still find it weird that nobody's calling them on it."

"Think of how long it took you to accept the truth, even after seeing it with your own eyes."

"Speaking of exposing them," he said, "how's your research into Holy Mountain going?"

"I start Monday," she replied.

"You haven't started yet? Why not?"

"No, I mean I start my new job there Monday."

"You got a job, what, inside the place? When you said you were going to research the place, I thought you meant you were going to dig through public documents and articles and tax forms or something, not commit corporate espionage."

She shrugged. "It's always easier from the inside."

He didn't like the idea and wasn't sure it was legal. Even suspended, he was still a cop.

"You planning on stopping me?" she said, seeing his expression.

"You planning on sharing what you learn?" he asked.

"That's the idea. I plan on sharing it with everybody, eventually. It's kind of what I do for a living," she said.

"All right," he said, and hoped it didn't sound like he thought he was giving her permission. "Let me know if you need anything. If you get into any trouble, I'll do what I can to help you out."

"Thanks," she said. "And what did you want to ask about?"

"The cop who's in quarantine. Will that make a difference?"

"If he's going to change, he would have by now," she said. "I've never heard of anyone resisting it for more than a few hours before and still changing."

"So why would they still be keeping him in quarantine?" he said.

"They probably don't know that," she replied. "You're the first one who's asked me about it. Want me to check into it?"

He was torn. She had just confessed to planning to infiltrate a company posing as an employee. And he remembered her stealing the files from his desk. On the other hand, something was up and he still felt responsible, regardless of his current status.

"Do I want to know what that entails?" he asked.

"Probably not," she said with a smile.

On the other hand, she probably had access to resources that he didn't.

He nodded. "Let me know if you find anything. But be careful. And don't get arrested."

A LIGHT RAIN was falling as Veer rode up Sandy Boulevard. Michael had given her a name, only one of three who had been wounded. From the name, she had managed to find an address, and the name of the man's wife. She had no idea what she could learn from the woman, but it was her only lead. She wanted to follow it up before dedicating her attention to Holy Mountain Research.

She found her destination, a small house in an up and coming neighborhood in the northeast and managed to find a parking spot a couple of blocks away and locked her helmet in the case on the back of the bike.

"Eileen Jackson?" she asked the woman who answered the door.

"Yes. You must be Vera Rosen?" When Veer had answered in the affirmative, she said, "Come on in."

"You're looking into the disappearances?" Jackson asked as she led Veer into the living room.

"Disappearances?" Veer was caught off guard. "I was hoping to talk to your husband about the attacks at the coffee shop. What disappearances?"

"You didn't know? I haven't heard from my husband since last week. The police won't tell me anything and so when you called this morning, I thought that was why you wanted to talk to me."

"I knew he'd been hurt at the Pied Cow, I didn't know he'd disappeared afterward."

"He's not the only one. His partner, Mel, is missing, too, and her husband hasn't heard anything either."

"What did the department tell you?"

"That he's under deep cover. 'He's okay, and will contact you when he's able,' but I know that's just cover-up speak for 'quit bothering us.'"

"You don't think he's really under cover?"

"He's always found a few minutes of privacy to contact me before. Even if he couldn't for some reason, he was just hurt in an attack. He should be in recovery, not on assignment."

"That makes sense, but..."

"That's not all of it," she interrupted her. "I talked to David - Mel's husband. She's one of the other officers who was injured."

Veer could guess where this was going. "And he hasn't heard anything from his wife, either?"

She shook her head. "Apparently they told him that she's in quarantine. They claim some kind of biological agent was used."

"I take it you don't believe them?"

"It makes even less sense. Say she really is in quarantine. Whatever she has is gonna get out over the phone? There's something going on, and I want to know what it is."

"That makes two of us."

"How can I help then?"

"Tell me everything," Veer said, pulling out her notebook. "Do you know who else was injured?" She gave her the name of the last of the injured police officers. And of Lauren Boyd, who she already knew had died at the scene.

"And of course the naked girl," the woman said.

The naked girl. Elizabeth Rowen, known as Lilith to her friends. Whoever she had been, whatever hopes and dreams and experiences she'd had had come down to this. Destined to be remembered only as "the naked girl" killed in a botched terrorist attack.

"He was working with the Werewolf Squad," Jackson continued. "They weren't just all getting coffee there. There was a reason there was nobody but cops and terrorists in that place."

"What can you tell me about this 'Werewolf Squad'?" she asked, hoping for additional insight.

"That's the crux of it," Jackson started. "Detective Michael Diaz is in charge of it. They're on the Pioneer Square attack, right? The ones who were trying to make it look like werewolves?"

"Right..." she said, her tone inviting the other woman to continue.

"It's just that..."

"What?" she asked, encouraging her to continue.

She still hesitated. "I... how much do you know about the squad?"

This was a tricky question, more so than Jackson even realized, and Veer wasn't sure how to answer.

"That's part of what I'm trying to find out," she stalled. "Why? What do you know?"

"It'll sound crazy," she said.

"Tell me anyway. You never know."

"You're leaving my name out of this, right?" she asked.

"If you want," Veer reassured her. "I can omit the details so it can't be traced to you."

"Then please do. It's just..." Veer could tell she didn't want to say it. That was a natural reaction. She thought of saying something herself, but established habit kept her from leading the source.

"Go ahead," she said. "No judgment here. I'm a journalist."

"Well, there's the name..."

When she trailed off again, Veer prompted her. "The were-wolf squad. Based on the Pioneer Square attack, right?"

"Except they were calling themselves that before the attack."

Veer knew this to be true, of course, but didn't realize anyone outside Michael's group did. She nodded slightly, but kept quiet, allowing the other woman to continue.

"And the force has set aside money for silver bullets."

This was new to her. She was aware that some members of the force were carrying silver ammunition, including Diaz, but she'd been under the impression that they had been making it themselves. For it to have actually been budgeted instead of coming out of their own pockets, or even petty cash... that implied a large scale sustained effort. It wasn't just Kevin and Shelly and Carl they were worried about.

"Is it even possible that... I think... I mean..."

Veer let her finish.

"I think werewolves are real. The terrorists in the square were really... Is it possible?" She looked at Veer.

Veer hesitated for only a second. This went against everything she'd done for the last three years, helping them to keep their secret. Always conceal and never reveal.

"Yes," was all she said.

The other woman looked surprised, then relieved. Then suspicious.

"You knew this already," she said. It was an accusation, not a question.

"I did," she replied, accepting the guilt and responsibility inherent in that statement.

"So why are you really here?" Jackson asked.

"For exactly the reason I said. I'm looking to find out what happened to the officers who were attacked."

"By werewolves," Jackson said. "Nick and his partner were

fighting actual werewolves." The other woman stated. Again, it wasn't quite a question.

"Yes," she repeated the simple confirmation, making that single word carry so much meaning.

"So... can they? Fight them, I mean? Can they even hope to survive such a fight?"

"They can," Veer said.

"How can you be sure?"

"Because," Veer said, "the werewolves have one great advantage: their secrecy, the idea that their very existence is ludicrous."

"So how does that help?"

"Because that's what I'm going to take away from them," Veer replied. There was steel in her voice. She tried to ignore the fact that it was a betrayal of almost everyone she cared about.

PEOPLE EITHER TURNED to look or stepped out of his way as Michael stalked past the booking area, through the officers' desks and up the three steps to the detectives' landing. His fury must have shown in his face or in his stance. Veer had given him the results of her research and interviews with the three police officers' spouses, and he wasn't happy. She would be starting her new job at Holy Mountain Research today. He had other concerns.

He was glad at least to see his own desk untouched. He spotted Alice in the war room with Aaron. That hadn't changed either. He didn't know why he expected everything to look radically different.

He flung the door open, startling them both. Alice looked confused while Aaron looked as if he had been caught collaborating with the enemy. He looked everywhere but at the two of them.

"Michael." He could tell Alice was making an effort to stay calm. "What are you doing here?"

"I could ask you the same question."

"I work here," she said icily. "Aren't you still on leave?"

He ignored the question.

"Do you know where Phil is?" he asked her. Aaron snapped his gaze to him as he said it.

She seemed surprised. "Phil? No..." He caught it, and she knew he caught it.

"And the three officers? Where are they?"

To her credit she didn't even pretend not to understand what he meant. "They're being observed."

"Where? By who?"

"You're not on this task force any more, Detective. You shouldn't even be in the precinct. You certainly shouldn't be speaking to me."

"Yes." He dismissed the complaints. "Where are they?"

"That's not your concern." She replied. "What's going on?"

"Their families are wondering. They've all been given different stories and know they're being lied to."

She paused for a second, before answering. "You've spoken to their families? You're not supposed to be..."

He cut her off. "Are they werewolves?"

When she didn't answer, he continued. "Dammit, I told you to keep an eye on them, not to lock them up. They're still cops - you can't just disappear."

"Nobody's been 'disappeared,'" she replied with a snort of derision. "I've already told you it's none of your business. It doesn't matter what you told me in the past. Your information is obsolete, and you're not the one who has to make decisions here. You can leave now."

He started walking towards the door, but turned back angrily, "What about their basic human rights? Shouldn't they at least get..."

"Human rights only apply to humans, detective."

At that he gave a long hard look, not at her, but at Aaron. His expression in return was unreadable.

"They're still cops," Michael said as he walked away.

"HELLO? ARE YOU IN THERE?" he heard Toni's voice call.

Carl crawled out from the small shelter into the dim sunlight. After the attack at the Pied Cow, he'd gone into hiding and had spent the last week living in the small shelter they'd found in Forest Park. He would sometimes venture into the city for supplies, late in the evening when visibility was lowest, so he'd have the least chance of being recognized.

Toni stood outside in the small clearing nearby. He was surprised to see Kim with her.

"We brought dinner," Kim said, indicating the large McDonald's bag she was carrying.

"Thanks!" Carl said when they were sitting on the grass, and he was unwrapping a burger. "First human food I've had since last night."

"Can you survive without it?" Kim asked. "Is it possible to only eat while in wolf form?"

"I don't know," Carl said. "I think it can sustain you, for a while at least, but I do get hungry still. I'm pretty sure I ate this morning in form."

"You already changed today?" Kim asked. She seemed disappointed.

Carl wondered why for a second, until Toni said, "We still

can. Carl and I have gone hunting pretty much every time I've come by and we've both changed separately as well."

"You can do that?" Kim asked. "How often can you change?"

"Don't know that either," Carl said. "Probably not more than a few times in a day. It takes a lot out of you when you do, so you have to eat and sleep some time. But what's up? Not that I'm not happy to see you, but why are you here?"

"I wanted other people to know where this place was," Toni answered for her. "Starting with Kim. If anything happens, someone, especially Kim, may need to disappear quickly and meet up with the rest of us. Thought this was a good rendezvous point."

"Oh," Carl said. They'd chosen this spot specifically because it was both abandoned and hard to find, "Why especially Kim?"

"The police came by, after... after the Pied Cow. With Lily killed, they wanted to talk to me. The Detective Diaz asked me what I knew about werewolves. He didn't know I'd been there. I told him that it was some kind of pagan thing that Lily was involved in and that I didn't know anything about it. Then he told me she was dead."

"Fuck," Carl said. "He came to your home?"

"It was Lily's home too, remember? They're still freaking out trying to figure out what had happened. Fortunately, I had an alibi. I talked to my cousin and he agreed to tag me in some pictures of a party he had at his house, and added a couple of pictures I was in from earlier parties. So, when the cops showed up, I was able to show them my Facebook to prove I wasn't at the Pied Cow. Still spent most of the day being questioned, though."

"Damn, I hadn't even thought of that," said Carl.

"Fortunately, she did," Toni reprimanded him.

"Lucky," Carl agreed. "But it's over now, right? They bought it?"

"For now," she said. "It's handy to have an anarchist cousin. He didn't even ask why I needed it, just did it for the fun of fucking with the cops. But if they look closely, they might figure it out, and with a dead cop... they'll probably look closely. I don't know what I'll do next time."

"Hence the contingency hiding place. Well, my castle is your castle," Carl said. "Think your cousin would be interested in joining us?" he asked.

"I could ask..." she said. "But I don't know. He's a great guy, and I like him enough, in small doses. He kinda tends to bring the drama, and..."

"And yeah, we probably have enough as it is," Carl said. Kim seemed grateful for his understanding. He turned to Toni and asked, "Any news about setting up a meeting?"

"Yep, Carrie set up a place for tomorrow morning. Figured I'd introduce Kim to your hideout, then we could all go hunting together and head out there in the morning. Still nothing from Kevin and Shelly?"

The thought of the three of them hunting together intrigued him. Hunting with Toni had opened his mind to new vistas. What might it be like with three people? Maybe someday an entire pack? He could have a family. He realized that if they were successful, children might be possible some day. He had considered that option forever sealed off to him. Now he imagined himself running through the forest, or openly through the high desert of central Oregon, teaching his children how to navigate the world, both as humans and as wolves.

But before any of that was possible, they had to succeed, they had to destroy the secret and overthrow centuries of established tradition.

"Yes," he said. "I mean, no. Yes to hunting then heading to

the meeting in the morning. No to hearing from Kevin and Shelley. Did you check their house?"

"Cyn and Tyler went by the address you gave us," Toni said. "Looks like the cops had been there, but nobody else for the last few days. If they've been arrested, they're keeping it on the QT."

"Which means they probably haven't been arrested," Kim added. "Their faces are still all over the place, just like yours."

"Dammit," he said. "Maybe I should just turn myself in. They're trying to make me out to be the next Osama bin Laden, maybe I can explain I'm not."

"At this point, I don't know how well that'll work," Toni said.

"I don't like it, but we'll stand by you either way," Kim said. He appreciated that.

"How'd things get so fucked up anyway?" Carl asked.

"Kevin," Toni said without hesitation.

"What?" he said.

"Our people were supposed to pounce, knock down, confuse, and run off," she said. "That was the plan if anything went wrong. Confusion and mayhem so you could get away. No biting. Definitely no killing. If Kevin and his people hadn't been there, and hadn't charged in and attacked the cops, it never would have gone so cockeyed."

Carl was pretty sure Toni had been the first through the window, and that Lily had attacked and stayed long enough to get shot but didn't say anything. He realized Kim was probably still grieving Lily and it wouldn't go well to put any of the blame on her.

"I don't know," he finally said. "We were all there. Myself included. Maybe I shouldn't have gone."

"Probably not," Toni said. She stood up and started undressing. "But too late now. C'mon, let's go get us a wildebeest."

HE FELT MUCH BETTER when he woke up. Toni was still asleep on the grass nearby, back in human form. There was no sign of Kim, but it could easily take her a few more hours to get back. He recognized where they were. Somehow, they had both made it back to the small clearing near his hideaway while still in wolf form. The sky was clear and full of stars. The first quarter moon was sinking out of view into the trees.

Toni opened her eyes and sat up. He moved over to her, but she pushed him away gently when he reached for her.

"Not now," she said. "I don't want to be in the throes of passion when Kim gets back."

He smiled at that. It wasn't like Kim didn't know, but he sat beside her, huddling close against the cold. They could have gone to get dressed. His shelter where they left their clothes was almost within sight, but Kim was new at all this and he didn't want her to feel embarrassed if she showed up and was the only one not dressed when she got there. He didn't know why Toni stayed.

They sat for a while in silence, watching the woods and the stars. A thin crescent moon hung overhead. Within a couple of days, it would be gone.

"Is it worth it?" he asked. "All this?"

"Her life for mine, you mean?" Toni replied.

"What?" He didn't follow.

"That's what you're thinking, isn't it? Was it worth Lily losing her life as I didn't lose mine?"

"Wait... No... where did that come from?"

"This whole thing started because the Alpha and his people wanted to kill me."

"No! No. Fuck that. Fuck this!" He leapt to his feet. "Fuck

all of that. This isn't even in the slightest bit your fault. This started because of me. I forced something on you against your will. I was selfish and short sighted and I fucked up and ruined your life and I'll bear that until the day I die, but wallowing in it doesn't do me or you or anyone else any good. It doesn't do any good when I do it and it certainly isn't any good when you do it because none of this, none of it at all, is even slightly your fault."

She sat for a moment, her knees pulled close to her chest, arms wrapped around them. She looked at him with an expression on her face he'd never seen before and couldn't begin to parse.

"He's right, you know," a voice from behind him said. He startled, then turned to see Kim coming toward them.

"Hi. Sorry I took so long," she said. "But Carl's right. What happened to Lilith wasn't your fault. She knew what she was getting into. We all did. You explained it to us during our initiation. We were there in that place because we knew things might go bad and we might have to fight cops, and when you fight cops people get hurt, sometimes die. Lilith could be flighty sometimes," and she smiled a sort of sad smile at a memory they weren't privy to, "but she wasn't an idiot. She knew what might happen."

"Do you want out?" Toni asked her.

"There is no out," she replied. "You can't bring us into this world then expect us to turn our backs on it. We can't go back, so what can we do?"

"You're right," Carl said. "The only way out is through. So, we go on. We have to continue the plan. Grow our numbers, continue in secret until we have enough people to reveal ourselves all at once so they can't deny us, or silence us. We gain the protection of law. Real law, as equals to the rest of humanity, not pawns of the police. We will not be invisible, we will not be quiet, and we will not peacefully lay down and die for the convenience of the Alpha."

"Hah!" Toni laughed out loud. He liked the sound. "As a St. Crispin's Day speech, it's not half bad."

"Who's St. Crispin?"

She rolled her eyes at that. "You can look it up on TV tropes later."

LATER THAT AFTERNOON, Carl had showered and was wearing a set of fresh clothes which Toni had somehow procured for him. He'd been delighted a few days ago to learn that a company he'd worked for three years previously still hadn't changed the code that opened the door to the basement. In the basement were two private restrooms, with showers. It had come in handy in the past when he'd been out drinking with friends - usually Shelly and Kevin - and wanted to find a restroom in an old town that wasn't filthy and covered in drunks' piss. Now it was a lifeline.

"Well, yeah, I mean I've *played* D&D," he told Toni as they walked through the glass doors. "But I've never actually been inside a gaming store like this before."

Amongst the merchandise displays, the store had several long tables set out, which were sparsely occupied by groups of people playing card games. In the back were a couple of small rooms, about 10' square, that could, conveniently, be reserved in blocks of up to six hours. As Toni had explained on the way over here, normally such rooms would be used for a D&D group, giving the players a place to meet up, and not incidentally encouraging them to spend time in the store, giving them every chance to buy more merchandise while they did. He wondered if all gaming stores did that. Either way, it suited their purposes. Carrie was already in the room when they found it. She was sitting at a round table with a cardboard screen standing upright in front of her.

Cynthia and Tyler were sitting next to each other across the table from Will and his friend Jacob. Daniel sat at the end of the table opposite Carrie.

As they entered, he noticed Carrie's screen was covered with a picture of a rather humanoid looking wolf attacking a group of people. In case the image wasn't clear enough, next to her sat a book with WEREWOLF! written across it in ominous looking letters, with an image of claws tearing out of the cover of the book. Carl was torn for a second between reminding them that they were supposed to be secret and saying something about the image they wanted to portray. Before he could say anything, though, Toni laughed.

"Perfect!" she said, stepping in and closing the door behind her. Carrie handed them each a sheet of paper. Carl looked at his - it was a character sheet, similar to ones he'd used in Dungeons and Dragons, though the format and stats were different from what he was used to.

"Hey, I wanted to be a druid," Toni complained with a smile.

"Just put 'em in front of you," Carrie dumped a large handful of ten-sided dice of all colors in front of them, spreading them down the table. "If anyone looks in, we're a bunch of people talking about werewolves, and making plans, and now we've given them a reason why."

"It's a public shop," Toni said. "What if someone wants to join the game?"

"Fuck it, let 'em," Carrie responded. "After all, we're discussing a conspiracy to expose a bunch of werewolves. Maybe they'll have some ideas we didn't think of."

"Oh my gods," Toni said. "You're totally gonna Ender's

Game some poor guy."

The door opened again, and Kim entered. Carl noticed she'd had a chance to shower and change clothes as well. He gave her a warm smile, which she returned. She moved to a back corner of the room and stayed standing. There weren't enough chairs for everyone, so he decided to remain on his feet as well, the better to address the group.

"Well, I think we're all here," Carl started. "I suppose things could've gone better."

"What the fuck happened in Pioneer Square?" Jacob jumped in. He'd obviously been waiting to ask. "That's not what I signed up for."

That took Carl aback. He hadn't been thinking about Pioneer Square.

"I... uh... no," he said. Not as eloquent as he'd hoped for, but he plowed ahead. "No. No, it wasn't. None of us did."

This was obviously not the answer Jacob had been expecting.

"What Kevin and Shelley did, well, it kind of fucked us. Especially me. We didn't know anything about it in advance, and now both the police and Alpha are hunting us as criminals. They know I knew Kevin, and the police think we're part of the same organization."

"Well can't you just explain that you aren't?"

"I don't think that'd work. Especially after they got involved with the mess at the Pied Cow." He didn't want to tell them about the one guy he'd actually helped kill. He didn't think the police would see it that way. "I was only an accessory to one murder, officer." Well, other than the one he actually committed directly. Maybe life under the Alphas wasn't so bad after all. Before trying to rebel, he'd never committed murder before, and he certainly had never been wanted as a terrorist.

"The police are searching for me, and anyone associated

with me is going to come under scrutiny as well. So... I guess
what I'm saying is, here's your chance. Walk away - go back, live
your lives, keep your secret, stay away from us. If you do that,
you should be safe."

"Hah!" Kim said.

"Relatively."

"What happens to us if we do?" Tyler asked. Cynthia
looked at him while Carl answered.

"If you leave, you mean? Nothing. Change into wolf form
once in a while. Go off on your own, nobody else ever needs to
know. Live your life just as you are now. Maybe take up solo
camping in remote areas as a hobby."

"Alone?" Cynthia responded. "You think we can see this
new amazing world, then just walk away? Leave it and everybody in it behind?"

"I can," Jacob said, rising to his feet. "I'm sorry, but I don't
want this. I don't want to be in a war. I'm not here to fight your
battles or die like Lily." He turned to Will and said, "I'm sorry, I
just can't."

"Okay," Toni said before Carl could say anything. "You
don't know us, and we don't know you."

"Sounds good to me," he replied.

As he reached the door, Carl spoke up, "One more thing..."
When Jacob stopped and looked back, all his muscles were
tense. Fight or flight, he was prepared for either.

"If we succeed, if it all turns out the way we hope, and
someday Were can live open and free, you're welcome to stand
among us, as a friend. There's no animosity, no resentment, and
nobody who is friends with me, or wants to remain that way
will hunt you down, harass you, expose you, or even call you a
coward. The point, the entire point of all of this, is that we're
free to make our own decisions. I won't betray that or think ill
of you for walking your own path instead of mine."

"Thanks," Jacob said, visibly relaxing.

"You have a gift, though, and you're stuck with it. Whether you keep it secret, try to go public on your own, or start your own group of wolves is up to you. Whatever you choose, be careful, and good luck."

"Thanks," Jacob said again. He held his hand out and Carl took it. "For everything. Seriously. Maybe we'll see each other again someday. And good luck to all of you."

"Hey, you're getting pretty good at the whole speechifying thing," Toni told him after he'd closed the door.

"I mean it," Carl said, to the group as much as to her. He realized this was her intention. "Seriously. We need there to be people like him out there. Allies, but not partners. Hopefully, he makes more wolves. It'll be a good thing. We won't know who they are, and they won't know who we are. I meant what I said about remaining friends. We've got enough enemies as it is, we don't need to fight amongst ourselves."

"What about this Kevin guy?" Carrie asked.

"We're keeping our distance from them. Whatever they're trying to do, we don't want to be involved in that kind of violence."

"So... no more deaths?"

"There might be. I can't say that for sure. The Alphas would kill all of us to stop us from doing what we're doing. Not to mention the police. But they're not after any of you. I meant it when I said there'd be no hard feelings if you want to distance yourself from me."

"Dude, we're in, okay? Stop saying that," Tyler responded. He looked at Cynthia as he said it, and she nodded in agreement.

"Yeah, stop trying to scare us off," she said.

"Agreed," Daniel said. "But are we really sure all violence is necessarily bad?"

"Yes!" said Cynthia quickly.

"It gets attention," Daniel said. "Isn't that what we want?"

"Not like that," Carl said. "We don't want anything like Pioneer Square ever again."

"But it's what got everyone out there talking about werewolves," he said, growing more animated. "More than anything we've done."

"Give us time," Toni said. "We can do this without violence."

"Non-violence is always the best way to resist," Cynthia said.

"Non-violence is always the method that oppressors prefer to be used by those they oppress."

An angry murmur passed around the small room.

"It doesn't matter," Toni replied. "Violence at this stage may get our reveal sooner, but it just means we'll turn all the humans against us as well as the Alphas. I don't want to trade being hunted by the Alphas to being hunted by the police. I want to make it so none of us is hunted by anybody."

"Yes," Carl agreed, and everyone else chimed in their assent shortly thereafter.

"Okay," Daniel said. "I see your point. I was just trying to think out loud on other options. That's why we're here, right?"

"Yes," Carl said, glad the issue was settled. "But I think we can take violence for anything other than self-defense off the table. We're not going to try talking to the police again either. As long as we stay away from any trouble, we should be safe."

Everyone nodded.

"So how do we do it, then?" Carrie asked.

"My proposal, and that's all it is right now," Carl answered her. "Is to take a page from the French Resistance model."

"Cells?" Daniel asked.

Before he could answer, Carrie asked "Like terrorists?"

"No. Well, yes, exactly, only without the terrorist part."

"So how does that work?"

"Everybody here becomes the leader of their own cell. Make more wolves. Have them break off into more cells and do the same. The eight of us here, we're cell Alpha."

"Or cell Zero?" Toni suggested. He'd meant to say that after she'd pointed out the unfortunate name. He had agreed, but slipped in the excitement now.

"Yes, that's what I mean. We occasionally get together, see how things are going, share any needed information or news, try to estimate our numbers, decide when to go public. If you want, you can call on Toni and me to run initiations, and there're lots of good reasons for doing so, or we can teach you how to. There's more to it than what you see on the surface. However you do it, growing our numbers is really the most important part. If everybody makes one new wolf a month, in six months there'll be almost four hundred of us. In a year, twenty-five thousand. That's way more than enough to go public with. If people spread out beyond Portland, that'd be even better.

"And even if we don't come anywhere near those numbers, a few hundred might be sufficient. They couldn't silence us then, and any attempt would only bring more attention to them."

"So, we each have a cell and take news back to our own little cells?" Tyler asked. "Do we ever all meet up?"

"No," Carl responded. "That's the point. We don't know who's in your groups, they don't know who's in ours, and only half a dozen people know the entire membership of cell zero. We shouldn't even know how many groups there are. And since I'm the most likely to be caught, it's best that I know as little as possible."

"You wouldn't betray us though, would you?" Kim asked.

"It depends. If the police catch me? No, I'd probably be sent to jail where the Alphas would have me killed to prevent me from revealing the secret. But if the Alphas got me first... they'd use torture to get what information they could. I don't know how long I'd last, but they say that everyone talks under torture eventually. I don't have such an inflated opinion of myself that I think I'd be the first one ever not to."

"Gah! How can you just talk so calmly about it?" Kim demanded.

This took Carl by surprise. "What... I... uh..." He was trying to remember exactly what he'd said, but his mind wouldn't engage.

"It probably won't happen," Toni spoke up. "We're hoping of course that it doesn't happen to anybody, but these people, the Alphas, they're not good people. Murder? Torture? Worse? These are possibilities. They need to be acknowledged. It's precisely because things like this exist that they need to be opposed. Because they shouldn't. Nobody should be killed just for being a Wolf without permission from the so-called 'right people.' That's why we want to expose the secret, because once everybody knows, once they see that the world doesn't end, there'll be no reason to kill or torture anybody to keep it."

"Maybe at some point, hundreds of years ago, the Alphas and their organization legitimately protected the wolves," Carl continued her point. "But now the only thing they protect is their power over them."

Nobody spoke for a while, until Will finally said, "I don't want to run a cell."

Carl looked at him, then noticed everyone else did as well. "I don't know how to recruit people or how to be a terrorist, even without causing terror," he continued. "Can I just stay a part of your group?"

This took Carl by surprise. This wasn't how he expected it to go.

"I can," said Carrie. "I mean, the recruitment and stuff. I know some people already who'd want to join. I'm not doing any terrorism. I don't want to kill anybody."

"Nobody is," Carl said, finally. "I just meant the structure. To keep them from finding us. I don't want anyone committing violence." He carefully did not look at Daniel as he said it. "We should be doing everything we can to keep as low a profile as possible until we're ready. In fact," he and Toni had discussed this part earlier, "if anyone does, you're out. If you pull anything like Kevin did in Pioneer Square, you're on your own. We won't help you, we won't protect you, and you're not welcome in the group anymore. Cynthia and Tyler both looked relieved at that. Kim looked proud of him. Daniel looked a little apprehensive. Like he was weighing the odds, considering the benefits to being in Carl's group against growing his own.

Carl didn't want to say anything, even to Toni, but he thought Daniel had a point. There was room for both approaches. He could become known for advocating nonviolence, and let Kevin, and maybe Daniel, take the big risks. Let them prove the existence of the Were. Once it was established, their job would be to convince everyone that they weren't all bad, that there were others who were different.

He was already toying around with how to say it, imagining himself being interviewed, "These recent acts of violence have convinced us to come forth and reveal our existence. We denounce those who commit violence in our name and want to reassure the world that that's not what being a werewolf is all about." Should he say Were? Or just wolf? The exact phrasing would be important, to convince people of the truth of what he was saying.

TWENTY-THREE
MOVEMENTS AND NOCTURNES

Gordon stared at his email. What could he even say after what happened at the Pied Cow? "Oops. Sorry I got your friend killed."

He thought he'd been clever when he invited Carl and Diaz to meet. He could be a mediator, helping both of them. From what Toni had told him, their goals were the same. Yet somehow everything had blown up. No, not "somehow." He knew exactly how. Diaz had tried to arrest Carl. The man was an accessory to murder. Under any other circumstances, there shouldn't even be a question. Toni herself had told him directly about how the guy had attacked her. Chained her in a basement. Someone had died. The man was a criminal and belonged in jail. Under any other circumstances.

Do the circumstances excuse anything he did? People had died. He watched them die. But he also saw what had happened at the coffee shop. The wolves ignored him as he cowered in the back. One paused, looked at him and snarled, but then turned away when he didn't attack it. Most of them had run off. Even Carl had tried to get away when he could have changed and attacked the cops who were trying to cuff him. He wasn't out to kill anyone. Did his intentions matter, or just the result of his actions?

Gordon had tried to get involved and people had died. He had tried to stop an attack on the streets and people had died. He had killed people, too, just like Carl. Was that part of being a werewolf? He had had a choice. He could have let the thugs live. He could have walked away. Hell, he could have called the cops, or run, or just distracted the guys long enough for the girl to get away. He hadn't done any of those things. He had tried to be a superhero, but this wasn't a comic book.

What was he, and whose side should he be on? That was the real question. Everything about his life had just been turned upside down and he didn't know where he fit in anymore. Were all of his disastrous attempts just him trying to be relevant? Could it all be simply ego-driven. Too many things had changed, and he didn't know who he was anymore.

He did know, though, that Carl and Toni were fighting against the structures that had caused the death of his daughter and nearly killed him. Twice.

"I'm sorry," he wrote. Just be honest and tell her how you really feel, he could hear Barbara saying. It was advice meant for a completely different circumstance, but that had never stopped her from repeating something. He smiled at the memory. He realized that he was addressing the email to Carl's alias, but he was really writing to Toni. "I didn't want to put any details in the last email because I didn't know who might intercept it. Because you didn't know what was going to happen - because I didn't tell you what was going to happen - everything went wrong. I thought it could be a polite, safe meeting."

He realized he was doing it again. So afraid of anyone intercepting it and using it against him he was limiting himself to vague statements that only Toni and Carl would understand.

He erased the last line, and replaced it with, "Everything went wrong, and your friend died because of it. I didn't know Diaz was going to try to arrest Carl. He had assured me he just wanted to talk." Did that last line sound too much like he was trying to avoid responsibility by throwing Diaz under the bus? It was true, though, dammit.

"I fucked up," he continued, just to make it clear. "I think I was..." he started, then went back and erased the first two words. "I was trying to be relevant, to fit in somehow. For everything that's going on, I'm afraid you're handling the transition into this new life better than I am. Given all the circumstances, I am impressed, and after the disaster that was our last meeting, I can understand why you'd be reluctant to trust me again. I'm not going to be making any plans, but if you do need anything, even a Mysterious Stranger again, or if there is anything I can do to help you, feel free to contact me. I am here." He signed it, "Gordon." If anyone read it, they would know exactly who he was and where his loyalties lie. So be it.

He thought for a moment of adding something about his own recent research but decided that it wasn't needed here. This was an apology. Admit fault, take responsibility, try to make things right. If they accepted it and contacted him again, he could go into any other ideas then. If they did not, well, then they didn't. If he didn't have anybody to share his discoveries in this new world with, that was his own fault.

Of course, that would imply that he had any actual discoveries. What he had was ideas. He also had questions. There was just so much he didn't know.

Against his own misgivings, he had tried changing more often. A few days ago, he'd changed four times in a day. It had left him exhausted, barely enough energy to get up off the floor. A hearty dinner and a good night's sleep had fixed that, though, and in the morning he'd felt better than ever. He'd tried experimenting. He took a video of himself changing and moving about his house in wolf form. He tracked his weight. He made multiple attempts to weigh himself in wolf form but had so far failed to do so. There were limits to the kinds of commands the wolf could understand, apparently.

In comic books, Wolfsbane, the werewolf character from the X-men, could change into a hybrid form. It gave her some of the powers of the wolf form but let her keep all her human faculties. He was a little wary of taking cues from comic books, but of all the werewolf literature out there, how much of it was pure imagination, how much was based on older myths and legends, and how much was real werewolves sneaking in references that only other werewolves would understand? Couching details in a popular comic book could be a good way for a secret werewolf to reach out to others of his kind, let them know what he knew. He'd experimented with trying to change part-way but had made no progress. There didn't seem to even be a halfway point in the change. Once it started, it happened completely.

He'd kept a journal in an attempt to document his mental state, so he could monitor any signs of radical changes. Each time he re-read older entries and compared them to newer ones, both seemed perfectly reasonable and sane to him. He wished he could speak to a psychiatrist, but they'd probably just think he was crazy.

He understood what he was doing. His life had spun out of control. He had this new gift, or curse, and all of his attempts to understand it, to analyze it and test his new abilities had just been his way of attempting to reestablish some measure of control. It was psychology 101.

He also realized he hadn't left the house for over 48 hours. A shave, a shower, and a long walk was what he needed.

THIS TIME, Kim was already back at the shelter when Carl got there. She was sitting on the grass in the small clearing in the fading light, wrapped in a wool blanket she'd brought, waiting for him. She'd come out on her own and they'd changed and run through the forest together for a while but hadn't hunted. He'd come back shortly after they'd gotten separated. Cynthia and Tyler had come to visit the night before, and Toni the evening before that. Kim had confirmed this was deliberate. They had decided to take turns coming out here. He wondered if this might be Toni's way of beginning the process of separating herself from him.

He sat down heavily beside Kim, outside the blanket.

"That was fun," she said.

When he didn't respond with enthusiasm, she asked what was wrong, and he voiced his worry.

"It's not that," she said. "For one, the police are watching her."

This was news to him. "Someone told them she knew you," Kim said. She pulled the blanket a little tighter around herself. "They can't prove anything, but we've spotted a couple of unmarked cars driving by. So, there's that, and after missing a couple of shifts, her work threatened to fire her if she missed any more."

He looked down and shook his head sadly. One more thing he'd ruined in her life.

Kim obviously realized what he was thinking. "She told me," she said, "about how she was turned. After I heard you talking last week, she told me the whole story."

He sighed. "So everybody knows, now?"

"No, she told me." She emphasized the last word. He recalled how she'd said the same thing once about her

boyfriend. "She asked if I thought the rest should know everything. I said no. It doesn't change who you are. We know who
you are."

"And who am I?" he asked her.

"You're Carl. The head of the Order of the Wolf, into
which I was initiated knowingly and of my own free will. An
ancient order that has protected new wolves since the earliest
days of October."

He laughed out loud at that last, then threw his head back
and laughed even louder.

"It wasn't that funny," she said, but the laughter was contagious and soon she couldn't stop herself. God it felt good, there
had been so little laughter lately.

"Any progress on finding a venue for the next phase?" he
asked when they'd finally settled down.

"Maybe," she said. "We've got a few more possible candidates, and Toni and I agreed that we want to do it the same way
as before - meet up at a local party somewhere first for a screening, see how they interact. It's a little more difficult this time
with you being America's Most Wanted and everything."

He stood up and was suddenly conscious of his nakedness.
Did the no-touching rule still apply, he wondered. He missed
Toni. He turned away from Kim so she couldn't see what he
was thinking and stepped toward his shelter. "I'm gonna get
something on," he said. He turned back after he'd pulled on his
pants. She was still sitting on the grass, wrapped in the blanket,
looking at him.

"Have you heard anything from Shelly and Kevin?" she
asked.

"Nothing. Nothing on the news yet, either," he said. "You?"
She shook her head.

"I got an email from Gordon Chandler, though," he told
her. He stooped back down to pick up his phone.

"Really? After everything that happened? What did he want?"

"To apologize. Said it wasn't meant to go down like that." He showed her the email.

"He seems sincere," she said, when she had read the entire email. "Do you trust him?"

"Hell no. But... I dunno, he was pretty helpful at the warehouse party."

"What are you going to do if he wants to go to the next one?" she asked.

He didn't understand. "What do you mean? Like should we invite him?"

"Is that your decision to make? What exactly is his position anyway?"

Carl laughed at that. It felt good to laugh. "Sorry, I thought Toni had filled you in on that too," he said. That thought cured his laughter quickly. He continued rather than dwell on it. "Everything we told you was one hundred percent true. But not everything was necessarily as we implied it to be." He told her about how they'd met Gordon at the Pied Cow, and how he had eavesdropped on their own conversation. How he'd been turned into a wolf by the rogue killer that the police shot and found him and Toni while searching for others of his kind, and how Toni had suggested the Mysterious Stranger bit at the party. Nobody said who he was, they let everyone draw their own conclusions.

"Hah." She laughed. "Maybe he can be trusted," she said. "Sounds like he's just trying to muddle his way through all this, too. It can be a bit overwhelming even with other people to talk to."

"I'm still worried about him telling the police where the next party is, though."

"That's something you're going to have to worry about

anyway," she said. "We know they're looking for us, so they'll probably try to send people to infiltrate the order."

"I thought about that. Unless they're willing to be turned, though, they can only go so far. They won't be able to wear a wire through the initiation at least," he said.

"Maybe have someone pick him up, and not tell him where they're going until we get there," she said. "That way, he won't have a chance to tell the police anything."

"I like that," he said. "I'd like him to be part of our group. If he doesn't have anyone else, I'd rather he be with us than the cops. Don't have to make the decision now, though. We'll see what everyone else thinks."

"I'll put it on the agenda for the next Cell Zero meeting," she said.

"We have agendas now?" Carl said, with a smile. "You guys are all good, taking turns visiting me? You don't have to come every day, you know, if you don't want to."

"I like it," she said. "I feel comfortable here. It's good to have a place to change safely. And someone to do it with."

He nodded at that.

"Are you okay here, though?" she continued. "We could probably find some place for you."

"I kind of prefer it here, too," he said. "Anywhere in the city, I'd be constantly jumping at any sound outside, and wondering which of all the people who pass by recognize me and are about to call the police. Here, I know that's not going to happen."

"How long are you going to have to stay here?"

"I think once we're ready to go completely public, I can come out. Probably turn myself in then and get a fair trial. I can handle living like this for a while, as long as people occasionally come out, and I can sometimes go into the city to shower and charge my phone."

"I've got a solar battery for camping. I'll bring it next time I come. Sorry, I should have thought of it sooner."

He smiled at that. "Not a problem. I can only accumulate so much stuff out here anyway. Cyn and Tyler brought me a nice foam pad."

"I'm leaving you this blanket when I go, too," she said, indicating the one she was currently wrapped in. "Wool's better here - it'll still keep you warm if it gets wet, unlike cotton. What about your place? Anything from there we can get you?"

"I doubt you could get in. I lost my key a while ago. Landlord's probably thrown everything out by now anyway. Haven't been around to pay rent." He didn't want to tell her he had already been behind on the rent even before anything happened.

"What, they didn't even call first?"

"That was my thought, til I realized any number they'd have would be three or four phones ago."

"Shit, that sucks."

He shrugged. "I honestly can't think of anything there I need. Maybe a few more changes of clothes. Furniture's all crap. No loss there." It was all true.

"What are you doing for water?" she asked.

"There're streams nearby," he said.

She made a face at that. He knew what she meant.

"Doesn't taste bad. As long as I change every day, I can't get sick from it."

"I never even thought of that. Another advantage, I guess."

"It really is. I don't want to live like this forever, but I can do a year."

"If it gets too cold..." she started. What could she say? He couldn't move in with her any more than he could crash at Toni's. The cops would find him in an instant. They had to assume they were all being watched. Fortunately, the bus went right to the park, so they didn't have to leave identifiable cars parked nearby.

AFTER SHE'D GONE, he'd taken another nap and was leaning back against the foam pad, still rolled up in the back of his shelter. It was a peaceful afternoon, sitting there by himself, listening to the rain outside. Still, none of it had gotten in. He said another silent thanks for whoever built this place, and again hoped they didn't come and want it back. He scanned Craigslist again, looking in the personals for any mention of Sandra Dee. No mention in the for-sale section of an Edwardian Desk, either, which was the keyword he and Toni had set up if they got separated and needed to meet.

He paged through the existing ads wondering how many other groups were secretly communicating the same way. He supposed if someone put a little effort into it, they could convey complex information without ever meeting in person. Something like "if the phone number starts with two-nine-seven, then take every ninth letter until you have two words that are seven letters long," and the second half of the phone number could encode a bunch of web sites - like 11 could be YouTube, so if the number contains 11 something, read the most recent comment by someone with that number at the end of their name and take every X number of letters to get the message. That could explain a lot of YouTube comments, come to think of it.

Kim had told him Toni intended to come by tomorrow night, with no one scheduled for tonight. He'd be fine for an evening alone. Some books would be nice. Maybe a Kindle. He didn't want to ask for too much, or they might just start getting annoyed with him. He thought about asking for a chair or something to put out in the clearing. So far, nobody had come anywhere near it, and even if they did a chair sitting out on its own wouldn't be suspicious would it?

Then he heard a noise.

He froze for several seconds then slowly set the phone down and tried to breathe as quietly as he could, listening intently. Were those footsteps? Some animal passing by?

Nobody should be coming by until tonight. But it was definitely footsteps - he could hear a voice - a male, but he couldn't make out what was said. If he didn't move, didn't make a sound, they might move on without noticing he was there.

"Hey, what's that?" he heard a female voice say.

Dammit. Were they getting closer? If they found him... what? Could he just tell them to get lost? Drive them away? Change into Form and scare them away? He didn't want to kill them unless absolutely necessary, but he didn't want to risk exposure, either. He only had the one change of clothes left. He didn't want to lose them in the transformation.

"Hey, yeah, it's like somebody built a little fort here..."

He could escape to another part of the forest. Five thousand acres of forest should be room enough to hide in. Toni had said there were probably dozens of these little structures hidden throughout the park. Maybe he could find another one...

"Maybe we should go," the boy said.

Yes, thought Carl, smart man. Go away, forget you ever saw anything.

"Probably just some homeless guy," the girl said.

If this was someone's home, wouldn't they, by definition, not be homeless? Carl thought, incongruously. He could hear them approaching still.

"What if they come back?" the boy asked. He felt a flash of anger at that. What if they came back? What if they were still here? He should step out. Scare them off. The problem was, what if they didn't scare? If he had to transform, he'd lose his last change of clothes. He thought of taking them off, transforming and scaring them off that way.

If he transformed before going out, they might mistake him for a normal wolf and run away. He could chase them until they got lost, they'd find their way out eventually, but would be unlikely to ever find their way back here again. Dammit, hikers were supposed to stay on the trails. They shouldn't even be back here. Whatever happened, he'd have to move. Even if they left now, he'd never be able to sleep peacefully, knowing they could come back at any moment.

Unless... no. He wouldn't kill them. Hudson had been bad enough, and he never wanted to do that again. In self-defense, to stop a guy who would have killed him, was one thing. But he wouldn't kill a couple of humans just to avoid having to abandon a lean-to in the woods. He slid his shirt off and reached down to unfasten his pants. They were still approaching. They didn't know he was there....

"Who's there?" he shouted, trying to make his voice as deep and gruff as possible. Doing his best Batman impersonation. He regretted it immediately. They knew there was a human here now. If he went out in wolf form, they'd know he was a Were. If he went out in human form, he wouldn't be able to defend himself without changing. If he did that, unless he killed them, they'd almost certainly go to the police, who would comb every inch of the park looking for him. Plus, he'd lose his last pair of pants. He just wished he had some way to hide his face.

He smiled. Of course he did. These two were going to have a good story to tell their friends, and hopefully it wouldn't involve either a werewolf or a wanted terrorist. He finished taking his pants off, then pulled them over his head, looking out through the fly with one eye. Then, wearing nothing else, he rolled out of the shelter and leapt to his feet.

"Arglebarglesnarb!" he screamed, waving his arms in the air, and jumping up and down.

He looked around.

There was nobody there.

They must have run off as soon as he'd spoken. He tilted his head back and laughed out loud. It felt good. They couldn't have gone too far, surely they could still hear him. The thought of them running through the woods, with maniacal laughter echoing behind them and unaware of the show they'd missed made it all even funnier, which made him laugh all the harder. And realizing he was standing naked in the forest in the rain, alone, still wearing his pants over his head to hide his face from nobody made him laugh even more.

"Arglebarglesnarb!" he yelled again, as loudly as he could, "Arglebarglesnarb!" he laughed at the ridiculousness of it all.

He wished Kim was still there to see it. He couldn't wait to tell her. Toni would be concerned, but Kim would think it hilarious.

The hikers would have a story to tell, too. He wished he could hear their version. He pulled the pants off his head and carried them back into the shelter. Laying on the floor, staring at the roof, he reflected that he was still going to have to move. He didn't know where. Maybe back into the city. Maybe he could find another shelter. He'd have a good story tomorrow for Toni, too. Without bothering to get dressed, he went back outside. Laughing felt good. Moving felt good. He felt good.

He dropped to all fours, and a wolf ran into the woods.

IN THE ENTRY for Holy Mountain Research, there was a sign hanging on the wall over the receptionist's desk with the quote "They shall not hurt or destroy in all my holy mountain; for the earth shall be full of the knowledge of the Lord as the waters cover the sea." Veer had looked it up after her first day here. It was a verse from the bible, the book of Isaiah. A rather ironic quote given what she'd been able to find out in the last week.

The advantage to being the department admin was that a lot of paperwork crossed her desk, and nobody questioned why she spent so much time at the photocopy machine. Probably at least half of what she was doing there was for legitimate purposes. The paperless office was still a thing of the future, despite so many promises over the years. That was the disadvantage to being an admin, of course: Admins actually had to do quite a bit of work.

She made it a point to arrive early and leave late each day. It not only looked good but afforded better chances for espionage. Each night she carried out with her a new sheath of papers, folded at the bottom of her purse, and each night she'd spend hours analyzing them trying to draw connections. Her collection was haphazard at best, composed simply of everything she could get her hands on. A lot of paperwork was filed away somewhere even she, with her temp's badge, couldn't reach.

She wanted to get into the basement. Despite what Victor had told her about it, she hadn't been able to come up with a plausible errand to run down there.

The work environment had been much as she had predicted. It was downright paranoid, with everyone carefully guarding what parts of the puzzle they knew. It was also insanely busy, even now with Thanksgiving rapidly approaching. There was a sense of urgency, as if the whole company was in the final sprint of a major game-changing project and every-body was in heads-down mode. It made it difficult to ask questions, as most of her "small talk" was met with vagaries and evasions at best. Of course, the environment could be used in her favor, too. It meant she could wander around freely, and nobody dared ask her what she was up to.

Security breaches were expected to be taken seriously, and it was stressed during her orientation that any breach was considered a fireable offense. Which meant in practice that if someone saw her where she shouldn't be, they'd be more likely to leave the area as quickly as possible than to stay and take the chance of being held responsible for her being there.

She was able to find some information. The location of the home office was a carefully guarded secret, she'd been told, and been warned not to ever reveal it when they gave her the address. Her biggest breakthrough came one night while digging through her daily take and found a report containing a great deal of information on a "Subject Zero" and the tests they had done to him.

Apparently, various amounts of his blood and saliva had been taken, and injected into a number of "volunteers," all with no effect. Three subjects had been bitten directly while in what they were calling his "alternative form," and two of those turned. The third was recovering from his wound and obviously kept under careful observation. There was a warning about forcing Subject Zero to turn any more as he'd "shown a reticence to do so," and they wanted to keep this one happy. "Our desire is to allow him to continue believing himself a volunteer," one memo put it.

The next day she came across the results of a vivisection. They had cut one of the subjects open while in form in order to observe changes to the internal anatomy. They had to do it while he was alive and awake, to avoid him reverting to human form. And they had to do it fast, cutting over and over as the wounds healed so quickly. Eventually, they had switched to silver knives, which allowed them more time as the wounds no longer healed, but the subject died as a result. Subject 87 he was called. They didn't even have his name in the file. She felt sick reading the dry descriptions.

It wasn't just damage. Several were deliberately infected with diseases in order to watch their progress. Among the Were, every one of them had been cured.

They experimented with other metals, cutting into the Were with sharpened bits of copper or gold. There were even more complex experiments aimed at trying to isolate what it was about silver specifically that retarded the healing factor. Much of it was highly technical and beyond her understanding. She was going to have to consult a chemist.

It was Tuesday on her second week that her break came. She followed one of the more senior people, a woman named Amanda, through the front door and noticed that she took her wallet out, waved it in front of the reader, and replaced the wallet in her coat pocket. When she got to her cubicle, she hung the coat on a hook just inside it. She never took the proximity card out of her wallet. She'd learned earlier that the ID badges they all had to wear were new. The proximity cards, used to open the front door and whatever other areas an employee was authorized to access, were separate. She didn't know if that was supposed to be for higher security, or if there were plans to eventually combine them that just hadn't been implemented yet.

The wise thing to do at this point would be to take what she had and go to the police with it. She had more than enough for Detective Johansen to come back here with a warrant. Veer could then write the story based on their findings. But her career wasn't based on always doing the wisest or safest thing.

Was Nellie Bly playing it safe when she got herself committed to a madhouse? Or when she traveled around the world alone, an unescorted woman in the Victorian era? She smiled at the comparison. Times had changed, but the thought gave her courage. She had to see the basement.

She couldn't get to the security access control database directly, but she could see the requests log. Two months ago, Amanda's supervisor had put in a request to give her access to the basement, and it had been granted. Veer had her plan. That afternoon, while Amanda visited the restroom, leaving her coat still hanging on its usual hook, Veer quickly went to it, found the card in her wallet and swapped it for her own.

Amanda left every day at 5:30. At 5:20, Veer went to her car, swiping out of the front door with her stolen card. She dropped the purse in the trunk, waited for Amanda to leave, and went back inside. The door log would show that Amanda had gone out, then came back in ten minutes later. Since Amanda was now using Veer's badge, it would show that Veer herself had left in between those times and not come back until the next morning. In the morning, she'd swap the badges again.

Amanda arrived at 8:20 every morning. Veer just had to make sure she arrived at about the same time. If anyone checked the logs, there would be nothing to tie any access to her. She felt a slight pang of guilt throwing the other woman under the bus like that, but they were doing illegal experiments on human beings here. She didn't consider any of them innocent.

She used her stolen card to reenter the building and made her way straight to the back elevator. She nodded a friendly greeting to a couple of employees who were still in the office. Neither of them responded. Inside the elevator, she waved the card in front of the reader and put in the code that Victor had given her, hoping that the number wasn't tied to any individual.

It was not. The basement button lit up when she hit it. The elevator began to move. She was committed now.

She tensed up as the elevator stopped. She didn't know what to expect, but stood near the row of buttons, and not coincidentally, partly hidden behind the front wall of the elevator. The empty hallway stretching out in front of her was almost anti-climactic. She permitted herself a quiet chuckle as she proceeded down it. She dropped the smile when the elevator doors closed behind her. She was in it now. Whatever it was.

She turned the corner and a lone security guard sat at a desk, slightly ahead of another door. He looked up at Veer's approach. She realized he would have to open the door to let her proceed any further. She began to think furiously, on the verge of panic, but didn't dare stop or even let him see her hesitate. She wasn't sure what to say to the guard once she got up there. The guard looked up expectantly as she approached. Veer nodded a greeting to him from halfway down the hall. She'd probably been on camera since she left the elevator.

"Should you be escorted?" the guard asked her as she approached. She had no idea if that was a rule. Certainly, she shouldn't be down with her at all, but that probably wasn't the right answer. What was, then? Remembering what she'd read earlier on the various reports, she took a stab in the dark. "I'm just here to collect some samples."

The guard hesitated a second. "You new?" he finally asked her.

"Yeah, just started..." Veer began.

"You gotta sign in."

"Oh, right, of course." Relieved, she signed her pseudonym to the paper list she had been presented. The security guard checked the name and photo on her badge and pushed a button on his desk and there was a loud buzz followed by a click from the door.

"It's open," he said, and turned away from her.

She stepped through the door. The lights were almost painfully bright on this side. Yet another hall stretched out in front of her, with multiple doors and glass windows to her left. She peeked in the first one, where a man in a lab coat and goggles was working on something under a vent hood. In another, a woman was writing in a small notepad while a centrifuge whirred on a table in front of her.

Down the next hall, there were again doors only along one side. These all had much smaller windows, each covered with a metal grate, with a keypad and what looked like a small speaker grill next to it. These must be the cells that Victor had mentioned.

She looked through one window and was startled to see a man looking back at her. He was wearing what looked like a hospital gown and a paper bracelet. Half a dozen bandages lined one arm. Samples. No wonder the security guard out front didn't bat an eye when she told him she was here to collect them. It must happen all the time. The room was simple - a bed and a sink and a small door toward the back, probably leading to a bathroom. It looked like a typical hospital room. But what was it doing here?

"Hey!" the man said, before she could say anything. When she stopped and showed she was listening he continued.

"What's going on? You said I could leave after a couple of days. You can't keep me here forever!"

"Sorry," she said. "I'm new. I don't know why the door's locked."

"Well let me out, then, and I'll find my own way home."

Why not? She waved the card in front of the reader and tried the same code as the elevator. The device gave a low squawk.

She tried it again, with the same result. "Doesn't work," she said, waving the card one more time.

"I'm sorry - looks like I don't have access either. What's your name? I'll see what I can do. Is there someone I can call for you?" she asked in sudden inspiration.

"Yeah, yeah, my girlfriend, Angela. Shit. They took my phone. I don't have her number." His voice rose in desperation.

"That's okay. What's her last name? Where can I find her?"

He gave her a name and a business downtown. They both worked at the same tech startup in old town. She quickly jotted down the names.

"I'll find her and let her know what's up, I promise. Can you do me a favor, though? Don't tell anyone I said so. I don't want to get fired."

"All right, but hurry."

There were more cells. Some were unoccupied. In one there was a woman, similarly dressed in a hospital gown and slippers. She turned quietly when she saw Veer and extended a middle finger, but didn't stop her pacing. Veer hit the intercom button by the door. "Hi. How're they treating you?" she asked cheerfully, by way of introduction.

"Fuck off!" the girl replied.

"Is there anything you need?"

"Yeah! You can let me the hell out of here!"

"I'm afraid I can't do that."

"Then fucking leave me alone!" She resumed her pacing again.

"Is there any one you'd like me to contact? To let them know you're okay?"

"Ha!" the girl replied, venomously. "You can't trick me that easily! I know what I am now. I know what you bastards turned me into. Better watch out, cuz I'm going to get free and murder every last one of you motherfuckers!"

"And what it is that you are?" Veer asked.

The girl just glared, then resumed her pacing, keeping her arm extended and her middle finger pointing directly at Veer the whole time.

She wanted to reassure her that she wasn't with these people, but it would be far too dangerous to reveal that now. She left her to her pacing.

Just as she turned away from the window, a door down the hall opened. She could feel her heart jump but did her best to remain calm. Act like she belonged here. She turned just enough and out of the corner of her eye saw a man turn the corner, stop, and immediately go back the way he'd come. She could hear his footsteps accelerating as he went. She'd been spotted and he'd gone for help.

How much time did she have left? The only exit that didn't have an alarm on it was the elevator. She looked back over her shoulder and the man was nowhere to be seen. Shit. She quickened her own pace, but couldn't resist a quick peek inside the last window. What she saw made her stop in her tracks.

She knew this man. Detective Philip Lee. He worked with Diaz. But he was so gaunt. He looked at the edge of starvation. He hadn't looked like that two weeks ago. What could possibly... the change. He'd become Were. Not only that, but he'd changed, possibly forced to change, over and over, repeatedly, without eating or sleeping. This must be what happened if you didn't renew the energy used in the transformation. If there was any doubt, it was gone now. She'd found the source of the black helicopter, and what happened to the missing cops.

Phil looked up at her weakly. Pleading. He lifted one hand briefly but dropped it back down. He was near death.

She couldn't leave him here. She tried her key again. Still didn't work. She slid it a couple more times then frantically yanked at the door handle. Whoever the unknown man had summoned could be here any second. You can't open the door, she told herself. Stop panicking and think like a journalist. Get out. Tell the story. It's the only way to help him now.

"I'll be back," she yelled into the intercom. She didn't know if he'd heard her. If he did, he didn't react. She took out her phone and snapped a couple of quick pictures, then stepped back and glanced down the hall. Just in time to see the two uniformed guards moving toward her.

When they saw that she'd noticed them, they doubled their pace. She glanced behind her. Two more steps to the corner. No telling what would be around it. She took the two steps, then broke into a run.

"Stop!" she heard someone yell behind her. She ignored them, sprinting down the hall towards the single door near the end, with no idea what lay behind it. She pulled the handle. It was locked, like the others. And like the other doors, it had a window.

Inside, she got a brief glimpse of what looked like a large operating room. Machinery scattered around the room looked like it would be at home in a hospital. Two tables of the four in the room were occupied. A pair of masked people in scrubs stood on either side of a woman strapped to a gurney. A man in one nearby watched them carefully. The look of fear on his face told her the rest of the story. This was where they did whatever experiments they were doing.

She swiped her card in desperation. It failed as she'd expected.

Both of the men in the room stopped and looked at her. She quickly stepped back and glanced down the hall. The approaching guards were between her and the only exit. There were no other exits at this end of the hallway. That's got to violate some kind of fire code, she thought. She would make sure to file a complaint later. She saw what they did to captured

Were. She had no illusions about what they'd do to her if she was caught.

The two guards were almost upon her when she turned to face them. They stopped. One of them reached for a gun. These people would be ready for Were. They almost certainly would be using silver bullets. She wasn't going to talk her way out of this one. With the firearm clearing its holster, she had only a split second to act.

SHE LEAPT forward and the human fell down screaming in pain as the wolf's jaws clamped down hard on its arm. She shook it violently, and the weapon it was clinging to fell to the floor.

There was another enemy behind her. She left this one, whimpering and stinking, no longer a threat. She spun, twisting her body toward the other. It had backed up against the wall, which gave her room to move. She spun around, then darted forward, ducking low to avoid the metal object in its hand. It was still trying to level it while simultaneously trying to back up into the wall.

She lunged in low. The stink of fear rolled off of the human. It tried to move away but was hampered by the wall behind it. Her jaws closed on its shin and she pulled back while holding tight. There was a loud noise, and something slammed into a wall behind her. She knew that this was the human's way of trying to fight her off. She would have none of it. She pulled harder and the human hit the floor with a cry of pain.

Something metallic clattered to the floor and slid away from them both. The human tried scrambling for it. Clenching its shinbone as hard as she could, she shook it violently. Something came loose with a wet pop and it went slack. The cry had become a whimper and she knew this one wouldn't be following her either. She dropped it and ran.

When she got to the door, she leapt against it, front paws extended in front of her to strike a bar in its center. Something shrieked around her as she did. She repeated the trick at the top of the stairs and found herself outside. More humans were nearby, but they were too far to pose a threat, and retreated further when they saw her. Running across the cold hard ground she sought the safety of the nearby woods. It was much too thin and sterile to be adequate shelter, but she knew nonetheless that she had to go through it. What she needed was on the other side. There were no further obstacles, but she knew she was still in danger. She got to her destination but couldn't get inside. The human could. She again reached out to it for help.

VEER FOUND herself lying naked beside her rented car. There was an alarm sounding in the distance. She had parked in the farthest reaches of the lot, past a wooded area with a path and picnic tables. If anyone had asked, she had planned to explain that she liked the short walk before starting her work day. Nobody had asked. She reached under the car to pull out the key she'd left there earlier and pulled on a T-shirt and jeans from the bag in the trunk. As she sped out of the parking lot, she saw four men carrying rifles running out of the woods.

On her way home, she began to contemplate her next move. They almost certainly had her on video, and from there it would not be hard to figure out who she was. There were two men who attacked her. Or did she attack them? As always, what happened in Form was hazy, like a dream after waking. She was pretty sure she'd bitten both of them. She hoped she hadn't killed them. She had left a set of shredded clothes behind, along with the stolen badge and a phone. The phone was a pre-paid model, registered to her alias, and would be locked anyway, but the badge could be a problem.

It had seemed like such a clever idea at the time.

The video would be the worst of it. She had to assume they knew, or shortly would know, who she was. They couldn't go to the police and couldn't expose her as a Were. The guards at the security checkpoints were obviously not the same as the mercenaries who had come after her, so they probably didn't have a large force, however well-equipped and trained. Of course, they'd already shown they were ready to physically harm, possibly even kill, others to achieve their goals. It would only take one assassin to stop her.

Her only protection would be publicity. A lot of it, and as fast as possible. She couldn't do this alone. The police might put an end to Holy Mountain Research, but the whole secret had to come out. There was only one way to do that, and she had to move immediately. She stopped by her house only long enough to pick up the rest of the documents.

TWENTY-FOUR
REVELATIONS AND DECEPTIONS

"Veer? You're looking... good?" Don said as she walked into the news room. He was outside his office, as he often was, talking to someone sitting at one of the desks arranged around the large open room. A man ran by her carrying a folder. Another pair were engaged in animated discussion, hunched over a desk. It had been too long since she'd been in this room.

"Thanks," she replied, acknowledging her editor's question with a wan smile.

"You ready to tell me what this big story is yet?" he asked her.

"Almost," she said. Before he could say anything else, she asked "Can I borrow an intern for a couple of hours?" She indicated the large stack of papers and folders she was carrying.

"Something to do with your story, I take it?"

"Yeah. I'll need to go through all of it, but there should be enough proof of everything. But first, I need some backup copies."

"Anticipating something happening to the originals?" he asked with a slight smile.

"They've already tried to kill me once, no, twice, and they don't know I have these yet."

His smile vanished. "Jesus, Veer, what the hell are you on to?"

"Well, this is the corporate malfeasance part."

"Malfeasance?"

"Maybe that's too mild a word. There's a local company who's kidnapped people and is doing illegal research on them."

"You can prove this?"

"That part, yes, that's what these documents are. I also have two on-record sources and possibly more, for the rest of it."

He whistled. "There's more?"

"What they're studying."

"And what's that?"

She motioned to his office. He nodded. Before they went in, though, Don called to a young man walking by.

"Here," he told him, taking Veer's papers and handing it to him. "We need all of this scanned in. This is your top priority today. Find someone to help you."

"Uh... this could take a few hours."

"Yep. Go."

"Where should I put the scans? That's gonna be a lot of data."

"Get some thumb drives. Send April to Office Depot if we don't have any handy."

"Four, at least," Veer said. To Don she said, "One for you, one for me, one I'm going to hide, and one I'll have to give to the police."

"You're going to the police with this?"

"Gonna have to. Don't worry, you'll get the story first."

"Speaking of..." he said and closed the door behind them.

"It's huge." She took the chair he gestured to. "It actually relates to the Stumpp story."

"You told me at the time there was more to it." She was surprised he remembered. "I take it you've continued to dig?"

"Heh," the laugh was involuntary. She pictured herself in wolf form, digging in the dirt like a dog, kicking up papers behind her.

"Sorry," she said. "Just conjured up a funny image. Not that funny. It's been a long day."

"Tell me about it."

So, she did.

"It starts with the Stumpp investigation. Remember how we thought at first that he was involved in some kind of organized crime?" she started. "It turns out, we weren't entirely wrong."

She continued for over an hour, laying out the case from the ground up. She'd done this dozens of times before with Don, telling him the story, using it as a rehearsal for how she'd write it. Using his questions and suggestions for improvement. It was this careful laying out of the facts, explaining the larger context, and telling the reader why the story mattered, that would keep print journalism alive for a little while yet in this age of internet listicles and one minute video clips.

She omitted the part where there were actual werewolves, and the fact that she had become one. She told him it was a secret society, international in scope, and that she had allowed herself to be initiated into it. When he asked for details, she just said, "I'll tell you. They're important, but won't make any sense until I get to the end."

"This sounds like it's going to take more than one article."

"Many," she said. "I expect I'll be writing them for weeks, maybe months." Nellie Bly's first major piece took a ten part series to tell properly, and that had involved a single organization mistreating captive people.

"It's going to be big. Once this news comes out, it's going to dominate the news cycles across the country. It's going to be the lead on every cable news show, headlined in every paper, and even the original series will be too much for me to handle alone. Parts of it are going to have to be written by your staff reporters. And there's stuff in those papers alone," she nodded in the vague direction of where the intern was busy scanning the documents, "that I haven't even seen yet."

"It's going to take something big to live up to that hype."

"It will," she promised. "Grant Talman? And the recent terrorist attacks? They're all tied into the same group. The attack on Pioneer Square and at the Pied Cow were both orchestrated by a couple named Kevin Banks and Shelly Petersen, who are part of a recent schism of the same secret society that Victor Stumpp is the local head of."

He regarded her quietly for a moment. "You know this sounds utterly insane."

"It gets worse. And, I know. That's why I haven't even mentioned most of this before. But I can prove everything I've said, and more."

He nodded. "If this was anybody else... So, this couple, you know who they are?"

"I've met them both on multiple occasions. Kevin was the one who stabbed me a couple of weeks ago."

"Wow. You know why they did this? What their motives are?"

"Yes."

"You're going to the police with this?"

"That's my next stop. I wanted copies first, and I'd like to keep the originals in your vault. If anything happens to me..."

"Why not..." She could tell he was about to ask about the police, then realized the answer, "You don't trust the police. Do you think they're involved?" And then a second later, with a look of horror on his face. "Are they?"

"I think so. They weren't, but it's possible that that has changed."

"Why? What happened?"

"Michael Diaz, the leader of the werewolf squad - that's what they're calling themselves - has been replaced."

"Only a temporary suspension, isn't it?"

"Yes, but he's pretty sure he'll be reassigned away from the squad when he returns."

"You've talked to him?"

"We've been working together closely on this."

"This is..."

"Told you it was big. I haven't even gotten to the best part yet."

He gave a short barking laugh. "What's the best part, then?"

"Holy Mountain Research. That's what all these documents are — records of abductions, details of illegal human experimentation, on at least a couple documented cases resulting in death of the subjects."

"Shit. Even without the conspiracy, that'll be huge news. Maybe we should start with that, add in the rest when we learn more or have more evidence?"

"Can't," she replied. "The conspiracy's tied up in it too much. The research won't make any sense without it."

"So, what's this research they've been doing? And what's with all the werewolf crap?"

"The answers to those two questions are related. And I have to show you, you won't believe me if I just told you. Ready to go for a drive? You're driving, by the way, the police still have what's left of my car."

"WHAT IS THIS PLACE?" Don asked as they pulled into the gravel parking lot.

"It's a wolf preserve," Veer told him.

"I had no idea there was one this close to the city."

"It's privately owned and run, and not open to the public."

"Privately owned by..."

"Victor Stumpp."

"Of course. And how many shell companies did you have to chase that through?"

"None, actually," she said with a laugh. "He owns it openly. It's a legitimate preserve, inspected annually by the Department of Agriculture and everything."

"I assume it's a cover for something, then... are they..." he trailed off.

She didn't answer. Experimenting on werewolves, was he going to say? Or something about human animal hybrids? He was on the right track but didn't want to make a fool of himself with speculation.

He didn't ask any more questions as she led him out the back door. She stopped halfway to the trail heading into the woods. She dropped her bag on the ground then took a few more steps and turned to Don.

"Normally, I'd go further in," she told him, "but this is far enough for our purposes."

He stopped, and just nodded, as if afraid to speak.

"Victor Stumpp," she began, "maintains this place for us..." It was too late to back out now. She was committed to her course at this point. There was no more 'us', just the Were, and the reporter they'd welcomed into their ranks, who was about to expose all of their secrets. "It's a protected place for us to change when we need to."

He still didn't speak. He'd pieced it together by now, she was sure. But he'd need that final confirmation before he'd believe it. She took off her coat and tossed it to the ground near her bag.

She turned to face him. "Don't be afraid," she said, "You won't be in any danger."

And with that, she changed.

THE HUMAN REEKED OF FEAR, but it stood its ground. She wanted to run, to hunt, to sprint through the forest. There was food nearby, she could smell it and sense its vague unease from her presence. The human, though, was backing slowly away. Something told her not to bite it. She leapt past it, cutting off its retreat, then turned around, circling and dodging, but it didn't move any further. She could smell the fear, but it wasn't acting like prey. She circled it again, sniffing. It reached out a tentative hand. It was her turn to stand still.

When the hand reached the top of her head, though, she jumped away, growling angrily. She stopped running when she got to the tree line and turned, facing the human again. It still stood, watching her. Curious. This was unusual. Different from any reaction she'd experienced before. And then she remembered what she was supposed to do. She approached him again but before she got too close, she once again called the human back into her.

BY THE TIME she realized where she was, Don was already running towards her. She stood up and accepted her coat that he'd brought to her. She shrugged into it and buttoned it shut.

"So, your... initiation..." he started.

She smiled and nodded. "Victor bit me."

THE LAST TIME Veer had been here she was stealing files from Michael's desk. She had been trying to find out what the police knew about a rogue Were who had moved up from San Diego and began killing people in Portland. It seemed a lifetime ago.

She walked the three steps up to the landing where Michael's desk still stood. She recognized the woman who approached her from the press conference she'd watched with Michael a week and a half ago.

"Detective Johansen?" Veer asked, then took the offered hand. "Thank you for seeing me."

"Not a problem, Ms. Rosen. I looked forward to meeting you."

"I understand you're the new head of the Werewolf Squad."

"Temporarily only. I'm sure this whole thing with Detective Diaz will blow over soon."

"That's good to hear. My understanding was that even when he returns to duty, he wouldn't be put back on the case." It was the closest she dared come to probing deeper. She didn't want to risk alienating this woman with a direct contradiction, but she must have known that what she was saying wasn't true. So, if she was lying, what was she covering up? "What will you do, then?" she continued.

"This is a lot bigger than a single case, now. When Michael comes back to work, there'll be plenty of it for everyone."

"Comes back to work," Veer noted the phrasing. As if Diaz was merely delinquent, or on vacation, not suspended.

Johansen led her into a conference room with a table covered in folders, many of which lay open showing photographs and various other reports. A large map hung on the wall at one end of the room. Pins marked several locations which she recognized from her own research. In many places, pins were stuck through the end of a string that led to a cluster of photographs or additional notes thumbtacked off to the side. They'd come a long way since the single folder she'd rifled through at Diaz's desk.

A man she didn't recognize sat at one end of the table perusing one of the files. He looked up when they entered but did not stand.

"Ms. Rosen, Detective Avison, a member of my squad," Johansen introduced them.

"Detective." Veer nodded a greeting.

Johansen shut the door behind her. "You wanted to see me about something specific?"

"Yes." Veer pulled the thumb drive from her pocket and handed it to the Detective.

"What's this?"

"Documents. Evidence. It's not everything, but it should be enough to get a warrant. There's a company in Hillsboro who is abducting people and using them in human experiments."

"Hillsboro is outside my jurisdiction. Why not go to their PD?"

"Because the people they're experimenting on are werewolves."

"Werewolves? Are you talking about Holy Mountain Research?"

"You know of them?"

"I do."

"And?"

"And I assure you the people there are volunteers. They're helping them..."

Veer cut her off. "I assure you, they are not."

The woman's tone grew icy. "It was you. Of course. The break in last night."

"I didn't break in. I was invited."

"And then they gave you these documents?" she asked, waving the drive.

"Nope," she said. "Those I stole. I broke no laws, though, unless you plan on arresting me for violating my NDA?"

"May I keep these?"

"That's why I brought them here."

"Is this the only copy, then?"

"Not by a long shot," Veer replied. The other woman seemed annoyed rather than relieved at that. Did that mean she was working with them?

"So..." she had to ask. "What are you going to do?"

"We'll evaluate what you brought us and take the appropriate action."

"There are people who are suffering there now."

"We will take appropriate action," she repeated.

Definitely in their pocket then. Damn.

"Does it matter at all to you that some of them are police, and one of them is on this very squad?"

She tried to gauge the other detective's reaction to this. He raised his eyebrows at that but didn't say anything.

"That will be all, Ms. Rosen," Johansen said and opened the door for her.

She had to say something. To at least try. "You knew, didn't you? None of this is news to you. How long?"

"I said we're done."

"I don't understand. How can you just let this happen? Those are innocent people there..."

"They have to be held somewhere. People are being killed out there and I will do what I need to to protect this city. If it turns out they are not being treated well, we will correct the situation."

"Correct the situation?"

"They are collecting a few blood samples and running some tests. As long as the subjects cooperate, they're not hurt at all. Has it occurred to you that they might be able to develop a cure?"

The thought gave her a chill. She would get no help here.

"I urge you, look at those documents before it's too late." She looked to Detective Avison as she said it, and he gave a slight nod. He may not do anything, but at least he understood what she was asking.

MICHAEL WAS SITTING on the couch, reading a paper while the news played on the TV, when he heard a motorcycle pull into his driveway. He checked his gun, still loaded with silver rounds just in case, and tucked it into the back of his waistband before going to the front window.

He pulled the curtain aside and saw Veer in his driveway. She was pulling a bag out of the back case on her motorcycle, replacing it with her helmet. He dropped the curtain and moved to the door.

"Hi!" she said, smiling with obviously forced enthusiasm when he opened the door for her. "Can I come in?"

"Of course." He stepped back, letting her in, and closed the door behind her.

SHE TOOK the bag back to the kitchen and started unloading it. He stepped past her to start a pot of coffee, tossing out the half pot that had been cooling in the carafe for the last couple of hours.

"You brought dinner?" he asked her, bemused.

"It seemed appropriate. It's what you did when you wanted something from me." That caught him off guard. How she could be so subtle and so clever and then be so blunt?

Her bluntness itself carried a message, he realized. She was laying her cards on the table. Yes, she wanted something, and she respected him too much to pretend otherwise. He could live with that.

"Hah," he laughed. The tension seeped away. "What is it you want, then?"

"For you to take back control of the Werewolf squad."

Which was completely not what he'd expected to hear.

"Wish I could, but the decision's not with me." She responded by fishing a small object out of her pocket and tossing it to him. He caught it and held it up. It was a USB thumb drive.

"What's this?" he asked.

"A week and a half of documents scanned from Holy Mountain Research," she said.

"Evidence of criminal corporate espionage?" he asked her.

"Yes," she admitted. "And evidence of more criminal activity by that corporation. It's worse than we feared. They're not only capturing Were, including Detective Lee, they're experimenting on them."

"Phil? Have you seen him? Is he all right?" he asked.

"Yes, yes, and..." she hesitated, as if afraid to say what had to come next. "Not really. They've been experimenting on him. Forcing him to change, over and over."

"So, he's definitely a werewolf after all?" he asked.

"Yes."

He tossed the drive back to her. "You need to take this to Inspector Johansen right away," he told her.

She tossed it back to him. "I gave her a copy already. I don't think it'll do any good, though."

"Why not?" he asked.

Again, she hesitated. Then she looked him directly in the eye. "Pretty sure she's working with them."

"Bullshit," he responded, almost reflexively.

She gave him a skeptical look at that.

"There's no way. I know Alice. I've worked with her for over a year. After Phil, she was my first pick for the squad. She's ambitious, but..."

"How ambitious?" she asked him.

"Not to the point of compromising her principles," he insisted. Was it true, though?

"What if she saw the cops who've been bitten not as victims, but as new enemies? How far would she go if she thought it was necessary to protect the public?"

He thought about it. How far indeed?

"No," he decided. "No fucking way."

"Well, I'm glad you're keeping an open mind about it."

"It's a serious accusation."

"As serious as several police officers being turned into were-wolves in the first place?" she retorted. "Cops are missing, and the police are covering it up. You're right, I don't have any proof she's directly involved, but if she's not working with them, she was remarkably unconcerned about what they were doing. Including torturing your friend."

He thought about that. Alice should be furious at the suggestion, not apathetic. Would she really let Phil, or the other two, suffer, just for... for what? For protecting the entire city from a multinational threat of supernatural creatures with unknown capabilities?

He thought about it and had to admit to himself that she might.

One thing, though... "No proof?" he asked, indicating the thumb drive in his palm.

"Her name hasn't come up so far," she said. "I haven't read all of them. I've found lots of details about what they're doing to their patients. They alternate between calling them that and subjects, depending, I assume, on who's writing. But nothing I've seen yet about where they're getting them from."

"Yet."

"Like I said - there's a lot of information there."

"If I had any real proof Alice was involved, I could go to Billings, suspension or no."

"Nobody else who can help? You must still have contacts, friends, information..."

"Not that they'll do any good. I can't get a warrant for a raid myself. Any attempt would have to go through Alice." He found himself thinking, though, of how it could be done. Could he convince Billings to take action, even over Johansen's objections? Not if he also already knew about Holy Mountain Research.

"Hell," he said, "it wasn't that long ago that I might have agreed with them."

At her shocked look, he continued, "We just aren't equipped to deal with werewolves. You pointed it out yourself: we can't disarm them. They can break out of handcuffs, any cell we put them in..."

"That doesn't mean you hand them over to torturers," she exclaimed.

"I agree with you," he said. "We're both on the same side here. But if we're going to get anywhere, we're going to need an honest appraisal of the obstacles in our way."

"Fine," she said. "I'm going to run this in the paper, expose the whole thing."

"Including the very existence of werewolves?" he asked, a little surprised.

"Especially that," she said.

"Victor's not going to be happy."

"No. He isn't. Nor are any of the other Were, including the Council of the Alphas."

"Okay, so first priority is to keep you safe."

"No, it's not."

He was expecting that. "It is. There are at least two powerful criminal organizations right now who would kill you for what you know. If either of them succeeds, there's nobody else who has as good a chance of exposing them. Even after the information is published, you'll need to make public appearances, go on TV, talk to people, keep the story alive so they can't just make it all go away again."

She thought about it. "I'm certainly not opposed to staying alive," she said.

He smiled. "Good. So, the question becomes what we do now."

"I've got a couple places I can hide. I've set them up some time ago just in case, along with a couple of fake identities."

He raised an eyebrow at that. "You know I'm still a cop, right?"

"So, you gonna arrest me over it?" she asked him. "There's no law against having a fake identity unless you're committing fraud with it."

"Getting an apartment under a fake name is fraud."

"Not unless I skip out on the rent. There's no actual law against lying to a landlord."

"What about forging government documents? No reputable landlord is going to rent you a place without ID."

"If I'm trying to hide, why would I want a reputable landlord?"

He couldn't argue with that. He decided to drop it. It didn't really matter. "If they're turning Were over to this company, then... we can check out one thing at least."

"What?"

"The safehouse. We have a werewolf, possibly one of Kevin's first 'recruits,' stashed there. He's agreed to testify if we can prove their existence."

"And Johansen knows where he is."

"Of course."

"Then he's in danger."

"Of course."

HE DROVE SLOWLY past the safe house. The lights were off, and the curtains drawn, which was not unusual. He didn't see anybody from outside watching the place, though, and that was unusual. If it was occupied, there should always be an unmarked car within sight of it. He circled the block once more.

"See anything?" he asked her.

"Nothing," she answered. "Place looks deserted."

"Okay," he said when they were around the corner. "No cameras out this way. Wanna get out now? I'm going in."

"They'll know you've been there," she said. It was an invitation to explain, not a question.

"Yes," he agreed. "They can either pretend they don't notice, or it'll force a confrontation, and they'll have to talk to me."

"All right. And if I'm with you, after being sent away by your replacement..."

He didn't like hearing her refer to Alice as his replacement, but she wasn't wrong.

"Then they'll definitely want to talk to me," he said.

"Okay," she smiled. "Let's go."

If he was expecting anything to happen, he was disappointed. He punched in the code to open the key box, then used the key to open the front door. The place looked like it hadn't been used for weeks.

"They've cleaned up," she said, and he thought of the few days she'd stayed here, when he first found out about a secret organization of werewolves living in the city.

She was right. If there had been any hints here, they'd been erased by professional cleaners. It had to be Alice, and Mitch Douglass was now almost certainly in a basement in Hillsboro.

"C'mon," he said. "Let's get to analyzing your documents and find the proof we need."

LAST NIGHT, Carrie had come out with Cynthia and Tyler and they'd brought him Thanksgiving dinner, comprised of cold turkey and leftover pie. They apologized for the meager feast. He was grateful, though, and told them it was the best Thanksgiving dinner he'd had since leaving Wisconsin. He didn't have the heart to tell them that it was true.

Nobody was scheduled to come out tonight. He had his phone and the Kindle that Kim had brought him along with the promised solar battery a couple of days ago. Tomorrow night would be the warehouse party, which Toni and he would travel together to. She'd said she might not be able to make it before then but would make sure he wasn't stuck out here all by himself. Most of his Cell Zero had come to visit by now at least once. He was looking forward to seeing Toni again, though. He wondered if this is what being in jail was like: the endless waiting punctuated only by occasional visits from friends. Except in jail, you couldn't just run around wherever you felt like it, whenever you felt like it, and your friends' visits were for minutes, not several hours. And you couldn't leave to sneak into town to shower or get a meal in a restaurant.

He'd finished the book he was reading and set the Kindle down. He took out his phone to check the news once again. So far, there'd been nothing, and no apparent progress on the police investigation. If they'd learned anything more, they hadn't told the press.

He flipped over to Craigslist and there it was: "Desperately Seeking Sandra Dee. Meet me Monday, Fred's place, SW 22nd and Morrison." Kevin or Shelly wanted to meet.

With the simple code they'd set up, the meeting was for tonight, so something important must have come up. Fred's place, he'd assumed was just a red herring, something to make it seem more legitimate to anyone reading. No time was listed, so they'd meet at the 6pm default. After dark, so he'd be harder to spot, but early enough that there'd be a number of other people around to blend into.

He thought about leaving a note in case anybody did visit that evening, then decided against it. They could wait for him, or not, as they saw fit. If they were worried, they could text. He'd have his phone with him, and there'd been good signal here. He hiked out to the road, then walked down to the bus stop to catch one going the right direction.

He was amused when he arrived to discover it was a grave-yard. There were only a few other people around, standing or walking through the graves. No sign of Shelly or Kevin. He figured they'd find him here easily enough, though. He was grateful for the light rain. Not only would it restrict visibility, he'd have an excuse for having his hood up and face down so it wouldn't look like he was trying to hide.

"Carl?" a voice from behind him said. He jumped at the sound and whirled around. An older man, Carl guessed close to forty, laughed unkindly. "Guess so," he said with a smirk that Carl wanted to wipe off his face. He didn't like this man and took a step back from him.

"Who are you?" he asked him, "What do you want?"

"Relax," the man said. "Kevin couldn't come. I'm here to take you to him."

"Where is he?"

"Come with me and I'll show you."

"Why don't you tell me first?"

There was something about the man's manner that bothered him. An almost arrogant self-assuredness. As if he was proudly possessing some secret that nobody else had. Well, Carl had a secret of his own.

"Sorry. Can't do that," the man replied.

"Why not?" he asked.

Now the man seemed annoyed, frustrated.

"Look, kid, just come with us, okay? You'll see soon enough."

"Us?" Carl wondered. Who was "us?"

He looked around. There were a few other people in the cemetery. One couple, a man and a woman, looked back at them with mild concern. Two other men, standing near the street not far away seemed to be trying to look everywhere but at them. Carl supposed those must be the others who constituted "us."

Footwear. Look at their footwear, he remembered from an old web site discussing how to spot police infiltrators at protests. All three men were wearing similar khaki pants, but also nearly identical combat boots. He was actually shocked at how obvious it was.

A white van with tinted windows started its engine just a little ahead of them, on the other side of the iron fence. That clinched it. He stopped in his tracks. The two men across the way started moving toward him. It was still possible they were working with Kevin. He could see him going out and biting an entire mercenary troop or something. Could it be possible that they'd broken the code somehow? He couldn't see how, but just because he couldn't think of a way didn't mean a team of dedicated experts couldn't.

Either way, he wasn't going with them, and he certainly wasn't getting into that van.

"Who are you?" he asked a few seconds later once the man had realized he'd stopped and turned back toward him.

"C'mon," was all he said. "We haven't much time." His hand moved toward his hip. The other two quickened their pace, to not quite a run.

And this had been his last set of clothes, too. Toni would laugh at him when he saw her next. Hopefully, she'd also bring him something to wear.

He leapt at the man just as he began to draw a gun, but it was the wolf who landed on him, teeth sinking into the shoulder.

THIS WASN'T a good place to feed. Humans were closing in. Two running toward him from behind, and another in front of him. He turned and ran, back away from the human on the ground and towards the other two. He veered at the last second and could feel their anger and frustration. One of them threw something, which he easily dodged, turning sharply to one side and quickly regaining his balance, before running off in a different direction, away from the hard-packed road and deeper into the sparse stony woodland.

Another pair of humans were approaching from the front. Again, he turned, but the ones behind him were gaining - they had spread out and began moving to intercept him. He turned again, straight towards the closer pair. One of them raised its hand, something clenched in it. He leapt, closing jaws tightly around the human's forelimb. He pulled and shook, ignoring its screams, until the hand went limp and it had dropped whatever was in it to the ground.

He turned, but before he could gather himself for another leap, something slammed into his side, penetrating into muscle. He tried to back away, but it stayed with him. He turned, trying to bite it off or pull it out when suddenly a fire burned through him. His whole body exploded into pain and his legs collapsed beneath him. He struggled to his feet, still wobbly, and snapped at a hand that was in front of him. It was hastily withdrawn. A second later, he was hit again, and immediately fire exploded from that side. His legs, already weak, collapsed again.

Again, he tried to rise, but once again the fire exploded through him and now a human was kneeling beside him. He wanted to bite, to tear, but he could barely move his head. The human yelled, angrily at the others nearby. There was a tiny sting and something small and sharp slid into his flesh. And then a warm, comfortable feeling was pulling him down into darkness. To escape the pain, he followed it.

TWENTY-FIVE
LIVE TO TELL THE TALE

Michael set the phone down and turned to Veer.

"All right," he said. "She's on her way."

"You're sure about this?" Veer asked him from her desk. She didn't turn to face him but kept her eyes on the computer monitor where she'd been furiously typing for the last hour. She wanted to finish up and get out of here as soon as possible. She looked over to the table where Michael was sitting, marking up and sorting piles of papers they'd printed out.

It should take Holy Mountain Research some time to find her, and at least a couple of days before Victor grew suspicious. By then, everything would be out. The truth would be known. Holy Mountain would be shut down, their captured Were brought out safely, and the secret exposed.

"Yes," Michael's voice said behind her. "Look, she's not a villain. She'll do the right thing."

"As long as her 'right thing' is going into Holy Mountain as soon as possible," Veer replied testily.

"When we show her that they really are torturing people

there." He stepped into view and picked up a piece of paper showing a chart of rapidly worsening vital signs. It was labeled "subject 3," who they had determined from other sources must be Detective Lee. To drive home the point, he had written "Phil" across the top in large letters.

"I suppose we'll find out," she said. She had agreed to this. It was too late to argue about it now.

She went back to her article. She wanted to be finished with the first draft before Detective Johansen arrived.

Half an hour later she was done and uploaded it to her shared folder at the paper. Don would know how to access it if anything happened to her. She went to the kitchen to start another pot of coffee. She was on her way back out when they heard a car pull into the driveway.

She went to look. It wasn't Johansen. She knew that van. "Crap," she said. Victor would have noticed her peeking out through the curtains.

"Take this," she said, hurriedly gathering up the most important of the papers and pressing the messy stack into his hands. "Find a place to hide them in the spare room." He would know where it was.

"Go!" she said as he hesitated.

He went.

She stepped to the door, just as Victor knocked.

"Hello, Veer," he said, his voice a deadly calm. He stepped towards the doorway. She stepped aside, inviting him in. There was nothing else she could do.

He went immediately into the kitchen.

"You've been busy," he said, surveying the remaining papers strewn across the table. His voice was still carefully neutral. Someone unacquainted with him might have thought this was a social visit.

"I have," she spoke after a long pause. She crossed to the laptop and pulled the thumb drive out and handed it to him. Its contents had long since been copied to the hard drive.

"What's this?" he asked her.

"Documents and files from Holy Mountain Research," she said. "Everything I've found. It's worse than you thought. They kidnapped people from Pioneer Square. They're experimenting..."

"It doesn't matter," he said.

She was getting sick of hearing that.

"They know of the Were. They're experimenting on them." She didn't say torturing them. She was afraid it might not make a difference.

"Don't you understand? The secret's out," she continued. "There's biomedical research. There've been public attacks. New Were have been created, and they know how to force them to make even more. It's only a matter of time before..."

"No," he cut her off. "This is all being dealt with. Contained. You don't understand..."

She had to convince him. It was her only chance. He wouldn't have come alone. Not this time. There was no telling who else was in that van. "No, you don't. This isn't the 16th century, Victor. Science, religion, music, philosophy, even politics - to say nothing of technology - would be unrecognizable to anyone from four hundred years ago, so why should the Were live by rules that they set down?"

"We are at a tipping point," he responded. "Right now, you could push the world either way. Back into hiding or into violence and chaos."

"It doesn't have to be that way."

"You just told me what happens." He indicated the thumb drive he still held in his hand. "When the humans find out about our abilities. What do you think would happen if they all knew? A million labs like this would spring up overnight."

"No - this can only exist because of the secrecy..."

"I have witnessed firsthand worse than anything likely to be here," he again indicated the thumb drive, "done to a people who everybody knew existed."

"It doesn't have to happen that way. If we're public..."

"Then people will fear us. Hunt us. Kill us. We will be forced to fight back. It will be a war unlike any seen before. The humans will fall upon us, and upon each other in their hysteria."

"We *are* human, Victor, we are..."

"No, Veer," he said with a sad shake of his head. "I had hoped by now you would understand. We are more than that. You've seen how easily they dehumanize each other. How much easier would it be for them to do it to us, who already aren't human? They will convince themselves we are monsters, a threat to be kept in check, so they can treat us as a resource to be exploited."

"It doesn't have to be like that. If it's explained properly," she started.

"You can't write about it," he said, his voice full of profound sadness.

"You don't have to do this," she said. "You can help me. With the secret out, the Council won't have any power over you. Over anybody."

He took a step back from her and glanced toward her computer. "So you are determined to expose our secret?"

She followed his gaze toward it, then brought it back to him. "I told you three years ago that I would."

"And there is nothing I can say to stop you?" It was almost a question. Almost a plea.

"No. I'm sorry, Victor," she answered.

"I'm sorry too." He reached into his jacket.

"Freeze. Right there. Don't do it," a voice came from behind him.

Michael stepped out of the hallway, his weapon in both hands. He kept it trained squarely on Victor.

"I mean it," he said. "Don't make me shoot you. I have silver rounds."

"Come loaded for wolf, I see," Victor said calmly. But he moved his hand away from his own gun. "But I wonder," he continued, turning slowly toward Michael, his hands up, palms outward. "Was it supposed to be for me, or for her?"

Michael hesitated half a second too long before answering.

"You're the one in front of me," he said.

Victor smiled thinly at that. He'd caught it too and knew that she did as well.

Her living room window exploded inward. Victor had a fraction of a second head start, as he was already listening for it. He fell to the side and the curtain billowed inward to the sound of shattering glass. A wolf leaped out from the curtain. It took Veer a moment to recognize the large black beast. Gregor. She'd only ever seen him in wolf form once before.

She took a step back toward the kitchen before she realized that he wasn't heading for her. His target was Michael. Kill a cop? Was he insane? If he wanted to start a war, she couldn't think of a better way to do it. She launched herself across the room, trying to get in between them. That's when she saw the second wolf. This one was all too familiar. Peter. She couldn't reach Gregor in time. But she could reach this one, and did, shouldering the wolf aside mid-leap. They crashed together into her desk, falling across it. A claw pierced her hip and tore upwards into her side.

She fell forward and out of the corner of her eye saw blood dripping in slow motion onto the cracked screen of the monitor.

How am I going to get that out, she thought. There were loud noises behind her. This was not the first time a firearm had been discharged in this house in recent memory. This isn't the first window to be shattered, either. What would the neighbors think? Concentrate Veer, she told herself. You're still in danger. Think!

It was hard to concentrate. There were several loud popping sounds and smoke billowed through the room. Detective Johansen stepped out of the smoke flanked by several people in blue uniforms and it seemed strange that she didn't have a cape billowing behind her. Why was there smoke? Was the house on fire? She should call the fire department. She rolled to her left when she heard a sound. Gregor was lying there, naked on the floor. There was so much blood. A booted foot splashed into it on the carpet. No, thought Veer, you'll make it worse. Victor was kneeling beside Gregor but wasn't helping him. He was being handcuffed. How did that make sense? He was going to get blood on his trousers.

Michael was across the room, his gun on the floor beside him, where he was slumped against the wall.

Still clothed, so he wasn't dead.

Wait.

No.

That didn't make any sense either.

Why was everything ringing? He... their eyes met. He tried to get to his feet, but the people at his side held him down. There was a bandage being pressed against his arm. Did Gregor bite him? Was he going to be one of us now?

Sudden pain tore through her side and her arm moved of its own volition behind her. How was it doing that? She spun sideways and a high-pitched scream filled the air. It seemed to go on forever. Her vision was narrowed to a single spot that wavered perilously around the room. Everything was tinted red. She could see Victor struggling toward her, but he fell under a pile of blue uniforms. They all seemed to be shouting. Everybody was shouting. But she couldn't hear them over the loud red fiery explosions of pain coming from her midsection and arm. There was a weight on it. She twisted and saw a cop trying to hold on and turn it at the same time. She couldn't figure out what he was doing.

She was in shock. No, not shock, what was the other thing? She knew this - the rushing river sound drowning everything. Survival... something. Survive. Was her survival in doubt? Was she in danger that she might not survive? She had to do something! Survival Stress... dammit. Fight or flight. That was the common name. Fight or flight. But there was more to it than that. An old joke from her sophomore human behavior ecology class: the four F's: Fight, Flight, Freeze, or Reproduce. That was them. The room was spinning around wildly still, and every once in a while a face would materialize in the fog. There was blood dripping from her side.

A man in blue stepped back, he was pulling out a taser. No, that couldn't be allowed. That could stop her. The room wasn't spinning. She was. She moved it again, and Victor's face appeared again. He was speaking. Calmly, in sharp contrast to the panic all around. He was speaking a single word, repeated.

"Run," he said. "Veer! Run!" His voice was insistent. Fight or flight. The survival stress response, that was the full name. There was a cop, she turned the room to bring him into view. Act. Act now. Fight or flight. Flight. Flight!

She twisted again, throwing the cop on her toward the one with the taser. She knew she wasn't strong enough to move him far on her own, but the wolf wanted in, was begging to be let in. Without even thinking, she'd been keeping it out. She stopped doing that.

SOMETHING cold and metal snapped off her wrist as she landed on all four feet. Run! The sound still echoed in her head. She ran. There was noise behind her. She ignored it. There was pain in her foreleg. She ignored that, too. She knew this path. She knew where to go. She'd run this route a hundred times. Only twice before out of necessity. But now she ran. She ran as much from the joy of knowing she could run faster than the rest of them as out of fear.

She didn't run for long, though. Her destination was nearby. She knew exactly where to go. Around the corner of the yard, into the hedge. But not through it. There was a hidden hole leading to another yard and away from hers, but that wasn't the one she wanted right now. Instead, she continued inside the hedge for a brief moment, then cut back out to jump through another hidden door. She crawled forward a ways, out of sight of the opening, and lay down. She could feel her insides sealing up, even as she drifted off to sleep.

STUMPP LOOKED ANGRY. Outwardly, he was calm, almost polite, but from his vantage point sitting on the floor at the end of the hall, Michael was glad he wasn't on the receiving end of that look.

"He's got a gun!" one of the officers patting him down exclaimed.

"I do," he replied. "It's in its holster, and you will find an Oregon concealed weapon permit in my jacket pocket. I was here by invitation and have broken no laws."

"Not entirely true," Michael spoke up.

Victor turned his look on him.

"Both he and his associate made attempts on Vera Rosen's life."

Now it was Alice's turn to look at him. "And what were you doing here?"

Michael didn't want to answer that yet, so he continued. "His associate was Peter Maxwell, wanted hit man and cop killer."

"Where did he go?" Alice asked an officer who had just returned from the back yard.

"No sign of either of them," he said. "We assume they jumped the fence, but we couldn't tell in which direction."

Michael had an idea where Veer might have gone, but he wasn't going to say anything in front of anyone here.

"Michael?" Aaron had come in and ran to him. He checked his wound, where the wolf's claws had raked his shoulder and arm. "Doesn't look too bad, but you're going to need to get it bandaged."

Alice looked down at him. "You sure it was him?" she asked.

"Positive." He didn't like her expression. "Why? Were you expecting him to be somewhere else?"

She didn't answer, which was answer enough. Aaron looked up at her, too.

"You were," Michael accused. "He was in that place, wasn't he? You knew where he was all along."

"He was neutralized. He couldn't..."

"He didn't look very neutralized to me! That man killed a cop! And you're letting him..."

"I'm not 'letting' anything. He was supposed to be secure!"

"So it's true! You've been working with them... you're, what... using the facility as some kind of black site prison for werewolves?" With Aaron's help, he got shakily to his feet.

"That's not important right now... where are you going?" she asked as he started heading to the door.

"Gonna go see the med team outside. I don't want to get my blood all over your crime scene."

She looked like she was about to say something. He cut her off, hoping to forestall any attempt to detain him.

"Unless you want to send me to your own little Guantanamo Bay there. Is that the policy on injuries now? If you're wounded by a werewolf, you get locked up and tortured like Phil?"

"Nobody's torturing anybody, they're just..."

"Performing medical experiments? Thank you, Doctor Mengele."

"Hey now, that's..." Aaron started.

"They're torturing people," he continued, ignoring him. "If I'm wrong about you, and you're duped, not complicit, there's a sheaf of papers shoved under the mattress in the bedroom that you will want to see sooner, rather than later."

"Go get them," she told one of the CSI officers nearby. This was a good sign. If she'd wanted to cover it up, she would have retrieved the papers herself. Michael nodded to her, and she replied, "Come down to the station when you're done."

"To give a statement?"

"To be debriefed."

This also was good. She was acknowledging him as a member of the force. You take statements from civilians. Police are debriefed. He turned back and headed toward the front door.

"You won't turn," Victor's voice came loud and clear from behind him. He turned back to see him standing, handcuffed, between two uniformed police officers. The motion of turning caused another jolt of pain up his arm. He tried not to let the older man see him wince in pain, but he wasn't sure he succeeded. This was the first thing Victor had said since his arrest. He raised his eyebrow at him.

"That's what you're worried about, is it not? That you'll become one of us?"

Michael stood in silence, allowing him to continue.

"You won't. He only scratched you with his claws. It has to be a bite to effect the transformation."

This was information Michael didn't have before. "Thank you," he said to Victor, and he meant it.

"But even if you had, no harm would come to you. You would be welcome among us."

At that, Michael turned and walked away from him toward the waiting ambulance.

He learned from the police outside that they still hadn't caught either Maxwell or Rosen, and had found no trace of either, which meant that Maxwell hadn't caught Rosen either. If they were both in wolf form, and there had been a fight... it would have been noticed. So, Maxwell was likely long gone, crawled back into whatever hole he'd been hiding in. And Veer... he had a good idea what hole she might be hiding in.

SHE WAS ALREADY AWAKE this time when he found her, leaning against the same post under her house, legs pulled up against her chest, huddled against the cold. He took off his coat and handed it to her. She smiled and said, "Thank you. I'd hoped to borrow it again. Anyone else coming?"

"I locked the door on the way in," he told her.

"Thanks," she said again, shrugging into his coat. He looked away and toward the hidden swinging door as he did so.

"You know," he said, keeping his voice low, "it shouldn't be too hard to rig it so it would lock after passing through it..."

"I've thought about that, actually. But I wouldn't want to risk some animal getting trapped, or it just closing when I don't want it to, and not be unlocked when I need it. Besides," she continued, "if it did that, how would you get in to find me?"

"Makes sense," he said, turning back to face her. She had finished with the coat and was leaning against the pillar again.

"How are you? That was a rather nasty cut," he asked.

She shifted the coat to show him her side. There was no trace of damage.

"One of the nice little perks," she said. "How about you?"

He pulled up his sleeve to show the bandage. "I should probably get stitches, but it'll heal. Eventually."

"How are things up there?" she asked him.

"Fucked," he responded. "I gave Alice the documents, but I'm not convinced it'll do any good. Maxwell got away, though he might be wounded. The other guy that came in with him got shot, and may be dead."

"Gregor?"

"Maybe. Older guy, white shaggy beard? Big black wolf?"

"That's him. Shit."

"You mentioned before he was giving Victor some trouble?"

"He's an Alpha, from San Diego. Also, probably Victor's closest friend. Definitely his oldest."

"That sounds bad."

"Probably worse than it sounds. The Council was already looking at Portland. And now, with one dead Alpha and another arrested, they'll be moving in hard."

"What does that even mean?"

"I don't know exactly. But we're probably in more danger now than ever before. Especially Victor."

"Victor... you think this Council of yours will try to silence him?"

"Count on it. They'll be racing the clock. It's long been

Were policy that we don't get taken by human authorities. If one of us goes to prison it would only be a matter of time before they change, and they won't allow that. Victor's strong willed, if he wasn't he wouldn't be an Alpha. That'll buy him some time. Maybe a month or two at the most."

"Any suggestions, then?"

"Protect him. They're not omnipotent, and they don't know everything. Gregor was surprised and dismayed that Victor didn't have any of his own people in the police, for instance."

"That's good to hear."

"Might be easier if it wasn't true."

He thought about that, but only briefly. "All right. I'll tip Alice that Victor's in danger."

"You have to protect him."

"I have no authority. If I try anything, it'll just pull resources away to deal with me and leave him in even more danger."

She nodded in response, conceding the point.

"They're going to be here a long time," he said, indicating the police presence above. "Even with the door blocked, they're likely to find us here eventually. You ready to go with them?"

"No. That will take too long. I need to get out of here, disappear for a while."

"They're going to want to talk to you," he said.

"They're going to want to arrest me," she corrected. "But I can't allow that right now. I don't have time. This needs to get out, and go public in a big way, before they can stop me. The only difference is that before it was just Victor. And now, thanks to your friends up there, we've got the entire council coming down on us."

"I'm still a cop," he said. He wasn't sure whether he said it for her benefit or his own.

"Yeah, and if you had any authority here, you could do something. So, are you going to help me or not?"

This was crazy. She was asking him to help her evade the police. He was a cop. She was asking him to betray his friends, and everything he was. If he did this, what would he be?

But he realized he was already working out how to do it.

TWENTY-SIX

SUSPICIONS, BETRAYALS, AND ACCUSATIONS

"They let him go?" Michael asked again.

"They didn't free Stumpp, he's out on bail. He'll still face trial," Aaron replied. They were sitting in a small coffee shop down the street from the precinct. Michael might not be allowed into the building, but they couldn't stop him from having coffee with a friend. Alice wouldn't be happy to know that Aaron was meeting him here, but he wasn't in a mood to care what Alice thought right now.

"It had to be Alice who tipped them off," Michael said.

"Or there was never anything there," Aaron said. "I was part of the search. We found nothing. The entire basement was storage. All the downstairs rooms didn't even have doors let alone reinforced doors with speakers. And the middle room just had a bunch of kitchen equipment, most of it still in boxes."

"They could have just purchased that in bulk and dumped it down there to throw off..."

"You're starting to sound paranoid," Aaron replied.

"What else could it be?"

"I didn't say you were wrong. I said you sound paranoid,

which is what they want. For the record, though, I think you're wrong."

"You've lost me."

"It was Rosen. From the beginning. The whole thing was a setup."

"No. No way."

"It's what they do, right? She told you that herself. Someone finds out about them, they can't keep him quiet, they discredit him. Smear his character. Set him up to do a raid on completely false pretenses, leave him looking like a lunatic publicly raving about werewolves and accusing everyone who fails to find evidence of it of being in on the conspiracy."

"No, it's too much. It would be too complicated."

"'It would be too complicated' is exactly how every magician and con man has fooled their marks since the beginning of history," Aaron said. "They rely on people thinking that nobody would go to that much trouble, it must be something else."

"She had hundreds of documents from that place," Michael challenged.

Aaron shrugged. "Forgeries, maybe, like the lawsuit claims. Could've been made years ago. Or who knows, maybe there was some company that did some research a decade or two back. The Alphas got wind of it, shut the place down. Ten years later they need to discredit some cop who's getting too close and someone says 'hey, I have an idea, do we still have those documents...'"

Was it possible? Could everything she told him have been a lie? No, not everything. Enough truth layered on top to make it all seem plausible. Running a long con, she'd have to play her part for months.

"No, it doesn't hold up," he decided. "For one, what about this Gregor fellow? He didn't have to be somewhere where he knew the cops would be. The whole setup at her house would have worked just as well without him."

"I don't know. Maybe he was set up, too? A rival faction, and Stumpp killed two birds with one stone?"

"There was no way Victor could have known I'd shoot Gregor before he got me."

"Are you sure about that? Can you remember every detail of who did what, and who was arranged where?"

He had to admit that he couldn't. Had the whole scene in the living room been staged for his benefit?

"I still don't buy it. It *is* too complicated. She fed me information, kept me going. Hell, if they wanted to keep me from finding the truth all they would have had to do was not change that first day in the preserve."

"Wasn't that Jablonski who changed? From what I understand, he wants to expose them."

"Wish I knew where he was right now."

"Think you could use him for that?" Aaron asked.

"Maybe. See if the DA would cut him a deal for talking. I have a feeling we could learn a lot from him. Probably long gone by now, though."

"Speaking of the disappeared," Aaron said, "I take it you haven't heard from Rosen?"

He shook his head. "Not that I expected too. If she's in hiding, she's not going to be doing a lot of calling out. I take it you haven't heard anything either?" He paused for a moment. "Would you tell me if you had?"

"Maybe. Probably. But we haven't. We've been keeping an eye on both Stumpp and on the paper. I suspect she'll eventually show up at one of them. If she does, we'll know where we stand."

"How so?" Michael asked him.

"If she goes to her editor, she's planning on printing the story, exposing them like she said."

"And if she goes to Stumpp..." Michael trailed off. The implications were obvious. If Veer went to Stumpp it would be to check in after the job and get whatever reward she had coming for conning them so thoroughly. It was thorough, if it was a con, he'd give her that. Not only was he completely discredited, his career ruined, but with the inevitable lawsuits from this Holy Mountain Research place the entire department would be slowed down, overly careful not to make any more costly mistakes.

For four hundred years they'd kept their secrets. He was beginning to understand how.

"HELLO, VEER," Victor said, rising from behind his desk as she came in. It occurred to her, for at least the dozenth time that day, that it was dangerous for her to come here. Well, once she'd passed Cate's desk and been allowed into the office it was too late for that thought. Time to dive in and hope for the best.

"Victor," she greeted him as if they hadn't been close friends for three years.

"So..." he started. This may be the first time she'd ever known him to not know what to say.

"Yes," she agreed. She didn't know what to say either. "I'm sorry," she started.

"No," he said. "You just did what you always said you would."

"As did you," she said, forestalling his need to return her apology. He had tried to kill her. He had tried to kill her and now she was worried about hurting his dignity by forcing an apology.

"It was well-written," he said, returning to his seat behind the desk. He indicated the paper lying open on the desk with her first article on the front page. "You made us come across quite well, even without using the biotech company. Thank you for that."

And that was it. She had exposed the secret he'd spent a lifetime protecting. The secret that he had been willing to kill her to keep, and now that it was out, he was thanking her for writing it sympathetically.

"So, what do we do now?" she asked. "What are we?"

"Now, we have a few matters to discuss, and I believe three roles we each must play today."

She chose the first one. "You were going to kill me."

"I was," he said. There was a sad tone to his voice.

What else was there to say? She could complain that they were friends, or demand an explanation, but she knew his reasons. His duty would always come first. If the circumstances were to repeat, he would do everything exactly the same way. He might regret it, but he wouldn't let his personal feelings stop him from doing whatever was necessary.

"That's one thing I'm happy to have failed at," he offered. She knew it was the closest he would come to saying he was sorry. "At least I won't have to do so again."

"What do you mean?" she had to ask, fearing the answer.

"It's too late, as you said. I am genuinely surprised you got your paper to back you. With the police raid finding no corroborating evidence at Holy Mountain Research, they are risking a reputation they have built up over more than a century. The council, of course, will do everything they can to discredit it, and you. It will, I think, be a close fight, and one in which I'll be happy to have no part."

"The council? Not you?"

"They're sending a new Alpha."

"They can do that? What happens to you?"

"We shall see. They want me to go to Maryland."

So that's where the Council was based. She filed the information away for possible later use. "And you're going?" she said out loud.

"Under the terms of my bail, I can't leave the state without permission. I doubt they will grant it for going to speak to the heads of a vast international criminal empire."

She laughed, though the situation wasn't funny.

"What will you do?"

"That remains to be seen. The new Alpha should be arriving by now. Peter has gone to meet them."

"Peter?" She realized the implications of that. "It won't be one guy traveling alone. He'll have an entire entourage with him. How will Peter..."

"He assures me he has a plan. I have full faith in him."

"Even if they all somehow mysteriously disappear, there's no way the council's not going to assume you're responsible."

"Assuming and taking action are two different things. In the time in between they will hesitate."

"Giving you room to maneuver."

"Exactly."

"To do what?"

"To begin with, there were some arrangements I needed to make." He picked up a manila envelope from his desk and handed it to her. "I had this drawn up this morning. You are now sole trustee of the preserve."

Her eyes widened at that, but before she could say anything, he slid another envelope over to her.

"And this one," he said, "Gives you power of attorney over all my known holdings in the event of my demise, incapacitation, or incarceration."

She looked up in shock. Three days ago, he was trying to kill her. Now he was turning over all his assets to her?

"Victor, you can't..."

"Who else?" he asked. Then his expression sobered. "I will likely be unable to protect the Were much longer. Someone else will have to. I wouldn't advertise either of those for a while, though. At least until all of this has blown over one way or another. I'm afraid getting past me was only the first obstacle in your path. Even, or perhaps especially, if I am taken off the board completely, you will still have the council to deal with."

She thought about that for a moment. She knew this wouldn't be easy. Without being able to use the documents from Holy Mountain, it was even worse. She had enough that Don was throwing everything into backing her, but Victor wasn't wrong. If the council was able to cover this up, it could bring down the entire paper with her. They had to win this one, there'd be no second chance.

Then she realized something he'd said. "What do you mean 'known' holdings?"

Victor smiled at that. "I may have squirreled a little something away in Switzerland, for a rainy day."

"Switzerland?"

"I'm a traditionalist."

"But if anything does happen to you..."

"I'll do my best to protect you and the rest of the Were."

"Does that include going public? Exposing the secret?"

"Not while I live. I am sorry, Veer. That will have to remain your task. However," he handed her a third envelope, thicker than the first two combined. "Keep this one hidden somewhere safe until you absolutely need to use it."

"What is it?"

"Information. Everything I know about the council and the

other Alphas' operations, which is, I might add, a great deal more than they think I know."

"You expect me to use it to blackmail the council?"

"No. I expect you to use it to expose them. I have already used it to blackmail them."

"So, I'm, what, your revenge?"

"Let's say a deterrent."

"Back off or it all comes down?"

"Something like that."

"It's all coming down anyway, Victor," she replied. "Wouldn't the best option be to let them come? To use their resources to contain everything?"

"To sacrifice myself?"

For half a second she was surprised at his answer. It never occurred to her that he wouldn't, if it became necessary.

"I have thought about it," Victor continued. "However, they would not hold the safety of my people as a priority."

"You don't think the Council would take care of them?"

"They would destroy as much as they thought they needed to. Kill without remorse, human and Were alike. They would burn all of Portland to the ground if they thought it would help."

"Then join us. Testify. Blow the whole thing open. Move your people under human law..."

He just shook his head. "It wouldn't work," he said.

"What are you going to tell them?"

"Absolutely nothing. When I was arrested, they told me I had the right to remain silent. I intend to exercise that right."

"They're going to want me to testify against you, you know."

"I know. There's nothing you can say that can hurt me."

"Only that you're a werewolf."

"This, they know already. Though it will be interesting to see them try to prove it."

"And that you're the Alpha of this region."

"Am I? Can you prove that?"

"Everybody..." she stopped. Everybody around him knows this. They offered him deference. They referred to him as "The Alpha." But both could be explained as deference to age and totally legitimate wealth. "And any criminal acts are just hearsay. And assumptions. I honestly can't think of you ever actually asking anyone to commit a crime in my presence. You've been protecting me against this eventuality the whole time, haven't you?"

"Myself as well. I would spare you being forced to testify against me, but I have also quite intentionally limited the number of people who can."

"It should be interesting."

"Can I assume you will be covering the trial, in addition to giving testimony?"

"Of course," she said.

"Excellent," he said. "Then I will see you in court. It will be nice to see at least one friendly face there."

She smiled sadly at that. "I'm afraid I won't be there as your friend."

"Even so," he replied. Then continued, "I understand you have some legal troubles of your own."

"Holy Mountain is suing me for slander because of the police raid. Not quite the same thing."

"Still," he said.

"The paper's lawyer thinks he can get them to back off. If they press it, they may have to admit I had stolen papers from them. Right now, they're claiming everything I have is outright forgeries."

"So, you threaten them with publicity if they pursue you," he said with a smile.

"They've got to have the originals somewhere still. We're

betting the last thing they want right now is a lot of public scrutiny."

"So that's exactly what you're going to give them."

"Eventually. It may take a while, but it's what I do," she said. She smiled herself when she said it. It felt good to share this moment with him, at least, whatever the future was going to hold.

———————

"WEREWOLVES, MAN. FUCK," Charles was saying as Gordon approached. There was a group of people gathered around the island counter in the office's break room. Gordon picked up the paper that was lying on it next to the coffee machine.

"What the hell is this?" he asked. He assumed it was some kind of set up. The banner headline read simply "WERE-WOLVES!" in capital bold letters.

"Sounds ridiculous, doesn't it?" Charles said. Half the office seemed to be gathered around the counter on both sides.

"It is ridiculous," Claire said. "There's no such thing as werewolves."

"They've got a lot of proof, though," Dave put in. "I read the article this morning. She makes a good case."

"You mean this is a real paper?" Gordon asked.

"Yeah, the paper's real," Claire answered him. "But the article's bullshit."

"No, it's not," Charles said. "It's been all over the news."

"That doesn't mean it's not bullshit."

"Vera Rosen?" Gordon said, noticing the byline.

"Yeah, if it's some kind of hoax, it's a big one," Charles answered. "They got her, the editors, the paper, the police..."

"The police?"

"Yeah, this Detective Johansen admitted they've had an entire werewolf squad devoted to catching them. And - get this - they've arrested Victor Stumpp."

"They arrested Stumpp?" he said, surprised. If they got the Alpha... Then he realized what he'd said and quickly followed up with "The computer guy?" He tried to sound as surprised as when Toni had told him about him over a month ago. He found he wanted very much to talk to Toni, get her take on this. She had invited him to play his mysterious stranger role at another warehouse party on Saturday. He was planning on going but got a text from her canceling at the last minute. He hadn't heard from her since. Whatever it was, it was probably related. If her wolves were ready and willing to go public, this article could just be the beginning, the breach that opens the dam.

"Yeah. Stumpp's also a werewolf, apparently," Charles was saying.

"What'd they arrest him for?"

"Being a werewolf, I guess."

"That's... is there even a law against that?"

"If there isn't, there should be," Dave answered. "I mean, can you imagine?"

"Imagine what?"

"Werewolves! I mean, if there is such a thing, they could be anybody, and once a month they go crazy and start killing people..."

"That's not how it works!" Charles said before Gordon could answer. He was grateful for that. He'd have to be careful not to seem like he knew anything.

"How would you know?" Dave asked him.

"I read the article."

"That doesn't mean anything."

"She says she's been a werewolf for three years," Claire said.

"Wait... so this Vera Rosen is a werewolf, too?" Gordon asked against his own better judgment.

"Either she's lying about being a werewolf," Dave said, "or she's telling the truth and can't be trusted because she's a werewolf."

"That's bullshit man," Charles responded with a vehemence that surprised Gordon. "That's... you can't say she's lying just because she's a werewolf. That's... that's like racism."

Several people glanced uncomfortably at Gordon. This, at least, was familiar. It seemed half the white people in the room would always look his way any time anything vaguely race-related was said.

"It's not... It's not the same thing," he started.

"Right. Because you don't grow up being a werewolf, and it's not the first thing everybody you meet notices about you."

"Hey, that's not... not everybody first notices..." Dave started, originally facing Gordon, then quickly glancing back away.

This was just too much.

"I gotta get to work," he said and walked briskly back to his cube, leaving them arguing behind him.

He put on his headphones and, unable to concentrate on work, started searching for coverage on the news sites. It was all over all of them. Some few seemed to be taking the whole thing seriously. Most, though, were treating it with either extreme skepticism or outright disdain. CNN seemed to be dismissing it out of hand, while the BBC was cautious but vowed to send reporters to find out what was really happening. Fox was still trying to figure out how to blame Muslims.

Charles appeared at the opening of his cube. Gordon thought about it for a second, then took off his headphones and nodded to the extra chair.

"I'm sorry," Charles said as he took the chair.

"For what?" Gordon asked.

"For... well... anything. Presumption, maybe."

"You still think I'm a werewolf," Gordon said accusingly.

"I think..." Charles stammered. "I think it doesn't matter. I think some people might be werewolves, and they probably have good reason to keep it to themselves and it doesn't matter if they are."

"What are you getting at?" Gordon said, testily.

"Just... just, I don't care if you are or not. Or if someone else is. I don't think they - whoever they are - should be treated any differently."

"You're not afraid they might change at the full moon and rip your throat out?"

"No. Apparently, that's not really a thing. And it makes sense - if they were really senseless killing beasts when they changed how would they possibly keep it a secret?" Charles echoed what Gordon had said to Toni back at that first meeting at the Pied Cow. "This article claims they can control when they change and even in wolf form avoid biting people."

"What if that's true for some, but maybe some are rampaging beasts?"

"What of it? So are some people. Somebody could come in here tomorrow and shoot the place up. It happens all the time, but we don't spend all our time worrying about it."

"But a metal detector would at least stop someone from carrying in a gun. There's no way to detect a werewolf," that he knew of, he didn't add.

"Yeah? I didn't go through a metal detector to get in here today. I'm sure at least a few people in this office are carrying right now, but I'm not worried about any of them losing control. Hell, I'm licensed, I just never bring my weapon into the office with me because I'm more scared of HR than I am of random murderers, werewolf or not."

Gordon never thought about anyone carrying weapons into the office before, but statistically Charles was probably right. He'd just never heard about it because they didn't generally talk about it, and in the five years he'd been working here there'd never been an incident where it came up.

Then he realized what else Charles had said. Even knowing, or strongly suspecting, his coworker was a werewolf, he didn't feel the need to arm himself against him.

"Thank you," he said and meant it.

IT WAS STARTING to get light. His vision was obscured by something and he struggled to catch his breath. There was something heavy in front of his face, it stuck to it when he inhaled. He nearly choked on dust and stench. But when he tried to reach up, he found he couldn't move his hands. He tried to roll to his side to free his hands. He could barely move.

"Hey!" he heard a voice call.

"Shit!" another responded. "He's waking up. Hit him again before he shifts!"

"Shifts?" Wait, were they talking about him? He couldn't see anything. Dare he change? He wasn't sure. And then there something heavy on his shoulder, holding him still and a pressure and then a burning feeling in his arm. Change. Yes, he should change...

AND THEN HE was being carried. His feet were dragging on the ground. He lifted his head and tried to stand up. Maybe he should change... but before he'd finished considering it, something hit him in the arm again, and his legs gave out.

HE WOKE up and found he still couldn't see. When he tried to reach for his face, he found he couldn't move his arm. There was a rumbling vibration around him. He was in a vehicle of some sort. "The new place is just up the road," someone said. He didn't know what they meant. He thought for a moment they were heading for the cabin but realized that couldn't be true. He decided to change.

THE WOLF'S world was fire and pain and humans yelling. He snapped and bit and snarled and they threw fire and darkness. An explosion and a sense of triumph from one of the humans and he found his legs stopped working. More fire and pain and then only darkness.

SLOWLY THE LIGHT CAME BACK, but he still couldn't see. There was something over his nose and mouth. When he tried to open his eyes, a blurry voice yelled "Turn up the gas, he's waking up again." There was a hiss and before he could think to hold his breath darkness took him.

HE WAS LYING ON A BED, or a table; there were men gathered around him. Something was over his mouth and a tube ran down his throat. He tried to spit it out. Voices, dim and distorted. Darkness again.

WHEN HE OPENED his eyes next the light was almost painfully bright. He squinted and raised his hand against the light and realized he could.

"Carl?" he heard a voice call. He looked around to see where it was coming from. He was lying on his back on a hard wooden slab in some kind of cage. How long had it been? It felt like days. His cage was one of many in what might have been a small warehouse. Each, like his own, had a pair of beds, a sink and a toilet. The floor was concrete with a drain in the middle. There were maybe a dozen other people, two or three to a cell, sitting or lying on their beds. It took several moments to realize that the voice, and the face looking back at him from the man sitting on the other bed belonged to Kevin. He looked so gaunt, and his expression was so sorrowful, so pleading, Carl almost didn't recognize him.

"Oh, god, Carl. I'm sorry. I'm so sorry." He lifted his arm as if to wipe away tears, and Carl saw it ended just before his wrist, in a bandaged stump.

"What... what happened?" he stumbled the words out. The question could have applied to Kevin's hand, or to his present circumstances.

"I'm sorry. They... they did things..." he waved his stump. "They hurt me. Over and over. And Shelly, they..."

He realized what had happened. They... whoever they were... had caught Kevin. The near-skeletal appearance, the mutilation... they'd tortured him. A lot. This pitiful creature was not the cocky, self-assured man he'd known.

"It's okay," he reassured him. Everyone talks under torture, he wanted to say, but didn't dare say the word out loud. "It's not your fault."

"It is!" Kevin wheezed. "I told them... I told them how to find you. And then they did."

"It's okay," he repeated. "I'm here now. They won't need to hurt you anymore."

Kevin broke down crying at that. "But they will. Oh, god, it never stops. Shelly..." but he stopped.

Carl wondered what had happened to Shelly. He had ideas. None of them were pleasant. He didn't want any of them confirmed, so he didn't ask. Perhaps that was his own cowardice.

"You don't know what they're like..." Kevin began.

Carl could guess, though. He'd heard stories. Second, third hand. Never anything direct, always rumors. He was not at all surprised that the Alpha ran a facility like this. Though he didn't expect so many to be in here. He was still having difficulty standing up, so he sat back down, and pulled the thin cotton blanket back over him.

He looked at Kevin again, the visible ribs, the missing hand, and wondered if that's what he'd look like in a couple of weeks. How did he even get like that? What could you possibly do to a person to make them that gaunt that quickly? The thought that he'd soon find out terrified him.

"It's not just cutting," Kevin said as if he knew what Carl was thinking. "Half the time they don't even ask me any questions. And then they... they... do things..." he trailed off again as if he didn't want to continue. Carl waited, nearly holding his breath, perched between wanting to hear the rest and wanting him to never continue.

He continued.

"Remember how I said that I would never face death quietly? That if it was inevitable, at least I'd go out fighting? Face down the fucking reaper with my eyes wide open?"

Carl didn't remember ever hearing him say anything like

that. "Yeah?" he said, his tone making it a question, urging
Kevin to continue.

"They... they took us out..." he stopped. Looked up at Carl
accusingly, then looked like he was going to ask him something,
or was steeling himself to confront him, then looked down
again and got quiet.

"This was at the old place, right before someone tried to
break in. They made us kneel," he switched back to his story.
Carl felt like he didn't even know this man, or maybe he was
seeing him clearly for the first time. All pretense stripped away
and only his core self flayed open and laid bare to the world.

"They had a gun and they... they showed me it was loaded
with silver bullets... They didn't even ask me anything. They
said they were done with me. And... I didn't look. When they
pulled the trigger, I just sat there, I closed my eyes and looked
away. I knew... knew in that moment I was going to die, and I
closed my eyes and turned away, just quietly... waited for it."

His body wracked then, with just a couple of sobs, but his
eyes were dry, as if he was no longer capable of crying.

Carl couldn't even imagine what that would be like. The
certainty that you're going to die, the giving up, and the despair
of knowing that you did. What would that do to a person? Was
that before or after they took his hand, he wondered.

He looked around the area and at the people in adjoining
cells. Many of them were wearing white gowns and slippers
like in a hospital, though about half were naked like he and
Kevin both were. He saw a couple different bandaged stumps
of missing limbs, but most seemed to be intact. A few had the
gaunt nearly skeletal features of starving people like Kevin, but
only a few. That gave him hope. Maybe they weren't torturing
everybody? They only wanted to hurt some of them? To what
end? Maybe it depended on what their "crime" was. Kevin had
staged a massive public attack. What had he done? Did they

know he was associated, and did it matter? But if different people were treated differently, was it even based on what they'd done? Was there some kind of secret court that met in some weird, twisted perversion of "justice"? Had it tried him and sentenced him without him ever even knowing about it?

He looked around at the others and wondered what they had done. There were so many. Were there always this many people here? If so, it was possible he got a lighter sentence than Kevin. He didn't do anything publicly after all. All he had done was... kill Andrew Hudson. Murder the Alpha's right hand man. But he hadn't done that alone, it was... no. They were going to ask him. He couldn't say her name. Couldn't even think it. If he thought about it, it would slip out.

He knew then they were going to torture him. They were going to hurt him and hurt him until he was a one-handed skeleton like Kevin and then when he'd finally told them how to find Toni, they would kill him. He wondered how long he'd last. He wanted to go find whoever was in charge and just tell them now. Get it all over with. But he owed it to Toni to hold out for at least a little while. As long as he could.

Kevin obviously had. That's why they were torturing him, right? To get to Carl. He looked at Kevin's arm again. Is that why they put him in the same cell? As a threat? This is what will happen to you? He was surprised Kevin held out as long as he did. He didn't owe Carl anything, but... what he had endured to protect him, even after Carl had abandoned him... If they ever got out of here, he owed him big time. He vowed never to let him down again.

He scanned across the room again. He didn't recognize any of the people here. There was a girl a couple of cells over from him dressed in jeans and a blouse.

"What are you looking at?" she asked him when she saw him staring at her.

He gestured to his own lack of shirt in indicating hers, but didn't speak.

"Yeah, cuz I don't wolf out while I'm wearing my clothes," she said.

Several of the prisoners in nearby cells glared at her.

"I do what they tell me to do," she said to Carl, ignoring them.

"Yeah, cuz all they ever do to you is take blood samples or scans," a sunken-eyed man wrapped in a blanket exclaimed.

"That's not true," she said, looking at Carl and ignoring the guy who spoke. "They sometimes make me do... things. Tests and stuff. And when they want me to change, I get undressed first, and when I change back, I still have clothes so I can put them back on. It's not really that complicated."

Carl looked around more. A couple of others were also wearing street clothes, he noticed, which just reinforced his idea that they were each being treated differently. They both avoided his gaze, though. He didn't see Shelly anywhere. Did they let her go? She must have gotten away. Right? He didn't want to, but he had to ask.

"Shelly?" he asked, tentatively, of Kevin.

Kevin looked down at the feet again. Again, that silent, tear-less sob. Carl said nothing. Finally, Kevin spoke.

"I killed her," he said. It was barely even a whisper. Then "I was angry because she killed me, so I killed her, but I didn't die. Just her."

Carl could make no sense of the statement, but still he waited quietly, allowing Kevin room to explain. This was too much. Too much to deal with. But he wouldn't abandon him again.

"They chained us both to the tables and they had this rod - it's silver. You'll see it." Kevin waved vaguely with his missing hand. "They... they told me this time it was for real, and said they were going to set one of us free. They were going to let one of us go, so we could spread the word.

"As a warning. They were going to let one of us go free and kill the other one, and they asked me which one they should free and I said me, I would have given anything. Anything at all, to get out of here, to make it all stop. Oh god, I said to let me go free and let her die and that was the last thing she ever heard.

"They took the rod and pushed it straight through her, and she changed and thrashed and howled and screamed in pain and then she changed back, and I was under the chains right next to her and she changed back, and she looked at me and said, "I'm sorry." I killed her and the last thing she said to me was that she was sorry, and I watched her die. I killed her and she told me she was sorry."

For a long moment it was quiet. Kevin looked at him expectantly, but he couldn't even begin to formulate a thought.

"No," he finally said. "You didn't kill her."

"Yes!" And Carl winced at just how weak his full fury sounded. There was the tiniest bit of his accustomed arrogance and that's what made it so much worse. "I did. I killed her. I killed you. I killed everybody in this room."

Then Carl realized who all the rest of them were. The other Were. All the ones that Kevin and Shelly had changed. All the ones the Alpha could catch, anyway. And they knew who Kevin was. The bastards put his cage right in the middle of them all then told them it was all his fault they were here. Whatever plan they came up with, they would find no allies here.

"No... " he began slowly. "No, you didn't. Maybe you turned them," he was about to add "but they had a choice", but realized that for the most part they hadn't, "but it doesn't matter," he amended. "You didn't build this place."

Several people were glaring in open hostility at him now. He raised his voice for their benefit. "This... the Alphas built this. It wasn't created in response to our movement, it was the other way around. We started it because, exactly because of this. We knew that this, or something like this, existed. Because we knew that they'd have to have a place like this to enforce their power. We fought," Carl caught himself, "are fighting against tyranny because tyranny inevitably leads to places like this."

"We weren't part of your rebellion and would never be here if it wasn't for you fuckers," a man in a nearby cage said. Carl had no answer to that. The man wouldn't care that something like this existed because before he arrived, he could never have imagined ending up here himself.

Kevin just shook his head. Carl knew what he meant. That hadn't been his motivation for fighting. Until he got here, Kevin wouldn't care if the place existed either.

Carl lowered his voice again and spoke just to Kevin. "Even if we die here, the movement will go on without us. They couldn't have gotten everybody you've turned, and I don't see any of my people here at all..."

"You will. You'll call them all in, in the end."

"I won't," he said, and when Kevin just shook his head sadly, he clarified, "I can't. Even if I wanted to, and I'm sure eventually I will want to more than anything. I don't know who they all are, or how to get in touch with all the ones I do know. They can trace the chain, go link by link through our entire web, but all it takes is one person dying before they can get the information, or getting away before they can capture them, and that whole branch is lost to them. We set it up that way on purpose."

"But some..."

"And even before that, they won't all come to the signal. Or some will see the vans and run off. Some will bring weapons or come in a group." He said the last for the benefit of anyone hearing him and planning to report it. He hoped it was true, but he didn't count on it. They should have arranged some kind of danger signal, he thought. Like, all the same things, but put the word Shinigami into the ad somewhere and that would be a warning that their code was compromised and not to trust it anymore.

"But it doesn't matter," he finished, "because even if we die here, you didn't kill us. You didn't kill Shelly, and you didn't kill me. They," he said with a vague wave of his hand, "did that. All the deaths, all the suffering, all of it, lies right at the feet of the Alphas and their desperate fight to hold onto power. And it's a fight they can't win."

"Fuck yeah," a voice said behind him. Carl jumped. At least a few of his fellow prisoners had been listening. He wasn't sure what to make of it, but at least a couple of them might be allies after all.

TWENTY-SEVEN

TESTIMONY, QUESTIONS, AND SILENCE

Veer pushed her way through the crowd outside the court-house. When she got to the metal detector, she showed her ID to a guard there, which earned her an escort to the main room where the trial was taking place, as well as a couple of glares from colleagues waiting to get into one of the two overflow rooms set up for the press.

As early as she was and despite her special access, she ended up sitting near the back of the packed courtroom. She'd have a better seat tomorrow, when she was scheduled to testify, but for now she was lucky to be here at all. Michael entered shortly thereafter and, spotting her already seated, took the seat next to her. She wondered what strings he'd pulled to be allowed in here.

"I don't think your bosses are going to like seeing you talking to me," she said.

"Well, if I had anywhere better to be, I guess I'd be there instead," he said, referencing his continuing suspension.

She just smiled at that. Michael opened his briefcase and

retrieved a yellow folder from a stack of similar ones. He opened the folder, using the briefcase as a lap desk.

"Is that from Holy Mountain?" she asked.

"Yep. I printed out the rest of the documents, going through them seeing if there's something we can use."

"You know the official story is that those are all forgeries, right?" she said.

"Yep. Turned out you weren't lying to me about anything else, though, so I figure they're legit."

That made her happy to hear. For the next couple of hours, he sifted, read, and marked, while she listened to the buzz of conversation around her in the crowded room, trying to gauge the general feel of the crowd and making occasional notes of ideas that she might possibly use in future articles.

Jury selection had taken the better part of the previous week. It could have taken even longer. Victor's lawyer at one point complained that there were no Were among the jury pool.

"I would suggest that perhaps the defense is taking the definition of peer a bit too far," the judge had finally told her. "If we knew who they were maybe we could consider it. However, isn't the fact that they have worked so hard to keep their existence secret the whole problem? We're not going to specifically look for werewolves for the jury any more than we're going to look for WWII veterans or software CEOs. You get a randomly selected group of people from throughout the county, just like everybody else."

Due to its extraordinary nature, they were rushing ahead with the Werewolf Trial, as it was already being called. Veer felt the name was unfortunate. Victor had been charged with racketeering and a single count of conspiracy to commit murder. "Werewolf Trial" implied it was werewolves themselves on trial.

Too many people were looking to the trial to prove or disprove the existence of werewolves. She'd have to figure out how to write the article to make clear otherwise. She wondered if the reporters at the Scopes "Monkey Trial" had had the same problem. *We exist regardless of the verdict in any one trial...*, she began writing it in her head. Or should that be *They exist...?* *Werewolves exist*, she decided, a nice neutral opening that neither highlighted nor attempted to deny her own involvement.

A side door opened, and Victor and his legal team entered, led by Dianne Solomon, who Veer had met after being arrested the first time. The murmur of conversation began to die down. Victor spotted her and gave her a slight nod and an even slighter smile before turning to take his seat. Just enough to reassure her that he'd be all right. On trial for his life, he was trying to reassure her.

He had a less kind look for Peter, who was led in through a side door shortly thereafter, flanked by two Multnomah County Sheriff's deputies. She had received the word just yesterday that he'd taken a plea bargain and was testifying against Victor.

Michael wasn't any happier seeing him here. "They let the cop killer off so they can catch the software guy," he said bitterly.

"Nine years isn't exactly letting him off," Veer replied quietly.

"He should be in jail for life. Allowing a manslaughter plea's bullshit."

"I agree," Veer said. "I don't like the idea of allowing the claim that while in wolf form he didn't have full control over his faculties."

"But that's not true at all, is it?" Michael said. "You told me..."

"That's why I don't like it," Veer replied. "It sets a dangerous precedent."

She was interrupted when the bailiff called them all to stand as the judge entered. The judge took his seat and the bailiff announced that the case of Oregon vs. Victor Stumpp was now commencing.

WHEN THE PROSECUTION had a large cage wheeled up to the front of the courtroom, Veer had an idea what they intended. She looked to Victor and saw that he looked more amused than annoyed by it, which surprised her. Peter was led to the cage, as expected. They made a show of padlocking the door behind him and he carefully removed his shoes, then shirt, and finally his pants, drawing out the process, leaving him standing in only his boxers before he turned back to the prosecutor and asked, "Are you ready?"

"Proceed," the prosecutor replied.

Peter stared at him, twisted his face into a snarl then growled. He took a step back, then lurched forward and transformed. Where he had been, a wolf now stood, pressing against the edge of the cage, snarling and snapping through the bars. The two deputies who'd been escorting him both drew tasers and stepped back away from the cage.

The courtroom gasped to see it. They'd read about Were of course - they'd all heard by now. After Veer's initial articles, a number of Were had come forth and revealed themselves, giving interviews and even demonstrations to various press organizations, but reading about it or seeing people talking about it, even watching video demonstrations of Were transforming was different from seeing it in person. Nothing could quite prepare the audience for what they saw.

Victor chuckled out loud at the demonstration, then sat, never quite losing the amused look on his face even when the prosecutor stepped close - but not too close - to the cage.

"Peter Maxwell!" the man yelled directly into the face of the wolf. "Come back now! Come back, Peter! We need you to come back now!"

"Laying it on a bit thick, isn't he?" Michael whispered to her.

She nodded. "I hate this. This isn't the image people should have of Were."

Finally, Peter returned to his human self, lying in the cage. The prosecutor handed him a robe, which he shrugged into before a deputy unlocked the cage and let him out.

"Victor doesn't seem too happy about it either," Michael said.

She looked to Victor. His lawyer, sitting next to him, seemed to be ignoring him while in intense conversation with Hudson's replacement, Cate, behind her. Victor looked like he was about to say something, but before he could speak, Solomon silenced her client with a hand on his arm. Then she stood up and addressed the court herself.

"What you just saw was very dramatic," she started. "And of course intended to prejudice your feelings against my client. For surely, if he himself is such a beast, how could he possibly be trusted? While Mr. Maxwell's behavior in wolf form makes for good drama, it doesn't really portray who we are. Since we're apparently doing demonstrations now, I'd like to show you a more accurate one." At that, she nodded to Cate and gestured for her to join her. So that's what they were talking about.

Cate stood up, took off her jacket and hung it over the back of the chair. She then kicked off her shoes and walked up to the front of the room. Solomon then turned to the two deputies who'd assisted in Peter's demonstration. "If you don't mind getting this out of the way," she said, indicating the large cage they'd used for Peter.

When they had wheeled it off to a corner, Solomon again turned to Cate and said, "When you're ready."

Cate reached down toward the floor, but before she could get there, there was a strange sort of twist and a wolf landed heavily. There was a loud gasp from the crowd and a quick murmur of fear rippled through it.

"Don't panic!" Solomon yelled over the growing sound of the crowd. "It's perfectly safe!"

There seemed to be a great deal of skepticism, but at least there wasn't a mad dash for the exits.

The wolf turned and looked toward the jury for a moment. Not threatening, just regarding them as if to say hello, here I am. Then she turned back toward the courtroom and Veer could swear she saw disapproval on her face. Then she lay down as if to sleep, but looked toward Victor. Victor obviously understood what she wanted and said something to his lawyer. She reached across to his seat, picked up his coat, and brought it to the wolf. When she got there, the wolf looked at her curiously for only a moment before stretching out into that strange shift, and a second later the wolf was gone and Cate was back in its place. She took the proffered coat and put it on before making her way to the witness stand.

"Thank you, Ms. Lowls," Solomon began. "Can you explain to us what we all just witnessed?"

"Like most Were," Cate began, "I can't recall exact details of what happens while I'm in Form. I changed into the form of a wolf, and then after a minute, changed back. It's a simple, natural process once you've learned how."

"If you can't remember what happens, can you tell us why you changed back?"

"Because you asked me to. We are still ourselves while in wolf form, to some degree. It is a generally accepted fact among the Were that you wouldn't do anything in Form that you wouldn't do as a human, and are still responsible for your actions."

There was some muttering at that, and Veer made a quick note to use it in her article: contrasting Cate's comment about responsibility with Peter's plea deal.

"Can you explain the difference between your behavior and Mr. Maxwell's, then?"

"I can only speculate as to Peter's motives..." she began.

"Please do so."

"Objection," the prosecutor said immediately.

"Sustained," the judge replied. "Please stick to matters of fact for which the witness has first-hand knowledge."

"Very well," Solomon said. "Can you then tell us why you remained calm while in wolf form instead of snarling and growling?"

"I only wanted to demonstrate what a Were transformation looks like. My aim was not to frighten anyone or convince anyone that we are more dangerous than we really are." Which, of course, answered the original question.

"If you're so harmless, why have you kept yourself secret for so long?" Those in the know glanced back at Veer at this statement. She wasn't expecting the sudden attention and found she didn't like it. She preferred to be known through her writing, avoiding the spotlight herself.

"Too long, perhaps," Cate began, which surprised her. "Though originally secrecy did not lack a good reason. It isn't taught in schools, and has nearly - nearly, but not quite entirely - been expunged from our history books, but the Were remember. We are an ancient people, and insular, yes, as any long-oppressed people will become. The last time our existence was widely known, non-Were made a great effort to kill every last one of us. Between 1590 and 1610 A.D., tens of thousands perished in the pogroms that spread throughout Europe alone."

"Objection your honor," the prosecution said.

"On what grounds?" the judge asked.

"The ancient history of werewolves is irrelevant. We are discussing the current situation."

"The history of Victor's people is not irrelevant," Victor's lawyer responded. "You wish to discuss the conspiracy. To do so we must show this conspiracy for what it truly is. The factual nature of it, rather than the shadowy hints the prosecution would deliver."

The judge allowed it, and she continued. "The Were are a quiet, peaceful people. And it is the rules set by those original convocations that ensure that continues. First among the rules is an absolute prohibition against violence. For violence brings attention from the outside, and that's one thing they absolutely do not want. For the same reason, we limit the number of new Were we create every year, and they are never created without their permission. There is a period of training making sure that each new candidate understands our rules and can be trusted to keep them."

"What about Grant Talman?"

"Talman was a rogue, a Were that did not follow the rules. How he came to be, we don't know for sure."

"If you had to guess?"

"My guess is he was already a killer, and eventually chose a Were as a victim. I believe that Gregor Theissen was working covertly with the San Diego police to find out, but whatever chance of success they may have had is lost forever since his death in Portland. But it is, I believe, illustrative of why we remain secret."

"So, your rules allow violence in self defense?"

"No, ma'am, not even then."

"But you said this Talman..."

"I said if I have to guess. I would guess that somebody broke the rules."

"If you can't use your... can I say power?... in self defense, what happens if someone else commits violence against you?"

She smiled at that. "There are many opportunities for escape open to someone who can turn into a wolf. Especially a wolf who heals very quickly from almost any injury."

THE NEXT DAY it was Veer's turn to testify. She placed the notebook and pen back into her inside jacket pocket, which she left lying on her place on the bench as she got up to take the witness stand.

"How did you first meet Mr. Stumpp?" the prosecutor asked her.

"He was the subject of an article I was researching."

"You were investigating werewolves?" he asked.

"No, I was investigating job off-shoring, exploitation, and corporate malfeasance. Instead, I found werewolves."

"And so you became one."

"Eventually, yes"

"Why?"

"For a variety of reasons."

"Such as?"

"Primarily to learn more about the Were, their society, and their culture."

"And you had no qualms about becoming a monster?"

"Objection!"

"Sustained."

"You had no... misgivings about turning into a werewolf?"

She waited again for the defense to object. When they did not, she answered. "Misgivings? Certainly. Fears, doubts, all that."

"But still, you persisted."

"I think the fear is perfectly understandable, if not justified. For centuries, stories, then books, then later movies and TV shows have portrayed Were as dangerous ravenous beasts. They literally call movies of them monster movies. So, your slip earlier is quite understandable, but in reality, the Were are not like that at all."

"But you admit some misgivings."

"I've seen the same movies you have," she said, with a smile. "And three years ago, I didn't know them like I do now."

"So why did Stumpp turn you into one?"

"You'd have to ask him."

"Surely you must have some ideas."

"I have lots of ideas. Some less fanciful than others, and some much more savory than the rest. Which do you want to hear?" She looked toward Victor and was not disappointed with his grin of amusement at her statement.

"All right, what can you tell me about this man?" He picked up a large photograph from the evidence table.

"Peter. He works for Victor."

"Yes?"

"Yes."

"What can you tell me about him?" he repeated his question.

"His name is Peter. He works for Victor," she repeated her answer verbatim. There were twitters of laughter throughout the courtroom. She felt a little apprehensive about that. She meant to be evasive, but not to undermine Victor's case by angering the prosecution. Despite the oath to "tell the whole truth," nobody actually wanted that. Years of experience with court cases had taught her that the best thing for all concerned, especially anybody you want to help out, is to answer questions as briefly as possible. If they wanted more information, they would ask for it. Any information volunteered beyond what was asked was more likely to do harm than good.

"In what capacity did he work for Mr. Stumpp?"

"Objection," defense counsel put in. "Mr. Maxwell is not on trial here."

"But Mr. Stumpp is, therefore his relationship is relevant."

"I'll allow it."

"I don't know the precise scope of his employment," Veer answered. "I have heard him referred to by various people as a troubleshooter, a gofer, and a plumber."

"A plumber, as in he eliminates leaks?"

"Or unclogs pipes," she answered.

"Have you ever heard Mr. Stumpp tell Mr. Maxwell to take care of any specific problem, or a specific individual?"

"No." Of course she hadn't. What kind of man did they think they were dealing with? She had always assumed Peter to be a hitman, of course, but Victor had never outright said it. He knew all along that this situation, however unlikely, was a possibility, and had prepared for it.

"WHAT CAN you tell us about this man?" the prosecutor asked him.

Gordon was tempted to say "Peter. He works for Stumpp," but decided it would be counterproductive.

"I only met him the one time, when he was trying to kill me," he said instead.

Until today, he'd always wondered if he hadn't possibly over-reacted in the hospital. Until he heard the police lab technician describe what she'd found in the needle and what it would have done to him if he'd been injected with it. He shuddered to think about it.

"How did you know he was trying to kill you?"

"Did you not hear the testimony from the lab an hour ago?"

"Before that, I mean. When he first came into your room, how did you know he wasn't a nurse?"

"I... I don't remember exactly. There was something wrong about it."

"So, having no idea if this man was a nurse or not, you leapt out of your hospital bed to attack him."

"He was going to kill me!"

"But you didn't know that at the time!"

"Objection!" the defense called again. "What is the relevance of this line of questioning?"

"It's relevant to the nature of the conspiracy," the prosecutor answered. "I intend to demonstrate that violence is a trait in werewolves."

Violence is a trait in werewolves. Gordon had heard that sort of thing before. The last president had spoken like that about African Americans. It was wrong then, and it was wrong now. He could not let this go unanswered. Perhaps Charles was right. He had a chance to get ahead of centuries of systemic prejudice here.

"No," he said, before the judge could answer to sustain the objection.

He spoke as calmly but emphatically as he could. "Violence is not a trait in werewolves. It is true that some werewolves are violent, because werewolves are human, and some humans are violent. I can't tell you exactly what it was that tipped me off," he continued answering the original question. "Perhaps some heightened wolf sense of smell detected the poison in the needle. Maybe a sixth sense recognized him as a fellow Were.

I've been told that's a thing some wolves can do. But it doesn't matter.

"Regardless of what it was, I did figure it out. I didn't attack him because I just attack people at random. I did so because he was an assassin sent to kill me. And even then," he raised his voice slightly, trying to keep from being cut off, "I feel I should point out that I didn't kill him. I didn't even really hurt him. I pushed by and used all my strength to escape, not attack. Because my life was in danger, not because I am now inherently violent."

"That would work for Mr. Maxwell, but how do you explain your subsequent attack on Mr. Samuels?"

"Who?" Gordon thought for a second he was asking about the pimp and his friends. He had hoped nobody would find out about that.

"According to reports, you did not immediately flee the hospital. Instead, you stopped and attacked a Mr. Bartholomew Samuels."

"No, I... oh." Right. He had done that. Kind of. "Oncology ward," he continued. "I didn't attack him, I..."

"According to his statement, you did. The hospital staff found him on the floor of his room, bleeding and in pain. He said a crazy guy came into his room, ranted about werewolves, then turned into a wolf and attacked him."

"I didn't attack him. I just bit him."

"I fail to see the distinction."

"I was trying to help. Look, he had cancer. He was terminal." He heard a gasp from the gallery. The reporter, Vera Rosen, who had testified right before him, had a look of... recognition?

"Unfortunately, he disappeared from the hospital shortly thereafter, so we may never know if it worked," the prosecutor finished.

ROSEN WAS WAITING for him outside the courtroom. He hurried over to her.

"C'mon," she said as he approached. She walked away from him, leading him through the crowd and to a large room down the hall. There were a dozen or so tables scattered around, though at the moment it was mostly empty, with just a few of the smaller tables occupied.

"Arbitration room," Veer explained. "Also, a good place to talk. If you're here, the arbiters," she indicated a handful of people at the other end of the room, "generally assume you're supposed to be. They tend to leave you alone for as long as you need, and..."

"Veer!" someone called, as he approached them inside the room. Gordon recognized Detective Diaz. Veer nodded to the table and the three of them took a seat.

"Mr. Chandler," Diaz acknowledged him as they approached the table.

"Detective," he returned the greeting.

"Gotta admit, I was surprised to see you here."

"Got subpoenaed. Traced me through hospital records."

"That's what I wanted to talk to you about: Samuels."

"Yes," Gordon said, unsurprised after her reaction in court. "Do you know him or something?"

"Maybe," she answered. "I'm almost positive he's the one referred to in the Holy Mountain records as subject Zero."

"Holy Mountain?"

"Biotech firm. They've recently learned about the existence of werewolves and have been doing research on them."

"Recently? How recently?"

"I'm guessing very shortly after Mr. Samuels' terminal

cancer completely disappeared and he was found wandering naked in the park."

"So it worked."

"You really deliberately turned him into a werewolf?" Diaz asked, angrily.

"You heard. The alternative was death. Terminal cancer. This way at least he can raise his daughter." He didn't say "unlike me." He could see from Diaz's downward gaze that he didn't need to.

"It worked. You saved him," Veer said. "Or at least cured his cancer."

"They probably still have him somewhere, then, assuming he's still alive," Diaz said. "When I was still with the squad, we followed up, but couldn't find him. His daughter hadn't heard from him since before you met him. Last I heard Child Protective Services had put her on a bus to Illinois to go live with her mother."

"Shit," Gordon said. "I hope she's all right."

At both of their quizzical looks, he explained, "She's not going to make it that far. I'm guessing she got off that bus at the first stop."

"Where would she go?" Diaz asked.

"No idea. Not Illinois, though."

"So... dead end then."

"And a young girl is out there somewhere, lost and on her own, ready to fall prey to..."

"Lots of young girls are," Michael said abruptly. He obviously noticed Gordon's look at that and stopped to explain. "I'm sorry. I don't mean to sound callous. There are resources that can help her, but unless she reaches out to them, the fact is there's not a lot we can do. Her mother may not be a kind woman, or maybe this Samuels guy was playing on your sympathies or just trying to make himself look like the good guy, but the fact is unless she has actually physically abused her daughter, that's where CPS will send her, regardless of what she wants, and that may actually be the best thing for her."

"Fine." Gordon nodded, accepting the explanation. He knew the detective was right. Portland Police weren't going to expend much effort trying to track down a single runaway girl who didn't want to be found. "Is there any way to find out what this Holy Mountain place did with all the people they had?"

"We've tried," Michael responded. "They moved them out and are claiming all the documents Veer found are fake. Either made up or test documents for the system."

"But they're not," Gordon said, looking at Veer.

"Definitely not. They corroborate what I saw with my own eyes."

"So they get away with it. It's my fault they know everything in the first place, and all I did was alert them and fuck up two lives. Fuck, maybe Stumpp has the right idea after all, about doing whatever it takes to keep your secret."

"Wouldn't have helped." Michael replied. "If Samuels was terminal, he'd be dead by now, and his daughter with his ex. Hell, who's to say this Holy Mountain group isn't right? I mean, you guys could be sitting on a universal cure to all diseases."

"How can you ask that after seeing what they were doing?" Veer exclaimed.

"Okay, maybe their methods are a little extreme, but..."

"It goes beyond a little extreme! They're chopping people up, vivisecting..."

"I'm sorry," Michael said quickly. "I misspoke."

But he's not entirely wrong, Gordon thought. How much could these people have contributed to us over the last few centuries if they hadn't spent so much time and energy having to hide?

THEY CAME for Carl the next morning. They pulled him off the bed he'd been barely sleeping on, shivering, naked between the plywood board and the single thin blanket. They still hadn't given him anything to wear. He barely registered Kevin cowering in the corner as they dragged him out the door.

The occupants of the other cells all looked away as he passed. Not one of them would meet his eyes.

"Where... where are you...?" he started.

A hard slap to the side of his face was the only answer.

He would have fallen to the floor if they weren't holding him up. Could he change? Could he escape if he did? He didn't know where he was, or where the exits were. He didn't dare change now - the wolf would be lost down here. He could always change later.

But Kevin had had that same option. For two weeks he'd had that option, as, presumably, had everyone else here. There must be a reason why they hadn't escaped. There were four of the guards, all armed with tasers and pistols. Would the bullets be silver? He suspected they might. They hadn't done anything yet. Maybe...

Before he could complete the thought, they passed through a door into what looked like a hospital room. It was as brightly lit as the rest of the place, but instead of the squalor this room positively gleamed. Machines with arms and tubes and blinking lights stood around the room, interspersed with half a dozen of what looked like operating tables, plus several more that were collapsed and pushed against one wall.

The whole place had a rushed together, half-setup feel to it. Kevin had said they'd only recently moved here. Could this be equipment they'd brought from a previous site and hadn't finished setting everything up yet?

They half led, half dragged him to a table and laid him on it. The metal was cold against his bare back. He had a moment of panic as they closed metal cuffs around his wrists, then ankles. For a minute, they seemed to be preparing something. Someone in a white coat checked a camera on a tripod before moving to a lower one on his other side and activating it.

"Subject nine-thirty-seven," the white-coated man spoke into a microphone clipped to the front of his white coat. "No current tattoos. Large scar on right shoulder." Where Kevin had originally bitten him. The one scar the wolf always left.

Okay, breathe, he reminded himself. The cuffs would snap right off if he changed, or the wolf paws would slide right through them.

The man moved the camera over next to Carl and manipulated it to where it was inches from his face, over his left eye.

"Keep your eye open, please, and look directly into the lens."

Carl closed his eyes.

The white-coated man - was he a doctor, Carl wondered - gestured to one of the black-clad armed men. "If you would?"

The man stepped up, placed one hand on Carl's forehead, holding him down and with the other roughly pried his eye open. The camera clicked several times, then the man let go and stepped back. Carl wanted to rub his sore eye, but his hand was still shackled to the table. If he changed now, there would be the doctor, or whatever he was, and the four armed assistants to deal with.

The man reached to a tray that Carl couldn't see and retrieved a metal rod, about two feet long, sharpened on one end. As he approached Carl, the assistants who'd brought him here each took a step back, their hands falling to tasers on their belts.

"Subject nine-thirty-seven," the man said again. "Test of regenerative property of eye tissue."

Wait... what?

Before Carl could react, the man stepped once more toward Carl, raised the metal rod and, without another word, plunged it into his left eye.

The shock and surprise masked the pain, but only for a second. The pain was excruciating and with barely a conscious thought, he changed.

HE FELT the cuff snap as he leapt off the table. There was a human directly in front of him. It was paralyzed in fear so he struck quickly, sinking his teeth into it before it could react. He brought it to the floor and tore and rent flesh. Half a second later, though, something hit him in the side and fire coursed through his body.

His muscles gave way. Something was wrong with his vision. There was something in his eye. He shook his head to try to get it out, but it held fast. Ignore it. Enemies nearby. His ears and nose worked fine. He could smell their fear. If he pounced, they should scatter. He struggled to get to his feet, but then the fire hit him again. Again, he tried to rise. Again, his muscles betrayed him as fire surged through his body. He howled in pain, and then his howls became whimpers. He felt something being placed around him, then he was being dragged. He hadn't the strength to resist. And then, blackness.

WHEN CARL WOKE UP, he was laying on his back on the concrete floor. Kevin was above him. He found he could see normally. He reached up to his eye. There was no pain. But he felt exhausted. And hungry.

Kevin helped him to the edge of his cot, where he sat with the thin blanket wrapped around him. It seemed even colder than before.

"Think we could ask them to turn up the heat in here?" he asked, trying to sound light-hearted. He was shocked by how weak his voice sounded.

Kevin looked like he'd been struck and fixed his gaze down on the floor. Carl wondered again what they had done to him.

"It's... " he began softly. "It's probably best not to ask for things," he said, with a wan smile and a quick sidelong glance at the stump of his wrist.

Carl lifted his hand back to his own eye. He closed the other one and found he could see, as well as before. It seemed intact, as if it had never been injured.

When he looked back to Kevin, he caught him quickly looking away.

He slowly looked back and met Carl's gaze.

"I'm sorry. I'm so, so sorry," he said. Carl was tired of hearing that. "Just... just tell them what they want. It won't be so bad if you just tell them what they want to know."

"But they didn't ask me anything," Carl replied.

"They will."

TWENTY-EIGHT
MANY MEETINGS

"Wow, you really are a dumbass, aren't you?" Jeans girl said.

He looked down at his legs. A series of cuts down the left leg were held together by a couple of stitches each. They looked like they might be infected. Was that possible? The cuts had been made with a silver knife. There was no trace on his right leg of a similar series that had been made with steel. After he had changed, then changed back, they had stitched up the cuts that hadn't healed, took more pictures, then dumped him back in his cell.

"If you just do what they say, they'd probably at least clean the wound first. Now you're probably going to lose your leg just because you keep antagonizing them."

"Oh, leave him alone," a man in another cell said. "I never bit anyone and they did the exact same thing to me."

"Why?" Carl asked him. He almost didn't recognize his own voice, it was so weak.

"They're trying to figure out how we heal," Jeans girl said. "They think they can cure cancer with it."

"Bullshit," said another prisoner. "They're just a bunch of sadistic assholes."

"Shows what you know," said the girl again. "Maybe if everyone cooperated with them, they could finish their work and let us go."

Carl looked to Kevin, who had been quiet throughout this conversation. In the old days, he'd have been the first to jump in with his theories. The old days. How long ago was that? Three days? Four? Ten? The lights in the underground room were on, brightly, all the time. The food arrived, what there was of it, at odd hours. Intentionally staggered, he'd guessed, and no way to tell whether it was supposed to be breakfast or dinner. Maybe the girl in the jeans knew something. She'd been here longer than he had, and she certainly seemed to not be suffering as much.

Twice, at least, he was pretty sure he'd bitten the black-uniformed guards. If he had, he didn't know what happened to them. Sometimes guards would disappear, and new ones show up. He didn't know if people quit or were being rotated through or were bitten by others.

Kevin had suggested that perhaps this wasn't the Alpha's doing at all, but that idea was discredited on his third - or was it fourth - visit to what he had come to think of as simply "the room." He had been strapped to the table and the net pulled over him. The net was made of heavy chain and attached to bolts set into the sides of the table. It was designed to hold down the wolf as well as the man. Once he was in position, he had an unexpected visitor.

"Hello, Mr. Jablonski," said a voice he couldn't quite place.

He turned his head to look and was surprised to see the Alpha himself.

"Wha... what?" He didn't expect him to be here.

"Do you know why you're here?" he asked.

"This is where they brought me," he responded. It's not like it was his idea.

Stumpp laughed. There was no mirth in it.

"Try again."

"This is where you take Were, when they... when they've broken the rules."

The Alpha looked disgusted at that. And somehow... sad? No, that couldn't be it. Carl half expected him to lash out. Maybe it would distract the men with the guns long enough to... to what? Escape? He still couldn't get out of the room. The words to the song he'd discussed with Toni on their first night together came into his mind. The hour of the wolf. *Dancing, dancing, dancing, under a full moon. It's the hour of the wolf and I'll be dying soon.*

"I want some information from you, Carl," the Alpha said. "We know you have a code word. A way of reaching your co-conspirator, Toni. Your friend Kim told us that much before she died. Oh yes," he said to what must have been Carl's startled look. "We have captured those you so foolishly sought to convert. Most of them eagerly came into the fold once we showed them we're not the laughable evil empire you made us out to be. Some of them were a little more stubborn and had to be dealt with. I'm afraid, though, that you are just about all that's left of your little group of rogues."

What about Kevin? They must have known he was involved... and there were others. Or were there? Could the ones he saw from his cell have been all that were left? If they captured any of his group, why weren't they here? Were they truly, as the Alpha claimed, all dead, or switched sides?

No. This is bullshit. There's no reason to believe any of this. Everything anyone here said can be considered a lie. That's the most important point to hold in his mind, he told himself. Everything they say is lies.

"What is the method you were to use to reach your girlfriend?"

"She's not my girlfriend," he almost replied out of reflex. But he kept silent. Give them nothing they don't demand. Don't believe their promises, don't believe their threats. If they were going to kill him, there was nothing he could say that would save his life.

"What is the signal?" Stumpp asked again. "Is it through Craigslist again? What is the code?"

Carl still didn't say anything. He was too scared to think of anything to say.

"When I was in Germany, at the end of the war, I was captured by Gregor," Stumpp said.

Carl didn't know what this had to do with anything, but at least nobody was hurting him or seeming to expect anything from him during it, so he kept silent.

"I would have made any deal with him to save the lives of my men. And I did. In the end, my entire platoon was released unharmed. I had no idea what the long term ramifications of my deal would be, but I took it and accepted the consequences. You, on the other hand, are no leader. I could tell that from the moment I met you. You haven't even asked about your people let alone tried to negotiate for their release. That's how I know that eventually you will tell us what we want to know. You can walk out of here now. Go anywhere you want. As long as you stay quiet, we're done with you. We're going to find her eventually. One of the others will tell us how, and then they will walk free while you suffer. It might as well be you who goes free. Nobody will ever know."

Thought you said they were all dead. He didn't say it out loud, though. He was expecting this. It was a lie. All promises, all threats, all deals. All lies. Once they had what they wanted, there'd be no reason to keep their word to him. Even if they did for some reason let him go free, he had no doubt he'd be found dead within days, either by an accident or by "suicide." Most likely they'd dispose of him here, before he ever left the building. His only hope was rescue, or escape. If Toni was the only one out there, she'd be his only hope for rescue. But she wouldn't come. How would she? What could she possibly do, even if she wanted to?

Escape was impossible. He'd tried to plan it since he got here. There had to be a way. Taking the deal would be signing his death warrant. *The grim reaper cuts, cuts, cuts, but he can't catch me.* There was a way, he had to find it.

"Bullshit," he murmured.

"Understand this is your final chance. When I leave here..."

"Bite me," he said, and chuckled quietly at the irony and the fact that he had cut off the Alpha.

"Very well," Stumpp said. "Eventually, you will talk. Your little rebellion is nothing. An annoyance, and an inconvenience, but in the end meaningless. We will deal with it as we have dealt with countless others, some far more clever. But your girlfriend killed Andrew, and that I will not forgive."

They thought Toni had killed Hudson? He forced himself to remain silent. The Alpha continued. "I'm leaving now. I won't be back. These men will get the information out of you. I've given them permission to do whatever they need to. Once we have her, you will be put down. There is no escape, no second chance, you will die, here, in this room, having accomplished nothing. Such a waste of life."

They hurt him then. A lot. Through the window of this room, he could see a clock on an office wall across the hall. He watched it as the second hand, then the minute hand, slowly crept across the face.

He lost track of how many times he'd changed. Sometimes

he'd wake up back in his cell, sometimes he'd wake up on the table, under the net.

He saw less and less of the white-coated men and more and more of the black-uniformed men.

He may have slept, briefly, from time to time, but he never felt rested. It was always too bright, and too cold, and the irregular meals he and Kevin were given were never enough.

He lay shivering in his cell. How many days had it been? He turned again to see Jeans Girl. Same jeans. Same blouse. Both the worse for wear.

"Is it worth it?" he asked her. "Just to keep one set of clothes, is it worth cooperating with everything they do? Telling them everything they want to know?"

"What are you talking about?" she asked.

But before he could answer, four men in black uniforms came and dragged him back to the room.

There, they hurt him. They cut him. They broke bones. He changed. He healed. They repeated the process. And over and over they asked him questions. "What's the signal? How many people did you convert? Where are they? How do you contact them?" And every time they asked about Toni, he would look at the clock and he would watch as the second hand made its way around and he would decide again, just 60 more seconds. I can last that long before I tell them. One more time around, then I'll speak.

Then he thought of her here, lying naked and broken on the table next to him and knowing that it was he who brought her here and he kept quiet. Not quite yet. Just one more minute, then she can't fault me.

Finally, one of the guards drew his pistol. They warned him not to change. They wanted to see how much he could heal without the wolf. If he changed, the man would pull the trigger on the silver bullet and he would die.

They forced him to say he understood. They hurt him until he finally said it out loud. Another concession, but not the big one. Not the one they really wanted.

They closed a vice over his shin and began tightening in. He could hear himself screaming in pain. The wolf was almost frantically beating at the edge of his consciousness now, demanding to be let in. He refused it, too. When they asked him again about Toni, he only whimpered in response. He screamed. He cried. He gasped for breath. But when they asked him to betray Toni, to once again be the cause of her suffering, he kept quiet. He knew he couldn't do so forever. Soon, he would tell them. He didn't even care if he lived after that, as long as the pain was stopped. He couldn't bear it anymore. He realized no matter what he said or did they were going to kill him eventually. It might as well be now. He thought of Toni and slipped into wolf form, knowing it would mean his death.

<hr />

THE FIRST PHONE call of the day was unexpected, and the results should have made him happy, but didn't. The second was even more unexpected.

The first was from Billings, informing Michael that the investigation into the shooting death of Elizabeth "Lily" Rowen had completed and it was found to be justified. With the force now accepting the existence of werewolves, they realized that the girl, though naked when they found her, had not necessarily been unarmed. Michael suspected that even so, the findings had less to do with the merits of the case, and more to do with political expediencies. They wanted him back at work and away from werewolf trials and, more importantly, the press.

It didn't help that his only close friend and confidant any

more was probably the most well-known journalist covering the werewolf story, and the trial.

Although the fact that the shooting actually had been self-defense may not have had anything to do with it, he had still accepted the findings. Not that he'd had any real choice. Back at work, he'd been reassigned back to homicide and ordered to stay away from anything werewolf-related. Alice's position as interim leader of the squad had been made permanent. He felt a little sorry for her. She'd achieved her position purely through her own merit, but it would look political. They'd removed the man who shot a werewolf and replaced him with a woman of color. It was an achievement and a well-deserved promotion, and it would be forever tainted by the situation. Politics ruins everything.

He couldn't say he approved of her way of doing things, especially her decision to work with Holy Mountain Research. He also couldn't say for sure that he wouldn't have made the same decision himself, if he didn't know everything he knew now. He hated not being able to trust her. But he couldn't. Not anymore. She may not have known everything they were up to, but she had willingly gone around the law to cooperate with them. Even more, and he hated to think it, but experience had taught him to evaluate all possibilities, no matter how distasteful, she almost certainly tipped her friends off before the raid.

Which is why, when he got the second unexpected phone call of the day, he agreed to meet Toni himself instead of immediately referring her to Alice.

"Thank you for coming alone this time," she said.

"What makes you think I did?" he asked. He hadn't seen anyone since he entered the forest and hiked down the path she'd told him to, but it would have been easy for them to hide, especially in wolf form. He hadn't brought anyone with him, that was true, but that didn't mean there wouldn't be witnesses.

Aaron had set him up with a small camera, hidden in his lapel, and a transmitter. He'd given the access info to Veer as well, so the two of them were watching and recording everything that went on.

If anything happened to him, at least somebody would know what. This woman was part of an organization that had killed a cop. He shouldn't be here. He shouldn't be talking to her. He should have called it in the second he knew where she was hiding. The entire forest should be crawling with SWAT and FBI and Homeland Security by now. But last time he had played it by the book and two people had died and three cops had disappeared. Despite Alice's assertion that werewolves could be treated like any other organized crime group, he didn't believe it. It was too new. There were too many important differences, and he had no way of navigating them by the book.

"We've been watching you since you entered the woods," Toni said.

"So, you didn't come alone?" he asked.

"Never said I would," she replied. "And after your botched ambush at the Pied Cow, you don't get to complain about that."

"That wasn't supposed to be an ambush,"

"Uh huh. You lured Carl to supposedly neutral ground, then tried to arrest him. How'd you think that was gonna go?"

"I thought he would come peacefully," Michael replied. "We didn't know there were a bunch of you waiting to attack us."

"We weren't attacking you; we were just trying to get Carl away."

"Three wounded and two dead seemed an awful lot like an attack to me," he retorted.

"And you killed Lily," Toni cried out. She was clearly holding back tears. He thought of the girl he'd shot, lying in the garden dead, an almost pleading look frozen on her face.

He was silent for a moment, then he spoke softly, looking her in the eye. "Is that why you brought me here? Revenge?" he said it quietly, but realized it was a real possibility. He scanned the nearby forest. He didn't see any wolves, but he knew they must be nearby, hidden in the underbrush, or possibly waiting up in the trees or behind the berms in human form.

The girl looked like she'd been struck. "Is that what you think of us?" she asked, her sadness turned quickly to anger. She was trying hard to stay calm and in control but in that moment he realized just how young she really was.

"I don't know you, or anything about you," he said. "I know that you and Jablonski weren't involved in the attack on the square," he added. It was an olive branch. She took it.

"We didn't want to hurt anyone at the Pied Cow, either. And we didn't bring you here to harm you. No matter what happens tonight, as long as you don't attack anyone, you walk free."

That was unexpected. "Then, what did you bring me here for?"

"I need your help," she said.

"You... what? How?"

"You're testifying against Victor Stumpp, right?"

"I was involved in the trial, yes."

"I got some information about one of his facilities that the police might want to know."

"What is it?"

"I found the place where the Alphas take captured wolves."

Holy Mountain Research.

"In Hillsboro?" he asked.

"Yeah," she said, suddenly alert. She took a step backward but didn't take her eyes off him. "You know of it already." It was an accusation.

"We raided it almost two weeks ago," he said, and noticed

her confusion at the revelation. "We didn't find anything. Whatever was there, it's shut down."

"Well, either you didn't look very hard, or they re-opened," she said. "Because they took one of my people there four days ago."

Four days? That would mean...

"Holy Mountain Research?" he asked. "On Evergreen?"

"That's not the name on the building," she said. "And it's on Brookwood, near the airport."

The second site. He had found references in Veer's documents to another site, but had assumed it was in Chicago, where Veer told him the home office was. Probably owned by a holding company, untraceable to them, they'd set it up in case someone looked into their activities. They'd probably been planning on moving to it for a while, and then had to move their timetable up when Veer got caught checking into them. So, they'd already begun the move before they were tipped off. Then Alice might not have told them after all.

"And you have evidence Stumpp's involved?" He asked her.

"Who else? It had to be either him or the cops that took Carl. And if you had him, you'd be trotting him out all over the place, announcing your so-called Great Success in capturing The Leader of the Werewolf Terrorists." He could hear the bitter capital letters as she said it.

"Can you show me where it is?" he asked her.

"Yes. Gimme your phone." He unlocked it and handed it to her, and she opened the map and zoomed in on a warehouse close to the airport. One of just a few surrounded by a large parking lot, and a creek blocking access to the back. Perfect. He held it up and read the address out loud, for the benefit of those watching through his camera.

"How did you find the place?" he asked her.

"After Carl disappeared, we were all looking for him. One

of..." She hesitated a moment, then continued, "One of our other cells found an ad - we have a secret way to communicate. Someone hacked it. The other cell found out, did the same thing in reverse, and when their guy got stuffed into a white van, they followed it. Unfortunately, they got snatched and their phones destroyed before they got close enough to report anything. They didn't know what to do after that, so their leader came to me, and I came to you."

The casual manner in which she said it startled him. Her eyes belied the calmness of her words. Her demeanor was also for the benefit of unseen watchers. This girl's been through a lot since I saw her last.

"They captured them? Are they holding them as well, then?"

"Gods, I hope so."

"Thank you. I'll see what I can do from here."

"Not good enough. Can't you just send in a swat team or something? They didn't do anything wrong."

It took guts for her to come to him for help. He wished he could help her.

"I'm afraid it's not quite that simple. For one, I'm not on the werewolf squad anymore. I've been expressly forbidden to have anything to do with werewolves. I'm here against orders."

"Yeah? Then who's on the other end of your camera?"

She'd spotted it and hadn't said anything until now. Young as she was, she'd be a formidable opponent. It was a good thing he wasn't planning to double cross her. He'd have to be careful not to give her the wrong impression, or make the mistakes he'd made with her boyfriend.

"The one guy from the station I know I can trust," he answered her, hoping it was true. "Let's all rendezvous back at my place and come up with a plan." He had a couple of ideas, but he didn't like them. "If they nabbed your people just doing surveillance, they're being careful and watching the area closely. There's nothing I can do on my own, but we should be able to come up with something."

"My car's back at my apartment," she said. "Unless you've impounded it already."

"Not as far as I know," he said. "But mine's just back at the trailhead."

"Okay," she said. "We'll take yours, but I'm driving."

"I'd rather."

"I don't care. I'm guessing you want this place almost as much as I do, but I still can't trust you."

"What do you think I'm going to do?" he asked, frustrated.

"I don't know what you're going to do." she replied. "That's the whole point. If I'm driving, I have more options. Worst case scenario, I floor it, swerve into oncoming traffic and dive out in wolf form."

"Fuck. And you think I'm gonna let you drive now?"

"Definitely," she said. "So don't do anything stupid and I won't."

He wasn't sure what to say to that.

"Look, I recognize your position here, too," she continued. "But of the two of us, so far only one has set up an ambush and killed the other's friend."

"You're not the only one who lost someone that day."

She looked away at that, then spoke a little softer. "I'm sorry. Does it mean anything that we didn't know Kevin and Shelly's group were going to be there, too?"

"Maybe," he said. "Was it one of them who actually killed Detective Boyd?"

"I think so," she said, looking at the ground.

"But you're not sure," he said. It wasn't a question.

"No," she admitted. She looked up and met his eyes. "Everyone claims they didn't, but there's no way to know for sure. Even if nobody's lying, it's possible they may not actually know."

That sounded honest, at least. He realized the implication: she had asked about it. Lauren's death was at least important enough to her to check into. He decided to extend a token of trust. When they got to his car, he tossed her the keys. "Please don't swerve into oncoming traffic. You'll probably kill innocent people in addition to me."

She nodded at that. Holy crap, she was actually thinking of the alternatives, he realized. Buildings, maybe the river? Perhaps charging into the MAX?

"If it comes to a fight, how many people do you have who'd help?" he asked her on the way. Using these kids to fight their way in was his least favorite idea. Unfortunately, he didn't have a most favorite.

It was a lot of information to give away, but she answered, "A dozen at least. Maybe as many as thirty. Not more than that." He realized she had the answer ready. She'd already thought this over.

While she drove, he kept an eye out for her friends. They were surprisingly easy to spot. One person driving, the other looking down at her phone. These were not experienced professionals, just a bunch of kids playing at being revolutionaries, in way over their heads.

But Phil was in that place, and they wanted to help get him out. He realized he had to decide soon how much he was going to use these kids. How much danger could he put them in, and how many of their lives was he actually willing to risk? The time to consider such things was now, because once things started happening it would be too late.

CARL WAS surprised when he woke up in his cell. It was the same thing Kevin said they'd done to him. Get him to accept death, see its inevitability, then snatch it away. This time.

When Kevin saw that he'd opened his eyes, he got up from his cot and helped Carl to his own. Carl pulled his blanket up and around him and realized how gaunt he'd become. He was so hungry. This is also what they did to Kevin. The wolf needs energy. You couldn't starve it.

It looked like they'd been mostly leaving Kevin alone since his arrival, though. He looked down. All the damage they had done to him was fully healed. He wasn't sure he was comforted by the fact. It just meant that there was worse to come. He looked around at the occupants in the other cells. Some were looking curiously at him, but none would meet his gaze. He was a warning to them, too: Any one of you could have it worse.

"Thank you," he said weakly to Kevin before curling up on his bed and trying to sleep.

He couldn't tell if he had, or for how long. He was so hungry. He wished they would at least turn the light off or turn up the heat. The blanket was too thin to block either the light or the cold.

He heard footsteps as the usual four guards approached their cell. Already?

"Hey!" Kevin called out to them. "Shouldn't we get fed? You haven't given us anything to eat since yesterday!"

When was it yesterday?

The guard laughed. "Oh, we got plans for that," he said. "Just waiting for confirmation." They continued on their patrol, banging on the bars of the cages of anyone sleeping, occasionally stopping to make rude comments to some of the other prisoners.

Half an hour later, they were back, another white-coated

man in tow. He set up a tripod he'd been carrying while the guards talked.

"You know, we've got security cameras all over, doc," one of the black-uniformed guards said.

"Yes," the man in white replied. "But I wanted footage I could count on, and from this level. If we must continue with this barbarism we might as well derive some scientific merit from it."

"Fine. Ready, then?"

"Go ahead."

"Funny you should mention food," the man said to Kevin, with a cruel smile, "See, we're not gonna bring you any."

"You can't just let us starve!" Kevin cried, clutching the blanket around him as he struggled to rise to his feet.

"Ah, we're not going to do that, either." The man shifted his attention to Carl. "Turns out, we don't really need your friend here." He pulled his gun and aimed it at Kevin. Carl knew it would be loaded with silver bullets. "We just needed him to get to you."

Kevin's eyes grew wide.

"So, there's your food source."

Carl, disgusted, stepped away toward the back of the small cell.

"What? You don't want it?" Kevin looked in panic toward Carl, then dropped his eyes when he saw he'd backed away. Had he actually thought Carl was going to...?

"No?" the man with the gun asked. "Well, here, I'll make it easy for you. But hurry, because I'm using silver bullets." At that, he fired, twice in rapid succession into Kevin's midsection.

Kevin, stunned by the impact, fell to the floor, clasping the wound, unable to stop the flow of blood around his fingers.

"There you go. Eat up before it gets cold."

Carl just stood, staring. Frozen in shock.

He looked from Kevin's frightened pleading and saw the scientist staring in equal horror and disgust. So, he wasn't happy with what these men were doing. But he wasn't doing anything to stop it. "I was just there. I wasn't the one who killed him."

"No?"

Kevin had changed. Where the man had lain, there was now a wolf, still bleeding and howling in pain.

"Well, maybe he'll eat you. This should be interesting." The wolf didn't react to his words, it just thrashed and howled, unable to understand why the injury wasn't healing.

A few seconds later, the wolf turned back into Kevin. He pressed against the wound with one hand, trying to stop the bleeding. Carl went to him then, tearing a strip off his blanket as he approached.

"Stay away from him!" the gunman shouted angrily. Carl ignored him. Either he would kill him, or he wouldn't. There was nothing he could do about it either way.

Wishing he'd learned more first aid when he'd had the chance, he pressed the strip of dirty blanket against the wound. Kevin whimpered in pain but didn't stop him.

"Very well, I was going to tell you this later," he was dimly aware of the guard saying, "But we only kept you alive to get to the girl. Fortunately, one of your friends already turned her in."

Carl snapped his head up at that, half expecting Toni to be marched into the cell then and there.

The guard snapped a fresh clip into his gun and raised it again. "And now that Stumpp has her, we don't need you anymore either." Carl realized the implications of that.

"No telling what he's doing to her right now, but I can imagine. He seemed pretty pissed off. Something for you to think about as you die, I suppose."

Carl heard two distinct reports from the weapon. Something knocked him backwards, and he fell as if in slow motion. He looked down and saw a pool of blood already pouring from his abdomen and drenching his fingers.

The wolf was coming upon him. He tried to push it away. Silver, he told it. You can't help. But it was too strong, he was too weak, and it didn't listen.

VEER'S MOTORCYCLE was parked in his driveway when they arrived, and she was waiting by the front door.

"Veer, Toni," Michael introduced them as they entered the house.

"I take it you were watching, too?" Toni asked her immediately.

When Veer nodded, Toni turned to Michael. "How many others?" she demanded.

"Just the two of them," he replied. He had to fight against his instincts to tell her not to worry about it, it wasn't her business, and let her know who was in charge here.

"Two of us?" Veer asked. "Who else?"

At that, Toni laughed out loud. Veer smiled back, as if they'd caught him at something.

"Aaron," Michael told her. He didn't bother to explain to Toni who that was.

"How many of your people were following us?" he asked her.

"A few. The two you saw and two other cars."

The two he saw. He had deliberately not mentioned seeing anybody.

"I got a text from Aaron on the way over here," he changed

the subject, as much to hide his embarrassment as anything else. "He'll meet us in a couple of hours."

"Long enough to get your anti-werewolf squad into place?" Toni asked, obviously suspicious.

"I trust Aaron," he said.

"You trusted Johansen, too," Veer replied.

He felt attacked from both sides now. At least he had an answer to that one.

"We still don't know if she was the one who..." he started.

Veer cut him off. "We know she's working with them."

"There's a huge difference between working with someone, even off the record, and sabotaging a police investigation."

"And can you be sure she hasn't crossed that line?"

"This is pointless," he said. "It doesn't matter because Alice isn't here. And whatever we decide to do, we're not going to tell her about it until it's too late to stop us."

"What to do is easy," Toni said. "Go in there. Get everybody out. Shut the place down."

"I'm afraid it's not that easy."

"Because you're not on the werewolf squad anymore?"

"Right."

"So, you're the cops, but you can't help me because you're not supposed to do anything with werewolves. And I can't go to the one who can deal with werewolves because she's in their pocket." She took a deep breath. "Okay, nobody said this would be easy. If you can't help me, I'm just wasting your time. Thanks anyway," she started heading toward the door.

"Wait!" Michael cried out after her. He caught Veer's look of encouragement and continued, "I didn't say I couldn't do anything, but we can't just rush in there guns blazing. Let's wait to hear what Aaron has to say."

"And what could he possibly say that will be of use?"

"I don't know yet. That's why I want to wait for him," he

was growing impatient. It had been two weeks, would another hour or two really make that much difference?

"He's gathering information on this Holy Mountain place?"

"Yes. I believe so."

"You're not even sure. Even if he does find anything, what's the chance of him bringing it to you instead of what's her nuts?"

"He'll be here."

"Because you trust him."

"Yes."

"I can't. There's too much riding on it. You have my number, right? It should still be good for another day or two. Gimme a call if he shows up. Assuming he doesn't have a SWAT team with him when he does."

She peeked through the door before opening it.

"Wait... where are you going? If you just wait to see what Aaron has found, I'll give you a ride back to wherever you want to go."

"Don't need it," she said as she stepped out the door. He followed her and stopped in the open doorway. A small green sedan pulled to a stop at the end of his driveway. She climbed into the back seat and gave him a friendly wave as it sped off. Michael unfortunately couldn't get a good look at the two people in the front seat, or the license number.

Something disturbed him about letting a terrorist leader simply get in a car and drive away, but he didn't see any other choice.

"Well, another triumph of diplomacy there," he said, turning away from the window.

"You got an address, didn't you?" Veer said.

"Yeah," he replied. "Which I assume Aaron is checking out now." He showed her the text from Aaron. "That's all I got. But he was watching the same transmission you were."

"They were waiting out there, and knew when she was ready to leave," he said.

"Looks like you weren't the only one transmitting," she replied.

"Yeah, and that car wasn't the one following us."

"She said there were a few," Veer reminded him.

"True, and they could have been each following the one in front, though that's harder to do successfully."

"Or tuned in to her phone's gps," Veer said.

"How would they get the signal? I have to jump through a dozen hoops to get that info."

"There's apps," she replied. "If the phone owner cooperates, it's just a matter of sharing the data. Hell, a lot of phones come with it already included, for theft or loss."

"Huh. Kids these days," he said with a smile. Still, the level of forethought and competence was something. He was impressed. "God, she's worse than you," he told her. "Nothing to do now but wait. You gonna stick around?"

"Yeah, I'll wait for Aaron. But if I see any hint he's trying to pull anything, I'm leaping out your back window."

"If he is, I might follow you," he said as he got up to start a pot of coffee. He hoped it wouldn't come to that. Unlike Alice, he had known Aaron ever since he'd arrived in Portland. If the consequences were not severe, Aaron would most likely choose personal loyalty where he could satisfy his own curiosity over merely following protocol. He hoped.

***

FOR AN HOUR AND A HALF, they waited, drinking their coffee and talking about everything other than werewolves and police. It was nice.

But hanging over them was the specter of what would

happen when Aaron arrived. Once he finally did, Michael was relieved to see Veer's and Toni's fears unfounded. He'd come alone.

"It's definitely the place," he said. "Black helicopter and everything."

"You didn't have any problems getting close?" Michael asked. Perhaps he had overestimated Toni.

"I didn't say that," Aaron said with a smile. "They had some pretty good security around the place. I saw a few cameras which I believe to be theirs. Though with the other businesses nearby, not to mention the airport, it's impossible to be sure. Pretty sure the license plate scanner was theirs, though."

"License plate scanner?" Veer asked him.

"Yeah, you know those trailers you sometimes see alongside the road with the display, 'The posted speed limit is thirty miles per hour and you're going forty-five?'"

"Yeah..." she asked hesitantly.

"We use them when we're looking for specific cars or trying to track somebody. It scans the license plate of every vehicle that drives by, and pings someone - usually sends a message with a photo attached - if it gets a hit."

"And civilians can have those?"

"Not generally, no, but it is possible with the proper access, which a military contractor would almost certainly have."

"How'd you manage to get close enough to see anything?" Michael asked.

"That's part of what took so long. I had a kid I know do a flyover with his drone."

"Don't the police have drones you could use?" Veer asked him.

"That'd require Alice authorizing it," he said.

"And you can fly that close to the airport?"

"Technically no," Aaron answered her. "But he did anyway.

Homebuilt, so it didn't have any of the fancy you-can't-fly-here software, and he took off the registration sticker before flying, which turned out to be a good idea."

"Why? What happened?"

"They shot it down."

"With what?" Veer asked.

Aaron beamed, as if it had been the right question. "RFI gun, apparently."

Veer whistled in response.

"Okay, why is that important here?" Michael asked. He was used to Aaron and wasn't surprised that Veer knew something about the field as well.

"An RFI device focuses, basically, a high-intensity burst of radio static at the drone. The drone needs the GPS signal and the input from the remote controller to know where to go, so the RF burst blocks both of those things. When it can't get it, it crashes."

"Some of the more sophisticated ones will land gracefully or start flying in a pattern searching for a signal, or even use dead reckoning to return home," Veer added.

"Yeah, this one didn't do that, it just went straight down. I had to pay the kid off - so someone owes me two hundred dollars."

"Okay, but why does it matter how it was shot down?" Michael asked.

"A device like that is specialized equipment," Aaron replied. "It's really only good for shooting down drones. Which means they were prepared for exactly that. It speaks to a well-funded paramilitary outfit."

"I'm kinda surprised the police don't have one, though," Veer said.

"Maybe they do. But I'd be the wrong department to be using it."

"The important thing is, it indicates we got our guys. How many groups like that can there be in Hillsboro?"

"I agree. I take it you couldn't get the drone back, then?"

"No, they beat us to it, and I didn't want to tangle with them on my own."

"Damn. If we had that video..."

"That I have," Aaron responded, and pulled a small laptop out of his bag. He opened it up and turned it on. "I could show you on the big screen if Michael here wasn't stuck in the 20th century."

"Not everything has to be wireless," Michael said. At that, he got up, crossed over the room and unplugged the video cable from the DVD player and handed the end to Aaron. "Will this work?"

Aaron plugged it into the laptop and began explaining as it was booting. "The drone was broadcasting the video signal the whole time. That's how you fly it, so we recorded off that signal - he already had that all set up, to record his races."

Once it was up, he started the video. Michael set down his coffee and leaned forward. He watched from the drone's perspective as it started on the ground and he could hear the propellers spin up. It rose straight up into the air, then hovered for a second before turning in place. For a moment it showed Aaron standing next to a young man, probably early 20s, seated in a folding chair with a radio remote in his hands and wearing what looked like a VR headset with an antenna. On the screen, Aaron waved.

After pausing on them for a few seconds, the drone turned away, rose even higher, and began heading over rural roads, with dense swaths of trees on either side. It passed over a small river - Dawson Creek, Michael guessed, he'd seen it marked on the map when Toni was showing him the location. Then, after another line of trees, a pair of buildings surrounded by a larger parking lot came into view.

The drone decreased its height as it got closer to the buildings. It looked like one was a small warehouse, with a few loading docks along one side. The other building may have held offices. There was a clearly marked helipad on the top of the warehouse, occupied by what looked like the same helicopter Michael had seen on Skyline. As the drone approached, they saw a figure on the roof. It emerged, peered up at the drone for a moment, then ran inside.

The drone dipped again, showing the sides of the building, then the front door, and swung around by the loading bays.

The signal turned to static. When it came back on, the drone was spinning out of control. It smashed into the ground, rolled a few times, then lay still, upside-down.

"Ouch," Michael said. "I guess that's where they hit it with the gun?"

"Yep."

"Okay, well, that certainly seems..."

"Hold on, the best part's coming up."

A minute later, two men walked into view. One leaned over toward it. His hand filled the camera as he lifted it. For just a couple of seconds there was a perfectly clear right-side-up picture of both of them, then he seemed to jerk something loose and the image went dark. Aaron backed the video up to the image of the two men and paused it there.

"Look familiar?" he asked.

"That's them. Definitely the same uniform, and I'm pretty sure the guy in the back was in the basement when I was there. This is them." Veer said.

"Excellent!" Aaron said. "Positive witness ID, that'll do for a warrant."

"What's the plan?" Veer asked. "How do we do this without them knowing we're coming?"

Michael knew what she was asking. Without telling Alice ahead of time. But the question was valid. He quickly filled Aaron in on his fears about her. He had obviously suspected something like this already, as he quickly accepted it and moved on.

"Let me ask Alice first, though. If she doesn't want to move in, or denies even having information, then I can back you up. We'll go to Billings and get a warrant for a SWAT raid, without letting her know first."

"And now that we know something about the layout and capabilities, we can plan it."

"Yeah, Charleston will have his own ideas, but I'd recommend going in hard, loud, from the front door. We should probably have a helicopter, too, if for nothing else to keep theirs from taking off if it's there or landing if it's not."

"So, charge in guns blazing," Veer said with a smile.

Michael laughed at that, while Aaron looked perplexed for a moment, then just shook his head.

"You planning on calling Toni, then?" Veer asked him. He was pretty sure she already knew the answer.

"Not a chance. She'd be too much of an unknown variable. I don't want her anywhere near the place. I'd prefer no civilians at all know about it until it's all well over."

THE WOLF SNARLED, whimpered, and struggled to his feet. After a few seconds, the intense pain began to subside. Somewhere in the back of his mind, there was surprise at that, and anger. In front of him a human lay bleeding and moaning. The hunger almost overcame him, but more humans, threats to him, were past that one. He turned at the last second and leapt forward. His jaws closed on a wrist, which pulled back. He held tight, even when his face slammed into the metal bars. He tried to push forward while still holding the wrist. The bars held fast. There was more screaming. Eventually the human wrist gave way, the wolf's teeth slid across bone, and dug in. He shook it, trying to pull it through the bars. He fell back down as a string of fire hit him.

When it had stopped, he was still too weak to go after them. He could barely stand. The humans were still a threat. One was wounded, and others smelled strongly of anger and fear. He was awash in it, coming from all around him. He couldn't reach through to get to them, but they could still hurt him. There was no escape, nowhere he could run to or hide. And he was too weak. He had to eat or he would die here.

Although something told him not to, he stepped carefully forward to take a bite of the only food available. The scent of fear emanating from it washed over him. He ignored it and the whimpers of pain as he began to eat. He ignored the voice somewhere in the back of his mind screaming at him over and over to stop, stop, STOP!

He continued to eat even after he'd had enough, storing energy for the future, pausing only to snarl or snap at any humans who approached or seemed to be growing less afraid.

When he had had his fill, he turned his attention to the humans. They backed up when he approached the edge of the cage. He paced the perimeter, seeking a way through. They weren't taking any action against him right now but were beginning to leave. He lay down, watching them warily as they did. When only two were left, showing no sign of either leaving or doing anything to him, he closed his eyes to sleep.

TWENTY-NINE
ALLIANCES AND BETRAYALS

Gordon didn't expect to see her again after the disaster at the coffee shop, and certainly not outside his office.

"What are you doing here?" he asked her in a hushed voice.

"C'mon," she said. "My car's around the corner."

"Look, I'm sorry about what happened. I had no idea things would go down that way."

"I know," she responded. "I just saw Detective Diaz. I'm not out for revenge, I need your help. If you don't want to help, you can get right back out."

He was intrigued enough to follow.

"Aren't you wanted by the police?" he asked her as soon as he'd climbed into the passenger seat of her car.

"Among others," she said. "That's why I have to be careful."

"Well, great disguise then," he said, indicating the hoodie she'd been wearing. "That's not suspicious at all."

"I'm not worried about being suspicious," she said. "I'm worried about being recognized. Lots of suspicious people around."

He conceded the point with a laugh. Then he realized

what she'd said. "Among others? Who else other than the police is after you?"

"The Alphas to start with."

"Stumpp? Why would he still be after you? The secret's out. Weren't all those recent testimonials in the papers from your group? And Stumpp's on trial - there's no way they could cover anything up now."

"Looks like they're trying anyway. They've already caught Carl and two others. We want to break them out."

"Sounds like working with the police would be the right thing to do, then. Look, I can talk to Diaz on your behalf..."

"Because that worked so well last time?"

"I'm sorry about that, I really am, but let me try to..."

"Besides, I already talked to him. Bygones and all that shit, but he can't help me now. He's not allowed to deal with wolves anymore and his replacement is working with the Alpha."

"Diaz is out?"

"Turns out, you shoot an unarmed nineteen year old white girl in Portland, you get reassigned," she said. He recognized the anger in her voice, held strongly in check.

"What do you mean his replacement is working with them? Openly?"

"Not openly, but close enough that even Diaz doesn't trust her."

"Okay, so what can I do to help you?" he asked.

"Come out with me and help us come up with a plan."

"Out where? And who's us?"

"'Us' is the Order of the Wolf - all those people you met at the warehouse, plus some that've joined since then. 'Where' is our secret base."

"What do you need me for?"

"Because there's a bunch of people who I don't know that I'm getting together. I'm no leader. I need someone with some respectability backing me up." She was almost pleading when she said it. Carl was a kidnap victim. The police should handle this. Except they may be colluding with his kidnappers. The same organization that had tried to kill him after he'd been turned into... into the same thing she'd been turned into. Neither of them had had a choice in the matter. And of all the people she might have turned to, she came to him. He couldn't just abandon her.

"All right. Let's go," he said out loud.

SHE PARKED at a wide spot in the road up hill in northwest Portland.

"You're hiding in Forest Park?" he asked when he saw their destination.

"Yeah. You can't get any further than this by car, and it's not that busy this time of year. We post lookouts so we can see anybody coming, and we can all easily fade out and hide in the park if we need to. It's the safest place for us I can think of right now."

They hiked maybe half a mile before leaving the trail, and another mile after that, along animal trails deeper into the forest, until they came to a large clearing.

"Welcome to Echo Base," Toni said, indicating the scene in front of them.

Several people were about, on a collection of folding chairs, blankets on the ground, and even a few canopies set up around the place. One of which sheltered a large folding table, with a few people gathered around it.

That was where they headed.

"This is Gordon," she told them. "He's going to help us." He recognized Kim, the young woman he'd first seen at the Pied

Cow, when she met Carl and Toni for the first time. He gave her a nod in greeting, which she returned.

Another man he recognized from the warehouse, Tyler something, approached the table. "These are all of our people who would come, Ethan, Loren with an O, and Tiffany with a bunch of Y's." Gordon wondered how that would be spelled. Tyffyny?

On the table was a rolled out vinyl mat that somebody had drawn a crude map on with overhead projector pens, a few of which were still scattered around it. It showed a couple of squares, buildings he assumed, surrounded by what might have been a bunch of trees, roads, and a stream.

"Sorry, that's the best we could get from Google Maps," one of the women told him. "At least we know where the loading docks and the entrances are." She indicated them on the map.

While they were looking at it, three more approached. "This is Nancy and Fred," the girl in front said. "They're from Kevin's group."

"Any news?" Toni asked them.

"Haven't heard from him since before Thanksgiving," Nancy said. Her companion nodded his agreement.

"Welcome aboard. Fill them in," she told the woman who'd made the introductions, "and I'll talk to them in a bit."

Gordon looked around the camp. These kids looked like they were getting ready to fight. Except they had no idea how. The place was full of fear and resolute looks. They were all looking to Toni to tell them what to do.

And she was looking to him.

They didn't look like terrorists. They looked like scared kids. Then again, what were most terrorists? Every one of these people was a werewolf, he reminded himself. An illegal werewolf, like he was. Unlike him, most of them had chosen to become what they were.

Another girl he recognized from the warehouse, Carrie, approached with a phone in her hand. She set it on the table. "Aaron's back. They got drone footage of the place and are talking about it now."

He recognized Diaz's voice over the phone.

"You bugged them?" he asked.

"Stuck a phone under his couch while I was there," she said. "I had to know what they were planning."

"Ha! I knew it!" Carrie said when they mentioned the license plate scanners. "Those bastards!"

Gordon shouldn't be here. This wasn't his place, with all these young people, breaking the law, clandestinely listening in on police plotting to... go around the law themselves?

He was relieved when he heard the two cops decide to get a warrant to raid the Holy Mountain site.

"So that's that. They're going in after all."

Toni looked skeptical. Nobody else around the table seemed to quite believe it either. Did they really not trust the cops could pull it off, or were they just disappointed that they didn't get to be the heroes? Their grand adventure just got canceled.

"What if they get tipped off again?" Toni asked.

He thought about it for a second. It sounded like they were taking steps to ensure that didn't happen. Of course, if this Aaron guy was the leak instead of Alice, they'd just fed him all the information again.

"If it's a huge operation, it'll take a while. It won't be just the people, but they'll have to move equipment, records, anything that can't be re-purposed or destroyed," he said.

"Right," Toni said. "Are you thinking we could get them while they're being moved?"

"That'd be when they're most vulnerable. It'll be slow and obvious. Do you have anyone with eyes on the building?"

"Couldn't," she told him. "Anyone who gets anywhere near the building gets snatched."

"How do they do that?"

"We don't know. After Karen disappeared, we stopped sending people."

"Why didn't you live stream?"

"Didn't think of it at the time, and now it's too dangerous."

Fair enough. He was surprised they sent a second after the first one disappeared. "What about a telescope from somewhere? Any high ground nearby? Can you see the place from the airport?"

Another one of her people pulled out a tablet and set it on the table. They zoomed in on the facility, and tried to find a spot of high ground, or a tall building that might be accessible.

"The library?" She pointed it out. "Maybe somebody could get to the roof?"

"It's a little far, isn't it?" Carrie asked.

"They don't need to see much - just if a large number of trucks suddenly show up. It would be nice to know what their normal traffic patterns are."

"Damn," Toni said. "We should have had somebody there from the beginning."

"Doesn't matter now. Hopefully it'll never matter. If they don't move them before the cops get there, then the police can extract Carl and the rest of the prisoners and we're all good, right?"

"Unless the police try to arrest him again."

"Look, if he didn't do anything wrong, then letting them do so should be safe. It's what you want, right? Protection of human law? Dealing with the police is part of it." He didn't think it was a good time to get into all the innocent people who get held for years or decades, or just outright killed for not following orders fast enough during a police raid. She was probably just as aware of that as he was. He was still convinced that justice was served far more often than not.

"Maybe," she said. "But I still want to be nearby if they raid the place, just to make sure."

"Interfering with police doing what they want to do could be the best way to get more people killed."

"We'll be careful not to do that, then."

He wasn't sure what she'd hoped to accomplish, but she was going to do whatever she was going to do. He just had to decide whether to help or simply to try not to get caught between her and whatever happened.

"THAT'S A PRETTY strong accusation you're making, Detective," Captain Billings told him when he'd made his request.

"I know," Michael answered. "And I have no proof, which is why I'm not suggesting anything other than letting me do this raid."

"Oh that's 'all' is it? Werewolves are her department. Hell, you recommended her for the position! How would it look if I took it away from her now?"

"I'm not asking you to..." he began.

"Yes, you are," Billings cut him off. "That's exactly what you're asking."

Michael took a deep breath. "Maybe you're right, but Phil's in there, along with at least three cops and an untold number of civilians."

"It's true we don't have hard proof," Aaron continued for him. "But Alice was in a position to inform them of the last raid. They're torturing people in there, including four cops under your command. We're not saying she's complicit in it, but she's unwilling to do anything about it either, or even review the evidence. She's had the same documents we just showed you."

"Documents which Holy Mountain claims are fake."

"They're not. I've seen the originals," Michael said.

"The existence of originals doesn't prove they're not fake," his captain responded. "We've already raided them based on those documents and could find no corroborating evidence. I don't see how I can justify a second raid."

"We have more information now. A separate source has seen them abduct people, and has given us the location where they've taken them."

"And who is this new source?"

Aaron looked uncomfortably toward Michael.

"It's... um..." Michael started.

"Tell me!" Billings growled.

"It's Toni Briggs."

Billings regarded him silently for a moment. Finally, he said quietly in a very even tone, "You've been in communication with Toni Briggs? Do you have any idea what kind of shitstorm that could cause?"

"Yes," Michael answered. "Which is why I didn't want to say anything."

Again, Billings was silent for a long moment.

"Say you did raid them. Can you guarantee we'll find Phil? Or any other prisoners?"

"Yes," Michael answered at the same time Aaron said "No."

Billings' look was halfway between angry and amused.

"Yes," Michael insisted. "At the very least, two people from Briggs' group were taken and are still there. Jablonski was taken there as well. We can't know for sure that our people were taken to the same facility or somewhere else, but it's a good guess that if they're not there, we can get anyone arrested in the raid to tell us where they are."

Billings thought about it for just a moment. "It could have been anybody..." he began.

Michael interrupted him, "No, there's only..."

"It could have been anybody," Billings spoke loudly over him, "And therefore the second raid will have to happen on the QT, without alerting anyone on her team, because we don't know who the leak is."

He got it. Same effect, but less politically volatile.

"Give me twenty-four hours to put it together. We've gotta coordinate with the Hillsboro PD, arrange a SWAT team, and alert the FBI. And I guess Homeland Security will want to feel involved. And I'll also call the prosecutor and ask for a recess in the trial..."

"What trial?"

"Stumpp's. You said he's involved in all this, right?"

"His name is mentioned in some of the documents, yes."

"Okay, you've got twenty-four hours to prepare. I'll let Alice know a few minutes in advance and issue my apologies then. And you'll be lucky if she ever speaks to you again after this."

WHEN CARL WOKE UP, he felt better than he could remember ever feeling before. Refreshed, and the ravenous hunger was gone.

Then memory hit him, and he reached down to his belly where he'd been shot. There was no sign of injury. They'd lied about the bullets being silver. Just one of their sadistic little games. Like Kevin had told them they'd lied to him about... Kevin. He raised his head and looked over. At the sight of what was left of his best friend he turned away and vomited painfully. There was nothing in his stomach to throw up. Again and again his whole body wracked with dry heaves. When he finally recovered and was able to stop, he turned back. The mutilated corpse had been left in the cell, limbs torn asunder, belly ripped open. He looked around.

All the others in their cells were either avoiding his look, obviously and intentionally, or glaring at him in anger or hatred. He glanced quickly at the remains. He couldn't blame them. They hated Kevin for bringing them all there and now they hated him for killing him. There was one uniformed guard standing nearby, a look of pure sadistic glee on his face.

Carl glared at him, hoping to put every bit of the disgust and hatred he felt into his look, as if he could burn the man to ash with his eyes.

"Kurt was a friend of mine," the man said. "You deserve everything that's coming to you, you monster."

"Who the fuck is Kurt?" Carl snarled back at him.

The man stepped forward, his hand going to his sidearm. But then he stopped. "It's not going to be that easy for you," he said, then walked away. When they came to get him several minutes later, he realized he may not get another chance. If they'd lied about Toni being captured or dead, and he decided to believe they had, then they'd keep torturing him until they got her. He didn't want to live knowing he'd brought her to this place. He didn't want her to believe that, either. If they forced her to kill and eat him like he did to Kevin, he didn't want her to experience that level of guilt. It wouldn't be her fault, and it would be no less than he deserved, but he knew she would feel guilty about it anyway.

He bowed his head meekly, doing his best impression of a thoroughly beaten man. There were only four of them, though, and none could turn themselves into a wolf.

AS THE FIRST man reached him, manacles in hand, Carl leapt, deliberately past him and towards the guard behind him. He changed as he leapt, and his teeth sank into the human's throat. He felt what seemed a long-forgotten joy as the warm blood spilled through his mouth and his teeth tore flesh loose. One gulp of meat only. He wasn't hungry and he still had more enemies to deal with. The freedom was palpable. The rule against attacking humans no longer applied, and he felt joy in its release. The remaining enemies were all backing away, smelling strongly of fear. He savored it as he turned on the next one.

That one went down under his weight but blocked his jaws with his arm. He bit hard and could feel bone but before he could do anything more, something slammed into side and his whole body was on fire and coursing with pain. He fell to the floor as his muscles gave way.

He tried to struggle to his feet, but the fiery pain engulfed him again. They were upon him then. There were more, many more than there had seemed. Something cold and metal bit into his foot, then another and another and he was being lifted and dropped onto a hard surface. The bursts of fire had stopped, but he was caught tight. The surface he was on was moving. The humans were pushing it, but he couldn't reach any of them, no matter how much he writhed and twisted. He couldn't escape and couldn't understand. He returned back to the darkness and let the human take over.

FOR A MOMENT, Carl wasn't sure where he was. He tried to lift his arm and couldn't. Something was biting, hard, into it. He turned his head to look and saw the manacle, bloodied where it was so tight it tore the skin. He was laying on his back on a gurney that was being wheeled down the hall. He had a pretty good idea where they were taking him. Guess the escape attempt didn't work.

He'd never changed back so quickly before, and he could feel the wolf's hesitation. But he called to it and it came.

HE SNAPPED at the closest human, relishing the sudden scent of fear that washed over him, almost drowning him in it. There was screaming and angry yelling and scrambling away from him as his restraints snapped. He pounced, and fell to the ground, his victim beneath him, its blood already filling his mouth. He shook loose a mouthful of meat and the human went limp. He swallowed but didn't pause for more. He had to get free. More humans were approaching.

He leapt, and they jumped to the sides as he'd hoped. He ran between them. They pursued. He ran on, with no idea what was ahead. The humans ran after him. The scent of fear began to give way to anger. He swerved, hoping to confuse them and scatter them more, to make them easier prey. One of the humans had stopped completely, which was good. When he swerved back, though, there was a sudden loud noise and something slammed into him, hard, knocking him over. He yelped in pain, then struggled back to his feet. But then something flew from another human and stuck in him, bringing its fire and locking his muscles. Again, he fell to the ground, his whole body in agony.

The other human stepped forward, and before he could bite it, planted his foot on his neck, pinning it to the ground. The fire ran through him again and again as the human shouted angrily at him. The pain wasn't going away, and he couldn't force himself to his feet. Every time he tried to roll or bite the human the fire coursed through him again. In despair, he called his human self back once more, retreating again into the darkness.

CARL CAME to himself with a scream. The pain was intense. There was a man standing over him, his boot on Carl's neck and a taser in his hand, the prongs of it embedded in Carl's side. He pushed the button on it and Carl screamed, trying to form words but failing.

"Yeah, that's what I thought, you bastard," the man snarled. He hit the trigger again. Carl tried but failed to stay silent as all his muscles seemed to contract at once. He panted, trying to catch his breath.

"Get up, I said," the man demanded.

You never said, Carl thought, but still couldn't speak. He tried to get his legs under him but couldn't. A surge of pain shot along his spine and he fell to his face, twitching.

"Geez, he's bleeding all over the place," one of his handlers said as they lifted him back onto the gurney.

"He shoulda thought of that before he took a giant bite out of the doc," another said.

"I'm just saying, you didn't have to shoot him like that," the first responded. "They got questions for this one."

"Let's get him into the lab then, so they can patch him up enough to answer them."

Carl was still trying to catch his breath. He felt weak. The way the guards roughly tossed him onto the gurney before pushing him down the hall hadn't helped. The taser prongs were still in him, and his belly felt like it was on fire where he'd apparently been shot. Silver bullet, it had to be, otherwise the wolf would have healed it. It was too much. He reached for the wolf, but felt it shy away. He could force it, insist it take over, but he didn't. It wouldn't do any good. At least the wolf had finally gotten to eat, he thought bitterly. At that, the sight of Kevin's mutilated body arose in his mind, and he retched, and immediately started choking.

"Shit! Hold him down. Turn him on his side," someone shouted and then there was a confusion of arms and hands as everyone tried to hold him sideways while simultaneously avoiding being directly in front of him.

For a moment, he caught a glimpse of the floor as the gurney hurried down the hall, leaving a smeared trail of vomit and blood behind it.

He passed out before they'd reached the room where he'd been held before, and again when they moved him onto the table and began pulling the chain net over him.

Pain brought him back to awareness as they began to operate. They were efficient, but not gentle. A needle was slid into his arm and taped into place. Darkness claimed him again. When he again regained consciousness, someone was cutting into him. "Dammit!" a voice said. "I said to wait til I'm done here!" Carl took a deep breath, gasping in pain.

"Your job is just to get the bullet out and patch him up enough to be questioned," the other man said. "We'll do the rest."

"He should be awake now," a woman somewhere off to the side said.

"Is that true? Can you hear me?" a man's voice said.

"Wha... huh?" Carl struggled to say.

"Can. You. Hear. Me?" the man asked, leaning down close over him to where Carl could see his face.

Carl didn't answer. The man stepped out of his field of vision. A second later, there was a surge of pain through his back.

"Aaah!" he cried out, tears running down his face. "What?" What did they want?

"Try this again. Can you hear me?" he said. Stepping back in front. He wiped a bloody finger across Carl's face.

"Don't worry about getting it out or repairing everything. Just keep him from bleeding to death before he gives up the code."

"The bullet's near the spine. If I don't remove it, he could end up paralyzed."

"I'm okay with that."

AND IT BEGAN AGAIN. They hurt him. They asked him questions. They hurt him more when he couldn't answer. And the clock slowly ticked away the seconds. And they'd ask him again. And again. And for some reason, the phrase Edwardian Desk came out, and he knew that was wrong and didn't even know what an Edwardian desk was and tried to throw in a bunch of nonsense words but the only thing he could think of was an Elizabethan Bed and then imagined Queen Elizabeth as played by Judi Dench laying naked in bed with a come-hither look and the thought made him laugh and when he laughed they hurt him more so he kept laughing because it made it hurt just a little bit less.

Then they asked him what he meant, and he asked what what meant, and tried to remember what he'd said but couldn't. And he imagined Toni lying beside him, her naked body on display to this monster's gaze, and she was broken and bloody and looking at him with a look of betrayal asking him why, why did he do this to her and he cursed more and screamed more and cried more but he didn't tell them the code.

The white-clad doctor was gone now, and nobody replaced

him. There were only the black-uniformed men and they seemed happy to have the doctors gone. He had killed some of them and injured others. They were angry and sadistic and weren't taking any more pictures or making any more notes, just hurting him and asking questions that he couldn't answer.

They broke his bones. He changed. They healed. They broke them again. He screamed. He cursed. He whimpered. But he didn't give them the code. Edwardian Desk. It was on the tip of his tongue, but every time, he promised himself he could endure just fifteen seconds more. Ten seconds more. Five more. Three. Tick. Two. Tick. One. Tick. Then, deep breath and instead of the words, all that came out was an incoherent growl. Was he in wolf form of human form now? He couldn't even tell. All he was was pain and rage and the tick tick ticking of the clock.

THE NEXT DAY, Gordon called in to work to take the day off. Hoping to meet with some of Toni's followers before she arrived, he took a bus to the edge of Forest Park and walked the rest of the way to their meeting place. He wanted to speak with them alone and get a feel for what they were like when she wasn't around. His hopes were dashed when Toni greeted him as he entered the clearing.

Nothing for it, he supposed. The place was less populated than it had been before, but there were still nearly a dozen people in various states of dress milling about. Toni stopped her approach and pulled out a phone and answered it. It must have buzzed, he didn't hear a ring. She held up a finger to him, then turned away and spoke into it.

While he waited for her, Gordon found a table under one of the awnings that had a few large containers of water on it.

He dumped out the backpack pull of snacks he'd brought there, and they all eagerly dug in. No, he noticed, not everybody. Several of them did. It was probably a good indication of who'd been here full time and who hadn't, if he was familiar with them enough to recognize them again. They could all forage for what they needed, but that much hunting would eventually be noticed, even in Forest Park.

She came over to him after she'd put down the phone.

"What's up?" he asked quickly, before she got a chance to ask him the same question.

"I don't know," she said slowly. "That was Nate, our guy at the courthouse. I guess they canceled the trial for today."

"Canceled it?"

"Yeah, all the lawyers and the judge went into the back rooms, then came out half an hour later and said they're taking a forty-eight-hour recess. Everybody's leaving. Weird." She gave a little shrug.

"The raid on Holy Mountain Research," Gordon said. "They've arranged it already."

"What? What's that got to do with it?"

"They're going to be getting new evidence. They requested a continuance to give them time to get it." He was guessing, but what else could it be?

Toni turned to a man sitting on a camping chair with two cell phones and a tablet. There were a pair of car batteries next to him attached to a USB hub that all the devices were plugged into. Tyler, he remembered the man's name. He had been hitting on a young blond girl at the warehouse.

"He hasn't moved all morning," Tyler said, checking one of his phones. He held it up to them to see, revealing a map of downtown Portland with a blue dot on 5th Ave.

Gordon turned his attention back to the map, such as it was, laid out on the large table.

"We really can't make concrete plans," Toni said apologetically, seeing where he was looking. "We've come up with a bunch of possible scenarios, but we don't know what's going to happen so we can't really plan for it."

"Without knowing what the cops are going to do, you mean," he said. "You aren't still listening in on Diaz?"

"No. That was only in his home, and we lost signal sometime last night anyway. Probably the battery finally died."

"Oh, hey, hey he's moving!" Tyler exclaimed, jumping up from his chair. He brought the phone over to them.

"Moving? Where to?" Gordon asked.

"Up Broadway..." he said. "Right on Clay... Heading toward the freeway looks like."

"Shit. It's right now," Toni said. She looked to Gordon, who nodded in agreement.

"Okay, everybody, go - it's on now!" she shouted "Spread the word, head to Caesar's Palace. We'll stage from there."

"What's Caesar's Palace?" Gordon asked her.

"Jeremy's mother's house," she answered.

He gave a short laugh at that.

"So, you in?" she asked him.

Being there would be dangerous. He could end up killed, or in jail. Just being seen with these people could cost him his entire career. He had tried to be a superhero once and had killed two men. He never wanted to do that again.

On the other hand, these kids were all rushing off to danger. He had no idea what he could do to help, but...

"Wouldn't miss it for the world," he said with what he hoped was a confident grin.

THIRTY

INTO THE HOLY MOUNTAIN

Michael didn't question her presence on this side of the yellow
tape. After all, technically, he wasn't supposed to be here
either. Looking around, nobody else seemed to be worried
about it. They all had their responsibilities and were busy
carrying them out. A light rain had been falling off and on all
morning and the dark sky was threatening to snow. He, Aaron,
and Billings were standing next to the FBI van, holding back
while the SWAT team advanced into the building. For lack of a
better place to be at the moment, Veer had joined them in
waiting for the SWAT team to secure the site. He assumed
Veer would go in with them once the signal was given.

Two FBI agents stood with them, all concentration on the
front of the building. With this many people sharing jurisdiction, a couple of extras wouldn't be noticed, as long as they
looked like they belonged, a fact of which Veer seemed
perfectly aware and willing to take advantage. Further behind
the perimeter, a pair of paramedics sheltered from the rain in
the front of their ambulance. With luck, they wouldn't be
needed. The police helicopter was still circling the roof,

keeping an eye on everything from the air as well as blocking the black helicopter from taking off.

The SWAT team had gone in loud and hard. Flash bangs to disorient those inside, along with a large amount of yelling and brandishing of weaponry. The whole operation was going like clockwork, and soon a voice reported over the radio, "The lobby is secure. We're sending some people out. Suspects. They should all be unarmed, but be careful."

A moment later a single-file line of people, widely spaced, with their hands on top of their heads began filtering out through the front door under the watchful eyes of two SWAT officers. Billings went over to coordinate with the police accepting them. While Michael was watching them, his radio squawked.

"Movement at two o'clock," a voice said. "Shit. They're fording the creek!"

Michael looked over that direction, and he saw them: four vehicles, trucks and jeeps, were coming through the underbrush. They had decided not to waste resources on that side of the building, as there was no easy escape and no approach from that direction. Looked like he was wrong about that. He sent two patrol cars over to check it out.

"Hold them there," he said. "Be careful and consider them armed and dangerous. We don't know who they are but they're not here by chance."

He didn't like splitting his forces like this, there were too few as it was.

"More coming from the road," another voice said, as if in answer to his question. What the hell was going on? He looked back that way and saw three more cars approaching at high speed. He recognized the one in front. This was not a meeting he was looking forward to.

"What the hell is going on here?" Alice said the minute she

stepped out of the car and saw him. She looked from him to Billings, but looked even angrier when she saw Aaron. Of course. He was supposed to be her subordinate. This was pure betrayal. He'd wished he'd thought to tell Aaron to stay out of it. He wouldn't have listened, of course. Aaron would own his own decision in this matter. He couldn't shield him from that, and Aaron wouldn't want him to.

"I made the decision," Billings replied. "I left you out of it because I believed there to be a potential conflict of interest."

"And I bet I can guess who told you that," Alice looked significantly at Michael and then at Veer. "And she's a civilian and shouldn't even be here."

"She's an embedded journalist," Michael responded immediately. There was precedent, especially on a high-profile raid like this one.

"And this woman should definitely not be here," Alice said. "Somebody arrest her."

Michael turned the direction she was indicating and was surprised to see Toni Briggs getting out of the third car. She must have followed the others in, hoping everyone would assume they were together. It got her this far, so he guessed she was right. In this case, though, he definitely agreed with Alice. She should not have come here. He was more shocked, though, to see Gordon Chandler climbing out of the passenger seat.

Two officers approached her.

"Wait!" Chandler cried out. He stepped forward, between Briggs and the officers. "We have information. It's important."

"All right, let them approach," Billings said. They both came forward to where the six of them stood.

"What is it?" Alice was the first to ask.

"We need to give it to Detective Diaz alone." Which was exactly the worst thing Chandler could have said. So much for any chance of patching things up with Alice or even avoiding the impression that he was usurping her leadership.

"Anything you have to say to me, you can say in front of everybody here," he said, hoping that they'd both understand his intent.

Chandler hesitated a moment, looking between them.

"Go ahead!" Alice said. "Aaron?" She glanced at him. He jumped as if startled and immediately followed her and Donald towards the building.

"I guess she's in charge of the inside operation now," Michael said. Billings just gave a sort of shrug. The raid was going on and if Alice was the leak there was nothing she could do to stop it or warn anybody at this point.

Veer followed him as he led Chandler and Briggs away from the rest of the group. He didn't bother keeping his annoyance at them both out of his voice. "Okay, what's the...?" he started.

He didn't get any farther than that. There was a deafening explosion from the building. He whipped his head around in time to see a cloud of smoke pouring out of the front door. A second later a series of gunshots sounded from within.

"Get down! This way!" Michael led the three civilians with him back toward the cover of the FBI van at a stooped run.

Billings was already there. A moment later, Alice, Aaron, and Donald joined them. Billings was holding a silent radio.

"What's going on in there?" Michael asked, but he just shook his head in response and peered into the growing cloud of smoke.

A moment later, a SWAT officer stepped out of the smoke. Two more appeared behind them, supporting yet another. They brought him to the perimeter where they were met by the paramedics.

"They planted explosives, brought the ceiling down on us.

We're all okay, but there's a giant pile of rubble blocking access to the basement."

"That's where the prisoners are," Michael said. "Can we get in through the back?"

"Back exits are both sealed," the officer responded.

"All right," Alice said, "Can we get some equipment in here to dig it out? Or would explosives do it?"

"The right amount in the right spot might do it," another responded. "But it's risky. It might bring the rest down. We'd need to get a demolitionist in here."

There was a single gunshot from inside the building. Then a few seconds later another.

"What was that?"

"Realizing they're trapped so they're committing suicide?" Aaron suggested hopefully.

A third shot rang out.

"Oh my god," Alice said. "They're killing the werewolves."

"What? Why?"

"They knew the explosions wouldn't stop us, they were just trying to slow us down. Now that they know they're trapped, they're destroying all the evidence."

"No!" Toni screamed. Michael had nearly forgotten her. She began running toward the door. She pulled a phone out of her pocket as she ran. "Go! Go now!" she shouted into it. "They're killing the prisoners. The cops are out. Nobody inside but Wolves and bad guys."

"Wait!" he called after her, but it was too late. She dropped the phone to the pavement and stepped through that weird twist in reality and came out the other side as a wolf. The wolf ran even faster, leaving a trail of shredded clothing in its wake. Across the parking lot, four cars started moving, going around the police trying to block them, heading at high speed toward the back of the building.

He made it back to Alice and Billings in time to hear the radio. One of the cops in the back was asking for instructions.

"Let 'em fight," Johansen suggested. At the look of horror from the men there, she elaborated. "Look, there's two groups of dangerous people in there. No civilians to get in the way..."

"You just said it yourself - they're probably killing the civilians as we speak!"

"You heard the girl. There's only bad guys and wolves in there. We go in there now, we can add a bunch of dead cops to that list."

"Hold back," Billings said into his radio. "Keep down, we've got shots fired."

"But..." Michael started.

Billings cut him off almost immediately. "No. It's too risky. We don't even know there are any civilians in there. Until we do, I'm not asking any of my officers to risk their lives."

"Fine, you don't have to ask me," Michael said.

Billings looked like he was going to say something. Alice looked away, obviously washing her hands of any decision he was making.

"Keep your radio open," Billings said. "Be careful."

He headed in.

WHEN SHE SAW where Michael was going, Veer immediately followed after him.

"It's dangerous," he said, over his shoulder. She noted he didn't say not to come.

"Less so for me," she replied.

He gave her a second to catch up. "Probably not. If they're used to dealing with werewolves, they're likely using silver bullets."

"Good point, and something I'll have to keep in mind as acceptance of our existence spreads. I've grown reckless, I'm gonna have to re-learn old self-preservation instincts." But she didn't stop.

His radio squawked just as they got to the front door. He immediately turned down the volume, but not before she heard Detective Johansen saying "The wolves... non-lethal means only unless you're attacked. Attempt to detain, but if any get past you, let them go."

That surprised her. "She must have had a change of heart," she said.

"Or Billings changed it for her," Michael said.

Inside, the place was a mess. On the partially collapsed upper floor, a fire was starting to spread. Toni's wolf friends had chosen the expedient route of driving their cars directly through the wall of the building. It was impossible to tell what damage was done by the explosives and what was done by the vehicles.

A pickup truck sat on the floor amidst a pile of smashed cubicle walls. Behind it a small green car sat half-buried in the collapsed upper floor. She recognized it as the one that had picked Toni up from Michael's house. The roof was crushed under the weight on top of it. Any merely human driver would have been killed. Toni's people may need the same lessons in self-preservation. Neither Toni nor any of her people were around at the moment, but a trail of shredded clothing littered the floor.

"Guess we know which way they went," she said to Michael, and led him toward the back of the room.

He followed her to a pile of rubble where the upper floor had collapsed down on top of the stairway entrance. The explosives had started a fire, or perhaps the fire had been deliberately set separately. The flames were spreading.

Michael radioed back about the fire. Most likely, due to the explosion, fire engines were already on their way, but until the building was secure, they wouldn't risk getting close enough to fight it. She didn't know how fast the fire would spread, or if the whole building would go up. They had to hurry.

Veer could see from the rubble that it could take days to clear it all. Holy Mountain's mercenaries had likely rigged it that way on purpose, but whoever set up the furniture obviously hadn't consulted with the military wing of the operation. A group of desks under the fallen upper floor, while partially collapsed, had created a short tunnel. It would be possible to crawl under them, and get to the stairway door, which she could see through the rubble, hanging lopsidedly off a broken hinge. Some of the rubble had been tossed aside, and there was more tattered clothing under the desks. No doubt about which way the Were had gone. Michael holstered his gun and drew his flashlight, preparing to crawl into the tunnel.

There was no way of knowing what would be on the other side. A wolf would have a far better chance.

"Hold on, I'm going first," she said, and pulled off her shirt. To his credit, he didn't argue. He looked away in embarrassment, which was cute, but she didn't have time for that right now. She'd considered just changing, but she was starting to run out of outfits she liked, and she hated shopping. She finished undressing and left her clothes in a pile on a broken desk. She might come back this way and it would be nice to have something to wear if she did.

"Here," she said, and took the phone from her pocket and tossed it to him. "In case I don't make it back here, hold on to that for me, will you?"

He nodded and dropped it into his jacket pocket. "I'll be right behind you," he said.

She bent down to the small tunnel, verified it was clear, and changed.

THE SMELL of fear and anger was nearly overwhelming. There were loud noises and human screams echoed from down the stairs ahead of her. She charged ahead.

There were corpses. Dead humans. She ignored them; they were irrelevant. The area outside the tunnel of rubble was clear. She ran down the stairs. She was looking for specific humans, dangerous ones who could hurt her. She ignored the frightened humans who ran past her. She could tell there was a large number of humans ahead of her. She went forward, leaving the lone human following her behind.

They were afraid, all of them, she could smell it. And the reek of them - humans in their natural state, smelling of sweat and urine. There was another human in front of her now, that had emerged from the crowd. This one wasn't afraid. Or, rather, it was, but a different kind of fear. Its fear was not the fear of prey about to be taken but that of a mother whose cubs were in danger. It was trying to tamp it down but without success. It stood between her and where she wanted to go. Was intentionally blocking her. This one was familiar, too. It wanted the human, so the human it would have.

"OH THANK the gods it is you," Toni said when Veer re-entered her own form. She seemed calm, poised, and completely unconcerned about her own nakedness. There was no hint of fear and only the remnant of a quickly fading memory told Veer otherwise.

"What's happening?" Veer asked her.

"We're trying to free the prisoners," Toni answered. "Do you know how to get these doors open?"

Veer looked around. There were about a dozen men and women in various cell-like cages. Several others - Toni's people, she assumed, from the fact they were all naked at this point, and either working on the doors or moving about looking for... something.

"Maybe," she said. "Are there any of the security people around?"

"Not alive, I don't think," Toni said, and Veer shivered at how casually she said it. "Sam?"

"Sorry," he said. "All either dead or fled."

"Where'd they go?" Veer asked him. "Is there another exit from down here?"

"There's a tunnel. A bunch of us chased some guards down it but we don't know where it leads."

"The Annex tunnel. This is site A," she said, remembering references in the documents she'd spent the last week or more cataloging. "Most likely, that would be the office building across the parking lot."

"I think they were trying to blow it up before we stopped them," Toni said.

"Okay, once we get these cages open, everybody head that way," Toni told everyone.

"They always radio to open the cages," a man said from one of them.

"There's probably a security room that monitors them, then," Veer said. "Most likely upstairs, unfortunately."

"Shit!" Toni swore. "And we can't get back up there now." She indicated the spreading fire which was already engulfing the stairwell. "Would cutting the power do it?"

"Maybe," Veer said.

"There's an electrical cabinet around the corner," a young man nearby said. "I could try flipping a bunch of breakers and see what happens."

"Do it," Toni said.

The man ran down the hall and disappeared around a corner. A moment later, the lights all went out. The dim light of the distant fire was the only thing they could see.

"The door's open!" someone called. "But I can't see anything."

"Everybody?" Toni asked loudly enough for the whole room to hear. "Are all the doors open?"

A chorus of yeses sounded from all around, accompanied by the sound of clanging metal. Nobody answered in the negative.

"Shouldn't there be emergency lights?" Veer asked of nobody in particular.

"They disabled them," said a voice in the darkness. "Sometimes they'd turn out all the lights and I could hear bumping around out there."

"They told me they were testing how well we could navigate without sight," another voice said. "They made me shift into a wolf, then run across the room."

"They had me do that too, in both wolf and human form," said another voice. "It was actually kind of fun." The last was met with a variety of disapproving noises.

"Everybody make your way to me, we're going to try to get to the tunnel. Follow my voice," Toni called again.

"Hold up," another voice in the darkness said. A second later, a bright light shone out of the darkness. Veer raised her hand to shield her eyes from it.

"Sorry," the man said, pointing his flashlight at the ground. There was a corpse in a black uniform at his feet. He played the light around and quickly found another one. A young woman nearby saw immediately what he was up to and bent down to it, pulling a flashlight off the dead man's belt. She handed it to Toni, who turned it on and shone it across the room. She focused the beam on a doorway in the corner leading to another hall.

She turned to Veer and asked, "Can you lead them through the tunnel?"

"Where are you going?" Veer asked her.

"I need to find Carl."

"Carl?" said a young woman dressed in filthy jeans and a blouse that may once have been white. "They took him to the big room in the back." She indicated the far hallway. "You might want to hurry. They weren't happy with him."

"Then that's where I'm going," Toni said.

"I'll come with you. I'm sure one of your people..." Veer started.

"Please. I need you there to talk to the cops. They'll listen to you."

"Okay," she agreed. "But don't stay too long. This whole place could come down on top of you."

"Thanks," Toni replied, and her relief was palpable.

"After me, everyone who's leaving," Veer addressed the crowd, "And be careful, we don't know what, or who, is ahead of us."

"Here," one of the men said, approaching with a belt that he handed to Toni. "Gun, Taser, radio. Should help." He must have taken it off one of the dead security guards.

"Good plan," she said. But she took the radio and handed the belt to Veer. "Gather up all of it. They'll have silver bullets in there. If we have to fight the Alpha's people, all this will be useful. Wallets and ID, too. Some of these guys might have families."

"Hah!" one of the girls with her exclaimed. "We forgot rule one of any adventure: remember to loot the bodies!"

There was a combination of strained laughter and horrified gasps in response. Adventure? Veer's first thought was to remind these kids that this wasn't a game, but then she recognized their reactions for what they were. This was the bravado of the soldier on the battlefield. They had just put their lives on the line. Some of them had killed these people. It was likely some of their friends were already dead. Joking in the face of that ghastliness was a way to cope.

"Everyone follow the reporter," Toni said, indicating Veer. "If you run into the cops, let her do the talking, or run if you have to. Meet back at your assigned rendezvous spot, and if you can't make it before they leave, head back to Echo Base when you can."

Veer wanted to know about the rendezvous spots, or what Echo Base was, but this didn't seem a good time to ask. She filed away the names for later use. She made a note of the discipline they had, how quickly they did what she said without questioning. Especially given the circumstances, it was impressive. She'd have to include that in her report.

She found the tunnel quickly enough. The door to it was broken and hanging loosely from one hinge. Somebody had come through here already.

"Go," Veer said to Toni. "Do what you have to do. We got this."

"Okay," Toni said. "I'll try to catch up to you in the annex and hope the bastards don't decide to hole up there, too."

"If they do, we'll deal with them," the man who'd brought her the flashlight said, hefting the pistol he was now carrying. Veer winced as he waved it, his finger inside the trigger guard. She vowed to give him a couple of quick lessons in safe handling before they got too much further.

Toni took off across the room while Veer headed toward the tunnel. The rest of the people from the cages soon caught up with her.

THERE WERE a dozen of them when Veer had gathered them all together.

"Hey, anyone want one?" one of the women who'd come in with Toni asked. "I'm Kim, by the way," she said by way of a hasty introduction. "And you're Vera Rosen," she continued before Veer had a chance to answer her. "Here, I found these in a supply cabinet." She passed out a stack of thin cotton blankets. They were the same types that some of the freed prisoners who weren't already wearing clothes were wrapped in. A couple gratefully exchanged theirs for much cleaner ones from the girl. Veer took one herself and felt better with it wrapped around her.

There was one more black-uniformed corpse halfway down the tunnel towards the annex. The man's throat had been torn out by big teeth. "Looks like this is the way they went all right," another of Toni's people, Daniel, said, with a coarse laugh.

Kim replied, "And they fought. And we won." We. Their side. These kids weren't children, they were soldiers. "I could weep for the lost potential..." She started automatically going over in her mind how she'd write it up. Not that, though, too sentimental. "This is what our society has turned them into. By considering Were secrecy more important than any human rights, or even basic dignity..." That would be a better beginning.

Daniel quickly stripped the guard of his gear and added it to the growing bundle the others were carrying.

MICHAEL GOT down on his hands and knees and was about to crawl after Veer when something hit him from behind. His face slammed into the desk and he could taste his blood. For a second he thought the fire had brought down more of the ceiling. But then he turned, trying to regain his feet, and saw a large paw, claws extended, coming towards his face. He jerked backward, raising his arm. A claw scraped across it, drawing blood. This was the second time recently he'd been scratched by a werewolf. He remembered Victor's words from last time and was grateful to him, both for the words and for telling him. It required a bite to turn him. He'd only been scratched so wasn't in any danger yet.

Any danger except for being killed, that was.

He was dimly aware of striking something with the back of his head when he moved. He was too squeezed down here, he couldn't maneuver. The wolf was on him now. He was on his back, pushing against the beast's head, but the jaws were getting closer. It was too strong. He couldn't roll out from under it and couldn't stand up against it. He was going to die here. He shouldn't have come. What chance did a mere human have against such creatures? Alice was right about everything.

"I'm sorry," he wanted to tell her. "I'm sorry I ever got in your way."

He regretted that he couldn't help Toni save her boyfriend who wasn't her boyfriend.

He didn't think the kid was really a terrorist, whatever else he was. In a way, he was glad, as the jaws approached and his strength began to give out, that he wouldn't have to make those decisions. He would never have to arrest the girl, or Veer, or face another press conference to reassure a frightened public when he had no more idea what was going to happen than they did. Whatever happened next, he wouldn't have to deal with it.

His part in the story was over. He hoped Veer would write something nice about him in her paper.

THE STEEL CHAIN net held Carl down and bit into him. He had been so cut and broken he wasn't sure where it ended and he began. Even if he had the strength to lift his arm, he was afraid not all of it would come with him.

They'd stopped, for now, with a dire warning from the man watching his vitals. He'd replaced the woman who'd been there earlier. They'd all changed, one by one. The guards, with their guns and their tasers. The white-coated scientists. The only one left was him. Even the questioner had changed. Though the question had not. He wasn't even sure what the answer was any more. Edwardian Desk. Elizabethan Bed. Victorian... what, Victrola?

He laughed at that. He realized he was laughing a lot lately. He wasn't sure that was a good sign about his mental health. The only thing he was clear on was that he mustn't tell them. He owed it to Toni. He thought there was something wrong with his eye. Everything was red and kept getting brighter and dimmer. He watched a shadow grow and fade with the light, behind his friend the clock. Somewhere a red light was flashing.

He realized there was only one person near him. Where did all the rest go? Was this it? Was he done? Did he answer their question? Could he leave now? He still couldn't move. He reached out to the wolf. Nothing. Was he already in wolf form? He reached out to the human. There was no answer there, either. How... he'd never had the wolf not be there. The only person remaining didn't speak. He didn't think he'd answered their question. Did he? He tried to turn his head again. Everything went dark.

He opened his eyes when he heard a loud noise. Did it wake him up? Had he been asleep? It was so hard to breathe. There was a gurgling noise every time he tried. If he inhaled slowly, though, and not too deep, it didn't hurt quite so much. Far away, there were voices, shouting at each other. And maybe gunshots. There was a light coming from the man standing near him. He waved it around the room and it played briefly across the clock. The second hand was just rounding the six. There was something important about that. Something he was going to do. He couldn't remember where the other hands had been before, though. Was the shouting getting closer?

"Okay, will do," the man said to somebody he couldn't see. It looked like he was speaking to his own chest. He dropped his hand from his chest to his side and it came back up with a pistol. He raised it. "About fucking time, too," he said as he pointed it at Carl's head.

There was a loud crash behind him. Carl tried to raise his head enough to see but couldn't quite manage it. The guard spun around and something dark and gray with fur and claws leapt out of a shadow and the guard and it both disappeared from his view. There was a brief scream and the sound of flesh tearing. He thought this time it wasn't his own. Light flashed wildly across the ceiling.

He tried to turn his head in that direction, but the farthest he could see was his own arm. It was a red bloody mess, under the steel chain. He could see bone poking out. It didn't even hurt. The gurgling sounds were getting fainter, and the voices louder. He closed his eyes again. *Everybody dies and I don't think I'm immune. It's the hour of the wolf and I'll see you soon.*

"Carl!" a voice cried. There was fumbling at the chain net. "Oh god, Carl!"

He opened his eyes again. Toni was there, standing by the table. She stood naked, silhouetted in a dim glow from somewhere beneath her. She looked like an angel.

"No," he said. "You can't... be here. I... never told them. They asked me... how to find you... but I never told them. It's not fair."

Every word was an effort to get out. There was a wispy sound to his voice that he didn't recognize.

"It's okay. It's okay," she said, and lifted the net off of him. It tugged at him as it went. But it didn't hurt at all. He must be getting better.

"They..." he took a breath, slowly but as deeply as he dared, "They didn't get you?"

"No," she said, with a pained laugh. She smelled scared. "I'm here to rescue you."

Rescue? He tried to say he didn't know if he could stand. He couldn't get the words out. But everything was okay now. Soon he would pass out and wake up in a hospital bed, covered in bandages and tubes. She'd be there at his side and make some humorous quip. They'd both laugh. He'd wince in pain and grasp his side, then chuckle quietly. Roll credits.

But right now, it was so hard to speak. He should say something. What did she just say? Here to rescue him. He tried to smile at the thought of getting to deliver the line. He started inhaling again, getting enough air to speak with. "Aren't you... a little short..." he managed to get out.

Wait. No, that was backwards. Crap. He started to inhale again. It was so much effort. The gurgling sound was gone, though. Was he actually inhaling? He wasn't sure. He needed to bring in air enough to say something else. He couldn't see her anymore. Where had she gone? Everything was so dark, and so cold.

He felt light. Was he the wolf again? He was, he was sure of it. He was it and it was him. They were together, a single being. He understood. He finally understood everything. He listened through its ears but heard her words, "Oh god, Carl. You are such a nerd!" He wanted to laugh. She caught the reference even though he said it wrong. He should inhale. Or did he do that already?

"Carl?" her voice sounded so far away now. "Carl? Carl!" she shouted.

Then... something else. It was so cold, and so dark. He tried to speak but he didn't think his lips moved. She was still there. Why couldn't he reach her? Was she crying? He'd never heard her cry before. Why was she crying? Not for him? Surely, not for him.

MICHAEL THOUGHT for a second that his heart was pounding loudly in his chest. Then he realized it wasn't his heartbeat, it was two pairs of gunshots. The wolf on top of him twitched, then fell down and lay still. As he rolled out from underneath it, it changed with that weird disorienting rotation that he didn't think would ever look familiar. A man lay naked in a spreading pool of blood. He turned from the sight to see Alice, her firearm in both hands in front of her. Aaron and Donald both stood beside her, shotguns at the ready. His first thought was to wonder where she'd gotten silver bullets to fit her service weapon. Why didn't he get any?

Then he wondered for a second what she was doing there. Then he saw the man in the black uniform sneaking up behind her.

"Look out!" he shouted, pointing behind her. She turned and the man leapt at her, hands outstretched. In mid-air he changed, twisting into a sleek grey wolf. It was beautiful, he thought, for just a second, then it knocked Alice down, the gun spinning out of her hand to slide away into the darkness, and shreds of his black uniform fluttered to the ground.

The wolf raised its head, tearing flesh from her arm as it did. He reached for his own weapon and the wolf spun toward him with another leap.

Alice leapt behind it as if she would transform as well, but she ducked into a low tackle. She couldn't hope to compete with the wolf on strength but redirected enough of its momentum to miss Michael. The two of them crashed into a pile of rubble. Something collapsed, and another section of the ceiling came down, burying them both beneath metal beams and furniture from upstairs. Fire danced above them, and the wolf lay beneath.

Michael got up on one knee and drew his revolver. He could see the wolf, pinned under a desk, its back broken, but it was already healing. When it had regenerated enough to move again, it would kill her. He didn't hesitate. He took careful aim at the beast's head and squeezed the trigger twice. Aaron and Donald wouldn't risk using their shotguns with Alice so close to the target. They both began pulling furniture and sections of floor off the rubble, trying to free Alice. Michael fired two more times, and holstered his weapon only when the wolf had turned back into a human. He sprang to his feet and went to help the others. They tossed the dead body of the mercenary to the side with as much care as they paid the desk.

With their help, Alice crawled out and climbed to her feet. The wound in her arm was bleeding profusely.

"We got her, Michael. Go," Aaron said.

"All right. Watch out for any more, no telling what's in here or where. Tasers if you can, though, some of them might still be civilians."

He heard Donald calling for paramedics and backup, and warning them that some of the security were werewolves now. "Arrest anyone who comes out," he said into the radio. "We can sort out later who's who."

He was wounded and in a burning building. Protocol and common sense demanded he get out immediately, not crawl under a pile of rubble to get to a basement that might have no way out. He got down on his hands and knees and started forward. He had almost made it to the door when the lights went out.

He found his flashlight and proceeded the rest of the way by its light. There was nobody, wolf or man, waiting for him in the stairway when he crawled out from under the rubble. He made his way down the stairs and into a hall. He could hear some noise from ahead but could see nobody in the red glow of the fire behind him. He drew his revolver and held it with his flashlight before him. The light played across a dead body. He slowly raised the light and it illuminated another, then another. Nearly a dozen in all lay scattered about the hall. Clad in black uniforms or white coats, torn apart or eviscerated. Either not all the mercenaries were werewolves now, or these had been killed before they got a chance to turn. Some were naked and obviously killed by gunshots. He assumed those were the prisoners. Phil was not among them.

The hallway opened up into a giant basement, filled with freestanding cages, most empty, with the doors all standing open. In some few of them were naked bodies, but only a few. A pair of dead mercenaries lay where they'd fallen, torn apart, he guessed, by a pack of wolves. On one side of a room was a short hall leading to an iron door, broken and hanging, leading to an unlit tunnel. On the other side, another hallway leading back around the room. He heard a noise from that direction. It may have been a woman's voice.

He took a cautious step forward. He reached the tunnel and shone his flashlight into it. It was a simple large, corrugated metal pipe whose floor had been leveled with concrete. It was a common style of underground access way around here. He cursed himself for not considering it earlier. There was another dead body here. This must have been where the survivors had gone. If he hurried, he might be able to catch up to them, but he wanted to make sure there was nobody left down here first. At least it was a way out, assuming that if he went farther into the basement, he could reach it again before the fire did. Or before the ceiling collapsed on him. He backed away from the tunnel and crossed the large room to the other exit he had seen.

Halfway down the hall, a trail of dried blood led to a pair of wooden doors, hanging wide open. He stepped through it into another room, considerably smaller than the one he'd just left. Sweeping across the floor he saw several, what, operating tables? Each with a bank of diagnostic machines similar to what you might expect to see in a hospital, all dark.

A muffled sob came from the far side. He swiveled his flashlight in that direction. One table was occupied, next to a black-clad corpse lying on the floor, nearly decapitated from having its throat torn open. These werewolves did not like the mercenaries. He moved quickly to the figure on the table, and recoiled from what he saw there. In all his years working homicide, he'd never seen such a disfigured corpse. All four limbs hung akimbo, broken. The man was terribly gaunt, past the brink of starvation, and his whole body was covered in cuts. Dangling from one side of the table was a net made of steel chain, stained with blood and bits of raw meat.

He realized this figure couldn't have been the source of the noise he'd heard. He swept his flashlight across the floor again and came to a stop when it hit Toni Briggs, huddled naked against the far wall. She had her knees pulled up against her chest like she was trying to draw herself into as small a position as possible and disappear altogether. She looked up at him with a look he couldn't begin to parse.

He holstered his pistol and rushed over to her, keeping the flashlight pointed at the floor. He took off his coat and tentatively handed it to her. She draped it over her shoulders as she stood up. She nodded but didn't speak.

"Can you..." he was about to say stand, before she did so, "walk?" he finished.

She opened her mouth like she was going to say something, then just nodded, keeping her eyes firmly on the floor. He led the way to the door.

"Wait," she said, just as they got to the door. She turned back toward the corpse.

He resisted the urge to reach for her. "We need to hurry," he said as gently as he could. "The place is on fire and could come down on us at any minute."

She continued staring in the direction of the corpse. With a shock, he realized who it must be. Carl Jablonski. The terrorist leader. He had confronted him just a month ago and he had disappeared completely after that. What had happened to him? He must have been down here the whole time, starved and tortured.

"I'm sorry," he said. "There's nothing you can do for him now."

"Yes," she said firmly. "There is. Do you have a phone?"

"There's no signal down..."

"Does it have a camera?" She interrupted him.

"Um, yes..." he started. Then he realized what she meant.

"Don't let them cover it up. The world needs to see what they did here," she said.

"There'll be a police photographer..." he started again. And maybe there'd be something left to photograph after the fire reached here, he didn't say.

"I don't trust the police," she said. Then, obviously still trying to hold back tears, "Please, just... please."

This was dangerous and stupid. The fire was spreading. They had to get out of here.

"Wait here," he told her. He walked back over to the body and took several pictures of it and the surrounding area, from multiple angles, trying to do a professional crime scene photographer's job with his cell phone camera, inadequate light, and no time.

She reached for the phone when he got back, and he handed it to her. She looked over the images, carefully trying to keep her expression blank. She only winced a couple of times.

"Let's get out of here," she said. There was no emotion in her voice.

He nodded. "Can't get back the way I came," he said. "But there's a tunnel..."

She nodded. "That's where the reporter took everybody else."

She dropped the phone into the pocket of the coat. He was about to object, but then figured he could get the phone back when he got the coat back later.

GORDON STOOD behind the FBI van with a couple of other men also in suits. Nobody seemed interested in talking to him or asking why he was there. He looked around. It looked like everybody was here. FBI, Homeland Security, Washington County Sheriff, both Portland and Hillsboro police. With all these different groups it would probably be easy for everyone to assume he belonged to someone else.

He heard over the radio being carried by a nearby officer that a group of men in black uniforms was seen running out of the back of the smaller building heading toward the woods. A minute later a squad car got there in time to see about a dozen wolves chasing them and disappearing into the woods. The building was supposed to have been empty, but he realized at once what had happened. When planning around the crude map in Forest Park they had discussed the possibility of an underground connection between the two buildings. It looked like his guess was right. It also looked like the private security contractors they were worried about had fled the area, and Toni's people had done the same.

So, when somebody else radioed that a group of people were seen in the side building, he came to the conclusion that these would be the prisoners they had been sent to free and that Toni would almost certainly be among them. He told the nearest officer, "Tell them it's okay; it's one of ours. I'm heading over there now."

The man dutifully broadcast to the rest of the group without even questioning who "ours" was. Gordon's suit was the nicest so that meant he outranked them, right? He got back in his car and drove the short distance to the smaller building. He parked around back, assuming the front door would be closed. The back one, though, had recently been used and was left unlocked. He did briefly consider that it might be somebody other than Toni and her friends coming up the stairs, when he heard them approach.

Toni's friend Kim was the first out of the door and Gordon relaxed. Vera Rosen came after, followed by about a dozen people he didn't recognize. Kim, Vera, and about half the remaining people were all carrying blankets wrapped around themselves and wearing nothing else. So there had been fighting. He scanned quickly around.

"Toni?" he asked anxiously.

"Should be along soon," Rosen said. "She sent the rest of us out ahead."

Kim addressed the rest of their group. "We're safe. Let's hold up here for a bit."

"Shouldn't we get the cops?" one of the men asked.

"I'm sure they'll be along soon when they see us here," Kim replied.

"I told them to hold off a bit," Gordon said. "Nothing to stop anyone from going over there, though, if you want to."

Kim shot him a look at that. She had originally met him while he was playing the role of mysterious stranger with unknown power and position. Toni had later told her the truth, but now that he seemed to have influence over the police, she was re-evaluating him again. He suppressed a smile at that and let her continue.

"If you want," she said, then addressed the group. "Before you do though, you have a decision to make. There's some things you need to know. First, I'm sorry we couldn't get everybody. We tried. We really did, but..." she trailed off. Caught her breath and tried again. "It's too late to change that, and you're going to have to decide quickly what you want to do next."

She continued, quickly sketching out the situation. She told them of the Alpha's group, of Kevin's, and of her own. And of the code of secrecy.

"That's changing now. Partly because we're changing it. A large part is because of the press coverage from Ms. Rosen here." She indicated Rosen with a sweep of her arm. "The... uh... secret is still up in the air, though," she continued. "We suspect the Alphas aren't going to take this lying down. Our goal is to prevent violence, but we haven't always been successful." One of the men let out a quick bark of laughter at that. She acknowledged the point with a quick nod and went on. "There is still some chance for justice for you. If you talk to the police, it might go well. Then again, it might not."

It sounded almost... not rehearsed exactly, but something she'd said before, or heard before. Gordon realized this was probably something they'd gone over, but Toni was supposed to be the one saying it.

"The Alpha is on trial right now," he put in. "And they're publicly accepting that he's a werewolf, so the secret's pretty much out of the bag."

"That's true," Veer added. "At least we're doing our best to make it so, but there's still some small chance they can cover it all back up again."

"I don't think that's even possible at this point," Kim said.

"They'll almost certainly fail, but that doesn't mean they won't try," Veer responded. "If they do, they will be utterly ruthless about it. Right now is probably the most dangerous time there is to be a rogue Were." Gordon suspected she may be right.

Kim nodded at that. "Which brings us to your other option. You can hide. Tell nobody but those closest to you, who you are absolutely sure you can trust. Keep it secret, stay off everybody's radar. If you do, you'll probably be safe."

"Probably?" one of the rescued prisoners asked.

"As long as nobody ever finds out, nobody will come after you. I won't tell anyone, and neither will anyone from our organization. But I can't speak for everyone, and I don't know what records the bastards who put you in there kept."

They continued discussing. He soon learned that the people he didn't know were almost all prisoners of this place, as Carl was suspected to be. The man he'd seen at the warehouse party, Daniel, seemed to have his own people, though they had all left by now. That must have been the first group out the back door. There was still no sign of Toni and he was beginning to get nervous.

In the end Daniel led four of the former prisoners out of the building, saying he'd see them to Echo Base. Kim herself stayed behind, to wait for Toni. Daniel took the collected weapons and other gear with him, dumping them into bags he'd found in the office. The wallets and ID badges, he piled on a table to be left for the police, after removing all the cash. Veer raised her eyebrows at the last, and he responded, "Well they don't need it anymore. It might as well be used to help their victims."

Kim addressed the rest of the former prisoners. "Anybody else, follow Daniel, we've got some extra clothes in the van and he can give you bus fare from there and a ride to the MAX if you want it." Daniel nodded at the last and led his charges out the back door.

None of them decided to go out the front door toward the police.

As soon as they all left, Kim turned to him and Veer and asked, "Can you talk to the cops when they get here? I'm going to go find Toni."

"I thought you had orders to wait here - nobody goes back inside?" Veer said.

"Yeah, I don't always do what I'm told."

Gordon wanted to go with her, but thought he'd be more useful here if the police did decide to investigate.

Veer apparently thought so as well. "I'll wait then. Be careful. There was another man, Detective Diaz, who was coming in behind me."

"Detective? He's a cop?"

"Yeah, but he's a...friend." There was some hesitation there, Gordon noticed. She was unsure of their relationship. He didn't say anything, though. She finished, "He won't shoot you on sight or anything."

"Well, that's a relief at least," Kim replied. "I see him, I'll let him know you're up here."

Gordon had a seat while Veer found the lounge's coffee maker and started a pot. She shrugged. "As long as we're stealing things, I don't think a bit of coffee will be missed."

AS MICHAEL APPROACHED THE TUNNEL, with Toni behind him, he glimpsed a light coming from the other direction. He held up his hand and motioned to Toni to get against the wall and stay there, then he killed his own light. For several long moments they stood there as the other light grew slowly closer. He could hear footsteps. Right before they got to the end, he stepped out, flashlight and gun both held in front of him and switched on the light, so it shone directly into the other's face.

It was a young woman, wrapped in a blanket. She held a cell phone in one hand, using its flashlight to light her way. The other hand she put up against the glare from Michael's flashlight. He deliberately kept it in her face. He wasn't taking any more chances down here.

"Kim?" Toni asked. "It's okay," she told Michael. "She's with me."

"Is he?" Kim asked, indicating Michael.

"For now," Toni replied. "What are you doing back here?"

"I came back to look for you. Are you okay? Where's Carl?"

At the last, Toni just shook her head slightly, but Kim got it. "I'm sorry," she said. "C'mon, the rest of the way's clear."

HE WAS SURPRISED to see Gordon Chandler waiting upstairs with Veer, chatting like old friends. Veer got up and poured a cup of coffee from a pot and brought it to him. He laughed out loud at the strangeness of such a normal act, and gratefully took the mug. Aside from Veer and Gordon there was nobody else in the room.

"Everybody else left already?" Toni asked him.

"Yes," Gordon said. "They all left through the back door, out of sight of the police. According to your friend Daniel, some of the mercenaries got away that way, too."

Kim nodded in agreement.

Michael glanced in the direction he indicated. Presumably one of those hallways, possibly both, led to the back door. Dammit, he should have taken this building into consideration in the planning. But it had been empty when they got here so they ignored it after that.

Across the parking lot, he could see the police cordon and a pair of fire trucks which weren't there when he left. The building was blazing now, but they hadn't moved in. He could see Billings watching it intently. He turned on his radio and checked in.

"Where've you been?" Billings asked. "What's your situation?"

"Got out through a tunnel in the basement," he replied. "We're over here in the annex." He waved out the window, and saw Billings turn to peer at him across the parking lot. "The main building should be safe enough for the fire crews. Everybody's either over here or fled already."

In the distance, it looked like Billings put down the radio for a moment to yell something at somebody nearby.

He picked it back up. "Need any backup where you are?"

"No, things are under control here. How's Alice doing?"

"Pretty well actually," Billings replied. "The medics are

treating her now, but she should make a full recovery. Looked bad when she first got here but seems to be better."

Vera smiled when she heard that, walking over to him where she could hear better. "Was she bitten?" she asked.

"Yep. We were attacked upstairs right after you left. Apparently the mercs are werewolves now. And, I guess, Alice is too?"

"Almost certainly," Veer responded, and took a sip of her coffee while doing a poor job of hiding her amused smile.

"She's not going to like that at all."

"I don't doubt it," she said, still smiling.

Speaking of werewolf cops... He turned to Kim, where she was talking intensely about something with Toni and Gordon. "You saw everybody who got out?"

"Yes?"

He gave her a description of Phil.

"I'm sorry," she said. "He wasn't there. They said that when they had to move a couple of older ones were really sick. They... they killed those they didn't bring over. I'm sorry," she repeated.

He sat down in the nearest chair on hearing that. Phil was dead. Murdered by Holy Mountain Research. Phil was a werewolf and now he was dead.

"It's not your fault," Veer said, obviously understanding what he was thinking.

"Isn't it?" he said. "He was there because I made him feel he couldn't tell anyone because..."

He looked up and saw the expression on her face.

"No. You're right," he said. "I can feel guilty enough about fucking up that relationship and now he's gone, and I'll never get the chance to apologize. That's enough to regret without having caused his death. That's all on Holy Mountain Research."

"I'm sorry," she said, and put a hand on his shoulder.

He looked back up and saw Toni heading toward the back door with Kim. "Hey," he called after her, then stood up to follow her.

"Sorry," she said. "I just... need to get out of here before all your cop buddies show up."

She was still wanted. Because of her boyfriend, who'd just been hideously murdered, by the same people who'd murdered Phil. She'd been taken against her will, that much had been corroborated by Mitch, who may or may not still be alive. Then she'd taken up with one of her abductors and mounted an entire rescue mission only to find him dead. There was a depth to that he couldn't fathom. He knew she wasn't a terrorist, just a traumatized child, barely into her twenties. But it wasn't his call. He was a cop, not judge and jury.

He already knew what his decision would be. "I'll need my phone," he said. He couldn't ask for the coat back.

"I'm gonna get the pictures off, first," she said.

"I can do that back at the station," he replied. "It would probably be best for you if you'd come..."

"Are you arresting me?" she asked, raising her voice. Veer turned to look, but Gordon and Kim both stepped forward, protecting her. He was the only one here armed, and with silver bullets to boot. But that wasn't strictly true. He was acutely aware how quickly they could transform and be upon him. He might be able to stop all three, but not without killing them, which was the last thing he wanted.

"No," he said, keeping his hands well clear of his weapon and making it obvious he was doing so. "But eventually, some-body will want to, and..."

"Tomorrow," she replied. "I'll come down tomorrow and bring your phone then. Deal?"

"Thank you. I'll do my best to help you."

"Thanks."

Veer turned to Toni. "You have a way of getting home?"

Toni turned to Kim.

"Cyn will have left by now," Kim told her. "But there should be some clothes and bus fare stashed."

"I can give you a ride," Gordon volunteered. "My car's right outside."

Rendezvous points set up. Clothes and bus fare stashed. Given how little time they would have had to plan, he was impressed at the organization. There had to be at least a couple rendezvous points set up, that different werewolves were at.

"Are all of your people out then?" Gordon asked her.

Toni looked to Kim, who nodded. "Everybody who went in made it out. No casualties." Michael noticed how much Toni seemed to relax at that. "Daniel's bringing some of the new ones, that Kevin and Shelly turned, back to Echo Base."

"That's good to hear," Gordon said.

"A lot of the guards got out, too, apparently. The way the others told it, pretty much everybody fled when the SWAT team went in. Some stopped to set the fire, and some started shooting their prisoners, but we put an end to that quickly once we got there."

He had seen the results of both the mercenaries shooting the prisoners and of her people putting an end to it. "I would have thought if they'd intended to burn the place, it would have spread quicker," was all he said.

"We put an end to that, too," Toni answered him. "Part of it started in the computer room. They had some kind of fancy fire suppression system, but they'd turned it off. Jeff turned it back on." She was proud of her people, he could tell. Despite everything, she was giving credit where it was due.

"Is that why you brought him along?" he asked, fishing for more information. She provided it.

"Maybe not that specifically, but he does datacenter infrastructure, figured he'd be useful in a place like that."

She'd chosen who to bring, not just grabbed whoever was handy and ran over. He felt a little guilty for pumping her for information at a time like this, and wasn't sure how much further he could push it, so he dropped it. Not his problem anyway. For a second, he was glad he was no longer heading the werewolf squad, if for no other reason than that it meant he wouldn't have to try to outmaneuver this girl.

"First thing tomorrow morning?" she asked.

"I hope to see you then."

Kim looked startled at that and looked like she was about to object.

Michael continued before she could. "It'll be better than being a fugitive," he said. "I promise to do everything I can to help you."

"Tomorrow, then," she said and headed out with Gordon and Kim.

He looked out the front door and saw a police car headed his way, as firetrucks moved toward the burning building.

"If they saved the server room..." Veer started.

"We've got a warrant for all the data in there," he finished the thought for her.

THIRTY-ONE

RED TAPE AND BEER

Six weeks later, Gordon braved the early February snow that had brought most of downtown to a standstill. It was the last day of closing arguments in the Stumpp trial. As a witness, he'd been given preferential position when getting into the courtroom. The weather hadn't seemed to dampen people's enthusiasm for the case. The documents gathered from the raid on Holy Mountain Research had been devastating. The fire that was supposed to have destroyed the server room had been put out by the automated suppression system. The prosecution spun this as a lucky happenstance, but Toni had told him what had really happened. Although the press was still mixed, the prosecutor had successfully used mentions of Stumpp's name in the Holy Mountain documents to paint a picture of Victor Stumpp as, rather than a man who had made a few hard decisions in protecting his people, a ruthless mob boss who was willing to imprison, torture, or even kill his own people to get ahead.

Gordon was not surprised when the jury returned with a guilty verdict on almost every count.

"I'd hoped to feel like I'd achieved some closure," he said to Vera Rosen after the trial. He didn't know why she wanted to talk to him first after the verdict, of all the people involved, but he didn't mind. He wanted to talk to her, too. He wanted the story told, and trusted her to treat Barbara and Toni both with at least some level of respect.

He also felt like he'd come to understand Victor somewhat, seeing him in court as witness after witness tore into the most private details of the life he'd led over the last seventy-odd years.

"I mean, how can you not come to empathize at least a little bit after hearing all that?"

"You don't blame him for Barbara's death."

"Not any more than you, or anybody else."

She seemed surprised, and maybe a little hurt, that he'd included her in that.

He continued anyway. "What I mean is, if we'd have known there were werewolves, or at least if the police had, they might have caught the guy sooner, or been able to do something. At the very least, recognize what they were looking for."

She didn't answer that. It may not be right to blame her for not coming forth sooner. She did reveal them in the end, and who was he to say it wasn't soon enough? Didn't he keep it secret once he found out what he was as well?

"I'm not going to spend my life hating you, it doesn't matter what could have been. There are a million things that, if they changed just a little bit, everything might have gone differently. And no, there is no closure. Barbara's still gone. There will never be closure. You would have liked her," he said, changing the subject again. "She was definitely a people person. Lots of friends at school. And curious. Always had to know everything about everything. No end of questions." He found himself wiping away a tear. It was getting hard to speak.

"I'm sorry if this is getting too personal..." she began.

"No. It's a good thing," he cut her off. "Seriously, it's good to talk about... everything. Maybe that's changed at least. I feel I can finally start to mourn. As for Stumpp... I know he's your friend. I don't hate him. I'm not even mad at him. Though I don't think Toni would understand how I feel."

"No, I suppose she wouldn't."

He was almost grateful that Toni had been in jail still when they had shown the recovered video in court. One of the internal security cameras had shown Stumpp yelling at the naked and chained Carl Jablonski. That was followed by the presentation of a series of horrific pictures that had somehow leaked to the internet. The source of the leak was never revealed, but Detective Diaz had confirmed that the pictures had come from his phone and he had taken them himself. The combination had all but clinched a life sentence for Stumpp.

Holy Mountain Research on the other hand had denied authorizing any experiments on werewolves and shut down its Oregon branch which it claimed had been corrupted by Victor Stumpp.

"I'm speaking to her tomorrow," Veer said. "That should be an interesting conversation."

"Probably not as bad as you might think. She'll separate your friendship with Stumpp from his actions. She tends to be remarkably pragmatic about such things. Hell, I could see you and her becoming friends before us. You were an active member of a group who tried to have me killed, while she and Carl helped me out, and helped me understand what had happened. Things maybe would have gone a lot differently if Stumpp had done that."

"He should have. I think Peter overstepped his bounds."

"Stumpp still sent him after me."

"He was acquitted of giving the order to have you killed."

She was grasping at straws there. He found he still didn't hate her for it. He didn't think he could let it go, though.

"Do you honestly believe he didn't?" he asked. It wasn't purely a rhetorical question.

She was quiet for a moment. He was grateful she actually thought about it before answering.

"No," she finally replied. "I don't think he meant that as the first option, but it was always on the table." She changed the subject. "You seem to know Toni pretty well."

"She's been staying at my place."

"Really?"

"She needed a place to go after she got out of jail. I had extra room."

"And she just accepted that you registered?"

"No," he said with a laugh. "Not even close. But she understands my reasons for registering. She doesn't like them, and called me a coward for doing it, but she understands them. Though I can't really understand hers."

"She's still publicly refusing to register then? Good for her."

"You agree with her that it's wrong?"

"I do."

"But you registered."

"I did," she admitted. "I've had to cross a lot of state lines recently. I didn't want to be in violation of federal law while doing so. So, cowardice, same as you."

"This isn't like Donald Trump's Muslim registry. Wolves can actually be dangerous. It's like carrying a concealed weapon everywhere you go."

"Not really the same thing," she said. "Though I'm not a big fan of registering firearms either. Though I did that, too, and even have a concealed carry permit, so there's my own hypocrisy."

That surprised him. "Not that it matters, I guess. I'm just

not sure what she hopes to accomplish. Everybody knows she's a werewolf. Aside from yourself, and arguably Stumpp, she's probably the single most famous werewolf there is."

"Exactly. And openly flaunting it like that will force the federal government to either take action or not. Which will force the state to either cooperate or not. If they take action, and arrest her for refusing to register, she'll gain standing to challenge the law in court. If they ignore her, it erodes support for the law. Either way, she wins."

"She'll be happy to hear that," Gordon said with a smile. He meant it. Though on second thought, now that Rosen had pointed it out, he was pretty sure Toni had already thought of it.

"What're your plans now?" she asked him.

"Move to Montana."

"Ha!" She laughed. Then saw his reaction. "What, seriously?"

He laughed at that, too. "Yep. Got a job there lined up already. Fresh new start, new area, new job, where nobody knows I'm a werewolf."

"Except the Federal government. And your new employer, if they check. And anyone who looks you up in the registry."

"Yes. Except for them."

MONDAY AFTERNOON, Gordon was home from his last day in the old office. He dropped the cardboard box holding all of his personal belongings from his desk on the kitchen counter.

"You're going to Montana?" Toni asked him, surprised. She had just come out of her room, which had been his office up until the last month or so. He hadn't worked up the courage to pack up Barbara's room, or do anything to it once the crime scene cleaners had finished. When the charges against her were dropped and she was released from the county jail, Toni moved into the office and he made do with the kitchen table for any paperwork he needed to do at home. Two lifetimes ago, when he bought the table there'd been three of them living here, and he had been hoping for a fourth. It didn't work out that way.

He reached into the fridge to get himself a beer. It was a habit he'd developed again recently, realizing he didn't have to worry about the calories. Or about setting an example for Barbara.

The calories he'd burn off every time he changed, which he'd been doing frequently. He and Toni visited Forest Park a lot. Even though there was no reason to hide, the old Echo Base location always seemed to have at least a few people hanging around. A couple of times they'd visited a wolf preserve she'd shown him out of town. It had apparently been set up by Victor Stumpp to give his werewolves a private place to change. It was anybody's guess who was running it now. In the times they'd visited it, there had been nobody around to question their right to be there.

"This is where I had my first date with Carl," Toni had said with a sort of strained laugh. There was something heavy there, and painful, beyond the obvious. At first, he'd thought when Toni said something like that it was because she wanted to be asked, but she had resisted his attempts to probe any further. Eventually he came to realize it was an indicator of trust she was giving him. She didn't want to talk about it, or couldn't bring herself to, but she allowed him to know there was something there. She didn't shy away from talking about Carl, though. In that, she'd adopted his stance on Barbara. She had told him she didn't want to flee from the memory by burying it and didn't want his name to become taboo.

That was something he shared with her, too. Barbara would always be in his memory, of course, and talking about it only strengthened that bond. There were some significant differences. She had told him how Carl had turned her against her will. They still formed some sort of relationship and he died before she could really figure out what it was. Then, before she had time to grieve, she'd been arrested for terrorism and conspiracy in the death of a police officer and spent two weeks in jail before the charges were dropped. He couldn't even begin to imagine what that would have been like.

He pulled a beer out for Toni as well. That act alone reinforced his reminder to himself that she wasn't Barbara, or a substitute for her. The fact that he kept catching himself thinking of her like that, though, was part of his reasons for leaving. A part he would never say out loud. Guess they both had their secrets.

"New job lined up," he said. "Moving there in a week."

"A week? I mean, congratulations, I guess." She hesitated. There was obviously something she wanted to say. But instead, she asked, "This a better job than what you have now?"

"Similar," he said, leaning on the kitchen island opposite her. "A bit lower pay, but cost of living there's a lot lower than Portland. But I think, well, after everything that's happened, a fresh start would be nice."

"No, I get it," she said. "And I'm happy for you. I really am. And..."

He gave her time to gather her thoughts, and say what she wanted to say. "Not to sound all mercenary or anything, but... well... I haven't managed to find a job yet. I don't know if, I mean, I appreciate everything you've done for me, I really do, and I know you don't owe me anything. But I don't know if I can find a new place in a week..."

"Oh, shit, I'm sorry." He felt like an asshole for making her ask it. "I should have started with that. I'm not selling the house, at least not any time soon. A few more years at least. Stay as long as you need to. Or as long as you want. Frankly, I'd prefer somebody I can trust being here instead of it sitting empty or rented to strangers. We can talk about rent once you're back on your feet."

"Really? That's... that's awesome! Thank you! A lot. I don't know what to say."

"Thank you works. I just wish I could do more."

"You've done a lot. You've really helped me out. Seriously. I don't know what I would have done without you."

She took her beer into the living room with her and sat on the couch. He stopped himself from yelling "No drinks on the couch!" Instead, he joined her. He did hand her a coaster, though, before setting his own down on the coffee table.

"Given any thought to what you're going to do now?" It was the same question Veer had asked him.

"Well, I'm still looking for work. Powell's finally officially fired me while I was in jail..."

"There's an 'and' in there..."

"Yeah," she said. "There's so much. I want to do something about Holy Mountain Research. They shouldn't be allowed to just get away with what they did. And then there's the Order of the Wolf. A lot of us want to stay together even though we don't need to be secret anymore. But there's a lot to be done. Like this stupid registry." Gordon smiled at that, recalling recent arguments, and his discussion with Veer. "And the associated discrimination. There's a lot of fear out there, and with the registry, that anybody can look up anybody, and no laws against firing people for being wolves, people are already starting to lose their jobs."

"You want to get werewolves as a protected class for discrimination?"

"They should be. Everybody should be. It's ridiculous. How does prejudice move so quickly? How long did racism take to get going?"

He laughed. "Long before my time, I'm afraid. I'm not that old."

"Well, it sucks and is stupid."

"Can't argue with that." He raised his bottle and took another sip. Since talking to Vera Rosen, he'd been kicking over an idea and decided to give voice to it. "You want to do something about it."

"Yes. And I will. I have no idea what, but I'm famous right now, and I should use that for something before it's over."

"At the very least, you should probably set up some kind of legal defense fund if you're going to keep pushing the registration thing. Maybe incorporate yourself as a 501(c)3."

"I have no idea what that means."

"Legal non-profit organization. Lets you accept donations from people and use them for your expenses."

"Well, that'd be nice, but I don't know anything about how to do that."

"Fortunately, you're friends with a rather kick-ass accountant."

"You'd help set it up? Ah, who am I kidding. I can't even find a job."

"Tell you what. Hold off on finding a job for a little while. You've got a lot of people who look up to you. Use them. Use their knowledge and their energy."

She looked pensive, but didn't respond, so he continued. "Write out your talking points. Why is registration bad? What else can be done? Find someone who wants to be an agent. Talk to Rosen tomorrow, then tell your new agent to call every TV station, radio, and newspaper, and go on all their shows and make them understand why registration is wrong, why prejudice is wrong. Get on Trevor Noah and explain it to his audience."

"I don't know if I can do all that. It's a lot of work, and I don't know the first thing about any of those."

"It'll be a lot for one person, yes. Fortunately, you have several. Don't get me wrong, it won't be easy, but I can help guide you through some of it, and Rosen will know ten times what I do. You won't have to do everything yourself. You're a good organizer, and a natural leader. I've seen it, and even Michael - Detective Diaz - told me he was impressed, and regardless of what you think of him, from a man like that, that means something. All you need is backing. You want a good board. I'll be on it, and if you want, I can talk to a couple of other people. I'd suggest Diaz and Rosen both, for starters."

"What's the board for?"

"They have final say on everything. Which is why you want a good one - someone who'll let you do what you need to, but keep you from doing anything stupid or unproductive. Also, they should be promoting the group and arranging donations - though a lot of that is up to you. Find someone in your group who wants to be a grant writer. I can get them some resources on learning how to get started."

"How will all this be paid for? Even with volunteers, there's going to be a lot of expenses."

He was glad to hear her say that. The first thing everyone starting a business did in his experience was to underestimate just how much it actually costs, in dollars as well as hours. "In the long run, donations, grants, crowdfunding. To get up and running, let me make a few calls, shake down some of my soon to be former clients, and we should be able to get enough to cover all the early expenses, and get you a small stipend until we can get you a real salary..."

"Are you... are you serious? Can this really work?"

"That's up to you. If this is what you want, it'll be twice the work at a fraction of the salary you're used to..."

She gave a snort of laughter. "What is this 'salary'? I've never heard of such a thing."

"Such as it is. You'll likely be working twelve hour days seven days a week for room and board in the beginning."

"This is awesome! This is perfect!" She jumped off the couch and gave him a big hug. "I won't let you down, I promise."

"I know you won't," he said, and lifted his beer. "To the future."

"To the Barbara and Carl Foundation for a Better Tomorrow," she replied, raising her own and intoning, "The fighting's over. Now begins the fight."

He gave a small laugh at that. The kids could work on their slogans later.

"Thought you wanted to get away from wolves," she said.

"The best laid plans..."

VEER STOPPED at the bottom of the three steps leading up to the Detectives' landing. Michael was arguing loudly with Detective Alice Johansen at the top while a couple of nearby police officers downstairs were trying to pretend their attention was anywhere else.

"Dammit, Alice, this isn't right!" Michael was saying.

"No, it's not, but it's what's happening, so just let me finish packing," Alice responded. She looked at him. "It's not like I'm innocent here. I gave the okay for that place to hold the werewolves. Their blood is on my hands as much as anybody's. Fourteen lawsuits make a pretty compelling argument."

There had been a slew of lawsuits following up on the evidence presented in Victor's trial. The survivors of Holy

Mountain Research were suing the company, the police, and the private security contractors. The police were suing both Holy Mountain and the security company, and Holy Mountain was even suing their own security firm. Since she'd seen the inside of both locations and retrieved a great many documents before they were destroyed, Veer was being called as a witness in over a dozen upcoming trials and was carefully following half a dozen more. The suit against her, at least, had been dropped when what had happened inside their facility had been revealed.

She didn't want to intrude on the detectives' argument, so instead joined the nearby officers in pretending not to notice them.

"But that's not what they're firing you for. I'll talk to Billings..."

"Billings can't do anything," Alice responded. "The chief can't do anything. You can't do anything. This comes from the mayor, and even she can't do anything. The people have spoken," she finished bitterly.

"I..."

"Until we can be certain they pose no danger, we can't have werewolves in the police force," Alice interrupted him. "Any bets on how long that'll take?"

"You were attacked on duty!" he said. "It's not your fault. They can't fire you for getting injured."

"They can. They did," she said. Michael opened his mouth as if he was about to say something. "And don't you dare resign in protest. The werewolf squad needs you now more than ever."

"I..."

"Yes, you were. Don't. It won't help anything and will just piss me off. Look, I'm not going to disappear. And I'm not going to just give up. You are needed here. You can work with the Were community - is that what they are? We are? Don't let them replace you with... with someone like me. Was that good, Ms. Rosen?" She picked up her box of belongings and turned to where Veer was standing. "Is that a good enough sound bite for you?"

Veer looked up and made eye contact. "I'm a print journalist," she said, and walked up the three steps. "I don't do sound bites. Though for a headline I'm thinking something like 'Hero cop fired after being wounded in line of duty.'"

"Hah! I'm no hero."

"That's for the public to decide. I'd love to tell your story and give them a chance to."

"Fine. Let's do that," she said. And Veer knew exactly what she meant. She wasn't just rolling over and playing dead. This would be the first step to getting her job back. Two months ago, Veer was hoping to get her fired. How quickly things can change. "I'll call you tomorrow." She picked up her box and walked past Veer to the stairway that led down to the underground parking garage.

Michael nodded his head toward the war room. Veer entered the conference room. The map remained but all the pins were different. One pin pointed to Forest Park labeled "Echo Base?" It was a ways off from the actual location. Veer had been there herself recently with Toni, but she didn't feel the need to tell him that. The location would be obsolete soon anyway. Gordon Chandler's house was quickly becoming the de facto Were central meeting place.

There were also pins marking a dozen incidents of violence throughout the city involving werewolves. Pro- and Anti- wolf rights protests. A fight downtown that had ended with one man transforming and biting another. Hospital intakes of people with bite wounds. She knew most of this already, and it wasn't what she'd come here to discuss.

"No werewolf cops?" she asked. "A bit extreme, isn't it?"

"I thought so. She was wounded saving my life, so they rewarded her by firing her and giving me her job."

"It was your job first."

"Fucked up situation all round. Also, and you didn't hear this from me, but it looks like they're talking about the same thing in the schools. It's beginning to look like the registry is just the beginning after all."

"Shit. Well, it'll give me something to talk about Monday."

"What's Monday?"

"Morning show in Chicago. I hear you've been doing some traveling yourself."

"LA next. Giving a talk on handling werewolves to the LAPD."

"Careful down there. That's Gregor's territory. They may not be too happy about you shooting their Alpha."

"Think they'd want revenge?"

"Want, definitely. Take, possibly. Maybe not all of them, but it would just take one loyalist."

"I thought the whole Alpha system was over now."

"Their rule isn't law anymore. But the networks are still there. They still have a lot of influence on a lot of Were."

"So, we're back to an organized crime ring."

"That's one way to put it, I suppose."

"Well, we have techniques for dealing with those." He thought of Alice telling him the same thing and wished she was here now to help. "Dammit," he continued. "Every time I talk to you, I realize how much more I don't know."

"I'd be happy to consult."

"I may take you up on that. I'm going to be talking budget with Billings when I get back from LA."

"You should talk to Toni before you go."

"Toni the terrorist? What about?"

"She's gone legit now. Started up an organization fighting for Were rights. She's looking for board members."

"Board members? I can't really see myself on the board of directors for a terrorist organization."

"She was never really a terrorist. Think about it. You're probably the foremost leading non-Were expert on Were now. You'd be a valuable addition."

"Hm. Might still be a conflict of interest."

"Or the opposite. Serving on the board of a Were rights group could be a powerful signal that the police are treating Were as humans with full human rights, and aren't going to be assuming they're all criminals."

"Maybe you have a point there. I'll think about it. See what the captain thinks. How well do you know Toni?"

"Better now. She's helping me with my book about the history of the Were unveiling. There've been lots of attempts before. This was the only one that was successful, and she's the only surviving member of its founding."

"Other than yourself."

"I just took advantage of their work, and yours, but I wasn't the cause."

"I think you underestimate your part. But I suppose we'll have a lot to talk about when we both get back."

"Yes," she replied. "I suspect that we'll be spending a lot of time together in the future. I still want that exclusive you promised me."

SETTING up the organization had gone better than Gordon had hoped. Rosen had proven helpful in many ways, including arranging some large anonymous donations that were just waiting for the IRS to clear the paperwork. She'd told him that some of the old guard were now very interested in officially fighting for werewolf rights, but didn't want their names associated with a rogue, regardless of her current status. She hadn't been able to talk Diaz into joining them, but he'd agreed to speak with them officially as liaisons to the werewolves, which could turn out to be even better. Rosen and Toni had been spending a lot of time together, which Gordon was happy about. She needed people around her who weren't her followers.

A couple of big names helped get them a lot of attention fast. Toni was already overwhelmed with the amount of work there was, despite all the help she was receiving from her Order of the Wolf. One of her early recruits, Kim, with Gordon's happy permission, had moved into the house and was working full time with Toni. They had helped him pack up his room which he assumed Toni would take over after he left. Packing up Barbara's room was far more difficult. He would be forever grateful for the help and support of the two young women.

Kim was acting as Toni's personal assistant. It was a role which neither of them had any idea how to handle, but they were learning. Kim had also talked about going to law school. He promised to check in regularly. There were already new laws being passed across the nation, and Toni was already busy organizing fights in court and various legislatures. He wasn't worried about her, but he was glad to get out of the fight. Mostly. The future was in good hands.

HE TURNED on the radio as he drove away, heading east on I-84. Everything he was taking with him was loaded in the back of his car. Everything else he owned was boxed up and filling the attic where Toni and Kim lived now.

The news was still trying to catch up with all that had happened. He skipped from station to station as he drove. Violence by Werewolves. Violence against Werewolves. Economic report on the cost of producing silver bullets for the military and the police. Breathless denunciations or justifications for Holy Mountain Research. More sound bites from an interview with Vera Rosen. He listened to a couple of clueless men discussing the first lawsuit filed by "Barbara and Carl," trying their best to minimize the importance and talk about the young, inexperienced, and hopelessly naive people who were running it. He listened as long as he could before getting disgusted and switching to a music station.

And as the traffic began to thin out and he hit the open highway, he turned up the volume and smiled as he watched Portland fade away in the rear view mirror.

ABOUT THE AUTHOR

Pat Luther has lived half his life in Portland, Oregon, and the other half chasing jobs up and down the west coast, with occasional forays further inland.

He's been a pizza boy, a Kelly girl, a corporate propagandist, and both a purveyor and debunker of conspiracy theories. He's worked on satellites and police databases and has lost more than one job when the forces of good forced an end to the project. He once helped save the world (you're welcome), and the 2008 financial collapse was almost, but not quite, entirely not his fault.

He's been a member of at least two different secret societies, neither of which actually involved werewolves.

http://pluther.us/
https://www.facebook.com/PatLuthertheWriter
https://twitter.com/plutheus

CPSIA information can be obtained
at www.ICGtesting.com
Printed in the USA
FSHW021355270721
83423FS